I0584548

MEN OF inked HEATWAVE

FLAME ❤ BURN ❤ WILDFIRE

www.chellebliss.com

CHELLE BLISS

USA TODAY BESTSELLING AUTHOR

MEN OF INKED: HEATWAVE SERIES

Book 1 - Flame

Book 2 - Burn

Book 3 - Wildfire

Book 4 - Blaze

Book 5 - Ignite

Book 6 - Spark

Book 7 - Ember

Book 8 - Singe

Book 9 - Ashes

Book 10 - Scorch

Book 11 - Torch

Book 12 - Inferno

Book 13 - Cinder

Book 14 - Dare

To learn more,
please visit *menofinked.com/heatwave-series*

PRAISE FOR THE HEATWAVE SERIES

"I loved this book!!"
-Corinne Michaels, NYT bestselling author

"This book will blow your mind."
-Chelsea Camaron, USA Today bestselling author

"Fast-paced, twist, turns, and a whole lot of FLAME" -Kaylee Ryan,
NYT bestselling author

"Absolutely had me wanting more!" -Author Angel Payne

"HOT. HOT. HOT."
-Ruth Cardello, NYT bestselling author

FLAME

A MEN OF INKED HEATWAVE NOVEL

WALL STREET JOURNAL & USA TODAY BESTSELLING AUTHOR

CHELLE BLISS

FLAME COPYRIGHT © 2019

No part of this book may be reproduced or transmitted in any form, including electronic or mechanical, without written permission from the publisher, except in the case of brief quotations embodied in critical articles or reviews.

This is a work of fiction. Names, characters, businesses, places, events, and incidents are either the products of the author's imagination or used in a fictitious manner. Any resemblance to actual persons, living or dead, or actual events is purely coincidental.

Publisher © Chelle Bliss September 17th 2019
Edited by Lisa A. Hollett
Cover Model: Dylan Horsch
Cover Photo © Aaron Rogers & Dylan Horsch

PROLOGUE

GIGI

Mistake: an error in action, calculation, opinion, or judgment caused by poor reasoning, carelessness, or insufficient knowledge.

LIFE IS A SERIES OF MISTAKES. I've made my fair share of them. Some were grander than others, but each time, I tried to learn a new lesson, driven not to make the same one more than once.

Falling for the wrong man has been my problem. Sure, I'd done stupid things like every young person. Things that could've changed the way the rest of my life had played out.

I didn't fear much. I also didn't think too far into the future, wondering how my newest mistake would alter the rest of my life. That's the thing about youth. We spend so much time in the now, we rarely think about the future because time seems infinite while we feel so indestructible.

Mistakes are how we learn and evolve. At least, that's what my father told me, trying to get me not to make the same mistake twice.

But I didn't listen. I'd made the same mistake twice. I'd loved two boys in my life—Erik and Keith.

Both said they loved me.

Both cheated.

Both broke my heart.

The only thing I got right with Keith, my high school sweetheart, was that I didn't sleep with him. Just before graduation, I caught him cheating and later found out it wasn't the first time he'd done me wrong. *C'est la vie.*

I thought Erik, mistake number two, was the real deal. I thought we'd go the distance, but again, I was wrong. Although I gave him my virginity, trusting him more than anyone in the world, he couldn't keep his dick in his pants either.

I seemed doomed, weaving a web of ex-boyfriends and cheaters to carry with me, altering the way I'd feel about men for the rest of my life.

I didn't want to be that girl.

I didn't want to be bitter and untrusting of every man for the rest of my days. I knew there was goodness in the world.

My parents had been married for over twenty years. Happily married at that. My mother was everything to my father. She could do no wrong in his eyes. He worshiped her. Treated her like a goddess. I grew up watching that goodness, seeing how a man should love a woman. But no matter where I looked, all I seemed to attract were cheaters.

After cheater number two broke my heart, I vowed to myself never to let it happen again. I'd either have to learn to keep things casual with the men in my future or hone my man-picker and try to weed out the slimeballs from the good guys.

How totally laughable is that?

But then I met the man, the one I thought was number three. The one I couldn't imagine getting it right with because everything about him screamed error in judgment.

He was different from any man I'd ever opened my heart to before. He was different from the boy I'd first given my body to.

...But that didn't mean he wouldn't become mistake number three.

CHAPTER 1
GIGI

"HE WANTS YOU." Tamara, my cousin, elbows me in the ribs while she gawks at a guy across the bar. "And he's hot, bitch."

I glance in his direction and look away quickly when our eyes meet.

Holy shit.

The guy isn't just hot, he's Freaking Fine with capital Fs.

But the last thing I need is more complication in my life, especially after what happened with Erik.

I tear my gaze away from him and roll my eyes at my cousin. "I'm not here for a hookup, Tam. I'm here to be with my girls, not some…"

"Hot piece of ass?" She finishes my statement and shoots me a smug grin.

"He's not *that* hot." I throw the thin red straw from my drink in her direction, hoping she'll change the subject.

I'm completely lying, of course.

This guy is hot as fuck. He's not a pretty boy…although he is handsome. He's a little rough around the edges and probably couldn't pull off the corporate look to save his life, but that doesn't make him any less hot. There's no way a guy like him rides his bike on the weekends and sits in a cubicle all day to pay the bills.

He lives *the life*.

He's all in.

Balls deep in the biker world by the looks of him. This isn't a getaway weekend to let his shit hang out and cut loose for a few days. Nope. This life—the drinkin' and ridin'—is part of his core.

On a hotness scale of one to ten, he's totally a twenty. But Jesus, he's a little scary too.

I've known plenty of bikers in my short twenty years walking this earth. Growing up with a biker dad who had biker friends, I've been around guys like the hottie my entire life. Since I worked at Inked during my summers, my circle of bikers grew, but they were all good guys...at least in their own fucked-up ways.

Mallory lifts the shot glass in front of her lips and stares over the rim at me. "You know how to get over a douche like Erik?"

I shake my head. "Don't say it," I warn her.

She slams back the shot and winces before the liquid has even slid down her throat. "Fuck, tequila is no joke," she grits out and coughs into her hand until tears are in her eyes.

"I told you," Mary, her identical twin sister, says and shakes her head in judgment. "You never listen."

"I'm fine. Anyway, what was I saying?" Mallory pauses as she slides the empty glass across the table. "Ah. I was telling you how to get over Erik." Her lips tip up. "Get under someone else."

Ugh.

That's totally Mallory, but not Mary. They are like night and day. Yin and yang. I'm not sure the world could take two Mallorys anyway, so it is a good thing they're so opposite. One's a wild child, and the other is a bookworm.

Tamara nudges another shot of tequila in my direction. "Have a drink. Maybe you just need a little liquid courage to go talk to Flame."

I raise an eyebrow, glaring at my not-so-innocent cousin. "Flame?"

"Well…" She glances in his direction again and shrugs. "He's hot as fuck, so Flame works. Like, he's so hot, you'll get burned." She laughs, finding herself funny even if no one else at the table does.

I tap my finger against the table, staring at her in disbelief. "You know what happens when I drink tequila, Tamara?"

Her smug smirk grows bigger. "I do, and I'm counting on it." She waggles her eyebrows.

Oh boy. Tamara is supposed to be my voice of reason on this trip. We lied our asses off to our parents about spring break. We told them we were staying on campus to catch up on homework and to study for final exams. They would literally shit a brick if they knew we were here, especially during Bike Week.

"Was Erik even a good lay?" Mallory asks out of the clear blue because her mind always seems to be thinking about sex, even if it isn't her own.

"He was good." I grab the tequila because if my mouth is full or I'm coughing from the burn, I can't talk about having sex with Erik.

I don't know if he was good or not. He was good for me, but he was also the only person I'd ever gone all the way with. Sure, I fooled around with other guys, but my experience wasn't as impressive as some people's.

My answer to Mallory's question isn't a complete lie, but hell if I know if anyone else would say he was good or not.

I wince before the tequila even touches my tongue.

"Good or great?" Mallory asks.

I tip my head back, letting the liquid slide to the back of my mouth before it makes its way down my throat. My eyes tear up immediately, and I almost regret choosing the liquor over talking about my lack of sexual experience with my best friends.

"Does Erik look like he'd be great?" Tamara asks Mallory, saving me from answering.

Tamara knows all about my sex life and everything that happened with my exes. We've always been open and honest with each other. I know she's been with a few more guys than me, but she doesn't judge me. But Mallory doesn't have a clue because she'd totally judge me. She judges everyone.

"He looks like he'd be a lame lay," Mallory says, totally judging Erik.

"Oh, stop, Mal. He does not," Mary replies and pushes a chunk of her long red hair behind her shoulder.

"I've been with enough guys to be able to spot a bad, good, and great fuck a mile away." Mallory turns her attention toward the hot guy who was staring at me. "And he—" she tips her head in his direction "—would be a great fucking lay."

Mallory has no problem putting herself out there with men. She's unapologetic about her sexuality and goes after what she wants. I envy her, but only a little bit. Not the part where she sleeps with any guy who is even mildly good-looking and wants to get in her pants. But the part where she's so self-assured and gives no fucks what anyone thinks about her or her activities.

Mary purses her lips and looks at her sister in disgust. "You can't tell by looking at someone. Stop with your bullshit, Mallory. Just because you're easy doesn't mean you're better than the rest of us."

Mallory sits up straighter and tilts her head, turning her attention toward her sister. "Sweetie, I'm not easy. Trust me. I make men work for this." She waves her hand in front of her chest. "I don't give it away to just anyone."

Mary, Tamara, and I laugh, but Mallory is shooting daggers at us, looking like she's ready to lunge across the table and wrap her skinny fingers around our necks.

"You guys can kiss my ass," Mallory snaps. "We're talking about Gigi and the sexy beast over there making goo-goo eyes at her. Is Miss Priss too good for a biker guy like that? Or maybe you're too much of a prude to even talk to a hot-ass guy like him."

I grind my teeth and glare at Mallory. Sometimes, I hate her. She can be such a bitch. If it weren't for the fact that she is Mary's sister, she wouldn't hang around us. But wherever Mary goes, Mallory's right there with her. They're a package deal.

"I am not a prude," I hiss and return her glare.

"Mal, by your standards, everyone around this table is a prude," Tamara says, coming to my defense.

Mallory tips her head back and cackles. "Tam, I know you're not a prude. My sister might as well be a nun, and sweet little Gigi over here—" she waves her hand in my direction, and I do my best not to slap it away "—is well on her way to sexual boredom."

The two shots of tequila I've already downed along with the beer I've been nursing are starting to work their magic. Between Mallory's annoying words, the hot guy across the bar, and the alcohol running through my veins, I'm ready to blow.

I curl my fingers around another shot glass, and I know I'm going to regret everything about tonight when I open my eyes tomorrow. But right now, I don't give a shit. I'm over the conversation, and I'm so totally over Mallory, I'll do anything to shut her up.

"Fuck you, Mal. I've been around men like him my entire life. I didn't grow up like you, in a mansion surrounded by overprivileged assholes. A badass biker guy like that doesn't scare me."

"Put up or shut up, sweetie." Mallory grins, thinking she's proved her point because she's always the unpredictable one in the group, while Mary and I play shit safe.

The chair scrapes against the floor and my knees wobble as I stand, but I can't stop now. If I falter in any way, I'll never hear the end of it from Mallory. The last thing I want to give her is more ammunition.

I lift the tequila to my lips, pouring it down my throat and barely wincing this time because it's already working its magic. "Don't wait up for me tonight."

Tamara's hand is on my wrist before I have a chance to storm away in dramatic fashion. "Do you think this is smart?" She stares up at me with wide eyes. "Don't listen to her. You know she's a bitch, Gigi, and she's just trying to piss you off."

I pull my arm away, feeling surer than ever that this is, in fact, the right thing to do. I'm going to prove them all wrong.

I can be wild.

I can be reckless.

I know how to have fun, and I can most certainly talk to a hot, badass biker guy without turning into a mumbling idiot.

"I'll be fine, Tam. I won't be back at the hotel room before the sun rises."

"Gigi, don't do this," Tamara begs, reaching for my hand again and missing.

"One second." I take another step backward.

Mallory's face is covered in a shit-eating grin, and Tamara and Mary both look horrified before I turn my back to them and make my way through the crowded bar.

Goddamn Mallory and her self-righteous bitchiness, making me do crazy shit. Well, it's not entirely her fault. A man named Patrón is just as much to blame as the bitchy redhead sitting at my table.

My eyes lock with the handsome stranger's, and all rational thought and any reason to stop what's about to happen go right out the window. God, he's beautiful. He has the sexy bed-head thing nailed with his light-brown locks going all different directions, begging to be touched and smoothed. The way his lips curve at the side, exposing just a hint of white teeth renders me a little stupid, and I almost trip over my own two feet, but I somehow stay upright.

Reaching into my back pocket, I grab my phone and unlock the screen as I take the final steps to the guy who's freaking hot.

This man isn't a college boy, looking to guzzle beer and make out at a frat party. Nope. Not this guy. He looks like the type who would have a different chick on the back of his bike every night of the week and make zero fucking apologies for it, offering nothing but a good time.

"Hey." I try to sound upbeat and excited instead of terrified and pissed off. "What's your number, handsome?" I lift my phone, moving my gaze from his face to the phone and back to him.

The corner of his mouth ticks, and I ready myself for a barrage of questions, but they don't come. "Hey, darlin'," he says smoothly.

Oh my God.

His voice is like velvet sliding over my skin, deep and gravelly. I stand there, unable to move, staring at his mouth, surrounded by that killer beard.

I've never kissed a guy with facial hair. I wonder what it would feel like to press my lips to his. Would the beard tickle? *Get ahold of yourself, girl.*

"Name's Pike." He tips his head back, tilting it a little to the side as his gaze sweeps over me.

I open my mouth and close it because, for a moment, I can't think of a damn thing to say. I can't stop staring at him and all thoughts, rational or not, just seem to vanish. I don't know how many seconds I stand like this, staring at him while he stares at me, but it's more than a few and entirely too long.

"Gigi," I finally mutter like I'm a complete and total imbecile, unable to say more than a few syllables. I can't seem to stop staring in his eyes. They're beautiful, but I can't tell if they're blue or green in the shitty lighting of the bar.

"Still want my number?" he asks, moving his hand across his face and partially covering his mouth to hide the smile he's sporting.

I nod because somehow, I'm still mute. *Way to go, Gigi.* In this moment, standing in front of this hot biker, who I now know is named Pike, I am indeed everything Mallory said I am.

Pike gives me a chin lift, and I raise my phone before he rattles off a set of numbers.

"Be right back." I smile, or at least, I think I do. With the tequila, it could very well be a grimace.

Thankfully, Pike doesn't ask me anything else. He just dips his head, those beautiful lips still quirked before I turn my back to him and hustle away as quickly as possible.

My eyes are wide as I stalk back toward the table where Tamara, Mary, and Mallory are all sitting, staring at me in complete disbelief.

"Tam, take down his number. If I die, you know where to start."

"Don't do this," she pleads and covers her face with her hands.

"Just take down his number."

"Don't listen to Mallory, Gigi," Mary tells me, but I shake my head.

"You want his number or not?" I stare at my cousin, ignoring the other two. "This is happening, so you can either have my back or not, Tam."

"If you fucking die," Tamara says as she fishes her phone out of her purse, "I might as well die too, because my daddy and your daddy will kill me. They'll find out about our fake IDs, underage drinking, and me letting you walk out of here with a scary as fuck biker."

I tap my foot. "Just open your contacts and type, Tam. I don't need a lecture."

She snaps her mouth shut and nods. Her fingers move fast as I read his number off the screen.

"His name is Pike."

"Of course it is," she mutters into her phone screen. "I still think—"

"Don't," I snap as I jam my phone into my jeans pocket while she stares at me with her mouth hanging open. "I'll be fine. You have his name and number. He's not going to murder me. I mean, look at him." I look over my shoulder, catching those beautiful eyes again.

"I'm looking, and he's fine," Mallory adds like any of us give two shits about her commentary or opinion.

I swallow hard, suddenly feeling like I haven't had a drop of liquid in my mouth for days. "Don't wait up for me. I'll see you when I see you." I turn on my heel and head toward Pike.

"Gigi," Tamara yells out, barely audible above the music and chatter of the people around me.

I don't stop, though. I walk straight up to Pike, taking in his vintage T-shirt, torn jeans, road-worn black biker boots, sexy bed head, and just fucking spectacular beard and eyes and say, "Wanna get out of here?"

He pulls the beer bottle back from his lips, eyes sweeping up my body before his lips curve again. "Thought you'd never ask."

CHAPTER 2
PIKE

"FANCY PLACE," the girl says as she walks into my hotel room, glancing around like she's waiting for something to jump out and bite her because it's a shit hole.

"I can take you back to your friends if you want." I can see she's not comfortable.

The chick—Gigi, I think she said her name was—drops her purse on the green carpet and turns to face me straight on. "I don't want to go. I'm right where I want to be." She sways as she speaks, clearly on the verge of drunk.

Why in the hell she asked me to take her to my hotel is beyond me. I'm not looking a gift horse in the mouth, though. When a hot chick asks me to get out of somewhere with her, I'm no fool; I take her wherever the hell she wants to go.

Drunk sex can be fun, but drunk sex with such a young chick may not be all it's cracked up to be. Besides being plain fucking stupid. I'm not an idiot. I've been with enough women, drunk and sober, to know when they want it and when they aren't quite sure.

Right now, the way she's looking at me, I'm not sure she wants what she's asked for. I grab the bottle of Jack Daniel's and pour two glasses, one for her and one for me, as she walks toward me. I push one in her direction, lifting the other one to my lips.

She takes the glass, staring at me as she moves slowly, lifting the rim to her mouth. "Pike, right?" she asks.

"Yeah, darlin'," I mumble into the amber liquid, gazing at her as she tips the glass back and takes a mouthful.

"I don't usually do this," she says, wincing as the burn slides down her throat and mine.

Those words, I believe. There's nothing in her body language that screams one-night stand. She didn't leap into my arms, attaching her lips to mine as soon as we walked through the door. I almost feel guilty having her here even if she asked me to bring her exactly where she's standing.

"Figured as much." I move to the bed, sitting on the edge, resting the glass of Jack on my knee as I look at this mint-ass chick with the wild brown hair, big blue eyes, and killer rack. But the thing that gets me most is those long-ass legs, smooth and shiny, dark from the sunshine kissing her skin.

"But I want to be here," she says quickly, moving to stand in front of me, but not close enough to where I could reach out and touch her.

"How old are you?" I ask, noticing the flawlessness of her skin as she stands near the bedside light.

"Twenty-two," she says, not meeting my eyes.

She's right at the edge of my limit. At twenty-six, anyone younger feels just plain wrong. I don't care how much they push their pussy in my face, I ain't looking for jailbait.

I take another sip, eyes locked on hers as she stares at me, shifting from foot to foot just a few feet away. "We can watch TV or just talk," I offer, trying to be a gentleman.

This wasn't exactly how I imagined the night going. When a chick like Gigi leaves a bar with me, I always assume there's pussy coming my way. And before tonight, I've never been wrong.

"You want to watch TV?" she asks softly, finally stilling and staring at me with her head cocked and one eyebrow higher than the other.

I shrug, staring at the beautiful creature before me. She's like a Greek goddess, wild yet subdued, with hair rolling down her shoulders, covering her breasts in long waves. "Wasn't how I planned the night to go, but I'm down with whatever. This doesn't seem like your thing."

Her foot starts tapping, fast and loud. "What's that mean?"

"Just what I said. We don't have to have sex. We can just hang out."

Why is this girl busting my balls so damn hard? Usually, a girl's already in my lap, lips on mine, riding my cock through my jeans and begging to be filled. But not this one. She's staring at me, putting more than a few feet between us, not moving a muscle or throwing herself into my arms. I'm trying to be a gentleman, but she's making it damn hard to keep my shit together.

She slams back the Jack, slides the glass onto the nightstand, and moves in front of me with her legs touching my knees. I glance up, and it's my turn not to move.

"I want you," she says softly, placing her hands on my shoulders. Her eyes warm as her fingers touch the tender skin on my neck near my collar, stroking slowly back and forth. "I want you to fuck me, Pike."

I don't know what I said that made her flip a switch. Thirty seconds ago, I could've sworn we were going to watch a movie, or at the very least, we'd be heading back to the bar.

But now... Now she's staring at me with hungry eyes and nothing but determination.

She moves forward, lifting her legs one by one, planting her knees near my thighs as she climbs onto the bed. I slide my hands to her waist, steadying her as she settles onto my lap, pressing her sweet pussy against my dick.

The kiss is sloppy, her lips tasting like Jack but her breath laced with tequila. Her movements aren't smooth, sending up red flags all over the place.

I glide my hands up her sides to her arms before hauling her backward. "Are you drunk?"

"No," she says quickly, gasping when I tighten my hands around her upper arms as she tries to get to my mouth again. "Are you?"

She's a sassy thing, ready to throw words back in my face without hesitation.

"Darlin', it doesn't matter if I am. I'm a sure thing. But it matters if you are."

She tries to wriggle free of my hold, but I keep her pinned, my hands on her arms with her body moving in my lap, making my hard-on worse. "It doesn't matter for me either. I just want to have sex."

The last thing I want is to be someone's regret. Tomorrow, when she wakes up, I don't want to be the biggest mistake of her life or even this week. I want to fuck a woman because she wants me, not because liquor gave her the courage to step outside her comfort zone for a walk on the wild side.

In one swift move, I have her in the air and then flat on her back in the bed. But I don't dare join her. I stand quickly, moving away from her as she blinks up at me in shock.

"What the fuck?" she hisses, trying to sit up but falling backward. "What's wrong with you?"

"I don't do drunk chicks." I run my fingers through my hair, pacing a path in front of the bed.

She grunts. "I'm not drunk."

By her behavior, I can tell this isn't her typical scene. Throw in alcohol, and this shit could blow up in my face big-time.

"Fuck."

"Well," she says, waving her hands over her body. "Hell yeah, baby. I'm waiting for that."

I grab the bottle of Jack, walking toward the table and two

chairs near the window. "I need a minute to think." I'm trying to buy some time and a way out without pissing off this chick completely.

She's not timid or meek. She's quick with her words, and I know if I say the wrong thing, she's liable to go off half-cocked, completely losing her shit.

"Pour me one," she says, trying to sit up again, but she falls back down, letting out a loud sigh.

I fill my glass, collapsing into the chair after I set the bottle back on the table. "No. I think you had enough for one night."

"You're not my father," she snaps, fisting the comforter in her thin fingers and squeezing her eyes shut.

"It's a good thing I'm not. I'd tan your hide for doing what you're doing."

She throws up an arm. "Now he has a conscience."

"I always have a conscience." I bring the glass to my lips and look toward the doorway, wondering if I should just leave her here or take her back to the bar.

I'm leaning toward leaving her, letting her sleep off the liquor. The last thing I want is for her drunk ass to be on the back of my bike, sliding onto the pavement because she's too fucked up to stay on.

"Mr. Badass Biker Dude has a conscience," she says before she starts to laugh. "Mr. McHotterson doesn't want to fuck me because I had a few drinks." She pauses, and her laughter turns into loud giggles. "Maybe more like five or seven drinks."

I slide my gaze to her, but her eyes are still closed as she lies flat, unmoving except for her laughter inflating her chest. "However many you had, it was too many."

Her eyes open for a moment, still unfocused as she looks to her side, watching me. "That's priceless coming from you."

I down half the glass of Jack, trying to get my shit under control because this girl is seriously getting on my nerves. "Coming from me?"

What the hell is wrong with me? An hour ago, I didn't give a shit if she was annoying or not. I wanted to fuck her until I passed out. But now she's lying in my bed, hurling insults and compliments in my direction because I'm trying to do the right thing.

"Well, yeah. You're a badass biker dude."

"What the fuck with that badass biker dude shit? I'm just a man looking to fuck."

"See." She waves a hand in my direction before dropping it to the bed like a ton of bricks. "Totally a badass biker dude thing to say." She closes her eyes again, and I stay silent, knowing the argument is useless. "I just wanted to get laid and get Erik off my mind. Is that so much to ask?"

She wanted to have breakup sex. She wanted to forget. I can understand that even if I've only had a handful of women who ever came close to breaking my heart.

I don't bother asking about Erik. I don't give two fucks about the guy, and at the moment, I don't give a fuck about the mouthy chick in my bed either. I sit here in complete silence, pouring myself another drink as she keeps on talking.

"There must be something wrong with me. Erik was awful in bed, or was I the one who sucked so bad I couldn't even get off?"

She's clearly way beyond tipsy based on the way she's spilling her guts. I'm not engaging in this conversation, but she has no problem continuing.

"If the badass biker dude won't even fuck me when I'm throwing myself at him, maybe I'm the problem. Two guys. Two cheaters. What else can it be but me?"

I'd love to tell her it's in no way her fault. She's beautiful even if she is a pain in the ass. I don't know a guy in his right mind who wouldn't explore her body for hours on end until he gave her a damn orgasm—or so many orgasms she passes out from lack of oxygen.

I lift the glass to my lips again, mumbling into the liquid as quietly as possible because I don't want to engage in her ramblings.

I'm thankful when she doesn't say anything else and nothing but her soft snores fill the room.

"Thank fuck," I whisper, glancing toward the ceiling and wondering what I did to deserve this shit tonight. "Dodged that fucking bullet."

All I wanted was a good time. And instead, I'm saddled with a girl I don't even know passed out in my bed, snoring away like she's got no cares in the world.

I'm tempted to leave, go back to the bar, and finish the night the way I'd planned. But I can't bring myself to do it. We may not know each other, but I can't leave her in this room alone. When she wakes up, the last thing I want her to think is something happened when it didn't.

I'm not a gentleman, but I'm also not a complete asshole. I don't need any more trouble in my life. I had enough of that growing up and trying to break free of my parents.

I tip my head back, downing the rest of my drink before climbing to my feet and making my way toward the closet.

"Way to go, Pike." I pull out the spare blanket, ready to bed down on the shitty couch near the door.

This may be one of the longest nights of my life. And I have a feeling tomorrow morning isn't going to be any better.

CHAPTER 3
GIGI

"OH SHIT," I whisper, turning my head to the side, seeing the hottie from last night passed out on the couch.

Did we do it?

That's a big nope since I still have on my clothes from last night and they reek of tobacco and the day-after drunk stench.

My head throbs as I start to sit up, and I instantly collapse backward, wishing I hadn't had the tequila. "The bad news is, I have a headache. The good news is, I'm still alive," I whisper again, staring up at the ceiling.

Maybe I can slink out of bed and make it across the room without waking up the badass biker. I place my foot on the floor, my body still flat against the mattress and comforter that probably hasn't been washed since before I was born. I push that thought right out of my mind as my toes dig into the dirty shag carpet, and I slide out of the bed like I'm doing a fire drill. It reminds me of the old stop, drop, and roll they used to teach us during fire safety week in elementary school.

I keep my head up, trying not to focus on the damn stickiness of the carpeting on my palms as I inch closer to the door while crawling on my knees. I hold my breath, trying not to wake the guy and wincing the entire time because it feels like there's a little garden gnome playing the drums inside my skull.

I glance at the guy as I reach for the door, still on my hands and knees, holding my breath. My fingers are an inch from the metal knob when I lift up into a crouching position, feeling my escape almost at hand.

I don't want to be here when the guy wakes up. He's probably pissed because we didn't do it last night. I came back here fully expecting to bump uglies because Mallory had pissed me off so much, and I figured it was spring break and the perfect time to do something reckless.

"Where ya goin', darlin'?" asks the voice from last night, still sounding like sin, but deeper from sleep.

I freeze. "I thought I'd let you sleep."

He reaches behind his head, arm thrown over the back of the couch, and grabs my wrist before I can turn the handle. "You in a rush?" His touch is light. "I figured we could get some breakfast."

My eyes widen and my mouth falls open. "You want to have breakfast?"

His fingers tighten around my wrist, but not painfully. He's holding me with such a light touch, it catches me completely off guard, and I do nothing to pull away. "That's what people usually do in the morning."

"But…" I swallow, hating to bring up last night but thinking it needs to be out in the open. "But we didn't do it."

"Do it?" He repeats my words, rolling his body without letting go of my wrist until we're eye-to-eye. "Seriously?"

I nod and shrug, feeling like a bigger moron than I probably look. And that shit is pretty hard considering I'm on my hands and knees, trying to sneak out of his room without even brushing my hair.

The guy laughs. "No, darlin'. We didn't *do it*, but I'm hungry, and I'm sure the hangover you're nursing needs some hair of the dog, along with something greasy."

I blink a few times, wondering if I'm hearing him right or if I'm still drunk and not quite understanding what he's saying. "You want to take me to breakfast?"

He lets go of my wrist and rubs his forehead, leaning over the couch with his elbows resting on his knees. "Clearly she isn't as smart as she seemed last night," he mutters to himself. "This is what I get for wanting to bang the hot girl."

I rise up higher on my knees, my back straight, still blinking at him with my mouth hanging open. "I'm the hot girl?" I ask.

He lifts his head enough to see my eyes. "Are you shitting me with this?"

"Pike, right?" I ask because last night is a little fuzzy, which is odd because I didn't have *that* much to drink. But it had been a while since I'd drunk something stronger than beer. He nods, and I continue as I finally climb to my feet. "I am not shitting you. Are you shitting me?"

He throws his body back into the couch and runs his hand through his still hot-as-fuck bed head. "About breakfast?" he asks.

"About everything."

His gaze intensifies as he stares up at me with those dreamy green eyes. "I'm hungry. Are you?"

"Yes."

"Then let's eat."

"Okay..." I whisper as my stomach growls.

It won't be so bad sitting across from Pike and sharing a meal. We don't have jack to talk about, but at least I'll be full and can buy a little time before I go back to my room and have to face Mallory.

"And, babe," he says and pauses, sitting motionless.

"Yeah?"

He's on his feet, hand on my jaw, eyes locked on mine. "You were one of the hottest chicks there. You're a little fucking loony and can't hold your liquor worth shit, but you're off-the-charts hot."

My knees wobble a little like I'm drunk on his gaze and the

words he just spoke. "Now you're really shitting me," I whisper, swallowing hard because I suddenly want to launch myself into his arms and finish what we started last night. "But I could eat."

The corner of his mouth twitches as his thumb grazes my bottom lip whisper-soft. "I could eat too."

Oh, fuck me dead. I know he's not talking about breakfast.

"So, breakfast..." My mouth's suddenly dry. My stomach isn't growling anymore; it's fluttering like a horde of tiny butterflies have taken flight inside it. I start toward the door, but he hauls me backward and in front of him again.

His eyes move down to the floor, but mine are firmly planted on his face. "You're probably going to need shoes."

I close my eyes, wishing I could start the last twelve hours over again. There's so much I would do differently, and maybe I wouldn't look like such a newb in front of this hot-as-fuck badass biker guy.

My face heats, and I want to crawl into a hole and die. "Yeah. Shoes would be good," I whisper, unable to take my eyes off him.

He releases me, but I don't move right away. It's like he's cast an invisible net around me, holding me to him. Maybe it's the fact that I haven't had any action in months, or the fact that every time he looks at me, I can see the hunger in his eyes...and he's not thinking about bacon and eggs.

"Sandals," he says as he sits on the couch and pulls on a boot.

"Yeah," I say, still not hauling ass because I'm too busy watching his every move. The way his muscles dance under his ink-covered skin is completely hypnotic.

"Do you need me to put them on your feet?"

"Yeah," I whisper again because my brain is fried, and I'm not thinking straight. "Wait, no." I wave my hands when he starts to stand. "I got it."

"Thank fuck for small miracles," he teases, putting his ass back on the couch as he grabs the other boot.

I silently chastise myself as I walk around to the side of the bed, finding my sandals placed neatly together, facing outward like he cared. I slide my toes between the plastic and close my eyes, trying to calm the fuck down. "Is it a far walk?"

"Nope. We're taking my bike. That a problem?"

Something about that makes me smile. Erik and Keith didn't have bikes. They both preferred their souped-up sports cars to the roar of a motorcycle. But they were boys, and Pike is all man.

"Nope," I repeat his words and tone. "Just let me make myself halfway presentable."

I don't wait for his approval before I take off toward the bathroom and shut myself inside. Leaning against the door, I allow myself a moment to freak out. Once I've whispered "Holy shit" for the tenth time, I move toward the sink and get a glimpse of my post-tequila face. I scrub away the smeared mascara with the little soap that is still in the wrapper next to the sink. As soon as my face is dry, I almost squeal when I find his toothpaste and place a drop on my finger, scrubbing my teeth and the rancid taste of last night away. "It'll do," I say to myself in the mirror, wiping away the toothpaste from my lips.

"Let's hit it," he says near the doorway, ticking his head toward outside as soon as the bathroom door opens. "I'm starving, and the day is wasting."

"What time is it?" I ask him as I brush past him and shield my eyes from the blazing sun.

"One."

"One?" I gasp, realizing I slept half the day away. "In the afternoon?"

He's right on my heels, laughing because I'm an idiot and making no moves to try to hide how stupid I can be, especially around him. "No, darlin'. The sun decided to come out at night just for you."

I slap his chest as soon as he's next to me. "Don't be a dick."

"Don't make it so easy."

"I don't make shit easy, Pike."

He reaches into his pocket and taps the cigarette packet into his palm. "No shit. I'm learning that quickly, and the hard way," he teases with a smirk, and it takes everything in me not to smack him again.

"Um, Pike."

"Yeah?"

I tuck a lock of hair that had fallen free behind my ear. "Can you not smoke?"

"Seriously?"

"Uh. Yeah. I don't like it, and it's not good for you."

He tilts his head but doesn't put up much of a fight before putting the cigarette back in the pack. "It can wait."

I try not to smile at my victory.

An hour later, we're jamming pancakes down our throats like it's an Olympic sport and we're both aiming for the gold medal.

"How old are you?" I ask Pike.

"Twenty-six. You?"

"I told you last night I'm twenty-two." Which was a lie, of course, but I'm not going to tell him the truth now after everything that's happened. I am a month shy of my twenty-first birthday, even if the fake ID in my pocket says otherwise.

Pike nods, shoving another forkful of pancakes into his mouth, chewing slowly as he stares at me across the table. I squirm in my seat because I expect him to call bullshit, but he lets it go. "Where ya from?"

"Miami. You?"

"Up north."

"Northern Florida?"

"A little farther."

I roll my eyes. I lied about my answer, but at least I was more specific than "down south."

"Are you a badass biker for a living?" I set my fork down, knowing if I don't stop eating soon, I'll need a nap and probably assistance wobbling out of this dive.

Pike laughs, and it's the most beautiful thing in the world. Serious Pike is hot as fuck, but laughing Pike takes my breath away. "Nah, darlin'. I'm not a biker in that way. I ride because I love it. I'm not in an MC or anything."

"So, what do you do?" I ask again because he's cagey, and I'm not getting much out of the guy.

"I'm a tattoo artist."

My eyes widen because I know the community is both big and small. Sounds like an oxymoron, but I know the probability of most tattoo artists in the South knowing my family is pretty damn high. Inked is one of the most well-known shops in the South after being featured in dozens of magazines over the years.

"That sounds fun." I lean back in the booth, fidgeting with my napkin.

"What do you do?"

"I'm between jobs right now, but I'm looking for work as a graphic designer." Technically, I'm not lying. I am between jobs, but I leave out the bit about my college classes. I will be doing graphic design, but not on paper or in a digital format. I'll be tattooing skin just like him.

"What's your medium?" he asks, running his last forkful of pancakes through the lake of syrup on his plate.

"I'm a traditionalist. I like drawing by hand."

"Me too. Those girls from last night old coworkers?"

"Shit. I forgot about them." I pull out my phone from my purse, but I don't look down at the screen. "One is my cousin, but we all work together and figured Daytona was the place to be this week."

I glance down, finally seeing the five missed calls and ten text messages from Tamara. My eyes widen at the level of crazy in her text messages.

Are you okay?

Hey asshole, I'm getting worried.

Are you alive or dead?

Fucker... You better reply to me!

I know you're busy sucking cock and all, but use those fingers to text me back, bitch.

Goddamn it. Should I call the police?

Your ass better be dead since you're not replying.

I'm going to kill you when I see you again.

OMG. If you're dead, your father is going to kill me, and then my father will kill me.

I'm too young to die. I hate you.

"They lookin' for you?" he asks as I chew on my bottom lip, typing out a reply.

At breakfast. I'm fine. Great, even. Don't worry so much. I'll text you later, and we can meet up for drinks.

"Nah. They're good. They know I'm always safe."

"You know that shit last night was *not* safe."

I lift my gaze to Pike. "I'm alive, aren't I?"

He nods. "If you'd have gone with someone else, you might not be. You can't just walk up to a stranger in a bar, ask if they want to get out of there, be shit-faced drunk on top of it, and think you're definitely going to walk away unscathed."

"But I did." I shrug as my phone vibrates in my hand.

Thank fuck. I was about to call Uncle James or Uncle Thomas.

"You didn't look like a serial killer."

Pike's face grows serious as he kicks back into the booth, crossing his arms over his chest, showing off that ink and those muscles. "And what does a killer look like?"

"Fuck if I know, but not you." I smile because he's right, but I feel a lecture about to start, and I'm not going to listen. "I'm alive and breathing."

"Because it was me you left with. Anyone else and shit could've been way different."

I lean forward, pushing my empty plate to the side, and stare at the hottie who's now preaching to me on personal safety. "You're not my father, Pike, and while I appreciate the lecture, it's not needed. I was looking for a good time, and while it didn't end the way I'd planned, shit turned out just fine."

We're headed to Froggy's in an hour. Meet us there, and bring the hot guy and his friends if he has any.

"Fair enough."

"Now, my friends are going to Froggy's if you want to go too. But I imagine after last night, you probably want to ditch me for someone else. So, if you can just drop me there, you can do your thing and I'll do mine."

"You going to pull that shit you did last night with someone else tonight?"

I shrug and give him my best poker face. "I don't know. The day is young, and the night is long."

Pike's jaw tightens and his eyes flash. "I'm coming," he says quickly.

"Don't put yourself out or anything. I don't need a bodyguard, especially not someone I don't even know. I've survived this long without you watching over my shoulder. I think I'll last another night."

Pike leans forward, our knuckles touching on top of the table. He studies me. "I know you don't need me to watch over you, but if you're going home with anyone, it's going to be me, darlin'. We never finished what we started last night, and I'm a man who likes to follow through."

"That's so romantic," I tease, rolling my eyes.

"You want romance, I'll give you romance. You want to fuck, I'm the man to fuck you. Whatever you want, I'll be the one giving it to you."

"Why?" I blurt out, wondering why this hot-as-fuck biker guy wants to saddle himself with me all day.

"Because you seem hell-bent on a good time, and there's no one more equipped to give you that good time than me. You want to let your hair down and get wild, baby, I'll be right there with you. The one thing I won't do—" he touches his hand to his chest "—is let another man be the one to give it to you."

I suck in a breath, feeling like he's punched me straight in the gut. I should hate him. I should tell him to go to hell. I can have fun with any guy here. And trust me, there're thousands of them here this week to pick from.

"Okay." He's hot as fuck, and like Mallory said... The best way to get over Erik is to get under someone else.

That someone else might as well be the hottie across from me, who's staring at me like he's starving even though he ate a stack of pancakes it shouldn't be humanly possible to consume.

He leans back and reaches into his pocket. "Let's blow this joint and get the party started, yeah?"

"I don't want to go to the bar."

The thought of drinking right now makes my stomach turn.

"I'll take you anywhere you want."

"Take me back to your hotel room."

CHAPTER 4
PIKE

I OPEN the door to the bathroom, tucking the edge of the towel around my waist and stop dead. Gigi's standing in the middle of the room with her towel still wrapped around her body, hair damp and wild as she pushes her fingers through her locks.

"Do you have a brush?" she asks.

My gaze travels up her body, taking in her long, tanned legs as she turns to face me.

"I don't." I barely get the words out because she's still in the damn towel.

She said she was going to get dressed before I headed into the bathroom to wash off yesterday's grime. When she left the bathroom, she had her dirty clothes pulled tight against her chest like she was using them as a blocker between us.

"Figured you wouldn't with that hair." She ticks her chin upward, smiling at the mess that's on my head. It's always in a state, and I gave up a long time ago trying to tame the style in any way.

I rub the back of my neck, trying to do something with my hands besides ripping the towel off her body and having my way with her. "I can run and get you one."

"No," she says, taking a step closer to me. "Don't go."

I still haven't moved from the doorway to the bathroom. It's like my feet are glued to the floor. Besides my chest heaving and my heart pounding frantically, the only other thing moving on my body is my cock.

She reaches for my face, but I grab her wrist, needing to set her straight. "Darlin', don't start something I'm not sure you want to finish."

The warning is gentle and soft, but necessary. After last night and standing here in our towels now, I want her so badly, I'm aching to bury myself deep inside her.

Her eyes burn with just as much need as mine do. "What if I don't want to stop?" she challenges, stepping even closer so her towel brushes against my chest. "Maybe I want this just as much as you do."

"Maybe isn't a yes, Gigi. I don't want there to be any miscommunication about what's going to happen. I'm wound so tight right now, I might break."

Her free hand moves to my towel, groping my cock through the rough fabric. I suck in a breath and close my eyes, tightening my hold on her wrist. "Gigi."

She moves her fingers up and down my shaft, causing my legs to tremble. "I want you, Pike. I've wanted you since the moment I laid eyes on you."

I open my eyes, peering down at her beautiful face and soft smile. "You don't know what you're asking."

"I'm asking you to fuck me." She tightens her grip, moving her hand faster until I'm so hard, I'm almost panting. "I know exactly what I'm asking, Pike. But if you can't give it to me..."

"I can give you everything." I lift my hand to cup her face and angle my mouth close to hers. "I want to taste your mouth." I run my thumb along her bottom lip. "I want to taste you everywhere."

She moves her hand to the top of my towel, pulling the material apart as my lips crash down on hers, getting the taste I've been dying for since last night. I slide my hand into her hair, holding her face to mine as I swallow her moans and my own. Her towel falls away, pooling near our feet as her skin touches mine. It's like a million little electric shocks go off at once.

Her hands are on my hips as I slide my other hand to her back, memorizing the dip of her spine as I move my palm to her ass. "So fuckin' soft," I murmur against her lips.

"So fuckin' hard," she murmurs back as her fingertips move up to my abdomen, toying with my V.

My stomach clenches at the way her fingers trail over my flesh, sending goose bumps scattering across my body.

She's hesitant. I can tell by her movements this isn't her usual thing. Most women would be grabbing at my cock, but not her. She's busy touching my body, exploring what I have elsewhere and not what's the usual main attraction.

I pull my lips away, knowing I have to give her another out. She's a big talker, but maybe the reality of what we're about to do has finally sunk in. "We don't have to do this."

She shakes her head, staring up at me with hooded eyes. "I want this. I just need to take it slow, okay?"

"I'm not looking for fast, darlin'. You take all the time you want because I know I will." I smirk, our faces only inches from each other.

There's something so intense about staring at someone this close. Something so intimate about it. Rarely have I ever done this with anyone. I never care about the emotion in their eyes or the tenderness they need. But Gigi is different. I am different with her.

She lets out a shaky breath, lifting up on her tiptoes to give me her lips again, and this time, I don't hold anything back. I slide my tongue along her bottom lip, loving the way she tastes of mint and strawberries.

Then she pulls away. "I have to be honest with you," she says, holding my sides but keeping her eyes locked on mine. "I haven't been with a lot of guys, and I was always in a relationship if I slept with someone. This is all new to me. I need you to know…"

"I don't need to know anything."

"But what if I'm bad?" She blinks up at me like she's surprised by my words.

"You can never be bad at anything. There's no such thing. Do what feels right and good. Do what comes naturally, and I promise you it'll be good for the both of us."

She nods, seeming satisfied by my statement. I've never understood that way of thinking. I've never had a bad time in the sack, no matter the level of skill or number of partners the person has had before me. I don't care if she's been with one or a dozen guys as long as her mind, hands, and body are only on me.

"No more talking." We've already said too many words, and I can't go another minute without my body attached to hers in some form.

Her tits press against my chest as I take her mouth again, claiming her long and deep with the kiss, showing her how I feel and how badly I want her, experience be damned.

She slowly slides her hands over my stomach, moving to my abdomen before gliding them across my trail of hair, finding my hard cock. The moan that escapes her lips along with the soft warmth of her skin makes my dick twitch in anticipation.

"You're big," she mumbles against my mouth because I don't give her a chance to get away this time. I knead her ass cheeks, humming my appreciation at the way her hand strokes along my shaft. When her fingertips find my piercings, she freezes.

"Oh. My. God." She pushes me away with one hand, cock still firmly in her grasp with the other. Her eyes are glued to my dick and are wide, her mouth hanging open. "I didn't know you had…"

I move my hips toward her, and my cock bobs, showing off the shiny jewelry that has often gotten a mixed reaction from the ladies.

"Can I?"

I don't think anyone's ever asked for a better view, but if that's what she wants, she can do whatever the fuck she pleases. "Anything you want."

She folds her legs, kneeling before me on top of the towel that had fallen near our feet. I place my hands on my hips, stopping myself from pulling her in and jamming my dick, piercing and all, across her pretty pink tongue.

"You've never seen a pierced dick?" I ask.

She shakes her head. "Not this close, but I have seen them. Never touched one, though."

"Figured all the college boys were into shit like this."

"Shh," she says, peering up for a moment with her eyebrows drawn together before she goes back to staring at my cock. "It's an apadravya, right?"

"For a chick who hasn't seen many, you sure got the name nailed."

She shrugs, toying with the metal. "I know a little about this type of stuff. It's always fascinated me."

I can't take my eyes off her fingers as they move around the tip of my dick. The girl is a conundrum. She's innocent. There's no denying that. It's not an act either. But she knows shit too. Shit someone with her level of innocence probably shouldn't know. I don't ask because I don't care. There's a hot chick on the floor, eye-to-eye with my junk, touching me. That's all that fucking matters.

Her tongue pokes out of her mouth, sweeping across her bottom lip, and I grip my sides harder, trying to control myself. "I've heard it's pleasurable."

"There's one way to find out." I'm about done with show-and-tell, but then I remember I have to be patient. Something I've never been known to be.

"Can I lick it?"

Oh. My. Fucking. God. This girl is too much. "Of course." I'm not a fucking idiot. "Deep-throat it if you want."

She gazes up the length of my body, looking small kneeling before me. "Let's not get extreme."

"A guy can hope." I smirk and then hold my breath as she leans forward, that cute-ass soft tongue coming out from between her lips, reaching for a taste of my cock.

I can't take my eyes off her. The curve of her breasts as she moves toward me. The slenderness of her fingers as they wrap around my shaft, milking me as she tentatively touches the tip of her tongue to the head of my cock.

My body rocks forward, wanting her warmth and the wetness only her mouth can deliver. I close my eyes because watching this sweet, pure girl take me into her mouth is too much for me to handle.

"Fuck," I hiss as she slides her tongue over the tip, across the shaft, taking me slowly, inch by inch between her lips.

The warmth is instantly gone. "Did I do something wrong?"

I blink down at her in confusion. "Don't stop, darlin'. It was the closest to heaven I've ever been."

She smiles, liking the praise, but then something passes across her face. "I've been told I suck. Not in the good way either."

"Whoever told you that should be shot. There's no such thing as a bad blow job." Technically, I'm lying. There is such a thing, but I doubt this girl could do anything wrong.

Her tongue's back on my dick a moment later, and I breathe a sigh of relief. If there's any more talking, I might lose my mind.

Her lips close around my shaft as she sucks me deep. No teeth with the perfect amount of suction and tongue. I'm in heaven, loving the way she uses her hand, not leaving an inch of my cock untouched.

"Just like that, baby." I tangle my fingers in her hair. I can't keep my hands to myself anymore. I want to touch her. I need to touch her.

"Darlin'," I say softly in a shaky breath as her tongue dances around the piercing, sending shock waves throughout my system. "Up, baby."

She blinks up at me with my cock still nestled between her lips, eyebrows drawn inward like she's confused.

"I want to taste you."

The corners of her mouth tip up, grazing the underside of my shaft with her teeth. I don't wince or grimace at the sensation because the last thing I want this girl to think is that I'm not enjoying myself.

I reach down, helping her stand before wrapping my arm around her back, hauling her toward the bed. My mouth is back on hers as our bodies fall backward, bouncing when we hit the bed. She lands on top of me, but she never stops kissing me as her hands slide across my shoulders, holding on to me.

I roll, pinning her underneath me, careful not to crush her with my weight. I kiss a line down her jaw to her neck, licking at the soft skin below her ear. Her fingernails dig into the skin of my upper back as she arches her back like she's offering her chest up to me and not satisfied with my mouth anywhere else.

Lifting up on one elbow, I stare down at her tanned skin, shining like a beacon underneath me. I slide my finger across the swell of her breasts as her breathing accelerates, and her eyes are fixed on me.

"You're so beautiful." I gaze down her body, letting my eyes linger on her wonderland of flesh.

"I could lose..."

I shake my head. "You're perfect the way you are." Suddenly, I'm a Chatty Cathy too, whispering sweet nothings to a girl I'll never see again.

She's fierce, yet unsure about everything sexually, almost like she's a virgin. I gulp at the possibility, hoping like fuck she's just had dipshit college boys in her life and that she's not entirely new to sex.

"Have you really done this before?"

She nods, giving me a small smile. "Yes, Pike. I'm not a virgin. I just…"

"Had shit boyfriends."

She nods again. "It was never like this."

"Like what, darlin'?"

"Slow and soft."

Fuck.

The last time I took it slow and soft was back in high school when I didn't know my ass from my dick. But here I am, going slow and soft for this girl because she needs it. Lying here naked with her, I'd do anything she asked without question.

"But I ache, Pike." She shifts her legs, rubbing her knees together and driving me crazy with desire. "I ache for you like I've never ached before."

"I'm going to make you feel good," I promise, leaning forward and swiping my tongue across her nipple.

She gasps, pushing her tits upward and against my mouth as I run my tongue around the outside edge of her nipple.

She burrows her fingers in my hair, pulling my head down against her skin. "Don't tease me, Pike."

I gaze down at her, noticing her rosy cheeks and the sheen of sweat across her skin. "I'm not teasing, I'm savoring, darlin'."

She growls a response, but I ignore her, going back to what I was doing and enjoying the fuck out of it. Her skin is warm and smooth against my lips, but her nipples are hot and hard on my tongue. Her body shakes as I close my lips around the tip, sucking with the right amount of pressure to drive her wild and have her on the brink.

Her nails claw my skin as her legs rub together, her body begging and needing more as she writhes underneath me.

I slide my hand down her side, making my way to her brown curls before slipping between her legs. Her knees fall to the sides, meeting the bed and giving me access to all of her.

The girl is wet. Almost dripping with need and I've barely touched her. I have to test her and figure out what she can take before I try to fuck her. The last thing I need is to hurt her, and she seems so sketchy and unsure about sex, I'm not sure I believe her depth of experience.

She rocks into my hand as I slide my fingers through her folds, parting her skin and stroking the pad of my thumb over her clit. She gasps, jumping like I shocked her at the contact.

I glance up, but she smirks with hazy, lust-filled eyes. "Don't stop," she begs me.

I mumble words against her skin, nipple still in my mouth, so I don't make a bit of sense and I don't care. I'm too busy exploring her flesh, tasting her body, and enjoying the fuck out of myself to speak or stop.

She tenses as I slide a finger down through her wetness and around the promised land, but as soon as I start to push inside, she relaxes and spreads her legs even wider.

She's tight, but not virginal tight. She may not have been with too many guys, but I'm not the first one to enter this territory. She doesn't even grimace as I push my finger all the way inside her body, relishing the warmth of her skin on mine. She moves with me, meeting every thrust of my fingers as her pussy contracts around me.

I pull out, adding a second finger, going slower this time and sucking harder on her nipple. She moans, pushing her ass upward and head backward like she's in heat.

"God, Pike. I want you so bad. Fuck me. Fuck me, please. I can't wait any longer. Don't make me beg."

I lift my head, fingers still buried inside her, rubbing her G-spot. "I'll never make you beg." I smirk, loving the way this girl reacts to everything I say and do. "Unless we're playing that game."

"Not now. Please."

I reach across her, grabbing the condom I'd left there last night when I thought I had a sure thing coming back to my room. Gigi moves both hands to my cock, jerking me as I place the wrapper between my teeth and tear it open.

"You want the honors?" I ask her, loving the way she touches me.

She shakes her head and pulls away, leaving my cock feeling cold and alone. "Not with the metal. You do it."

I lean back, watching every movement. I make quick work of the condom after years of practice, barely noticing the piercing as I roll it down over the tip and shaft, readying myself for what I know is going to feel like heaven.

She places her feet on the bed, spreading her legs open as I slide between her thighs and line up our bodies. I can't take my eyes off her face as I lean forward on my elbows, ready to fuck this girl, but knowing I have to take my time.

I lower my mouth to hers, kissing her soft and gentle as my cock nudges her opening. She moans again as I press inside slowly. Inch by inch, I sheath my cock in the warmth of her pussy, causing my eyes to roll back from the tightness and pressure I haven't experienced with anyone else in a long time.

Her fingernails are on my skin, raking across my back as I push all the way inside until I'm fully seated. She gasps into my mouth, and I swallow down her pleasure, taking it as my own.

I rock my hips, thrusting in and out as slowly as I can with as hard as I am. Sweat breaks out across my skin as the mix of pleasure and torture washes over me. She locks her ankles around my ass, holding me to her, not giving me much leeway to be aggressive.

I roll my hips, moving any way I can in this position. She pulls her lips away, staring up at me as I rock into her. I thought our moment was intense before, but it's nothing compared to this. Being buried balls deep, staring into each other's eyes, I'm momentarily winded from the intimacy.

My heart pounds as I realize I could like this girl. Not just like her, I could spend more than one night staring into her big blue eyes, listening to her babble about whatever she'll talk about. I could spend forever between these legs, fucking her, and never get bored.

I push my thoughts out of my mind, needing to stay in the moment and not think about tomorrow. We never promised each other more than this. More than a fuck at a shitty-ass motel in Daytona. She's a career girl with hopes and dreams that probably didn't include a guy covered in tats, working nights at a tattoo shop.

Get a grip, Pike. My mind keeps straying, and I have to remind myself to let shit go. Gigi grounds me, bringing me back to the moment when her tongue runs along the skin near my collarbone.

"Harder," she pleads, digging her heels firmly in my ass.

I pull back, breaking the bond her ankles have around my back and slam into her.

"Yes!" she screams, bucking against me, grinding her pussy against my body. "Fuck yes!"

It doesn't take but a few more minutes for me to teeter on the edge of orgasm. With one hand, I reach between us, rubbing her clit as I thrust inside her, deep and sharp, quickening the pace each time.

She gasps for air as her body locks up, following me over the cliff into bliss. "Jesus," I murmur as I nearly collapse on top of her.

"Again," she says almost immediately.

"Little tiger," I whisper, staring down at the most beautiful girl I've ever seen.

"I hope you're up for more, big boy, because I'm nowhere near done."

"I could go all night."

She pushes me backward, climbing on top of me. "Let's see if you mean what you say."

I slide out from underneath her as she paws at me like she's going to pull me back to the bed. "I'm going to need to get rid of this condom and get another."

"Take your time. I'll just stare at your ass and touch myself."

I turn, looking over my shoulder to see she's a girl of her word. "Fucking incredible," I whisper, running to the bathroom because I'm nowhere near done fucking her.

CHAPTER 5
GIGI

FIFTEEN MONTHS LATER

THE DAY I stepped off the stage with the diploma in my hand, I felt like I was finishing a chapter and starting a new one. The grown-up part of my life I'd been waiting for since I was a little kid.

The only thing I'd ever dreamed about was working at Inked. My artistic skills, I clearly got from my dad. He'd sit with me for hours when I barely reached his hip, watching me draw picture after picture as I tried to copy his work. He was a patient teacher and an even better father. There isn't a time in my life I remember art not being part of my world.

My poor mother didn't have a creative bone in her body. She was a numbers girl, and math bored the crap out of me...much to her disappointment. She dreamed of me growing up and becoming some dull corporate suit, slaving away for someone else instead of being tied to Inked.

After four years of college and four summers interning at Inked, I am finally ready to take my rightful spot, or should I say chair, at the shop.

"I don't understand why you need to move out," my mom says as I sit down at the kitchen table with a cup of coffee, trying to get time to pass a little quicker.

I can't wait to get to the shop. My uncle Bear decided he would be my first official customer, and I couldn't be happier. But I could probably ink a piece of shit on him, and he'd still love it.

"I love living here, Ma, but I want to have my own place. You're great and Dad is the best, but I haven't lived under your roof and with your rules in four years. I just think it's the next step I have to take in my new life. Living here feels like taking a step backward, and I'm all about moving forward."

"Can't you stay a few weeks? I've missed you." She leans against the counter and sips her coffee, looking just as beautiful as ever.

"I'm picking up my keys before work today, but it'll take me a few days to get everything in order, so I'll be here until the place is ready to move in."

"Take your time, baby," she says softly before letting out a long and very dramatic sigh. "Make sure it's perfect before you officially move out."

I want to tell her that I moved out four years ago, but I don't. My mom is a big softy, and by the way she's looking at me, she's about to cry.

"Did you move back home after college?" I ask her.

She shakes her head. "I love my parents, but there was no way I could ever live under their roof again. I knew once I left for college, I'd never go back."

"Even if they were great parents, could you have gone backward after having a taste of freedom?"

She slides onto the chair next to me and places her cup on the table. "I don't think I could've gone back." Her lips pull downward because she realizes where I'm coming from, and no matter what she says, I won't change my mind. "Maybe we could build a guesthouse out back for you."

"Mom, come on now. I already signed my lease. And I'm sorry, I love you both, but living in the backyard won't work for me."

It's a sweet gesture and completely my mom, but in no way,

shape, or form will that type of living arrangement ever work for me. I'm already going to be spending all day working with my dad. The last thing I want is to see him every night, checking up on me, and living under the Gallo microscope.

"I worry about you living alone."

"I'll be fine, Ma. Tamara is going to live with me for the summer, and when she's home on break too. If all goes well, when she graduates next year, she'll move in with me too. Where's Dad?" I change the subject because there's no way I'm living at home, and I know the mention of my cousin's name will get Mom off my back...at least for a little while.

She wraps her hand around her coffee mug and stares out the window overlooking the backyard. "He went in early. There's a new artist starting today, and he wants to train him before everyone gets there."

"Maybe I should be there too. Why didn't Dad ask me to go?"

Mom laughs. "Baby, you grew up in that place, and you've been working there for four summers. I'd hardly call you a new employee." She laughs and brings her gaze back to me. "I'm pretty sure you could train this boy yourself."

I push away from the table, about to stand, when she covers my hand with hers.

"Stay a little longer. You don't have to be there for thirty minutes, and I feel like we never have quiet time like this together."

"I don't want to be the last one there on my first day, Mom. How about we go shopping on my day off and buy some stuff for my new apartment?"

I'm grasping at straws here, but the last thing I want to do is sit here another twenty minutes, listening to my mother hem and haw about how I shouldn't move out. I figure if I ask her to help decorate my new place, she'll feel more invested, or at the very least, like she helped me.

That's the thing about Suzy Gallo. She's not one to sit idly by when her loved ones are in need. It doesn't matter that I only need help to pick out the perfect throw pillow or the best pots and pans, she wants to be included.

Right on cue, her face lights up. "I would love that. I know all the best places we can go too. We'll make a day of it."

"It's a date, Mom. I'm off Friday, if that works. But if not, I completely understand."

"Luna and Rosie have cheerleading camp starting on Wednesday," Mom says, looking pained and moderately horrified that her two daughters are cheerleaders. "So, I have all day on Friday to be with you."

"Perfect." I push away from the table and walk toward the sink. "I better run. The landlord is probably waiting for me, and I want to make a good impression."

Mom follows me, leaving her coffee mug where it was sitting on the table. She leans against the counter, staring at me as I rinse and place my mug in the dishwasher. "I'm proud of you, sweetheart. I'm proud of the independent woman you've become."

My insides warm. "That's because I had two kick-ass parents."

Her smile falters.

I know she wants to chastise me for my crude language, because she's never been one for cussing.

"We want nothing but the best for you."

I lean over and kiss her cheek because, hell, I love my mother. "I couldn't have asked for a better mother. I mean it, Mom."

She wraps her arms around me, hauling me close. "I love you, baby. I can't believe you're old enough to move out. I never wanted this day to come, but now that it has, I couldn't be prouder."

That's my mom. She's full of all the goodness in the world. She never has a mean thing to say about anyone or anything. She wears rose-colored glasses when it comes to life. There are times where she's a little overprotective and worried about everything for no good reason, but I wouldn't change a thing about her.

"I have to run, Mom." I pull away from her embrace even

though she tries to squeeze me tighter. "I don't want to be late on my first day."

Mom laughs. "Well, at least you know the owners. I'm pretty sure they won't fire you if you're a few minutes late."

"Mom, I don't want to be treated any different."

"Different from whom, baby girl? Besides Kat, everyone is family and works by their own rules."

I shrug. "The new guy. I don't want to set a bad example, ya know?"

She nods. "Go and have a great first day at work."

It's all silly. I'd worked at Inked for four summers, but interning is entirely different from earning my seat at the shop. Today feels like the first day of my adult life. No more school. No more classes. No more homework. Only freedom and time lie before me.

I had the same feeling the day my parents dropped me off at college. I watched their SUV pull away, and I waved at them frantically, filled with excitement and possibility. I had so much freedom, I didn't know what to do with myself the first few days. I didn't have a schedule. No curfew. No reporting my whereabouts to anyone. The only rigidity I had in my day were classes, but they were a breeze and mildly interesting.

But this, my first job and new place, will be the first time I get to make all the rules. I set my own hours at Inked, have my own place, and don't have to walk around my apartment in anything at all if I don't feel like getting dressed.

By the time I make it to the leasing office, Mr. McNamara is waiting at his desk, paperwork ready and keys lying right next to the pen. "Are you ready to sign, Miss Gallo?" he asks as I slide into the seat across from him.

"I've never been more ready for anything in my life, sir."

Five minutes and a dozen signatures later, I have the keys in my hand. I thought graduation was the sweetest moment of my life, but I have to admit, being officially handed the keys to my new place tops even that.

"Shoot me over an email of any issues you find in the apart-ment. I'll get them fixed right away and add them to your paper-work, just in case. I did a walk-through this morning and found everything to be in working order, but it's still important you do the same in case you spot something I didn't."

"I'll be back after work later and will check everything out. I won't be staying here for a few days, though."

He smiles, but I know I'm rambling, and this man couldn't care less if I am going to use the apartment or not. The only thing he cares about is getting his rent check on time every month.

"Whatever you'd like, Miss Gallo."

I thank him with a firm handshake, something my dad taught me to always do, and excuse myself because I only have a few minutes to make it to the shop and not be late.

I blast the radio as I drive to Inked, weaving in and out of traf-fic, belting out the lyrics to "Truth Hurts."

The day just started, but it can't possibly get any freaking better. I have the keys to my new place, and I am headed to my new job. I've dreamed about this moment for so many years, it feels surreal to finally be living it.

CHAPTER 6
PIKE

"ANY QUESTIONS?" my new boss asks after giving me the rundown on how he likes shit to go.

I can't blame the man. He is the owner. He spent years with his family building up Inked to be the most sought-after tattoo parlor in the state of Florida. Their reputation is what drew me to this place. Well, that and starting over after shit went south in the last place I settled down.

"Nothing yet."

"My kid is starting today too. She's been interning during her summer breaks, but today, she officially has a chair. So, you won't be the only newbie in the place."

"Cool."

Fucking great. The first week at any new place is hard, but add in the owner's kid, and shit can become a whole lot more complicated in a hurry.

"She's bossy as fuck, but just remember she's not your boss, I am."

I nod because what he's saying is technically true, but I'm pretty sure the kid will have his ear. If I fuck up and get off on the wrong foot with her, she can and probably will make my life miserable. I have to decide if I want to make friends with her, whoever the hell she is, or if I want to steer clear of her entirely to lessen the chances I'll get my ass canned in a heartbeat.

"I put you and her next to each other. I figure you two can help each other out. I know you're not new to this business and the craft, but sometimes people become intimidated working with so many family members."

I rub the back of my neck and try to pull on a smile. "It won't be a problem," I mutter, but nothing about the way I say the words is convincing.

"I'll be right next to you two, so I can be close if you have issues or questions."

Maybe I'm in over my head here. Working at a place like this, one with a crazy-good reputation, has always been a goal. No one wants to work at a run-down shop, scraping by and waiting for new clients to walk in the door. Inked has a two-month wait before someone can plop their ass in a chair and get the tat they've been craving.

The front door opens, and a beautiful woman steps inside, carrying a box of donuts and talking so fast on her phone, I can barely make out the words she's saying.

"That's Izzy, my sister. She's a ballbuster, so watch out for that one." Joe, my boss, laughs. "She may look small and weak, but the girl will no sooner have your balls in her hands, making you wish you could black out from the pain."

My eyes widen. "I'll steer clear of her, then."

I can't stop looking at her, though. There's something familiar in the way she talks, hand moving through the air like the person on the other end can actually see her. She's wearing a skintight white skirt, a pair of kick-ass boots with a heel long and pointy enough, she could do some damage with the fucking thing if she wanted. For an older woman, she's smoking hot.

Joe laughs louder. "There's no such thing. Once you're on her radar, you're on it. There's no hiding. So, prepare for that because, guarantee, she'll have her sights set on you at some point. I just hope, for your sake, she lets you get your feet wet before she decides to make a pet project out of you."

"Sounds great," I mumble, finally tearing my gaze away from the person who's going on my list of people to avoid while working here. "I'm sure we'll be great friends."

"Just don't get too chummy. She'll have you on the ground, begging for mercy, but it's her husband who will have you pleading for your very life."

Sounds fantastic. "Got it."

Izzy places the donuts on the front counter before telling the person on the phone she'll talk to him later. As soon as she ends the call and tosses her phone next to the donuts, her eyes are on me. "Well, well. I see the new kid finally showed."

"Ma'am," I greet and avoid correcting her on the fact that I'm nowhere near close to being a kid.

I'm twenty-seven and have been on my own for over a decade, with no one around to look out for me even longer than that. But I do the smart thing and keep my mouth shut.

"Ma'am?" Her mouth gapes open. "For real? What do I look like, your mama?"

I can't hold back the smirk as I run my fingers through my hair, trying to do something…anything…not to put my goddamn foot in my mouth. "No, ma'am. My mama looks nothing like you."

I can feel the judgment in them as she tries to make a decision if she likes me or wants to rip out my throat already with her blood-red fingernails.

"He just had to poke that bear," Joe mumbles behind me.

"I brought donuts for you assholes. That goes for you too, *kid*." She smiles.

I know she's going to call me that forever, just like she'll always be ma'am to me because that's how I was raised. As a Southern man, you don't have good manners unless you call a lady a proper name out of respect. I may have shit parents, but my grandmother taught me to be a gentleman. Because if I didn't, she'd smack me right upside the head.

I glance back at my boss, but he only shakes his head slowly like I need to let the conversation die and take what she's saying like a man. I make a quick note that Izzy, who's also Joe's sister, is the one who rules the roost.

"Where's my baby girl?" Izzy asks as she walks by us. "I thought she'd be early."

"She had to pick up the keys to her new place before work, but I'm sure she'll be here any minute."

I head to my station, unpacking a few personal items and the tools I brought with me that I've carried from place to place for the last nine years.

"She's really moving out?"

"Yep. I can't convince her to stay."

I keep my head down and do my best not to listen, but I also want to know the family dynamics so I can figure out which land mines to avoid in the future. Plus, I never had a family that could stand one another in even small doses, let alone work together every day. The entire thing is fascinating and completely foreign.

"She's independent and grown, Joe. You had to know this was coming. Once she had a taste of freedom, how could she ever move back?" Izzy says, grabbing the only donut with sprinkles and then proceeding to pick one off and throw the pink sugar into her mouth.

Joe sighs. "I know, but she's my little girl. I thought I had a few more years of waking up to see that beautiful face." He leans back in his chair, crossing his arms. "You know what I miss the most?"

"Her attitude?" Izzy laughs.

"Hell no. I blame you for all her piss and vinegar, sister. I miss sitting with her at the kitchen table, drawing together and talking about life."

Izzy leans against the counter, still picking apart the donut and eating it in small bites. "You can still have those moments. They just won't be random."

Their gazes move toward the front of the shop as an engine roars, and a sleek black pickup pulls into a parking spot out front.

"She's here," Izzy says, tossing the massacred donut into the trash can and brushing her hands together. "Finally, some new life in this place. The kid here—" she tips her head to me "—and the other kid are just what we need to liven things up around here."

I grumble under my breath, busying myself again. I have my first client booked in thirty minutes, and it's a piece that'll take me all day plus another session to finish. My back's already aching thinking about the hours upon hours I'll be hunched over the woman's back, giving her the angel wings she's requested.

"Sorry I'm late," the female voice says, coming through the front door.

"No problem, doll," Izzy, her aunt, says.

I doubt I'd get the same response if I'd shown up late today too. But that's what you get for being family. Special privileges are the way it goes. Who knows if this girl has any real talent or if she rode on the coattails of her father, not earning the chair based on her skills.

"Thanks, Auntie," the girl says as she makes her way toward her father and me. "Hey, Daddy."

Joe rises from his chair as I watch his boots move across the floor in front of me toward a pair of sexy boots much like Izzy's. "Are you ready for your first day?" he asks her.

"I've been ready for this day since I was a little girl."

I'm sure she has. Most kids dream of following in their father's footsteps. I, for one, did not. My dad was the only attorney in a small town. He was also a bastard and not someone I ever wanted to be like. As soon as I could, I got out and as far away from him and my mother as possible.

"I have someone I'd like you to meet," Joe says, and I know it's my cue.

I stand slowly, running my hands down the front of my jeans before I finally lift my gaze upward.

No fucking way.

My eyes widen, and so do hers.

"Gigi, this is Pike." Joe motions toward me with his hand. "Pike, this is my little girl, Gigi."

Fuck me.

She looks like a deer in headlights as her mouth opens and closes, but no words come out.

She can't be here.

I run my fingers through my hair, staring at the beautiful girl I'd tasted and fucked more than once, but then she vanished without even leaving me a phone number. All I had was a first name and memories after Daytona last year. Hell, they were some great fucking memories too.

I narrow my eyes as I sweep my gaze from her face and down her body, remembering exactly how perfect her skin is underneath the scraps of cloth she's wearing. I don't linger on her body too long before I bring my eyes back to hers. "It's a pleasure to meet you, Gigi."

"Mm-hmm. You too, Pike," she says like the words are acid, stinging her tongue. She's staring at me as the shock wears off and the reality of what we've done in the past is hitting her square in the face.

"Do you two know each other?" Izzy asks as she walks to our side, staring at us, but neither of us looks at her because we're too busy gawking at each other.

"Don't be silly," Joe says, wrapping an arm around his *little girl.* "Pike isn't from around here. He's new in town."

I fucked the boss's daughter. Way to go, big man.

"Are you sure you don't know him?" Izzy asks Gigi.

Gigi shakes her head, eyes still locked on me. "Never met the gentleman," she says easily, lying without hesitation.

She doesn't know Pike the gentleman. She's well acquainted

with Pike the man. She'd spent days in my bed, pleasuring me and taking what she wanted without apology.

"Iz, I had a question about the schedule. You got a minute before we get slammed?" Joe asks.

"Sure," Izzy says, drawing out the word but not moving as quickly as Joe does. I can feel her eyes on us for a moment before she finally steps away and follows Joe into the office.

Gigi and I stand here, staring at each other, listening to the slow march of her family members' feet across the tile until they're on the other side of the shop.

"It's far too quiet in here," Izzy yells before loud music fills the shop.

Fuck my life.

"Are you stalking me?" Gigi whispers, getting right up in my face.

"Don't be fucking crazy." I wave her off and walk back toward my chair.

Gigi's right on my ass, practically glued to my back. "Don't fucking lie to me. You came here on purpose."

I turn to face her, leaning my head down so our faces are close. "Babe," I whisper, staring straight into her eyes so she knows what I'm saying is one hundred percent the truth. "Let's get a few things straight. You're a great fuck and you have a hot little bod, but I'm not chasing a piece of ass all the way across the state because I need another taste. I'm also not planting roots and finding a new job just to get closer to that piece of ass either."

She blanches. "You're crude."

"I thought that's what you liked best about me. At least, that's what you said when you were riding my cock and moaning my name, baby."

CHAPTER 7
GIGI

HIS WORDS ARE like a punch to the gut. There's truth to what he's said, but that doesn't mean it isn't devastating. I'd thought about Pike for months after spring break last year. Months of lying awake in my bed, replaying all the naughty things we did together, touching myself to the memories.

I knew Pike wasn't a gentleman, but the words he just threw in my face prove that simple fact.

There was nothing about him that screamed manners in the time we spent together. But there was a sweet side to him when he wanted to show it, which wasn't very often in the short amount of time I spent in his bed. He was a conundrum to me. I knew very little about the man.

Even though we spent days together, we didn't talk too much about our personal lives. I knew a few basic details about the badass biker with a cock so damn good, he could charge admission for a single ride.

I raise my hand, about to strike him, when he grabs my wrist and holds it in midair. "You're an asshole, Pike," I hiss, ripping my hand from his grip. I take a step back, knowing I need more space between us. "I don't know what game you're playing, but I'm not interested in spending more time with you."

He smirks. The bastard actually smirks when I say those words. His gaze moves toward the office where my father and Izzy are talking. "Babe," he pauses and steps closer. "I don't play games. I don't need to." He lifts his hand and runs the backs of his fingers across my cheek, but I don't move away. "And based on the color of your cheeks and the way you're looking at me, I'd say you'd like to be back in my bed and riding my cock."

I slam my palm into his chest, knocking him backward because kneeing him in the balls isn't an option. At least, not now, but I'm not above using that move to bring him to his knees. Pike's not fazed in the slightest. He just stands there, still smirking like an asshole, looking just as delicious as he did fifteen months ago.

"I will not be *riding your cock* ever again, asshat. You scratched an itch when I needed you, but I'm so over this—" I wave my hand between us. "Whatever we had, no matter how short, is all we'll ever have. Don't even look at me sideways, or I'm going to make you wish you hadn't packed up your life for a fresh start. You may have skill, but that doesn't mean my daddy wouldn't fire your ass in a heartbeat. Especially if he knew…"

"How good I fucked you?" He raises an eyebrow.

The growl creeps up my throat and slides out from between my lips before I can stop the sound from leaving my body.

"Everything okay?" Aunt Izzy asks, stepping back into the room.

I nod and turn my face toward her. "Just talking about the shop," I lie.

Her eyes move between Pike and me, and I can tell by the look on her face, she isn't buying what I'm selling. "It looks like a little more than that," she says, running her fingers across her chin.

"Auntie, it's just a little friendly competition between us. We're both starting on the same day, and neither of us wants to look like the bigger asshole…even if that's going to be Pike. You know how men are. They never like to be showed up by a woman."

Izzy walks between us and faces Pike. "Is that all this is?" She stares at him, watching his every facial feature for a tell. I know my aunt, and she misses *nothing*. One misstep and Pike's days could be numbered before he's even had a chance to finish unpacking his tools.

"That's all this is, ma'am."

Oh shit. There are things my aunt hates and then things she loathes. Being called ma'am is a surefire way to set the woman off like she's got a wick coming out of her ass, ready for ignition. She's going to blow like a Roman candle on the Fourth of July.

Her entire body stiffens. "Pike, sweetheart," she says, but her tone isn't friendly, "don't ever call me ma'am. I get where you're coming from, being a Southern gentleman and all."

I snort, but it dies as she glances over her shoulder at me for a moment.

"But around here, I'm Izzy, Iz, or boss. Do not ever, and I mean never, call me ma'am. Got it, kid?"

I pull my lips into my mouth, biting down on them to stop the laughter that's bubbling up the back of my throat. First, because Pike's getting his ass chewed out in the nicest way possible by my aunt, and second, because Izzy just called him a kid.

"I'm sorry, Izzy," Pike says without sarcasm. "I didn't mean to offend you."

"Your looks may get you a free pass with some women, but I'm not so easily charmed by a pretty face or that Southern drawl. Her daddy—" she pitches her thumb toward me "—will be even less impressed if you do something to piss off his daughter. So, word to the wise, kid, either steer clear of Gigi, or learn to make friends with her. You do something to make her mad, and it'll be your made bed you'll have to lie in as the door kicks you in the ass on the way out."

Pike nods, those beautiful green-blue eyes that have haunted my dreams for months showing no emotion. "Got it. Loud and clear, boss."

Izzy smacks her hands together and moves away from Pike. "My work here is done. We have a full schedule today, so it's time to get your asses in gear and your shit set before they walk through the door. No more time for girl talk. You two can finish your bullshit later. Got me?"

I'm staring at Pike, smirking because my aunt shut his shit down, but when I look at her, any glee I felt dies. She's staring right at me, looking like she knows something isn't on the up-and-up.

"There's no bullshit to finish later, Izzy. We're solid, and I don't have time for anything else. Bear's coming in this morning to get that piece he's always wanted."

"Who's Bear?" Pike asks.

"A real badass biker, Pike. You may want to take notes on how one acts instead of being a wannabe." I walk toward my chair and away from Izzy's penetrating stare.

"You two ready?" my dad asks, walking into the main room, completely oblivious to everything that's been happening. "I prepped your station last night, sweetheart. Figured it would make your first day less stressful."

I pop up on my tiptoes and kiss my dad on the cheek. "Thanks, Dad. You're the best." I wrap my arms around him and hug him tightly. I peer over his shoulder, catching Pike's eye and sticking my tongue out at him.

Not the most grown-up thing to do, but I don't care. I'm not into impressing Pike. I've already taken what I wanted, and now whatever we had, which was only a few days, is done. Over. Caput. Finished. There was no dipping my toes back in those waters again, no matter how fabulous the orgasms were.

And they were ridiculously great.

Every orgasm I'd had before Pike, I gave to myself. It had always been me and my hand until Pike rocked my world and showed me how it could be. Or should I say, how it should be.

"I'm here, baby girl," Bear yells as the bell above the door chimes so loud it's like my aunt purposely wants to scare the shit out of everyone every time it rings.

"Back here, Bear," I yell back, trying to be heard over the bell and the death metal my aunt feels is appropriate for this early hour.

By early, I mean noon. Nothing happens in the shop before noon. My family has a different idea of time. In college, I took the earliest classes possible so I'd have the rest of the day free. Now, I'm trying to reset my internal clock to be on Inked time.

"I'll grab Bear," Dad says as he pats me on the shoulder. "Get your shit together because Bear may love you, but don't put it past him to be on your ass on your first day."

I nod. "I'll be fine. I'm ready for whatever he's going to throw at me. You know I've spent my life handling men like him." I smile, because my father's friends aren't for the faint of heart, and I've perfected wrapping them around my little finger.

Bear's no exception. He and my dad go way back. They've been friends for almost thirty years, back to my dad's single life when he was an even bigger badass than he is now.

When I was little, Bear married my great-aunt Fran, my grandfather's sister. No one was happy about their relationship at first, and I remember more than a few screaming matches, but people calmed their shit after a while and gave them free rein to be happy. I love Bear and Aunt Fran together. She is absolutely perfect for him because I don't know if anyone else could *handle* Bear the way she does.

Bear may be a biker, but he is the very best kind of person. He is sweet beyond compare—but only if he likes you and you have a set of tits. He is a horndog. It doesn't matter how old he is or that his beard is almost completely gray, he's never lost his thirst for the females. But he is a one-woman guy, and that woman is my aunt Fran.

"Got a handout for your first client. Must be nice to ride on everyone's coattails," Pike says when we're alone again.

"Why don't you just fuck right off?" I glare at his reflection in the mirror. "I can't help it if my family owns this shop. I'm sorry that pisses you off so badly, but I earned this spot just as much as you did, Pike. So, get the fuck over yourself." I plop down in my chair, pulling the bottle of black ink out of the cabinet I stocked last week, ignoring whatever face I'm sure Pike's making at me.

"There she is," Bear says as he walks into the back, holding out his arms, waiting for me to jump into them like I did when I was a little girl. "Come and give me some love, baby girl."

"Hey, Uncle." I smile at Pike so he'll eat shit. I want him to know that I plan to have everyone eating out of my hands, whether they're related or not. The only person who's not going to like me is Pike, and for that...I don't give a shit. "I've missed you."

Bear hugs me tightly. "Not as much as I missed you."

Pike's gaze flicks upward as he slowly shakes his head, muttering something under his breath. I can't wipe the smile off my face, because knowing he's annoyed has me over-the-fucking-moon ecstatic.

I pull away, still holding on to Bear's arms. "You finally ready to let me scar you for life?"

Bear's eyes light up. "Been waiting for you to leave your mark on me for years, kid."

"Still putting it on your shoulder?" I ask.

"Well, it's either there or my ass. I figured I'd save your young eyes and stick with the shoulder."

I love my uncle, but there's no way in hell I'd tattoo his ass. I know it comes with the job. Men and women will walk through the door and ask for ink in places no human should have to see, but I am not prepared to go there with Bear. I'd never be able to sit across from him at another family dinner or holiday and not think about his pasty white ass.

"I have your design all ready." I grab my sketch pad from my bag and flip through the pages until I find his design. "I'm so excited for you to finally see it. I can make any changes you want." I tear out the page and hand it to him.

Bear holds the paper with both hands, gaze sweeping up and down and back up. His mouth twists at the corners, and his pink lips disappear, replaced by his white teeth. "Damn. You did good."

I let out the breath I've been holding because I wasn't sure if Bear would like the design, and I knew he wouldn't hold back. I may be his niece, but one thing Bear isn't is a liar. He doesn't sugar-coat shit. He doesn't spare anyone's feelings, and it's one of the things I love most about him.

I don't like people who are full of shit. Family or not, I want to be told the truth, and if Bear says it, I believe him.

"Do you want black or some color, Uncle?"

"Whatever you want, kiddo. Just not fucking pink." He shakes his head. "I fuckin' hate pink. No purple either. Not into having pansy-ass colors on my skin."

"No chick colors. I got it, Bear. You want it bigger or smaller than it is?" I ask, taking the paper from between his fingers.

"It's perfect. Let's get this show on the road. I have to be home in time to take your aunt Fran to dinner, or she'll have my balls in a sling, sweetheart."

"Get comfortable and take off your shirt. I'll be back in a minute, and we'll get started."

Bear sits down and pulls his shirt over his head before leaning back and throwing his hands behind his head, staring right at Pike. "What's your name, boy?"

I snort as I walk toward the back room to put the design on transfer paper.

"Name's Pike."

"Pike, huh? Where ya from?"

"Tennessee."

I stand close to the door, listening to them shoot the shit and trying to get whatever details I can on Pike.

"That your hog outside?" Bear asks.

"Yep."

"It's nice."

"You look like a man who knows his way around a machine, and that is one of the best."

"Had to cost you a pretty penny. I'm impressed someone your age could save enough for a classic like that."

"I don't spend my money on bullshit. I like a few things in life, and riding is one of them. I don't cheap out when it's something I want, and I wanted that bike since I was a kid."

Bear laughs. "A kid with an attitude. I don't know if this shop can take more, but you're going to fit right in here, Pike."

"So, Gigi's your niece?" Pike asks, and I move closer to the hall.

"By marriage. I've known her since she was born. She's like one of my own, and I can tell by the way you've been looking at her since I walked through the door, you better turn your eyes elsewhere."

"Ain't looking at her, man. She's not my type," Pike lies because from the way Pike fucked me, I'd say I was very much his type.

"She's every man's type," Bear tells him, calling him on his bullshit.

I laugh as I grab the paper, but I don't walk out of the back room yet. I'm enjoying this exchange way too much to interrupt.

"And I know her daddy, and he won't like you staring at his daughter like you want to devour her. So, word to the wise, kid. Look elsewhere. Don't shit where you eat, and do not—and I mean, absolutely do not—make goo-goo eyes at my niece, or you'll be packing up quicker than that young pecker of yours can come."

"Noted," Pike replies.

I cover my mouth to hide my laughter as I stroll back into my station, holding the design, ready to give Bear the best tattoo I can. I also plan to fuck with Pike as much as possible to make the day even more kick-ass.

CHAPTER 8
PIKE

MY CLIENT, Piper, has headphones on, and she's trying her best to last one more hour in my chair before she calls it a day. She's sweating profusely and on the verge of hyperventilation with her eyes squeezed tightly shut.

"It doesn't look like she's going to make it," Joe says, standing behind me and watching over my shoulder.

I don't look up. Every second is precious now, and I'm doing my best to finish the outline of the massive piece before Piper quits. "She said she can take it. I've asked her every ten minutes if she wants to tap out and finish another day."

"She pukes, you're cleaning that shit up," Joe tells me. "You have two hours before your next and last client arrives." He walks away, going to the front of the shop where everyone is standing around, shooting the shit.

Everyone except Gigi. She killed the design on Bear's shoulder and finished four other small pieces on various clients. Each design was better than the last. I'd assumed she'd gotten the chair because she was related and for no other reason. But I was wrong. The girl has talent and tons of it. I have nine more years under my belt than her, but she is so skilled, I would've guessed she'd been doing tattoos for years.

I glance up as Gigi feverishly types away on her phone, tongue poking out, sweeping across the corner of her mouth. She's barely said two words to me since our little chat before the shop opened. It's probably for the best anyway.

Of all the damn shops I could've planted new roots in, why in the hell did it have to be the one where I'd fucked the boss's daughter? I was psyched when I got the call that there was a free chair at Inked because they needed extra hands to keep up with the demand for their services. This is a dream job for me. Every artist wants to be at a place that's brimming with life.

That was my main reason for coming to Inked. That and starting over, getting away from the bullshit of the last five years, and finding a new place to call home.

"I'm done. Stop," Piper groans as she pulls off her headphones, almost making me fuck up a wing tip.

I lean back, looking over the massive piece, knowing the shading will take a fraction of the time the outline did. "We can finish it when we do the shading."

Piper's facial features relax immediately as she sits up, holding her T-shirt against her chest. "I need a month before I can come back and go through this shit again."

I scrub my hand across my face, catching Gigi's eye as she watches us across the room. "Take all the time you need. When you're ready, we'll finish what we started. I've got nothing but time. Let me just cover this piece, and you can go."

Gigi's eyes narrow. I don't know if the words I just spoke were for Piper or Gigi. I don't plan on going anywhere, no matter how badly Gigi says she wants me to. What happened last year between us feels nowhere near finished either.

That's the biggest problem.

I didn't do a damn thing to the chick. At least, nothing she didn't beg for me to do to her. Yet, she's treating me like a piece of shit. A distant memory. A huge fucking mistake.

Piper pulls her shirt over her head as soon as I finish covering the back piece, facing away from me but giving Gigi the full view of her tits. "Can you put me down for one month from today? I want to have something solid in the books before I leave."

"I'll grab you a water and put you down." I stand, stretching my back and legs because they're stiff and ache like a motherfucker.

Piper follows me back to the front, standing on the other side of the counter as I pull up the scheduling software I've had five minutes of training in how to use.

"That piece is going to be killer when it's finished," Izzy tells Piper, chatting with her as I fumble my way through the screens, trying to find next month.

"I'll be happy when it's over. I always forget how much this shit hurts until my ass is in the chair and the needle is pulling at my flesh."

"But it's totally worth it. And Pike does some of the best damn line work I've seen in a long time. You'll be happy when the work is finished and you can show it off to the world."

Piper shakes her head. "This one is for me. I don't plan on showing it off."

"Oh?"

"My husband died last year, and this tattoo is for him."

Izzy gasps. "I'm so sorry. I didn't know."

I glance up as Piper gives Izzy a pained smile. "It's not something I share. I'm still not ready to talk about everything that happened. He always wanted me to get this tat, but I was too much of a pussy to do it until now."

"Well, it's beautiful," Izzy says, placing her hand over Piper's. "The tattoo and the sentiment."

Finally getting the computer program to work, I tell Piper, "There's a spot open on July 5th at noon if that works."

"It's fine." She nods quickly. "We'll be done after that?"

"Yes, ma'am."

I get the side-eye from Izzy, and Piper's face falters for a moment. What the fuck is it with the chicks around here? Why is ma'am such a shitty word? Where I come from, every woman is a ma'am. You'll get yourself smacked upside the head if you call a woman by any other name. But here, in the middle of fucking nowhere Florida, the women act like you're physically hurting them every time you speak the word.

"Just Piper, kid," she throws back my way, just like Izzy did.

"I keep telling him," Izzy says, giving me a satisfied smile.

I scribble the date and time on a business card before handing it to her. "I'll see you in a month, Piper."

"Thanks for helping me push through it today, Pike," she says as she heads toward the door.

I nod, smiling at the pretty lady whose face displays all the layers of pain and grief for the world to see.

"You have just enough time to grab something to eat," Joe says as he stands across the counter in the same spot Piper just was. "Why don't you take Gigi and go grab some dinner?"

"I'm fine." The last thing I need is to be alone with her tonight.

"You both need to eat. I have a client coming in, and no one else is free. Just take Gigi. She knows this area, and maybe you two can be friends. It's always nice to have someone at work to talk to who isn't related."

I don't want to tell him that she and I have nothing much to talk about. We could fuck like monkeys, but beyond that, I'm not sure we have much to say to each other. Based on our earlier conversation, I'd say there are no words left to be spoken.

"I can just grab something next door."

Joe shakes his head. "I want my kid to eat, and it's important to me that you two are friends."

"Joe, let the kids work their own shit out," Izzy tells him, grabbing on to his arm and handling him with her words and body. "You can't force them to like each other."

"Gigi!" Joe yells out like his sister didn't say anything to him.

Gigi's in the front, standing behind her father and glaring at me within a few seconds. "What's up, Dad?"

Joe dips his head in my direction, not turning around to see his kid. "Go with Pike and grab something to eat. Show him some of the local places that serve the good shit. No fast food."

"Go with Pike?" Gigi whispers. "Why?"

"I want you two to be friends."

"Are you fucking serious?" she whispers, eyes turning icy fucking cold, but she's staring at me and not her daddy. "For God's sake, why?"

Joe glances toward the ceiling, muttering under his breath. "Just do as I ask," he tells her.

She lifts her phone and shakes it in his direction as he turns toward her. "They have food delivery now, Dad. You don't actually have to go anywhere. I'll just order us something to eat."

If he knew what he was asking, if he knew what we'd done, he wouldn't be forcing her to leave this place with me. But I never plan on breathing a word of what we'd done to anyone. I'd have my ass booted from the shop, and my name blackballed from every tattoo place in the state.

"Just let her order in," Izzy says, looking at me and then at Gigi. "You know kids today, Joe. They don't like to actually do anything for themselves." Izzy laughs nervously.

By the way Izzy's acting, I reckon she's read something in our body language and has assumed we aren't the strangers we've made out to be. She seems like someone who can figure things out quickly and see through bullshit quicker than most.

"Grab me a burger from that place down on County Line. You know it's my favorite, and they don't deliver up here."

"That's fifteen minutes away," Gigi whines.

"It's a good fucking thing you both have over an hour, isn't it?"

He shuts down any argument either of us can make on why we shouldn't head out alone.

Gigi curls her lip as she glances at me. "Fine. We'll go, but you've used up your asks for this week."

Joe takes a few steps toward his kid. I haven't moved an inch, just stood there, staring at them both. "I'm not asking as your father, baby girl. I'm telling you as your boss."

My eyes widen, and so do Gigi's.

"So, grab me my usual," he says, looking down at his kid, standing a foot away from her.

"Fine," she snaps.

"Oh lord," Izzy whispers and shakes her head. "Clusterfuck. Total and complete clusterfuck."

I rub the back of my neck as I walk around the counter. "I can go alone," I tell Joe, not needing Gigi's pissy attitude because her daddy forced her to go with me. "I can find the joint and grab your food."

But any other words I have on the tip of my tongue die quickly as Joe glares at me. "No, you won't. She's going too. I don't know what bad blood you two have, if it's from both being new and starting on the same day, but this isn't a competition. This is a business, and you two have to work together. Whatever bullshit, imaginary beef you have ends here and now. Do you understand me?"

I nod because I'm not arguing with the boss. No way. No how. If he wants me to take a ride with his kid to hell and back to get him a bottle of water, I'll fucking do it. It's not like Gigi is hard to be around. Keeping my dick out of her might be an issue, but it isn't a hardship spending time with a pretty chick who could do more with that mouth than sass.

"I understand, Dad," she says softly. "I'll play nice."

Joe's lips turn up and his shoulders relax. "Now, get moving. I'm starving. Ask everyone else if they want anything before you go."

"I'll grab my keys."

"Oh no." Gigi shakes her head, still glaring at me like she wants to rip off my head. "I'm driving."

"Why?"

She crosses her arms, tilting her head to the side, eyes traveling up and down my body. "Let me guess," she says, her tone all full of piss and vinegar. "You have the bike, yeah?"

"Yeah."

"We're getting food for everyone, and I'm not fucking holding it while we weave in and out of traffic just because you want to take your bike."

I shrug. "I have a compartment."

"It's a big nope for me. We're taking my truck."

"Whatever makes you happy." I'm not going to stand here another ten minutes arguing about which form of transportation we're going to take. "I could give two shits how we get there as long as we get there."

"Smart kid," Joe says.

"Or the dumbest one ever," Izzy whispers before shaking her head at me.

Hopefully, whatever scenarios Izzy has swirling around in her head, she comes to me about before blowing up my life. She and Gigi are close. I can tell that from the short amount of time I've seen the two interact. If Gigi spills the beans, my ass will be on the back of my bike, searching for a new job and a new town...again.

"I'll meet you out front." Gigi tips her head toward the door. "Black truck."

I don't stick around. I need some air and to get my head on straight before I go anywhere with this chick. She has me all kinds of tangled up inside. My brain is going a million different directions, most of which are bad, but they all end up in the same place...with Gigi back in my bed, moaning my name, and begging for more.

Fuck.

The door doesn't close behind me as I step outside into the damp Florida air. I don't notice I'm not alone as I start to pace.

"I don't know what's going on, but whatever it is, you better find a way to fix it or move the fuck on," Izzy says.

I jump, clutching my chest. "Jesus fucking Christ. You scared the ever-loving hell out of me."

She marches up to me, craning her neck to look me in the eye. "Did you hear me?"

I nod. "Uh, yeah. I said you scared the shit out of me, Iz."

"Listen, kid." She points to the window of the shop. "Gigi's gunning for you. She doesn't like you, and she doesn't hate many people. So, whatever you did to fuck shit up, make it right. I don't want to lose you already, but she's family."

"Yeah. Yeah. I know how it goes." I run my hand through my hair and sigh.

"It's not my business. She's my niece and you're both adults, but mark my words, fix whatever you fucked up, or you won't be here more than a week."

I don't deny that there's history. I won't lie to Izzy again. She's smart. I won't be going into detail about all the ways I'm acquainted with her niece. I won't tell her how I know the way she tastes, how she kisses, and the perfect curve of her ass.

"I'll fix it." I jam my hands into my pockets, trying to figure out exactly how I'm going to do that.

Maybe I need to remind Gigi of how perfect we are together. I don't get why she's so fucking pissed. I did not stalk her across the state. Hell, I knew her first name but nothing else about the girl.

She lied to me, in fact.

First, based on the fact that she just graduated from college, her first lie was about her age. She told me she was twenty-two and was about to graduate last year. Second, she told me she was from Miami and stayed there to work. I know there were a million other lies she told me that week, but I wasn't exactly open and honest about my life or my past either.

We both knew what we were doing. The week in Daytona was all about pleasure. About being in the moment. Our pasts and futures didn't matter. The lies we told were of no consequence because there was nothing more than that moment, in that hotel, tangled in sheets and coated in sweat.

But now...our paths are intertwined. My fate and future lie in the hands of the boss's little girl, the same chick I'd banged until my legs barely worked anymore.

"Do whatever you need to do to make shit right," Izzy tells me before walking away and disappearing inside the shop, leaving me out front with my dick in my proverbial hands.

She said do *whatever*, but I wonder if the whatever includes being with her niece.

I know the spark is still there.

I caught Gigi staring at me more than once. Not with rage, but curiosity. Watching my hands as they touched Piper's back, maybe remembering the way they felt sliding across her skin.

Whatever there is between us...I'm not going to leave her alone until I find out.

CHAPTER 9
GIGI

FUCK. I love my dad, but come on. Why does he have to be so gung ho about the happy family vibe at the shop? What does it matter if I like Pike or not? I don't remember my dad going to this much trouble when they hired Kat. But what I do remember is my aunts going bananas about a young little hottie working so close to their men.

But now my dad wants us to be all kumbaya, holding hands, and one big, happy freaking family. If he only knew...

He'd fucking kill me, and then he'd murder Pike.

"We going to talk about this?" Pike asks from the passenger seat of my pickup truck.

"I think we said everything we needed to say already." I stare straight ahead, keeping my eyes on the road instead of on the hottie next to me.

Why the hell does he have to smell so good?

Pike shifts his body, but I don't dare sneak a glance. I know his eyes are on me and nowhere else. I can feel the weight of his gaze like a warm blanket, covering my skin. "Darlin'," he says with a hint of a Tennessee twang in his voice. "I have a lot more to say to you."

"Well, you talk, and maybe I'll listen while I drive." I shrug one shoulder, wrapping my fingers tighter around the steering wheel. "It's not like I have a choice, do I?"

"I like a captive audience," he says sarcastically. "First, I didn't follow you. I'm not a stalker."

"That's what you say, but how do I know?"

"Gigi, how the fuck would I even find you?"

I shrug again. "Anything's possible."

"You told me your first name. You also told me you were from Miami, and the last time I checked, we're hundreds of miles away from there."

"There are other ways."

"What other ways?" He turns and his knee is almost touching mine, but I have nowhere to go. No way to fight back because he's making all the sense in the world, and it's aggravating as hell.

"I don't know. My uncle's a private investigator, and I'm sure he could've found me with very little to go on."

Pike laughs, and I can see him shake his head out of the corner of my eye. "Listen, babe."

I growl, which only makes Pike laugh. *Ugh.*

"You like darlin' better?"

"I don't like either. My name is Gigi or Giovanna," I correct him.

"Giovanna is kind of an uppity name, which right about now, suits you."

"I changed my mind." I reach for the radio because I'd rather listen to anything other than his sexy as all get-out voice.

He tightens his fingers around my wrist, peeling my hand away from the buttons on the console. "I didn't have anything to go on. I figured what we had was nice, but it wasn't anything that would go the distance. The last thing I'd do is stalk you to try to get another piece of that fine ass."

My gaze slides to his face for a moment before going back to the road. "Nice?" My voice is high, almost shrill. "What we had was *nice?"* I ask, grinding my teeth and ripping my hand from his grasp.

"Well, not really." He pauses, and he's lucky as hell I can't lunge across the seat and wrap my hands around that beautiful neck of his. "It was fucking spectacular. The shit you did..."

"Stop." I shake my head, grinding my teeth so hard, my jaw aches. "I was there. I don't need a play-by-play."

Pike laughs again, practically making my blood boil. "I'm just saying, I didn't track you down. I figured you had your fill and were through. So why would I bother to track you down?" He pauses, but I don't reply before he continues. "I don't chase pussy. Never have. Never will. It's not my style, darlin'."

"Thanks for that little nugget of truth, Pike."

"You're acting like I did you wrong. You were the one who just up and left without even so much as a goodbye."

I cringe when he says the last few words. I did do that to him. I told him I was running out for some coffee, and I didn't look back before I got in my car, picked up the girls, and headed back to FSU. But in all fairness, when I rolled over that morning and saw his phone with a text from some skank that read, "When you're done with the little girl, I'll be waiting for you," that shit set me right off. I knew I was just another piece of ass to him in a long line of pussy waiting to take my place.

For half a second, I thought we had something more than a casual fling, but that text reminded me I was nothing more than another notch on his bedpost.

"I waited in that hotel room for three hours before I figured you weren't coming back. I felt like a fuckin' fool too."

"I'm sorry."

I didn't take into account how he felt or if he'd even give a shit. I figured a clean break, no goodbye, no last kiss, and no more questions was the best way to end things with him. It was a coward move, but I'd never done anything like that in my life. I didn't know how to act or if there was a proper way to say *thanks for the cock, big man.*

"Who does that kind of shit?"

"Oh, please. I'm sure you've been with plenty of chicks who didn't kiss you goodbye."

"I've never had anyone run away without at least saying thanks."

My gaze moves from the red light to his face. He's staring at me with a hardness in his eyes, fingers moving across his beard. "Thanks?"

The corner of his mouth tips up, showing the white of his teeth nestled behind his facial hair. "Why not?"

I throw my head back and laugh. "I think you would've been the one saying thanks to me, buddy."

My words only make Pike laugh. God, he's so annoying. "I figured I gave you all the thanks you needed with so many orgasms you could barely walk when you went for that fake-me-out coffee."

I narrow my gaze on his handsome, smug face. "It's not like you're the only man on the planet who can give an orgasm. You're not God's gift to women, country boy. Hell, I can give myself an orgasm anytime."

"Do you think about me?" His smile grows wider.

I twist my lips, staying silent as I turn my eyes back to the road. I'm thankful we're two minutes from the burger shop because I need out of this truck and need distance between us. "Babe, when I'm touching myself, like really getting into it, fingers stroking away, and I'm craving to be filled…"

"Don't say things like that unless you want to be flat on your back, begging for my cock, sweetheart."

"You're so full of yourself." Fuck, he's so right.

We're trapped in the small cab of my truck, and he's so close to me, I can smell the musky soap on his skin. All the memories from that week come flooding back to me like the naughtiest and most vivid dream, but I push them aside, staying in the present with the more annoying version of Pike.

"Tell me you haven't thought about me once since you left Daytona, and I'll leave you be, chalking it all up to a good time and nothing more."

"I haven't thought about you once," I lie. "Have you thought about me?"

"Every. Damn. Day," he answers quickly, and I immediately regret asking him that question.

If I were being truthful, which I'm not because I'm not giving him any ammo, I've thought about him every damn day too. How could I not? After a week like we had, the way we had it, I couldn't think about anyone else but him.

He ruined me. I never thought I'd say those words, and I can barely admit them to myself sometimes. But he did. He ruined me completely.

Mallory had asked me before I met Pike if Erik was any good in bed. I said he was okay or maybe I said he was good, but now I know better. Pike did things to me that made my toes curl and my legs shake like I was having a seizure.

"We're here." I open the door and hop down from the truck's cab, leaving Pike behind as soon as I shut off the engine.

I move quickly, pulling open the door to the burger shop, trying to put as much space as possible between Pike and me. But no matter how quickly I move, he isn't far behind.

"We're not done," Pike says, almost plastered against my back in the impossibly busy restaurant.

I turn, glancing up and over my shoulder at him. "We are."

He leans forward, putting his face so close to mine, I can feel his warm breath tickle my skin. "I'm calling a truce for now, but that doesn't mean I don't want you in my bed again, lips on mine."

I suck in a long, deep breath, feeling a little dizzy, remembering how his lips felt like velvet even with that beard. "It's never going to happen." Quickly, I twist my head, staring up at the menu and silently cursing myself because I very much wouldn't mind being in his bed with his lips on mine again. "Asshole," I mutter softly.

"Welcome to Burger, Burger, Burger," the guy with the dopiest outfit ever says on the other side of the counter. The name is cheesy, the uniforms are even cheesier, but the burgers they make are the best in the county. "What can I get you?" he asks with a grin so large, I know it's fake as fuck because ain't no one that happy to be working in this joint.

"I'll take a Double Swiss and Mushroom, a large onion ring, and a medium diet lemonade."

"Diet?" Pike says in my ear. I elbow him because he's close, and I don't feel like getting into it with him in front of everyone.

"What do you want to eat, Pike?" I ask, not turning around, but instead giving the same fake-ass smile back to *Jim*—or at least, that's what his name tag says.

"Besides you?" Pike whispers in my ear, which earns him a second elbow to the gut. "I'll get what she's having." His voice is strained, the two good shots I got in clearly having an impact.

"For here or to go?" Jim, the cashier, asks with his smile still firmly planted on his pimply face.

"To go."

"Here," Pike says over me, and Jim nods. "We also do need a few other things to go." Pike's fingers graze my ass, and I jump but stop myself from smacking him when I see the yellow sheet of paper in his hands. He rattles off the order for everyone at the shop before handing Jim a wad of cash.

"You could've just asked me for the list," I snap.

Jesus. When did I become so bitchy?

Pike brings out the worst in me. That week in Daytona, I felt more like myself. I didn't have to be anyone else but who I was. Although I told a few lies because I didn't know Pike at all, I was truly me. I didn't have to put on a good face or act like some happy party girl, ready to do anything Mallory wanted so I didn't have to listen to her shit.

"My way was more fun." He smirks, eyes blazing as he stares at my snarled lips.

"We'll bring it out to you when it's ready," Jim says because, clearly, we're done and stopping the flow of traffic.

I stalk toward an empty table, plop down in the chair, and stare out the window.

"We can be civil," Pike says, sliding into the chair across from me. "I want this job, and I'm not looking to get canned before I've barely had a chance to start. Your dad won't fire you, but he'll toss my ass out in a fucking heartbeat. I'm not trying to piss you off."

"That's news to me, Pike, and by the way, I didn't get the job because I'm related. I've been working my ass off at the shop for years, earning that damn chair."

"Your line work is amazing," he says, complimenting me on something that isn't sexual for the first time. "Especially with the short time you've been tattooing. It's impressive, actually."

"Thanks. My dad taught me well."

"You're lucky," he says, leaning back in his chair and kicking one leg out so it's practically touching mine. "My father didn't teach me shit except how to be an asshole."

"Ah, it's genetic, then," I tease, reaching over and pulling a handful of napkins out of the container just so I have something else to do besides stare at him.

"Ha. Ha. Very funny. I'm not an asshole." He pauses. I risk a glance at him and quickly realize I shouldn't have. The teasing, happy-go-lucky guy from a few moments ago is gone, and in his place is a man filled with sorrow and maybe...regret. "Well, not one like my father, at least. We're nothing alike. Thank fuck for small miracles."

"I'm sorry." I can't imagine growing up with a horrible father.

Joseph Gallo may be overbearing, but he is so damn loving that the amazing outweighs the bad. Sure, there were times I wanted to scream at him about his ridiculous rules, but I knew why he was being so over the top. He loves me. He also thought he knew better than me, which he probably did, although I'll never admit it.

I won the lottery the day I was born. I knew that much. I have a father who adores me and a mother who is the sweetest human being on the planet. I have an entire tribe of people who are mine, looking out for me, loving me no matter what shit I pull...and there's been a lot.

Pike shrugs one shoulder and then runs his fingers through his impossibly messy, yet somehow perfect, dirty-blond hair. "It is what it is. I put as much distance between him and me as possible."

"But what about your mom?" I ask, unable to imagine not being able to go home again.

"She's no better than him. Just a different type of asshole, but still an asshole."

"That's harsh."

"If you knew them, you'd understand why I'm not being harsh enough."

I stare at Pike, losing myself in his soulful eyes, wondering what made me the lucky one to be born into a great family, when there are others who got a shit deal the day they were born.

"Two burgers, two onion rings, and two drinks," a girl says at the side of our table, wearing the same hideous outfit as Jim and looking no less ridiculous.

"That's us." I reach for the tray because she's staring at Pike with wide eyes like a deer caught in headlights. She's not a deer and Pike's not a car, but she's no less mesmerized by him.

Yeah, girl, I know.

I take the tray from her hands, placing it on the table in front of us, but she doesn't move. She barely blinks, ignoring the fact that I'm sitting right here, like she's stuck to the floor, frozen in place.

"Can I get you anything else?" she asks him in an almost robotic voice.

"I think we're good," Pike says and looks at me, pleading with me with his eyes like I'm going to be able to chase this girl away. "You need anything else, darlin'?"

"I got everything I need," I reply, grabbing the burger from the paper basket, trying to ignore the weird girl who can't seem to do anything other than stare at Pike.

"Well," she says softly, blinking her eyelashes so quickly I'd think she has something stuck under her eyelid. "If you need anything, just ask for me." She smiles and points at her name tag. "Angie."

"Thanks, Angie," Pike says with a big smile, tipping his head to her. "I'll let you know if we need anything else. My girl and I are hungry."

Her top lip curls as Pike looks over at me, breaking the happy trance she was in and reminding her that he isn't alone. "Enjoy," she says flatly before stalking away from our table, thankfully leaving us in peace.

"Is it hard being you?" I tease him.

"Hard because people are nice?" he asks, grabbing his burger and holding it in front of his lush, soft lips.

"Hard because women seem to throw themselves at you."

"Sometimes it's great, while other times, it's a pain in the ass." He takes a big bite, chewing slowly, staring at me across the table as I do the same.

We sit like that, chewing and not speaking, but his eyes say everything that needs to be said. I could lose myself in his eyes. The deep green like the Gulf of Mexico before a storm.

"Like the night I met you, that was one of the great times."

I'm mid-swallow, and the burger almost gets lodged in my throat, but I fight to get it down. "And when it's not so great?" I ask, wanting to talk about anything except us.

"Fuck," Pike mutters, burger in hand, cocky smile playing on his lips. "Who am I kidding? A face like this has its perks with very little downside."

I grab an onion ring and playfully throw it at his face, but Pike catches it before it can connect. "You're being an asshole again."

"Darlin', I'm always an asshole, but that's why you like me," he says with a straight face.

"Keep dreaming, buddy," I snarl and take another bite of my burger, chewing on my food and his words.

Do I like Pike?

I liked him enough to sleep with him...repeatedly.

I was attracted to him. That much was true.

I liked Daytona Pike way more than I like Inked Pike. But Daytona Pike also had an expiration date, whereas Inked Pike seems to be ready to settle in and stick around, putting down roots in my small town.

I can't chase him away. That would require me being open and honest with my father about what happened in Daytona and what went down between Pike and me.

Shit, my father didn't even know I went to Daytona, and the one thing he hates most is lying. I did my fair share of that in college, though. If they knew half the shit I'd pulled... Well, it's not like he could ground me. I don't live under his roof anymore and can make my own rules. But that doesn't mean my ass wouldn't get chewed out for the danger I'd put myself in.

I can't even imagine what he'd say about me sleeping with a stranger, let alone going to his hotel room where I could've been raped or murdered. I'm sure my father would immediately go to the worst-case scenario and all the ways I could've fucked up my life by sleeping with a stranger.

I didn't get an STD or end up with a lifelong reminder, waking me in the middle of the night to be fed. What I did get was the best damn sex of my life—and now a constant reminder sitting in the chair across from me.

"Finish up. We have to get back. I have a client in thirty minutes," Pike says as he glances at his phone.

I take two more bites, trying to keep my eyes on the table

instead of on his muscular, ink-covered arms, flexing with each movement. When I lift my gaze to his face, he's watching me and knows exactly what I'm staring at. I'm totally busted.

"I'm done." I toss the burger back into the paper basket before shoving an onion ring in my mouth. "I'm ready when you are," I say while chewing, hoping to pull off being as unsexy as possible.

I know I need to put space between us. The spark, the chemistry, the pull I felt toward him in Daytona is still there. That scares the shit out of me too. I'd never felt that invisible force pushing me toward someone when I was with Erik or Keith, but it's so strong with Pike, I'm not sure I can escape it.

"You're still hot," he says like he sees through my plan. "Still give me wood, darlin', even with that mouthful of onion rings."

I'm out of my seat, tray in one hand and the to-go bag in the other before Pike can say another word. But I'm not alone for long. I don't even make it to the door before I can hear his heavy footsteps and feel the warmth of his body nearby.

"Fuck my life," I whisper into the glass door before pushing it open and stepping outside into the inferno that's a Florida summer day.

"Next time, we take my bike," he says, rounding the truck and opening my door before I can do it myself.

I stare up at him. "There won't be a next time." I stop myself from reaching out and running my fingertips along the coarse hair on his face.

Pike smiles, tipping his head and putting his face close to mine. "News flash, Gigi. Daytona was only the beginning."

CHAPTER 10
PIKE

"WHY COULDN'T you move to Nashville?" my grandmother asks as I stalk around my apartment searching for my boots. "There are plenty of places to work around here, sweetheart."

"Gram, it's still too close. I needed to put distance between myself and that shit-ass town."

"That mouth of yours, Pike. I know I didn't teach you to speak like that."

"Sorry, Gram." I pull on my boots as soon as I find them next to the couch.

"Nashville is two hundred miles from your daddy. It's not like you'd run into him."

My grandmother was the only saving grace I had as a child. She still is. How she's the same woman who raised my father, I'll never understand. Where she's sweet, he's cruel. Where she's soft, he's hard. It's like he decided to spite the world and do the opposite of anything Gram wanted for him.

"I know, Gram, I know."

"Just promise you'll come visit this old woman before I die," she says, laying on the guilt like she always does.

The woman has been talking about her death since I was in middle school. At first, she used it as a means to control me. It worked like a fucking charm until I got smart enough to realize she wasn't dying anytime soon. Then, she used it as a way to guilt me into doing shit like being around my parents when I wanted to be anywhere else in the world than breathing the same air as them.

"I promise I'll come see you before fall."

"That's three months away, sweetheart. A woman of my age could meet her maker at any moment."

"Why don't you come here? I have a spare bedroom, and I can show you around where I live. Have you ever been to Florida, Gram?"

"No, and I have more humidity and heat than I can handle here. I don't need to come to Florida so I can get more."

I laugh as I step onto my patio with a cup of coffee, closing the screen door behind me because the bugs out here are ridiculous and bigger than most rats I've seen crawling around near the gutters of Nashville. "Don't be dramatic."

"I'm always dramatic."

"From your lips to God's ears."

"Lydia is here to take me to the store. Call me tomorrow, and let me know how you're settling in."

"Okay, Gram. Tell Lydia hello." I lean over the railing and rest the coffee mug on the top. "Talk soon. Don't die on me today."

"No one is promised time, Pike. Remember that," she says, hanging up without saying goodbye like she always does.

She'd just turn me off. When I was younger, it bothered me that she never said goodbye. She was the only person I knew who never uttered those words. She said they were too final and not meant for casual conversation. That was the hard part of Gram, but everything else about the woman was soft and loving.

"Beautiful morning, isn't it?"

I turn my head, coffee cup close to my lips, finding a buxom blonde in a silk robe. She's leaning against the railing of her patio which touches mine, only separated by some iron spindles. Her hand is wrapped around a mug, but the robe is open, nearly exposing her breasts.

"It's something." I don't let my gaze linger too long because I don't know this chick or if she has a man inside her apartment who'd be willing to go five rounds because I looked at his girl wrong.

"New here?" she asks, sliding closer but still leaning.

"Moved in last week."

She extends her free hand, but I don't move a muscle. "I'm Cadence, but my friends call me Cady like Katie."

She wiggles her fingers, not getting the clue that I'm not interested in niceties, especially at this hour. "Well, Cady like Katie, it's nice to meet you."

"I won't bite," she says with a small laugh.

I've known plenty of women like Cadence, and they always bite. They take their pound of flesh in the end, and I am not particularly looking to have any more scars.

"Pike." I take her hand, giving her a quick handshake and nothing more.

"Well, Pike, I'm always around if you're looking for company."

"Sorry, Cady, I'm a taken man," I lie because it's easier than telling her I'm not interested.

She doesn't look like a woman who takes no for an answer. The way she's staring at me, I can tell she wants a piece of me for breakfast.

"Such a shame," she whispers and withdraws her hand from mine. "But if you change your mind..."

"I know where to find you."

"Nice ink, by the way."

"Thanks." I leave out the part about being a tattoo artist. The last thing I need is Cady's ass planted in my chair at Inked, tits hanging out, coming on to me in front of the entire Gallo family.

She gives me a once-over, eyes hungry and still burning as her gaze slides down my arms to my crotch. "You have a good day now, ya hear?"

"You too." I hold my breath, not daring to move until her screen door closes behind her.

I'm halfway back into my apartment, one leg still outside, when the patio door on the other side opens, and a familiar voice catches my attention.

"I know, Tamara. Can you believe this shit? Pike just shows up out of nowhere."

Well, fuck me.

If Gigi thought I was stalking her before, wait until she realizes I'm living next door to her. Out of all the places in this small-ass town, why in the fuck did she move in to my complex and right next door?

I pull my leg into the apartment but stay near the door and out of view. I don't dare shut the door because the last thing I want is for Gigi to see me or catch me listening to her.

"Yeah, he still looks delicious," she tells Tamara over the phone.

I fucking knew it.

"Tam, be serious for a minute here. Don't worry about Pike's big dick. Think of all the ways this shit can go south and bite me right in the ass."

There's nothing she can say now to wipe the big-ass grin off my face. Nothing. She can call me an asshole all she wants and pretend she doesn't want me, but I know the truth. She clearly told Tamara everything and is laying it all out for her again.

"You're so fucking funny." Gigi snorts but quickly sobers. "What if my dad finds out about Daytona? He'll fucking have my head."

Ah. The girl has a secret. Besides sleeping with me, her dad has no idea she was in Daytona last year for Bike Week. He'd probably shit a brick. I know if I had a daughter, I wouldn't let her anywhere near the place. Not when there're guys like me around. No fucking way would that ever happen.

I peek around the corner, getting a full view of Gigi's ass in the most spectacular pair of cutoff jean shorts ever. She's holding a coffee in one hand and her phone in the other, leaning against the railing near the corner.

"I can't sleep with him again."

I stand a little straighter.

"Because we work together, and Pike isn't the type of guy who settles down. I don't want to be someone's booty call forever, Tam. I want love. I want a relationship. I want what my parents have. What your parents have."

That's where she's wrong, but damn it, I can't set her straight right now. It would ruin everything that we built on yesterday. By the end of the day, she wasn't ready to rip out my throat. We'd made progress, and I wasn't going to do anything to fuck that up. And I most certainly wasn't going to scare the piss out of her by walking out on the patio and interrupting her most telling conversation.

"I'm not going for another ride on that cock just because I haven't been laid since the last time."

My eyes widen, and everything around me seems to disappear. Her words slam into me like a ton of bricks.

She hasn't slept with anyone else?

"My fling with Pike was a one-time thing because Mallory wouldn't shut the hell up about how I was a prude. I've embraced my prudishness now. I have exactly two notches on my bedpost, girl. Erik was a cheating asshole, and Pike is Pike. Best fucking sex of my life or not, I'm not rolling around with a man who can't commit."

To say I'm dumbfounded is an understatement. Very little surprises me in the world anymore, especially the shittiness. But goddamn, I was only the second guy Gigi had ever slept with, and she hasn't been with anyone else since.

How is that even possible?

I know three things for sure in this moment.

First, Gigi isn't exactly what she seems. She's not a party girl and has never been one to sleep around. I was the exception and outside her norm.

Second, I still have a shot with Gigi. She wants love. She wants romance. I could do those. I could be whatever she wants me to be. She is that badass. She is soft and hard, sweet and salty, and everything I want in a chick. She has balls and a mouth on her that could break a man's heart or have him panting with need.

And third, I need to find a way to make Gigi mine without getting my ass shot by her badass father. I know I could break down Gigi's walls, but Joe... He is another story entirely.

"Trust me. The women basically throw themselves at Pike. They go all stupid around him. It's ridiculous." Gigi pauses for a moment. "I did not go stupid around him. Shut up, Tamara. He scratched an itch, and that's it."

I don't know what Tamara is saying, but I sure as fuck wish I could hear her. Having one side of the conversation is fine, but damn...I want it all. I wonder what she told her cousin. How open she'd been about the things we'd done and how fucking fantastic it had all been.

"I'm not full of shit," Gigi barks.

Oh, but she is. She hasn't been honest about a damn thing with me since the moment I met her, and she continued the lies yesterday. Her mouth was saying she hated me, but now, talking to Tamara, she's saying the opposite. I knew by the way Gigi stared at me that she still wanted me.

"Anyway, when are you getting here? My mom's flipping out because I'm living alone and I told her you're staying with me for the summer until school starts again."

Fuck. Tamara could be a wrench in my plans to win Gigi over. But maybe not. From the sound of it, I think Tamara believes Gigi and I should be together, even if only sexually. I'll take what I can get, trying to win Gigi over piece by piece, orgasm by orgasm. Whatever it takes. I've never been a quitter, and when I see something I want, I go after it...full throttle.

"I'll have the place ready, but I'm only giving you two weeks to get your ass here. I don't know what the hell you're still doing up there."

I now have a timetable. I have two weeks to see what I can do to win the girl over before her cousin crashes the party. Maybe I can use the time to my advantage. If her parents, specifically her mother, don't like her living alone, maybe if they knew I lived next door, they'd feel better about her living arrangements. Knowing there was a friendly face and coworker right next door in case shit went bad wouldn't be a bad thing, would it?

"Dump Hank. He's a loser, Tam. You could do so much better, and you know it. You said you were breaking up with him a month ago, but there you are, staying at FSU for him." She pauses again, and I'm still plastered to the wall just inside the doorway. "You have two weeks to break his heart and get your ass here, or I'm telling your daddy you're there getting your brains banged out of that pretty little head."

I reach out, slowly sliding the patio door closed and engaging the lock. I keep my body out of sight, not knowing if she's looking but taking no chances either. I need to get to the shop, and I want to be out the door, on the back of my bike, before she has a chance to leave. The last thing I need is for her to find me here, thinking I'm following her ass around.

I have to find a way to let her know I'm living here without her also knowing I was listening in on her conversation.

It's a giant clusterfuck, but a damn good one too.

I'm halfway to my bike when a door opens behind me, and I freeze.

"Pike?" Gigi calls out. "Is that you?"

Fuck. I rub the back of my neck and turn to face her. "Hey." I wave with my other hand, keys dangling from my fingertips like a dope.

She looks stunning in the early morning sunlight, the rays shining around her hair and illuminating her like an angel. But the look on her face isn't sweet.

"What the hell are you doing here?" she asks as she stalks toward me, arms swinging at her sides with each hurried step.

"Headed to the shop." I wait in the empty parking spot next to my ride.

"No." She crosses her arms, the anger coming off her in waves. "I mean, what are you doing here at Sunshine Vista?"

"I live here," I answer flatly, laying out the truth.

"Here?" She points to the cement.

"There." I point toward the building. Our building.

She narrows her eyes. "Which one?"

"On the end."

Her eyes widen. "Right fucking next to me?"

My eyes widen too. "No shit. Really? What a crazy-ass coincidence."

Please for the love of God, I hope she didn't hear my sliding door close, figuring out I was listening to her conversation. I'd like to get to work with my balls intact and my voice in a normal octave.

"You say you're not stalking me. But for real, Pike, it sure as fuck seems like you are."

"I signed the lease two months ago, and I moved in last week. You?"

"I'm just moving in this week," she tells me, balling her fists at her sides, and I slide backward because she looks like she's about to throw down.

"Why here?"

"There're only two apartment complexes in this small-ass town. The other place was..."

"Gross," she finishes my sentence, and I nod.

"Wasn't going to plant my roots in a shithole like that. So, I wasn't stalking you. This was the only place within a twenty-mile radius that was worth renting. Nothing more. Now, you want a ride to work today or not?"

"Not," she hisses.

"Suit yourself."

"Pike, how would I explain why I'm on the back of your bike when we get to the shop? Think about it for a minute."

I slowly nod and swing a leg over my bike, sitting my ass down on the seat. "I wasn't thinking about much other than having you on the back of my bike, those sweet thighs rubbing against mine and your tits pressed against my back."

She tips her head toward the sky and groans, followed by a slew of curse words I haven't heard strung together in quite as creative a way before. "It's so not happening ever again," she tells me as she brings her gaze back to mine instead of the fluffy clouds floating above our heads.

Yeah, it will, darlin'. I don't utter those words out loud because she'll just deny how she's feeling and tell me I'm fucking crazy. But I heard her talk to Tamara, and I know the truth.

"Just go. I'm not ready for work yet. I have to do my makeup. I just ran out here to grab my makeup bag from my car."

My lip curls. "You don't need any of that shit on your face, babe. You're looking beautiful right now with the sunshine streaming through that brown hair of yours, kissing those cheeks."

Her cheeks turn a bright shade of pink, and the attitude that had been running all through her body seems to evaporate. "You're full of shit." She waves me off. "Go, and I'll be a few minutes behind you. Don't say anything about being here."

"Lips are sealed, darlin'."

"Gigi," she says as I throttle the engine, ready to take off.

"Sure thing, darlin' Gigi." I smirk, unable to hear her scream even though her mouth is open over the bike. I slide on my sunglasses, lift my chin to her, and walk the bike back slowly out of the parking spot.

She doesn't move from the spot she's standing in. Her eyes are on me, hands on her hips, body looking smoking hot in those jean shorts, showing off the perfect amount of leg. She looks like a goddess with her brown hair blowing in the soft breeze, watching me like a hawk as I pull away.

CHAPTER 11
GIGI

"WE'RE all going out after work to celebrate," Izzy says as I walk into the office to grab a cold drink after my last client of the evening finally leaves.

"I don't know," I mutter, reaching into the small fridge near the doorway. "I have a lot to do at the apartment, Auntie."

"We're celebrating you and Pike joining our team. So, there's no getting out of this one, kiddo."

I twist the lid off the soda as I turn around, gawking at my aunt as she sits at the desk. "I'm not new, and I don't think Pike will be here for very long."

She draws her eyebrows inward. "Why do you say that?"

I lift a shoulder. "Just a feeling I have."

She taps her fingernails against the wooden top. "Are you ready to tell me how you really know Pike?"

"I don't know what you're talking about."

I will deny the shit that happened between us for as long as humanly possible.

She pushes back from the desk and stalks toward me, crossing her arms, which is never a good sign. "I've been watching both of you for two days. Want to know what I see?"

"Not particularly."

She gets right in my face. "I see two people who know each other and know each other well."

I laugh, but it's a shrill, nervous one. My aunt's eyes flash, and I know I have to divert. "I don't know him. He's just hot, okay? It's been a while since I've been with anyone, and he's the only guy in the shop I'm not related to. It's that simple."

She stares at me, lips twisting like she's chewing on what I'm saying but not buying a word. "He is hot. I'll agree with you there, but there's more to the story. There's something you're not telling me. And about Pike..." She grabs my shoulders, moving closer. "He's sticking around, kid. He signed a one-year lease on that chair, and he's planting roots."

"Planting roots," I mumble because Pike has said those same words so many damn times over the last two days, I could scream.

"That man has been trying to get a chair here for three years, but we weren't ready for new blood. Now, we've got a spot for him, and he's staying as long as he wants unless he does something to fuck up majorly. But if he does, he still has to pay for that chair for the duration of his contract. So, settle in, sweetheart, the hottie's here to stay."

Three years? That kind of kills my theory that he tracked me down, following me halfway across the state to get me into bed again.

"Fuck," I hiss under my breath, and Izzy doesn't miss it.

"So, you might as well tell me how you know him and why you want him gone before those roots are firmly planted here."

I know if there's one person I can trust to understand everything that happened and how I feel about it, it's Aunt Izzy. She wouldn't judge me for sleeping with a stranger, but she'd probably give me a lecture about safe sex and other uncomfortable topics I didn't feel like talking to her about. Then, she'd probably lay into me about being in Daytona for Bike Week, which I don't feel like hearing. Not yet, at least.

"It's no big deal. We just ran into each other somewhere. He has an unforgettable face," I lie because it's easier than the truth.

I don't want to make waves for Pike. He didn't do anything wrong. I took what he gave, and then I ran away without so much as a goodbye. If anyone should be pissed, it's him. But he's not. He doesn't seem angry with me about the entire ordeal. Maybe I should tell him about the fact that I hadn't done anything like that before and I wasn't sure how to handle saying goodbye to a man I never planned to see again. But here he is, and he's not leaving anytime soon.

Izzy hasn't moved, and she's still staring at me like she's a human lie detector, ready to call bullshit. "That's it?"

"Yep." I stare her straight in the eye when I speak because doing anything else will be a dead giveaway.

"What bullshit are you two cooking up?" Uncle Mike asks as he walks in the room, scaring the shit out of me.

"Just talking to Gigi about today. Making sure she's comfortable and happy."

Mike collapses on the couch behind me, kicking his feet up on the small coffee table and putting his hands behind his head. "She's not new, Iz."

"Thank you." I wave my hand toward him, proving my point to my aunt.

"Well, she is, but she isn't," Izzy replies.

I roll my eyes. "I don't know why we have to go out to celebrate tonight."

Uncle Mike laughs. "After you have kids, you'll understand that you'll make any excuse necessary for a night out."

I cross my arms, feeling like my entire family is ganging up on me in some way. "I'm sure Auntie Mia would rather you be at home."

His laughter gets louder. "Mia will be asleep, and so will the kids. I'm sure she'll be lying in the middle of the bed, enjoying the extra space for a few more hours. Pike's finishing his last piece, so we're out of here in thirty. Want me to close out the register?"

"I got it," Izzy says before bringing that hard stare back to me. "We're not done, baby girl. I know you better than anyone, and there's something you aren't telling me."

"Oh, I love a good secret," Mike says from the couch.

"There's no secret, Uncle."

"Want me to hold her down, and you can tickle it out of her, sis?"

I put my hands on my hips and spin around to face my uncle. "I'm not five anymore. That won't work."

"Kid, you know your aunt. She's like a rabid dog when she gets something stuck in her craw. You might as well spill your guts now and make it easy on yourself. And in my mind, you're always going to be a little girl."

"There's nothing to tell. I'll go clean up my station so we can get this celebration happening earlier rather than later. I have a lot to do, and time's wasting away." I march out of the room, not giving them another chance to say anything more.

Pike, Anthony, and my dad are cleaning their stations, talking about bikes because what else would they be talking about.

"Gigi, Pike just told me something interesting," my dad says as soon as he spots me.

I stop dead like my feet have been nailed to the floor. My heart starts to pound out of control, pumping so fast, I'm pretty sure it's about to burst. "What?" I ask, wincing because I'm not sure I want to hear whatever my dad is about to say.

Pike's gaze locks on mine, and I'm ready to blurt out something, anything, to lessen the blow. Why in the fuck would Pike tell my dad about seeing me in Daytona? I thought he wanted to be here, and although starting on a lie isn't great, telling your boss you fucked his daughter is just plain stupid.

"He got a place over at Sunshine Vista. So, you two are neighbors now. That'll make your mom feel better, knowing someone is close by that can look out for you."

A slow grin spreads across Pike's face, and I immediately want to smack it off.

My eyes widen as my gaze moves to my father. "Look out for me?"

"Well, yeah." My dad nods, smiling because he doesn't know the truth. "Your mom doesn't like that you're going to be living on your own, and this will make her feel better."

"He could be a serial killer, Dad. We don't really know Pike that well, and anyway—" I smash my hands together, pulling at my fingers to keep my anger in check "—I'm twenty-one and can look out for myself."

My dad shakes his head. "You're also a girl who's living alone. I don't care if you're thirty, your mom is always going to be your mom. You know how she is, and with knowing Pike lives close, even if you don't ever need his help, she'll sleep better at night."

I love my father, but he still has some backward ways of thinking. He has three daughters and has taught us all how to defend ourselves and be independent, but here he is, talking about how my mom will sleep better knowing I have a guy nearby. A dick has nothing to do with safety. Knowing I've got a bullet for whatever dumb fuckers try to fuck with me is all the security I need.

"She should sleep better knowing I'll have my Glock in my nightstand, ready to shoot anyone who tries any shit."

Dad shakes his head, scrubbing his hands down his face and muttering a string of curse words under his breath. "First, you know she can't find out about the Glock."

"Dude, you never told Suzy about getting Gigi a gun?" Anthony says, staring at my father with his mouth hanging open.

"Nope, and we're going to keep it that way," Dad tells him.

"You know how to shoot with that?" Pike asks, leaning back in his chair, eyes only on me.

"You want to find out?" I smirk.

Pike throws up his hands. "Maybe we can hit the range."

"That's a hard no." I turn back toward my dad. "I don't need a man to keep me safe. Not when I have Lola."

Anthony almost chokes on the water he's sipping. "You named your gun Lola?"

"Of course. What did you name yours?"

"I never named a gun, and I don't have any in the house anymore. Max would skin me alive if she found one with the kids in the house."

All the badass men in my life pretend to be in control, having shit on lockdown in their lives. But it's all a lie. The women in their beds have all the power. Anthony won't even keep a weapon in the house because he can't win an argument with my aunt because she holds the reins, as well as his balls.

"Well, Dad taught me how to shoot a long time ago. When I went away to FSU, he bought me Lola as a graduation present."

"Classy," Anthony says, earning him a glower from my father. "Couldn't get her a normal gift like money or a car?"

"He doesn't do anything normal," I add.

"That ain't no lie. Tamara hates guns," my uncle says, but he couldn't be further from the truth.

I chuckle because Tamara, Anthony's daughter and my cousin, so doesn't hate guns. She loved going to the range with me, especially when we needed to let off some steam around exam week. The girl actually has killer aim, a born natural for someone who never spent much time shooting.

"Lily has a gun," Mike says. "It's good for a girl to know how to defend herself."

Izzy walks into the main room, arms folded, head cocked, ready to go off. "You assholes act like we're weak. I never needed a gun to bring a man to his knees. Don't start acting like we're delicate flowers in need of rescue. You taught your girls how to fight just like you taught me. Lord help any man who fucks with a Gallo girl."

"You got a gun, Pike?" Anthony asks, diverting the conversation from the weakness of the Gallo women and back to guns.

"Nope." Pike shrugs. "I have my fists, and they're the only weapon I need. Used to have one when I was a kid, but haven't felt the need in years."

I roll my eyes again. That was such a bunch of macho crap spewing from his mouth.

"I got you covered, Pike, ya know…in case you need rescuing." I smirk.

Pike's body shakes with laughter. "You're a funny chick, Gigi."

"We're leaving in ten. Whatever isn't cleaned tonight will have to be done in the morning," Izzy announces to the entire room. "There's a cold drink with my name on it, and you Chatty Cathys are wasting time."

"We're moving as fast as we can, Mom," Anthony tells her, earning a glare back for his attempt at trying to make a funny.

Ten minutes later, Izzy's shooing us out of the shop, locking the door behind us.

"Want a lift?" Pike asks as he walks next to me into the parking lot.

I gawk at him. "Are you serious?"

"Well, yeah."

"Do you want a lift? Because I'm not going on the back of your bike tonight."

"Does that mean you'll get on the back another time?" he asks with his face covered in shadows, but his white smile is clearly visible.

"No."

"Why don't you ride with Gigi, Pike?" Izzy asks, and I know she's testing me. Seeing if I'll lose my shit, which I'm pretty close to doing. "Since we're going to be having a few drinks, one of you needs to stay sober enough to drive. Might as well use one car since you're going to the same place."

I open my mouth to argue, but Pike jumps right on in. "Good idea, boss."

"Just put your bike behind the shop. No one will mess with it," she adds, staring at me as I glare at her, but she's sporting the biggest smile. "Gigi will follow you back there."

I look to my dad for a rescue, but he's climbing on his bike, either completely oblivious to the conversation or he agrees with my aunt and just isn't saying anything.

"Works for me," Pike says, throwing a leg over the seat, looking all too happy about the turn of events.

"I'm sure it does," I mutter to myself before climbing in my truck and letting out a stream of curses as soon as I close the door.

My aunt, God love her, is testing my patience and doing what she does best...sticking her nose where it doesn't belong and meddling in other people's lives.

What else could possibly go wrong?

CHAPTER 12
PIKE

THERE ARE things I know for certain, and others I'd only assume. I know Joe Gallo loves Gigi more than just about anything, except for maybe his other daughters and his wife. The way he looks at his eldest daughter, it's like the sun and the moon rise and set on her very existence. I don't remember my parents, either one of them, ever looking at me the way he looks at her. I was more of a nuisance to them than a source of pride. I could do no right in their eyes, and they made sure to let me know how they felt on a daily basis.

Even from the short amount of time I've spent at Inked, I also know the Gallos are a tight-knit crew. They love being around one another, busting the others' balls about whatever they could find. I can't imagine having so many people willing to have my back about anything and everything.

The closest I got to having something like that wasn't from blood relations. When I turned eighteen and left Tennessee, I landed straight in the middle of a group of bikers who were hell-bent on making me one of their own. Spent three years riding with them as I worked at various tattoo shops all over Florida, trying to better my artistic craft and my line work. They treated me better than the two people who gave me life. They didn't judge me, didn't expect anything but loyalty, and had my back no matter what shit went down. And there was shit. Plenty of it too. I was an angry kid with a massive chip on my shoulder, pissed off and ready to take on the world, no matter the consequences.

The guys adopted me in a way. As much as any group can when the person's not a child anymore. I was always open and honest, telling them the biker life wasn't for me. I had dreams, and nothing, not even my first real family, would derail me. When I finally found a shop that would hire me full-time, I started spending less and less time with the MC. They weren't happy, but they understood where my heart was, and it wasn't riding up and down the coast of Florida, wreaking havoc and raining down mayhem.

They weren't in my life on the daily, but I never said goodbye. I still met the guys every year at Bike Week, catching up like old friends who had a long history together. It was our own little fucked-up family reunion, because we had one another if no one else.

Over the last two days, I also realized Gigi's Aunt Izzy, the one with the giant attitude, liked to be in the know about *everything*. There wasn't a person's business she wasn't all up in. That included Gigi and now me since we were clearly throwing off some sort of vibe neither of us could hide, but we weren't about to fess up to anything either.

"This is my last beer," Mike says after he orders his second and another round, slipping a fifty to the waitress. "I finally feel as old as I am, and staying out late, partying my ass off, won't make for a happy Mike tomorrow."

From the little I know about Mike, he had dreams of being a fighter. He even lived out that dream, climbing to the top, getting the title, before marrying and calling it quits.

I'd thrown down with some pretty scary fuckers in my time, but no one quite as big as Mike Gallo. The man made every doorway seem small. But even with his imposing size, he has a kind smile and says shit that makes the smile slide easily across my lips.

"We're all leaving after this," Izzy announces, mothering us like she did all day at the shop. "This makes the second round, and anything more than this and none of us can drive."

"I'm good with the one," I add because although I'm not above mixing business with pleasure, I don't know these people well enough yet to match them drink for drink.

"Good, then you can drive Gigi home," Joe says from across the table with his daughter sitting right next to him, giving me the side-eye.

"I'm fine, Dad. It's only beer," she tells him and motions toward her half-empty glass sitting in front of her. "It's not like I'm about to chug the next one."

The first time I met Gigi, she had more than a beer in her system. The girl could drink and had an appetite for alcohol, like almost every college kid in the country.

"I'll make sure she gets home safely." I know it's going to aggravate her to no end that I'm willing to be her escort home.

"It's amazing I survived college without a ride home after a beer." She rolls her eyes, pushing her beer farther away with her top lip curling. "It takes more than that to get me tipsy."

Joe covers her hand as it lays on the table in front of them. "Just do your old man a favor. Give me peace of mind tonight and let Pike drive you."

"Why? Because he's a man?" she grumbles. "That's such bullshit, Dad, and you know it."

"Just be happy you have two sisters and not two brothers, Gigi. Your life could be worse. So much worse," Izzy adds, sliding her fingers through the water drops running down the side of her glass.

"Whatever," Gigi mutters, glaring at me across the table like I'm trying to give her a hard time when I've done nothing but keep my mouth shut, letting our secret stay hidden.

"So, Pike," Anthony says, placing his phone on the table next to his beer. "What's your story?"

I blink a few times, staring at him in confusion because the question is loaded and totally open-ended. "My story?"

"Yeah." Anthony lifts his hand as his eyebrows pull downward. "You got any siblings? Parents still alive? What brought you so far away from home?"

"One brother. Ten years younger than me. My parents are very much alive and still in Tennessee, hopefully where they'll stay until they take their last breath." I push my beer glass to the side and lean over the table, clasping my hands together.

"Your folks planning a visit?" Izzy cocked an eyebrow, staring at me, waiting for more details than I gave. She was fishing. Always fishing.

"Nope. I haven't spoken to them in years." I catch Gigi's eye. "My grandmother raised me since I was thirteen."

"Years?" Gigi mutters. "I couldn't imagine going that long without talking to my parents."

"That's because you have good parents. No, great parents, Gigi. You grow up with shit parents, living the way I did, you ride away and don't look back. The last thing I need is to waste any more of my life on people who couldn't give a shit if I'm alive or dead."

Gigi's eyes widen in horror at the harshness of my words. "That's awful."

It isn't the first time I've seen the pity on someone's face when they realize I'd had a bad hand dealt to me before turning everything around and making it what I wanted.

"If I'd grown up with an ounce of what you've got—" I dip my head toward her father and waving a hand toward her aunt and uncles "—I probably wouldn't be sitting here, having a beer in another state, determined to plant new roots far enough away I could never run into my past either."

The pretty little waitress sets the beers down on the table, her eyes moving from one person to another but not saying a word because she can probably feel the vibe at the table has shifted.

"Keep it, doll," Mike says when the woman tries to hand him his change.

"You're too kind, Michael," she says as a giant smile spreads across her pouty lips. "If I didn't love Mia so much…"

"It still wouldn't happen, babe. While you're pretty and sweet, you're way too young for an old fart like me."

She snorts. "Always a charmer."

I'm thankful for her interruption. Most of the table is busy shuffling around the beer glasses, hopefully forgetting everything I said moments ago. Everyone except Gigi. Her eyes are pinned on me, sweeping over my face with the small little creases across her forehead more pronounced.

"What about your brother?" Gigi asks as soon as the waitress wanders off because the woman can't leave shit alone.

I shrug. "He was seven when I left home. It's not like we had a close relationship."

"But if your parents were that bad, don't you worry about him being with them when you're not there to protect him?"

I laugh and shake my head. "My parents were shit to me, but not that kid. They love him. Treated him like the king of the castle. He could literally do no wrong in their eyes. He's fine right where he is, and it's not like I could've just taken him when I left. The road is no place for a kid."

Before I took off, I thought about taking Austin with me, but I wasn't sure how I was going to feed myself, let alone a kid. I knew he'd be fine with my parents. They loved him way more than they ever loved me. They made sure I knew how much more on a daily basis too. My grandmother promised me she'd check in on Austin, and the moment their attitude went south and they started treating him like anything other than a little prince, she'd let me know. Then and only then would I go back for him, taking him wherever my ass ended up.

"Where have you been for the last nine years?" Gigi asks, leaning forward, resting her fist underneath her chin and studying me like I was a rarity instead of the norm.

"Here and there."

"Pike's been working at some of the best tattoo shops in Florida since he was twenty," Joe tells her, figuring my answer wouldn't satisfy his daughter.

"If they were so good, why is he here?" she asks like I'm not even at the table or able to answer.

"Because I only wanted to be at the best place, and that's Inked."

I hope it's enough for the conversation finally to shift away from me.

"And for the two years in between?" she asks like a bloodhound, suddenly interested in my life for the first time since I met her.

"He was hanging with the guys in the Disciples," Izzy throws out there like it is common knowledge and something I put on my resume, which I didn't, and I thought I'd covered my tracks enough that no one would find out. My gaze slides to Izzy, and she shrugs with a shitty smirk. "You didn't think I'd hire you without having my husband run a full background check, did you?"

"So, you all knew, but hired me anyway?" I lean back in my chair, stunned as I look around the table, all eyes on me.

"When we let someone into the shop, we're not only letting them into our business, we're giving them access to our family. No one gets hired without a full work-up, no matter how fucking great their work is," Joe tells me, his face hard and unreadable.

"I was never a prospect," I reply, feeling like I need to explain my checkered past.

"We know," Izzy says, crossing her arms in front of her chest, leaning back like me. "You wouldn't be in that chair if you had been."

"How do you know?" I'm pretty sure the things she's saying

and thinks she knows aren't public knowledge or part of any record. At least not something someone could find out without digging into my background, finding the filth I wanted to stay hidden.

"Babe," she says, a shit-eating grin spreading across her face. "My husband may be an investigator now, but he was a DEA agent working the MC scene all across the South. If there's something he needs to know about a person or any club in the country, he's going to find it and not stop until he does."

"He asked around about me?"

Izzy nods. "He went right to the source, had a sit-down with Tiny."

My shoulders slump, and I let out a long, exasperated sigh. "He went to Tiny?"

Izzy nods. "Yep. Got all the dirt."

I raise an eyebrow because I'm sure he got some dirt, but he didn't get the steaming pile of shit that was my time hanging with the Disciples. "Tiny isn't much of a talker."

"Tiny and James go way back, and my brother Thomas and he go even further. They picked Tiny's brain, got the dirt they could get, and were satisfied enough with what he had to say that I got the okay to offer you that seat." Izzy pauses for a moment, shifting in her chair, leaning forward with her elbows resting just off the table. "And just so you know, the Feds watch those clubs every second of every day. You're in the files. Your name is there, pictures of you at their compound, riding with them, causing the havoc only the Disciples cause. If Tiny hadn't vouched for you, telling my husband you were just a kid who needed a home and help, you wouldn't be sitting where you're sitting."

"Still don't like that shit one bit," Joe says, glancing down at his daughter as she gawks at me like she didn't know a damn thing about my past.

She may not have known about the Disciples, but she knew why I was at Bike Week. It's not like we met at the ice cream shop, sharing wanton glances as we licked our cones. We met at a biker rally. One of the biggest ones in the country for fuck's sake.

"I was never in the life, and I don't plan on ever being there either. Those guys took me in when I had nowhere to go. They gave me a bed and a place to belong at a time when I had nothing and no one. They were a solid in my life when all I had was chaos."

"They don't do that shit out of the goodness of their heart," Izzy says, clearly knowing a lot about the life from her husband. "I spent enough time around those guys to know that life comes with strings."

"You know a lot of bikers?" I ask, trying not to laugh because the woman may be scary, but she didn't seem the type to be hanging out at compounds, sucking the cocks of random bikers for kicks.

"Someday, if you stick around, maybe I'll tell you about the time I spent with the Sun Devils. But that day isn't today, kid."

My eyebrows shoot up. "I know enough about the Sun Devils that I'm not sure I want to know about what shit went down between you and them."

"The fucking Sun Devils," Joe groans. "I hate those fuckers. They caused enough shit with this family that if I ever see one of them again, I'll..."

"They're all put away, Joe. Calm your shit. They can't touch us now," Izzy tells him like he doesn't have a reason to worry, which isn't entirely true.

"They have a far reach, Iz. Even behind bars, those fuckers have eyes and ears on the ground. I'm waiting for the next time they come after this family. And besides, it's not like they have life sentences."

I swallow down the lump that's lodged in my throat, thinking about the Sun Devils and the carnage they'd spread across the South back in the day. "They came after the family?"

Joe nods, eyes steely and cold. "Kidnapped Izzy and, hell, Angel too, but in the end, they landed in the place they deserved.

Should've known better than to mess with two DEA agents' family members, but they weren't always the brightest fucking bunch. They let their thirst for vengeance cloud their judgment and sealed their fate in pulling the shit they did."

"Happens a lot with men like that," Anthony adds as he lifts his beer glass to his lips.

The table goes on chatting about the Sun Devils as I sit there, staring at them in shock and amazement. I can't wrap my head around the fact that the MC went after the Gallos. They seem like the nicest people in the world, maybe wound a little tight and possibly a little too loving, but why the fuck would they come after them and kidnap two women who weren't even part of the world? It makes no sense. But then again, shit inside the MC world rarely made a bit of sense unless you were part of the life with axes to grind and anger to burn.

"I'm ready to go." Gigi stares at me across the table. "You ready?"

I nod, swallowing down the last sip of beer and pushing my seat back, standing. "Let's hit it."

"You two be careful on the way home," Joe says like he's said it a million times before.

A weird feeling crashes over me as Gigi waves goodbye. One of belonging. One of family. All about something I never had before but wished like hell I did. No one has ever given a shit if I got home okay or made it in one piece. The only person who cared was my grandmother, but she wasn't even that concerned, figuring I was a man who would somehow get myself through anything.

But Gigi grew up Gallo. She grew up surrounded by love, not knowing what it's like to have no one at her back. She is luckier than she could ever know, and I am kind of jealous of the life she's lived. The love she has. The acceptance that is freely given.

I'd give anything to have just a small sliver of that goodness in my life. I may not have been given it by birth, but I'll do whatever I have to do to get a little piece of it in my life now.

CHAPTER 13
GIGI

"I LOVE the last piece you did tonight," Pike says with his wrist on the steering wheel, looking like he's driven my truck a thousand times. The flash of oncoming traffic lights up his features, sending shadows across his face.

I stare at him in the relative darkness, taking in the slight bump on the bridge of his nose and the lushness of his lips. "I love when clients want me to design a piece. When they give me free rein to run with their thoughts and turn it into something original and meaningful."

"You nailed it. The coloring was spot-on too," he praises, and warmth blooms inside my chest.

"Thanks." I turn my head just as he turns his to look at me because I don't want him to know I'm staring at him. "I could use a little more practice at shading."

"Nah. It took me a couple years to get as good as you are now. In five years, you'll be featured in all the big magazines. Mark my words, Gigi."

"That's really nice of you to say, but you don't have to suck up to me. I don't plan on blowing up your world anytime soon, Pike."

He rolls the truck into the empty parking space in front of our apartment building and stops, turning to me as he cuts the engine. "I figured if you were going to, you would've done it already."

"Oh," I whisper, glancing at him when he shifts, sliding a little closer to me. "What are you doing?"

"Just wanted to talk alone for a few minutes." Pike stares at me in the soft glow of the parking lot lights, and I practically have to will myself not to leap into his lap.

Even after fifteen months, the pull to him is so heavy, the attraction so deep, I have to remind myself he's not for me. We have very little in common except for where we live and what we do. He comes from a different life. One without a loving family but with the Disciples in his past.

"You can talk from over there." I tick my chin toward his side of the cab, because if he gets any closer...

He scoots closer, and I hold my breath. "What's going to happen?"

My fingers work the fringe on the bottom of my denim shorts, and I remind myself to breathe. "I just don't think it's a good idea."

The one thing I know about Pike is he won't do anything I don't want. If I tell him to back off and it's not going to happen, he'll leave me alone. But then I remember the way his mouth tastes, the sensation of his lips against mine, and how much I want to feel his body pressing mine into the mattress.

"Sometimes, the best things never are."

"What if we get caught?"

He cocks an eyebrow. "Your parents have surveillance set up?"

I shrug, laughing nervously because the way he's looking at me is nothing short of hot and needy. "I wouldn't put it past my mother. My father is overprotective, but my mother is downright smothering."

His gaze drops to my lips as I speak, and heat sparks across my body. The needy ache I've felt for him since the moment I laid eyes on him again at Inked amplifies, and I'm pretty sure nothing but his touch will help chase the feeling away.

"Darlin'," he says, and my belly tumbles. I keep telling him how much I hate that word, but damn it, it's a lie. It's so much better than babe, and when Pike's saying it, there's nothing sweeter and it's a total turn-on. "Get your ass over here and kiss me already."

I gawk at him. It's like he's reading my mind because my body language doesn't exactly scream sex right now. I haven't moved an inch, too scared of what will happen if I do. The last time Pike and I kissed, we barely came up for air for almost a week. With my current dry spell, I'm confident it'll be much the same, but I don't have the luxury of time.

When I don't move, Pike slides closer until our knees are touching. "I'm going to kiss you, Gigi."

Oh God. Oh God. Oh God. Yes! Yes! Yes! I want to crawl into his lap, wrap my arms around his neck, and kiss the hell out of the man until I'm gasping for air.

"Pike," I whisper, my eyes locked on his mouth as his tongue pokes out, sweeping across his bottom lip. "I…"

The words don't make it out of my mouth before his hand is on my jaw, caressing my cheek with his thumb. "Tell me no, and I'll stop."

"Pike," I repeat like my brain is fried and his touch alone has rendered me completely and absolutely stupid.

He leans forward, eyes locked on mine, hand on my face as the shadows pass over his face when he moves his mouth closer.

"Yes," I whisper so quietly, I can barely hear myself over the loud thumping of my heart against the insides of my chest.

When his lips connect with mine, so velvety soft and warm, I can do nothing but open to him. The man is hard everywhere. Hard arms. Hard features. Hard eyes. Hard cock. But the one place he's soft is his lips. His mouth is demanding, just like the rest of him, as his lips press against mine. He tightens his fingers behind my neck, pulling me toward him, and my body moves on its own. Without thinking, I crawl into his lap, straddling him in the front seat of my truck in the very public parking lot of our building.

My arms go around his neck like they were always meant to be there as I settle into his lap, pressing my chest against his, loving the demanding way he's kissing me.

I could get lost in him.

I did actually.

Fifteen months ago, I'd been in this same position, tasting his lips, figuring I'd never see him again.

Wrong.

He slides a hand around my back, gripping my ass roughly as his tongue moves across my lips, and my skin starts to tingle everywhere like his mouth is the lighter fluid and his touch is the match. My body's on fire, burning for the man below me.

I grind my hips as I open my lips, giving him anything he wants. It's been so long since I've been touched like this. So long since I've felt this kind of need for anyone. In all honesty, I haven't wanted another man since the day I drove away from Daytona, telling myself Pike was nothing more than a fling.

Pike's fingers slide up the back of my neck before tangling in my hair, securing me to him even though I'm not going anywhere. I'm right where I want to be.

"I missed this," he murmurs against my lips, sending a jolt of white-hot electricity down my spine like a lightning bolt of need coursing through my system. "Missed how sweet you taste."

I moan and tighten the hold I have around his shoulders, latching my lips back on to his to stop him from talking. We talked all day. What we didn't do was kiss. Now isn't the time for chatter. Now's the time to get what I've been thinking about since the moment I laid eyes on him again.

A man clears his throat, and I freeze, my eyes flying open and going wide. We stare at each other, our mouths still touching, but not breathing.

"Excuse me," the man says, not giving two fucks that we're currently getting hot and heavy in the parking lot. "I'm looking for a Mr. Pike Moore."

Pike's lips move to the side, sliding off mine slowly, and I want to crawl through the open window and knee this guy in the balls for interrupting us. "I'm him."

The man reaches down, fishing something out of his pocket, and Pike's body stiffens under me. His hand is wrapped around my arms, hauling me off his body and to the other side of the truck, shielding me from whatever the man is about to do.

"I'm Special Agent Russo from the FBI. I was wondering if I could have a minute of your time." The man flashes his identification before snapping the leather wallet shut.

Pike growls. Flat-out growls like he's about to attack. "It's almost one in the morning, I'm sitting in the truck, having a nice time with my girl, and you pick now to bust my balls?"

The agent's eyes cut to me and then back to Pike. "Sorry for the bad timing, but I've been waiting around here all day for you, Mr. Moore."

"Bad timing," Pike mumbles, his hands balling into tight fists against his legs. "Understatement of the fucking year."

"I only need a moment of your time," the agent says, making no move like he's going to leave and let us finish what we began.

Pike's gaze moves to me. "Go inside, darlin'. I'll only need a minute."

"I'm not leaving." No man is going to tell me what to do, and like fuck am I leaving Pike out here alone with an agent without finding out what the hell he wants.

"It's about your dad."

If I thought Pike was stiff before, he's hard as granite now. His movements are slow, letting the man's words wash over him, soaking into his soul. "Is he dead?"

"He wasn't the last time we had eyes on him."

Pike moves his hand to the steering wheel, making no attempt to get out of the truck as I sit next to him, not moving and barely breathing.

What the hell could the agent want with Pike if it has to do with his father? Whether Pike likes the man or not, I can't imagine a cop showing up, asking me questions about my own blood.

"I don't talk to my father, so I don't know how I can help." Pike's eyes burn as they come to me. "I'm busy with my girl, so if you could come back tomorrow, maybe, and I mean maybe, I'll talk to you."

"Sir," the agent says and shakes his head. "I'm not leaving until we talk. If I have to haul your ass downtown to FBI headquarters to do it, so be it."

My hand clamps over my mouth as I gasp, and I try to cover my horror at the entire situation. "Is that really necessary?" I mumble against my palm with wide eyes.

The agent nods. "Actually, let's take a drive. I'd like to speak to you in private. It'll be safer downtown."

"Like fuck," Pike hisses, hand tightening around my steering wheel like he's trying to choke the life out of it.

"Don't go."

I stick my nose where it doesn't belong, but that's always been my way.

"Ma'am, do you want to take a ride in the back of my car too? You can wait in the holding cell where we keep the *good* criminals." He winks.

Pike's out of the truck before the guy can straighten his face again. "Leave her the fuck alone. If your beef is with me, keep it with me. Ya hear me?"

I lunge to the side, trying to grab on to his arm but miss, falling face first into the seat. "Let me call my uncle," I mutter into the fabric as I push myself upward to a sitting position.

Pike turns, his eyes flashing a warning that needs no words. I'm to call no one. "I'll be fine. Get your ass inside and lock the door." Pike ticks his head toward the apartment building like I'm just supposed to obey.

Is he for real? If the situation weren't so dire and the agent didn't look like such a giant douche, I'd laugh right in Pike's face. "Pike, I don't think…"

"He'll be fine, ma'am." The man dips his head, giving me a bullshit smile like I'm just going to take his word on that. He already said shitty things to me and hasn't been the nicest to Pike even though he's supposedly only wanted for questioning.

"Are you arresting him?" I blurt out as I slide across the truck, crawling to my feet just behind Pike.

The agent's gaze sweeps over Pike as he pulls at the cuffs of his dress shirt that are barely peeking out from his suit jacket. "Not yet, but stranger things have happened."

Well, isn't that reassuring?

"Just go inside, Gigi," Pike orders as I start to reach for my phone. "Call no one."

I let out a loud huff before jamming my phone back into my shorts pocket. "Fine."

"Let's go, son."

"Don't call me that. You're not my daddy," Pike says coldly.

"The longer you wait, the later it'll be when you get back."

Pike turns to me and grabs my hands, tangling his fingers with mine. "I'll text you when I'm back, darlin'. Don't worry. I'll be fine."

"I'll go with you." I take a step toward Pike before he tightens his grip, stopping me.

"Stay here in case I need you. Please," he begs with knitted brows.

What the fuck am I supposed to do from here? How can I help him if I'm thirty minutes away? He's crazy if he thinks I'm just going to stand by, twiddling my damn thumbs until he sends me a text message.

"Okay," I lie. "I promise," I lie again.

He exhales as his shoulders finally relax. "Thank you." He leans forward, placing his lips on my cheek and whispers, "I promise everything will be fine."

I don't know if I want to scream or cry as he releases me, backing up toward the agent, our eyes locked on each other. I want to beg him not to go. Beg him to stay here, but I know it's useless.

Pike folds himself into the back of the guy's unmarked car, staring at me through the window as the dickhead slams the door. I lift my hand and wave, wishing I could tell him everything will be okay. He may have whispered the words, but I know he didn't believe a word he spoke.

The agent smirks as he climbs into the front, revving the engine like that piece of shit Capri is a hot rod.

I walk toward the car, following as it slowly rolls toward the exit of the apartment complex. Pike turns in his seat, peering at me through the window, barely visible in the darkness.

I waste no time, grabbing my phone and dialing the only person I know who can help in this situation. The only one I know who can keep his mouth shut.

"It's fucking late. This shit better be good."

I wince. "Um, Uncle James. I need you." I look into the darkness as the taillights of the agent's car disappear.

CHAPTER 14
PIKE

THE SOUND of metal on concrete snaps me out of the haze from sitting too long in a quiet room at four in the morning. Fuck, I need to be at work in eight hours, and I'm nowhere near my place and need to get some damn sleep so I'm not useless tomorrow.

So far, the asshat agent hasn't said much but has come in to bust my balls every few minutes just as I'm nodding off. I assume it's all part of his genius master plan, trying to deprive me of sleep so I'll tell him whatever he's fishing for just so I can leave.

"Sorry," a new guy says, plopping down in the chair, almost spilling the coffee he's holding in one hand. "Didn't mean to wake you."

Fucker. "Can we just get this shit over with so I can get out of here?"

They took my phone as soon as I got here. I'm pretty sure there's probably dozens of texts from Gigi, possibly a few missed calls, all growing in levels of panic. I wasn't looking forward to having her chew my ear off for ordering her ass inside and telling her to mind her own business, even if I said it in a nice way. Or at least, the nicest way I knew how.

The man flips open a folder, fingers a few pages, staring down at the words. "Your father is Colton Moore?"

"Yes." I grit my teeth together, slouching over in the chair and rapping my fingertips on the metal table. "I thought we established this."

"I'm the new shift." He peers up for a moment as he turns a page. "Have you ever worked for the firm of Moore, Justice, and Sanders?"

I glare at this dumbass. "Do I look like a lawyer?"

"I guess that's a no," he says, pulling a pen from a pocket on the front of his shirt. "Have you ever spent time in his office?"

"Recently? I mean, my ass is in Florida, so that would be a no."

Is this guy fucking serious with these dumb-ass questions?

"Ever, kid. Have you ever spent time in his office?"

"When I was a kid, sure. He is my father."

He scribbles something on the paper, flipping to the next sheet. "Have you ever heard the name Dominic DiSantis?"

My face doesn't move because I've heard that name a million times in my life. Dirty Dom. That's how my father always referred to him, especially when talking with other friends and clients he'd bring back to the house. The man was a criminal and my father was his attorney, but half the shit my dad did for him wasn't covered under the umbrella of a normal attorney-client relationship.

They thought I was too young to understand when they'd talk in my presence. Just figured I was some dumb kid who was too busy pushing around the same shitty toy truck I'd had for three years to know what they were saying, but I heard every word and took it all in.

"I've heard the name," I tell the guy who is staring at me across the table, waiting for me to lie.

I'm pretty sure he already knows the answers to the questions. A quick background check would've told him I haven't lived in Tennessee in almost a decade, and being Colt's kid, of course I heard names I probably never should've heard.

He raises an eyebrow. "Care to elaborate?"

I raise mine right back. "Care to tell me why?"

The man sighs, leaning back in the chair, pushing the folder of papers toward the middle of the table. "Dominic DiSantis is a mobster."

I nod because anyone who's anyone and pays attention to the national news knows this shit. He was popped a year ago and is awaiting trial for money laundering and a whole long-ass list of shit I'm pretty sure he did.

"He's currently locked up and awaiting trial."

"Tell me something I don't know." I kick back, putting my hands behind my head, acting as chill as I can so I don't lose my shit. "Why did you haul me down here to tell me something I already know? This is bullshit, verging on harassment."

"Your father was on retainer with Dominic."

"I know," I bark, losing my patience.

"We believe your father may be involved in Mr. DiSantis's criminal enterprises."

I lean forward, resting my arms on the table and glare at this buffoon. "Whether my father is or isn't, I don't know how you think I can help. Do you know how close I am to my father?" I pause for a second, and just as he's about to say something stupid again, I continue. "I haven't spoken to my father in over ten years. I lived with my grandmother as soon as I started middle school because I couldn't be around the asshole another minute. He may be my blood, but that doesn't make him my family. I know you want to nail him and DiSantis, but there's nothing I can say to help you."

The agent crosses his arms, studying me. "Whether you've talked to him in ten years or not, you know things, were privy to things no one else was. If you're not willing to help us, maybe we should visit your little brother at summer camp and see if he's willing to help us."

I force myself to stay in my seat because all I want to do is lunge at the asshole and wrap my fingers around his neck until he begs for me to let go. "Leave Austin out of this."

"We're running out of options, Mr. Moore. Either you help us, or we'll have no other choice but to speak with Austin."

"Talk to my mother. I'm sure she'll flip on him if you offer her something she wants, like a new life and an unlimited bank account."

"She's dead, son."

I blink a few times, thinking I must have heard him wrong. "Excuse me?"

"Died this morning. Gunshot to the back of the head after she dropped Austin off at camp. We figured it was an execution, sending a message to your father from Mr. DiSantis."

My head spins with the news as it slams into my chest like a ton of bricks. *My mother is dead.* She and I had a tenuous relationship at best, but I wasn't her favorite and always seemed more like a burden than a blessing. She never once stopped my father from putting his hands on me. Never once stopped the man from treating me like an outcast in my own home. If she had a maternal instinct, it didn't appear until Austin was born.

I never went to summer camp. I never got shit as a kid. There wasn't a new toy in my room until the ones I had were so worn out they basically fell apart. I don't remember being hugged or snuggled, even if I was sick or bleeding. The two of them were worthless. The day my grandmother caught my father, hand raised, ready to strike me, she took me in and I never looked back.

"You think DiSantis killed my mother, and you track me down, harassing me for hours, and don't even bother to mention that shit until now?" I ball my hands into fists, wanting to punch this fucker straight in the face. "And you make me leave my girl alone and vulnerable so you can haul me down here, not even thinking it's a good idea to clue me the fuck in on the day's events?"

"We have no reason to believe your girlfriend is in danger."

"Pardon me if that isn't reassuring. Did you think my mother was in danger, or did you let her take one for the team?"

"Son..."

"Don't fucking call me that!" I yell, pushing back from the table and rising to my feet. "Don't ever fucking call me that. I want to talk to your superior."

The man's up, studying me as I pace around the room, running my hands through my hair to do something with them besides knock his lights out. "I don't think..."

"That seems to be the norm around here," I taunt, wishing he'd get pissed and swing on me just so I could land a good one on him.

He turns his back to me as the handle to the door turns and opens, and a man appears. "Agent Carson, the interview is over."

"Damn right, it is," I bark out, leering at the two men across the room from me.

"We weren't finished," Carson replies, turning and tossing his pen on the table that sits between us. "Just a few more minutes."

The other man shakes his head. "Can't let that happen. We have an issue."

"What kind of issue?"

"The Director called and isn't so happy about us bringing Mr. Moore in for questioning."

Carson stiffens. "How the hell does he know?"

The man gives a small shrug. "I guess the kid has a few connections. Calls were made. Favors exchanged, and we're to let him go or else..."

Connections? Favors? No one knows I'm here except for Gigi. *Fuck.* She didn't listen to a damn word I said. By now, the entire Gallo family probably knows my ass is downtown, sitting in FBI headquarters for some unknown reason. I'll have a lot of explaining to do and a lot of begging if I am going to be allowed to stay at Inked and at least finish out the contract on the chair I so badly want.

Fucking perfect. If shit wasn't fucked up enough already, my mom dead, my brother motherless, and my father who the fuck knows where, my job is in jeopardy because Gigi couldn't let me handle my own shit.

"What the fuck? The Director knows how important this case is." Carson throws out an arm in my direction. "And we're just supposed to let him go?"

The other man raises an eyebrow. "You want to call him at this hour and tell him you think he's wrong?"

Carson glances toward the ceiling and lets out a loud grunt. "Fuck. This is bullshit."

"It's *all* bullshit," I mutter, still pacing so I don't go ballistic about the entire situation, including the two assholes in the room with me.

"We're sorry about your mother, Mr. Moore," the new guy says like somehow his condolences are going to make anything better.

My mother cut ties with me years ago. The last time I talked to her, I was already living at the Disciples' compound, which she snubbed her nose at, reminding me that she thought I was a piece of trash before and always. That was the last time I said goodbye to her, and that time, I meant that word completely.

I should be crying, shedding a tear that the woman who gave birth to me is lying somewhere on a cold metal table, stiff and not breathing. But I can't bring myself to cry. I care, of course I do—she is family—but there's no love between us. There never will be now.

The thing I care most about is the fact that Gigi's out there and I don't know who's had eyes on me. If DiSantis was watching my parents close enough to off my mom, is he watching me too? Has he seen Gigi and me together? Would he use her to keep me quiet?

"You can go, Mr. Moore. If we need you further..."

I wave him off, pushing past Carson. "You know where to find me the next time you want to drop a bomb in my lap and harass me."

"The department truly is sorry," he says as I brush against him, wishing I could knock them both over as I make my way toward the sterile gray hallway.

"Save it. Just give me my phone and let me go."

"The receptionist at the front desk will give you your things before you leave."

I pause for a minute, waiting for someone to offer me a ride home, but they say nothing. I stalk down the hallway, happy to be heading toward freedom and to make my way back home to check on Gigi. I have to figure out what to do about her. Do I distance myself from her entirely? Distance myself from her family too? I don't want my father to put her and her entire family at risk because he's a money-grubbing asshole.

I'm staring at the floor, watching the black-and-white checkered pattern pass in a blur and thrilled as fuck to get out of here, even if I have to hitch a ride home with a stranger.

"Pike!" Gigi screeches.

I lift my head, catching sight of the beautiful brunette running toward me like we haven't seen each other in years. "Are you okay? Oh my God. I was so scared. I thought they were never going to let you go." Her gaze darts over my body, checking for some sign of wear and tear. "Did they hurt you? I was so worried, I didn't know what to do. I'm so sorry." She looks over her shoulder toward a man who doesn't look happy and is scarier than any dude in this place. "I had to call someone. Don't be mad at me," she finally pleads, sucking in a breath because she hasn't given herself a chance to come up for air and stop talking long enough to breathe.

"I'm not mad, darlin'," I whisper, mindful of the man looking a little like a caged lion and totally pissed off to be here at this hour. I want to wrap her in my arms, steal her away from this place, and put her where I know no one will find her, but the way the man she came with is staring at me, at us, I know I'd better keep my hands to myself.

Gigi turns toward the tall, dark-haired man behind her. "This is

James," she says and pulls me toward him, locking her fingers with mine. "My aunt Izzy's husband."

My eyes widen. "You called Izzy's husband?"

She nods, smiling at me like her decision made all the sense in the world. "Izzy's not stupid. She knows something is going on. Plus, James worked for the DEA, and I figured if anyone had connections with the FBI, it would be him. What else was I supposed to do? Just leave you here?" She squeezes my fingers and gives me the sweetest smile, like it's going to make all this shit okay.

Fucking great.

"Well, yeah." I pull my hand from her grip because Uncle James hasn't taken his eyes off our connection, and there's no happiness on his face. "I would've figured something out sooner or later."

James stands taller, crossing his arms as he spreads his legs farther apart. "You two about done?"

"We're done." I look the man in the eye because he deserves my respect. No matter what, he pulled my ass out of a jam, getting up in the middle of the night to help a person he didn't even know. "Can you just take us home?"

James shakes his head. "You two are going to my place. Izzy's waiting, and she's probably climbing the walls right about now. If I don't bring you there, she'll have my ass. And besides losing sleep, I don't need her chewing my ear off all morning about dropping you off at home."

"I'm sorry," Gigi says again.

"It's fine," I lie because what else am I supposed to say? Nothing about this night has been fine. From the moment the asshole interrupted our kiss until the moment I walked out of the interrogation room, nothing has been fine.

"We're coming, Uncle James." Gigi turns to me, grabbing my hand, giving my fingers a light squeeze. "Okay?" She stares up at me, looking for my confirmation.

I nod. I'm not sure if it's something I want Gigi to know because she'd flip her shit and rightfully so. Maybe I need to explain the situation to James, get his thoughts on what my next move should be and how we can shield Gigi from any potential blowback.

James practically punches the door open, walking into the thick night air with Gigi and me following behind him. She glances at me, giving me a small smile every few steps before staring at her uncle and frowning.

I know she has a lot to say. I know she wants to ask me everything, but she's holding back...for once. I have a lot to say too, but I'm not sure I can put everything into words just yet. There's so much swirling around my brain, I can barely make sense of it all.

"Pike, sit up front. You and I are going to talk," James says as we approach his kick-ass Challenger parked just outside the doorway since the place is deserted.

"Um," Gigi mumbles, wanting to say more but shutting her mouth when James turns his gaze toward her. "Got it. I'm in the back."

I fold the seat forward, letting her crawl into the impossibly small back seat, thankful I don't have to contort myself in crazy ways to sit next to her. I slide in under the watchful eye of James and stare straight ahead, feeling something strange wash over me.

"Seat belts, kids."

I don't argue with the man. I'm not stupid. I'm not even in the mood to tell him I'm not his kid because I'm almost certain he'd knock me upside the head, and I'd still have to put on my seat belt before he'd drive away. Right now, all I want is a place to lay my head, sort out my thoughts, and say goodbye to this day.

"How do you know DiSantis?" he asks before we're even out of the parking lot.

"I don't." I shrug, staring out the front window as the oncoming cars pass in a blur. "My father worked for him."

"That's it? You never did any side jobs for him?"

"That's it. I was a kid last time I was around him, fifteen years ago, maybe. I forgot about the guy until I saw he'd been arrested splattered on the front page of the newspaper."

James adjusts in his seat, leaning forward, holding the steering wheel with one hand. "The Director and I go way back. We have a history together. He told me what he could about the case, why they hauled you in for questioning, and what they're hoping to gain."

"I don't have anything to offer." I shrug, placing my elbow on the door, resting my head in my palm because I'm so exhausted, I'm fighting to stay awake in the darkness.

"They told me about your mom," James says softer, his voice laced with sorrow. "I'm sorry for your loss."

Gigi gasps behind me, and I straighten. "Oh my God. Pike, I'm so sorry." Her voice wavers like she's on the verge of tears, but there's no time for crying.

I ignore her, because there's more pressing shit than fretting over a woman who gave no shits about me. "I'm worried about Gigi and anyone who's around me right now. I could use your help in figuring out what my next move should be, sir."

"Why are you worried about me?"

This time, James ignores her. "We have a lot to figure out and not a lot of time to do it. For the time being, the safest place for the two of you is at my house. You'll stay there until we know what we're dealing with. Got it?" James raises up, looking in the rearview mirror as we wait at a traffic light. "You hear me, Giovanna? I don't want any lip either."

Fan-fucking-tastic.

The night just went from bad to clusterfucked beyond belief.

CHAPTER 15
GIGI

I YAWN for what might be the hundredth time in the thirty-minute drive home from the FBI headquarters. To say I'm tired is an understatement. I don't remember being this exhausted in my entire life. I never even pulled an all-nighter studying for college exams.

I've sat in relative silence as James and Pike talked around me, ignoring my every comment like I wasn't talking or even in the same car with them. They are both infuriating, cut from the same manly cloth, and it's annoying as hell.

"Be ready for the real grilling to start," James says as he pulls into the drive and his headlights land on Aunt Izzy.

She's pacing back and forth in the driveway, her head coming up as she's bathed in light from the car. The look on her face isn't friendly or even playful, but serious as a fucking heart attack and like she's ready to pounce at any second.

"Well, this should be fun," I mumble and wonder if I should've called Uncle Thomas instead. But I know Angel is shit at keeping secrets, and right now, I needed silence.

"Just let her say what she needs to say, answer what she wants to know, and you'll live to see the sunrise," James says, trying to make light of what totally isn't a funny situation.

I drag my hands down my face, trying to clear my mind and wake myself up for what's probably going to be hours of explaining and getting my ass chewed out.

"You handle your aunt while Pike and I talk in my office," James tells me as he cuts the engine and unlocks the car doors.

"Handle her?" I cackle, feeling loopy from exhaustion. "You know that's an impossibility, right?"

James's eyes slice to mine. "You're exactly like your aunt, kid. You two think alike. If I didn't know better, I'd think you were her daughter. You know how she thinks, so handle her. Tell her what you want, leave out what you can, and then get your ass to sleep." James turns toward the door as Izzy raps her fingers against the window before throwing her arms up in a *what the fuck* kind of way.

"I think I'm getting the better end of this deal," Pike says as he pushes open his door, climbs out, and pulls the lever to let me out of the crazy-small back seat.

"You so did," I whisper, brushing up against him as I crawl out, almost smacking my head before I find my footing. "I'll find you when you're done."

"You two better get your asses inside. You have a lot of explaining to do," Izzy announces before I've even stood straight and stretched my legs.

"I have a feeling I'm going to be done before you, darlin'," Pike says as the corner of his mouth quirks up.

I scowl because there's nothing even remotely amusing about the entire situation. From Pike being hauled downtown, the fact that his mother is dead and I have no fucking clue how or why, and that my aunt and uncle are now all up in my shit and Pike's too.

"Sweetheart," James says, grabbing Izzy by the waist and hauling her body against his. "Go easy on the kid. She's had a long, stressful night. She's tired."

Izzy glances at me over James's shoulder. "Good. She'll break easier that way."

"For fuck's sake," I mutter, rolling my eyes. "I'll tell you everything, Auntie, if you just let me sleep for a little while."

"Fat chance, missy. March your pretty little ass in the kitchen, and we'll have some coffee while we talk about all the shit you've left out."

Pike squeezes my hand, peering down at me. "Tell her what you want, Gigi. I have nothing else to hide. I'm pretty sure my ass is going to be fired anyway."

"Why?" I furrow my eyebrows as I glance up at him, my mouth hanging open.

"No one wants trouble coming to their door, especially from someone they don't know and just hired. Go with her. It'll all be better in the morning."

"Find me, okay? Promise me," I plead.

Pike nods, releasing my hand and pushing me toward my aunt. "Go."

Izzy's out of James's arms and around the Challenger within seconds, stalking toward me like a woman possessed. "Stop wasting time," she says, reaching for my arm and hauling me away from Pike like I'm a little girl again.

I glance over my shoulder, mouthing "I'm sorry" to Pike as I follow my aunt up the stairs to the front door of their house. He only waves, giving me a small smile like this is just another day and not one where his mother dies and his life may be at risk.

"Sit," Izzy says before I'm two steps into the kitchen, pointing at a chair near the island. "Coffee or water?"

"Coffee." I slump over, wishing she'd just give me a pillow and one hour to get a little sleep. But I know my aunt, and she ain't giving me nothing until I give her something in return.

She pours the coffee, her back to me, and I can almost hear her thoughts and the line of questioning she's about to hurl at me.

"Before we start." I clear my throat, staring at her back, wishing like fuck I was anywhere but here. "Can you not tell my dad?"

Izzy sighs, placing the coffee carafe back on the warmer. "They already know."

I gasp, eyes widening, and suddenly feel more awake than I ever have in my entire life. "What?"

"There was an agent waiting at your parents' house when he got home from the bar tonight. He knows Pike was hauled in for questioning. But we left some things out like the fact that you called James in a complete panic, begging for someone to help a guy you claim to hate."

"I don't hate him," I mumble, crossing my arms over my chest, trying to figure out how to crawl out of this miserable mess.

"I know, baby girl," she says, sliding the coffee cup in front of me. "I used to look at your uncle James the same way. Girl," she laughs, shaking her head as she leans across the counter, facing me. "That man had me all kinds of crazy and my head all twisted."

I laugh because she says that like she's normal now and Uncle James's effect has worn off. He's the only man who can shut my aunt up when she's on a tirade, which is more often than not, especially lately.

"So, start at the beginning and tell me how you know Pike." She pins me with her gaze, and I swallow the lump that suddenly forms in my throat.

I glance down at the mug, wrapping my hands around the warm ceramic, wondering just how far back I should go and how detailed I should be. I'm not about to get graphic with my aunt because she's my aunt and I sure as fuck don't ask about her sex life, even if I have heard about it.

"Well…" I pause, stalling but knowing she would wait an eternity to hear the answer. "I met him last year."

Her eyes flash. "Where?"

"In Daytona."

"When?"

"Last year."

"No, smartass. When were you in Daytona? I don't remember you ever mentioning it to anyone."

I shift, squirming in the chair because Tamara and I swore each other to secrecy and hadn't broken our promise for fear of our parents flipping the fuck out. "We went there for spring break," I squeak, cringing at my voice and the look that shifts across my aunt's face.

"You went to Daytona for spring break last year?"

"Yeah." I nod slowly, holding her steely gaze.

"In March?"

I nod again because I figure there's nothing else I need to say, and I know more questions are coming.

She moves her coffee mug to the side, flattening her palms against the cold granite countertop. "Wasn't that Bike Week?"

I nod again, biting on my lip to stop myself from saying anything more.

"Are you fucking stupid, little girl?"

I shake my head, figuring words aren't necessary and knowing she is going to say enough for the both of us.

"You went to Daytona for spring break, which just happened to be Bike Week, alone, and didn't bother to tell anyone?" She sucks in a breath, looking like her head is about to pop off. "Do you know how goddamn dangerous that was?"

"I wasn't alone," I whisper, staring back down at my mug as I play with the handle.

"You were with Tamara, weren't you?" she says flatly because usually, wherever I go, Tamara isn't too far behind. We're a package deal especially since Lily decided to go to Miami instead of FSU like Tam and me.

I nod again.

Izzy pushes away from the countertop, cursing into the air as she starts to pace again. "Of all the stupid shit you two could do..."

"We were safe. We made it back in one piece. Nothing bad happened, Auntie."

"Thank fuck," she blurts out, stopping on her heel and spinning her body to face me. "I've been to Bike Week. That shit ain't no joke, Gigi."

"You went there?" I ask, fascinated that my aunt ventured into the biker world, but I shouldn't be surprised. She did end up married to one of the most badass men I've ever known besides my father. "To Bike Week?"

"I was almost raped at Bike Week. If it weren't for your uncle Thomas and uncle James, I don't know what would've happened to me." She hangs her head for a moment and takes a deep breath. "But I was older and should've been wiser. You weren't even twenty-one yet, and Tamara isn't even twenty-one now, so explain to me what the fuck you two were doing at Bike Week?"

"Lying on the beach." I don't even believe my own shit because my voice rises like I'm asking a question instead of stating a fact. Dead giveaway and my aunt doesn't miss a fucking beat.

"Gigi," she says flatly. "Stop the bullshit. Lay it out, and I want the truth."

"We went for spring break, but we honestly didn't know it was Bike Week when we planned the trip. We found out as we pulled into town and noticed all hell had broken loose and everyone was covered in leather and tattoos."

"Even if you didn't know it was Bike Week, why did you lie about going to Daytona in the first place?"

I shrug. "We figured Dad would get pissed and Uncle Anthony would throw a fit, so we just thought it would be easier."

Izzy chuckles softly, and I almost think she's going to let it drop, maybe let me go to sleep, but I'm dead wrong. "You should always let someone know where you are. You could've at least told me. A place like that at a time like that was risky, and you're lucky you two made it out unscathed."

"Yeah. I know that now." I'm trying to pacify her. "I'll never do it again."

"And how does Pike fit into—" she clears her throat "—lying on the beach in Daytona?"

"We ran into each other there," I lie and lift the mug to my lips, hoping to cover some of my face so she doesn't know I'm still not telling her the entire truth.

She straightens, crossing her arms in front of her as she stands there in a black tank top and yoga pants, her hair pulled into a tight, high ponytail. "So, you two ran into each other and then you looked like you saw a ghost when you ran into him again?" She narrows her eyes. "You think I'm going to believe that line of horseshit?"

"It's not horseshit," I mumble into my mug, staring at the black liquid because meeting her eyes is a little too much, especially when she's ready to start frothing at the mouth.

"You know the man better than just a quick passing hello. I wasn't born yesterday, Gigi. You better start telling me the truth, or I'll tell Joe about Daytona."

My eyes widen. "You wouldn't."

She drops a shoulder, a grin playing on her lips. "Sweetheart, I'll do whatever I need to do. It won't be my ass getting chewed out by him when he finds out."

I groan, knowing I'm not handling Izzy, but she sure as shit is handling me. Like a pro too. "Fine, we did more than run into each other."

"Did you drink together?"

"A little." I wince.

"Did he know you were underage?"

I shake my head. "We had fake IDs."

Izzy closes her eyes, pressing her fingers against her temples and rubbing. "Motherfucker," she whispers, drawing in a loud breath. "How many drinks did you have with Pike?"

"Which time?" I try to be funny even though I was also being honest.

She twists her mouth. "Stop being a smartass."

I shrug again. "The first night I met him, I think I had one drink."

"So, you weren't drunk?"

"Well…" I give her a nervous smile. "I may have been drinking before I met him. I said I only had one drink with him."

"On a scale of one to ten, ten being black-out drunk, where were you?"

"Before the drink with him or after?"

"For fuck's sake," she says, shaking her head, cursing again under her breath. "After you had the drink with him."

"A nine. I remember everything except for passing out, which I did because tequila." I laugh, trying to break the tension in the room, thinking Izzy will laugh because she's usually the fun one in my family.

She pulls her lips into her mouth, closing her eyes again, and groans. Clearly, I was wrong about the funny, and my aunt's sense of humor died somewhere between earlier tonight—or was that yesterday?—and right now. "You passed out with him, or were you with Tamara?" She's leaning over the counter, tapping her long black fingernails on the granite. "You can tell me, or I'll ask Tam when she comes home."

"I passed out with him." I don't want her questioning Tamara, and she'll find out anyway because Tam will crack like an egg under Izzy's pressure.

"Of all the stupid shit," she says, pushing off the counter and pacing again. "Did he hurt you?" Her eyes slice to mine.

I shake my head. "No, Auntie. He was a gentleman."

"A gentleman who took you back to his hotel room." She laughs. "You're priceless, kid."

"So, you've never had a one-night stand with a stranger?" I throw that right in her face because I've heard all about the night she met James at my parents' wedding. They weren't sipping coffee all night before she snuck right the fuck out of his room.

"We're not talking about me," she deflects. "Now, you had a drink with him, passed out, and then what? Don't leave anything out, or Pike will be out of this house and have his shit packed before your tired ass wakes up."

I take a deep breath and start at the beginning, telling my aunt every detail, minus all the crazy-amazing fucking we did. She doesn't need to know the details because she isn't my girlfriend, and it is already horrifying enough that I am telling her I slept with him. After what feels like I've been talking forever, I stop, finally looking at her in the eyes again. "That's it."

"Did you give him your phone number? Promise him anything?"

I shake my head. "He didn't even know my full name. Just knew me as Gigi, and I told him I was going for coffee one morning and never went back."

My aunt's face changes, and her eyes light up. "You said you were going for coffee?"

I nod, laughing a little and feeling guilty too. "I did. He said he waited for me for hours before realizing I wasn't coming back."

"You so should've been my kid," she says, holding her stomach, still laughing. "That's totally something I would've pulled back in my heyday."

"We're not talking about your heyday." I use air quotes on the last two words. If there's anything more horrifying than telling your aunt about a guy you banged, it's hearing about the guys she banged when she was your age.

"I was young once."

"You still are." I suck up. Something I've always done with my aunt and has typically worked.

"You're a shit liar, baby girl."

"Don't fire Pike," I beg because her mood has changed, and this may be the only time I can beg her for mercy. "I promise he didn't do anything wrong."

"I need to talk to your uncle before I can make you a promise about Pike and his future at Inked."

"That's bullshit. I'm either an adult, or I'm not. You can't treat me like a girlfriend one minute, laughing about the way I left a guy with his dick literally in his hand, and then in the next breath, tell me you can't make me a promise until you discuss something with my uncle. Why not just throw Dad in there too?"

"Pike's future is going to be a family decision, Giovanna. We all own Inked. I don't get the final say in anything that happens to that man without the others getting to say their piece."

"Fucking great," I groan.

"I won't tell them about your spring break activities, but they will know what happened tonight and the world of shit surrounding Pike."

"You won't tell them that we were making out tonight, will you?"

When her eyes widen, I slap my hand over my mouth, realizing I hadn't told her about that and she had no way of knowing. *Fuck. Good going, dumbass.*

"I won't tell them about that either if you want Pike to still be breathing, but they're going to have questions, and you're going to have to woman up and answer them."

"Fine."

"But there will be lots of questions—especially now that Pike's worried about your safety."

Sounds like a fan-fucking-tastic time. I've always wanted to tell my dad about the lies I've told him and the guys—even though they've been limited—that I've banged. I'm totally looking forward to the most uncomfortable situation of my life. *Not.*

I would rather have my hair pulled out strand by strand while being tied to a chair of nails sticking in my ass than talk about any of this shit with the men in my family, especially my father.

"Speak of the devil," Izzy says as the door creaks behind me.

My eyes widen and I freeze, unable to move as if somehow I'll disappear and won't have to have this talk now instead of later.

"Giovanna," my father says, his voice washing over me like I'm a little kid again, waiting to be punished for my stupid shit.

I don't turn around because Joe Gallo is a sweet man, but every guy, even my dad, has his breaking point. I'm pretty sure I've punched right through that ceiling without even trying. "Hey, Daddy."

"You and me, outside."

"Just talk here and grab a cup of coffee. I'll go see what's taking Pike and James so long." Izzy catches my eye, giving me a small wink before she sashays right the fuck out of there, not even worried that my dad's going to blow a fucking gasket.

"Daddy..."

"Save it, baby girl."

I bow my head, staring at my coffee, and ready myself for the biggest ass-chewing of my life.

CHAPTER 16
PIKE

"WE HAVE A PROBLEM," James says into the phone, staring at me from across the desk with his lips set in a firm line. "You're the only man I could think to come to about the situation."

I bite the inside of my cheek, rubbing my hands against the wood of the chair my ass has been planted in for hours, taking James's questions in rapid-fire succession.

"I know what fucking time it is, but I couldn't wait until your old ass decided to get out of bed."

My mouth falls open. No one has ever talked to Tiny, the President of the Disciples MC, that way. At least, I'd never heard them do it, because Tiny would've pounded their face in until they were black and blue, sucking their food through a straw for the next two months.

James laughs. "You never were an early bird, ya old fuck."

I blink a few times, wondering who the fuck James is to Tiny, and how they know each other well enough that they can laugh while insulting the hell out of each other.

"I have your kid Pike here." James pauses, eyes sweeping over my face. "Yeah, he's in one piece, alive and breathing, sitting right in front of me."

I begged James not to call Tiny. Pleaded with him not to get the Disciples MC involved, but he told me not to be a fucking moron and picked up the phone like it meant nothing to call in a favor.

"Just sit there and keep your mouth shut," James told me before he dialed Tiny's number from memory, surprising the fuck out of me.

So, here I sit, watching James as he takes my business into his own hands, giving help where I didn't ask. But this isn't just about me; this is about his niece and the pile of shit she landed in just by being near me.

"He has an issue with DiSantis and needs somewhere to lie low." James taps the pen he's holding against the pad of paper he'd been taking notes on like he was working my case too. "Couldn't think of anyone with enough manpower and weapons, outside of law enforcement, who would look after the kids except you and the boys."

I shake my head, surprised James is asking Tiny for help. Not just Tiny, but a motorcycle club that has many wearing the badge shaking in their fancy, polished boots.

"It's serious. Pike's mom ain't breathing no more because of the shit his father's in with DiSantis."

I close my eyes, rubbing my fingers into the corners, wondering where the fuck my normal life has gone. Now, my mother's dead, lying somewhere cold with a bullet lodged in the back of her head. My brother's God knows where, hopefully with my grandmother, and my dad's gone missing because he's a fucking coward and a criminal.

"My niece is involved too, Tiny. She'll need safe haven and a guarantee you'll protect her with your life. I'm trusting you more than I've ever trusted anyone who isn't blood by asking you for this favor."

That shit ain't no lie.

Gigi said her uncle worked for the DEA but had since retired, now owning a private investigation firm. But from the sounds of it, he's not entirely out of the game.

"I'll owe you, and you know I always pay my debts," James tells him, still staring at me with a look I can't quite place, and I'm not sure I'd want to even if I could.

"I'll drive them over after nightfall. You're going to have to keep them out of sight until this shit blows over. I don't want them traceable. No eyes can fall on them. The FBI has already questioned Pike, and I don't want them getting their hands on him again. No man, no matter how much he hates his father, should be put in this position. Just keep them safe, and I'll come for them when shit blows over."

"James." I want to argue with him because I'm not sure hiding out with a badass biker crew at their compound is the best idea.

He covers the phone with his hand, mouthing, "Not now. Just keep quiet."

I raise my eyebrows and twist my lips, biting back the words I want to say so badly.

"We'll be there around one. Be ready for us. I'm dropping them off at our meeting place and heading out. I'll have two cars following, making sure no one is on our tail. I want them untraceable."

James leans back, laughing with Tiny before he presses his finger to the phone screen, ending the call. "Go get some sleep. You have a long day and night ahead of you," he tells me, not even wanting to discuss the plans he made on my behalf.

I don't move because I'm not ready and I'm sure as fuck not used to being ordered around. "How exactly do you know Tiny? Because from what I can tell, neither of you run in the same circles."

"You know I worked for the DEA, yeah?"

I nod.

"We most certainly weren't friends back in the day, but there was a mutual respect because I wasn't out to pop him or his club for the dumb bullshit they were pulling back then. The Sun Devils were our target, and they were the mortal enemy of the Disciples. Let's just say Tiny was happy to see that MC put behind bars."

"Wait, he helped you?"

James shakes his head. "Fuck no. He's not a narc, but when I started my own company and needed information, I went to Tiny, made peace, and paid him for intel I couldn't get through any legal channels."

"That's it? You paid him for information, and now you're sending us there, thinking Tiny's going to protect us?"

James studies me as he leans forward, putting his palms together, elbows on the desk, and his mouth resting on the tips of his fingers. "When I went to Tiny about you because Izzy asked me to look into your past before she took you on, I'd never heard the man speak so highly about someone who wasn't a brother." He drops his hands to his desk, squaring his shoulders, eyes still on me. "He talked about you like you were his own kid. A man like Tiny doesn't do that unless you crawled under his skin and made him feel shit he hasn't felt in years. You're up to your neck in shit, and by default, so is my niece. You need to hide out, lie low until shit with your father and DiSantis blows over. I can't think of a better place to put you than a spot that has enough brute force and an arsenal to handle an attack if the man is stupid enough to go after you inside their compound."

"I'd think a man like you would have us under FBI protection instead of the Disciples."

James gives a slow shake of his head. "Even though I worked for the government back in the day, I know how corrupt the system is and how easily people can be bought. I'm not putting my niece somewhere unless I know they can handle the blowback."

I've got nothing left to say. What he's saying is true. If DiSantis wants me dead, I'm a sitting duck unless I hide out, and there's no better place to disappear from radar than at the Disciples' compound.

"Now the sun's up, the day's already fucked because I've been up for hours, and I'll have to listen to Izzy for an eternity as she tears me a new asshole. We'll roll out just after sunset. You tell no one where you're headed, and I mean no one. Not even your grandmother, Pike."

I nod. "I won't tell a soul. Gigi's safety is all that matters."

"If DiSantis's men come..."

"I'd throw myself in front of a bullet if it meant she'd be okay."

She wouldn't be in this shit if it weren't for me.

"I'll hold you to that. If you don't, I'll make you wish you had taken that bullet instead of what I'd do to you."

I stand, rubbing my hands down the front of my jeans, feeling the day's events finally starting to wash over me. "Understood, James."

"Now, go. I have shit to do," he says, not moving from his chair and lifting his chin toward the door.

I turn the knob, swinging open the door, and come face-to-face with Gigi's father. Our eyes lock, and I wait for his fist to make a beeline for my jaw, but he just stands there, staring at me. "We'll have words when this is done," he says, all joy gone from his voice.

"Yes, sir."

"Now, get gone so I can talk to my brother-in-law." He ticks his head toward the empty hallway. "It's best if I'm not around you right now."

By the hardness in his jaw and the coldness in his stare, I'm guessing he knows what went down with Gigi and me in Daytona. This isn't a conversation I want to have with him after being up all night. It's actually not a conversation I want to have with him anytime, but it's one that's going to come whether I like it or not. It's also not a conversation I've ever had to have with a woman's father because relationships weren't really my thing and the women I've slept with were usually older and not so attached to their fathers.

"Got it."

"Izzy's waiting for you in the kitchen," he says, brushing past me and stalking into James's office before slamming the door right in my face.

I expected nothing less. If Gigi were my kid and I were face-to-face with a guy who'd done the shit I did to her, I'd want to rip his fucking throat out with my bare hands. I couldn't fault the man.

I make my way down the long hallway and head toward Izzy's voice. If she weren't talking, I'm not sure I ever would've found the kitchen because the house is probably the biggest one I've ever stepped foot inside.

"There you are," Izzy says as soon as she sees me rounding the corner. "I was beginning to think James was never going to let you out of that room."

Gigi's sitting at the kitchen table, quickly running her fingertips over her cheeks. "I'll show him to his room," Gigi says to Izzy with her back to me.

Izzy raises an eyebrow, eyes moving from me to Gigi. "Your dad is still here. Watch your step, little girl. If you want Pike to still be breathing when the sun sets, don't get cute and try to crawl into his bed, curling yourself around the man for comfort."

So, Gigi did spill our entire sordid, although brief, history together. I'm surprised she kept her shit together this long, even though it's only been two days. I'm sure it was impossible for her to maintain the lie about not knowing me, especially after she lost her shit tonight once I was taken in for questioning. Even more, she was probably shaken up after hearing the shit James and I said in the car. All that together was just enough to have Gigi blabbing every last detail.

"Got it, Auntie." Gigi finds her footing before turning around, showing me her tear-stained cheeks and red, puffy eyes.

"You okay?" I ask as my eyes sweep across her face, knowing I'd caused her tears.

She nods. "Let me show you to your room," she says, ignoring the look I'm giving her and the fact that she's been crying. She dips her head toward another hallway, adding to the maze that is James and Izzy's house. "We'll talk after we get some sleep. I want to know that you're okay."

I walk inches behind her, following her wherever she's taking me because I don't care if it's a closet, as long as there's enough space for me to stretch my legs and close my eyes. "I don't know how I feel just yet. Shit's pretty fucked up, and now you've been pulled into the same mess."

She stops near an open doorway, leaning against the wall, staring up at me with glassy, bloodshot eyes. "I'm sure Uncle James has a plan."

Reaching out, I wipe away a tear that's resting near the edge of her lashes, ready to fall. "Do you know what his plan is, darlin'?"

She shakes her head, not moving away from my touch when I let my hand linger.

"He's sending us to the Disciples' compound to lie low."

Her eyes grow big as saucers. "He's what?"

I nod, just as fucking shocked by that reality as she is. "He said it's the safest place. Can't say I disagree with him either, but the compound isn't a place for a girl like you."

She wrinkles her nose. "A girl like me?"

I sweep my thumb just under her cheekbone, loving the softness against my skin. "You're good, Gigi. Pure, even. The Disciples' compound is no place for a lady."

Gigi's eyes sparkle, and she snorts in the most unladylike way. "I've been around bikers my entire life, Pike. I think I can handle whatever happens at their compound without losing my shit and rockin' myself in a corner."

"These aren't recreational bikers, Gigi. They're hard-core. They live the life. All full of violence, mayhem, booze, drugs, and so much pussy, it'll make your head spin."

She wraps her hand around my wrist and pulls my arm away from her. "You used to live there, yeah?"

I nod.

"We'll be safe there. And right about now, I could use a big fucking drink, so the compound sounds like a good place to get lost and forget all this shit."

"I don't think James is sending us there to party, babe."

She draws her lower lip between her teeth, biting the tender flesh gently. "Then he should send us to a convent. I'm not going into that compound to sit in a dark room day and night, playing the role of a scared little girl. I'm letting my hair down, immersing myself in whatever they have to offer for however long they're offering it. You don't like it? Then you can sit in that dark room alone."

Oh fuckin' boy. This girl is clueless about so much. She's probably binged every motorcycle show available online, thinking she knows how bikers are. But even Hollywood glorifies the life. If she thinks she can handle watching a guy do blow off some chick's ass while she's stretched out on the pool table for everyone to watch, so be it. She's going to get a hard lesson in the real MC life, and it may be eye-opening if not entertaining.

"Just know I'm not leaving your side. You're out of your room, I'm on you like glue."

She grins. "I'm counting on that, Pike."

"But first, we gotta live long enough to get to that compound." I grab her by the shoulder, moving her away from my doorway. "Now, you need to get gone so I can get some sleep before your father finds you outside my room and I end up next to my mother."

Gigi stares up at me, eyes glistening in the bright light. "You want to talk about her?"

I shake my head. "Another time. Maybe once we're settled, but not tonight."

"Okay, but I'm always here to talk," she says sweetly, and I want to wrap my body around hers, surrounding myself with the goodness and warmth only she can offer.

"Night, darlin'." I fight the urge to plant my lips on hers, letting all the day's shit leak out into that kiss.

"Night, Pike," she whispers and takes a step back, staring at me like she's pleading with me to give her what I want to, but I can't because I want to live to breathe another day. "I'll be right next door."

"Got it." I dip my chin, waiting for her to disappear through her doorway before I take a step inside the bedroom, ready for this day to be fucking over with.

Tomorrow starts a whole new shitshow. One filled with Gigi's family, Tiny and the Disciples, and us running for our lives, ducking for cover in a den of sin.

CHAPTER 17
GIGI

"DON'T you think this is excessive?" I ask Uncle Thomas, which earns me a hard stare in the rearview mirror. "I mean, seven cars behind us is a bit extreme. Even you have to agree with me." I turn to Pike, but he doesn't say a word because he's not rocking any boat, especially not after the way my uncles and father gave him shit before we left Izzy's house.

"Seven cars and twenty men is not excessive when you're dealing with a man like DiSantis," Uncle James says as he sits beside Uncle Thomas in the front seat of the car.

Pike's hand finds mine in the darkness, and he squeezes my fingers. "They're just being safe."

"Don't give me no shit, little girl," James barks.

That's my new name...little girl. I thought I'd grown out of it about the time I started to grow tits, but now it's back, and I have a feeling it's not going anywhere either.

"If I get word that you try to leave that compound..."

"You'll spank me?" I sass, smirking as soon as his eyes cut to mine in the mirror again.

Uncle James and Izzy get their freak on. I know all about their sex life now, after finding his profile on a BDSM website I'd used for research when I had to write a paper for my sexual psychology class at FSU. The textbook only went so deep, and the library was absolutely no help because many of the books they carried were by men who preferred the missionary position and knew nothing of real kink. So, I went right to the source, clicking my way through the biggest kinkster site I could find.

A few clicks later and I was on Master James's page, looking at shit I could never unsee and learning things I never wanted to know. That's not something you can just wipe out of your head. Can't erase the images and words with any amount of alcohol, and I should know because I tried and failed.

"Fucking hell," Thomas mutters, shaking his head. "You have a mouth on you sometimes."

"I'm just practicing for my stint at the Disciples' compound. I figure I can't walk in there all meek and mild. I have to be balls to the wall, ready to sling some shit with the best of them. Yeah?"

Pike's eyes flash as I glance at him with a big smile. "Fuck," he groans, which only makes my smile even bigger.

"It's best if you just stay in your room," James says, like that's going to fucking happen.

So, I keep poking because I have to do something to pass the time, and this drive has officially turned into the longest one of my life. "Why didn't you just lock us up instead, Uncle James? I mean, if you want us to be prisoners, why not just keep us home, locked in our rooms like the little kids you think we are?"

"I get you're pissed, kid, but I don't need your lip right now when I'm trying to do everything to keep you and Pike alive. You don't like the situation?" He pauses, but I don't fill the silence. "Too fucking bad. Sometimes, as adults, we have to do shit we don't want to do so we can live another day. You think a jail cell is going to be better than the compound?" He barks out a bitter laugh. "You have a lot to fucking learn."

"Three minutes out," Thomas says into the phone, sending a voice text to everyone who's following behind.

"Still all clear," my father's voice says back.

And I mean everyone. Not only are my other uncles and Dad in the cars behind us, but so are the guys from ALFA. Even Uncle Bear tagged along for the ride because he's down with anything that could end up with his ass shot. The man is crazy, searching for danger and driving my great-aunt Fran absolutely batshit crazy.

"I promise I won't cause trouble," I say softly, knowing my fate is sealed and our imprisonment within the walls of the compound probably won't be as bad as I'm making out.

"Just stick by Pike. He lived at the compound for a few years and knows what situations to steer you clear of."

"So, you want me at Pike's side at all times?" I clarify because it's sounding like I have the stamp of approval to be in Pike's bed.

"Gigi," James warns, knowing where I'm going, because of course he does.

"She's trying to get me killed," Pike whispers.

I squeeze his fingers, trying to hide my laughter because this shit is heavy. I'm using the only coping mechanism I have...my humor and my sarcasm.

Who wants to be running for their life?

Not me.

Who wants to hide out because there might be a bullet with their name on it?

Again, not me.

The only upside to this entire situation is that I'll have Pike at my side. But if he thinks he's bossing me around like I'm his woman, he has another thing coming.

"Let's go over a few things before you step out of this car."

"Of course." I roll my eyes, getting a hand squeeze from Pike because he's not happy either, but somehow, he's remained silent.

"Absolutely no drugs."

"Uncle James."

"I'm serious, Gigi. They're into some heavy shit there. Stuff is just lying around, easy to get, and even easier to take. If I get word that you're sniffing coke or taking some shit you shouldn't be taking, I'll have your ass back in this car so fast…"

"I promise, Uncle. I've never taken anything before, and I don't plan to start now."

Pike raises his eyebrows because my admission has to be shocking to everyone in the car, especially him. I mean, what person my age hasn't at least dabbled in drugs besides me? Probably no one except Tamara. It has to do with the way our parents raised us and the fear of them finding out and the ass-chewing we'd both get over it after a very lengthy and boring-as-fuck punishment.

"No drinking either," Uncle Thomas adds.

My mouth drops open, and I gawk at the back of their heads, blinking like somehow it'll make those words any easier to swallow. "You've got to give me something. I'm old enough to drink and it's legal, so I don't understand the issue."

"Cut the girl some slack," Uncle James says, which shocks the hell out of me and Thomas too.

"Are you serious right now? She's going to be in the middle of a crazy scene, and you're giving her the okay to drink?"

"She's grown, Thomas. We can't stop her from drinking."

"Or doing drugs," I add because fucking with them is too easy, and maybe if I fuck with them enough, Thomas will relent on the drinking. "But I promise I won't get drunk."

"Just don't do anything stupid. Stay inside and out of sight."

"I'll sit at the bar day and night." I smile, earning me a few curse words from all three in the car.

"They're here," James says, ticking his chin out the windshield at a long-ass line of bikes and an unmarked, windowless van parked in an abandoned lot.

"Guess we're doing this," I whisper, glancing at Pike as he stares back at me.

"We're going to be okay," Pike says sweetly, squeezing my fingers gently. "I promise."

I believe what he's saying, and from the huge army waiting for us, I believe they'll do what's necessary to keep us safe. Unless DiSantis brings an actual army, they'll have a hard time outnumbering the men waiting in the parking lot and probably even more still back at the compound.

"Out," Uncle Thomas barks as soon as he throws the engine into park, letting it idle. "We're making this quick. Drop and dash."

Uncle James helps me from the back seat, looking no less badass than the other men standing in this parking lot. "Behave, Gigi," he warns before releasing my hand. "I love you and don't want anything bad to happen to you. Something goes sideways, and we're all going to be in the shit."

I swallow the lump his words cause to lodge in my throat. The last thing I want is for my entire family to be in the proverbial shit because I slept with a guy who has a questionable father and a possible order for his assassination.

"I'll be good. I promise," I rasp.

He gives me a quick nod before stalking toward a giant man with a potbelly, no doubt caused by all types of excessive drinking. I assume it's Tiny because that would make total sense as there's nothing small about him.

My father is at my side before I can follow Uncle James. "This is it," he says, balling his hands into fists as his eyes dart to Pike and then back at me. "I've said what I needed to say."

I don't correct him and tell him it was more of a lecture than a good old-fashioned chat. My dad chewed my ear off for hours about my trip to Daytona and throwing myself in the path of countless bikers and into the arms of one in particular.

"I'm sorry this is happening, Daddy. I never meant to cause any trouble."

His face softens. "Baby, sometimes trouble finds us, no matter how hard we try to stay away. This isn't your fault. It's not Pike's fault either."

I blink up at him in surprise. "You're not pissed anymore?"

His jaw ticks, which answers my question before he even opens his mouth. "I'm not happy about any of this. Pike and I will be having a long talk when you two are back home."

So, he is still pissed, but at least he isn't talking about murdering the guy anymore. In my book, that's progress. For my dad, that's a huge step. The man has the patience of a saint sometimes, but when it comes to men and his daughters, he has zero. I've probably had it easier than my sisters will because I'm like the trial kid where they can fuck up and see what works, tweaking their plans for the next in line. Luna and Rosie aren't going to stand a chance, but they're crafty little shits even at their age and will adapt easily before my father knows what hit him.

"Go easy on him, Daddy."

My father's eyebrows draw together, causing the wrinkles on his forehead to deepen. "You want me to go easy on Pike?"

"Yo, we gonna do this, or what? Eyes are everywhere, and I don't feel like being a sitting duck," Tiny yells across the parking lot.

"Gigi," Pike calls, motioning for me to move my ass before things start to get heated.

"I'm coming." I wave and stare back up into my father's piercing eyes. "Pike's no different from you, and I'm no different from Mom." I pop up on my tiptoes, planting a kiss on my father's cheek and throwing my arms around his shoulders, squeezing him tightly. "Well, maybe I'm a little different from Mom because I have two kick-ass parents."

"Baby," he whispers, wrapping his arms around my back and holding me so tight, I can barely breathe. "Go. Stay safe. Don't do anything stupid."

I nod, pulling out of his embrace ever so slowly. "I love you, Daddy."

"I love you too, baby girl. One call a day to me on the burner phone. You understand?"

"I'll call around noon every day. I promise." I start to walk backward. "But don't worry so much. I won't do anything stupid, and these guys—" I pitch my thumb over my shoulder toward the horde of badass bikers "—will keep us safe."

"Tiny, Gigi. Gigi, Tiny," James says, looking between the two of us as I walk toward them, almost faltering when I get close enough to realize the true size of Tiny.

"Holy fuck," I whisper. "Well, aren't you a big fella." I wink, throwing that out there because I know bikers, and they love a compliment.

Tiny's lip twitches ever so slightly, but the man keeps up his tough-guy exterior with his arms crossed, making him look even bigger and downright scary. "She'll do fine," he tells James like I'm not even standing here.

James extends his hand to Tiny, and the men shake as I turn my gaze toward Pike, who's also shaking hands with a man about his age and his size, but with a bald head and a tattoo across his forehead that does nothing except make him look so frightening, I can't imagine getting pussy is real easy.

"You." Tiny juts his chin at me as soon as we make eye contact. "Ass in the van. We gotta roll."

"And Pike?" I ask, because where he's going, so am I, whether Tiny or any of these other bikers agrees.

"He's in the van too. Can't have you bein' seen before we get you within our walls."

"Sure thing, boss man." I smile at the big guy, because if it's the last thing I do, I'll get the old bastard to smile back.

"She's a handful," Uncle James tells him, shrugging his shoulders and throwing out his arms like he doesn't know how to handle me and is sorry to put me off on someone else.

"I got a kid her age, but mine isn't so...pleasant. Anyway, Pike will keep her ass in line, and if he doesn't, I'll make sure she's under control."

I roll my eyes at their conversation, and Pike mutters, "Good fuckin' luck," at my side.

"Let's get this shitshow on the road, boys." I wave my hand in the air and look at Pike with a smirk. "This is going to be one hell of a time."

Pike keeps step with me as I stalk toward the van. "This isn't a vacation, darlin'."

"Don't give a fuck. We're spending time in a biker compound, and I plan to enjoy the fuck out of it because I'm not spending all day in my room worrying about some asshole trying to kill us. Now turn around, put a smile on your face, and wave to my family." I spin on my heels just outside the back door of the van, my eyes sweeping across the line of cars brimming with my family and the ALFA guys. I wave a little too happily, which earns me more than one glower. "Bye, I love you," I call out, knowing they'd all cuss me out if they could and probably will the next time they see me.

My father's near the car, talking to Uncle Thomas, shaking his head at my antics, knowing shit isn't going to be as PG as he hopes. "Just behave, kid," he yells out, knowing damn well there's a snowball's chance in hell that's going to happen. "Now, get your ass in the van, and get the fuck out of here."

I salute him before crawling inside, nestling against the side wall of the filthy van. They could've at least cleaned up a little bit seeing as they were going to be transporting two people in here instead of whatever the fuck was here before us.

"We're only twenty minutes away," Pike says as he settles next to me, legs outstretched and his shoulder touching mine.

"Good, I could use a drink." I plaster a smile on my face because I don't want my father or uncles to know I'm terrified.

"Already?" he asks, staring at me as the doors slam shut.

"Already?" I gawk at Pike, happy I don't have to put on a good show anymore. "We're in some deep shit, Pike. What the fuck do you mean, already? Don't you want to drink that shit away?"

Pike shakes his head. "I have to stay focused. Shit can happen at any time, and I don't want to be three sheets to the goddamn wind when all hell breaks loose. They come for you, I need to be ready. I'll throw myself in front of whatever they hurl in our direction, shielding you so you can walk away without a scratch."

My mouth's hanging open as I blink at Pike like I'm trying to focus, but everything's crystal clear. "You'd give your life for me?" I whisper as Tiny slams the front door, shrouding us in darkness.

"I'd give everything for you, darlin'."

CHAPTER 18
PIKE

"THIS PLACE IS like Disney World for crack whores, career criminals, and lost souls," Gigi says casually at my side, almost making me spit my mouthful of beer across the bar.

"Keep your voice down." I wipe my lips with the back of my hand, glancing around to figure out if anyone overheard.

"They can't hear above this classic rock, Pike. Half of them are probably hard of hearing, and the other half are so trashed, they're probably unable to form coherent thoughts."

"You're on a roll tonight, sweetheart." I lift my mug, glancing over my shoulder at a few guys who are sitting close, most likely assigned the task of keeping an eye on us while we're under their protection.

I'll have to talk to Tiny about that. While I appreciate his concern and security, when we're within these walls, hidden from view, we don't need extra eyes on us, watching our every move. Gigi most certainly doesn't need any men loitering near her, making her feel any more uncomfortable than she already does.

"They your friends?"

I shake my head. "Nope. Never seen them before. I haven't been around here in years. Based on the lack of patches, I'd say they're prospects."

"Oh. I saw that on television," she says, confirming everything I assumed she thought this place would be. "How long do they have to do that?"

"As long as Tiny and the guys want them to."

"There's no time limit?"

"Babe, this isn't a job. Bikers don't put time on anything unless there's money involved."

"Where's the little fucker?" a familiar voice says, and we both turn, watching him finish tucking his cock into his pants before he zips his fly.

"I guess you're the little fucker, yeah?" Gigi giggles, peering at me over her shoulder.

I set my beer down, climbing off the stool to greet Morris before he sets eyes on Gigi and tries to get his hands on her too. "Morris. Lookin' good, man."

"Morris?" Gigi asks, not hiding her shock that the guy with the crazy-ass salt-and-pepper hair and goatee to match doesn't have a biker name like the rest of the guys.

Morris shakes my hand and pulls me in for a bear hug before slapping my back so hard, I'm almost winded. "Who's this fine piece of ass you brought with you, kid?"

"This is Gigi, my girl, Morris. Don't start no shit, and there won't be no shit."

A slow, wide smile spreads across Morris's face, showing his white teeth with a big enough gap between the two front ones it's hard to mistake him for someone else.

Morris throws his hands up as he steps away from me, and his eyes sweep over Gigi again. "Wait a second, isn't she the chick from..."

"Yeah, man. Don't say it. It's a long-ass story."

"Hello," Gigi calls out, waving her hand at Morris and me

because we're talking about her like she isn't sitting right there, and she hates nothing more than being ignored.

Morris slides next to her, moving onto the barstool so smoothly, it's like he practiced the maneuver a thousand times. "You're even more beautiful than the last time I laid eyes on you."

She blinks at him in confusion, moving back slightly when he reaches for her hand and brings it to his lips. "I'm sorry, I don't remember..."

"You probably don't remember a lot, mama. You were pretty trashed the night I met you—and damn fucking mouthy too." Morris laughs, placing a soft kiss on the top of her hand and getting a growl from me.

Gigi laughs, looking like a little kid next to the old man who will stick his dick in just about anything as long as he can get off. "It was spring break. I was letting loose."

"And so you did, sweetheart." Morris grins, eyes only on her and not on me at all.

Gigi grabs her drink as soon as Morris releases her hand and rests her chin in the palm of her free hand, elbow propped against the bar. "Why Morris? Why don't you have a tough name like the rest of the guys?"

Morris grins at Gigi, motioning to the prospect behind the bar for a drink, but he never breaks eye contact with her. "Because every MC has a Tiny, Rooster, Reaper, and so on, but only the Disciples have a Morris."

Gigi's nose wrinkles. "That's the reason?"

"Doll, I'm one of a kind. Who wants to be lumped in with those sorry fuckers when you can be the only one?"

Gigi shrugs, lifting the drink to her lips, and his eyes follow the movement. It's time to shut down the flirtfest Morris is having with my girl, so I slide in behind her, wrapping my arm around her middle and hauling her ass backward so she's pressed flush against me.

"You happy to see me, baby?" she asks playfully, tossing a glance over her shoulder.

"I figured I needed to remind Morris who you belong to, darlin'," I whisper in her ear, causing her to shiver, but my gaze is on Morris. "I don't want this dirty old man to get the wrong idea."

"My head only has room for wrong ideas," Morris says with a laugh. "Now, let's celebrate you comin' home, asswad, and get shit-faced drunk, telling stories about back in the day."

Gigi bounces on her stool, sending shock waves through my system from the way her ass is rubbing on my cock. "Fuck yeah. That's the best idea I've heard tonight."

"Gigi doesn't want to hear about all that boring shit, Morris," I hiss, because he's trying to start trouble.

It's what he's best at after all. If shit's going down, Morris is smack-dab in the middle, stirring the pot, making sure the shit stays moving.

"I very much want to hear about the *good old days*, baby. Hush your mouth." Gigi throws a wink at me over her shoulder.

"I could spend all night telling Pike stories."

"Don't you have a woman to satisfy?" I raise an eyebrow.

Morris shakes his head, grabbing the beer as soon as the redheaded prospect sets the bottle in front of him. "She's passed out. Figurin' the session we just had, she'll be out for a couple of hours if she even wakes up at all."

"You're a dirty old man, Morris." Gigi grips my knee like she's going to keep me quiet.

"He's old, all right," I mutter, reaching for my beer with the hand that isn't locked around her waist because nothing is going to make me let go of her.

"I think this calls for tequila," Gigi says to Morris, scooting backward, knowing exactly what she's doing because she's always thinking ahead.

"My kinda girl." Morris smirks.

"Maybe we should just go to bed." I want her out of the common room because the real shit hasn't even begun. The night's young, and the guys aren't as shit-faced as she thinks.

"No, Pike. We're not going anywhere until *we* catch up with Morris here. So, settle in, cowboy, and get comfortable."

Morris is laughing so hard, he's almost falling off his stool. "I can see why you like this one so much, kid. She's mouthy and bares those kitten claws."

"Morris, baby," Gigi replies, laying her hand on his arm. "I'm not a kitten, sweetheart."

Morris tips his head toward her, grinning like I've never seen the man grin before. "See, mouthy as fuck."

I look toward the ceiling, cursing under my breath. The long night just became longer because once these two get going, there's no stopping them until someone's passed out.

"Three tequilas," Gigi tells the prospect as he walks by, delivering a handful of beers to the guys at the other end of the bar.

"Long-ass fucking night," I whisper, pulling on my beer, swallowing down the bitter liquid along with the sour taste this entire evening is leaving in my mouth.

"Have a fucking sense of humor, Pike. Did you lose your balls somewhere around Orlando?"

Gigi chuckles, turning her head so her lips are so close to mine, I could silence her with a kiss. "Let me have a little fun, Pike. I know you have a past. Hell, so do I. I don't know a lot about you, and I want to hear what Morris has to say. Don't shit on my parade. Ya dig?"

"I dig." That's not the end of the conversation even if she wants it to be. "Just remember whatever he says—" I jut my chin toward him "—is probably bullshit."

"I never bullshit," Morris interrupts, staring at me over the lip of his beer bottle. "Well, almost never."

"If you learn something you don't like tonight, you tuck that shit away and forget about it. I'm not the same punk kid I was when I lived here, surrounded by these men, five years ago. You dig?"

"I dig." Her eyes sparkle and drop to my mouth, and she pulls the corner of her bottom lip between her teeth, making me want to haul her ass into the back room and slide something else between those beautiful lips. "Now, Morris," she says, turning away from me quickly because she knows exactly what's on my mind. "Start at the beginning. How did Pike end up living with the Disciples? Didn't know you guys welcomed anyone into your world."

Morris snaps his fingers at the prospect who's still fumbling around behind the bar and hasn't delivered the tequila Gigi ordered. "We don't usually take in strays."

I roll my eyes because I know he's going to lay the shit on way thicker than it really went down. The reality of the situation is much more boring than he's going to tell her. He's going to glorify the entire thing, probably saying he rescued me from the side of the road like a wounded animal.

"We were pulling this job up in Jacksonville," he starts, at least getting that part right, but I know it's about to go sideways. "Some crazy-ass shit went down, guns came out."

"For fucking real?" Gigi gasps.

"For real, kid. Then this dumbass—" he ticks his chin toward me "—decides he's going to jump in front of one of the bullets, because his slow Tennessee ass can't move fast enough to get the fuck down."

Gigi turns, looking at me with wide eyes. "The scar on your shoulder?"

I nod, gritting my teeth because one of the fuckers shot me, not giving a fuck that I was an innocent bystander in the entire thing. I was filling my tank with gas, minding my own business, when they decided to open fire. I didn't have a chance to duck before I took one in the upper right shoulder.

"When shit died down, Pike was still standing there, holding his arm, glaring at me like it was my fault he was bleeding. We had words, and the fucking punk didn't care that I had a gun in my hand because he kept barking at me about how I put a hole in his body." Morris laughs, running his fingers through the tip of his goatee. He pauses when the kid finally sets down three tequila shots but is still moving like he has lead in his shoes. "About fucking time," Morris barks, shooing the guy away when he lingers a little too long. "What are we drinking to, kids?"

Gigi hands me a shot but doesn't give me her eyes. "To new friends and old times," she tells him, lifting her shot in the air. They clink glasses as I watch Gigi throw back the tequila like she's been doing it for years. "Now, finish the story. What happened after he had words with you?"

"I figured the kid had a pair of balls on him so freaking big he could be something to us. So, I had two choices."

"What were they?" she asks, not giving him a chance to finish.

"I could end his life right there, or bring his sorry, bleeding ass back here to get patched up and figure out what to do with his mouthy ass afterward."

"Aww," she coos. "You totally rescued him."

"He fucking shot me." I scowl.

Morris places his hand on his chest, trying his best to look innocent. "I did not shoot your ass, kid. Wasn't my bullet you jumped in front of that night."

"Don't mind him." Gigi jerks her thumb at me, and I tighten my hold around her waist, reminding her these men aren't playthings.

Morris may not have been the one who shot me, but someone in this room fucking did. They didn't give two shits that I was innocent with piss-poor timing, filling my tank when they decided to play cops and robbers at the gas station in a seedy part of town.

There isn't a man in this room who hasn't drawn blood from another human being without so much as a backward glance at the carnage they inflicted or the death they left in their wake. They give zero fucks about human life. Their world revolves around money, drugs, pussy, and the brotherhood—and not in that order either.

"And..." She leans forward, hanging on his every word.

"So, this kid..." He laughs, shaking his head like he doesn't even believe what he's about to say. "He's yelling at me, poking me in the shoulder while I've got my gun in one hand like I'm just going to stand here and take his shit. I didn't know what to do, so I punched him right where he got hit, sending his ass to the floor in a flurry of curse words that would make the devil himself blush."

"You fucking punched him in his injured shoulder?"

Morris shrugs. "The kid wouldn't shut up about how I shot him. Figured I'd give him something to be angry with me about, plus, I needed him to shut the fuck up for a few minutes so I could get his ass into the back of the van."

"Did you know you were going to keep him?" she asks.

"What the fuck?" I hiss, shaking my head. "I wasn't a puppy, Gigi."

"Shut up," she tells me. "Morris and I are talking."

"Three more tequilas," I tell the prospect, figuring the only way I'm going to get her to stop talking to Morris is to get her so shit-faced drunk, she'll pass the fuck out.

"Welcome to the party, Pike," Gigi teases, wiggling her ass right against my dick.

I flatten my palm against her stomach, moving my mouth near her ear. "Be careful, darlin'. I'm not above throwing you over my shoulder and hauling your ass into my room and putting something in that sassy little mouth of yours."

"Is that a promise or a threat?" she asks with a wicked gleam in her eyes.

"Both."

I've never been more serious in my life.

"Such a big talker," she teases.

I do the only thing I can. Moving quickly, I throw her over my shoulder like a sack of potatoes and march toward my old room.

"Put me down!" she screeches. "Help!"

No one pays any attention to her pleas for help. I even get a few high fives as I carry her ass to the back, ready to do exactly what I promised.

CHAPTER 19
GIGI

HE HAS one hand on my ass, only moving the damn thing when he smacks the hands of the other assholes in the room.

I wiggle, trying like hell to get out of his hold and off his shoulder, but that only causes him to tighten his grip around my leg.

"You're not getting out of this one, darlin'," he drawls, stalking on heavy feet, making my tits smack against his back with every step.

"You're an asshole."

"Speaking of asshole," he says, running a finger along the crease of my ass as we finally make it to the hallway.

I stiffen, squeezing my ass cheeks together as tightly as possible. "Don't you fucking dare!" I screech, lifting my head and catching sight of all the guys in the compound, laughing and watching us with total amusement. I give the biker assholes my middle finger, scowling at them for reveling in the spectacle Pike is putting on, even though I know I'm not helping it. "You're not touching my ass!"

"I promise you'll love it." His hand massages my cheeks, but I have them on lockdown, just like they're going to stay. "I'll make you want it always."

That's the problem. I know if Pike does it, I'll love the hell out of it. There hasn't been anything he's done to my body that I didn't want more of, craving it since the second I ran for coffee and never went back. He's skilled and generous, unlike anyone I've been with before...although my list is super-short and kind of embarrassing.

I reach down, trying to get my hands on his ass so I can pinch him hard enough that maybe I'll be able to break free. "The only thing I want is for you to put me down and let me finish my drink," I grit out, stretching as far as I can, but it's no use. His body is too long for my short everything even to get near anything worth pinching.

"You're done drinking," he says like he's the boss, which is laughable.

I go limp, knowing there's no use. I'm going nowhere except where Pike is taking me. "Where the fuck is your room? Another county?"

Pike laughs, making my body shake with his. "We're almost there, baby. You in a hurry to have my cock in you?"

A door opens, and Pike comes to a dead stop. "Calling it a night?" a man asks, and I crane my neck, trying to see, but damn my size.

"Takin' my woman to bed. Won't be back out until the mornin'."

"Morris put your shit back out and cleaned. Should feel like home for you, kid. You enjoy yourself."

I growl. "Hello, wanna help me here?"

The man laughs, moving around Pike, and crouches down to my level. "Looks like you're doing just fine, sweetheart," Tiny says.

"You're all fuckers," I hiss, which only gets me a small laugh and a headshake from Tiny as he goes back to standing on the other side of Pike and away from me.

"You got your hands full with this one, son. I hope you know what you're doing."

"Just reminding her who she belongs to, Tiny. You have a good night," Pike says.

Who she belongs to? Ugh. My father says shit like that all the time about my mother. Come to think of it, every man in my family says macho bullshit like that, and I roll my eyes every time.

Pike starts moving and I lift my head, catching Tiny's smile, the first one I've seen him crack since I met him tonight. Badass MC biker president or not, he gets a middle finger too before Pike turns a corner, opens a door, and we're suddenly in darkness.

"Will you put me down now?"

"Nope," he replies as he switches on the light, making everything in the tiny space visible. "Well, fuck."

I press my hands to his lower back, lifting my head up farther than before, and try to take in the sparse room covered with all things Pike. There are posters and artwork lining the walls, a twin bed along a black-painted wall, some furniture that had to be secondhand, and not one goddamn window for any type of natural light. "Is this a closet?"

My closet at my parents' place is twice as big as his *bedroom*. I couldn't imagine living in here on a daily basis without going a little mad from the lack of sunlight and the fact that it's the size of a prison cell.

"It has everything we need, babe." He finally relaxes his hold on my leg, allowing me to slide down his front, relishing the way his hardness feels against my body.

When my feet touch the floor, Pike's hands are on my hips and his eyes are on mine. He's so beautiful like this. Hair wild, his green eyes burning with need, and those lips begging for mine. "Pike." I'm trying to kill a little time because now that we're alone, I know there's no turning back.

Pike shakes his head. "Been thinking about this since you left me," he says, and my breath catches in my throat. "Been thinking about the softness of your skin..." He runs his finger along the top edge of my jean shorts and across the sensitive skin on my stomach.

Goose bumps form everywhere, scattering across my flesh like they're reaching for his touch. "Pike," I say again, but my voice is needy. Even I can hear the way his touch affects me, and I'm sure it isn't lost on him either.

"Tell me to stop, and I will," he says, licking his lips, and my gaze drops to his mouth, remembering all the ways he brought me pleasure. He bends his neck, bringing those lips to my mouth, whispering, "I need you, darlin'."

I'm a goner. It's easier to pretend I hate him when he's not about to kiss me, staring at me like he's been in a desert without water and I'm the oasis.

"Kiss me," I whisper, staring into his eyes, losing myself a little more.

I barely get the words out before his lips crash down on mine, his hand sliding to my ass and pulling me flush against him. In the last fifteen months, I haven't forgotten how he tasted or the velvety softness of his tongue, no matter how hard I tried.

I slide my hands up his arms, tangling my fingers in his hair, holding him to me like he's my lifeline. My knees weaken as his tongue sweeps into my mouth, giving me exactly what I've craved and wanted since Daytona.

Pike turns, slamming the door behind us, but I don't even flinch at the noise because I'm too lost in the way he's kissing me to care about anything else around us. The world could crumble, and I wouldn't move from this spot, away from his body, away from his lips.

His hands are on my ass, lifting me in the air. I wrap my legs around his waist like they were always meant to be there as he walks us backward.

The kiss deepens, becoming more demanding as his hands move to my back, sliding up my tank top, finding my bra strap. I'm in his lap, his cock to my pussy, separated only by our clothes as he sits on the bed, working quickly to unclasp my bra.

I pull back, gasping for air as I stare at the handsome man underneath me. "Did you bring protection?" I whisper.

Pike nods as he grabs the bottom of my tank top, and I lift my hands because I want this more than anything right now.

"You knew I'd sleep with you?" I ask through the material as the cool air hits my skin and the bra goes with the shirt, both thrown to the floor behind me.

"I hoped," he says. His hungry eyes travel across my skin for a moment before he pulls my head back down, pressing his lips to mine.

I move my hands to his sides, reaching under the thin T-shirt, wanting and needing his warmth and hardness.

I've touched myself hundreds of times since I last was in his arms, trying to recreate the feeling only he'd given me. I'd failed miserably. Nothing could replicate the way he touched me, how he kissed me, or the way he made me melt into his body.

As I lift his shirt, our mouths separate and I lean back, taking in his ink and the lines of his taut stomach and firm shoulders. I only get a glimpse before Pike flips me, putting me on my back, and crawls between my legs, settling in like he's always meant to be there.

The sense of shame and uncertainty I had every time I was with Erik isn't there with Pike. I have no doubts he likes what he sees and loves everything he feels. I'm not ashamed of my nudity, and any worries I had about my inexperience were wiped away after our time together in Daytona.

Pike lifts up on one arm, staring down at me like I'm a goddess. "Dreamed about having you under me again, darlin'."

I run my fingers through the coarse hair of his beard, staring up at the man I know is about to give me so much pleasure, I'm not sure I'll ever recover. "Me too," I confess, because there's no reason to pretend otherwise.

He runs his hand down my neck, along my collarbone, over the swell of my breast. My eyes drift closed, and I sigh, letting every sensation wash over me, memorizing each touch in case I never feel them again.

Warmth covers my nipple, and I open my eyes, peering down my body and finding Pike with his mouth attached. A small moan escapes my lips as our eyes lock, and the pleasure his tongue's delivering shoots straight between my legs, making me squirm.

Without moving his mouth, Pike shuffles over, resting his front to my side. His hand is at my shorts, working the button and zipper quickly, and I lift my ass because I want nothing more than to feel whatever he's about to give.

My shorts and the fancy lace undies I wore just in case this would happen are thrown to the end of the bed, discarded without even a glance. He moves his hand to my mound, cupping my pussy, making the ache turn into a burning throb.

"More, Pike," I beg. My insides are like a raging inferno, and only his fingers can extinguish the flame.

He doesn't tease me or make me beg any more than I already have as he slides his fingers between my legs, and I rock into his touch.

"Greedy," he murmurs against my breast, and I can't argue with him.

I'm greedy as hell when it comes to him. I'm even needier, which should make me worry, but I want an orgasm so badly, I don't bother to think too much.

My knees fall to the bed as his fingers slide back and forth, capturing my wetness. I lift my ass, wanting more than he's giving, growing increasingly impatient with each pass of his fingers.

He slides one finger slowly inside, filling me, but it's not enough. I want more. I need more. I want the delicious ache of being filled, stuffed, owned. I arch my back, pushing my bottom toward his hand, letting him know I want more than he's giving.

I don't have to wait long before he adds another finger, stretching me more than I've been stretched since the last time I was in his bed.

Pike is exceptional at finger-fucking. Like, the best of the best. Or at least, the best I've ever had. He knows how to work every spot, sending me soaring over the edge faster than I ever have before.

My fingers fist the soft blanket, squeezing until my knuckles turn white as if it'll help the orgasm I want so badly to come easier.

"My girl wants this," Pike whispers against my skin, eyes moving to my face with a smile.

I seal my eyes shut, pushing my nipple against his lips, hoping he'll get the hint. He doesn't. He keeps staring, fingers working in and out of me, his thumb brushing against my clit with not enough pressure to have me singing the high notes, praising his work, and for the waves to rock my body.

"My girl needs this," he says, pressing the pad of his thumb flat against my clit.

I inch my bottom upward, rolling my hips, trying to get his thumb to move in the way I need to give me the damn orgasm.

"Enough with the *my girl* stuff and put your mouth to better use."

Pike's smile widens, and he slides down my body, fingers still inside me, thumb not giving me what I want. He settles his shoulders between my legs and pushes my legs farther apart. "Been waiting forever to taste you."

"For fuck's sake," I groan, bucking against his fingers because they've stopped although they're still inside me. "You have two seconds to put your..."

Heaven. That's what it feels like when Pike swipes his tongue over my clit, rolling the tip around to trace the outside.

"Fuck yeah..." I drop my head back, closing my eyes and letting the sensations wash over me.

The warmth of his mouth.

The wetness of his lips.

The hardness of his fingers.

It all works together in perfect harmony and is everything I remember.

He curls his fingers, rubbing my G-spot as he seals his lips around my cunt in the most perfect way. "God, yes, right there."

The goose bumps from earlier return as every fiber of my being seems to be standing at attention, wanting this as badly as I do.

I open one eye, staring down my body again and loving the sight. There's nothing sexier than Pike nestled between my legs, eating like he's a starved man, fucking me like it's his sole purpose in life, and me...lying back and taking it all in.

Pike is right. I am a greedy lover. I won't apologize for it either. I'd lie here all night with him like this, orgasm after orgasm crashing over me if Pike would let that happen. But then again, I don't know of any man who is that giving.

My toes curl and my legs strain, trying to make the orgasm quicker. "Don't stop!"

His mouth is gone, and I groan my frustration. "Let it happen, darlin'. Don't force it."

I raise up on my elbow, glaring at the man whose lips are glistening from all his hard work. "Hey, Dr. Ruth, can you get back to suckin' and fuckin' without so much talk?"

"She's bossy too," he whispers, smiling up at me, mumbling something else to himself before his lips are back on my clit.

I collapse back onto the bed, trying to relax and let it happen naturally, because Pike's right...it's always better when it isn't forced.

Within seconds, my toes curl again, but this time, I don't strain, chasing it. His fingers move faster, his lips suck harder, tongue flicking against my flesh as my muscles tighten on their own and all the breath in my lungs vanishes.

"Yes! Yes! Yes!" I scream, wrapping my fingers around the blanket again as my body shakes out of control. "Fuck yes!"

Pike doesn't slow. He doesn't allow the orgasm to wane. He pulls me from one orgasm straight into another, leaving me gasping for air and limp.

I'm in so much fucking trouble, and this time, there's no way out.

CHAPTER 20
PIKE

"WHAT'S YOUR NAME, HONEY?" a woman leans on the bar next to me, ass sticking out like she's looking for attention. Attention I won't be giving her beyond answering her question.

"Pike."

"You new around here?" she drawls, pushing her tits forward with the arm that's tucked under her chest.

"Nope."

"I've never seen you."

"Midge, leave the kid alone," Tiny says, stalking past us and around the bar. "He's an old-timer, but he's been gone for a while. He's not a brother, but a friend, and completely off-limits."

She snarls, but by the time he looks at her, her face is neutral. "I was just saying hello and introducing myself." She smiles at Tiny and straightens, allowing her tits and everything else to go back to normal, thanks to gravity. "I'm Morris's old lady."

"No shit?"

Morris never seemed like the type to settle down, especially not with someone so close to his own age.

"He doesn't know it yet, but I will be." She winks.

I hate to tell the lady, but Morris isn't settling down for no one. I don't care if she was a *Playboy* centerfold, the man couldn't stick to one pussy if his life depended on it. He is all about variety and excess, rarely dipping his wick in the same well twice.

"Get lost, Midge. We got shit to talk about, and you have work to do." Tiny glares down at the small woman with so many wrinkles, she looks like she was taken out of the dryer after staying in there too long.

"Yes, sir, big man," she says, throwing me a smile before stalking off with a sway of her hips.

Tiny glances toward the ceiling and sighs. "She ain't nothing but fucking trouble."

"Why keep her around?"

"She ain't got anywhere else to go, and she's a damn fine maid too."

"You finally hired someone to clean?" I look around the place, noticing it's not any neater than the last time I was here.

The floor is dirty, my boots stick to the tile in some spots, old alcohol acting like glue. Beer bottles are everywhere, but it's been a long night and the guys were celebrating my return, even if most of them didn't give two shits. They'd use any excuse to have a party.

"She cleans for beer and cock."

My eyebrows go up. "Interesting arrangement."

Tiny grabs a beer from the cooler, holds it out to me, and I take it before he grabs another one. "Where's the girl?"

I twist the top and take a swig, needing something to quench the thirst Gigi caused because the girl is insatiable. "Sleeping."

Tiny grins as he lifts the beer to his lips. "I like her."

Again, I raise my eyebrows. Tiny doesn't like many people. Most of the time, I never thought he liked me. "You do?"

He nods. "She's a good fit for you. Unlike that other skank... What was her name?"

"Which one?" I laugh a little, but there's truth in what I'm saying.

I may not have been a brother or a prospect, but I had just as much pussy in my bed as every guy in this place. Somehow, the men here let me take advantage of all the perks without risking my life or requiring the oath bullshit they all swore to one another.

"What are you doing up?" I ask him because it's almost morning, but I haven't slept a wink.

"I'm not up. I'm headed to bed, but I had a few loose ends to tie up." He leans against the bar across from me, taking another swig of his beer. "I have eyes and ears out all over the state. No one's looking for you or the girl. Hopefully in a few days, you two can get back to your lives without looking over your shoulder."

"I'm sorry about this, Tiny. If I would've known James..."

Tiny waves me off. "If you're in any kind of shit, I want you calling me. If you need help, pick up the goddamn phone. I thought we made this clear to you when we saw you in Daytona. You may not live here anymore, but you'll always be part of our family."

"I don't know what I did to deserve any of this." I grip the neck of the bottle, swiping my thumb down the glass. "I don't see you taking in any other strays."

Tiny laughs. "You're a good kid. If I had a son, I'd want him to be just like you, Pike. Instead, I got a daughter because I've done bad shit in my life and the big guy found a way to pay me back. You needed help and had a pair of balls and a mouth back then." He laughs louder, shaking his head. "Hell, ya still do. I thought I'd convince you to be one of us, to join the brotherhood, but when I knew it was hopeless, I couldn't just toss your ass out into the street."

"You really could've. My parents didn't give two fucks what happened to me, and they're my own blood, Tiny. You have no duty to help me or even protect us right now."

Tiny's laugh dies and he moves closer, leaning into my space. "Family is more than blood, kid. Shit goes down in your life and you need backup, you call me. Now, you have James in your life and his people, which is good, but I'll always be here for you."

"James seems decent."

Tiny's laughter is back. "He's an asshole. One of the biggest fucking dicks I've ever met, but he's solid. When he speaks, it's the truth coming out of his lips. Shit went down years ago between us, but we made our peace. And when I need help, something I can't call on the guys to do, I call James and his guys."

"I don't want to know."

Tiny nods. "Trust me, you don't, but if that girl is his family, James will pull you into the fold."

"I work for her dad."

Tiny's eyes widen. "My man's fucking the boss's kid? You got a bigger set of balls on you than I thought."

"Or I'm dumb as a fuckin' brick. It's debatable at this point." I crack a smile, trying to make light of the situation, but none of it's funny. "And her life may be in danger because of that very fact. I'm pretty sure her father wants to rip my dick off and shove it down my throat, but we gotta make it out of here in one piece for that to happen."

"I'll make sure you live," Tiny promises, and I believe he'll do everything in his power to keep us alive.

"Thanks, T."

"Now, as a father to daughters, let me give you a little advice."

"I'm listening."

"Treat her good and make her happy. A father has many weapons, and if the guy is a douche and treats her like shit, he doesn't need to bring out the big guns to drive them apart. But if the guy is good and makes her happy, in bed and out, not even a nuclear weapon or her father's unhappiness can make her leave you. You make it right with her, her father will fall in line."

I shrug. "He's pretty pissed, and if I didn't know better, I'd think he was part of an MC too. He's friendly, but I know there's more to him than meets the eye."

"City was never in an MC," Tiny says.

"City?" I ask because that's not a name I know him by.

Tiny raises his hands. "Joe Gallo, dumbass."

I tick my chin toward Tiny. "How the hell do you know Joe?"

"He did a tat of mine back in the day, and I know all about him and that family from working with James and Thomas. He's solid. Never been in an MC, but he has been around the biking world for years. He keeps to himself. Dedicated to his family and isn't afraid to go to any length to protect them."

"Yep. That's him."

"I wish you fuckin' luck with that one," he says before he tips his head back, polishing off the rest of his beer.

"Thanks for the encouragement," I grumble because I know the shit hasn't even started. Once we step foot outside this compound, the danger gone, a new risk awaits, and it'll be directed only at me.

"Get some shut-eye. You look like shit."

I run my fingers down my beard, smiling at the old bastard. "Still lookin' better than you," I tease him as I climb off the stool and toss the rest of my beer in the trash as I walk toward the hallway.

When I open my door, Gigi's passed out, blankets half off her body, breasts sticking out, and taking up the entire twin bed like she's slept there her whole life.

I undress, pulling her over to one side, careful not to let her fall before I climb in next to her and tug her against my body. Her skin smells of sex and vanilla as I nuzzle my face into her neck, tightening my arms around her.

"Pike," she whispers.

"Shh, darlin'. Go back to sleep," I whisper back.

She turns in my arms, lying flat on her back, and blinks up at me. "Where were you?"

"Just talkin' with Tiny."

"Is everything okay?" She fights back a yawn but loses, covering her mouth with her hand. She closes her eyes, turning again and burrowing her face in my chest then throwing her leg over my hip.

"Everything's good." My fingers find her spine, tracing the straight line down her skin. "Don't worry. We're safe."

"Are you sad coming back here?"

"No. It's like going home again, although a fucked-up home, after being gone for a while. I'm comfortable here, but I worry about you being in a place like this."

She laughs against my skin. "Clearly you've never been in a frat house."

"Can't say that I have."

"The guys are bigger and scarier, but there is just as much drinking and naked bodies at a frat party as there was here tonight."

"How many frat parties have you been to?"

"A lot," she whispers. "Too many to remember."

I tighten my arms around her, and I don't like hearing about her in a place with so many drinks or naked people, but I know we both lived lives before we met. The thought of another man touching her makes my stomach knot.

"No more though, yeah?" I ask, letting my jealousy shine a little.

She laughs softly. "There's no time for frat parties. I figure this is like the last big hurrah, being at the compound. I'm going to use the time to party my ass off because adulting is going to suck and it's forever."

"You party as much as you want while we're here, but I'm going to be with you every step of the way. So, don't get any crazy ideas."

She pulls her head back, staring up at me with a smile. "What do you consider a crazy idea?"

"You're here with me and only in my bed. No one else."

Her smile grows wider. "Would you be jealous?"

I sigh, figuring I have to lay shit out because she's testing me. "Darlin', we both have pasts, but we're living in the now. I don't know if I have one hour or one hundred years, but whatever time I got, I want you where you are right now."

She blinks a few times, staring at me like I'm speaking a foreign language she can't understand. "I'm down with the now, but what makes you think you want to spend one hundred years with me where I am?"

"We got something special."

"Orgasms don't make a relationship." She rolls her eyes.

"They don't hurt either." I smirk. "But I've also been around enough wrong women to know when I've found the right one."

"Pike," she says softly, reaching her hand up between us and resting her fingers on my beard. "I'm not as...experienced as you."

"Really?" I say even though I knew that fact the first time she was in my bed. It's not hard to tell the difference. I knew back then Gigi Gallo wasn't an easy girl and didn't give her body away to just anyone. Why she decided to offer herself up to me in Daytona, I'll never know, nor do I give a fuck. It happened, and I haven't stopped thanking my dumbass luck for being in the right place at the right time since then.

She pulls at the hairs near my chin, toying with the tips. "I've only had a few boyfriends, and those relationships were complete disasters. How do I know we won't be the same?"

I press my lips to her forehead, wishing we could stay here, this way, forever. "There's no way to tell if we'll work out, but that doesn't mean I don't want to do whatever I can to hold on to what-ever this is. All I can promise is that I'll treat you good, be loyal to you always, and give you as many orgasms as you want."

"As many as I want?" she whispers into my neck, fingers still playing with my beard.

"As many as you want," I repeat.

"I never had one with someone else before you," she confesses. Her voice is so soft and quiet, I almost don't hear her.

The statement doesn't shock me. So many women never get off with their partner, and half the time, the guys don't even try. They think that by getting theirs, they did enough, and if it doesn't happen for the chick, it isn't their fucking problem. I've never been that way. Can't even begin to understand that way of thinking.

"But you did with me, yeah?"

"Every time."

"That has to count for something. What if you don't stay with me, and no guy ever gets you off again?" It's a lie, but one I can use to my advantage since she has very little experience, and all of it before me was absolute shit.

"I do have a vibrator, so it's not like I'd never come again."

"I got a hand too, but it doesn't mean I'd be happy jacking off for the rest of my life."

She tips her head back, a smile back on her face. "Can I watch?"

My eyebrows draw together as I stare back at her. "Watch what?"

"You know." She waggles her eyebrows. "Watch you jack off. It would be the hottest thing ever."

"You going to give me that ass?" I ask, waggling my eyebrows just like she did. "Because that would be the hottest thing ever."

Her nose scrunches. "Um, no."

"A little more tequila and I bet you'd say yes."

She lets out a loud huff and flattens her lips. "You let me watch you jack off and give me enough tequila, and I'll think about giving you my ass."

I roll her to her back, and I'm on top of her quickly. "See, darlin'. We work well together. Communication and negotiation are important in every relationship."

"You just want my ass, Pike."

"I want all of you, Gigi." I slide between her legs. "But right now, I want that sweet cunt squeezing my cock until we both pass out."

"That I can do," she promises.

CHAPTER 21
GIGI

THE COMPOUND IS MASSIVE. Not just the main building—everything is supersized. The ten-foot-high walls around the perimeter seem excessive, but I wouldn't be shocked if there was a moat on the other side of the gate either.

"Don't get any ideas, girl," cautions one of the men who's been following me around like he's my shadow.

I pull my hand back, letting the dusty green curtains fall back into place, and scrunch my nose. "Where would I go? Seriously, it's like Fort Knox out there."

The guy pulls a toothpick from his lips, sliding the same hand through his blond hair. "You look crafty and as if you'd claw your way over that wall like a superhero or some shit."

The double doors leading into a room that's set up like something you'd see in a corporate office creak, and the men file out, but there's no Pike, Morris, or Tiny. The looks on the men's faces don't give me much solace that this shit is over and we can finally go home. They called an emergency meeting an hour ago, telling me I wasn't allowed to attend even though my life was on the line and anything they said in there could either save me or end shit in a bad way.

To say I was pissed was an understatement. Even though I am a girl, I never have been treated like one by my family. We are all equals. It doesn't matter what you have between your legs, your opinion and thoughts count for something and are always taken into consideration.

The Disciples don't feel the same way. There is a macho hierarchy where the women cook, fuck, and suck dick, but beyond that, they aren't needed or wanted.

Thank God Pike didn't pick up on that shit when he lived here. He has enough of an attitude; I couldn't take the sexism on top of the rest of him.

The men scatter in opposite directions, pulling their guns from their waistbands as they walk. *Great.* Whatever they talked about has them on edge, because I haven't seen weapons out in the open in such numbers except for on television.

"What do you think's happening?" I ask Mr. Toothpick because he's the only one who's bothered to talk to me today besides Pike.

He shrugs. "My ass is out here with you, so I'm not in the know."

"They didn't clue you in?"

"They clue me in when they want me to be clued in."

The man talks in riddles, and he wouldn't be half bad-looking if he cut his long hair and trimmed his beard so it wasn't so scraggly.

"Gigi." Morris's voice booms through the open space, drawing my gaze. "Get your ass in here."

I smile at Toothpick. "Guess I'm going to be clued in before you," I taunt him because it's the only form of entertainment I have, and I'm feeling bitchy.

He snarls, waving me off. "Lucky you," he mutters and slides the toothpick back between his lips.

Morris is standing in the doorway, leaning against the frame, eyes on me like my ass is moving too slow for him. "You out for a stroll?" he asks, confirming I am, in fact, moving too slow. But I have one speed, and it's sloth.

"The scenery lacks a certain charm." I smile, looking up at the big guy I've grown fond of in the short time I've been at the compound.

I can understand why Pike liked him even if he thought the guy shot him. I'm not sure I'd ever get over everything that happened, like him punching Pike in his injured shoulder, but men are cut from a different cloth like that.

"I'll make sure to call HGTV and see if we can get a makeover," Morris jokes, following me through the double doors.

Tiny's at the far end of the table, Pike next to him, both men staring at me as Morris closes the doors behind us. "Is everything okay?" I ask, walking slower than before because the looks on their faces say shit is far from okay.

Pike pulls out the chair next to him, and Tiny motions for me to sit. I do it quick, like my ass is suddenly on fire and only the chair can put out the flames.

Pike throws his arm around the back, turning his head to face me. I give him a timid smile. "What happened?"

As Pike opens his mouth, ready to tell me what I want to know, Tiny clears his throat. "There was an attempted hit on Pike's father last night."

I gasp, because this shit is far too real. His mother is dead, and his father was in hiding, just like us. But somehow, it sounds like he didn't come out unscathed.

Tiny leans back, eyeing me. "As far as we can tell, he's alive."

"That's good, right?" I ask, swallowing the lump that's back in my throat.

"DiSantis isn't taking his time. The next twenty-four hours will tell us if Pike or you are a target. So far, there's been no movement toward either of you. I spoke to James this morning, and he said it's quiet over there. He's had his boys sitting outside your apartments, parked outside Inked, and ears everywhere in that shithole town listening for chatter."

"And?"

Tiny drags his hand down his face, maybe not used to being questioned about anything. He probably lays shit out and people just take what he has to say and soak it in. But I'm not built that way. I question everything, and just when the person thinks they're done, I want to know more.

"We're ready in case they come here, looking for either of you."

"You really think they're here?"

Tiny shrugs. "Don't know. I'm sending out some guys to see if there's anyone new around, asking too many questions. The next few hours are critical."

"And if they hear nothing, can we go?"

"If we hear nothing, James and I will make the call on if your ass can walk outside those walls tonight."

"Okay," I whisper, knowing there's no point in arguing about who gets to determine our fate.

"DiSantis isn't a fool. I'm sure he did his homework, and if he's after Pike, he figured he'd come here for cover from the hell storm he's raining down."

"I can do another day standing on my head." I lean back into Pike's arm that's still flung across the back of my chair. I stare at Tiny, looking to him for some comfort.

"Just lie low. Maybe stay in Pike's room as much as possible. If shit goes down, I'd rather you be in a room with no windows than out there." He jerks his head toward the door. "I'm sure you can find ways to keep yourselves occupied." He winks.

I let out a nervous laugh. "Nothing gets me hotter than knowing I may be taking my last breath."

Tiny swipes his hand across his lips, muttering obscenities. "Take a nap, play Scrabble or some shit, but keep yourselves out of sight."

"Scrabble?" I scrunch my nose. "Poker maybe." I tap my chin, thinking of ways to entertain ourselves. "Strip poker works too." I turn to Pike, who's pale as a ghost. "You okay, baby?"

He gives me a small smile, hiding whatever passes across his eyes. "I'm great, darlin'."

His answer comes too easy, and I wonder what I'm not being told. Maybe he's in shock, mourning the loss of his mother and the possible death of his father.

"Now, you two get gone. I have shit to do, and the sooner this is over, the better," Tiny announces, pushing back from the table and climbing to his feet.

"You know you're going to miss me," I tell Tiny, standing and craning my neck to look up at him.

"Kid, the next time I see your face, I expect it to be under happier circumstances."

"Me too, Tiny. Me too."

Pike's on his feet, arm around my shoulders like he needs to be physically touching me at all times. I turn my head, looking at his face, soaking him in. "Why don't we grab a bottle of Jack before we head back?"

If the day goes to shit, I'm going to need something hard to chase away the fear that's settled into my bones. I've been good at keeping it under wraps. I've pretended to be sleeping, when half the time, I'm paralyzed by fear, waiting for the bad guys to come crashing through the doors, ready to take us out.

"I think we should stay clearheaded," Pike says, moving me toward the doorway right behind Tiny. "If something happens and I'm shit-faced..."

"We'll stay sober." I reach up and touch his hand that's closed around my shoulder.

Tiny puts out his hand, stopping us from walking to Pike's room. "Here." He pulls a gun from his waistband and holds it in front of us. "Take this. If you don't need it, great. If you do, at least you have it. You remember how to shoot it?"

"I'll never forget," Pike says as he wraps his hand around the handle, holding it like he's done it a million times.

"Shit goes south, you shoot at anything coming your way."

Pike nods at Tiny, and I'm feeling a little left out again. "Do I get a gun?"

Tiny's eyes twinkle, but his expression doesn't change. "Absolutely not."

"This is bullshit."

"As is life," Tiny teases.

Pike moves one hand to the small of my back, the other one still holding the gun. "Come on. Let's let the guys do their shit so we can get out of here sooner rather than later."

"Fine, but I'm grabbing the Jack." I stalk away from him and push past Morris before Pike has a chance to usher me toward his room.

"Fuckin' women," Morris mutters loud enough for me to hear even though my legs are moving faster than before. "Now she's Jackie Joyner-Kersee."

I don't know who Jackie is, but she has to be badass if he thinks I'm anything like her. I'm so not chill right now as I stride across to the bar, throwing myself over the top, and reaching underneath to find a bottle of Jack. Once I have it in hand, I slide back down, turning to face the three of them, all of whom are staring at me with a look of amusement.

"Good luck," Morris says to Pike, slapping him on the back as I throw them a quick glance before striding down the hallway, cracking the top of the bottle open.

"You comin'?" I call out when Pike's not right behind me, hanging on me like he was a few minutes ago.

Tiny and Morris laugh their asses off, but I don't turn around to see if Pike's following me or not. I'm cranky and starting to go a little stir-crazy, missing the sunshine on my skin. All I can hope for now is that today's our last day in captivity and we walk out of here breathing.

––––––––

Half a bottle of Jack and four hours later, I'm sitting on the edge of Pike's bed, wrapped in a blanket and nothing more. He's naked, pacing near the door like he's a caged animal, gun on the dresser.

"You okay?" I ask him, watching the muscles of his body flex and relax with each step.

His body is long, sleek, and sculpted. His legs are longer than his torso, all brought together with the most spectacular ass I've ever seen on a man.

"Just thinking."

I lean back, still staring at his nakedness because I can. "About?"

"How my family has fallen to shit because of the stupid, greedy things my father's done. But then there's you—" he motions a hand toward me "—and that part of my life feels like it's finally falling into place."

"I'm sorry about your mom and dad."

I can't imagine something happening to mine. I wouldn't even be able to get out of bed, let alone form coherent thoughts. My world revolves around my family. Always has, and I can't imagine that ever changing. I didn't even leave the state to attend college because I wanted to be close enough to go home whenever I missed everybody. Which ended up being more often than I'd expected.

Pike shakes his head. "I feel like I should be crying or at least be sadder than I am. They're my parents after all. They brought me into this world, but Gigi, they weren't good to me. There wasn't a day that went by where I didn't feel like I was a burden to them. Do you know how it is to be a little kid, playing with your old-ass toy truck that is falling apart, knowing you're not wanted." He looks at me, and I shake my head. "Of course, you don't. You have the Gallos. They love you. They worship the ground you walk on and would do anything for you if you asked."

"I'm sorry."

Those are the only words I have because I know I was lucky the day I was born. I could've very easily been born into a shit-ass family where I was just another mouth to feed. But I wasn't. I hit the proverbial jackpot. Not only do I have amazing parents, but my aunts and uncles are the bomb too.

"I'd give my left nut to have something good like that in my life."

I'm on my feet, walking toward him. "I wouldn't like that because I'm kind of partial to your left nut." I'm using humor because it's the only thing I can do. "Your right one just doesn't do it for me."

Pike grabs me as the blanket I have wrapped around myself falls to the floor. "You're such an asshole." He laughs, holding me tightly, skin against skin.

"But you love me."

"I do," he replies, running his fingers down my spine. "More than I have anyone in a long time."

"Pike." I'm breathless, wondering if he meant to say that, wondering if he'll take them back. "Is it a little too soon to say those words?"

He peers down at me, a swirl of emotion in his eyes. "I didn't just meet you, darlin'. After you left, I dreamed of no one but you. When I saw you walk into Inked, I couldn't believe my goddamn eyes. We've only spent two weeks together in total, but I feel like I've known you since the day you walked up to me and asked me for my number—and let me say, you never gave me yours."

"Well…" I don't know what to say to all that. If I were honest, I've thought about Pike a lot since the day I walked out the door for that nonexistent cup of coffee.

"You're young. Maybe you're not ready to say how you feel, but I've lived enough to know when there's something good in my life and something I don't want to let go of again."

"Um," I mumble, my vision blurring because this beautiful man, one who doesn't always share his feelings, is spilling his guts like water over Niagara Falls.

"I'll give you all the time in the world to figure out if it's how you feel too, but until then, you're my girl and only my girl. You're mine, Gigi Gallo."

My stomach flutters at the way he says those words and at the intensity in his gaze. I've heard my father utter those words a thousand times to my mother, and every time, I'd roll my eyes. But now I understand how it made her feel. I understand why those words made her smile and go all gooey in the knees, because in this moment, I am finding it difficult to stand.

"Okay," I whisper.

"Okay?" He raises an eyebrow.

I nod. "I'm yours." I brush my hand across the beautiful back dimples he has just above his ass. "But as long as we're staking claims, you're mine too, Pike Moore. No other women are in your bed or on the back of your bike. If we're doing this, we're doing it right."

Pike's sadness from earlier is gone, replaced by a big, toothy smile. He slides his hand up my back, cupping my neck. "In the shittiest week of my life, you've somehow found a way to make me the happiest man alive."

I don't get a chance to reply and tell him I feel the same before his lips crash down on mine, stealing my words and my breath.

CHAPTER 22
PIKE

MY EYES FLY open as a cold hand covers my mouth. "Pike," Morris tries to whisper, but being quiet has never been his thing. "Men are on the perimeter."

I blink up at him as I lift myself, letting his words slide over me, penetrating the haze I still have from the dream I was just in a minute ago.

Gigi shifts in my arms. "What's wrong?" She goes stiff as soon as she lays eyes on Morris, who's hovering above us.

"Get your asses up and be ready." Morris moves toward the door, but he's still staring at us, a worried look on his face. "Shit's about to go down."

Gigi rises next to me, holding the sheet over her chest. "Fuck. For real?" Her eyes are wide, and I can see the fear all over her face.

Morris doesn't answer as he disappears into the hallway. The only sounds are his heavy footsteps and those of his brothers moving around the compound as the door clicks behind him.

"Get dressed and go into my closet." I move my chin toward the door on the other side of the room. "Don't come out under any circumstances. And when I say any circumstances, I mean, don't come out until you hear me, Tiny, or Morris calling your name."

She scurries to her feet, gathering her clothes off the floor where I'd thrown them last night. "Don't come out under any circumstances," she repeats my words, pulling her shirt over her head and then moving for her pants. "Pike, what if…"

I shake my head, zipping my jeans. "No ifs. If you don't know the voice, don't come out. Stay quiet, and no matter what, don't cry. I don't want these fuckers finding you."

"Don't get yourself shot, okay? No jumping in front of bullets for me."

I stalk up to her, grabbing her neck and hauling her lips to mine. "Darlin', I'll do whatever it takes to get you back to your family and keep you breathing."

"I'd never be able to…"

I don't let her finish the statement before my mouth closes over hers, taking what I can get for what might be the last time. If shit goes south, which it could and probably will, I may never have another chance to kiss her beautiful mouth and feel her in my arms again.

I break away, even though I want to hold her like this forever and forget the shit that's going on outside this room.

"Go." I run my finger along her chin, memorizing every dip of her lips. "Get in the closet. Go all the way to the back and hide behind my things."

She nods, walking back slowly, dragging her hand down my arm until just our fingertips are touching. "Be safe and don't be a hero."

I've never wanted to be the hero, but I want to be hers. I'm not sure I've ever wanted to be anything more that in this very moment. No one would get by me and get to her. Not as long as I still have air in my lungs and the ability to move.

"Go, Gigi," I order her, pulling on my boots, gun by my side on the bed, my body facing the hallway.

A wave of emotion passes across her face as she opens the door to the closet and steps inside. I lift my chin at her, and she gives me a pained smile before finally closing the door, disappearing into the darkness.

I grab the gun, but I stay on the edge of the bed, knowing whoever comes through that door is going to get one of my bullets. I won't hesitate to pull the trigger, and the brothers here know better than to walk in here unannounced or without calling the all clear.

Gunfire rings through the building, sounding like fireworks on steroids and coming so fast it's like a hurricane of metal and fire.

A million thoughts cross through my mind as the shadow of boots passes by the door, heading toward the main room where the majority of the bullets are flying.

These guys, the ones I thought of like family, are hauling ass toward the gunfire, shielding us from their spray.

We're the intended targets, but they're willing to put their lives on the line so we can breathe another day. They live for shit like this. They crave danger, not giving a fuck if they live or die as long as they enjoy every minute of the time they're here, walking this earth.

I hold my breath, knowing someone's going to come through the door if anyone has survived. I pray—something I haven't done since I was living with my grandmother—hoping like hell we get out of here unscathed. Not just us, but the men putting their lives on the line as I sit in the dark, protecting my girl and waiting for hell to come to me.

I've lived through a hail of bullets before, but I had never been the intended target. I've been shot, and I sure as fuck am not looking forward to feeling the hot metal slice through my skin again. But I also want to live, having more to live for than ever before.

My father's sins were following me. His curse was the only thing he gave me besides his name. But after tonight, after the gunfire ends, no matter which side comes out on top, his time in my life will end as well.

The shouts of the men I know are barely audible over the gunfire as it grows louder, coming close to us. I prepare myself, lifting the gun toward the door, poised to shoot anyone who enters. My hand doesn't shake, even though I've never shot a man before. I've held a gun hundreds of times growing up in Tennessee, but never have I been more prepared to use it to kill another person than I am right now.

My body stiffens as a door slams nearby. Clearly, someone's searching and got through the front line. I lift my other hand, gripping my forearm to steady the gun because if I shoot, I sure as fuck ain't missing.

"Keep lookin'!" a man yells. "I know he's here."

He is me, and I'm thankful they haven't said anything about Gigi. I'm their intended target and not the scared girl hiding in my closet probably losing her shit but following my orders nonetheless.

A single shot rings out in the hallway, sounding more like a firework popping and echoing through the tiny corridor. The knob on my door turns, illuminating my room with just enough light to see the outline of a man. I squeeze the trigger, not hesitating to fire as he lifts his arm, ready to take me out too. But my shot is quicker, and the man falls backward, a clean shot right in his head.

"Don't shoot," another man says, but my ears are still ringing from the shot I just fired. "Pike." I can't see him because he hasn't shown his face, probably not wanting the same fate as the dead bastard on the dirty-ass floor.

The gun's still pointed at the door, my hand not as steady as it was, but I'll take out any other bastard that tries to walk inside. I keep my mouth shut, not knowing who's calling my name or their intentions.

"It's Morris. Don't shoot," he says. "They're gone. All dead but a few already out the door and running for the hills."

"They're gone?" I ask, not moving a muscle because I can't.

"Just this one cocksucker got by us, but you handled his ass.

Three more made it out, but men are after them, making sure they don't get wherever they're going."

"Morris?" I ask because my mind is hazy and all I can see is the puddle of blood oozing out of the man's body.

"Yeah, kid. It's me. Put the gun down. The shit's over." He's still hiding, taking no chances with me.

I don't blame him. It's not every day a man takes the life of another. Morris knows I've never done it and how it changes a man.

My hand drops as I take my finger off the trigger, but I'm not ready to put it down. It's like the metal has fused to my hand, becoming one with me. I'm in shock. I know it. I know my body is trying to catch up with what my mind already knows. I shot a man. I took a life.

"Is it down?"

"Yeah," I call back to Morris. "Come in."

He steps over the man's body, flipping the switch on the wall and bathing the room in light. "Nice shot," he says as soon as his eyes land on the man with a bullet clean through his forehead. "I always knew you had it in you."

"Can I come out?" Gigi says from the closet, no doubt hearing our voices but unable to wait for the all clear. The girl only has so much patience to follow orders, which is maddening, but at least she stayed in there long enough to keep her ass alive.

"Come out, girl," Morris tells her before I can. "It's over."

I'm on my feet and at my closet before she has a chance to see the dead guy on the floor. I grab her face, keeping her eyes on me. "You okay, baby?"

She nods, eyes glistening as she stares up at me. "I'm okay," she whispers, but her voice wavers. "When I heard the shot go off…" Her lip quivers, and her voice breaks, not finishing the statement.

"I'm fine. We're fine." I hold her gaze, trying to keep my shit together so I can convince her that what I'm saying is true.

"Yo!" Morris yells, making Gigi jump. "We got a body over here."

Gigi tries to look around me, but I hold her face, forcing her to look at me and nowhere else. "Don't look. You don't want to have that burned on your brain."

"Did you do it?" she asks, her voice whisper-soft, the quiver still on her lips.

I nod, rubbing my thumb across her cheek. "It was him or us, and I wasn't about to end what we have. I told you I'd do anything to protect you, and I did what I needed to do."

"You killed a man."

I nod again because I did. I pulled that trigger without an ounce of hesitation, thinking of him as the enemy and not a human being. I didn't give a fuck if he had a wife and kids. He wanted to kill us, and for that alone, he deserved the bullet he got.

The tears in her eyes build and fall when she blinks. "You protected me?" she whispers as her hands find my sides, gripping me like she needs to touch me to stay upright.

"I'll always protect you." I know my words are true. "I told you that, darlin'."

Boots are behind me, shadows moving around the room as the guys bend down, hauling the dead guy from the doorway. "Take him outside with the others," Morris says. "We'll deal with them together. And get Midge in here to help clean up this mess." There are a few grunts of understanding, followed by Morris's shadow growing in size on the wall behind Gigi. "I'll give you two some time to talk and some privacy."

I nod, not turning around because I'm not taking my eyes off my girl. She needs me. More than she needed me before this shit went down. She heard too much, knew too much, and that shit would mess with her head.

When I peer over my shoulder, there's only a small amount of blood visible near the doorway. The majority of the guy's brains and blood landed in the hallway just outside my door and out of sight.

I reach down, lifting Gigi into my arms, carrying her toward the bed. Her head moves to my shoulder, arms around my neck as I cradle her tightly, wishing she'd never had to experience this. I brought this to her door. My father brought this to mine.

"We're safe now." I sit on the edge of the bed, resting her ass in my lap, still holding her close. "No one's going to hurt you."

"I've never been so scared in my life, Pike." Her fingers toy with the hair on the back of my neck, sending a shock wave of feelings through my system. "Not just for me, but for you. I was so worried that…"

"Shh, baby. It's over. Stop thinking about it. I'm breathing. You're breathing. There's nothing else that matters right now."

"What about the guys?"

"I don't know what happened out there, and I'm not ready to find out. Tiny will call for us when he's ready to tell us what we need to know and what he wants to tell." I brush my lips across her forehead, needing to feel her softness and be reminded of all the good there is in life to replace the bad I've just done. "All that matters is you're okay."

"Do you think they'll come back?" she whispers, toying with the collar of my T-shirt, grazing my skin with her fingernails.

"I don't know if there'll be anyone to come back. If any of them made it out, the others went after them on foot. They don't have much of a chance on all this land with the Disciples on the hunt."

"I guess that's a good thing."

"It's a good thing for us, but not for them."

We're both thankful to be alive. I may have lived within these compound walls for years, but we'd never been attacked and I'd never been in what sounded like a battle zone. My body trembles slightly as the adrenaline that has been coursing through me starts to wear off.

"Do you think we'll ever get to go home?"

I run my hand up her back and nuzzle my face in her neck, needing her smell, her softness to keep me grounded. "We will, darlin'. DiSantis isn't stupid enough to lose all his men trying to kill someone who doesn't know dick about his business. I don't know how many came here tonight, but based on the sounds, I'd say he lost too many to try to come after me again."

"Kid?" Tiny calls, knocking on my door but not entering the room. "You two decent?"

Gigi laughs, and the sound is like angels singing, making all the shit that happened seem like it was part of a distant past.

"Yeah, Tiny. We're good."

The door creaks, and Tiny sticks his head in the room. "Just talked to James."

"Oh shit," Gigi whispers, and her laughter dies. "We may have survived the gun battle, but now we have to figure out how to make it through my family."

"He's on his way with a few of her uncles and her father. They'll be here in a few hours. Get your shit together. You two are heading back."

I gawk at Tiny as he wipes his bloodied hand with a towel. "But what about DiSantis?"

Tiny shrugs with a smile. "Fucker's dead. Someone went after him tonight before the hit went down. Took a blade across his neck just before lights-out. He ain't gonna bother you again."

I let out a heavy breath like a weight has been lifted off my back that I didn't know was there. "That's it? He's dead. It's over?" I repeat like the words haven't sunk in.

"Yup. Dead as a fucking doornail. You have three hours before the guys get here to collect you two."

He starts to close the door, but I have shit to say and not a lot of time to say it. "Tiny," I call out, causing him to stop. "Thank you for tonight and everything."

Tiny nods, still wiping the blood because there're so many dead bodies out there, I'm sure there's blood on everything. "You are family, kid, and we take care of our own. I meant what I said earlier, you need backup or safe haven, you come here. Nowhere else."

I nod. "Nowhere else."

"Now get some rest. You made it through one hit squad, but you're about to be in front of another. I have a feeling you're going to get an earful on the way back."

"I won't let them say anything to you." Gigi gazes up at me from my lap.

"You're cute, darlin'. If they want to lay into me, let them. I can take it. It's not like they're going to be shooting bullets at me. I can handle a little angry talk. Let them get it off their chests, and I'll take it like a man. They're probably worried out of their minds."

"A little angry talk?" she says, laughing with every word. "I know you're used to badass bikers, but these are Gallo men. They may not wear patches or ride a hog, but I'm telling you now, they're just as fuckin' scary. A little angry talk." She bursts into a fit of giggles, knowing her family way better than I do. "We're going to get our asses chewed out for a living, and you're going to wish you were lying in that heap of bodies outside."

"Come on. We're alive. How bad can they honestly be?"

CHAPTER 23
GIGI

I SLAM back two shots of Jack as Morris yells that two cars are approaching. The same two cars that are carrying my family. The same two cars that not only carry my family, but men so pissed off, I'm pretty sure they broke every speed record to get here.

I know what awaits me. I've seen my dad and Uncle James angry before, but it was never pointed at me. I figure if I am going to make it through the long-ass drive home, I need a little liquor to make me more agreeable and less likely to argue back.

"You ready?" Pike asks at my side, holding out his hand to me.

"I don't think I'll ever be ready." I try to smile, but it's impossible knowing my dad is nearby, probably foaming at the mouth.

"It won't be that bad," he says with a straight face because he only knows my dad and uncles as the chill guys they can be sometimes and not the raving lunatics they can be when someone in the family is in danger.

"I'll remind you that you said that." I grab the bottle of Jack and try to pour myself another drink before Pike takes it from my hands.

"This won't make things better."

I try to pull the bottle out of his grip, but it won't budge as we play tug-of-war. "I beg to differ."

"Get your asses moving," Morris yells out, standing at the open door of the building, glancing back at us as we're locked around the bottle of Jack.

"Fuckin' fine." I let go, knowing it's a lost cause and we're out of time.

"The girl lives, sees death, but the attitude never leaves," Morris mutters, glancing up at the dark sky and shaking his head.

I walk away from Pike, stalking toward Morris, the guy I've grown fond of over the last few days. "Thanks for everything, big guy."

He blushes as he tips his head down to look at me. "Don't be a stranger, kid. Make sure to keep that boy in line, ya hear?"

I laugh, nodding at him as I wrap my arm around his middle. "I promise to make sure he walks the straight and narrow."

Morris's arm is around me immediately, holding me tightly. "Maybe I'll come visit. I could use another piece."

"I'd love that."

"You two done?" Tiny says, stalking by the doorway, heading toward the headlights.

I release Morris and practically run up to Tiny, hurling myself against him. He stumbles back like he's in shock and not used to being hugged. "Thank you for everything, Tiny."

Tiny pats my back but doesn't give me the rib-crushing embrace Morris just did. "Anytime, girl. Now, give me a minute with the boy."

I stare up at him, craning my neck all the way back to meet his eyes. "Can you make sure they don't kill Pike?"

"Can't promise anything when it comes to James," he says, amusement lighting up his face.

"It was worth a shot." I shrug and pop up on my toes to just reach his cheek.

Tiny doesn't move as I kiss his cheek and then step away. He looks a little shell-shocked, which is funny because he's so big and burly, but my little kiss seems to have knocked the badass right out of him and left him speechless.

Two cars pull in, gravel flying from the speed and hurling in all directions as they slam on the brakes. We're like deer, frozen in the headlights.

I was scared as hell in the closet, listening to the screams and gunfire going off everywhere. You'd think facing my family would be nothing after that, but nope. I'm just as scared as I was a few hours ago.

"Just stay calm," Morris calls out as Pike walks up next to me.

"You ready for this?" I ask, looking over at him, ignoring the sound of the car doors opening and boots hitting gravel.

"I don't know," he says before his eyes go to where my family stands.

I turn my head slowly, soaking in my uncle James, who looks like he's about ready to tear a man's jugular clean through his neck. My uncle Thomas, who looks just as pissed and no less scary. And then there's my daddy and Bear, looking like caged animals, shifting slightly like they're unable to stand still or all their fury would cause them to combust.

"Hey," I call out, putting on a smile and trying to act like our asses didn't almost get shot tonight. "I missed you guys." I slowly move in their direction, gaze going between all four men, trying to see if I could make their badass exteriors crack.

My dad rushes toward me, putting his eyes on no one and nothing but me. My slow walk turns into a full-on run until we're close enough that I leap into his arms, and he catches me like he used to when I was a little girl.

"I love you, Daddy." I feel like a kid again and finally safe in my father's arms.

"Baby girl," he whispers, holding my head with one hand and squeezing my body with his other arm. "I've never been so scared in all my fucking life and never more thankful than I am right now."

I bury my face in his neck, holding on to him like I don't think I've ever held him before. "I'm sorry," I whisper. "I'm sorry I had you worried."

"We'll talk about it in the car," he says.

Oh goodie.

Car talks have never been my favorite. I'm like a trapped animal and a captive audience with no escape or talking my way out of whatever my dad wants to put down. I freaking hate every minute of the car chats. They are the most sucktastic things ever because they are so effective at breaking me.

"Joe," Pike says, walking up behind me, but my daddy's body goes stiff underneath me.

"Get your ass in the car with James and Thomas. I want to talk to my *daughter* alone."

Goodie times two.

"Yes, sir," Pike says without even arguing.

He probably knows it's a lost cause. There isn't any arguing with a Gallo man on a good day, but in a moment like this and with the anger on my dad's face, there is no way in hell Pike or I would win that argument.

My feet are back on the ground as Pike turns his back and is walking toward James and Thomas where they chat with Tiny and Morris.

"Let's get out of here," Bear says, giving me a wink instead of saying anything else.

I'm sure he wants all the details, but he isn't going to ask about shit when my dad's in a mood. And I'm pretty damn sure my dad's mood isn't going away anytime soon either.

"Daddy, can't Pike come with us, please?" I pitch my thumb over my shoulder toward the five guys.

"I want to talk to you alone, and James wants to debrief Pike." My father shakes his head. "They know the way home."

I hang my head, dragging my feet through the gravel as I make my way toward the car. I know I'm going to get my ass chewed out, but I'll live. It won't be the first time my father has read me the riot act about something.

But Pike may not be so lucky.

I turn toward Pike as I open the car door, giving him a small wave and pained smile when our eyes lock. He waves back, tipping his chin like shit is cool, but he's freaking clueless.

I don't know much about his dad and know even less about his entire family. But what he's about to deal with will, no doubt, be nothing he's prepared for or expects.

"We're out!" my dad yells across the parking lot, not bothering to wait for a response before he's climbing in the passenger seat.

"This should be fun." Bear catches my eye in the rearview mirror, always trying to make light of heavy shit.

No other words are spoken as Bear revs the engine, taking off the same way they came in…fast. I twist my fingers, staring out the window at the endless trees flying by in a blur as we exit the compound.

Maybe my dad is too pissed to even talk. Maybe he's too happy I'm alive to rip me a new asshole. Anything is possible. How can he be mad when we didn't do anything wrong, nor did we do anything to cause the clusterfuck of chaos that landed at our feet?

The silence is killing me. I figure maybe this is an instance where I've got to rip the Band-Aid off quickly and get it over with. Waiting just makes it worse, and I can't sit here in silence for the next two hours. "So…"

"Don't so me, little girl," Dad says.

I widen my eyes at his clipped tone. "Okay," I whisper, slouching down in the seat and crossing my arms over my chest.

"You could've been killed." He turns in his seat so he can look at me. "You almost were…"

"But I wasn't."

His eyes harden. "Were there bullets flying within fifty feet of you?"

I shrug. Now, I'm pissed. And when I'm pissed, I dig my heels in and turn on the smartass. "I didn't have my tape measure."

He surges forward like he's going to leap over the seat and wrap his hands around my neck, choking the life right out of me. His eyes aren't hard anymore; his glare is blazing hot. "What did you just say? Say it again."

"Dad, you're being a little crazy and unreasonable. Where's my big, badass father?"

"Your big, badass father is dealing with a lot of feelings after men just tried to bust into an MC compound, raining down fire, in an attempt to take out my kid and end her life."

"They weren't trying to kill me," I say softly because I know he's about at his wits' end and he doesn't need my shit.

"I know. They were trying to kill Pike, who—" he pauses, twisting his lips up, and I know what he's about to say before the words spill from his mouth "—you didn't tell me was actually your boyfriend!"

He yells those words, the sound echoing through the car like a bomb blast. "He's not my boyfriend, Daddy."

I keep up with the Daddy bit because it's always worked in the past and usually helps to defuse his anger. This isn't the first time he's been pissed at me, but it is the most pissed he's ever been that I can remember.

Bear shakes his head, muttering something under his breath, and he catches my eye in the mirror. I don't know what he's trying to tell me, but I know instantly I fucked up.

"That's right," Dad says, nodding his head, eyebrows drawn down, and his top lip curling like he's smelled the biggest pile of shit. "He's not a boyfriend. He's a guy you fucked."

Uh oh. This isn't good. Damn. I can't backpedal my way out of this one. There're no more secrets at this point, and I lied right to my dad's face about Pike when Aunt Izzy confronted me at Inked.

I don't move. It's as if my ass is glued to the seat, and every muscle in my body locks up as if I'm paralyzed. The only thing I can do is stare at my father with wide eyes and say, "I'm sorry."

He tips his head back, staring at the ceiling of the car. "She's sorry." His shoulders rise and fall. "No big deal, Dad. I met a guy at Bike Week and slept with him even though he could've raped me and left my ass for dead."

"I'm grown and I was careful."

"Adults die too, Giovanna. How many times did I tell you under no circumstances were you allowed in Daytona during Bike Week?"

"It was a mistake. We went for spring break."

"And did you tell me you were going to Daytona for spring break?"

"Did you tell your parents everything when you were twenty?" I pause, returning his hard stare because I'm sick and tired of being treated like a little kid. "Oh, wait. No, you freakin' didn't. You were out riding your bike, bangin' broads without giving any fucks."

He turns his head like he didn't quite hear me. "You want to repeat that shit for me?"

"No."

He grinds his teeth, and I wince at the sound. "I didn't fucking think so," he growls.

"She finally says something smart," Bear mutters.

"When we get back, I forbid you to see him again."

He forbids me? I raise an eyebrow, ready to dig the hole I've already dug a little deeper. "So, you firing him or me? 'Cause other than that, I don't know how I'm not supposed to see him. Care to explain, Daddy?"

My father slides a hand down his face before his fingers crumple into a fist near his chin. "Did the bullets scramble your brains or some shit?"

"Nope." I shake my head. "I'm seeing clearer than I have in a long time."

"The way your mouth is talking, I'd say you're still in shock."

"Not in shock. I'm feeling more alive than ever. So, who's leaving?"

"Izzy won't fire him, and you're not going anywhere. You two can work together without dating."

"Okay." I nod, thinking over my next words carefully. "So, the guy who was just ready to take a bullet for me, the guy who put his body in the way, hiding me so he'd die instead of me…" I close my eyes, remembering the way my body shook when the door to Pike's room opened and I didn't know which person had died. "I'm just supposed to tell him to kick rocks because my *father*, who's also his *boss*, doesn't want me to see him again." I open my eyes and roll them because I know it'll piss off my dad something fierce. "Hey, Pike, thanks for almost dying for me and being willing to throw yourself in front of a bullet, but my *father* doesn't think you're good enough."

"I didn't say he wasn't a good person."

I cross my arms again, lifting one shoulder, staring my father straight in the eye. "Just not good enough for me, right?"

My father's entire face scrunches up like he's about to shit a brick and it's painful as fuck. "His life is dangerous, Gigi. Look at all the shit you've been through in a couple days of him being in your life."

"It's not trouble he brought to his door. It was *his* father's fault, and if it weren't for the men in Pike's past, he'd probably be dead and maybe me too." I pause and our eyes are locked in a silent tug-of-war, but I don't give him a chance to talk because I'm not done making my point. "Didn't something happen to Mom when you two were dating? Wasn't she almost…"

"It was different," he says quickly.

"Shit happens, Dad. Life happens. No matter how hard you try to protect someone, you can't stop the bad from getting through all the time. Pike's innocent in this, and the decision of if we're going to see each other again falls to Pike and me. And frankly—" I swallow because if he hasn't leaped over the seat yet, my next words may be the nail in the coffin "—it's none of your business."

He blinks like I've slapped him, and his mouth moves but nothing comes out.

"I'm not trying to be mean, and if I am, I'm sorry. But imagine if Grandma or Grandpa said you couldn't see Mom anymore."

"I love your mother."

"Maybe I love Pike."

My father laughs. "You just met the kid."

"How long after you met Mom did you know you had feelings for her? Real feelings…"

"Well…" He looks at Bear because Bear was there in the beginning, and I have zero doubt he'll call my dad on his shit if he tries to lie. "Honestly, I don't remember a time when I didn't love your mom."

"Then why does it matter that I just met him?" I use air quotes on the last three words because we both know I didn't just meet him, but I have had fifteen months to think about him and the way he makes me feel.

"I…" He pauses, staring at me like he doesn't know what to say and hates to tell me I'm right.

"The man would've died for me tonight, Daddy. How many guys would do that? Let me tell you. Not many. Guys my age are a bunch of pansy-asses who cry when they get a paper cut. Chivalry is fucking dead. Pike would've taken that bullet and died with a smile on his face knowing I was going to live to breathe another day."

"I…" he says again, but I don't let him finish before I go on because I have shit to get off my chest.

"Here's this guy with a mother who's dead because his father is an asshole. The same father who treated him like shit as a little kid and a mother who wasn't much better. For growing up the way he did, he turned out to be a freaking great guy. He's envious of me, you know. He sees how close we all are, how much we love each other, and he knows exactly what he missed out on growing up and even now. So whatever misconceived notions you have about Pike, you may as well forget them all until you get to know the real man underneath."

"She's kind of telling you how it is, City." Bear glances at him with a slight shrug. "Pike's not too far off from the man you were at that age. You had a good family behind you, but you weren't a choirboy."

My father glares at Bear. "You're not helping. Whose side are you on?"

"Don't ask me to pick a side because I'll always pick the girl."

My smile's so big, my cheeks hurt. This is why I love my uncle Bear. He can totally call my dad out on his shit, reminding him of the man he is and used to be. It doesn't hurt that he's always willing to have my back. Always. It doesn't matter that we're not blood; he's been in my life since the day I was born and is just as much my uncle as any of my father's brothers.

"It's a fucking conspiracy," my father mutters, turning around to face the windshield.

"Just give him a chance, Dad. Give me a chance to live my own life and find my own happiness."

"I don't like it."

"I never asked if you did."

CHAPTER 24
PIKE

"THREE LARGE BLACK COFFEES."

"Would you like sugar, sir?"

"I said black," James barks out the driver's window, arm slung over the door, looking chill as fuck but sounding like he's wound so tight, he could break at any moment.

"Black means no cream, but it doesn't mean no sugar," the woman on the other end of the drive-thru tries to explain, but James is in no mood.

"No cream. No sugar. Just coffee."

"Iced or hot?" she asks.

James looks at Thomas like he can't get over this shit, and Thomas laughs at James's misery. "Hot," he growls out the window, practically foaming at the mouth.

"Please pull around, sir."

"What the fuck happened to ordering a simple cup of coffee?"

Thomas shrugs. "Life's moving fast, old man."

"Get the fuck out of here with that old man shit."

Thomas glances down, staring at his phone. "Well, this should get interesting."

"What?" James asks as he inches the car forward in the long line.

"Mom's requiring Pike to be at today's family dinner."

"She what?" I ask, shocked and a little scared.

"Joe isn't going to be happy about that," James states the fucking obvious.

From the moment our eyes met at the compound, I knew Joe hated me now. I'm not even sure hate is a strong enough word for all the things he's feeling toward me. I can't blame the guy. I'd fucking hate me too.

"I'd give my left nut to be in that car with them." Thomas laughs. "Gigi's more like Izzy than Suzy. She's probably reading him the riot act."

"Maybe one of them isn't going to make it back alive," James jokes, sliding up to the drive-thru window, trying not to make eye contact with the lady behind the voice.

Seconds later, Thomas's phone rings, and Joe's voice comes through the car speakers. "Do you believe this shit?"

"You know Ma."

"Why on God's green earth would she want him there?"

James turns to me, shrugging and rolling his eyes while the guys talk about me like I'm not overhearing the entire conversation.

"You know Ma is always the peacemaker and sticks her nose in everyone's business."

"This is my kid," Joe says.

"And you're her kid," Thomas reminds him. "I think that trumps your thinking."

"Does she realize Gigi could've died?"

"I'm sure she does. Our wives told her everything, Joe," James tells him, and I know there're no secrets left in this family. "You know they can't keep a secret, and Ma could pull the truth out of anyone, especially them."

"Fuck," Joe hisses. "Drop Pike off at my house, and he can ride with us."

"Do I get a say in this?" I ask from the back seat, wishing I could get out and run, but it's impossible without a door in the back of this Challenger.

Thomas turns, glaring at me to shut the fuck up but without actually saying the words. He doesn't need to either. I get the message loud and clear.

"We'll drop him off and go. We'll only have a few hours to sleep before we have to be there," James says. "She doesn't care that we've crossed the state and come back in the same day."

"You know how she is... There's never a good reason to cancel a dinner. Bullets. Near-death experiences. Hell, not even a hurricane would stop her," Thomas tells them.

I tip my head back, staring out the back window at the sky painted with pinks and purples as the sun starts to rise over the horizon.

All I want to do is talk to Gigi and crawl into bed, leaving all the bad shit behind. But I have a feeling I don't get a choice in whether I attend family dinner since the big men in the front seat aren't finding a reason I can't go. The fact that Joe wants me at his house and is going to drive me there himself seals the deal.

"We're grabbing a quick cup of coffee, but we'll be at your place a few minutes after you," James says, handing the money over to the woman.

"I'll be there waiting," Joe says before disconnecting the call.

"Well, that wasn't so bad," Thomas says, turning his head to stare at me as I lift mine, forgetting the beautiful sunrise because although that wasn't so bad, it wasn't good either.

I laugh. "So bad? I'm pretty sure the man wants to kill me."

"Here's your *hot* and *black* coffees," the woman says, holding three cups in her hands, waiting for James to take them.

He hands one to me, then to Thomas, and takes the final one for himself. He doesn't say anything else to the woman. He's had a shit night like the rest of us and doesn't want to get into another argument over something as simple as a cup of coffee.

"That man," James says, placing his coffee in the cupholder before he rolls the car forward, "is a devoted father. He'd lay down his life for his family. Just like we would in his shoes."

"I would've taken a bullet tonight to save Gigi."

"We know that, kid. Hell, even Joe knows that. He knows every-thing that went down at the compound. Trust me, he's thankful that you helped get her out of there alive, but the man's out of his mind right now. Joe doesn't scare easily, but he's been a raving lunatic the last few days. He'll come around. Just give him some time and space to let him get his head on straight."

I rest the Styrofoam on my knee, letting his words settle deep. "Then maybe you should just drop me off at my place. Give everyone some space without me around, crowding shit."

Thomas shakes his head. "Ma wants you at her house, you'll be at her house."

I close my eyes, trying to picture the mother of these rough and tough men. She must be a powerful force if, even at their age, she's still the boss.

"And if Joe walks around there all broody and moody, she'll set his ass straight if she likes you."

"Why don't you two hate me?" I ask, lifting my head and prying the lid off the coffee.

Thomas laughs and shakes his head. "We've been in shit just as big as you were last night. You didn't cause what came at you, but we played a role in the hell we brought to our door. Our women were almost casualties too. We know how things easily spin out of control. That's life, kid."

"Hell, Izzy's been knee-deep in our bullshit so many times," James says, gunning the engine as soon as he's on the highway with nothing but open road before us. "But that was shit we brought on ourselves or she put into motion. Life happens. Shit happens. We rolled with it, and so did you. The family, including Joe, will get over what happened. And if you're lucky, they'll welcome you into the fold if that's what you're looking for."

"I want Gigi in my life." I figured I'd lay shit out for her uncles since they are here and I'm not going anywhere. "She's the best thing to ever happen to me. But the family..." I pause, wondering how to explain the shit I've been through and the lack of familial support I'd grown up with. "That isn't something I'm used to dealing with."

"I didn't grow up Gallo," James says, looking at me in the rearview mirror for a moment, "but they treat me as if I did. From the moment I stepped foot in her mother's house, I was welcomed as part of the family. Doesn't matter how you were raised, kid. Once you're in, you're one of them. One of us. Win over Ma Gallo and Suzy too, and you're in the fold."

"Gigi's mother is going to hate me." I'm never the guy a girl brings home to meet her mother.

Thomas laughs, smacking his leg. "You're just like Joe, and Suzy's crazy about that man. Suzy may seem straitlaced, but don't let her fool you. She'll take to you like glue if she sees her daughter's happy. You'll remind her of the man she fell in love with. The guy with the chip on his shoulder who's head over heels for a girl."

All of this is out of my comfort zone and territory I haven't ridden through before. I've never dealt with an entire family. I never gave a shit if people liked me, especially not a woman's parents. But this is different. I have to win over countless people, starting with her mother and then her grandmother before I could get everyone on board.

"You looked death in the eye last night and came out alive," James says. "Facing our family will seem like a cakewalk."

"Yeah," I mutter, staring into the blackness of the coffee, not believing a goddamn word. Sure, I was scared when the gunfight was going on and the door to my old room opened, but I knew how to respond. Family...isn't something I'm used to.

"Just relax. We'll be at Joe's soon."

"Oh goodie," I mumble and sip my coffee.

Thomas and James laugh, clearly getting a kick out of my

misery and knowing full well shit isn't going to be as easy as they make it out to be.

An hour later, I'm climbing out of the back of James's car, and I catch sight of Gigi on the front porch, hugging a blond woman tightly. I assume it's her mother because that's the only thing that makes sense, but there's very little resemblance between the two.

Joe's next to them, glaring at me like I'm the enemy, and not over the shit that went down, or the fact that he probably knows everything about what happened between Gigi and me in Daytona. Well, not everything because I'd be a dead man, but he knows enough that he has to want to at least break my legs.

"Pike!" Gigi yells as soon as she sees me. She moves away from her mother, running down the front steps, across the driveway, and leaps into my arms. "I was so worried about you." She holds me tightly, locking her hands behind my neck and staring up at me. "I thought maybe my uncles would leave you somewhere on the side of the road."

"I'm fine, darlin'." I push the hair away from her eyes, needing to see her face. "Your uncles were nice."

I didn't say they were friendly because, under the circumstances, it wasn't like hanging out with my buddies, but they weren't assholes either. They laid shit out for me, telling me how it is and how to get in everyone's good graces.

She smiles up at me. "They were nice?"

I nod. "They weren't mean."

"Huh. That's shocking." Her smile widens. "I want you to meet my mother."

"I'm sure she hates me, Gigi. Maybe I should just go back to my place."

Gigi shakes her head, tightening her hold around me. "Not happening, big guy. My mother is a cream puff. She's going to go bananas for you."

"Bananas?"

"Yeah." She smiles again but bigger this time. "My mom is

sweet where my dad's rough. She's going to love you as much as I do."

I glance toward her parents. They're in a heated conversation. Her mother's eyes are on me, but her father's only paying attention to his woman. She slaps Joe's chest, eyes raking over me as a smile spreads across her face. She looks harmless. A mess of blond hair, fair skin, and a tiny little figure. Gigi gets her size from her mother, but everything else about her is all her daddy.

"I want to kiss you so badly right now." I rest my forehead on hers, trying to control myself because her father could very well end me right here.

"We'll sneak away once things settle down. Maybe at my grandmother's, we'll go for a walk or something. But for now, my mother's waiting, and I think her patience has just about worn out."

"Lead the way, darlin'."

She releases her grip on me and grabs my hand, pulling me toward the front porch as soon as her feet touch the ground. Joe ticks his chin toward Thomas and James before James peels out of the driveway like his ass is on fire.

Suzy, Gigi's mother, doesn't even glance toward the noise. Her eyes are locked on me, soaking me in, probably thinking the worst.

"So, you're Pike," she says with a small smile.

"Ma'am," I reply, squeezing Gigi's hand because this is almost as terrifying as the gun pointed at my head.

Her mother comes down the stairs, meeting us at the bottom. "Thank you for keeping my baby safe."

"Um, you're welcome." I nod because I don't know what else to say and I wasn't expecting those words or her kindness.

"Now, don't freak out. I know you're a badass biker and all, but this mama bear wants to give you a hug."

Gigi snorts as her father starts cursing. "Told ya," Gigi says, describing her mother perfectly.

"Hush it," Suzy tells her and holds out her arms for me.

I pause, gazing down at my girl, but she's smiling and jerking her chin toward her mama. "You better do what she says. She isn't as sweet as she seems, especially if you don't do what she asks."

"Seems to be a theme in this family." I let go of Gigi's hand and move into her mother's waiting arms.

Suzy's hug isn't soft. Her hold is pretty damn firm, especially for her size. "I can hear you two," Suzy says with a small chuckle. "I can also understand why my daughter likes you." Suzy pulls back, gazing up at me, eyes sweeping across my face. "You're just like her daddy."

My eyes go to Joe, who's now pacing on the porch, brooding about the fact that I'm being welcomed and still looking like he's ready to leap over the railing and murder me at any moment. "I don't know about that."

Suzy takes a step back, hands still on my arms, gazing up at me. "Sweetie, if you don't see the similarities between you and her daddy, you must be blind. Her first love was her father, and now my baby has found a man who's the spitting image of him." Joe's eyes are on me as she speaks, and his cursing gets louder. "Don't mind him. He has a lot of trouble dealing with his children growing up and sprouting wings."

"I do not." Joe stalks down the stairs, heading right toward us. "I have a problem with my daughter falling for a guy who's—"

"Exactly like you?" Suzy interrupts him.

Joe grunts. "I wouldn't go that far, sugar."

"He's a biker, has tattoos, piercings too. Probably a lady-killer with a chip on his shoulder and bossy as all hell."

"Yep." Gigi smiles.

"So, tell me, dear husband, how are you two different?" Suzy crosses her arms in front of her chest, staring at her husband, waiting for his response.

Joe waves his hand in my direction, and his eyebrows draw down. "He's..."

"What?" Suzy taps her foot, looking a little annoyed at this point, and the sweetness has all but disappeared.

"Shorter." Joe shrugs.

Suzy grabs his arm, plastering her body against his. "That's the best you can come up with, sweetheart?"

"Sugar…"

Suzy shakes her head. "Whatever you're feeling right now doesn't matter. Look at your daughter." She tips her head toward Gigi. "She's happy, Joe."

"Well…" Joe's eyes go to his daughter then to me before going back to his wife. "I won't say I'm happy about any of this."

"Would you ever be happy with any man she'd bring home? I remember you didn't like the other two either."

"They were spineless shits," he says quickly.

"And Pike is not."

"He's just so…so…"

"Like you," Suzy says with a smile, winking at her husband.

Gigi chuckles at my side, tangling her fingers with mine as she tugs me toward the front door, leaving her parents standing at the bottom of the steps. "We're going in. We've had a long night and could use a nap before Grandma's."

"Pike can take the couch in my office. Separate rooms," Joe says, "if you want Pike to live another day."

"You're cute, Dad." Gigi laughs as we walk into the house. "Don't listen to him," she tells me. "He's a bit overdramatic."

"But he's right, and this is his house, darlin'. If he wants my ass to sleep on the porch, that's where I'll sleep. We're under his roof, and he gets to set the rules."

"Fine." She rolls her eyes. "I'll show you where his office is."

"Thank you. Now, tell me about your grandma. I've had enough surprises this week to last me a lifetime."

Gigi nods her head down a hallway, and I follow her as she starts to walk. "She's fierce."

"Great," I mutter because the fierceness in this family has already been off the charts.

"She's tough too."

"Even better."

"But…" Gigi stops outside a closed door and leans against the wall, tangling her fingers with mine. "If you win her over, you have an ally for life. It doesn't hurt that she's the boss of everyone, including her sons."

"So, you're saying I have to win her heart?"

"You have to win her mind." Gigi smiles.

I've got this one in the bag. Winning over the ladies has never been a problem. I'm sure another fierce and tough Gallo won't be too hard…

CHAPTER 25
PIKE

WITH THE WAY Gigi described her grandma, and based on the size of her children, I expected the woman to be tall, sizable, and downright scary.

"Baby, I was so worried about you," her grandmother says, wrapping her arms around Gigi and squeezing her tightly.

"I'm fine, *Nonna*. Pike made sure of it."

Gigi's already working the woman, trying to put in a good word for me because, like she said, she's the boss. The ride over here was tense. I sat in the back of the SUV with Gigi, getting an icy glare from Joe in the rearview mirror as her two sisters chatted in the seats between us.

Her grandmother's eyes are on me as she embraces her grand-daughter in the driveway. "This is the boy I've been hearing about?"

Gigi pulls away, glancing over her shoulder at me, a smile on her lips. "Yep, but don't believe anything *he*—" she dips her head toward her father who's stalking by and ignoring us all "—says. You know how Daddy has a tendency to fly off the handle and overreact."

Her grandmother laughs with a slow shake of her head. "He's

just worried about you, and sometimes his emotions get the better of him. Cut him some slack, sweetheart. Your daddy will come around, but you have to give him some time to adjust to the reality that you're no longer a little girl, but this beautiful and confident woman who's standing here today."

I smile because I already like this woman. She gives sound advice, and it doesn't sound like there's an ounce of judgment in her voice.

"I guess." Gigi shrugs and steps to the side, turning toward me. "But he should've come to this realization the day I graduated from high school."

I haven't moved a step. I'm too engrossed in their conversation, the way they look at each other and like each other. One taller and younger, one shorter and older, but of the same blood with the same eyes and mannerisms.

"You never stop being a parent, Giovanna. There's no off-switch once your children sprout their wings and fly away from the nest. We always worry. Always want the best for them. When they hurt, so do we. He's just doing what he thinks is best for you, even if he may be totally off base. Forcing something on him that he's not ready to face won't make changing his heart and mind any easier. Just give him time, and he'll come around and see the light. What's your mother say?"

I turn toward the SUV where Gigi's mother is on bended knee, speaking with the two younger girls. I can't imagine what it had to be like growing up a Gallo. Sure, they were all up in each other's business, which could be annoying, but there is so much love between them that the good had to outweigh the bad.

Gigi sighs. "Mom seems to be cool about Pike. She says he's the spitting image of Daddy."

I catch her grandmother's eye as she laughs. "Oh, that had to go over big with your father."

"Can you talk to him for me?" Gigi begs. "Please. You're the only one who can talk sense into him sometimes."

The woman's laughter grows louder. "Child, when it comes to a man loving his children, there's no talking sense into him. You have to give him time and make him see the light." Her grandmother's eyes rake up and down my body before landing back on my face. "So, you're the one causing all the fuss?"

"Ma'am." I dip my head, giving her a playful smile because my lady-killer smirk doesn't feel right. "I've heard so many great things about you."

"All lies, I'm sure." She waves her hand through the air and steps closer, squinting up at me as she cranes her neck. "Well, aren't you a looker?"

The smile on my face only gets bigger, because Grandma may be old, but she's a tiger. "You aren't so bad-looking yourself." I throw her a wink.

"And a charmer." She laughs. "You've caused quite a commotion in a family that's seen serenity for a long time."

"I'm sorry." My voice goes up as I speak, making it seem like I'm asking a question when I'm making a statement.

"Don't be." She shakes her head. "You're both alive and well. Life has a way of reminding everyone of the preciousness of everything. Sometimes we need to have things shaken up a little to bring everything back into focus. Now, let me get a better look at you." She lifts her hands and wiggles her fingers.

Gigi ticks her head toward her grandmother, widening her eyes when I don't move right away. I take a few steps, closing the space between us as the woman stares up at me like she's trying to see something that isn't there.

"Quite handsome," she says, and she takes me by surprise when she wraps her arms around me, embracing me like she did Gigi. "Strong too."

I laugh, biting my lip to stop myself from saying something inappropriate. "Thank you." Again, the words come out like a question as the woman's hands splay across my back.

"Hush, child. Let an old woman enjoy herself for a minute."

Gigi shrugs, throwing her hands upward as she giggles silently behind her grandmother.

"Oh boy." Suzy walks by us with her two daughters in tow, taking in the hug. "Welcome to the lion's den, Pike. I hope you're ready for what you're about to walk into," she calls out, not bothering to look back at us.

My body stiffens at her words. I've never met anyone's family. Especially not all at once. I knew half the people inside, already working with them for a few days or riding with them back and forth from the Disciples' compound. But there were a few who were still a mystery to me. I've had the Gallos in small doses, but this is going to be supersized and in my face.

"Don't listen to her. We're as good as they come. Now, wrap your arms around me, and give Grandma a hug."

All the worry I have vanishes, and it's replaced by the goodness of the woman wrapped around me and her granddaughter, who is beaming at me like I walk on water. I do as I'm told, holding the woman tightly in my arms.

"Much better. Now," the woman whispers near my ear. "I'll give my blessing because I see depth in those eyes, but if you hurt my granddaughter, you won't have to worry about her father, Pike. I'll find you first and make you wish you'd never been born."

There's the fierceness I'd been warned about. The toughness I'd been told to expect. "Yes, ma'am."

"Grandma," she tells me like I'm already one of the family.

"Grandma," I repeat, glancing down and taking in her beauty, wondering what she looked like when she was younger. Is Gigi the spitting image of the hellion in my arms?

"Now, my sauce needs stirring, and there are more than a few curious women inside looking forward to laying eyes on you." She takes a step back and puts her hands on my chest, groping me through my T-shirt. "They're excited, while their husbands are not."

I tip my head back, drawing in a breath. "You're really selling me on walking through that door."

The woman laughs. "What lies on the other side of that door is all the goodness I brought into my life. I created it—not alone, mind you—and there's no better group of people on this earth. Once you're in, you're in forever. See this chip?" She touches my shoulder, drawing my attention downward. "Don't let it falter, but keep that shit in check and mind your elders."

"I know my place, ma'am." Her eyes narrow, and I immediately know my mistake. "Grandma."

"Not such a quick learner, but you'll get there," she teases and takes a step back. "I heard you almost took a bullet for my granddaughter."

"He was willing to die for me, *Nonna*." Gigi steps forward and tucks herself under my arm.

"I was only doing what was right, darlin'."

Her grandmother smiles at her, eyes moving between us, taking us in as a couple. "My granddaughter needs someone who's strong both in mind and body. She's not a weakling and will never be controlled, but if a man's willing to take a bullet for her, just like her daddy would under the same circumstances, she's not going to let that pass without snapping up the goodness and keeping it close."

"It's not like that, Grandma. I liked Pike before this all happened."

I glance down, eyes wide because I don't want to talk to her grandmother about our time in Daytona. I didn't want anyone to know, but it seems there are very few secrets in this family.

"I've heard all about spring break. I remember your aunt Izzy causing some chaos there a while back. Trouble seems to run in our blood along with our affinity for badass, bossy men."

Well, there it is. Grandma knows all about everything and everyone.

"Now, if we don't get our asses inside, the sauce will burn, and you know how much Grandpa hates when his meal is shot to hell.

We wouldn't want your aunt Fran fixin' the meal in my absence, would we?"

Gigi looks up at me. "Aunt Fran is Bear's wife, and she's not the best cook."

Grandma starts toward the door, and we follow. "You're being nice. She's the world's worst cook, but she has a good heart and a nosy spirit about her."

When the front door opens, there are so many eyes on me, I almost trip over the top step. There's not a man in the bunch. Four women I've never seen before are gawking at me like I'm an exotic animal on display and only there for their amusement. The grandmother laughs, shaking her head as she walks past them, disappearing into the back of the house.

Gigi grips my side, still tucked under my arm. "Pike, this is my aunt Max," she points at a very beautiful, tall, and lanky black woman. "She's Uncle Anthony's wife."

"Girl, get it straight. He's my husband," Max corrects her and takes a step toward us, staring up at me. "You're causing a lot of trouble around here."

"I never meant to…"

Max waves me off. "Don't say it. It's been far too quiet around here for far too long. We needed a little excitement." Then she turns her eyes toward her niece. "You did well with this one." She angles her head at me, talking like I'm not standing right in front of them. "I can't wait to see your dad lose his shit."

Great. Not only am I here to be gawked at, but they're all banking on me pissing off her father for nothing more than sheer entertainment. The last thing I want to do is make Joe mad. It doesn't mean I'm going anywhere, but I don't want the man gunning for me my entire life.

"He already lost it, Auntie."

The two women laugh.

My gaze moves to the three ladies still staring at me, covering their mouths and whispering to one another. I catch a few words here and there. The only words I can make out are *fresh meat.*

"Your daddy was the biggest badass I knew, sweetheart, but his heart is even bigger. Give him time. He'll come around."

Gigi rolls her eyes. "I don't think you understand the depths of his..."

"Love?" Max finishes her statement. "He's not angry, Gigi. He's mourning the loss of his baby. I can understand how he feels. Every day, I see the misery in Anthony's eyes as Tamara grows up and pulls away."

Gigi gasps. "Oh my God. Where's Tam? I haven't talked to her since before all hell broke loose."

So, this is Tamara's mother. The cousin Gigi had gone to Daytona with after lying to their parents, and the same Tamara Gigi had a conversation with on the phone about my cock.

"She's in hiding." Max laughs. "Anthony knows about Daytona."

Gigi's eyes widen. "I'm sorry we lied."

"Eh." Max shrugs. "You two were just blowing off steam, but I wish you'd been honest about where you were going and what you were doing."

"Dad and Uncle Anthony wouldn't have let us go."

"You're a grown-ass woman, Giovanna. Your fathers can't tell you how to live your lives forever."

"Then why's Tamara hiding from her dad?"

Max laughs. "I didn't raise a stupid child. A strong one, for sure, but not stupid."

"Enough chitchat," a small, older woman says, pushing by Max and getting the evil eye. "I need to get my hands on this boy."

"Auntie Fran, go easy on him," Gigi says as the woman plasters her body against me, resting her head on my chest.

"Shh. Don't ruin this for me, girl. When you're my age, there're very few thrills left in life."

I stare down at the woman, staying still as she feels me up like she's blind and trying to figure out the dips and curves, memorizing my body.

"Bear's wife." Gigi shrugs because Fran isn't stopping the attention she's giving to my muscles.

"Don't ruin this for me," Fran says again, her fingers digging into my pecs. "God, to be young again."

I laugh because what the fuck else am I supposed to do with this small, older woman hanging on my body? Talk about awkward. But then, there's been no real normal around me in days. This is just another experience with this family, and I can't say it's a bad one either.

"If I were ten years younger…"

"He'd break you, Fran," a redhead says from behind her, and all the women giggle.

Fran's hands move to my arms, holding tight and squeezing until her fingernails practically dig into my skin. "No, he wouldn't. I have the biggest baddie of them all, and I'd say I broke him." She nuzzles her face deeper into my chest. "I think I could handle this kid."

"Um." I hold out my arms. I'm not going to hug the woman draped across me like I'm a blanket and she's in need of heat. I'm already treading in deep water, and any movement, even if it's innocent, could send me spiraling to the depths on my ass.

When Fran doesn't unstick herself, Gigi starts talking, ignoring my new body ornament. She points toward the pretty redhead. "This is my aunt Angel. She's Thomas's wife."

"It's nice to meet you," she says with a friendly smile.

"You too." I smile back, wishing I could at least shake her hand, but there's Fran.

She moves her hand toward a woman with long wavy brown hair and big, beautiful eyes. "This is Mia." Gigi steps closer, looming over Fran but having zero effect. "She's a doctor and my uncle Mike's wife."

I'm impressed. Mike doesn't seem like the type of guy who'd

marry a doctor. I'd read all about him, knew about his career as a fighter before giving it all up for love. Looking at her, I can understand why he walked away from the ring.

"It's a pleasure to meet you." I tip my head because it's all I can do with Fran still twisted around me like I'm her new favorite accessory.

Gigi's grandmother appears in the hallway, shaking her head as soon as she sees Fran. "Give the boy some space, ladies. He's not here for your entertainment. Especially you, Fran."

"I'm not moving," Fran says, latching on tighter, and I wonder if I'm going to have to pry the woman off my body.

"Fran?"

My gaze moves across the room to Bear, who's staring at Fran, arms crossed over his chest and jaw set tight. "You have thirty seconds to let that boy go, or…"

Fran doesn't budge, and she doesn't even look in his direction. "Or you'll what?" She looks up at me with a playful smirk and a quick wink, looking like she's loving every minute of hanging on me and antagonizing the big guy.

"You're not going to be able to sit comfortably for a week."

"You promise?" she teases, finally turning her head away from my body.

"Woman, you have ten seconds to let go of that boy and get your ass over here…"

"He's such a big talker," she says, looking up at me and not paying any more attention to her husband. "He's all bark and no bite."

"You want teeth, baby?"

She continues to ignore him. "I should really trade him in for a newer model."

She barely gets the words out before his arm is around her waist and then her body's in the air, landing on his shoulder. "Woman, I think you need me to remind you of who this fine ass," he says with a smack right on her behind for everyone to see, "belongs to."

The move reminds me of the way I hauled Gigi out of the bar area at the compound in front of all the guys. I gave zero fucks if I pissed her off, but I had a hell of a time doing it. Just like Bear is having while Fran grabs at his ass like a woman starved for cock.

"Sorry about that," Gigi says, "Fran can be a..."

"No worries. I think she's great. Everyone is so far."

"Well, you know my uncles, but let's see how they are after all the shit that went down. You ready to face them?"

I nod, but I want to say hell to the fucking no, I'm not ready. The ladies are always easier. The men, not so much. This group of moody and broody guys knows all about my past, the last week, and that I slept with their niece. "I'm ready."

CHAPTER 26
GIGI

"THAT WASN'T SO BAD, was it?" I ask Pike as we walk toward the line of trees in the backyard.

"Compared to what?" He looks over his shoulder like he's checking to see if anyone is following us.

"It could've been worse." I shrug, gazing up and into his beautiful green eyes.

"There's still time."

I wave him off because if they were going to cause a scene, they would've done it already. "They like to put on a big show, but they're all pussycats."

Ten years ago, they maybe would've chased Pike out of here, but they've become more chill with age. Plus, they know the harder they try to drive him away, the more I'll run toward him.

"Why don't you say that to their faces?"

I curl my fingers around his hand as he brushes some hair away from my shoulder. "Do you like them, at least?"

"Who? Your family?"

I nod.

"They're like a small army, but yeah. You were a lucky kid to have so many people surrounding you as you grew up. I never had anyone except my grandmother who I could count on and who gave a shit about me."

"I care about you now." I curl into his side as we stand in the shade and out of view of all the nosy Gallos who are probably plastered to the back windows, trying to keep an eye on us.

He pulls our hands in front of us as his face grows serious. "Now that everything's over, I wouldn't blame you if you want to go back to the way things were."

"The way things were?" I ask, confused and a little dumbfounded.

"Yeah," he says like we're talking about the weather and not about *us*. "We went through some scary, heavy shit together. We didn't know if we were going to make it another day, and sometimes that affects how we think. Now that we're alive and no one's coming after us, maybe we should take a step back and make sure this is what we both want."

I jerk my head like he physically struck me. "You want to break up?" I take a step back, tearing my hands from his. "You're saying that shit now? You've met my family, saved my life, and were willing to take a bullet for me, and now you're saying you want to break up and not be together anymore?"

Pike steps forward, reaching for me, but I move quickly, evading his touch. "I didn't mean it that way. Be reasonable, Gigi. Think about it."

My eyes widen. "Be reasonable?"

"Um, yeah."

"I can't believe after everything we've been through, you're saying this shit to me now."

"I don't regret anything. I would still take a bullet for you or do anything necessary to keep you safe."

I fold my arms in front of me, cocking one shoulder upward, and raise an eyebrow. "But now that the bad shit has passed, you don't want to date me?"

"I don't want you to have any regrets," he says softly, closing the space between us, but I don't allow him near enough to touch me. "You're young. You have your whole life ahead of you. You have a perfect family who wants only good shit for you. What the hell do you want with an older guy who has baggage and commitment issues?"

"You have commitment issues?"

"Darlin', I never stay in one place longer than a few years. My parents fucked me up. I'm always searching for something bigger and better. Looking for that place I can call home and find out where I belong. I've been traveling around for almost ten years, and I still haven't found it."

I wave my arms around, trying my best not to sock him straight in the jaw. "What the fuck was this last week?" My hand flies toward the house. "You just spent an hour charming my family, building the foundation that's necessary to be welcomed into the fold. Now, you're saying you don't have a place, and you want to up and run away like a pussy."

"I'm not being a pussy, Gigi. I'm giving you a chance to think about if this is what you want. The shit we went through the last few days can fuck with your head and make it hard to think. We were living in the moment, hoping to have more, but now it's over. Shit's gonna settle, and I don't want you to look back and regret the time you spent with me before you up and marry some guy worthy of you."

I scrunch my nose because compared to any pile of horseshit I've ever smelled before, this was far worse. "You've got to be shitting me right now! Why the fuck did you come here if you felt this way?"

"It's not like I had any choice in this," he yells back, throwing his hand toward my grandmother's house. "But I like you, Gigi. Hell, I love you. I'm truly, madly, deeply in fucking love with you, and I don't want to be another mistake in your life. You deserve more than a guy who's good at ink, with a fucked-up family, and not much to offer other than how I feel."

I inhale and slowly exhale, letting all his words seep in. I know this man loves me. He's said those words before. Sure, we were probably about to die, but the possibility of not taking another breath doesn't make a man say shit he isn't feeling.

"Have I ever asked you for anything?"

"No," he says.

"Have I ever forced you to do anything you didn't want to do?"

"No."

"Ever asked you about your bank account and what you could bring to our relationship besides yourself?"

"No."

"You're right, Pike. I'm a lucky girl to be surrounded by all this." I tick my head toward my grandparents' house. "But I could give two shits about money or anything else. My parents taught me about the real important things in life. They taught me about loyalty, love, and most of all, family. I don't care if I'm piss-poor as long as I have someone with me who'll love me and do everything in his power to keep on loving me."

He tips his head back, staring up at the trees. "I'm not a saint. When I look at you—" he glances back down at me "—I see everything that's pure. I see an untouched soul who's had a life of good. And in the short time I've known you, I've brought you a whole lot of bad. I don't want that for you. I don't want you to have a moment's sadness in your life. I never want to see the look on your face I saw the night in my room after I shot that guy. I don't want to know I'm the one who put that look on your face."

"Are you done yet?" I ask, tapping my foot and giving him a dirty look because I'm barely keeping my shit under control.

He nods, not adding more fuel to the wildfire he's already started. I stalk up to him, pressing my fingers into his chest, letting my fingernails dig into the skin underneath his black T-shirt.

"Now it's my turn to talk and for you to shut the fuck up."

He throws up his hands. "I won't…"

I dig a little harder. "My turn, Pike." I glare up at him, and the corners of his lips twitch. "You didn't bring the bad into my life. That was your father's sin, not yours. Stop blaming yourself for shit you couldn't control." He nods, but I keep going because I'm not giving him a second to argue. "As for the look on my face, I didn't care that the bastard who wanted to kill you was lying on that floor, blood oozing from his body."

He scowls. "You didn't?"

I shake my head, twisting my lips. "I kept looking at him, imagining what would've happened if your gun hadn't gone off first. How that could've been you lying on that floor, bleeding everywhere, having taken your last breath." I lean forward, dropping my hand and resting my forehead where I've just poked the hell out of him. "It would've killed me seeing you like that. Do you know how close you came to dying?"

His arms wrap around me, one hand flattening on my back. "But I didn't die, Gigi. We lived. We're standing here, under the sun, listening to the birds sing, just as alive as we were last week when things were normal and you were never in danger."

I slide my fingers under his shirt, running my hands along the soft skin at his sides. "We're standing here because you made sure I lived to see another day. If it weren't for you, I could be dead right now."

He shakes his head. "If it weren't for me, you never would've been in that situation."

"Shut up, Pike." I listen to the slow, steady beat of his heart underneath his shirt. "I've never told another man besides my father that I loved him. I've had a few boyfriends, not many, but they never got the words from me."

"Never?" he asks as I tip my head up, seeing the shock all over his face.

"Never. You know why?"

"Why, darlin'?" he asks softly.

"Because they never got me. All they cared about was getting in my pants. Even Erik, my last boyfriend, I never saw a forever with.

He was nice and all, but he didn't have what it takes to be with me for the long haul. My father and uncles would've chewed him up and spat him out. Hell, if someone would've come after us, I'm pretty sure Erik would've hurled me in front of a bullet to save his own ass."

Pike's hands are on my shoulders, pushing me backward so he can look at me. "That's what I'm talking about. You haven't had any good relationships in your life, babe. You can't compare what we have to those guys...and I use that term loosely. Every man you're with should be willing to die for you because you're his girl. You need to explore, sow those oats, before you decide you want a nobody like me in your bed every night."

"Pike, do you really love me?" I whisper, gazing up at him, my nails starting to press into his skin because he's beginning to piss me off again.

"I do," he says quickly.

"Then can you just shut the fuck up and see where this goes? I'm not ready to walk away. I don't want to date someone else, I don't want to find out what good and bad is out there because I've already found something good, someone good, and I don't want to let go because even if I find someone out there who'll love me, they'll never be you."

His hands cup my face, and I melt into his touch, wanting more, always wanting more. "I've never wanted anyone as badly as I want you. I've never felt so at peace with someone as I do you. I've never been surrounded by so much love as I have been with your family, even if they don't like me."

"They like you." I wish he'd shut up and kiss me already, but he doesn't.

"They're tolerating me, hoping I go away."

"Not everyone in that house grew up the way I did. They have pasts and skeletons in their closets too. It didn't change the way my family feels about them. The Gallos judge people on who they are, not what they did or how they grew up. All that matters is that we love one another. The men in my family are protective and overbearing, a little like you, and I know they'll love you and welcome you with open arms when they realize how good we are together."

"Gigi..."

"Pike, just kiss me already. And so help me God, if you try to break my heart again, I'm going to knee you so hard in the balls, you won't be able to sleep with another woman for months."

Pike smirks. "I kind of like my balls, babe."

"Me too." I smile. "Now, you better kiss me, or I'm going to leap into your arms and cause a scene that'll have my dad out here so fast..."

I don't get the rest of the words out before his mouth crashes down on mine, stealing away the threat I was ready to carry out if necessary.

My hands slide behind his neck as I plaster my body to his, kissing him with all the force I can muster on my tiptoes. I've been waiting hours for a moment alone to feel his lips on mine, tongue sliding inside my mouth, giving me his small moans and the warmth of his body.

"Don't you ever threaten to leave me again," I murmur into his mouth, needing him to say the words.

"Never again," he whispers, pulling back and gazing down at me. "You're mine now, darlin', and I hope you understand what that means."

"I'm hoping it means a lot of dirty shit." I wink, pulling his head down because his lips are looking lonely.

"Gigi. Pike. Dinner," Nonna yells from somewhere in the distance. "Get your bodies untangled and get your asses in here."

Pike rests his forehead against mine, trying to catch his breath as we both gasp for air. "We better go." I know Grandma's still watching and isn't going to go anywhere until we "untangle" ourselves and start marching our asses toward the house. "But we're finishing what we started as soon as we get home."

"Your place or mine?" he asks, waggling his eyebrows with a playful smirk.

"I don't have a bed."

"Darlin', I only need a wall."

Oh. My. God. Fuck yes!

CHAPTER 27
PIKE

"GIVE ME TEN MINUTES, and then come over. I'll leave the front door unlocked because I have a surprise for you."

I can't stop the smile on my face as I lean forward, brushing my lips across hers and squeezing her ass. "What kind of surprise, darlin'?"

She bats her eyelashes, smirking. "What kind of surprise would it be if I told you?"

"You're a tease."

She giggles when my fingers find the bottom edge of her jean shorts and my lips slide down to her neck. "Hey," she says, pushing against my chest. "If you don't stop doing that, I won't be able to let you out of my sight, and the entire night will be ruined."

"If I fucked you right now, it would ruin the night?"

She lets out a loud huff. "Well, no, but I want this time to be special."

"Baby, every time with you is special," I murmur against her skin before running my tongue from her ear to her collarbone. "I don't know if I can wait ten minutes."

She tries to wiggle out of my hold, but I grip her thighs, wanting to sink between them even though we're outside. "You waited fifteen months, I think you'll survive another ten minutes," she says, pushing against my chest again. "Please, Pike."

I loosen my grip, allowing her to put space between us. "Well, since you said please. But get your surprise and come to my place. I have a bed."

"And walls too." She winks.

"Walls too, darlin'."

"Okay, I still need ten minutes. I'll grab the surprise and be over."

"Perfect." I try to grab her again, wanting to taste her lips or skin, but she isn't having any of it.

She backs away, shaking her head. "No touching."

I raise an eyebrow. "I hope that isn't part of the surprise because touching is required for what I have in mind."

"There will be touching," she says, still moving toward her front door. "But not until I say so."

"Not until you say so?" My mouth falls open, but I'm totally playing. I know this girl, and she doesn't play hard to get. I also know just the right buttons to push to have her begging for more than my touch.

There's a wicked gleam in her eyes. "Of course. I'm the boss."

"Naturally," I tease, but she is.

I learned today that every woman in her family is the boss too. It doesn't matter how big or tough the man is, his wife has the final say in how things go down. I loved their strength and that their husbands didn't care as long as their women were happy.

"Now, go." She shoos me with one hand and takes her keys out of her back pocket with the other. "I'll be quick."

I throw up my hands and turn toward my door. "I'm going. I'm going."

"Catch ya in ten," she says before disappearing into her apartment.

I step inside my place, flipping on the light and kicking off my boots, thankful as fuck to finally be home and still breathing. I wasn't sure I'd make it back, and after a long-ass day of travel and Gigi's family, I'm happy as shit for a little peace and quiet.

I strip off my clothes as I walk toward the bathroom, needing a shower and a reset after all the bullshit that went down the last few days. I don't waste too much time under the spray because my girl's coming over with a surprise that I'm hoping includes very little clothing and a whole lot of fucking.

After a quick wash, I dry off, pulling on a pair of sweat pants and nothing else. I don't see the need when I don't plan on having clothing on my body for very long.

I glance at the clock, realizing it's been ten minutes, but Gigi's nowhere to be found. I press my ear against our adjoining wall but only hear silence. I wait another minute, pacing a path down my hallway, back and forth between my bedroom and living room.

"You comin'?" I text her because I've never been a patient man.

I take five trips up and down the hallway, turning my phone over in my hand, waiting for her reply, but I get no response.

I'm out the door, knocking on hers. "Gigi!" I yell because it's not like her to promise one thing and do another.

It isn't like she could lie down and accidentally fall asleep. The girl just moved in and doesn't have any furniture in her place.

I try the handle and it's unlocked, but I hesitate for a second because I also don't want to walk in and scare the hell out of her, getting myself kicked in the balls in the process.

"Gigi!" I yell again, pounding louder this time, and when there's no response, I open the door, figuring a kick in the balls is worth knowing she's okay.

My foot connects with something, and it skids across the floor, slamming into the wall. I look over, realizing it's her cell phone, and my heart immediately slams into my chest like a brick.

"Gigi!" I yell again, but I only get my echo back and not another sound.

I frantically look in each room of the tiny space, searching for my girl, but find nothing. My hands are sweating and my heart's beating double time as I push open the door to her bedroom, catching sight of a person's back.

A back that isn't Gigi's.

I lunge for the man, turning him around, laying eyes on his mask-covered face. His eyes widen, the only part of his face that's visible before I rear back, hurling my fist through the air and connecting with his jaw.

"Pike!" Gigi screams, and I move my eyes toward her voice. She's in the corner, hands at her neck, huddled in a ball, and tears staining her cheeks.

I lay into the man who's staggering in front of me, whaling on him with my fists until he falls to the floor. I kick him in the ribs once, making sure he's out cold before I run to Gigi, kneeling in front of her. Her eyes are wide, and her cheeks are stained with tears.

"Are you okay?" I ask her, lifting her into my lap, checking over her body.

"I'm fine. He was hiding in here when I walked in," she says quickly, whimpering at the memory. "He… He…"

"Did he hurt you?"

She shakes her head and curls into my chest, gripping on to my T-shirt with her long fingers. "He put his hand over my mouth and hauled me back here, but he didn't have a chance to hurt me before you showed up."

"I'm so sorry, baby. I should've been here sooner."

"I'm okay," she whispers like she's trying to convince herself or maybe just me, but by the way she's shaking, I'd say she's anything but okay. "We have to call the police."

"I will in a minute." My priority is making sure she's okay before I let her out of my arms.

"No, Pike. I don't want him waking up and coming after you. My heart can't take any more," she whispers. "Please." She crawls out of my lap, staggering, but catching herself on my shoulder. "I have some packing tape we can use to tie him up."

"You're crafty," I tease because right now, we could use a little lightness in our fucked-up week.

"You have no idea." She smiles, wiping away the tears from her cheeks. "I'll grab the tape, and you check the guy." She's out of the room before I have a chance to rise to my feet.

"Let's see who you are, motherfucker." I hunch down next to the man's face, staring at the asshole who went after my girl.

Gigi's back, holding a roll of packing tape, eyes pinned on the lifeless body on the floor. "You didn't kill him, did you?"

I shake my head and laugh, reaching for the man's mask. "Darlin', I may be strong, but my punch didn't kill him."

"Thank God," she mumbles.

When I pull the mask from his face, I'm knocked backward, falling on my ass.

"What's wrong?"

I shake my head, blinking like my brain doesn't believe what my eyes are seeing. "It's my father."

BURN

A MEN OF INKED HEATWAVE NOVEL

USA TODAY BESTSELLING AUTHOR

CHELLE BLISS

BURN COPYRIGHT © 2019

No part of this book may be reproduced or transmitted in any form, including electronic or mechanical, without written permission from the publisher, except in the case of brief quotations embodied in critical articles or reviews.

This is a work of fiction. Names, characters, businesses, places, events, and incidents are either the products of the author's imagination or used in a fictitious manner. Any resemblance to actual persons, living or dead, or actual events is purely coincidental. This book may not be resold or given away to other people.

Publisher © Chelle Bliss December 10th 2019
Edited by Lisa A. Hollett
Cover Model: Dylan Horsch
Cover Photo © Aaron Rogers & Dylan Horsch

CHAPTER 1
GIGI

"WHAT DO YOU MEAN, that's your father?" I blink, my mouth hanging open as I gawk at Pike.

Holy freaking hell.

Pike glances up at me with those stormy green eyes, kneeling next to the guy who just tried to choke me to death. "Like, he's the guy who knocked up my mom."

"I know that, smartass," I snap. My body's wound so tight, the slightest touch would cause me to shatter into a million pieces.

He turns his gaze toward the asshole who attacked me. "What a fucking mess." Pike flicks his index finger against the guy's cheek, but he doesn't move. "But the bastard's out cold at least."

"Why was he in my apartment, choking me?" I rub my neck, soothing the spot where his hands just were.

The reality of what happened starts to settle over me.

I was attacked.

Hell, if Pike hadn't have shown up when he did, I could have been... The thought is too much for me to even finish.

Pike rises to his feet and reaches for me, pulling my hand away from my neck. "I have no fucking idea why he was in your place, putting his hands on you." He cradles my face in his palms, and I move into his touch, needing the contact. "All I know is he'll never do it again."

I lock eyes with him, knowing he'd never let anyone hurt me. Especially a man whom he loathes.

My heart flutters and my knees wobble as the adrenaline from the fight starts to wear off. "Now what?" I ask, grabbing on to Pike's forearms, needing his support to stay upright.

Pike's eyes flash with concern as he slides his other arm behind my back, holding me. "Let's get you out of here."

I bat his hands away as he tries to lift me, and I finally find my legs again. "No. No." I motion toward the jagoff. "We can't just leave him here like this."

Pike draws in a slow breath. "He ain't going anywhere, and I think it's best if you're not here when he wakes up."

I shake my head and point at the bastard. "I'm not leaving you here with *him*."

The corner of Pike's mouth turns up. "You worried about me, darlin'?"

I nod, unable to smile because there's a guy knocked out on my floor and what was supposed to be a kickass night has now turned into a clusterfuck. "If you're staying, I'm staying. You may need backup."

Pike bends his head back as he mutters a slew of curse words under his breath. I stand there, watching him talk to the ceiling.

How did I end up in this batshit crazy situation?

The answer is simple... Tequila.

"Should we get rid of him?" I let out a nervous laugh because I've watched way too many crime movies. "What am I saying? He's not dead."

Pike narrows his eyes as he dips his chin, studying me. "Who are you, and what have you done with Gigi?"

I punch his shoulder before sobering quickly. "This is no time for jokes. I don't know what we're supposed to do when something like this happens."

Pike strokes my cheek with his thumb. "And you think I know what to do in a situation like this?"

I lift a shoulder. "No, but the only people I know who would know what to do when bad shit like this goes down are my uncles. We could maybe..." I wince at the very thought of calling Uncle James or Uncle Thomas.

Pike closes his eyes, slowly shaking his head. "Fuck." His jaw tightens as he snarls. "The last thing I want is your family involved in my mess *again*."

Ugh. It's the last thing I want too, but I don't see another way out of this. We could call the FBI. They are looking for his dad, but after the way they treated Pike last time, I'm pretty sure that isn't an option he'd entertain.

I press my palm to his chest, looking into his big green eyes. "Then you better grab a shovel and be ready to dig a deep hole, because nothing happens in this town without my family knowing."

He shakes his head again like he can't believe the crazy shit coming out of my mouth. "Call James, then."

I'm out of his arms a second later, and I grab my phone off the floor. I can finally breathe for the first time since I stepped inside the apartment and the jackass lunged at me.

Thank God my dad and uncles taught me how to defend myself, or else... I shudder, trying to shake off what could've happened if I hadn't kept my head together and if Pike hadn't shown up when he did.

I dial the number which I've had on speed dial the last week. I cringe on the first ring, knowing Uncle James is going to lose his shit.

"What's wrong?" he asks as soon as he answers.

No hello. No, hey kid, how ya doing? Nada. Nothing. Just, what's wrong?

Sweet baby Jesus.

"So, um...don't freak out," I warn.

"Just spill it, babe. I don't have all night."

"Umm. Pike's father is here," I blurt out, spilling the problem just like he asked. It's better to rip off the Band-Aid and get it over with, right?

"Is he secured?" is his only response.

I shrug like he can see me. *Secure?* I guess that's what you'd call him. He isn't going anywhere in a hurry. That much is true.

"Yeah. He's knocked out cold and taped up."

"Taped?" James pauses.

I meet Pike's eyes as he waits near the bedroom before answering, "Yeah. It's all we had, Uncle."

"Stay put, and for the love of God, don't call anyone else." There's a shuffling noise in the background followed by the sound of metal-on-metal. "Keep him there until we get there. We're nearby."

"Do you really have to bring Uncle Thomas?" I sigh, dropping my shoulders forward, knowing it's about to be a shitshow.

"Gigi," he says in a tone that tells me I'm not supposed to question him because he's the boss.

"Fine, Uncle James," I draw out, staring down the hallway again as Pike leans against the doorway of my bedroom. "We'll be here waiting. Need the address?"

"Already know it," he clips out.

Of course he does. He knows everything.

I don't even get a goodbye before the call ends. "He comin'?" Pike asks before I have a chance to lower the phone away from my face.

"They'll be here shortly. They're *nearby*." I use air quotes.

Pike lifts his arm, making a spot for me against his body as I walk back toward my bedroom. I slide underneath, tucking myself against him. "Do we just stand here?"

Pike gazes down at me, jaw tight, and the creases in his forehead deepen. "Maybe we should wait outside for them."

I curl my fingers into his T-shirt and rest my head on his chest. "James said to make sure he doesn't get away."

Pike dips his chin toward the motionless body. "Do you see the amount of tape I used on that asshole? He's not going anywhere, darlin'."

I grimace at the perfectly hog-tied man. "I wonder what they're going to do with him," I mumble.

"Don't give a fuck. They can throw his ass in the swamp for all I care."

I stiffen as the weight of his words slams into me. "Pike," I whisper, turning my gaze upward. "He's your dad. I'm sure you don't mean that."

"He was a sperm donor, Gigi. He's never been a dad. Never once has the man shown me any affection. Not once has he ever said a nice thing to me. He never gave a shit about me. So, why the hell should I care what happens to him?"

He has a point and every right to feel the way he does. Who am I to tell him otherwise? "Well..." I place my head on his chest again, thinking about his words. "I'm pretty sure they won't throw his ass in the swamp."

"Your uncles are pretty badass."

I lean my head back, smiling up at him. Pike's a lot like them. All rough edges with a soft center.

"We're going to have to do something about this apartment," Pike says, trying to distract me from the reality that's lying near our feet.

"What do you mean?" I glance around, taking in the white walls, tile floor, and not much else. The place is empty. A completely blank canvas waiting for me to get my ass in gear and decorate.

"You need furniture," he states the obvious.

"I know. I just got the keys before we were hauled off to the Disciples' compound, and now this." I wave my hand toward his father. "Someday, things will calm down enough for me to make this place a home."

He curls his hand around my shoulder and holds me tighter to his chest, stroking my exposed flesh with his thumb. "I'll help you."

We're standing in what's going to be my bedroom, his dad lying motionless and bound, talking about moving like it's just another day and nothing out of the ordinary has happened.

The man could've killed me.

I could be the one lying on the floor, not moving, not breathing. If Pike had waited just a few more minutes, I probably would be.

Jesus.

My skin crawls at the reality. I was so busy going through the motions after Pike stormed in, beating the hell out of the guy, I hadn't really let that sink in.

Pike's fingers continue to stroke my skin as I start to have another internal freak-out. "Next day off, we'll get a truck and grab whatever you need at the store."

"I can do it myself. It's not that big a deal." Nothing seems like a big deal anymore after what just happened. What's a little furniture compared to dying?

Pike takes a step back, staring down at me as he rests his hands on my shoulders. The look on his face is serious and fierce. "Babe," he snaps.

"Yeah?" I find the edge of his shirt with my fingers, shoving them under the soft material as I tilt my head back, looking up at him. "What?"

"*We're* doing it," he tells me like he's the boss.

I narrow my eyes. "I didn't see your name on the lease, and last time I checked, I can do things on my own."

His eyes match my own as we eyeball each other in a virtual pissing match. "Have you always been this hardheaded?"

I nod, smiling. "Pretty much," I mutter.

Pike wraps his arms around me, turning our bodies so he's

facing his father and I'm not. "You're fuckin' crazy," he tells me like I don't already know this.

I bury my face in his chest, wishing I'd just gone to his place like he'd asked. We wouldn't be standing here, waiting for my uncles, with his father hog-tied on the floor.

But then again, would his father have been here when I did eventually come back to the apartment?

I tighten my fingers around the material of his shirt, staring blankly at the wall as I shiver. "It's a good thing you love crazy, then."

There's a pounding on the front door, making us jump. "Open up, kid!"

"Seriously, did they fly here?" Pike asks.

"They said they were close, and I guess they weren't lying." I pull out of his embrace, squaring my shoulders like I'm preparing for battle. "Here we go. You ready?" I ask and get a quick nod from Pike.

When I open the door, Uncle James and Uncle Thomas are standing next to each other, lips pinched, foreheads crinkled, looking badass and pissed off like they always do. It's their thing, and they've perfected it.

"Where is he?" Uncle Thomas asks, pushing past me without as much as a hello.

These men.

"In the back." I pitch my thumb over my shoulder, but only Uncle James is still in front of me.

James's eyes sweep across my body as he steps inside. "You okay?"

I nod, not saying anything because I don't know exactly how I feel. I'm physically okay, but being attacked has a way of changing a person on the inside.

I feel different.

I'm numb. That's the only way I can describe how I've felt for the last handful of minutes. Maybe I'm in shock. It's not every day I see my life flash before my eyes. "Yeah," I answer slowly and softly, but not believing my own words, which means he doesn't buy them either.

James squints and reaches out, running his finger along my neck where Pike's Dad's hands had been. "We'll talk about this later."

"Later?" I gulp, but I shouldn't be worried. I'm the victim here, and even if I weren't, Uncle James would always protect me.

"Later. Got shit to do." He drops his hand and stalks right by me, heading toward the back of the apartment as I follow him.

When we enter the room, Thomas is crouched down, rolling the big jerk to his side. "You did good with the tape, kid."

Pike rubs his neck, giving Thomas a halfhearted smile. "I wish I could say it was the first time I'd ever tied someone up," Pike confesses before his eyes dart to me.

I rock back on my heels at that little revelation. Pike's tied someone up before? I'd be fooling myself if I thought his life was easy breezy. After all, he did end up with the Disciples after getting shot. I knew it wasn't all sunshine and rainbows, but there are so many bits and pieces of his life I am missing.

I mean, at no time in my life have I ever had to tie someone up. Never. Not even one of my little sisters when they were being a total pain in my ass…which, let me tell you, was often.

I should've known it wasn't his first time because he didn't even pause for a moment as he wound the tape around his father's arms and legs, securing him easily. But I was so inside my own head about what had just happened, I didn't give it a single thought.

James steps closer, getting his first look at the man's face. "Damn, you got a few good shots in too. Nice touch."

"I wasn't going to let him hurt her again." Pike reaches out, wraps his hand around my arm, and pulls me toward him.

I tuck myself against his body, groaning into his T-shirt. "I'm fine."

James grunts before he pulls a knife from his back pocket and cuts the tape away from the guy's hands and feet. "I'll carry the top. You get the bottom, Thomas."

"I'm too old for this shit," Thomas mutters under his breath before he bends over and grabs Colton's feet.

"I can do it," Pike offers, stepping forward as he moves me out of his embrace.

Thomas lifts his head, his eyes blazing with anger. "Are you saying we're too frail to carry a man?"

Oh dear God. My eyes widen as I rock backward on my heels, sucking in a breath.

"No, sir," Pike replies quickly, realizing his error, and he steps back toward me. "I figured it's my mess and I should help clean it up."

"Don't listen to him." James climbs to his feet, waving off Thomas before leveling Pike with his steely gaze. "This is not *your* mess. This is *our* mess. You stay here and look after Gigi. Take her to your place for the night. This isn't the first guy we've carried, and I'm sure it won't be the last. We'll deal with your father alone."

Not the first guy we've carried. My mouth falls open. Those words make me look at my badass uncles in a whole new light. I always knew they'd done things, but I never put much thought into what exactly that meant...until now.

"What are you going to do with him?" I ask, watching my uncles as they glance at each other.

"We're not going to make him disappear or anything." Thomas laughs like the very thought is absurd, and for a moment, I'm relieved.

"Yeah, that would be *illegal*," James adds, dropping his voice in a weird way, causing me to blink.

My mind may not be working right, but I don't miss the awkwardness. Are my uncles really the type of men who could make a person disappear?

"What?" I blurt out because they are truly scary right now. I don't know how I've never seen this side of them before, but now it's slapping me right in the face.

Holy shit.

"Everyone's living, sweetheart," Thomas says gently, trying to calm my fears. "We're going to haul his ass down to the FBI head-quarters and drop him. They can sort his shit out."

Maybe I overreacted, jumping to conclusions and taking their words a little too literally. I never really thought they had bad in them, but then again...they were well acquainted with men like Tiny.

"I know. I didn't really think you were going to throw his ass in the swamp for the alligators to eat." I snort, knowing I sounded like an idiot.

"We'd never do such a thing." James gives Thomas the side-eye as he reaches down to grab the guy's arms. "Thomas, legs, man. Let's get this shit done and over so I can get home before the sun comes up."

Thomas groans as he grabs ahold of the asshole's ankles. "I fucking hate the FBI. They're going to have a million questions. Can't we just drop him at the sheriff's office and be done?"

James grunts. "I already told the Feds I don't have time for their shit. They just want him and said they could give two fucks what we had to say."

I gaze up at Pike as they carry his father toward the hallway. "Do you want to go with them?"

Pike wraps his arm around me, moving our bodies to follow them. "No way, darlin'. I'm not leaving your side tonight."

"I'm okay," I whisper even though I feel the weight of the last half hour starting to press down on me like a wet blanket.

Pike stops, places his fingers under my chin, and brings my eyes to his. "I'm not leaving you. I don't want to say it again. I'm right where I want to be." He ticks his chin toward my uncles. "Plus, they officially scare the shit out of me. They're good men, Gigi. You're lucky they have your back."

"I know," I whisper and want to remind him they have his too, but I don't have a chance before Thomas's groan has us turning our heads.

"I forgot how dead weight is so fucking hard to carry," James groans.

Pike and I watch in sheer fascination as they carry him through the doorway, almost knocking his head against the frame.

"Are you done moaning, or do you want to draw the neighbors' attention while we carry him out of our niece's apartment?" Thomas lurches to a stop, Colton's feet in his hands.

James glares at Thomas, muttering something under his breath. "I'm done, old fucker. Get moving."

Thomas grunts, trying to get a better hold on the guy's ankles and almost dropping him as they clear the doorway. "You're chattering on like a lonely old woman."

"Are they always like this?" Pike asks as we follow them outside, keeping our distance.

"Sometimes, they're worse," I tell him, tucking my thumb into the waistband of his pants as we walk.

"We don't need you two watching over us. Take her to your place, Pike." James moves his head toward Pike's apartment. "Get settled and get some rest. We'll talk tomorrow."

"Fucking great," Pike mutters, glancing down at me. "That should be fun."

"They're all bark and no bite, baby." I smile up at him, hoping my words are true. "They're gentle giants."

"Who have carried bodies before," he reminds me as if I could actually forget their earlier words, which I haven't.

I place my hand on Pike's chest. "Don't worry about them. You're one of us now."

Pike's eyes flash, but whatever my words stir in him is instantly hidden. Like it or not, Pike is now in the fold. My family is just as wrapped up as he is in whatever his father brought to our doorstep.

"Let's get you to bed," he says, skipping over my statement.

I sigh but nod, because nothing sounds better. "This evening was supposed to end like that, but way sexier."

"There's always tomorrow, darlin'." He stops near his doorway, his gaze trained on James and Thomas as they carry the asshole toward the car. "And I'm not sure about being one of you, especially after your father hears about tonight."

I stare at my uncles as my stomach tightens. "You let me handle my father."

"I need to be a man and deal with him myself, Gigi. It's the only way I have any hope of earning his respect."

"Fine," I whisper. My dad's liable to pop a freaking vein when he hears about tonight, but so be it. "But just so you know, it's going to suck."

"I never thought it would be easy."

CHAPTER 2
PIKE

"SAY THAT AGAIN." Gigi's father turns his head, giving me his ear like he didn't hear every word I'd just spoken.

I cross my arms, standing on the other side of his desk, and look him straight in the eyes. "My father was in Gigi's apartment last night," I repeat, giving him what he wants.

Joe pinches the bridge of his nose and grimaces like he's just eaten a steamy pile of horseshit. "And..." His jaw ticks.

This isn't going to go down the way I'd hoped. I don't know what I was thinking. I knew it wasn't going to be easy, but fuck, I'm not sure I've ever had a tougher conversation.

I remind myself I'm talking to Gigi's father and not my boss. He's worried about his little girl, which is understandable and expected.

"He attacked Gigi, but she was able to fight him off. I knocked him out before he could do anything worse." I swallow hard, trying not to think about what could've happened if I hadn't...

He closes his eyes and grits his teeth. "And..."

Jesus Christ.

Almost-silent Joe is far scarier than ranting-and-raving Joe. I know how to handle men with bad tempers and loud mouths, but the silent types…those are wild cards.

"And we called Thomas and James afterward. They took him to the FBI, where he is now, and where he will stay for the foreseeable future."

Joe stares up at me, his blue eyes burning with nothing short of rage. He closes his hand into a tight fist against the armrest of his chair and flexes. "So, my kid was attacked because…" His voice trails off.

I'm sure he's fighting the urge to beat my face to a bloody pulp. He wants me to say it's my fault. He wants me to tell him I brought this trouble to her doorstep.

And, in all honesty, I did.

"Because my father's an asshole," I blurt out, giving him what I can but not what he wants. "I don't know why he was at her place, but he was, and I handled it."

"Giovanna!" Joe yells so loudly, my ears ring. "Get your ass in here."

"I don't think…" My words die in my mouth from the murderous look he throws my way.

He stands quickly, leaning over his desk with his knuckles against the wood, coming eye-to-eye with me. "That's the problem, Pike. You don't think. My kid could've been killed last night because of you. No. Scratch that." He shakes his head, grinding his teeth together until they squeak. "She could've been killed twice since you walked into her life."

I jerk back my head like he punched me in the face. His words sting, but they're true.

"Daddy," Gigi hisses like he's gone off the rails. "What the hell is wrong with you?"

He turns his head toward the doorway but doesn't back away from my space. "What's wrong with me?"

She nods.

He lifts a hand and touches his chest. "What's wrong with me?" he repeats in a deeper and scarier than shit tone.

She pushes her long brown hair behind her shoulder before crossing her arms, giving him the same look he's giving her. "Yeah, Dad. You're in here freaking out so loud the entire shop—which is full of customers, by the way—can hear you. You're like a raving lunatic."

Joe stiffens and gawks at Gigi. "I'm a lunatic?"

She nods again, pinching her lips as her glare holds steady. "You're acting like one."

I scrub my hand down my face, muttering to myself. "Fuck me."

Joe takes a step back, hands balled at his sides, chest heaving like he's about to blow a gasket. "I'm sorry I'm losing my shit, but you were almost killed twice because of—" he turns his gaze toward me and snarls "—him."

"Give us a few minutes, darlin'," I tell her when she's about to open her mouth and probably say something she'll regret later.

Her icy gaze sweeps over me, searching my face like she's not sure it's a good idea. This conversation needs to be handled man-to-man. Joe and I need to have a straight and to the point conversation about what went down and my feelings for his daughter.

Gigi shakes her head as her eyes go back to her dad. "I can't deal with this." She throws her arm out, waving her hand at us. "You two work it out. I don't want to hear any more yelling, and, Dad..." She waits, cocking her head at him until he finally looks at her. "Don't walk out of this room until you've calmed down and have started acting like a rational human being again."

We gawk at her as she stalks out of the room, high heels clicking down the hallway toward the shop, showing just how badass she is.

"Fuck, I liked her so much better when she was five," he groans and collapses back in the chair.

I try to imagine Gigi as a little thing all full of sass and sweetness. God, she had to have this man wrapped around her little finger from the moment she was born.

"Someday, when you have children of your own, you'll understand how I'm feeling, Pike. From the moment you walked into her life, you've brought nothing but danger and misery." He shakes his head slowly, eyes narrowed on me like a hawk. "I can't give my blessing for whatever you two have going on. I just can't do it."

I suck in a deep breath, figuring there's no better time than now to lay it all out for him. "We've seen a lot of shit in the last week. We've lived even more, Joe." I take the seat across from him, leaning back, trying to be chill as fuck. "I can't stop bad things from happening, but I can promise to keep her safe. I'd do anything in my power to protect her. Hell, I'd take a bullet for her without even blinking."

"You know most men don't have to worry about taking a bullet for their girl? Normal people don't worry about being gunned down." He raises an eyebrow.

He's right, but I can't change the cards I've been dealt. I can't change the past I was born into. All I can do is try to control the damage from the insane shitshow I tried to leave behind me.

"Would you rather see Gigi with some stiff suit who goes to an office all day, working long hours, probably fucking his secretary because he's a sleazy asshole? You'd want her with someone who doesn't have a loyal bone in his body?"

Joe studies me, not speaking for what seems like forever. "Of course I don't want that for my daughter, but I also want someone who doesn't have his past chasing him into his future."

I run my fingers through my hair, keeping my voice calm and low. "It's my father's past. Not mine," I correct him. "You're judging me for things outside of my control. Things that happened when I was a kid. A goddamn kid, Joe!"

He flinches as I bark out the last statement, but that doesn't stop me. I have to hold my ground now or risk being run over for the rest of my life.

"I don't know what it's like to grow up Gallo, surrounded by people who love you. People who are only looking out for your well-being all the goddamn time. People who will always have your back." I run my sweaty palms down the front of my jeans and take a deep breath. "I never had anyone besides my gran who gave two shits about me. Do you know what it's like to be that alone? Not knowing love or safety, even as a child?"

I pause for only a second, and when he starts to open his mouth, I continue.

"I do. I never had anyone but myself to fall back on. I never had Sunday dinners, big family Christmases, birthday parties, or things most people get to experience in life. I had shit and I came from shit, but now, I'm trying to break free. Start over. Become someone better than my past. Someone different."

I hold up my hand because I want him to hear it all, and the last thing I want is him interrupting me.

"The fact that you'd hold their sins against me, telling me to stay away from your daughter because of things outside my control, is pure and utter bullshit. I thought you were a better man. I thought you were a fair man. I thought you were…"

"Stop," he growls.

"I'm not finished." I raise my chin defiantly.

"You spoke. Now, it's my turn," he argues, rubbing his face. "Kids never stop giving stress and heartache. I don't care how old she is, I'll always worry about her." He twists his hands together, eyes trained on me. "Am I just supposed to turn that off?"

I lift a shoulder and shake my head. "She never should have been wrapped up in my father's business. All I can say is I'm sorry." I glance down as I grip my knee, trying to stop it from shaking. "No matter how much I try to leave them behind, all their hate and bullshit—somehow, it follows me." I gaze at him again. "You worry about Gigi constantly. There's never been a day when my parents have worried about me. Never been a day when they gave two shits if I was alive and breathing. Never been a moment when they wondered how something would affect me and my brother. They are vile, worthless, and selfish people, but no matter how hard I try to break free, their bullshit follows."

Joe passes his hand over his lips, his fingers rubbing the stubble along his jaw. "You had a bad life."

"I have a great life now, but I had a shit childhood," I correct him.

"No one should have the sins of their father follow them. No one should have to worry about whether or not they'll be able to take their next breath because of a deal their father made."

I hold Joe's gaze. "With him in FBI custody, DiSantis dead, and my mother not breathing, I'm hoping it's all behind me."

A shadow passes across Joe's features as he shakes his head. "I'm sorry about your mom."

I want to say I'm not sorry because, well, I'm not. It's cold, callous, and a shitty thing to think, but the woman never gave a damn about me. Why should I give a single shit about her?

"Will you be heading up to Tennessee to handle her affairs?" he asks when I don't reply.

I blink a few times, eyebrows drawn down, wondering if that's what I'm supposed to do? Is that what a person does in my situation?

"Possibly," I tell him because I have no idea what someone does after a family member dies.

"Take as much time as you need," he offers with so much kindness in his voice, I'm completely thrown off.

Then it clicks.

He's trying to get rid of me.

"I have to talk to my gran, but I'm sure I'll only be gone a couple of days. My brother and Gran should be able to handle everything without me. They've been getting by without me for years."

Joe leans forward, resting his elbows on the desk. "Does he live with your grandmother?"

I nod. "He does since my mother…"

"Gotcha. Well, let me clue you in on a few things. As a man with a few brothers, I can tell you your brother is not okay. Your brother needs you more than anyone else has ever needed you."

He does? I haven't given much thought to Austin since hearing about my mother. "You think?"

"Death has a way of changing someone. Especially when it's the death of someone you love. You may not have any good feelings for your parents, but maybe Austin does. He's trying to work through those feelings, and it's not easy for him at his age. Hell, it's not easy at any age. He'll need your strength to help him through this time."

"We haven't been tight in years." Ten years, to be exact. I hadn't seen Austin since I'd blown town, leaving my parents and everything else in my life behind.

"You're blood. Tight or not, he's going to need you. This is going to give him a reality check. Don't you remember when you were his age and you thought you were untouchable? This is going to have him facing his mortality."

I lean back, exhaling and coming to terms with shit I hadn't thought about. "Yeah," I whisper.

Their darkness clung to me, became part of me. I'd spent ten years trying to break free from that time in my life. From the hate they gave freely and only showed to me.

Why? I have no fucking clue. But at this point in my life, I don't give a fuck anymore.

But at Austin's age, I was angry. I wanted the world to feel the pain I felt.

"You're going to need more than a few days to sort him out. Don't rush back on our account. We'll handle your appointments. Izzy will reschedule your clients, so you don't have to worry about anything except spending time with your family."

"Thanks." I dip my head, trying to be gracious but knowing

he's not going to all this trouble out of the goodness of his heart. "Now, can we talk about the giant elephant in the room?"

Joe lifts his chin, twisting his lips as he pulls at the collar of his black T-shirt. "I'm not happy about it."

"About us being together?"

"About everything," he answers in a flat tone. "About what happened in Daytona. About the bullets and your father. About everything," he repeats.

I lean forward, resting my elbows on my knees, and look him right in the eyes. "I can't change what happened, but I can make sure nothing like that ever touches her again. I can love her like no one else ever can or will. I can make her happier than anyone else has before. Hell—" I pause for a moment and lean back. "I already have."

He draws in a deep breath before sighing. "When I thought about my little girl growing up, I never pictured her with a guy like you. I thought she'd find a college boy, settle down, and have a family. I never pictured her running for her life, hiding in a goddamn closet as bullets were flying."

I can see he's not going to get over that little event. It's burned into his brain, and when he looks at me, all he sees is someone who brought that to his daughter's door.

"Shit happens." I don't have the flashy cars and big bank account, but fuck, I do the best I can with what I have. "I may not have grown up surrounded by expensive things and the love of my parents, but I'm a good man, Joe."

He grunts as I sit up straighter, winding myself up for the big finish.

"I work hard. I do the right thing. I protect those I love, even if it costs me my life. I would've gladly jumped in front of a bullet for your daughter. I'd do anything to keep her safe and happy. I'm sorry if that's not good enough for you, but the only person who will decide if Gigi's going to be my girl is Gigi. No one else." I touch my chest. "Not me." Then I point at him. "Not you. Not your wife. Not anyone else in this shop. Only Gigi." I pitch my thumb toward the door, driving the point home.

Joe snaps his head back like I've slapped him. "You're suddenly very wordy, kid." The corners of his mouth curve up ever so slightly, and for a minute, I feel like I'm getting somewhere.

There're two ways this conversation can go... He'll back off and give us space, or he'll come down harder, trying to push a wedge between us just to show how much pull he has over his daughter.

I'm not trying to fuck with their relationship to save ours. That's the last thing I want to do. Gigi has something special with her father—hell, with her whole family—and I'd never let her throw all that away for someone like me.

"I can't punch your ass out, so I gotta fight you with the only thing I have." I shrug, giving him a smug grin. "You can say whatever you'd like to me about our relationship, about me, about your displeasure at the entire situation. I'm grown. I can handle it. But just to clue you the fuck in, she's grown too."

Joe's eyes widen, but I don't let his shock stop me. "I respect you, man. I respected you before I ever stepped foot in Inked. I respect you even more after watching you with your family. The depth to which you love them is something I strive to find and hold on to in my life. The last thing I want is you as an enemy."

He opens his mouth again, but I shake my head. "I tried to end things with your daughter after we left the Disciples' compound. She wasn't having any of it. You know how she is. She's going to dig her heels in and do whatever the hell she wants, no matter what either one of us says or thinks."

I tilt my head, waiting for his response. He seems surprised by my words, almost taken aback by them as he watches me without moving a muscle.

I can take his anger.

I can deal with his disdain for our relationship.

The one thing I know I can't take is his silence. "I..."

"Shut up," he rasps.

I snap my mouth shut as I lean over my legs. The man has finally found his words, and I am not about to stop him from talking.

"Suzy lost it on me this morning." He digs his fingers into his forehead and frowns. "She told me to get my head out of my ass and let Giovanna live her own life. Don't get me wrong. Suzy's not happy about what went down in the last week. She's petrified. But she said the same thing you just did, only without all the veiled threats and profanity."

"We good in here?" a female voice asks.

We turn our heads to the doorway, finding Izzy watching us. "We're good," he answers, waving her away with his hand.

"You sure?" Her eyes are on me now like she's not buying the line Joe's selling.

"Yeah," I tell her. "We're almost done."

"You both have clients out here waiting while you two girls talk about love and relationships. Wrap it up, boys," she warns before she stalks down the hallway, heels clicking against the tile just like Gigi's did.

Joe swivels his chair from side to side and sighs. "I don't like the entire situation. All I want is for my daughter to be happy."

"She is."

"For her to have someone she can count on. For her to have someone who will love her more than himself. I'm not yet convinced that man is you, Pike."

"It is," I argue. *Fuck me.* I just about jumped in front of a goddamn bullet for her. How much more does the man want?

"All I know is that you *met* my kid in Daytona, and now you're here. But you're right..."

Finally.

"I can't control her. I can't tell her what to do anymore. She's grown. She has a mind of her own and has since she was a little girl. I don't have to like what's going on between the two of you. I never will. But I know the harder I pull her away, the tighter she'll cling to you."

He runs his hand back through his hair, grinding his teeth, and I stay silent. I've said all I needed to, and now it's up to him to say what he needs to in order to be at peace with the situation.

"Go back to Tennessee and let things calm down around here. Let me get over the panic of almost losing my daughter. Give me time to sort my shit out, and we'll see how I feel then. I've always tried to be fair. I know not everyone grows up blessed with good parents and a big family. I know you've been given a shit hand to start out, but now's your time to make your own path and change the course your life has been on."

"It's what I've been trying to do for ten years now, Joe. Coming here, to Inked, is my chance to start over and find my place in this world. I want to leave all the baggage of my past in the past. I want what I've never had."

He stands, cracking his knuckles. "I may not approve of you with my daughter, but that doesn't mean I don't respect you for what you're trying to do with your life."

"Enough!" Gigi hollers, stalking into the room and coming to stand by the side of the desk near her father. "And, Daddy—" she turns her gaze toward him, straightening her back "—just so you know, I'm going to Tennessee with Pike."

He opens his mouth, but she shakes her head, narrowing her eyes.

"I don't want to hear it." Gigi reaches for my hand, and I give it to her, squeezing it tightly. "Izzy's going to reschedule my clients. I could use a few days away from the craziness to get my head on straight. Pike needs someone with him when he buries his mother, and I'm going to be that person. Got it?"

Joe blinks a few times, stunned. "Yes, baby girl."

"Good." She smiles, turning her attention back toward me. "Let's finish up today, and then we'll go. I'm sure your gran and brother need you up there as soon as possible."

"I suppose so," I mumble, rubbing the back of my neck, blown away by the backbone on my girl.

"Then it's settled. We'll leave in the morning," she tells me.

"Maybe Pike wants to visit his family alone," Joe inserts, still trying to put that space between us.

Gigi drops a shoulder, cocking her head to the side, gaze sweeping across his face. "Would you want Ma with you if something happened to Grandma or Grandpa?"

Joe nods, frowning. "I couldn't imagine handling anything without her."

"Point proven." She raises her palm like she knows he's about to say something else. "I don't want to hear how it's different, Daddy. It's not. No one should have to go through something like this alone."

"All right," he mumbles, shocking the shit out of me—and her too, by the way her head jerks back ever so slightly. "You go up there with him."

"Thank you." She pulls me toward the door, leaving her father still standing by his desk. When we're in the hall, she turns back to face him. "And, Daddy..." She pauses.

"Yeah?"

"I wasn't asking your permission."

My eyes widen, and I bite my lip to stop myself from laughing. This chick is all sass and attitude.

She's not scared of anyone.

Not even her father.

CHAPTER 3
GIGI

"DO you want to have two visitations or only one?" Pike's granny asks over the phone.

I keep my eyes on my truck, trying not to be too nosy, but it's not easy as we walk through the parking lot of the fast-food restaurant. I sip my soda, pretending not to listen to their conversation but hearing every word.

He'd spoken to her before we left Florida and there didn't seem to be any tension between them, but now, with the talk of his mother's funeral, the uneasiness in their voices is hard to miss.

"No. I don't even know why we're having one. Why the hell would we do two?" Pike glances at me as he runs his hand through his light-brown hair, letting out a low grunt.

I give him a tight smile, straw between my teeth, somehow stopping myself from telling him to chill out. This is about his mother after all, but the hatred runs deep. Even after her death, the way Pike feels about her hasn't changed at all.

"Don't start with me, child. There are people in this community who would like to pay their respects. Now, pick. One or two?"

"One," he growls.

"How hard was that?" Her voice is full of sarcasm.

Pike scowls. "Can't we discuss this when we get there?"

"The funeral home needs to finalize their calendar. You never know who's going to die today and steal our place if we don't get on their schedule now."

Pike fishes the keys from his pocket and presses the button, unlocking the doors. "Don't give a damn when we do it. Don't give a shit how many time slots we have. I just want to get it over with." He leans against the back of the truck, resting his arms over the bed, staring off into the distance.

I stand next to him, sucking down the last drops of my soda, eyes on him. The closer we get to his hometown, the crankier he becomes. This short conversation with his granny has him on edge, and I'm pretty sure it's only going to get worse. Pike has a cold streak, and right now, he's the freaking Arctic.

"This isn't about you, Pike. What about Austin?"

Snap. Gran has a point.

Pike closes his eyes and sucks in a breath at the mention of his little brother. "I get it. I do. If it's important to him, ask him and not me."

I grimace, turning my face so he can't see. Man, he needs to calm down, take a step back, and look at it from his brother's perspective.

"We have enough sad things going on over here. You better get your head on straight before you walk into this house. Leave your past at the door and think about your brother. He's a kid, and he's just lost the one person who loved him the most. You got me?"

The lines across Pike's forehead deepen. "Loud and clear. We'll be there in a few hours and can discuss everything then."

"I can't wait to see you. But do me a favor…" She pauses for only a second. "Leave your attitude in Georgia."

I let out a little laugh, covering my mouth with my hand as he glances at me.

"Fuck," he hisses, lifting his face toward the sky and closing his eyes. "What a damn mess."

I slide my hand across his back and step closer. I'm not sure what to do in a situation like this, but I want to be there for him. "Everything's going to be okay," I tell him, trying to comfort whatever demons are chasing him.

He leans his head down toward me, eyes blazing with so many emotions. "It's all so fucked up."

Beyond fucked up. "I know."

Nothing's been normal since the moment Pike walked back into my life. I've experienced more crazy things in the last week than I had in my entire twenty-something years being alive. He's definitely not wrong when he says things are so *fucked up*. Everything has been.

Pike wraps his arms around my waist, pulling me tight against his body. "I'm sorry I brought you along. You don't need to be witness to all this."

I stick my hand under his T-shirt, running my fingernails across the skin of his lower back and smashing my cheek against his hard chest. "I want to be here," I murmur into his T-shirt.

His lips are against my hair. "You deserve happiness and the fairy-tale family you have, Gigi. Mine is awful. The Moores are nothing like the Gallos. I never meant to pull you into the drama and bullshit."

"We aren't perfect either, Pike," I remind him. "No family is. Sure, we seem like a freaking Norman Rockwell painting on the outside, but we fight all the time and crazy shit happens in our lives too."

"Darlin', your family almost shits rainbows."

Oh no, he didn't. I tip my head back, nose scrunched up, and glare at him. "Do you really believe that?"

Pike nods, his strong hands splayed out across my back. "Never met a family quite like yours. They love each other. They'll do anything for each other. They argue sometimes, sure, but there's lots of love there."

I step back, gawking at him. I shouldn't be surprised that with the parents he had, the man has no perception of an average family. "That's how family works."

"That's how *your* family works."

I cock my head and cross my arms. "And you know the inner workings of families because…"

I shouldn't have said it. It was wrong of me to throw his fucked-up childhood in his face, but I couldn't stop myself. I can only hold my tongue so long before I snap. Talking about my family is the quickest way to get me to start spewing words before thinking.

He shrugs. "I don't know. The short time I've been with the Gallos, I just…"

"Choose your words very carefully," I warn him, ready to give him an even bigger piece of my mind.

I can put up with his shitty attitude.

I can even put up with his anger.

The one thing I can't put up with is him throwing digs at my family.

He takes a deep breath and lets out a sigh. "You look at my family and think, wow, they're so messed up, right?"

"Not really," I lie.

I'm not sure "messed up" is even a strong enough term to describe the Moores. I'll never know his mother, but in the small amount of time I spent with his father…he tried to freaking kill me. His granny and Austin are complete unknowns, but they won't be for too much longer.

Pike eyes me like he knows I'm not being truthful. "You're a shit liar." He shakes his head with a small smirk on his lips. "Maybe the worst ever."

I laugh with a shrug. "I didn't want to hurt your feelings."

"Let's go." He motions toward the cab of the truck. "I want to get there before nightfall."

I take a step backward, but his hand captures mine before I get too far. I squeak as my body jolts, and he pulls me against him again. "Promise you won't hate me after this trip," he begs, his eyes searching mine.

"I won't." I blink a few times, confused. "Why would I?"

He places his palms against my face as he traces the edge of my jaw with his thumbs. "When you see where I come from and the few family members I have left, you may not like what you come across. Sometimes it's easier to cut dead weight than wade through the mess, even if there could be something great on the other side."

"Are you the something great?" I tease him.

"We're the something great." He doesn't even crack a smile when he says the words.

I can't stop my stupid smile from spreading. I place my hand on his chest right over his heart. "We've already been through some ugly things together, Pike, but I'm still here."

He rests his forehead against mine, hands still cupping my cheeks. "Thank fuck for small miracles," he mutters.

I don't speak, letting him feel whatever he's feeling. I just breathe him in, seeing the sadness marring his features.

He opens his eyes, locking on mine. "I take back what I said earlier."

"What?" I whisper, gripping his T-shirt in my hands.

"I'm glad you're coming with me. I'm not sure I could face this alone," he confesses.

And just like that, arctic Pike is gone and the guy I love is back.

"There's nowhere else I'd rather be. I'd never let you go through this alone," I reply.

Not that long ago, I wanted nothing more than to send him back to Daytona. I couldn't believe he showed up at Inked out of the clear blue and that it wasn't intentional. But after everything we've been through, his arrest, our stay at the compound, and then almost getting killed, I feel territorial about him.

I have an insatiable need to make sure he's okay and to be at his side, which I've never experienced.

Pike's fingers are on my chin, lifting my mouth to his. The

kiss is whisper-soft but filled with all the sweetness of the moment. I could stay like this forever, peppering him with gentle kisses.

Life is simple in that moment.

There's nothing trying to pull us apart. No one chirping in our ears about how we're wrong for each other or trying to end our lives.

"We better go." He pulls his head back, ending the kiss. "Granny's waiting, and if she's bitchy now, the longer she waits, the bitchier she'll become."

Just great. "She sounds like Maria."

"Constance may be worse," he says, finally dropping his hand and breaking our connection.

I back away, moving slowly and keeping my eyes on him as I make my way around the side of the truck. "Then why are we still here? It's bad enough I'm meeting your grandmother under these circumstances, I don't want to make her wait any longer. I need her to like me, Pike."

"Why?" he asks as he slides into the truck, and I climb in next to him. "All that matters is I like you."

I turn, blinking at him like he understands nothing about me even after everything we've been through. "Are you new?"

He furrows his eyebrows as he turns the key in the ignition, facing me. "Am I new?"

I nod quickly. "Uh, you know family's important. Like, *the* most important thing to me. Not just my family, but yours too. If your grandmother hates me…" I pause and shake my head because the look he's giving me says he doesn't really understand me at all. "Let's go." I motion toward the windshield. "I'll explain as you drive. We're wasting daylight."

"We're only three hours away," he tells me like that's supposed to make all the difference in the world.

I cross my arms over my chest, pinching my lips together, and eyeball him.

"Okay. Okay." He slings his arm across the back of my seat, pulling out of the parking spot faster than I expect.

Sheesh. Pike Moore doesn't like being told what to do.

I lean against the door, turning my face toward him, wishing I could smack the shit out of him.

"What?" He gives me the side-eye.

I slowly shake my head, telling myself he's going through a lot of shit, and take a deep breath before I say something I know I'll regret. I should give him a break. Let him throw whatever fit he's throwing to get the emotion out. I know there's a lot he's feeling and not sharing.

"Back to the family part," I explain in a calm, even tone. "It's important to me that your grandmother, and even Austin, likes me. Just like it's important to me that my family likes you."

"I think we burned that bridge." He doesn't even look at me when he says that.

"Which one?" I narrow my eyes, feeling my heart starting to race.

His eyes cut to mine as we sit at the red light, waiting to pull onto the highway. "Your family, especially your father, will never like me."

"That's not true," I argue.

He's facing forward again, checking the side mirror before the light turns green. "The conversation I had with your father yesterday was anything but friendly."

"He'll get over the shock of what happened and move on."

Pike lets out a bitter laugh. "I've known a lot of men like your father, and one thing they don't do is get over shit and move on, especially when it involves their wife or kids."

I stare out the windshield, trying to relax my jaw but failing. "My father isn't like most men," I grumble.

"You got that shit right," Pike says quickly. "He's worse."

I snap my eyes to him, dropping my hands to my lap and clenching them into tight fists. "I've known that man my entire life.

He *will* get over this, and as soon as he knows you like I do, he'll even like you too. But if you keep acting like a shithead…"

"You're fooling yourself, darlin'." His eyes flicker to mine. "Your dad and I will never be friends. He'll never look at me as anything more than the guy who almost got his little girl killed."

I grind my teeth, annoyed with the entire conversation. "I know you think you know my dad, but you don't. Sure, he's protective…"

"Protective?" Pike laughs. "That man is way more than that."

"Let me finish," I growl, glaring at him. "The one thing I know about my family is that they know forgiveness. No one will judge you for things you didn't do or couldn't control. What went down wasn't your fault. My dad knows that. Deep down, he understands. He just needs some time to cool off and come to his right mind so he has a chance to figure it out for himself."

Pike shakes his head, throwing his arm over the steering wheel like we're out for a Sunday drive. "I know you have this need to be liked, babe, but I don't feel the same. I'm me. I can't change who I am. I can't change where I come from or what happened before I walked through the doors at Inked. If he doesn't like me, I'll be okay. It won't change how I feel about you."

I take a deep breath, letting his words settle before I dare open my mouth. My entire body is stiff, and being trapped in the truck, unable to move, isn't helping my anger either. "You think I can go through life with you and my father at each other's throats?" I gape at him.

Pike shrugs. "Don't know, but I guess we'll find out."

I run my hand down my face, groaning into my palm. "What a clusterfuck," I mutter. "I never should've let you talk to him about what happened."

"Nah, darlin'. I had to be the one to talk to him. I had to man up, and I did. He may not have liked what I said, but I said it. It's over. We're moving on."

I widen my eyes. "We're moving on, and it's over?"

What the fuck?

Pike nods, not looking at me as he keeps his gaze trained on the traffic in front of us.

"Are you fucking serious with that?" I ask, my voice all high-pitched and full of bitch.

"I can't control how your dad feels."

I close my eyes and whisper, "Fucker."

"I'm a fucker?"

I don't dare look at him. I'm too pissed to look at his face. I just stare straight ahead and snap, "Yep. Wake me if you want me to drive."

What the hell am I doing with someone like Pike? He's so much like my father, it's almost maddening sometimes. He's moody, difficult, and bossy. Nothing has been easy since the day he walked back into my life.

Daytona was easy. We were hundreds of miles away from everyone and everything. There weren't parents getting in our business or bad guys coming after us.

Pike's going through some shit. Some really dark shit. He's dealing with the death of his mother. He's about to face his past, including a little brother and grandmother he hasn't seen in years.

All I can do is be there for him and hope the guy I knew back in Daytona, the funny asshole who caught my eye, comes back to me.

I close my eyes, wanting nothing more than to get away from him for a little while. Since it's impossible, I do the next best thing. I go to sleep.

———

"We're here, darlin'." The backs of Pike's fingers brush against my cheek so softly I barely feel them.

I moan as I try to move. "Already?"

"Afraid so."

I blink a few times, trying to clear the haze from my mind. Gone is the endless gray of the road, replaced by an explosion of colors—lush green grass and a yellow-orange sky as the sun sets behind the mountains.

"Here they come." Pike dips his head toward the windshield as I stretch.

My gaze follows his to an older woman and young man as they walk out of a white house with a beautiful wraparound porch. I reach for the visor, pulling down the mirror to make sure I don't look as shitty as I feel.

"You're beautiful," Pike says as I wipe the mascara smeared under my eyes.

"You should've given me a heads-up," I whine in a panic.

"I tried, but you wouldn't wake up. Based on how fast Granny's walking, you still have a minute or two."

"Fuckin' men," I mutter, flipping up the visor, knowing my face is as good as it's going to get.

That is when I get my first real good look at his brother, Austin. He's a younger version of Pike, but with darker hair and no tattoos. He's holding his grandmother's arm, helping her down the walkway in front of her house like a little gentleman.

"Man," Pike says, taking in his granny and brother. "I never realized how long I'd been gone until right now."

I reach across and grab his hand, locking our fingers together. Sure, he was a shithead, but I came here to support him, and support him I will.

"You ready for this?" I ask him, rubbing his wrist with my thumb.

"Don't have a choice." He shrugs.

"I'm here for you," I tell him, wishing we were here under happy circumstances.

There's a faint smile on his lips as he squeezes my fingers and reaches for the door handle with his other hand. "I wouldn't want anyone else by my side."

I slide out of the pickup truck, following Pike, and I hang back as he walks toward his grandmother.

Austin's gaze moves from Pike to me. When our eyes lock, a smug smirk plays on his lips before he throws me a wink like I'm going to kneel down at his feet and profess I've fallen for the wrong Moore.

Lordy.

I raise an eyebrow and stare at the kid. I mean, don't get me wrong, he's freakishly good-looking, but he's a baby.

"Granny, this is Gigi," Pike says, drawing my attention away from Austin.

I smile at the cute old woman with a bloom of white hair and soulful dark brown eyes. "It's an honor to meet you, ma'am," I declare with a big smile on my face, tucking a lock of hair behind my ear.

She steps forward, the wrinkles around her mouth deepening as she smiles. "Come closer, honey. I can't see so good with these old eyes." She motions for me, and I step forward, closing the space between us. I glance at Pike, who only gives me a nod.

She grabs my hands, holding them tightly, and peers into my eyes. "Such a natural beauty," she whispers. "I like a girl who doesn't have to put on a mountain of makeup to be seen."

I don't want to break the news to her that most of my face wore off somewhere between Florida and Tennessee. I've never worn a ton of makeup, but rarely do I leave the house this naked either.

"Thank you, ma'am."

"Connie, please." She pats my hand, making me feel welcome during such a difficult time.

"Connie," I repeat as Pike strides toward his brother, leaving us alone.

Connie doesn't let go of me as her gaze follows Pike, watching the brothers exchange words neither of us can hear. "My heart is happy now," Connie confesses, smiling at her grandsons. "It's nice to see them together. It's a shame it had to happen because of their mother's death."

"Yeah," I whisper back as they embrace each other for the first time in years.

"They need each other," she tells me. "Siblings are never complete when they're apart."

I get what she's saying. After I left home and headed off to college, I felt funny without my little sisters around. My entire life had been filled with them. I rarely had a moment alone, and then overnight, I had all the silence in the world.

"Maybe out of all this tragedy will come a bond stronger than they've ever had before. They really only have each other left," she says.

I turn my gaze toward Connie, our hands still connected. "They have you too."

"Honey, I'm an old woman. I don't have many days left on this earth, and it would give me peace knowing I'm not leaving them alone."

Sadness comes over me as she speaks. I don't often think about time. Death and dying are something I barely put any thought into. But standing with Connie, listening to her dreams for Pike and Austin, my mortality hits me square in the face.

"I'm sure the boys will get closer now that they're older," I reassure her, but who knows how Pike feels.

He's barely spoken about his brother. It's like they're strangers even though they spent years under the same roof. I couldn't imagine feeling the same way about my sisters.

"Let's give them some time together. Sweet tea?" she asks, pulling me gently toward the house.

They're so deep in conversation, neither of them notices as we walk away, leaving them alone. I hope whatever they're saying, they're finding a path back to each other.

"Please." I glance at Pike and Austin one last time before I follow her inside.

We're nothing without our family, and right now...they need each other.

CHAPTER 4
PIKE

AUSTIN NEARLY COLLAPSES against me as soon as he's in my arms. "I'm so happy you're here," he whispers, holding on to me like I'm the only thing keeping him upright. "I feel so alone."

My heart aches for the first time since hearing about my mother's death. I'm not sad for the wicked woman, but I'm torn up for my little brother.

"I'm here for you." I hold him tighter, giving him the strength he needs.

"You don't know what it's been like." He pulls back, eyes glassy and swimming with tears. "No one knows."

He's no longer the little kid I'd left behind when I drove away from this small-ass town and the life I had here.

"I've missed you," he blurts out before I can reply.

I'm still soaking in the realization that my brother is a grown man and not a little boy anymore. "I've missed you too," I confess for the first time in my life.

My parents may have never treated me well, while they smothered Austin, but I never held any animosity toward the kid. He didn't rub it in my face or do anything to earn my hatred. That shit all fell on my parents. He was the only one in the house who was nice to me and paid me any attention, which I know drove my parents crazy.

"Stick around for a few days, yeah?"

I nod, unable to find my voice as the guilt of all the years I've missed washes over me. All the moments I wasn't here for him. All the milestones I didn't get to see. Memories I should've been a part of but wasn't and never will be.

"You look…" Austin's voice trails off as he rocks back on his heels.

I raise an eyebrow with a small smirk, hoping to lighten the dark mood. "Like shit?"

He runs his fingers through his dark hair, glancing down at his feet to hide his smile. "Your words, not mine."

There's an awkward pause. I'm not sure what to say after so many years, and I'm pretty sure he feels the same.

I glance toward the patio where Gigi and Granny just were, but they're gone. "Life has a way of wearing on our skin. You'll learn that as you grow older."

"If that were true, I'd look like an old piece of leather." He grimaces. "I ain't ready for all that."

"You're only seventeen, Aus. Your skin's too new to show the wreckage." I knock him on the shoulder, trying to be playful even when it's not the time.

"Thirsty?" he asks, finding his footing and straightening his back.

I nod. "I could use something to drink."

"Granny grabbed a six-pack from the corner store, but she said I can't have one." He rolls his blue eyes, rubbing the back of his neck. "She's absolutely no fun, brother."

"You don't need fun in your life right now. Fun around here means bad shit and even worse people." I point my finger at him. "The last thing you need is that kind of *fun*."

Austin smacks my finger away and throws his arm around my shoulder. "A drink with my brother isn't the bad type of fun. I just want to kick back, shoot the shit over a beer, and find out where the hell you've been for the last ten years."

"You don't want to know," I argue.

"Sure I do. You just disappeared. Poof. Gone."

I wince as more guilt floods my belly.

He turns his head, giving me his eyes, and I brace myself for his next words. "It was like you were the one who died, but you were alive, forgetting all about me."

The confirmation I'd abandoned him cuts me deep. I had never put much thought into how my leaving town would affect him. He was seven when I left, and I didn't think he'd even notice.

I mean, we barely saw each other. At least not like most siblings. My parents made sure of that. They did everything to keep us apart from the day I moved in with Granny.

"Let's get that beer and go down by the river, yeah?" I ask him, figuring Granny won't put up too much of a stink.

"You get the beer, and I'll meet you down at the spot?" He moves his head toward the path still cut in the thick brush lining the driveway. "It'll be easier," he says as his hand falls away from my shoulder.

"Be there in five," I tell him before he disappears into the woods, and I go into the house. Nothing has changed since the last time I was here. It's like time stood still in this place, while I moved on with my life.

"Where's Austin?" Granny asks, leaning over the kitchen island where two glasses of sweet tea sit in front of them.

"He's down by the river, waiting on me," I say, glancing at my girl, who looks comfortable sitting in my granny's kitchen.

Granny raises an eyebrow, knowing exactly what happens down by the river. "He's only seventeen, Pike."

I shrug before walking behind Gigi and putting my arms around her shoulders. "I'm pretty sure it's not going to be the first beer he's ever had."

Gigi glances over her shoulder at me, grabbing on to my hands. "Don't drink too much, okay?"

I kiss the top of Gigi's head as Granny eyes me. "I won't. Just a few, darlin'. We'll be back before you know it. Are you okay staying here with her?" I ask Gigi.

Granny crosses her arms, tilting her head and narrowing her eyes. "I'm a *her* now?"

I laugh. "Granny, I know how you are. I just want to make sure you're being good to my girl."

She shakes her head and wrinkles her nose. "She's the first woman you've ever brought home. You can bet your ass I'm going to be on my best behavior, but that doesn't mean I'm not going to have some questions about my grandson or the beautiful girl in my kitchen." Her lips slide into a smile. "We'll be fine. I promise."

"Just go," Gigi agrees, trying to hold back her giggles at the ridiculousness of the conversation. "I think your granny and I will get along perfectly, babe."

"We're just going to have a little girl time. You need to go have some boy time with Austin," Granny tells me, leveling me with her gaze.

"We're hardly boys," I correct her, "but we do need to have a man-to-man talk." I kiss Gigi's cheek before heading toward the fridge. I open the doors to the mostly empty refrigerator and grab the six-pack, turning to find both women studying me in sheer fascination. "What?"

Granny smiles. "It's just nice to see you here again. Go be with Austin. Don't come back until later. We'll get dinner started."

"What the hell are you going to make?" I pitch a thumb over my shoulder toward the empty fridge. "There's nothing in there."

"Pike, I've made more with less. Now, go." Granny shoos me toward the door.

It's a short walk to the river's edge where Austin's sitting in an old Adirondack chair. He's hunched over, elbows on his knees, holding a stick in one hand, smacking the water with the tip.

"Sorry I took so long." I set the six-pack between us and sit in the lawn chair next to him. "The girls…"

"Did you call Granny a girl to her face?" Austin asks.

I shrug, laughing because he knows as well as I do how much she hates it. "Maybe." I reach for two beers and offer him one. "She can try to beat my ass now, but I'm a little too big and too fast."

Austin laughs too, taking the beer from my hand. "She's too old for all that. Now she just gives you the look when you've fucked up. You know the look?"

I nod, knowing damn well the way she can put the fear of death in you with just a single squint and crook of her lips.

"I get it a lot," he says, twisting the top off the beer before throwing the cap in the mud. "She's slower now but still scary."

I kick back, relaxing in a spot where I spent a lot of time during my childhood. "Granny's all bark and no bite. I couldn't say the same for some people in our lives."

Austin grimaces. He is young, but he wasn't blind. "I don't know why they were always so good to me and treated you like shit." Pain flashes in his eyes. "I'm sorry."

"You didn't do anything wrong. Don't even think about it, Aus. We all go through shit in life. That was mine to deal with. I've moved past everything. I got away and landed places where people wanted me. I may have been born into the family by blood, but I found my new family by choice."

He looks off into the distance as he rests the bottle on his leg. "Where did you go?"

I follow his eyes, ogling the same patch of trees. There has been pain for both of us. Mine was caused by the people he loved the most, and his was by my absence and our mother's death.

"I just took off," I confess softly, digging the heels of my boots into the thick mud near the shore. "I wanted to be anywhere but here."

He glances at me, eyebrows drawn inward. "And went where?"

"I headed south." I shrug, wondering how much I should tell

him. But then I figure, I shouldn't hold anything back. "I left with five hundred bucks in my pocket. Slept in some pretty shady motels as I made my way to Florida, blowing through most of my cash before I hit the Georgia-Florida line."

He turns in his chair, giving me his full attention. Attention I don't really want but have no choice but to take. "Then what did you do?"

"My life took an unexpected turn near Jacksonville."

He raises his eyebrows. "Jacksonville?"

"Yeah. I was minding my own business, filling my bike's tank with some gas, when all hell broke loose."

"What happened?"

"Got my ass shot that night," I say, smiling as I think back on the stupidity of the entire thing.

His eyes widen as soon as the words are out of my mouth. "Shot?" he gasps.

"Some bikers had a beef with some jackasses nearby. I got caught in the cross fire."

"Jesus," he mutters, shaking his head. "Where did you get shot?"

"My shoulder." I rub the spot where I'll always have a scar. "It wasn't too bad, but I was pissed. I got into it with one of the guys, and he ended up punching me in the shoulder, making me kiss the cement."

"What the fuck?" Austin's mouth hangs open. "For real? The asshole punched you in your wound?"

I nod, knowing how fucked up it sounds. "I passed out from the pain after that. I don't remember anything until I woke up at their compound."

Austin swallows as his knuckles turn white from gripping his beer so tightly. "Were you scared?"

I shake my head, lying my ass off because if you aren't a little scared in a situation like that, then you're really a dumbass. "Well, I wasn't happy when I woke up. My shoulder was fixed and the bullet removed, but I had no idea what they had planned for me. When I saw the guy who punched me, it took three men to hold me back from getting my retribution." I chuckle, remembering the shock on Morris's face when I lunged at him.

Austin gives me a cocky smile. "I would've punched that fucker square in his jaw. He'd be eating nothing but smoothies for a month."

I laugh at my brother's greenness. If he knew Morris, ever laid eyes on the man, he'd realize there was no way he'd have the kind of power to actually break his jaw. "I never did get to give him payback, but after I talked with him, I understood why he did it."

"I don't think I could ever get over something like that," he mutters.

I throw back half the beer, letting the cool liquid coat my throat, trying to come up with some words of wisdom. "As you grow older, you realize some things aren't worth holding grudges over. At some point, you've just got to move on, or else you'll always be stuck looking back."

Austin leans back in his chair, eyes going back to the forest with the sun cascading through the leaves. "I guess so," he whispers. "What happened after that?"

I let out a sigh, knowing there's so much to the story. I could talk about my time with the Disciples for days and never really get into everything that happened. "They invited me to stay after they found out I had nowhere to go. I ended up living there for a few years, hanging out with the guys, feeling like I was part of a family for the first time in my life."

The only family I'd ever known.

"Wait." He slices his eyes to mine. "You lived with a biker gang?"

I nod, lifting my beer to my lips and pausing. "Only for a little while."

"You said a few years," he corrects me, throwing my own words back in my face.

I shrug. "That's a little while. As you get older, years aren't as long. It went by in the blink of an eye."

"Did you go on runs and kill people too?" he asks.

I shake my head. "Never. I never prospected with them. Never wanted to be in a biker club. They gave me a place to live and I did some stuff for them to pay my way, but damn, it wasn't as bad as you're making it sound. You watch way too much television."

"*Sons of Anarchy* was my favorite show, dude. Now I find out I have my very own Jax Teller in the family."

I bark out a laugh at his statement. "Austin, I am not and have never been Jax Teller. I wasn't in the Disciples. I didn't wear their cut. I was like the live-in help. They gave me a room, food, and let me hang around, but that's about it."

"They have all those wild parties?" He raises an eyebrow because he's seventeen and probably thinks about sex as often as he breathes.

"No," I lie and try to keep my face as neutral as possible.

"Liar." He rolls his eyes. "You're telling me they don't have half-naked women all around their compound?"

"If they did, I never saw it." That is my story, and I am sticking to it. In no way do I want to make the life sound even a little bit like something a horny teenage boy would enjoy.

"Whatever," he mumbles against the top of the beer bottle. "How long did you stay with them?"

"A few years, honing my skills as a tattoo artist. I loved to draw. It was always my thing. My escape. But drawing in a book and doing it on flesh are two different things."

"I remember you always sketching something or other."

"The guys in the club let me use them as my guinea pigs. They got free tattoos until I was pretty fucking good at it."

"So, you got room and board, and they got free tattoos?" he asks, repeating my statement.

"Something like that," I say.

"It was a nice trade-off. Plus, I'm sure the tits and ass were a bonus too." He laughs, knowing I'm full of shit.

I'm going to go right on by that because he doesn't need to know about all the tits and ass.

God, there was so much, too. All shapes, sizes, ages. Thirsty bitches who wanted nothing more than to fuck and suck their way through the members of the club.

I was young and didn't care about anything else except for getting off. I wasn't looking for long-term. I wanted casual, and the ladies around the club were perfect for something like that.

"I never really had much trouble getting tits and ass, kid." I wink at him. "That's one thing Mom and Dad gave us...good genes. We're damn good-lookin'."

"I don't know about your ugly mug, but I'm fucking hot." He touches his chest, giving me a smug grin. "Ask any of the chicks around here. They're all chomping to get a piece of me."

I roll my eyes, remembering when I was just as cocky as he is now. That's youth. Life has a way of reminding you you're not as great as you think you are. "Tell me what you really think of your-self." I laugh at my little brother as he kisses his bicep.

"Nah. I'm sure you can see the perfectness that's me. Now, I want to know what happened and why you left the Disciples."

I slam back the last of my beer and reach for another one. Even-tually, we're going to get off of me and move on to the shit that went down after I left.

"It was just time to go. I headed out after tattooing at a local shop for about a year, moving a few hours south where I could find a chair. I still saw the guys, caught up with them every year at Bike Week in Daytona, but I had my sights set on bigger and better things than anything I could get with the Disciples."

"So, you're living somewhere south of Jacksonville?"

I shake my head. "I live north of Tampa now."

His eyebrows furrow. "What? How?"

"So, I lived near Daytona for a while, doing tats in a decent shop, but I wanted to work at the best shop in Florida. They were always in every tattoo magazine, featured for their killer work and designs. I wanted to work there from the day I put my first mark on someone's skin."

"And they're in Tampa?"

"They're about an hour north. Middle of fucking nowhere, but not like here. There's still civilization around, but it's a quieter way of life than Daytona with all the tourist bullshit."

"And the hot chick?" He tips his head toward the path leading back to Granny's. "How does she fit in?"

"I met her in Daytona, but her family owns Inked. She works there, and now I work there too."

"No shit. You're fucking the boss's daughter." His mouth hangs open.

"Watch it. That's my girl you're talking about."

"Well…" He turns the beer in his hand, swiping at the water drops with his thumb. "You are sleeping with her, yeah? She's not just a friend who tagged along?"

"She's my girlfriend, yeah."

"So, after all this time, you found what you were looking for? You achieved your dream, and the girl is the bonus."

"She's the real dream," I confess as my throat grows tight. "But I didn't know that when I walked into Inked. I thought I'd achieved everything I'd ever wanted when I got my spot. But Gigi…" I shake my head, unable to stop myself from smiling. "That girl and her family, they're really what I've always wanted. Just never knew it until it landed in my lap."

Austin kicks at the dirt near his feet, setting down the empty bottle before grabbing another. "You do have a family here, you know," he heckles, flicking his eyes at me.

"I've never forgotten about you and Granny. Time has a way of getting away from someone. And…" I pause, running my hand down the front of my jeans. "I figured it was easier for everyone if I just disappeared."

He narrows his eyes. "Easier for who?"

I blink, at a loss for words.

"You or us?" he adds.

It's like he's punched me square in the chest without even lifting a finger. The words sting. "I guess, for me," I answer honestly.

Austin leans forward, resting his elbows on his knees, casting his eyes downward. "I needed you. I wanted you here. I was only seven when you left, but I used to love coming to see you." His eyes flicker to mine. "I didn't care what Mom and Dad said, you were and are my brother. I still remember when I walked into her house and Granny told me you were gone." He shakes his head, blowing out a long breath. "It was like someone kicked me in the face."

"I'm sorry." I rub my forehead, wincing as his words connect with every emotion I've shoved down so deep I never let myself feel any of them. "I was a shit brother for leaving without saying goodbye."

"You *are* a shit brother." He drives that knife in a little deeper and twists.

I study his dark brown hair, wide build, athletic body, all of which look nothing like mine. "I hope to change that. I need to make amends for the time we lost."

"You do." He doesn't even flinch when he says those words. "It sucks that Mom dying was the reason you finally came home, but I'm happy you're here."

"I'm sorry about Mom." I rest my head against the back of the chair, watching the clouds passing over us. "She and I had a complicated relationship, but I never would've wanted this for her or you."

"I was there," Austin confesses, drawing my gaze. "No one knows. Not even Granny."

My body stiffens. "You were where?"

"In the house," he says quietly.

Jesus. "When she died?"

He nods slowly, his lower lip trembling. "We both hid. She told me not to come out, no matter what happened. They found me first and used me to lure her into the open."

"They found you?" I gape at my brother, trying to imagine the sheer terror he had to have felt.

He nods again, frown firmly planted on his face. "I was hiding in the closet, and they dragged me out. I tried to fight them off, but I was outnumbered. I told them she wasn't there. I told them I was alone, but they didn't believe me." He slumps forward and sighs.

"Fuck," I hiss, wishing I could take the memories away from him.

"They punched me in the face before kicking my feet out from under me. They held a gun to my head in the middle of the living room and waited, knowing Mom would eventually come out."

I shake my head, imagining the entire situation. The scared seventeen-year-old boy with a gun to his head, and a mother who adored him, lured into the open.

Sickening.

"It only took a few minutes, but she came downstairs, pleading with them to let me go." He turns his head away and wipes at his face with the back of his hand. "I think they hit me with the butt of the gun. I was knocked out cold. I didn't see what happened, but when I woke up…" He pauses and swallows, his Adam's apple moving like it's fighting an unwinnable battle. "Mom was lying in a pool of blood with the back of her head missing." He goes back to staring at the trees, trying to be nothing but strong at a time when I'd be falling apart.

"Jesus fucking Christ," I mutter and take a deep breath. "I'm sorry for all of it. For you having to find Mom like that. For having to go through the entire thing alone."

"Maybe now that you're here…" He looks at me with so much hope in his eyes, my heart aches. "I'll never have to go through something like that by myself again."

"Yeah," I reply, knowing it's a promise I can't keep.

CHAPTER 5
PIKE

GIGI'S BOOTS come into view as I sit on the porch, trying to digest everything Austin told me. "What are you going to do about Austin?" she asks.

I lift my gaze, traveling slowly up her bare legs to her cute little tank top and finally landing on her face. "What do you mean, what am I going to do about Austin?"

She crosses her arms and furrows her brows like we're speaking two different languages. "After this. What's going to happen to him?"

What's going to happen to him? I haven't put much thought into where my brother will go after the funeral is over. "I figured he'd stay here."

Gigi's face morphs into something unreadable. "You know your grandmother is getting older, yeah?"

"I'm not blind."

"Maybe she doesn't want to raise another child at her age," she tells me.

"Child?" I laugh as I lean back in the chair. "He's seventeen. He's hardly a kid, and in a year, he'll go off to college or wherever the hell else he wants to go."

"Pike," she says, shaking her head like I've just said the most insane thing in the world.

"Gigi."

"He can't stay here."

I jerk my head back. "He can't? I stayed here, and I turned out just fine."

"Nope," she says bluntly, tapping her foot, clearly pissed off at me...again. "Your grandmother cannot control a seventeen-year-old boy who's going through some shit after losing his mother. Someone needs to watch out for him so he doesn't end up surrounded by bad people. Imagine if you were a different type of man and got involved with the MC. Where would you be now?"

I put my hands behind my head, trying to keep calm while she grows angrier. "No one can control someone else. If he's going to fuck up his life, he'll do it whether he stays here or goes somewhere else." I shrug off her comment.

"He won't fuck it up if someone guides him."

"He's grown now."

She moves her hands to her hips, and I know she's gearing up for a fight. "He's a kid."

"If he hasn't learned how to act or stay out of trouble by seventeen, there's no help for him anyway, Gigi."

Taking Austin with me and being responsible for someone other than myself scares the shit out of me.

She blows out a shaky breath. "I can't believe I'm hearing this from you."

"What the fuck do you want me to do?" I growl, but I know what she's saying isn't totally off base.

"You're a coldhearted bastard sometimes." She's trying to run my life, something I've seen all the Gallos do to one another on a daily basis. "You should take him home," she says finally, getting to her point.

I shake my head, thinking I had to have heard her wrong. "Say that again."

She leans her ass against the railing and sighs. "It doesn't make sense for him to stay here. He needs you right now. You have a place, a stable job, and although sometimes you're a dick, you're basically a good guy."

"Thanks for the compliment," I mutter.

"Shut up," she growls. "Why would you leave him here?"

"She's right," Granny says from the door, hiding behind the screen and eavesdropping like she always used to do.

"Fuck," I groan. They're going to double-team me.

"Now, Pike," Granny says, sitting down in the rocking chair next to me. "Your girlfriend—" she dips her head toward Gigi, who is standing there with a smug grin "—is bringing up a valid point about Austin."

I rub my forehead, readying myself for the assault from two sides. I never imagined my grandma would want Austin to come live with me. Never in a million freaking years.

Hell, we barely know each other.

The kid liked toy trucks the last time he and I breathed the same air, and now he's driving a real one.

"You can't seriously think it's a good idea?" I scoff.

Granny nods, giving me a sweet smile, which always made me crumble in the past. "He needs guidance."

I lean forward again, resting my elbows on my knees, scanning the wood planks beneath my feet. "I can barely guide myself, Granny. I don't think Austin coming to live with me would be a good idea."

No fucking way am I taking this kid home with me.

"Your daddy's in jail, and your mama's in her casket. He needs a man in his life to show him the way. He needs to know how to survive in this crazy world I don't understand. I'm old, Pike. Too old to be raising a teenager." Granny takes a long sip of her tea, giving me time to process what she's just said.

I study Gigi as she glances down at her feet, avoiding my eyes completely as Granny continues.

"If Austin were a girl, I would keep her. Show her how to be a lady and not put up with any boy's shit, but he isn't. Lord knows your father didn't teach him how to be a man. That leaves you, and I know what kind of man you are."

Without my granny, I'm not sure where I'd be or, hell, who I'd be. No matter what I was doing, I always wondered about the possibility of disappointing her, and that single thought stopped me from doing some stupid shit in the last ten years.

"No. It's not happening," I tell her, standing from the chair. "This conversation is over."

"We'll see," Granny brags, but I don't turn around to see her smug smile.

Fuck my life.

CHAPTER 6
PIKE

"WILL YOU COME IN WITH ME?" Austin asks me as we stand in the hallway of the funeral home.

Gigi squeezes my hand, silently pleading with me not to be an asshole. "Sure," I tell him, making my girl happy, but me miserable at the same time.

The last thing I want is time alone with the woman who made me feel like nothing but garbage for most of my childhood.

Do I wish she were alive? Sure.

I'd never wish death on someone unless they were trying to kill me or mine. But am I torn up over her taking her last breath?

Not in the least.

Austin brushes his hand across his dark hair, making sure it's perfect for the tenth time since we walked through the door. He looks ten years older in his black suit and nothing like the kid I left behind.

Gigi pops up on her tiptoes, brushing her lips across my cheek. "Be there for him," she whispers. "He needs you."

I peer down into her blue eyes. "I will," I reassure her, speaking softly so no one else can hear.

Granny turns toward Austin, playing with his tie to make sure it's perfect just like his hair. "It's okay to cry," she tells him as he lifts his head.

"I'm not going to cry, Gran."

She touches his face with her fingertips and gives him a pained smile. "I know you're grown, Austin, but it's okay to feel things."

He grabs her wrist, gently pulling her hand away from his cheek. "I'll be okay."

I release Gigi and straighten my jacket for whatever fucking reason. I hold my breath as the funeral director moves in front of the double doors.

"Please let me know if you're unhappy with anything," he declares solemnly.

If we're unhappy with anything?

Is anyone ever happy at a funeral?

"We will, sir," Austin tells him, sounding very much like an adult.

Austin keeps surprising me. He's handled the man with grace and respect, something I couldn't do, and I'm not even torn up about being here. He not only looks older than he is, but he acts like it at times too. Sure, there're still remnants of the little boy there, but he's seen things I can't imagine.

He found her.

I take a deep breath, following behind my brother as we step into the room filled with wooden chairs placed in neat, even rows. In the front, surrounded by flowers, is a white casket, half open and with my mother's face clearly visible.

Austin freezes, his shoulders going rigid. "I don't know if I can do this." His back is to me, and his gaze is firmly locked on our mother.

I step next to him, placing my hand on his shoulder. "I'll be right here with you."

Austin sucks in a deep breath, closing his eyes for a moment and muttering something so quietly I can't make out the words.

When he exhales, he opens his eyes and looks over his shoulder at me. "I don't think I could've done this without you, big brother."

Every time he calls me brother, the guilt of leaving him grows roots, settling in my bones.

I wish I could go back.

Change the way I left things. I should've kept in contact with him. It wouldn't have changed where we are standing, but it would've made my presence mean more than it actually did.

When he doesn't move, I squeeze his shoulder again. "I won't leave you," I promise him.

"I'll hold you to that." He takes a step, moving out of my grasp.

I follow behind, my eyes going back to our mother's motionless body.

Austin's steps are long and slow as he closes the gap between himself and Augusta Moore.

High-class socialite.

Piss-poor mother.

His knees buckle as soon as he's within a few feet of her, landing on the tiny kneeling bench in front of her. His hands shake as he places them on the edge of the casket. "Fuck," he hisses, brushing the backs of his fingers across his face, no doubt wiping away tears he said he wouldn't shed.

I slide into a chair in the first row, careful to give him space to feel what he needs to feel.

I face forward, the words *Loving Mother* nestled in a flower arrangement resting on the lid catching my attention.

Now that's laughable.

"She looks so good." He turns his face. "Don't you think?"

I look at her, trying to make Austin happy, and I finally see my mother's face clearly for the first time in years. "Yeah." My throat starts to close as the realization that the woman who gave birth to me is gone. Dead.

My mind buzzes with so many things.

So many fucked-up emotions I didn't expect to have wash over me, coating me like a second skin.

Sadness.

Remorse.

Longing.

Regret.

"Just remember, baby. I'll always love you," she says as she slides my favorite pajamas over my head. "Never think otherwise."

I throw my arms around her neck as soon as she starts to pull away, planting a wet kiss against her cheek. "I love you too, Mommy," I whisper against her soft skin. "Forever and always."

"Forever and always." She wraps her arms around me tightly, nestling her face against my neck, tickling me. "Now, crawl into bed, and I'll read you a story."

I practically leap out of her grasp, climbing up on my cool race car bed, tucking myself under the covers. "I want the baseball book." I smile up at her as she walks toward my nightstand, the book I want already waiting.

She sits down, tapping my nose with her thin finger, giving me a big smile. "As if any other book exists."

I giggle because I love this part of the day.

It's only her and me.

No Dad because he's been extra grouchy, ignoring me more than usual.

But Mom...she makes me happy.

I reach for my neck, loosening the tie, suddenly unable to breathe. How could a woman so loving turn on a dime?

"Who's Ashton?" my father asks Mom as she reaches for the coffeepot.

I look up because my father's voice is angrier than usual. The toy truck in my hand is in midair, and I can't stop myself from staring at my mother as she stands so still, it's like she's frozen.

"Ashton?" she whispers, giving my father a funny look.

My father steps behind her, holding up a piece of paper and shaking it in her face. "Don't play stupid with me, Augusta. I already know, but I want to hear it from your lying, cheating lips."

I widen my eyes when he reaches for her, wrapping his hands around her arms, forcing her to face him. Although Dad's not nice, he's never laid his hands on her before.

"Colton, you're hurting me." She glances down at his hand and winces. "I have no idea who Ashton is."

Dad's face grows redder, and his jaw pulses, the same way it does when he's about to lay into me for being a pest. "Do you know what this is?" He shakes the piece of paper in her face again.

She stares him straight in the eyes, not even bothering to look at the white sheet. "No."

"I knew that bastard wasn't mine. Had the DNA test to prove it two years ago, but could never figure out who you fucked"—he says that word so loud, she flinches—"until now."

I stand quickly, dropping my toy truck to the carpet, and run toward the kitchen. "You let go of her!" I shout, grabbing at my dad's arm.

His angry gaze slices to me, his teeth showing with his lips curled. "Get the hell away, little asshole." He pushes me with his elbow.

I topple backward, catching myself with my hands before my butt hits the floor. "Don't you touch her!" I yell, climbing to my feet to rescue her.

I have to.

His foot is in the air, connecting with my stomach before I have a chance to straighten. I fly back, my ass landing hard on the tile floor as I gasp for air and tears fill my eyes.

"Don't," she pleads. "I'll tell you whatever you want to know. Just leave him alone."

Tears trickle down my cheeks as I curl into a ball, trying to catch my breath.

No one comes to my rescue.

No one seems to care, not even my mom, that I can't breathe.

"Who is he?"

"He doesn't live here anymore."

"Augusta, so help me God." He raises his hand again, and she flinches.

"He used to deliver our mail."

My father's eyes narrow, and his entire body rocks back like he's the one who's been hit. "You fucked the mailman?"

My mother smirks, holding his angry glare. "Many times," she taunts him. "So, so many times."

"The boy that has my name is the fucking mailman's kid?"

My mother's smirk breaks into a wide smile. "He is."

"And this one?" My father's eyes fall down to her stomach, where my little brother's growing.

"He's yours."

My father wraps his fingers around her neck, and her face turns red. "If I find out this one isn't mine, Augusta…"

Tears trickle down her cheeks. "Please," she gasps, clawing at his fingers. "I can't breathe."

"That one," he snarls, turning toward me, "is nothing. Not to me. Not to you. He's nothing. Do you hear me?"

"He's…"

"He's what?" my father challenges.

"He's my baby."

"He's nothing to you. If you want to keep either of the children, he's nothing to either of us."

I wipe at my face, sniffling as my nose starts to run.

I'm not nothing.

I'm their little boy.

I'm the one Mommy loves the most.

My father moves his head so close to hers, their noses are touching. "So help me God, if you want to keep breathing and for your bastard to live too, you'll do as I say."

"But I can't…"

"You will!" he shouts.

She nods as her eyes find me for a brief moment, and I think everything's going to be okay.

But then he shakes her body, lifting her off the floor by her throat. "I'm not playing with you, Augusta. Don't test me."

Her eyes leave me, and her gaze goes blank. "I swear, Colton," she gasps.

He places her feet back on the floor and releases her neck. *"Traitorous bitch,"* he mumbles and turns to face me. *"Nothing but a no-good bastard."*

I'm a good boy. I always follow the rules and listen to Mommy, careful not to upset my dad. Today, I did nothing wrong, yet he looks angrier with me than he ever has before.

"Mommy," I whisper, lifting my arms, looking for her embrace.

She steps forward, and I smile, thinking she's going to wipe away my sadness and give me the snuggles she's always been so good at giving.

She doesn't reach out for me.

She doesn't even look at me.

She steps forward, grabbing the piece of paper he'd dropped on the floor, and walks out of the room.

"Pike?" Austin whispers.

I sit there unable to move, memories I'd locked down so deep flooding back.

Colton Moore isn't my father.

The news I'd long forgotten crashes over me, leaving me with more questions than answers. I'll never be able to find out why or how. How could she turn her back on me so easily? Sure, she was trying to protect me, but she could've gotten away from Colton and made a new home for us. She could've done anything more than she did.

"Yeah?" I blink, chasing away the tears filling my eyes.

He studies my face, still kneeling in front of our mother's casket. "You okay?"

I nod, not trusting my voice.

"You want to say anything to Mom?"

More than you want to hear.

"Kneel with me," he pleads, motioning toward his side. "I want you here with me."

Austin's the only person besides my grandmother who ever

made me feel wanted in my family. He looked up to me from the time he could talk, always trying to get me to play cars when I was too busy being pissed off at the world.

I move to be at his side because my kid brother deserves my attention.

Austin grasps my hand as soon as I'm next to him. "She wasn't an awful mom all the time, Pike," he comments like he's reading my mind. "Was she?"

I shake my head, choking back the suffocating sadness. "Not always, kid."

I'd blocked out anything good we'd ever had before walking into this room. It was easier never to think about the happy times, the moments where I felt loved, before my father took it all away.

She allowed it to happen.

She didn't fight back.

She didn't try to run.

She gave up on me.

He squeezes my fingers as I take in our mother's pale, serene face. "She loved you, you know."

"I don't know, Aus. It doesn't feel like she ever did."

"She told me," he whispers, even though we're alone. "Sometimes, when Dad wasn't around, she'd talk about you."

My entire body jerks back. "Austin, you don't have to lie to make me feel better. I'm a big guy, and I know exactly how she felt."

He shakes his head, eyes dark and serious but still swimming with tears. "I remember how she treated you, Pike. I was there. I was little, but I saw." He bows his head and gives it a slight shake. "It wasn't right, and I'll never understand why. But sometimes, she'd talk about you like you were everything in the world to her."

"You were everything to her, Austin. Mom adored you. Dad too."

"I'll miss her," he admits sadly. "No one will ever love me as much as she did."

I wish I could say the same, but I can't. I miss the version of my mother that was tucked so deep in my memory, it took seeing her dead body for me to remember.

She's the one I'll miss.

But this shell…the awful woman who turned her back on me, I won't give her a second thought.

"I love you, Austin." I look over at him, placing my hand on top of his. "I'll always love you. I can't replace Mom, but I want you to know you're not alone."

He gives me a halfhearted smile, pulling my hand in front of his and placing them both against the casket. "If she did nothing else right in her life, she gave us each other."

———

"I'm so sorry for your loss," Mrs. Daniels, my high school English teacher, declares as she shakes my hand. "She was a lovely woman."

"Thank you," I repeat for what feels like the hundredth time this afternoon. I'm on autopilot, and my voice is robotic.

"Mrs. D," Austin greets her from my side, taking her hand as soon as she offers it to him.

I take a deep, shaky breath when Gigi grasps my hand. "You're doing great, baby. Just another hour."

I smile at the next person, Mr. Porter, the town butcher. "The town has a hole in it now that your mother's gone, son."

I shake his hand, giving him a fake smile because he must've known a different woman than I did. "Thank you," I repeat.

"She was so selfless and kind."

Augusta Moore was neither selfless nor kind. At least, not to me. But the people of this town see her differently. And no matter how hard I try, I can't wrap my head around any of their compliments.

"I'm sure someone will step into her shoes easily enough, Mr. Porter."

The creases in his forehead deepen as he bristles. "Son, your mother was the biggest donor for our feed the homeless program. She had an especially soft spot for the children, and I don't know how we're going to feed them all without her generosity."

Wait. Hold up.

My mom cared about homeless kids? Everyone in this small town thinks of my mother as a saint. She somehow became the Mother Teresa of Tennessee after I left.

The funeral is supposed to be my closure, but I'm walking away with more questions than I had before.

CHAPTER 7
PIKE

"ARE YOU LEAVING TODAY?" Gran asks as she pours herself a cup of coffee.

"We are."

We're alone. Gigi and Austin are still sleeping, and the sun hasn't even kissed the sky. I didn't sleep at all last night. There was too much on my mind to find even a minute's peace.

Gran walks over to the table, setting down her cup across from me before sitting. "You takin' Austin with you?"

I turn my coffee cup in a circle, wrestling with that same question I've been asking myself all night. "I think so."

"There's no thinking involved, Pike." Granny studies me across the table, tapping her long fingernail against the rim of her mug. "You either are or you aren't. You know that's the right thing to do in your heart."

"Do you know about Ashton?"

Gran sucks in a breath. "That's a name I haven't heard in a while."

"So, you know." I glance down, realizing the only grandmother I've ever had isn't even mine, but she knew.

She knew.

"Baby," she sighs softly, reaching across the table and placing her hand on mine. "Get that thought right out of your head."

I look up, that fullness I felt in my throat yesterday back and stronger than ever.

"You're every bit as much my family as Austin is. You and I have a bond. A bond I've never shared or felt for anyone else except you."

"How long have you known?" I whisper.

She glances down and blinks. "Since you were a little boy. Maybe about six. When I found out about her affair, your mother was pregnant with the baby she lost."

"How do I not remember her losing a baby?"

Granny pats my hand, giving me a sad smile. "You came to stay with me for the week. I told you they went on vacation."

I turn to the window, gazing across the empty pasture. "I remember that."

So much of my childhood is a blur. It's like I blocked everything out, jumbling up events to protect myself from the hurt and anger. There are years missing, events just gone from my memory.

"Your mother would never admit it, but I'm pretty sure your father..." She pauses and grimaces. "I mean, Colton—had something to do with her losing that baby."

"I don't remember, Gran, but I know he'd laid his hands on her before. I saw it with my own eyes."

She shakes her head, twisting her lips as she bows her head. "I don't know how I raised such a rotten bastard."

I reach out, wrapping my fingers around her hand, and wait for her to look at me again. "You did everything you could. You are loving and kind. Sometimes, men are born bad, and no matter what you do, you can't make them into something they're never meant to be."

"You're a wise one, child. Always so wise for your years. You were forced to grow up before you should've. I should've fought harder to bring you home with me. You know I tried for years.

Colton had a fit every time I brought it up. But as you got bigger, he knew he couldn't control you anymore, and only then did he allow me to take you. I wanted you. I wanted to love you like you should've been loved by your parents."

"I'll forever be grateful to you for giving me a home, Gran."

"That's what family does, Pike. Or at least, what they're supposed to do." She reaches into the pocket of her robe, fishing out an envelope and sliding the paper across the table. "I was holding this for the right time and I don't think it'll ever come, but this is as close as I'll get." She taps on the front where my name is written in my mother's handwriting. "Your mother asked me to give this to you if anything ever happened to her. I hope it gives you some peace."

Her hand disappears from the envelope, and she gets up, walking away from the table.

"Gran," I call out, wishing she'd stay.

"Read it, Pike. I'll be on the porch when you're done," she commands without even looking back.

When I flip the envelope over, I can see the back has been torn open. No doubt, Gran already read every word before she decided to give it to me.

I pull out the single sheet of folded paper, my mother's fancy, loopy cursive covering both sides. I unfold the sheet, hold my breath, and start to read.

My Dearest Pike,

I'm sorry.

It's such a simple statement. I wish I had the chance to say these words to your face, but they still need to be said. I was an awful mother and an even worse person for turning my back on you.

I should've been stronger.

I should've fought harder.

For you.

For me.

For us.

I was a coward, too fearful of Colton and too scared to try to run away. A man like him would stop at nothing to find us, making every nightmare I dreamed come true.

Your happiness was the casualty.

The love you deserved was stripped from you, making you shoulder the guilt and blame like you'd done something wrong. I saw the change in you over time.

The hurt.

The anger.

The loneliness you endured due to my fateful decisions.

I love you, son.

I loved you more than you'll ever understand or believe.

The regret I carry with me every day gnaws at my insides, staying with me like an invisible scar.

Colton took one child from me, but I wouldn't let him take you and Austin too.

For that, you were the victim, but I did what I needed to do to keep you alive, hoping I could make amends someday.

As the years passed, you grew distant and hateful, rightfully so. By then, I knew my words would seem hollow, and I left you alone, figuring your hate would be easier for you than the truth.

Colton Moore is not your father.

While you carry his name, you share no blood with the vile man who threatened my children so long ago.

Your father is Ashton Miller, a kind, joyful man who resides a few towns away but has no idea you exist.

Do whatever you want with that information. Hold it close or reach out to him. Finding out he has another child may make him happy, but maybe you've had enough family in your lifetime and don't want to open yourself up to more hurt and rejection.

I wish life could've been different.

I wish I could've been stronger and given you the love you deserved.

At least you have Austin, a boy who's loved you since he took his first breath. His view of you isn't tainted by Colton's hate.

I hope, in my death, you'll embrace your brother and take him under your wing, doing everything you can to protect him from your father or anyone else who would do him harm.

Do not hold my sins against him.

Don't hate the little boy who looks up to you and adores you. He needs you now as much as you need him.

I'm not looking for your forgiveness.

It's too late for that.

I want you to know you are loved.

You were wanted.

But my fear and weakness stopped me from being the mother you deserved.

I hope you find peace and happiness. I wish I could be there to see you as the man you are today. No doubt, strong and hard.

Open your heart to someone.

Let love in. Find peace.

That's my dream for you, my son.

Find the happiness I could never give you.

Love always,

Your Mother

I fold over the sheet of paper and sit there, processing the words as my fingers drift across the black cursive.

The words are nice to read, but they're too late to bring me any solace.

I tuck the note in my pocket, not wanting Austin to find our mother's words. If he found out about Ashton, I'm pretty sure the news would devastate him.

I step outside, and my gran looks up, studying me. "You takin' Austin home?" she asks again, skipping right over the letter.

"I am," I blurt out, not giving myself a chance to overthink the entire situation.

"Good." She smiles and pats the armrest of the chair next to her. "Now sit with this old lady and talk to me. Tomorrow, it's going to be quiet around here."

I ease back into the chair, resting my coffee mug on my knee. "Why don't you come back with us?"

Although I hate this place, I love my grandmother. I should've come home and visited her over the years, but staying away was easier on me. It was the only way I didn't let the bad creep back into my heart.

Absence doesn't make the heart grow fonder, but it sure has allowed me to pretend like my past never happened.

"Don't be silly." She waves me off. "I love it here. There's nowhere else I'd rather live. But make this old woman a promise."

"Anything."

"Don't stay gone so long this time."

"I was an asshole, Gran."

She nods. "You were, but that's in the past. I don't think I have another ten years left either. Maybe I can see you at Christmas."

"Why don't you come to Florida? The weather's great that time of year. I can show you where I work and live. Show you the life I've built for myself."

She smiles again. "I'd love that."

Austin strolls outside, scratching his bare chest as he stretches. "Did I hear Christmas?" he stutters through a yawn.

"You did. I was just talking to your brother about visiting you both for Christmas this year."

Austin's eyes snap to mine. "Visiting us both?" He raises his eyebrows. "I'm coming with you?"

I nod. "But only if you want to."

He fist-pumps the air, letting out a loud howl. "Hell yeah! Beaches. Babes. Why wouldn't I want to come with you?"

I don't want to burst his bubble, but I live nowhere near beaches, and the babes... Well, they're pretty much like the chicks in Tennessee. "Don't know," I admit.

He'll learn soon enough that the romanticized version of Florida isn't reality.

He starts to walk back toward the door, moving faster than he did when he strolled out. "I'm going to pack." Before he reaches for the handle, he leans down, planting a kiss on Granny's cheek. "I'll miss you, Gran."

"Mm-hm," she mumbles, smiling up at her grandson. "You seem devastated at the news."

"But you're coming for Christmas, right?" he asks.

She nods at him. "I'll be there with my bikini."

He grimaces. "Let's not get crazy, Gran."

She chuckles, shooing him inside, and then turns her gaze toward me. "You're doing right, Pike. I'm proud of you."

I relax back into the chair again. "I don't know about that, but I figure I can't mess him up more than his parents already did."

"And Ashton?" she asks, finally getting to the letter she gave me.

"He doesn't know about me, and I think it's best it stays that way."

She gives me a slow nod, twisting her lips like she wants to give me her opinion, but she won't. "That's your call."

"I know." I take a deep breath, pushing off the chair, needing to get my ass moving. "I better get my girl up so we can hit the road."

Gran's on her feet, arms around my middle before I can make a move toward the door. "I like your girl, Pike. She's good for you. A little high-maintenance, but sweet as apple pie." Her eyes twinkle as she whispers, "You hold on to that one."

I wrap my arms around her, leaning forward to kiss her forehead. "I have every intention of keeping her, Gran."

"That's my boy. Now, scoot. I have lunch with the ladies from church."

"Gran, what do you want to do about Da—" I stop myself, remembering he's not my father. "What do you want to do about Colton?"

She reaches up, cupping my cheek in her small hand. "Nothing, son. Leave him be. He made his bed. Now, it's time he lies in it."

"You know how he was arrested?"

She shakes her head, dropping her hand from my face.

"He attacked Gigi in her apartment. We live next door to each other. I can't figure out why he did it."

"That's something you'll have to ask him. I stopped trying to figure him out a long time ago."

I'm not sure anyone will ever understand Colton Moore. All I know is he's not worth my time or energy.

He's nothing to me.

CHAPTER 8
GIGI

"ARE YOU READY FOR THIS?" Pike asks as we sit in my grandmother's driveway with Austin in the backseat, headphones in his ears.

"You think my dad's going to lose it?" I know the answer, but I ask him anyway.

Of course Joe Gallo's going to go off the rails. It's something he does often, and I still haven't gotten used to it.

Pike gives me a forced smile. "I don't know."

I look over my shoulder at Austin and wince. "I know my dad, and he's not easygoing, ya know? He's going to freak out."

Pike laughs, rubbing his forehead.

I cover my face with my hands and groan. "Maybe we should go."

Pike pulls my hand away from my cheeks. "We have to face him sometime. We can't hide Austin forever."

"What about me?" Austin asks, scooting forward and sticking his face between us. "Where are we?" He looks through the windshield, taking in my grandparents' house. "Whoa. Someone hit the mother lode."

Pike turns his upper body so he's face-to-face with Austin. "This is her grandparents' house. I expect you to be on your best behavior. You understand?"

Austin gives him a lopsided smile, throwing up his hands. "Chill, bro. I'm not a little kid. I know how to act around old people."

I glance toward the ceiling of the truck, knowing this is one giant mistake. "Oh Lord."

"So help me God, if you embarrass me…" Pike's sounding more like a parent than I ever imagined.

It's cute, even.

Austin cocks his head, scrunching up his face. "You need to relax a little. I'll behave. I can charm the pants off almost anyone." He gives Pike a smirk followed by that damn wink.

I bite my lip and shake my head. "Clusterfuck," I mutter to myself.

Pike squeezes my hand, giving me a small smile. "It'll be fine, darlin'."

Austin takes out his earbuds, winding them around his phone, eyes flickering between the two of us. "What's the problem? You two are tense as shit."

"My father's the problem." I turn to look at Austin. "He's not happy about Pike, and now…"

"I'm the bonus prize no one wanted?" Austin raises an eyebrow, his voice filled with sadness.

I frown, hating for him to feel like he's unwanted. "You're wanted. You're just a giant surprise."

"He'll love me," Austin brags, puffing out his chest like he's the shit, his emotions all over the place. "Everyone loves me."

"Let's get it over with. We can sit here all day and talk about how your dad's going to react, or we can go inside and let the chips fall where they may."

Austin reaches for the handle and climbs down from the truck. "Don't worry. We'll be BFFs before the end of the day," he promises.

I'm out of my seat, following him up the driveway, jumping in front of him before he has a chance to knock. I turn to face him, blocking the door with my body. "Listen, I know this is all new for you, but this is important. This is make it or break it time. You understand?"

Austin turns his baseball cap backward and then pounds on his chest with one fist. "I'm bringing my A game, sis."

I roll my eyes. *This kid.* He reminds me of every cocky jock I was ever around in high school, loving himself and thinking he's God's gift to the entire world.

"Don't worry. He'll behave." Pike gives Austin that don't-be-an-asshole look I've seen my father throw my way more than a few times.

We walk in, Pike and Austin behind me, and I hold my breath, knowing there's going to be a shitstorm of questions hurled in our direction.

I'm not even five feet into the foyer when I catch my father's eye. He's sitting in the living room with a clear line of sight to the front door. He sat there on purpose, waiting for us to walk through so he could give Pike the stink-eye.

Typical.

My dad moves his eyes from my face to Pike, and then they land on Austin. He's out of his seat, stalking toward us, jaw set tight, eyes narrowed.

Oh boy.

"Sweetheart," my mother says, stepping right in my father's path and coming out of nowhere. She's like a ninja. He's plastered against her back, glaring at Pike like he just robbed a bank or some shit.

"Hey, Mom." I grab her quickly, hugging her, and throwing my father's glare right back. "I missed you."

"Who's the young, handsome devil with your handsome devil?" she whispers with a giggle.

I release her and glance over my shoulder. "That's Austin, Pike's brother."

"Oh." Mom's body stiffens before she releases me and goes right to him. "My poor baby," Mom says, holding out her arms to Austin like he's one of her own. "I'm Suzy. Gigi's mom."

Austin looks a little freaked out as my mom grabs him and squeezes tightly. "Ma'am," he squeaks, losing his badass edge pretty quick.

"Are you okay?" she asks him.

My mom worries about everyone, and it's totally adorable when it's not aimed at me.

I turn back around, letting my mom do her thing, and bring my gaze back to my father. His body is stiff, arms straight, hands in tight balls at his sides. Is he pissed off? For sure.

I cross my arms, dropping my shoulder, and cock my head, throwing the vibe right back at him. *Whatcha going to say now, big guy?* I raise an eyebrow, waiting for him to open his mouth, but he just tightens his jaw and swallows whatever angry words are sitting on his tongue.

"After the funeral," I say, reminding him that the two men behind me just lost their mother, "Pike felt it was best to bring Austin home for his last year of high school. Family first, right?" I throw his own words right in his face, but I do it with a hint of a smile.

Suck on that, Dad.

"We're so happy you're here," Mom tells Austin. "Family is the most important thing to us, and you're just in time for Sunday dinner. I hope you're hungry."

"I'm starving." Austin rubs his stomach. "Pike's fridge didn't have much in it that was edible."

"I wasn't expecting company," Pike mumbles as he grabs my hand, ignoring my father's angry presence. "You okay?"

I nod. "You?"

"Great," he replies, but not in a way that's convincing at all.

"What's going on out there?" My grandma's voice comes from the kitchen.

"We have an extra guest," Mom calls out, and within three seconds, my grandma is in the foyer, pushing my father out of the way.

"The more, the merrier." Grandma eyes Austin and then looks at Pike. "I can see the resemblance. They build them cute up there in Tennessee."

"Gram," I groan, covering my face in embarrassment.

She touches my cheek, looking at me with nothing but joy. "Sweetie, I'm old, not dead. Guess who's back?" she says to me, holding on to my shoulder.

"Who?" I glance around, seeing no one out of the ordinary besides Austin.

"Tamara and Lily finally came home for summer break." She pitches her thumb over her shoulder toward the lanai. "They're out by the pool."

My eyes widen, and for the first time in days, I'm freaking excited. I've missed Tamara since she wouldn't leave her shit-in-the-pants boyfriend behind, and Lily... I haven't seen her in what feels like forever.

"Can I talk with you?" My father motions toward my grandfather's study, killing all my joy. "Alone," he adds.

I squeeze Pike's hand, trying to smile. "Give us ten. If I'm not out, send in a search party. One of us might not come out alive."

"I'm sorry." Pike blows out a breath, glancing at my father over my shoulder. "This is all my fault."

"It's not your fault. *Stop*. I'll handle my daddy. Trust me." I brush my lips against his before turning around to face a very angry Joe Gallo. "Let's go, Dad," I demand, walking toward the study without even waiting for him.

"Joseph," my mother warns, trying to come to my aid and throwing out his full name like he's about to be in trouble.

"Giovanna."

Ah. He's busting out my full name. That means shit is serious. "Yes, Dad?" I fold my arms again, throwing him all kinds of shade as he closes the doors to the study.

He blows out a loud breath, scrubbing his face with his hands. "Do you really think being involved with a man who has a criminal family and is now in charge of a kid is something you should be getting into in your life right now?"

"Are you for real right now?" I bite out, dropping a shoulder.

He mimics me and crosses his arms too. "As real as you're gonna get."

"So..." I grit my teeth, staring him down. "Pike's father is an asshole, and his mother's dead. None of which Pike was involved in. The kid out there—" I point toward the foyer "—who's seventeen, by the way, has no parents left. What's Pike supposed to do?" I throw up my hands, exasperated. "Just leave him behind to fend for himself?"

My father glances up toward the ceiling as his jaw ticks. "Of course not. Pike did what any man should do in that situation. My issue isn't with what he does in his life. My issue is the choices you're making in your life."

I laugh, putting my hands on my hips. "How old am I?"

"Twenty-two."

"So, I'm an adult, yeah?"

His eyes flash with anger. He knows where I'm going and that I'm right. Lord, the man hates being wrong. "Of course, but I'll never stop being your father."

"Then you should support me instead of getting pissed when I don't do what you want. You know what you've always told me?"

His shoulders slump. He knows I've stored away every word he's ever spoken for moments like this. "What?" he growls.

"You told me to be strong and be my own person. To follow my heart and never let anyone lead me astray. You taught me, hammering it into my head, that family is the most important thing in the world. We stick by one another no matter what bad shit happens and never turn our back on someone in need."

He raises his chin. "You sure I said all that?"

I nod. "I could go on if you'd like."

He shakes his head and throws up his hands. "Damn it. I wanted something different for you."

"Different?" I arch an eyebrow, challenging him. "Different from what?"

"I wanted your life to be simple and filled with nothing but happiness."

"News flash, Dad, I am happy."

He rolls his shoulder and moves his neck from side to side, grunting. "But this isn't simple. Let me remind you what hasn't been simple."

I roll my eyes. *Here we go.*

"Pike's been arrested and taken to FBI headquarters to be questioned—"

"For something he didn't do," I interrupt.

He holds out his hand to silence me. "He, along with you, sweetheart, was forced into hiding."

"They weren't looking for me."

Again, he gives me the hand. "Men shot up the compound, and from what I hear, Pike put a bullet in a man's head."

I grimace. "He saved our lives," I tell him, because fuck him and this conversation.

That goddamn palm is back up as he continues talking. "Pike's mom gets assassinated somewhere in there."

"Again, not Pike's fault."

He bristles. "Then, you come home, and Pike's father is in your apartment and tries to kill you."

I blow out a breath, squaring my shoulders. "Pike saved me."

"If it weren't for fucking Pike, you wouldn't have needed saving."

I flinch because my father rarely swears at me, but he just dropped a doozy. "This isn't his fault," I groan.

"And now…" He steps forward, dropping his voice. "You come home from his mother's funeral with a teenager in tow."

"Family first, Daddy."

He crosses his arms again, clearly not amused by my words. "Are you going to be a stepmom at twenty-two, Giovanna?"

I shrug. "Austin doesn't need a mom. He needs a friend and to know that there are still people who care about him. Maybe—" I glare at him. "Maybe instead of making him feel unwelcome, you should get to know the kid whose mother was just murdered while he was in the room."

My father's body jerks. "He was in the room?"

I nod. "They knocked him out, but when he woke up, he found her body."

My father sucks in air between his teeth. "Damn."

"Uh, yeah."

He rubs the back of his neck, head bent toward the floor. "I can't imagine."

"So, instead of being Mr. Judgy McJudgerson, maybe you should try to find out what happened before you fly off the handle first."

"I feel bad for the kid, but I still don't approve of your relationship with Pike."

I step forward, getting right in my dad's face. "Do you hate that I fell in love with a man who's exactly like you?"

"He's nothing like me," my father snaps.

I throw my head back and laugh. "He's so much like you, I should probably get my head examined. I love Pike for all the same reasons I love you, damn it."

"Just don't do something stupid like run off and get married. You two are still so new. It's already complicated enough with Austin. I don't want you to get your heart broken again, baby."

"Dad, we eloped in Tennessee." It's a lie, but I figure he deserves it now.

"What?" His eyes widen, and all the color drains from his face.

"I'm kidding," I snort, putting him out of his misery when, really, I should let him suffer longer.

The vein down the middle of my dad's forehead bulges. "That's not funny."

"It was to me." I smile. "Pike's a really great guy, Dad. You liked him a lot before the bad shit went down. You even pushed me to be friends with him, remember?" I nudge him with my shoulder.

He mumbles under his breath before he clears his throat. "I was an idiot."

"No. *Now* you're being an idiot," I correct him, resting my hand on his bulky forearm. "Be nice to Pike and Austin. They could really use some friends right about now, Daddy."

"Sweetie." My mom's voice comes from the other side of the door before her knock.

"Yeah, sugar?" Dad moves his gaze toward the door, and I use the moment to relax because this has been freaking exhausting.

Mom opens the door, looking between us. "Come out and spend time with the family. Your mother is asking for Gigi, and she told me to tell you to leave the child alone already."

I smirk, but I quickly sober when my father glances at me. "We're done, Mom," I tell her, shutting down the conversation, whether he likes it or not.

She motions toward the door, excusing me. "Give us a minute alone, Gigi."

I nod, smiling at my dad as I close the door behind me.

You're in so much trouble, Daddy.

Someone's going to get their ass chewed out, and for once, it isn't me.

CHAPTER 9
PIKE

"YOU'VE HAD a rough few days. Poor baby," Fran says, kneading my shoulders as she stands behind me. "I'll make you feel better."

The woman is harmless.

Her husband, however, is not.

"Fran, get your hands off that boy," Bear growls, eyes locked on her from across the table, looking like he's about to drag her out of the room. "He doesn't need some old lady pawing at him."

Her fingers push harder, working my stiff shoulders like a pro. "You love when I do this for you," she tells him, earning herself a slow headshake from Bear.

He cocks an eyebrow, and his jaw tenses. "He has his own woman to do that."

Gigi stalks into the kitchen, shaking her head as soon as she sees Fran's hands on me. "Aunt Fran, you just can't keep your hands to yourself, can you?"

"You takin' over?" Fran asks Gigi.

Gigi glances down at me and winks but looks up at Fran a moment later. "I was going to see Lily and Tamara, but if your hands are tired, I will."

Well, there went my rescue.

"I'm good, doll. I can do this all day."

I can just imagine the shit-eating smirk on Fran's face as she said those words. And based on the scowl on Bear's face, I'm not far off.

"I could use some air." I pat Fran's hand on my shoulder as I push back from the table, finding a way out.

"I'll be waiting if you need another rubdown." Fran winks at me, and my face instantly heats.

"Like hell you will, woman. Get over here and give me those lips." Bear taps his leg, and Fran moves around the table, doing as she's told. "Good girl," he says, rewarding her with a deep kiss as soon as she's firmly planted in his lap.

"How'd it go?" I ask Gigi, pulling her off to the side before she can sneak out to the patio with her cousins.

"Fine." She rolls her eyes. "You know how he is, but I think we made headway."

"You made headway, or he did?"

"We did." She shrugs and snickers. "Well, I did."

I look over her shoulder, watching as her father stalks through the living room, clearly not happy. "Maybe I should talk to him."

She slides her hand up my chest, resting her palm on my shoulder, drawing my attention back to her. "Don't do that. I really took care of everything."

I'm sure she thinks she did, but I need to have another man-to-man talk with her father. This shit needs to end. "Thanks, darlin'," I tell her, brushing my lips lightly against hers.

"Where's Austin?" she asks, all sugary-sweet and totally trying to change the subject.

I shift my gaze toward the pool, catching sight of the Casanova lying between the two girls. "He's outside with your cousins."

"Shoot," she grumbles and shakes her head. "He better not get any ideas."

I laugh. "He's seventeen. All he has are ideas."

She chuckles, pushing me away before dashing out the door.

"Gigi!" The two women run toward her, almost knocking her off her feet as they hug.

Austin's eyes find mine, and I mouth *behave* before sliding the door closed again, leaving them be.

"Pike, can we talk?" James asks.

I nearly jump out of my skin because the man just appeared out of nowhere. "What's up?" I try to sound casual, like he didn't just scare the living shit out of me.

He motions toward the dining room and waits for me to make the first move, lifting an eyebrow like he's talking in code. "I have some news," he blurts out.

James always has news. The man never stops digging, and with all his contacts in the legal and criminal worlds, I'm sure he always has something crossing his desk.

"Thomas, you comin'?" James yells across the room to where Thomas is watching the Cubs game with the other guys.

I barely have my ass in the dining chair before James starts to speak. "Your father was arraigned two days ago. No bail, so he's going to be behind bars until his trial."

I place my palms on top of the table, trying to be relaxed, but happy as freaking fuck. "More than one charge, I hope?"

James nods. "So many, but the biggest are money laundering, conspiracy, attempted murder, and murder."

I raise my eyebrows. "Murder?"

"He killed a man back in Tennessee before stealing his car and heading here," James replies before blowing out a long breath.

"He's a heartless SOB," I mutter, but this is Colton Moore, and he's always been cold-blooded.

"That he is," Thomas agrees, resting his hand on my shoulder like I need comfort.

"We haven't been able to find out why he was in Gigi's apartment or why he came to Florida. We're sure it has something to do with you, but we haven't pieced it together yet."

"Maybe he wanted to kill me too." I shrug. Anything's possible, especially when it comes to him.

Thomas takes a step back, crossing his arms as he studies me. "Maybe he thought he was in your apartment."

"It's possible." I nod.

James pulls out the chair at the head of the table and sits. "I got word from Tiny and Morris. They're headed this way for business."

"Okay," I draw out, leaning forward and thinking there has to be something more to the story because there always is.

James glances at Thomas briefly before he explains, "They'll want to see you. They know you were at your mother's funeral. They held off on coming to this coast until they knew you'd be back. Should be here in a few days."

I nod, always happy to see the guys, especially since they saved our asses without asking for anything in return. "I'm sure Morris will reach out."

James rests his hands on the table and pushes back, straightening his shoulders. "They're going to ask for payback," he tells me, like his words aren't a big fucking deal.

And they are…they're a *huge* fucking deal.

"Payback for what?" I ask, looking between James and Thomas.

"They lost a lot in that gunfight with DiSantis's men. They're going to want something for that."

I squeeze my hands together, not liking the sound of this. How could they willingly come to my rescue, pretending to be my friend, and then ask for something in return? "What's their price?"

James throws up his hands as he shrugs, not looking rattled in the least. "Fuck if I know, but I'm sure it's going to be big."

"I don't have jack to my name," I admit, and I don't. I have enough to live, but by no means do I have a pile of money sitting in the bank for moments like this.

Thomas laughs, shaking his head at me like I'm an idiot. "They don't want money. They'll want a favor. When they ask, if they ask you and not us, talk to us before you give them an answer. Got it?"

I cross my arms over my chest, trying not to take offense. "Didn't know I had to run my life decisions by you two."

I know I'm an idiot. I shouldn't be smarting off to the two guys who have saved my ass more times than anyone else ever has in my life.

"Pike." Thomas leans over the table, crowding my space. "You lived with these guys. You know how they operate. You want a cell right next to your pops?"

I shake my head, gritting my teeth. "No," I growl, keeping my eyes on James and not the scary-as-fuck guy looming over me.

"Then talk to us before you make a move," Thomas whispers so quietly, the hairs on my arm stand up like even they want to get away from him.

"What's wrong?" Izzy's in the doorway to the dining room, gaze sweeping between the three of us. "You three together never means good things."

"What's happening?" Joe questions, coming to stand behind her, eyes flickering around the room just like his sister.

Fucking great. I rub my temples, wishing this family weren't so far up one another's asses all the time. Don't get me wrong. It's nice…sometimes. But other times, moments like this, it's all just too much.

James slides out of his chair and moves toward his wife, trying to usher her out of the room. "Nothing's going on. Just having a chat with the kid."

Joe stalks in and sits in the chair James just vacated. "Can I talk to Pike alone?" His ice-cold eyes never leave mine.

"You two going to be okay in here?" Izzy asks, always looking out for everyone. She's such a ballbuster, but the woman has a good heart.

"We'll be fine," Joe answers for us both, waiting for them to leave, eyes still burning with anger.

"I'm sorry," I blurt as soon as we're alone. "I shouldn't have brought Austin here."

Joe slowly rubs his hands together, grinding his teeth like he's almost choking on whatever he's about to tell me. "I talked to Gigi, and she really laid into me about how I feel about you and how I talk to you."

I raise both my eyebrows, but I don't move another muscle. "Yeah?"

"Yeah." He moves his hand to his face as he passes his fingertips across the stubble of his jaw. "It wasn't pretty, but she reminded me of a few things. Listen..." He pauses, swallowing down what I assume is his pride. "Ever since I found out about you being with my daughter, I haven't been nice to you. I have to keep reminding myself that she's not a little girl anymore."

I give him a halfhearted smile. "She reminds me of that every day."

It's his turn to raise his eyebrows.

"I mean, she keeps telling me she can do whatever she wants. She sure as hell doesn't listen to me," I add.

"I taught her to be strong and independent. I also taught her about loyalty and love."

"Your daughter is truly the most spectacular woman I've ever met, Joe. She's everything," I admit.

"I'm going to back off, but if you fuck up—" he points at me "—don't think I won't kick your ass," he threatens, scratching at his face like he's having an allergic reaction to the entire conversation.

"You can try," I tease, winking at him, hoping to get back to the easy relationship we had when I first started at Inked.

He doesn't even crack a smile. "Now, about your brother."

Here we go.

"We could use some help at Inked. We need someone to run the front desk. I realize he can't work late once school starts, but maybe he can work a few hours in the evenings and on the weekends."

All I can do is blink.

"You'll be able to keep an eye on him, and he'll get to know the rest of us."

Who is this man? I don't know what Gigi said to him in their little chat, but whatever it was, it must've been a freaking killer.

I blink again, waiting for him to say he's totally fucking with me. "You really want him to work at Inked? I mean, he may be a total shit human being."

His eyes don't even twitch as he asks, "He's your brother, yeah?"

I nod slowly because he is, but… "He's my family, and now that our parents can't raise him, he's fallen on to me and is my responsibility. But I barely know the kid, Joe. Like I said, he could be a total fuckup."

"Are you serious, bro?" Austin thunders, standing just a few feet away, listening to our private conversation. "I'm just a responsibility?"

Fuck. I rush from my seat, trying to get to him, but he's already on the move.

"You know what, fuck you!" he shouts, and everyone in the room flinches. He waves his hand around the room toward Gigi's family. "And fuck them!"

The wide-eyed looks from every Gallo make my stomach turn. They've been nothing but kind and don't deserve this shit.

"Austin, watch your mouth," I grit out, trying to get my hands on him, but he's too damn fast.

The little shit dodges to the right, stalking toward the front door. "I'm out of here. I don't want to be a burden to anyone, especially my own flesh and blood," he rages before storming out the front door, slamming it so damn hard, the photos on the walls rattle.

Before I can chase after him, a hand is on my shoulder, stopping me. "I'll go talk to him," Tamara offers, looking up at me with a sad smile. "He needs some time to cool off. That's all. It'll be okay."

I nod, knowing he's not going to listen to me right now. If I were in his shoes, I wouldn't listen to me either. I fucked up. I didn't mean for my words to come out that way, and I sure as fuck didn't expect for him to hear them.

"I'm so sorry," I say, looking around the room at the people who've been nothing but nice, making me feel welcome.

Gigi's at my side, wrapping her arm around me and placing a hand on my chest. "It's all going to be okay," she says softly and so damn sweetly.

"Pike." Joe motions for me to come back to the scene of the emotional crime, but there's a different look in his eyes. It's not murder or hate, but...understanding and sadness?

I move toward him, but Gigi stays with me, watching her father, assuming he's going to pull the asshole card.

Joe rubs the back of his neck, eyeballing his daughter before glancing at me. "I've dealt with a lot of teenagers in my life. Sure as hell dealt with emotional ones too. Have three girls, and you'll know the sheer and utter chaos they create." He gives me a smile. "Your brother's going through some shit. Your words hurt him. Let him cool off and he'll come back, but you need to make sure he knows exactly how you feel. Don't hold back, and don't give him enough rope to hang himself either. Be firm yet kind. What happened here can never happen again."

I nod, feeling the knot in my stomach grow tighter. "I know. I'm sorry."

"Don't apologize for him. You did nothing wrong, son."

Son. I blink. Did Joe Gallo just call me son? No one, and I mean no one, has ever called me that. Not even Colton Moore. It was always some mix of bastard and fucker with a few other slurs thrown in to remind me what an insignificant piece of shit I really was. But here, in this moment, with this man who isn't my biggest fan...he called me son.

I swallow, somehow finding my words. "How long do I give him?" I croak, trying to keep the emotion from my voice. Because... *it's just a word, dumbass.*

"Let him come to you." Joe ticks his head toward the dining room where we'd just been sitting.

"Let's eat, have a drink, and wait him out. Tamara will bring him back."

"What if he doesn't come back?"

Joe laughs, slapping me on the shoulder. "Where the hell's he going to go? We're in the middle of nowhere with nothing for miles except bugs and trees."

Gigi tugs at my hand, drawing my attention away from her father as he walks away, leaving us alone. "What set him off? He was just outside flirting with the girls, and then that." She waves her hand toward the door, wrinkling her nose.

I glance down at my feet and shake my head. "I fucked up."

"I can see that." She moves in front of me, touching my face with her fingertips, making me look at her. "But how?"

"I said dumb shit like I always do, but this time, he heard me."

She grimaces. "Stop being so hard on yourself. We all mess up sometimes. I'm sure once he calms down, you'll be able to explain."

I close my eyes, leaning my head forward until our foreheads touch. "Your family has to hate him."

Gigi snorts and pulls away from me so I can see her. "Please, temper tantrums are nothing new around here. He may have used a little bit more colorful language than usual, but it'll be just a distant memory in a few weeks."

I force a smile on to my face, but it's totally fake. "Yeah. Maybe."

"Hey." She bumps my shoulder, probably feeling my *I don't believe a word you're saying* vibe. "My family knows he just lost his mom and his father too. That has to be weighing pretty heavy on him. I'm sure I'd be a complete asshole if I were in his shoes."

I shake my head, drawing in the longest, deepest breath, trying to calm myself. "You're right," I tell her, which gets me an eyebrow raise.

"Can you say that again?" she asks, a crooked smile crossing her face.

"Why?"

She pulls her phone from her back pocket, shaking it in my face. "I want to get that for posterity."

Fuck me. This chick.

CHAPTER 10
GIGI

"I'M GOING TO CHOKE HIM." Pike runs his fingers through his hair as he hunches over his legs while we sit on the couch in his living room. "I swear to God…"

"Stop." I rub his back, rolling my eyes. "They're on their way back. It's not *that* big of a deal."

Austin wasn't the first person to throw a fit and storm out of my grandparents' house. Lord knows he isn't going to be the last. There isn't a person in my family who isn't overdramatic, and Austin seemed to fit right in within the first hour.

Pike lifts his head, eyes blazing. "Not that big of a deal?"

I push his face back toward the floor. "He's a teenager. They do this stuff all the time. I'm sure you did too."

Pike grunts, his back muscles tensing under my fingertips. "Not if you didn't want to get your ass beat."

The frown on my lips is immediate. "Promise me you're not going to hit him."

His eyes are back on me, neck craned, those beautiful brown eyebrows drawn inward. "Do you seriously think I'd hit him?"

My shrug is barely there, but Pike catches it. I grimace and try to make up for it by saying, "Never."

Pike straightens as my hand falls down to the couch near his ass. "Listen, darlin', and listen good."

I nod when he pauses, straightening my back too because I know this is going to be a short but deep conversation.

"I have never put my hands on anyone in my family. I will never put my hands on my brother." He squeezes my hands in his. "Even if the little fucker hits me first, I'll never lay a hand on him."

"I believe you," I confess because I've never seen Pike be physically menacing to anyone unless he hated them and they totally deserved the anger.

"I'd never touch you either. You could stab me in the thigh with a butter knife." I wince because who the fuck would do that, but he just keeps on talking. "There isn't anything you could do to make me hurt you."

"I know." The man would and almost did take a bullet for me. He's never, even when I've been a complete asshole, shown any type of anger or hostility toward me that's caused me to so much as flinch. He's always sweet in that Pike kind of way.

A few of his fingers brush the hair away from my cheek as his eyes search mine. "I need you to know what I'm saying is true. Never. Never. Never would I lay a hand on you. I'm not built that way."

"I know," I repeat, and I'm being one-hundred-percent truthful, but the look in his eyes tells me he's not believing a single word.

"No. You need to believe what I'm saying. I saw too much bad shit in my life." He shakes his head, pain all over his face. "I'd never want that type of shit to touch you. There's nothing worse than a person you love laying their hands on you in anger, making you not only feel the pain of the strike, but the bite of their words."

My stomach clenches. "Pike," I whisper, moving my cheek into his touch. "I know with everything I am, you'll never hurt me. I promise." I place my hand over his. "I can't imagine what you went through as a kid, and I never want you to feel that way again."

"In ten years, I've never allowed anyone close enough to me to give me that kind of hurt." His eyes sweep across my face as he traces the edge of my chin with his thumb. "Only you, Gigi."

"Only me?" My mouth hangs open. *Only me.* That's a pretty damn big deal. Pike isn't the first man I've let get close to me. I have two assholes in my past and the scars from the horrific end to those relationships to prove it too.

He nods ever so slightly. "I never wanted to give anyone that power over me. I swore I'd never let anyone else in, but you..." His voice trails off.

I lock on to those green eyes that first captured my attention. "I'm glad you let me in," I whisper.

The door creaks open, and neither of us moves. "Stay calm," I mouth to him with my back to the door, seeing the vein in his neck start to pulse.

A second later, Pike swings his gaze to the front door, and his fingers tighten near my neck. Two distinct sets of footsteps stomp on the tile, followed by two different giggles.

"Hey, bro," Austin barks before laughing again. "Sup?"

"Aussie, what'd I tell you about how to talk to him?" Tamara chastises him, slurring her words a bit.

I close my eyes and count to five, knowing when I turn around, I'm not going to like what I see.

How do I know? Pike's about as hard as a piece of granite and barely breathing.

"I love when you call me that," Austin tells Tamara before there's a loud *umph* and my body dips from the weight.

Pike follows the movement with his eyes, looking over my shoulder like every promise and word he just said is about to go right out the window.

Uh oh.

"You can sit here, TamTam," Austin offers playfully, and I hear the sound of his hand slapping something.

"Do *not* sit on his lap," Pike growls, his eyes narrowing but not moving from his brother.

"When did Mr. Badass Biker dude turn into such a party pooper?" Tamara teases, her shadow covering me as she stands somewhere behind my back.

"Calm down, big guy." Austin snorts. "We're just having fun, and Tam's my new BFF."

I close my eyes again, trying not to lose my shit because if we both do...it's game over.

"Actually, she's my only friend."

"When school starts, all the girls are going to be all over you, Aussie. You're going to have to fight them off," Tamara tells him.

I let out a sigh, turning to find my cousin leaning her hip against the couch just above Austin as he kicks back, one ankle resting on the knee of his other leg. "A guy can dream, TamTam," he mutters.

What. The. Fuck?

Five hours ago, these two didn't even know each other. Now... now, they have cute nicknames for each other?

TamTam and Aussie.

Puke.

My gaze travels up Tamara's body and lands on her flushed cheeks from too much sun and... "Have you been drinking?"

Tamara shrugs, unable to hide her lopsided smile. "We may have grabbed a few twenty-fours."

My eyes widen, darting from Tamara to Austin. "What the hell? You're both underage."

Tamara taps her purse slung over her shoulder. "I still have my ID from Daytona." She winks.

I glance toward the ceiling and mutter, "Dear God," before sucking in a breath. I'm going to lose my shit. "He's in high school, Tam. High school!" I glare at her.

She wrinkles her nose, leering at me. "Hey, Ms. Prude. I know you had a hell of a lot more than a twenty-four or two when you were his age—or mine, for that matter." She throws her chin at Pike, and I know she's talking about *that night*. "Hypocrite much?"

Oh. My. God.

I suddenly sounded like my father or mother. Take your pick. They were both the same when it came to underage drinking and partying. But now the words are coming out of my mouth about a kid who isn't even my own. I shake my head, trying to remember I'm not the mom of these two assholes. "I'm not a hypocrite."

"You so are," she argues with a smug grin as she rests her bent arm on Austin's shoulder. "Never thought I'd see the day you'd turn into Suzy."

Pike's hand is on my leg, squeezing tight enough to draw my attention away from the giggling idiots. "Let it go," he says softly. "Just let it go."

Tamara moves, wedging herself between my back and Austin's side. "What are we going to do tonight?" she asks like nothing happened earlier and it's just another day.

"We're going home," I tell her, leering over my shoulder at her.

Her eyes widen, and she jerks her head back. "The party's just getting started, li'l cuz. What's at home besides *nothing?*"

She has a point. I still hadn't had time to buy any furniture. Hell, there isn't even a spoon or a coffee cup in the kitchen. Everything is in my parents' garage, waiting to be picked up. Well, not everything. I still have to buy things. So many things too. But who has time to shop when death and mayhem are falling all around? Not this girl.

"Fine, I'm taking you to your parents', then," I demand, pushing her away from me when I try to stand.

But I don't make it to my feet before Pike's hand is around my wrist, pulling me back onto the couch. "Stay here tonight."

I blink. "Here?" I repeat.

"Please," he begs.

"I have Tam to consider."

"So? I have Austin."

"Sleepover!" Tamara shouts, fist-pumping the air.

Austin nods with a smug grin I wish I could wipe right off his face. "Nothing sounds better."

Sweet Jesus. Nothing about this sounds like a good idea. "I don't think…" I mutter.

"I'll feel safer if you're here," Pike says, cutting me off as I snap my lips shut because I feel safer here too.

"Pike," I breathe.

"I need you here tonight," Pike admits, his eyes pleading with me to say yes.

"Ew," Tamara gags. "I don't want to listen to you two bumping uglies all night."

I shoot my cousin a death look. "You better shut it before I shut it for you."

She sticks out her tongue, proving we're never too old to act like immature kids. "Whatever," she mutters, snuggling a little too close to Austin.

"You like wearing orange?" I snap at her.

She wrinkles that cute-ass nose on her beautiful face. "I hate it, but it looks great with my complexion."

There isn't a color that looks bad on her with her deep olive skin, a perfect mix of her Italian father and African American mother. She looks perpetually suntanned, while I, thanks to my fair-skinned blond mother, don't.

"If you keep touching him, you're going to wind up behind bars since he's seventeen."

Austin throws his arm around Tamara. "Nah, babe. I checked the laws. We're good."

Tamara's gaze slowly slides to Austin. "It's never happening, kid."

Austin shrugs. "I can wait a year."

Tamara smacks his chest, giggling again because she's drunk and an idiot. "You're such an asshole."

"Stay here so I don't murder him," Pike whispers, his mouth right next to my ear.

I giggle, sounding just like my moronic cousin, and turn my head so our lips are almost touching. "Don't worry. She likes her men a bit older, baby." I waggle my eyebrows because by older, I mean *older*. "She's just being a pain in the ass."

"Tamara can take the spare." Pike frowns, catching himself because we all know it's not spare anymore. "I mean Austin's room, and Austin can sleep on the couch."

"And Gigi?" Austin asks, raising an eyebrow, chin lifted, just trying to give Pike a hard time.

"I'll sleep with Tam," I say quickly, ending whatever game Austin is trying to play.

Pike grunts. "Fucker."

"Ooh. Let's make popcorn and watch a romantic comedy, yeah?" Tam asks, popping up from the couch and clapping her hands. "Like old times, Gig." She bumps my shoulder with her hip, knowing I'm an absolute sucker for anything romance.

"I get my own bowl," Austin announces, lifting his shirt with his fingertips and scratching at his six-pack. "I don't share."

"Shocking." Tamara winks at him.

"What can I say?" he asks, lifting his shirt even more, flashing the entire room. "I'm greedy."

I roll my eyes.

"Everyone can have their own bowl," Pike says easily, like he's not so freaking tense he could shatter. "Guys on the floor, girls on the couch."

Austin looks cross-eyed at Pike.

"I don't want any hands wandering," Pike grumbles.

Tamara leans forward, bending at the waist, and loses her shit in a fit of laughter. "Listen..." She slaps her knee, snorting. "Austin is cute and all."

"Cute?" His eyes widen like he's truly offended. "I'm hot, TamTam."

"Whatever," she teases, waving him off, "but I like my guys with a little more..." She pauses, eyes sweeping over him and the six-pack he's still showing. "Hair on their chest."

"Baby," Austin quips, that smug grin right back on his lips. "I got all the hair you could ever need."

I snicker at the insanity of the entire situation, and I figure it's best I just throw her business out there so there's no room for misinterpretation. "She likes 'em *old*, Austin. Real old."

Tamara rears her leg back and kicks the side of my calf. "Don't be an asshole. Pike isn't a youngster."

I rub the spot that will no doubt bruise from her bony-ass toes. "Pike's *only* five years older than me. How old was that one guy?" I ask her, forgetting his name because he wasn't around long enough for me to even memorize it.

"Marcus?" she asks, tapping her chin with her index finger.

"No. I remember Marcus. That other one. The one with the gray hair."

Austin's face pales, and he looks like he's going to puke. "Tam. Why you hittin' the old shit?"

She smacks him right upside the head without giving two shits if it hurts him or not. "Shut your hole, li'l boy. And his name was George."

I snort. "George."

"Yup." Austin slowly shakes his head, touching the spot where she just smacked him. "George sounds like an old-ass fucker." He moves, flinching as she reaches back, ready to hit him again. "Don't do it, woman," he warns her, but there's a playful smirk on his face. "You'll be sorry, old-man fucker."

"Dear God," Pike mutters at my side, and when I turn to face him, he has his eyes closed, nostrils flaring like he's just smelled the biggest pile of shit.

"Can we just watch the damn movie?" Tamara asks, crossing her arms and dropping one shoulder, clearly not liking us talking about her choice in men.

"Your dad know about the old guys?" Austin asks, not reading her body language at all.

"Nope, and if he finds out—" she bends down, getting right in his face "—you better sleep with one eye open, Aussie." She ruffles his hair when the look of horror flashes on his face. "Now." She clears her throat and straightens, putting on a big smile. "Where's the popcorn?"

This is going to be a long-ass night.

CHAPTER 11
PIKE

"THE KIDS ARE STILL ASLEEP," I whisper in Gigi's ear as I cage her in with my arms.

She leans forward, resting her hip against the kitchen counter, her fingers wrapped around the coffee mug as she gawks at me. "Kids?"

I nod. "Yep. Tam and Austin are out cold. I'm sure we have a little time before they wake up."

"Time for what?" She lifts an eyebrow.

I waggle mine, sliding my hand to her hip and squeezing. "You know."

She glances at Austin on the couch, his mouth hanging open with his arm slung over his face. "We can't. What if they hear?"

"Fine, at least take a shower with me," I plead, knowing once I have her naked, all bets are off.

She eyes me for a moment, studying my face, but I'm not giving in. "Well, I do need a shower, but Tam and I are going shopping soon."

I grab the coffee from her hands, setting the cup on the counter. "She's dead nuts asleep. You aren't leaving anytime soon, and I know how to be quick."

"You better behave," she tells me, poking me in the chest.

I smirk. "When don't I behave?"

She rolls her eyes. "Always."

In one quick motion, I find the elastic at her waistband, dipping my fingers inside enough to find the patch of skin that always drives her wild. "Scout's honor."

I tug her down the hallway toward the bedroom before she has a chance to protest. She pauses just outside Tamara's doorway, glancing around the corner to make sure she's still sleeping.

Tugging her arm again, I pull her toward my bedroom. "Stop wasting time, darlin'."

I push the door closed with my ass and hook my fingers into the top of my sweat pants, quickly removing them.

She shakes her head, giggling a little bit and blushing like she hasn't seen my cock before. "We *seriously* can't do this."

I pitch my thumb toward the door, my pants down around my ankles and my cock standing at full attention as I move us into the adjoining bathroom. "They won't hear a thing. Turn on the water."

She reaches over me, doing exactly what I ask. Before she has time to make another excuse, my hands are at her sides, lifting her tank top over her head, exposing her beautiful breasts. "God, I've missed these."

She cups her breasts, taunting me as she runs her thumbs over her hardened nipples. "You make it sound like you haven't seen them in ages."

My cock bobs, doing its own thing, as happy as the rest of me to see my girl naked again. "It feels like forever. Last time, it was dark."

She reaches down, her eyes on me, and pulls down her shorts, kicking them off to the side. "Lock the door. I don't need them walking in on anything."

I reach back, not taking my eyes off her as I engage the lock, making sure no one can walk in on us. "They have their own bathroom."

She gives me a look. One I can't really place, but I know something I said is wrong. "They better not be fucking in their bathroom too."

"God. No," I tell her, because I'd had that talk with Austin last night once his dumb ass finally sobered up. He wasn't laying a finger or cock on Tamara Gallo or any Gallo, for that matter. Ever. "That's not what I meant. Now give me your mouth. You're wasting time."

She steps back into the warm spray, motioning for me to follow her. I don't hesitate as I step into the tiny shower, the hot water streaming over my skin as I wrap my arms around her waist and pull her body to me.

"I've been waiting for this," I murmur against her lips, having missed her mouth. Her warmth. Her touch.

She pulls away, kneeling down as her hand wraps around my cock, stroking it. "I've been waiting for this." She licks her lips, inching toward my cock as it takes everything in me not to grab her head and shove my dick right into her mouth.

Her lips close around the head of my cock, and I thrust my hips forward, begging for more. She moans, her hand working up and down the shaft, and I close my eyes to stop myself from coming. Seeing her kneeling before me, sucking my dick, is more than I can take. The last thing I want is to be a two-pump chump, coming in her mouth before she's barely had a chance to get started.

The heat of her mouth mixes with the warm spray of the shower, setting my entire body on fire. I comb my fingers through her hair, touching her head gently as I rock my hips forward, wanting her to suck me deeper.

She hums her enjoyment, probably getting off on the fact that my legs are almost shaking. With one hand on the wall, I try to steady myself, locking every muscle in my body to stay upright.

"Am I doing this okay?" she asks, stopping her sweet sucking and causing me to open my eyes.

"Perfect, darlin'. Just fucking perfect."

She smiles up at me, stroking my cock with one hand and placing her other hand between her legs.

Sweet Jesus. I can't wait. I can't. But goddamn do I want to. I drop my head, back pressed against the wall, watching her fingers play with her pussy as her lips close back around me.

If this isn't heaven, I don't ever want to go. The beautiful creature before me, all sweet and good, has a dirty streak that makes my dick hard without even trying. But having her on her knees, water cascading over her breasts, fingering her pussy, is nothing short of the most perfect moment of my life.

"Stop," I moan, barely able to take it anymore. "I can't…"

She looks up, my cock between her lips, eyes wide. "What's wrong?" she asks, but it's barely audible as she speaks around my dick.

My hands are under her arms, hauling her upward until she locks her legs around my waist. "It was too much. Too perfect," I tell her when her eyes flash with worry. "You said you'd behave, and you lied."

She smirks, biting her lip.

Reaching between us, I grab my cock, lining it up perfectly with her greedy, beautiful cunt. "No moaning." I motion toward the bedroom with my head, reminding her we're not alone.

"Kiss me, then," she breathes.

I take her mouth with mine, sliding my cock into her slowly, taking what's mine.

CHAPTER 12
GIGI

"WELL, SOMEONE LOOKS SATISFIED," Tamara teases over the brim of her coffee mug, sitting at Pike's kitchen table and quirking an eyebrow.

"Shut up." I wave her off, feeling the heat creep up my neck and settling on my face.

Her eyes never leave me as she sips her coffee and tilts her head. "I'm really impressed. I thought you'd be a loud one for sure."

My fingers bunch around the dish towel on the counter before I hurl it in her direction, catching her off guard. It slaps her in the face but luckily misses her coffee. "Nice," she taunts, tossing the cloth onto the table in front of her. "You're so fucking chatty sometimes, I figured when you were getting it, you'd be all *oh yes* or *harder*."

I narrow my eyes on her because the way she said those words was pretty fucking loud and sexy as hell too. "I never sound like that." I stick out my tongue, going back to the cup of coffee I started an hour ago.

Her finger taps against the mug as she studies me, but I do my best not to look at her. "So, you're the silent type?"

I roll my eyes as I reach for the coffeepot, topping off what's left in my mug. "You don't need to know how I am in the...you know."

Tamara laughs, shaking her head at me. "You're so lame. Beyond lame."

Leaning forward, I wrap my fingers around the mug, gawking at my smartass cousin. "Do you screech like a howler monkey?"

She smirks. "Since we're going to be roomies, you just may find out."

I hold in the gag that's building in the back of my throat. "What happened to your guy?"

She shrugs, twisting her lips. "I kicked his ass to the curb. I was done playing with boys, and it's time I find myself a real man again."

"A real man?" I lift an eyebrow, looking at her in her pink bunny pajamas as she talks about the difference between men and boys. "Cute pjs."

"Shut your mouth." She glares at me before barking out a laugh. "They're comfy, and I didn't have time to get all the shit out of my car. They were the first thing I found." She leans forward, resting her elbows on the table and lets out a loud sigh.

"So, what really happened to him?" I'm talking about her boyfriend, and she knows it.

"He was getting a little too territorial, and I'd had enough. Sometimes, it's cute, but then other times..." She looks up at me with her hazel eyes blazing. "I knew when I wanted to suffocate him in his sleep, it was time to go."

I nod, knowing once murder comes into play, it's time to pull up stakes and move on. "You finally came to your senses."

"And you know what they say?"

I shrug, because she could be going anywhere with this statement. Anywhere.

"Tattooed boys are my favorite toys." She smirks.

I roll my eyes again. "You're such a weirdo."

"Pike has tats," she reminds me like I've forgotten.

"And?" I snort.

"He's a great toy, isn't he? Better than what's his name?" She taps her chin like my list of guys is so damn long she can't remember.

Bullshitter.

"Erik," I croak, even though she hasn't forgotten.

"And that dipshit Keith. Neither were real men. But Pike..." Her gaze shifts to behind me, and I know he's there. I feel his body heat and presence before he can say a word. "...is all man."

Pike grunts, pulling the cup of coffee from my hand and lifting it to his lips. Before I can warn him, he takes a large gulp and immediately winces. "Jesus, darlin'. This tastes like shit."

I reach out to take the mug from him, but he dumps the contents into the sink before I can rescue my cold coffee. "I was enjoying that," I whine.

"It was cold and the amount of sugar in it..."

"I like my coffee sweet." I snarl because I needed caffeine, and twice now, he's denied me. First with sex, not that I'm complaining, and now, by throwing it out like it wasn't any good, which it was.

He doesn't speak as he turns his back to Tamara and me, busying himself with making us a new pot of coffee.

"He's so hot," Tamara mouths, totally checking out his ass. Her eyes are hungry as they travel upward, taking in the bare skin of his back, which does, in fact, have ink too. "So freaking hot." She hoists two thumbs in the air, lifting her eyebrows with the biggest damn smile.

"What's on tap today?" Pike asks, turning around just as Tamara's putting her hands down, and he's completely oblivious to the fact that she was just treating him like a piece of meat.

"We're going shopping," I tell Pike, leaning against him as the coffee starts to brew behind us. "If I can ever finish a cup of coffee."

His hand is on my waist, squeezing ever so gently. "I'll take you guys."

"No," Tamara declares, shaking her head quickly. "I want a girls' day. We have so much to catch up on."

Pike glances down at me, and I shrug because nothing had been set in stone. "So, you two are going to talk about me?" he asks with a tiny smirk.

"Pretty much," Tamara answers, rising from the table to come stand at the other side of the countertop. "And it's going to be pretty damn hard to get all the juicy bits if you're there."

"There're no juicy bits," I lie because, holy freaking hell, there's so much to tell her.

Her eyes rake over him again, but now she's checking out his chest, the tats, all the way down to his happy trail. "Girl, if you don't have a juicy bit to share, then you're clearly doing something wrong."

She is such a ho. "Go get dressed before you embarrass yourself."

"Mornin'," Austin drawls as he saunters into the kitchen, his eyes little slits as he scratches at his stomach like he has a rash. "What time is it?" He blinks slowly as he takes in Tamara in her super-short shorts and bunny tank top that hugs every curve and nipple the girl has.

"Noon," she answers, eyes moving to him for only a second before coming back to my guy. "They've been up for a while."

My hand is around whatever's in front of me, sending it flying through the air and, again, hitting her straight in the face. She pulls the oven mitt away, tossing it back, but I catch it. "Why don't you go get dressed, Tam?"

Austin's just standing there, watching us, eyes wide and totally zeroed in on her hard nipples. "Don't get dressed on my account," he teases with a grin.

I'm pretty sure if I looked close enough at his face, he'd be drooling.

Pike slides a new cup of coffee in front of me, the steam rising above my face. "Austin and I have some shit to do today too."

Austin's eyes finally leave Tamara's tits and look at his brother as he plops onto a stool near the counter. "Like what?"

"Got to get you a new ID, and Joe said something about hiring you on at Inked if you're interested in a job."

"No shit," Austin whispers in disbelief.

"My dad said that?" I gape at Pike, blinking rapidly. "You sure you heard him right?"

Pike nods, those green eyes sweeping across my face. "Those were his exact words."

"Before all the fucks or after?" Tamara asks, reminding us all about the meltdown.

I give her the side-eye, and she shrugs.

"Fuck," Austin mutters, dropping his shoulders, remorse clearly evident in his posture. "I'm so fucking sorry. So. So. So. Fucking sorry."

"Maybe try talking without so many fucks, kid." Tamara chuckles. "I mean, we all love the word, but I'm thinking at the shop, it may not fly around so freely."

I snort. "We're not a library," I remind her. It is a business, of course, but it's still a tattoo shop. "But you should probably expand your vocabulary if my dad hires you."

"I fu...screwed up, didn't I?" Austin's eyes are begging me to tell him he didn't, but I have to be honest.

"Kinda. But..." I give him a small smile, hoping I can at least make him feel a little better. "We've all screwed up before. It's not the end of the world."

"Go shower, and we'll head to the shop and see how bad the damage is," Pike tells him, getting a quick nod from Austin before he takes off back down the hallway.

"You're really sure you heard my dad say he wanted to hire him?" I scrunch my nose. "Because that sure as hell doesn't sound like something he'd offer."

Pike rubs the back of his neck, lifting one shoulder. "He said they needed someone part time to cover the desk because you're too busy with your own customers now."

I blink, because sure, it made sense, but Austin? My dad isn't the biggest fan of Pike, and now, after Austin's outburst, I'm not sure he would even give Austin the time of day.

"I figured we'd drop by the shop, feel out your dad a bit, and see what happens from there."

I go back to my coffee, sipping slowly, thinking over all the ways this could end in disaster. I liked being there when Pike and my dad were in the same room so I could be the referee, but today it isn't possible.

"I'm going to get ready so we can go shopping, okay?" Tamara asks, interrupting my train of thought of all the horrible ways their stop by the shop could end.

"Yeah. I'll be ready in thirty," I tell her, bringing my attention back to Pike as she disappears down the same hallway Austin just went down.

"Hey, sweet cheeks," Austin says from his room, that Southern drawl coming out just a little.

"Change in Pike's room!" I yell.

Tamara and Austin burst into laughter, knowing full well they were just trying to get a rise out of me.

I fell for it too. Hook. Line. And sinker.

"You think I shouldn't go?" Pike bumps his hip into me when I don't take my eyes off the hallway, making sure both parties are separate so there're no shenanigans.

"No. Of course you should go," I lie. "What's the worst that could happen?"

Everything.

Pike smiles, nodding like he believes the bullshit coming out of my mouth. "We won't be long. We'll be back to help you carry whatever you need inside."

"It's going to be a lot," I warn him, wrapping my arms around his neck and soaking in those deep green eyes.

"Darlin', I'd carry the weight of the world on my shoulders for you."

———

"Which one is Morris again?" Tamara asks as we sit at lunch, trying to find more energy to keep shopping.

We've managed to buy almost everything I need for the kitchen, which isn't much because, like my mother, I suck at cooking. We bought pillows, bedding, towels, and just enough other things to make the place livable and as comfortable as a dorm room. In time, I'll make it more of a home, but for now, it would do.

"He's a guy in the Disciples. One of Pike's good friends."

Her dark brown eyebrows wrinkle as she studies me over her double burger. "So, he shot Pike in the shoulder, but they're friends?"

I know what she's thinking. It's bananas and something I'll never understand about men.

"Yep," I snap the P.

"If a bitch even looks at me sideways, I'm never going to be her friend. If she shoots me..." She shakes her head, that pile of brown hair moving with her, still not comprehending the way a man's brain works. "I'd kill her."

I shrug, shifting through my fries to find a crunchy little one. "I don't understand it, Tam, but he's really a nice guy."

She blinks at me, dropping her chin. "He's a nice guy?"

I nod. "He's super sweet and funny."

"He shot Pike," she reminds me as if I didn't just tell her that five seconds ago.

"I know, but it was on accident."

She blinks those hazel eyes again, placing her burger back on the plate. "You sound like him now. He shot Pike, but it's okay because it wasn't on purpose and he's nice."

"Uh, yeah," I say like duh.

"Where's my cousin, and what have you done with her?"

I snort, knowing I sound like a complete psycho. "Stop it." I throw a fry in her direction, one that's limp and wasn't going in my mouth anyway. "I'm just telling you what happened."

"Is Morris hot?" She lifts an eyebrow, her old-man radar going off. "'Cause he sounds badass."

"Are you out of your freaking mind?" I gawk at her.

She smirks. "You said he's funny and sweet. Plus, if he's any kind of a badass biker dude like Pike, I'm all in, baby."

I reach up and rub my temples, instantly regretting it when my greasy fingers slide across my skin. "Morris is old enough to be your father."

She grimaces but quickly rebounds. "Does he have a son?" she asks in a super chipper tone. "Because if he does—" she waggles her eyebrows "—I want to meet him."

"What is wrong with you?" I ask her, going back to pushing around my French fries.

"I need to move on with my life. What was it that Mallory told you?" She lifts a finger, staring upward, recalling those words from almost two years ago. "The best way to get over someone is to get under someone else. Maybe we can go over to the compound one night for a party."

I drop the fry from my fingers and push my entire plate to the side. Leaning forward, I whisper, "Are you out of your fucking mind?"

"No," she insists calmly. "I'm just looking for a good time, and nothing sounds like more fun than a biker party."

I close my eyes, sucking in the deepest breath, trying not to lose my shit in the middle of the restaurant. "You've watched way too much television. Biker parties are…"

"You're trying to tell me there's not dick for days?"

"Dick for days?" I giggle. "Did you just say that?"

She nods slowly, tossing her dark locks behind her shoulder. "I'm not looking for anything serious, babe. You know me. I've been in enough shit relationships to last me a while. I just want some cock, goddamn it."

The lady next to us starts choking, clearly hearing every filthy word coming out of my sweet cousin's mouth. Within seconds, she has picked up her plate and is moving across the restaurant with the plate in her hands.

"Nice," I tell her, rolling my eyes.

She shrugs. "Whatever. That lady could probably use some dick too."

"There's something seriously wrong with you," I whisper, trying to hold back my laughter. "I really missed your dumb ass."

"I missed you too." She smiles. "This is going to be the best summer ever."

Heaven help me.

CHAPTER 13
PIKE

AUSTIN HASN'T SAID three words to me since we got in the truck, finding the scenery way more interesting. "We need to talk about yesterday."

He doesn't look in my direction. "I think you said enough."

I deserve the shitty attitude. I know how much words hurt, sometimes more than any fist. "I'm sorry for what I said, Austin. It was such an asshole thing to say. I didn't really mean for it to come out like that."

He lifts a shoulder. "It doesn't matter," he mutters as he rests his cheek against his palm.

"It does. It matters a hell of a lot." I flick my gaze to him, wishing he'd at least look at me, but he doesn't.

When the girls were around, he was a funny, smartass guy, but as soon as they walked out of the apartment, he went cold.

"I'm not stuck with you. I wanted you to be here with me," I admit, trying to dig myself out of the verbal grave I've been buried in since my talk with Joe. "Gran would've been more than happy to have you live with her, but I thought we'd spent enough time apart that nothing else made sense other than to bring you home."

"Yay, me," he cheers in the most unenthusiastic voice, one full of sarcasm. "I'm a lucky guy."

"I know I was an asshole," I admit.

"You always have been," he shoots back immediately.

I bite my lip, stopping myself from telling this little fucker off. "I deserve that."

He finally glances in my direction. "Even though you weren't there, I looked up to you, man. Even with all the bad shit, I was so freaking happy to see my big brother again. And what did you do?"

"I fucked up."

"Do you know how it feels when you know you aren't wanted?"

It's my turn to give him the side-eye because it's the only thing I knew as a child. Felt that shit every damn day.

He closes his eyes, knowing how he's just fucked up. "It sucks," he groans.

"I never want you to feel how Mom and—" I pause and almost say Colton, but I catch myself "—Dad made me feel every day. If I could take the words back, I would. It was the most asshole-ish thing I've ever said."

"I highly doubt that." He snorts.

Pulling into the lot of Inked, I know I have to smooth shit over before we walk inside. If Austin's on edge and a total shithead, he's only going to bury me deeper. Plus, I don't want my brother to feel unwanted, even though I didn't expect to have a seventeen-year-old living with me right now. "I know you're almost a man."

"Damn right," he blurts out.

I resist the urge to roll my eyes. "And I'm not Mom or Dad." God, that word is like acid on my tongue, burning every time I say the single syllable. "But we're in this together. I had Gran looking out for me around your age before I took off, and I want to be there for you before you do whatever it is you're going to do after this year."

He doesn't reply, just stares out the window, checking out the shop at the end of the truck's hood.

So, I keep going. "Do you want a job?"

"Do you want me to work here?" He ticks his head toward Inked, and his brown hair flops over into his eyes. "You work here, right?" he finally asks, looking at me again.

I nod, blowing out a long, long breath. "I want you here. I work a lot in the evenings, so this would be the only way for us to spend more time together."

He twists his lips and narrows his eyes, but at least I have his attention. "You mean so you can keep an eye on me."

I shake my head and grimace. "You're not a little boy. We need to get to know each other all over again, and that isn't happening when I'm working all night."

His gaze goes back to the tattoo shop, eyes sweeping over the front window and the flurry of activity inside. "What do I have to do?"

"Work the front desk, welcome customers, answer phones. Gigi used to do it, but now she has her own chair."

Austin drops his arm, straightening in the seat. "You think he'll still hire me?"

"I don't know, kid. The guy hates me."

He gives me a *no shit* look. "You are fucking his kid."

I glare at him. "Never say those words again."

"Fine." He rolls his eyes. "You're dating his daughter. Better?"

I point toward Inked. "She's related to everyone in there. Her aunt, father, and uncles own the place and work there. And I work there. If you're a shithead…"

"I know how not to be an asshole, Pike. I've had a job since I was fifteen, and I am a damn good employee."

"Where?" I ask.

"Over at the Sanders' farm. I worked after school and on weekends to save some money for a bike."

"A bicycle?" I ask, raising my eyebrows.

He shakes his head. "I'm $1000 away from having the keys to my own Harley."

"Maybe you should get a junk car first."

He gives me the same look I gave Gran when she said the same thing to me. Jesus Christ, I am turning into an old person.

"Cars are too expensive, and I've wanted a Harley since..."

"Since I took you for a ride on mine," I reply, remembering him as a little kid with his hands wrapped around my waist, screaming at the top of his lungs as he sat on the back.

He smiles. "Yeah."

"Harley it is, then." I'm not one-hundred-percent comfortable with the idea, but who the fuck am I to tell him no?

"Can we go inside?" He reaches for the handle but doesn't open the door, waiting for me to answer.

We're not two steps inside when Mike, Gigi's uncle and the ex-fighter, steps right in front of us, locking eyes on my little brother.

Austin cranes his neck back as far as it can go, taking in the height and width of the freakishly large man. "H-hi again," Austin stutters with wide eyes.

"You're not going to pull that again, are you?" Mike threatens more than asks, his voice deep and, as always, scary as shit.

"No, sir." Austin swallows.

A slow smile spreads across Mike's face as he places his hand on my little brother's shoulder. "You have things to work through, but you save them for when you're away from the customers and on your own time."

"Yeah," Austin whispers. "My own time."

I chuckle to myself, watching my brother virtually piss his pants as Mike squeezes his shoulder hard enough to make him wince.

"Smart kid."

"Austin," Izzy says in a singsong voice, walking quickly into the front of the shop, knocking her brother out of the way with her hip. A moment later, her arms are open and around my brother's shoulders like she's missed him.

Hell, the woman never hugged me. She's never looked at me the way she looks at him. No matter what I've done, I've never told the entire family to go fuck themselves. But here we are, and Izzy is being…motherly?

She pulls back, but her hands stay on his arms, never breaking contact. "Are you doing okay? We were worried."

"I'm fine now, ma'am."

My eyes widen immediately, waiting for her to rip him a new asshole like she did me the first time I called her ma'am.

She laughs, slapping his arm. "It's just Iz or Izzy, kid."

He gives her a lopsided smile, probably thrown off by her hotness even if she's old enough to be his mother. "Iz," he whispers, turning a bright shade of pink but clearing his throat when it must dawn on him that he's acting like an idiot.

"Hey, Pike," Izzy throws out over her shoulder, barely even looking my way.

"Hey," I reply, rubbing the back of my neck, knowing I'm never going to get the warm and fuzzy welcome from anyone in this family.

"Joe, Austin's here." Izzy smiles at Austin, still acting like she's the sweetest thing ever. Which she isn't. "Pike too."

I walk around Izzy and Austin, heading to my chair, figuring I might as well get comfortable for a little while. I'm sure Joe's going to grill him, read him the riot act about his behavior yesterday, before making his final decision.

"Yo," Anthony murmurs, dipping his chin at me as soon as he sees me. "The girls going good?"

"They're great," I tell him. "What's going on?"

"Just waiting for them to finish so we can get out of here. I hate these monthly meetings," Anthony grumbles.

"Monthly meetings?" I raise an eyebrow, having forgotten it's Monday. When Gigi told me to take Austin to the shop today, I didn't even think about the fact that Inked was usually closed.

"Yep. All the owners meet every third Monday to talk about the financial affairs and store business. It's Mike's idea. He's such a pain in the ass."

I snort but quickly wipe that look off my face when Mike walks in the back. "What are you two bitches talking about?"

"Your meeting." Anthony kicks back, resting his feet on a nearby stool as he folds his hands behind his head. "Are we done? You've already gone on and on for almost two hours."

I grab my phone, swiping across the screen to the text app, letting them talk.

Me: Hey, darlin'. How's shopping?

"As soon as Joe's done talking to Austin, we'll leave," Mike says, dropping into a chair so hard, I'm shocked it doesn't buckle under his weight.

Gigi: Tamara's on the prowl.

Me: For dishes?

I scratch my face, staring at the screen, ignoring the two guys bickering across the room from me.

Gigi: A man!!! A badass biker man. WTF is wrong with her?

I have nothing. I don't even know how to respond to something like that.

Gigi: Other than that, it's going well. We'll be back in a few hours.

Me: We'll be ready.

"Gigi?" Mike asks, making me lift my head.

"Yeah. They're shopping."

Joe strolls into the room with Austin at his side. "We'll start training you as soon as you're ready to start working."

"I'm ready as soon as you are, sir." Austin smiles up at the big guy.

"You can work as many hours as you want until school starts, and then we'll cut back. Nothing's more important than your schoolwork."

Austin blanches for a moment before wiping that shitty look right off his face. "I agree," he lies.

I didn't even think about homework, classes, report cards, and all the shit that's involved in dealing with a seventeen-year-old. Was Austin a good student? I don't have a clue, but something tells me he wasn't on the honor roll.

Izzy walks up behind Austin, giving him a quick hug around his shoulders. "We're happy to have you as part of the family."

I should take offense. No one's given me a hug, but fuck it. I'm not a kid, and the fact that they're so willing to open their arms and business to my brother is enough for me.

"Me too," Austin babbles, practically beaming as her tits smash against his biceps.

I climb to my feet, jamming my phone back into my pocket. "Ready to hit it?" I ask Austin, more than ready to roll.

"The girls done?" Joe asks, the smile that had been on his face vanishing as soon as he looks at me.

I nod. "They'll be headed back soon."

Joe eyes Anthony for a moment before looking at me. "Anthony and I are going to follow you back. I have a trailer filled with furniture Suzy's been storing up for this day. Beds, couches, and all that bullshit."

Anthony's on his feet, rubbing his hands together like he's ready to get moving. "Between the four of us, we should be able to at least get everything in before they get back. It'll be a nice surprise."

"I'm game," Austin exclaims, being totally agreeable and nothing like the grumpy fucker who was just in my truck. "Wanna come, Iz?"

Wanna come, Iz? It takes everything in me not to roll my eyes. The kid is such a flirt. It doesn't matter how old a woman is, he is totally going there.

"I have to pick up my sons from football practice, and then I'm meeting my husband for an early dinner. He has to work late tonight." She ruffles Austin's hair, making him blush. "But thanks for the offer."

He bobs his head, jamming his hands into his front pockets. "Anytime."

"Mike, you comin'?" Joe asks him as he reaches into his back pocket, fishing out his cell phone.

"Can't. With Lily home, Mia wants the family to go down to the beach for dinner and to watch the sunset."

"That's so sweet. I'm dreading the day Carm and Rocco head off to college. Dreading," Izzy groans, shaking her head. "I won't know what to do with myself."

"Trace will no doubt keep you busy," Anthony tells her with a snicker. "That boy is a wild man."

She rolls her eyes. "He's like his daddy. He's going to put me in an early grave."

"We'll meet you at the apartment," I say, done with all the sugary sweetness that was the Gallo family.

Joe nods his head. "Be there in five."

"See you tomorrow," Austin tells Izzy and Mike with a wave of one hand, following me out of Inked. "I like them."

"Yeah?" I ask, sliding into the driver's seat of Gigi's pickup truck she let me borrow since they were taking Tam's car. "They're not the worst people ever."

Austin laughs, slamming the door after he settles into the seat. "I feel awful about being such a dipshit yesterday."

"You should," I grumble, turning the ignition.

"Asshole," he mutters in response. "You ever..." He drags his hand down his face as he cranes his neck toward me, hesitating for a moment before speaking. "Ever wish we'd had a large family like that?"

I wince, not sure how to answer the question, but then I explain exactly what I feel and leave nothing out. "I wish we had a family like that." I point to the people in the shop in front of us. "Would I want a large family if they were dysfunctional like our parents?" I pause and shake my head. "No fucking way."

"I like the Gallos. I could've totally dug being in a family with those people growing up. Imagine all the birthdays, holidays... Hell..." He smiles. "Think about Christmas."

"I know, Austin. We were shortchanged, but at least we have each other now," I tell him, backing out of the parking spot.

"Can you do me a solid?" he begs, his voice suddenly serious.

"What?" I glance over at him before I put the truck in drive.

"Can you not fuck it up with Gigi for a little while so we can at least have a great Christmas this year. Okay, brother?"

I stare him straight in the eyes, but without any anger, just pure honesty. "It's a two-way street. Don't do anything like that shit," I say, referring to yesterday's performance before dinner, "and I think we have a solid chance of making the guest list."

He nods, smiling as we head off toward home.

CHAPTER 14
GIGI

"WE CAN'T SLEEP HERE TONIGHT," Tamara announces hours after our fathers leave. The apartment is an absolute mess.

I look around, taking in the level of mass destruction in the living room and dining room, not even wanting to peer down the hallway toward the bedrooms. "It's bad, Tam."

Boxes are everywhere in various states of unpacking, and the washer and dryer are going at full steam as the new sheets and towels we'd purchased are being cleaned. Every few feet, there's something that needs to be moved or cleaned, and absolutely nothing has been completed.

Tamara groans, collapsing on the couch. "I didn't think this would be so much work." She throws her arm over her face, being super dramatic, but I wouldn't expect anything less from her. "Moving in to a dorm room was so much easier. I can barely move another muscle."

"We can just push everything onto the floor and crash on the couches."

Her arms move upward so her hazel eyes are visible. "Do you even know where the toilet paper is?"

I glance around at the various boxes and bags scattered everywhere and shrug. "I know where the paper towels are," I say, trying to put her mind at ease that she'd at least have something to wipe her ass with.

She scowls. "My lady parts are way too sensitive for paper towels," she argues.

I snort, smacking her legs with my hand as I collapse next to her. "I know where your *lady parts* have been, and I'm pretty sure sensitive isn't a word I'd use to describe them."

"You're a bitch," she snaps, laughing with me because she knows she's full of shit. "We should totally have another sleepover with Aussie and Pike."

I roll my eyes, leaning back into the couch and pulling her legs onto my lap. "We should give them space tonight. They could use some alone time."

Now it's her turn to snort. "They need alone time?" She laughs louder, hitting my shoulder with her bony elbow, knocking me to the side. "They're not chicks. They've got dicks, dude. They don't need alone time. I can guarantee they'd love to have us over again."

I straighten, rubbing the spot she's just assaulted. "This is our first official night together in our new place."

"Fuck that," she sasses and slides her legs off me, climbing to her feet quickly. "We can have that night tomorrow. I don't want to work anymore."

She's such a whiny bitch sometimes, but I still love her. I sigh and grab a glittery pillow that's itchy as hell and not very comfortable, clutching it to my chest. "We don't have to work. Let's just veg and watch some Netflix. We'll start straightening up tomorrow. Leave the boys alone tonight."

"I gotta piss," she announces, being the classy bitch she is.

That's my Tamara.

"The paper towels are in the laundry room!" I yell to her as she marches down the hallway, stomping her feet, having her own little temper tantrum.

I pull out my phone, wondering how it's going next door since the guys left an hour ago. I haven't heard any yelling, so I assume it's going great, but after the last few days...anything could be possible.

Me: Whatcha doin'?

A second later, three dots are on the screen like Pike had been about to text me when I sent the message.

Pike: He's in his room. I'm on the couch. Fun times. You?

I glance up, taking in the chaos all around me.

Me: Tamara's giving up, and I'm tired.

Pike: Want some help?

Me: No. We got it. It's not your mess.

Pike: One sec. Austin's yelling for me.

Me: K

"Oh, Gigi!" Tamara yells from the hallway, her steps lighter than before. "Guess what?"

"Your lady bits aren't as sensitive as you thought they were?" I laugh until I see her face because I know the asshole is up to something. "What?" I groan.

She twists around, putting her hands behind her back as she stands only a few feet away from me. "The guys want us to come over. We're having another sleepover!"

"You didn't!"

"I so did," she sings, looking mighty damn pleased with herself.

"Asshole," I grumble under my breath, fisting the pillow in my hands and throwing the glittery monstrosity at her face.

She ducks, and the pillow sails past her, sliding across the tile. "Come on. You can snuggle with Pike, and we can use real toilet paper. It's a win-win."

"If I have to listen to any more Aussie and TamTam shit..." I make a gagging sound and lean over like I'm throwing up.

"You're just jealous," she tells me, crossing her arms over her chest. "You wish you could have such cute nicknames."

I glare at her because she's unbelievable, and then my phone vibrates next to me.

Pike: Come over.

"What'd he say?" Tamara asks, stepping closer, trying to get a good look at my phone.

"We'll go. Just…" I look down at her chest, remembering this morning. "For the love of God, wear a damn sports bra."

She glances down at her tits, which are propped up by her arms. "Why?"

"Those suckers are like laser beams, and Austin's only seventeen." I motion toward her nipples, which are hard like she's perpetually cold. "He doesn't need to be seeing them."

She drops her arms and cups her breasts in the palms of her hands. "These cannot be contained. A sports bra is too constricting." She bounces her tits like she's testing their weight.

"You know what's constricting?" I glare at her.

"What?"

"My fingers wrapped around that beautiful neck of yours," I threaten.

"Fine," she says. "I'll wear a damn sports bra."

"Thank fuck," I mutter, glancing up at the ceiling. "Don't give that kid any ideas. He's young, Tam. Too young."

"We're just friends."

"You know that—" I motion toward her with my hand before smacking my own chest "—and I know that, but that horny little toad next door does not."

"They'll be locked and loaded, baby. Don't worry," she laughs, turning on her heel and stalking toward her bedroom. "I'm putting my pjs on now before we head over."

Me: We're coming. Give us five.

Pike: I'll be waiting, darlin'.

My insides go all squishy when I read *darlin'*, just like they do every time he says that word.

Tam is right. Spending the night curled up with Pike is so much better than sitting in the middle of this disaster, listening to her whine all night.

Ten minutes later, we're on Pike's couch, my legs curled up against me and my back to his front. Tamara and Austin are on the floor, legs stretched out, looking like the oddest set of twins.

"Nope," Austin tells her, grabbing the remote from her hands. "You ladies picked last night. It's guys' night."

Tamara pulls the remote back toward her, but Austin doesn't let go. "That's bullshit. We're your guests."

Austin blinks but doesn't give in. "You asked to come here, babe, not the other way around."

Snap. He shut her down good.

Her eyes narrow, and she doesn't say a word before pulling back, causing Austin to lean forward. And then, like the asshole she is, she lets go, making him fall on her. "Whatever, bitch," she tells him.

I glance up at Pike as he gazes down at me with those pretty eyes. "I hate them," I mouth.

"Me too," he mouths back.

"Shut up, ass." Austin lifts himself upward but not before totally checking out her rack.

Gross.

"Eyes there," she reminds him, pushing his face toward the television. "Unless you don't want to be able to see out of them for a week."

He scrunches his nose. "They're not that amazing, TamTam. They were in my face, for Christ's sake."

Telling Tamara her tits aren't *the shit* is like saying her face is ugly. Those are fighting words. Seventeen or not, he will pay for that remark.

She lets out this loud growl, rearing her arm back like she's going to sock him right in the face. But Austin flinches, and Tamara instantly breaks out in giggles, pointing at him. "Sucker," she snorts.

"I hate you sometimes," he grumbles, lifting the remote toward the television.

"No, you don't." She smiles as she stares at the screen.

"We're watching *Aquaman*, and I don't want any lip," he tells her, sounding all serious.

Watching that movie is not going to be a hardship. In fact, Tamara has said she'd climb Jason Momoa like a tree on more than one occasion. She even had a poster of him above her bed in her dorm room.

"Shut up!" she screeches, clapping her hands like she just heard the best news ever. "Jason Momoa is a total dreamboat."

"If you like old dudes," Austin grumbles, pressing the button to start the movie.

I settle into Pike as he wraps his arms around my middle and his lips move to my neck. Closing my eyes, I moan softly as the wet warmth of his mouth connects with my skin, sending goose bumps pebbling down my arms.

I turn my face, placing my mouth so close to his lips, I can feel his warm breath. "Stop," I plead, the tingle between my legs making me wish we weren't saddled with the two assholes still grumbling at each other on the floor like they're brother and sister.

"Shh," he whispers, his warm breath skidding across my skin, using his nose against my jaw to push my face back toward the television.

My body stiffens as he places his mouth near my ear, his breath tickling my flesh and turning that tingling into a full-on throb.

"Let me enjoy your skin," he pleads in such a husky tone, my body shivers before I can stop it. "Just be still, and no one will ever know what we're doing."

I instantly lift up my hand, pulling a nearby blanket on top of us. "Man, I'm so cold," I say because I'm lame.

Tamara looks back, eyes raking over us before she winks and turns back toward the television. It's not the first time we've been in the same room together when one of us was literally necking. That's the bitch about college... There's zero privacy.

"Who's your favorite superhero?" Tamara asks Austin as the opening credits are just about to finish.

"Iron Man. You?"

"Aquaman all day, bitch."

I tune them out as Pike's hand slides down my front, resting on my stomach. My breath hitches as his mouth attaches to that spot near my shoulder that always makes it impossible to breathe.

Pike's cock presses into my back, straining against his sweat pants and making me pant. I want him so damn bad.

"Think we could sneak out without them knowing?" Pike whispers when I shift, and his cock twitches right above my ass cheeks.

I shake my head, unable to speak without sounding like a needy whore.

"Damn," he hisses. "This is going to be the longest movie of my life."

I giggle, my body shaking as Pike growls, pulling his bottom away from my back.

"We gotta stop," he bites out softly. "Or I'm going to die."

I pull myself forward, putting as much space between us as possible. "Stay over there," I mouth to him, kicking my feet into his lap.

He scowls as he wraps his long, strong fingers around my feet and rubs, causing me to moan loudly.

Austin turns his head, eyes flickering at Pike's fingers on my feet and grimaces. "Weirdo," he mutters before turning back around.

Pike winks at me, and all I can do is laugh.

I don't know when I fall asleep, but I am awakened when strong hands slide under my bottom, lifting me into a pair of warm arms. My face flops into the warm muscles of his chest, and I groan, hating the idea I'd be left on the cold couch without Pike to keep me warm.

"Off to bed?" Tamara whispers.

I don't even have the energy to reply, but Pike does. "I'm taking her with me. You two behave," he commands ever so quietly to Tamara and Austin before taking another step, holding me firmly in his grasp.

I don't open my eyes until he places my body on the cool sheets of his bed and covers me with his body heat.

"I've been waiting all night for this," he whispers in the darkness, his face level with mine. "All fucking night to taste you."

A lazy smile stretches across my face as I spread my legs. "Taste away."

He crawls down my body, placing soft kisses on my skin, giving equal love to each breast. I moan, shoving my fingers into his hair as he sucks my nipple between his lips.

"Quiet," he murmurs around my flesh, reminding me of the two in the living room.

The warmth of his mouth is gone, and then the hard muscles of his shoulders slide between my legs, opening me to him.

Pike studies my skin in the faint light. "You're so beautiful," he whispers, glancing up at my face for a moment.

I push his face down, done with the compliments, needing his mouth back on my body. The coolness from the room is replaced by the damp heat of his tongue, causing my hips to jolt off the bed.

He hums his approval and wraps his hands around my thighs, stopping me from squirming. When his lips close around my flesh, I moan loudly, throwing my hand over my mouth to stop the sound.

Pike doesn't stop, sucking harder and rubbing his tongue over the perfect spot.

"Yes," I moan into my palm. "Oh my God."

Another moan escapes as Pike's lips send vibrations through my system, making my toes curl.

"I'm going to come," I whisper, biting down on my lip.

His fingers are at my opening, pushing inside and stretching me. Just when I don't think the pleasure could get better, goose bumps break out across my flesh.

This is it. I can't stop the wave of pleasure from crashing over me again and again, building in intensity with each thrust of his long, thick fingers inside me.

I gasp for air, my body growing rigid as the orgasm takes over, making it impossible to even think. I rock forward, possessed by the passion only his lips can deliver.

"Goddamn," he whispers as he pulls away, and I collapse back into the mattress. "That was too quick."

"I'm sorry." I smile, too sated to care how fast or slow I came.

"Let's do that again, but slower this time." He grins, placing those lips back on my skin.

Damn, I love this man.

CHAPTER 15
PIKE

MORRIS: *8 pm at the Neon Cowboy*

I flick my eyes to my phone, reading over the message a second time before I look up. *Shit.* They're here. James and Thomas said they'd come. The Disciples wanted payback.

Me: I'll be there

I type the message, hitting send before I have a chance to think. If I had taken a minute, or hell, a few seconds, I would've remembered James's words.

I had forgotten they were coming. Days had passed. Night turned into day, bleeding into almost a week before Morris had finally reached out to me.

Morris: Bring the sweetheart with you

"Who are you talking to?" Gigi asks as we sit in the living room at her grandmother's house.

It's Sunday. Family day. It's the weekly celebration of everything Gallo. Austin's been welcomed back as if last weekend never happened.

"Morris," I mutter softly, trying to avoid the attention of everyone else in the room.

Gigi's eyes widen as soon as his name is off my lips. "We should tell…"

I touch her hand, stopping her from saying any more. I know the protocol. The last thing I'm going to do is fuck things up with this family again.

I get to my feet and lean over to kiss her cheek. "I'll be back. Let me talk to the guys," I whisper in her ear, earning me a quick nod.

I catch James's eye, motioning toward the dining room with my head, and he slaps Thomas's shoulder before they both are right behind me.

"Disciples reach out?" James asks as soon as we're in the dining room, far away from the rest of the family.

"Yeah. Neon Cowboy tonight." I tap my knuckles against the table, the muscles across my shoulders already growing tight. "He wants me to bring Gigi."

James looks at Thomas, unspoken words passing in their gazes. Thomas and James slide into the chairs across from me, looking calm and collected like I didn't just tell them that payback was on the horizon.

"What do I do?" I ask, flexing my fingers, trying to contain my nervous energy.

Thomas rubs his chin, studying me. "If they want Gigi to come along, most likely, they'll tell you what the favor is, but it won't happen tonight."

"Are you sure?" I ask, my voice serious and deep. "What if she's part of the favor?"

James's eyebrows shoot up. "Fuck no," he howls quickly. "You know these guys. They wouldn't ask for her. They know they'd have to go through all three of us, and then I'd rain down fire upon them."

I nod immediately, knowing Tiny, Morris, and everyone in the Disciples as well as I've known anyone in my life. "They wouldn't."

"Take her," Thomas orders. "Don't stay too long. Keep shit short and simple. Do not, and I mean do not, go anywhere with them without calling us first."

"We're not fucking around, Pike," James barks like I'm an idiot and can't follow directions.

"I'm not a dumbass," I bite back.

James narrows his eyes and flattens his lips. "Call us from the Neon, and don't be an asshole."

"Who's going to the Neon?" Joe asks, eavesdropping.

The man has been so far up my ass for the last week. I'm surprised he doesn't have a drone following me around, making sure I'm not fucking up somehow.

"Pike and Gigi are just going for drinks later," Thomas tells him, leaving out the most important information.

I close my eyes because why couldn't the man just say I was going alone. Joe didn't need to know everything. What the hell is wrong with this family? Can't anyone do something without everyone being up one another's asses?

That would be a hard no.

Joe's arms are down at his sides, hands fisted tightly, probably dreaming about punching me right between the eyes. "Tonight?" he growls.

"They're meeting Morris," James offers, climbing to his feet as soon as Joe moves forward like he's going to land that punch. "Hold up, big guy. It's not a big deal. Morris saved her life, remember." James blocks Joe from reaching me.

Joe swings his eyes from James, to me, to Thomas before landing back on James. "It is a big fucking deal. This is my kid we're talking about, and they are—" his eyes go stone-cold, jaw tightening as he glares at me "—criminals."

If looks could kill, I'd be a dead man. Hell, I would've been good and buried, my body rotting in the ground by now. "I'll keep her safe," I tell him, trying to smooth shit out because the last thing I need is more trouble.

"If she's going, I'm going," he demands.

Thomas lets out a loud laugh. "Yeah, 'cause everyone wants their daddy to tag along."

The shade of red on Joe's face matches that of the spaghetti sauce I'd just shoved down my throat. "Would you let your daughter go alone?" Joe pauses, staring his brother down. "Oh, wait. You have a fucking son."

Thomas isn't thrown off by his brother's anger. "Fine." Thomas throws up his hands. "We'll all go. We'll gather the ALFA guys and sit at our usual table so we can keep an eye on them. How's that, big guy?"

I shake my head, knowing immediately this entire evening is going to be nothing but a giant clusterfuck. The biggest epic failure. Dread washes over me, coating my skin and clinging to my back like a second shirt.

"Sounds like a great time," I mutter to the table as I rub my forehead with my fingers. "Fan-fucking-tastic."

"Hey, dipshit," Joe heckles, and I know he's talking to me.

I glance up, looking at him straight on. "What?" I growl because I've had just about enough of his shit.

"That bar used to be my bar. I know exactly what happens in a place like that, and I'm not letting you take my kid in there to meet the Disciples without being nearby."

"Where am I going?" Gigi asks, standing behind her father, appearing out of nowhere just like he did.

There's seriously not a room in this house with any privacy. Even if you think you've found a spot, someone will show up, reminding you just how public everything is and how nosy they all are.

"Pike—" Joe motions toward me "—is taking you to the Neon Cowboy tonight to meet Morris." He says the words in such a shitty way, like I'm taking her to the worst place imaginable.

Gigi's eyes light up, and she practically jumps in the air. "Oh my God. I freakin' love Morris." Her body's humming with excitement about seeing the old guy again. "He's such a hoot."

There's no happiness on Joe's face. "Jesus Christ," he mutters, glancing upward toward the ceiling. "Have you all lost your minds?"

"Daddy." Gigi smiles up at him. "You know you like Morris."

"I put up with him. Like is too strong of a word."

The bastard doesn't even like me, and I almost died for his kid. I'm pretty sure I'd actually have to take that bullet before he'd let go of that chip on his shoulder. But then again, probably not.

"We're all going," Thomas tells Gigi, and I wince, closing an eye because I know my girl, and she's going to...

"Like hell you are," she bellows, hands going to her hips and eyes burning with fire. "You are not going to embarrass me."

"We would never do that, baby girl."

Gigi cranes her neck, glaring up at her father. "You are not going. Neither are they." She tips her head toward her uncles but never breaks eye contact with Joe. "I've put up with your overprotective nonsense for my entire life." She lifts her hand, pushing her fingertip into his chest. "I will not do it anymore."

He glances down at where their bodies are touching but doesn't otherwise move. "You're not going alone," he tells her.

Gigi lets out a loud, dramatic groan. "I won't be alone. I'm going with Pike, and Jesus Christ, stop being so mean to him. He's kind, loving, and an overprotective jerk just like you, so lay off."

My gaze moves to Joe's face, and he's eyeing me, anger coming off him in waves.

"No one will keep you as safe as I would," Joe replies, barely moving his lips as he speaks.

He's about to blow. No man talks without moving his mouth unless he's so mad, he's about to beat someone to death. I'd sure as hell be the victim, but I'd put up one hell of a fight before I took my last breath.

"You know you have two other daughters and a wife, right?" she throws back, not missing a beat. "I'm sure one of them needs your protection. I have Pike, Daddy." She pulls her fingers back before sliding her palm against her father's chest. "I love you with all my heart. You're the best father a girl could ever want. I won the lottery the day I was born, getting you and Mom as parents. But, Dad..." She curls up against him, looking so small against the big man. "You have to let go sometime. Pike will never replace you. I love you, and I love him."

Joe's eyes cut to me, first hard. But then, like something comes over him, they soften for a moment. "You love him?" He sounds like he's choking on those words.

She peers up, nodding. "I love him, and I love you," she tells him again. "Just let go, Daddy. Let me grow up and find my own way. You taught me well. I know how to be safe and not be stupid, and when all else fails, Pike will be there."

"Goddamn it," Joe mutters, curling his arm around his daughter's back. "I never thought this would be so hard."

"I'll always be your little girl, but you have to let me live my own life too," she pleads, embracing her father, head still on his chest. "I promise I'll make you proud."

"Sweetheart," he whispers, kissing the top of her head. "You already make me so damn proud. I love you more than anything else in the world."

"More than Mom?" Gigi asks, teasing her father, because the girl always has to bust balls.

Three hours later, Gigi's under my arm as we walk into the Neon Cowboy, a bar I've only been to a handful of times since I moved to the area. It's your typical country biker bar with loud music, cold beer, and not much else.

Gigi's talk with her father convinced him and her uncles to give us space. I swore on my life that I'd keep her safe, and if I didn't, I expected to pay with my own life.

"There she is," Morris says, pushing his body away from the bar the moment he sees Gigi. "Beautiful as always, sweetheart." He holds out his arms to her like he's her long-lost father, and my girl, she just runs to him.

"I've missed you," she tells him, giving him the biggest bear hug as he lifts her feet off the floor, reciprocating.

Fuck me.

"Pike," he mumbles, still hugging on her and barely glancing in my direction.

"Let her go, Morris," I tell him, and not in that *hey, how you doin'* kind of tone either. When he just looks at me, pretending he didn't hear every word out of my mouth, I reach out and grab her arm, hauling her back against me.

"Don't be a buzzkill," is her response, as she throws a glare over her shoulder at me, shrugging out of my grip. "So." She hooks her arm around his and starts walking to where Morris left his beer. "What's new with all my badass biker friends?"

I walk behind them, reminding myself not to lose my cool. This is Gigi being Gigi. She's going to test my limits, and in all reality, Morris hasn't done a goddamn thing. *He saved our lives.* It's something I reminded myself of a hundred times on the way over here. Nothing will happen to us. Not after everything the MC lost to protect us.

"After you two left and the smoke cleared, we swore in some new members." Morris motions toward the bartender, holding out three fingers and pointing toward the spot in front of him.

Gigi's eyebrows go up. "Really?"

"Yeah. You'll have to come celebrate with us and meet the new guys. We're having a huge party on Labor Day weekend if you want to come."

Like hell.

"Hell yeah," she exclaims, answering for both of us as she grabs the beer the bartender has set down for her.

"Darlin'." I slide next to her, placing my hand on the bar next to her, leaning my body against her. "We have plans with your family on Labor Day."

She looks at me over her shoulder with a straight-as-fuck face. "No, we don't," she argues. "We're going to the compound, baby."

I curl my fingers around the wooden edge of the bar, and I grind my teeth, trying to keep myself from losing my shit. *Stay calm, Pike. Breathe.*

"We'll be there. Can I bring two guests?" she asks Morris excitedly.

"No," I snap, as Morris says, "Yes."

Gigi grabs her beer, lifting it toward Morris, ignoring me again. "We'll be there, old man," she says, waiting for him to clink his beer to hers.

"It's a date." He winks, hitting her glass before lifting his to his lips.

I'm almost foaming at the mouth. What the fuck just happened? I promised her father I'd keep her safe. I promised James and Thomas we wouldn't go anywhere or do anything before I spoke to them. And Gigi just blew it all up in a matter of sixty seconds. Invitation given and accepted without so much as a moment's thought of all the ways shit could go wrong.

"Clusterfuck," I mutter.

She turns her head again and blinks. "What's your issue?" she whispers.

"Don't have an issue," I tell her after glancing up at Morris, who's watching me like a hawk. "No issue at all. Just don't want to disappoint your family."

"They won't miss us. It's two months away, damn it."

That's all she says before giving Morris her full attention again. I lift the beer to my lips, muttering a slew of curse words against the glass. I warned her about the Disciples. Did my best to tell her they're looking for payback and Morris was here to collect. She blew me off, telling me I was imagining shit because there's no way *the big guy* would expect anything from me.

Absolutely clueless.

"I'm not bringing Austin," I tell her.

Morris's eyes widen. "You have your brother?"

I nod. "Brought him back with me after the funeral."

"No shit," Morris mutters, shaking his head, setting his beer down on the bar like he's in shock. "Didn't think you'd take him in."

"He's my family," I tell him, but Morris knows me as well as anyone. He knows family hasn't meant shit to me in the past. Why would it? They never gave two fucks about me.

"You're changing, softening," he explains, but without any judgment in his voice. His gaze dips to Gigi and then back to me. "The girl's changing you."

Gigi punches his arm playfully. "*The girl* has a name."

"I know, beautiful," he teases, throwing her a wink, and she eats that shit right up. "He stayin' forever?"

I nod, tightening my one arm around Gigi's middle, plastering my front to her back. "Never had much of a family, Morris, and now…" I flick my gaze down as Gigi looks up. "Now, I have people I love and care about in my life, and I'm not turning my back on them for nothing or no one."

Morris doesn't even twitch. The fucker is made of stone. "I can see that," he says in an even tone.

"Can you two excuse me for a moment?" Gigi asks, dipping out of my grip. "I need to use the…" She throws her thumb over her shoulder. I nod, thankful to get Morris alone.

"What the fuck?" I hiss as soon as she's far enough away. "Coming here for payback and then inviting us for a party?"

He shrugs like it's no big fucking deal. "Just because I'm here out of duty for the club doesn't mean we're not still friends."

I take a step closer to him, pushing away my beer. "You were supposed to be my friend first. I didn't think you'd come for payback for saving my life."

He nods, elbow on the bar, leaning against the edge. "Sure as fuck gotta. We lost a lot of men that night. It's going to take us a while to get back to earning what we were before that shit with DiSantis."

"I don't have any money."

Morris smiles, slow and lazy. "I heard your pops broke in to Gigi's apartment, almost killed her."

I blink, shocked he knows what's happening over here, but I shouldn't be. Just like the cops, the MC knows everything. They have eyes and ears all over the state, from dirty cops to other bikers looking for an opportunity.

"Had my guy on the inside have a little talk with your pops. He was looking for something." Morris strokes his chin, studying me. "Looking for something really important."

"I don't have any of his shit," I spit out, wondering how I ever could've thought Morris was a friend.

He reaches out, and I lurch backward, avoiding his touch. "I'm not going to hurt you or your girl. I love you like my own son, and that one—" he lifts his chin in the direction Gigi walked "—is the best thing that's ever happened to you."

"Then why the fuck are you here?"

"Word on the street is that your father has a storage locker filled floor to ceiling with cocaine and cash. The dumbass told my buddy on the inside he would split it with him if he'd find someone to track you down and get the fucking key."

"I don't have his fucking key," I grind out. The man never gave me anything besides misery.

"He hid it," Morris explains, resting his hand on my shoulder. "In some small box that was your grandfather's. I guess he put it in the box years ago. After your mother was killed, he figured he would get the key from you and cash in enough coke to live the rest of his life somewhere off the grid."

"Motherfucker," I mutter, realizing he hadn't been after Gigi, but the key and me instead. I have no doubt he would've killed me to get his hands on that key. No fucking doubt at all.

"The assholes who killed your mom," Morris says, pausing for a moment until I narrow my eyes. "They were after the key too."

I suck in a breath, knowing my brother went through hell,

almost dying at the hands of the same men. Over what? Fucking drugs.

"You going to have that hanging over your head forever? Do you want to unload that kind of inventory and risk the beautiful thing you're starting with your girl?"

"Fuck no," I howl, squeezing my hand in a tight fist, wishing I could punch something...anything.

"You know which box I'm talking about?"

I nod.

Morris tightens the grip on my shoulder. "Find the key, give it to me, and we'll call it even."

"I don't fucking want it, but..." I peer up at him, looking him right in the eyes. "But if you're going to help Colton with the money..."

Morris shakes his head and barks out a laugh. "That bastard can rot in jail, kid. Fuck him. He doesn't deserve anything more than the dry ass-fucking he's going to get for the next twenty years."

The visual, while gross, brings a smile to my face.

"Bring the key, and we're even. I don't want anything else from you. I'd never hurt you or Gigi, but the longer you have the key, the more danger you'll be in. There're eyes and ears everywhere," Morris warns, knocking his knuckles against the table to drive the point home.

"I'll bring it to you," I promise.

CHAPTER 16
PIKE

"I DON'T KNOW why I couldn't come alone." I stare out of the blacked-out windows in the back of the SUV, annoyed and aggravated that I couldn't deliver the key by myself.

"We told you. You're not going alone. Disciples or not, that's not how things are done in this family," Joe says at my side.

"It's just a simple drop," I argue.

Never in my life have I needed babysitters. I did as I was asked. I told James and Thomas exactly what Morris, Tiny, and the Disciples wanted as payback. A key that led to probably millions of dollars of illegal drugs and cash. All of it gained through violence and death, and nothing I wanted or needed.

The fact that they threw a fit when I said I was going alone was laughable. I should've taken off on my bike, delivering the key to the MC days ago. But no. That's not how this family rolls. They do everything in packs like wolves.

James grunts. "Pike, you need to start dealing with the fact that you're no longer alone in anything you do."

I glance up, meeting his eyes in the rearview mirror. "There wasn't a need for this to be a family affair," I grumble, resting my chin on my knuckles as the trees swish by so quickly, they're a blur of green.

I've always been alone. It's how I've operated from the time I was a little boy. I am used to looking out for myself, not worrying about anyone else around me.

"There's always a need," Thomas tells me, turning his neck to glower at me over his shoulder from the front seat.

"Gallos don't go into danger without backup," Joe adds with a straight face, as serious as a heart attack.

"But I'm not a…"

"Shut your mouth," Bear barks in my ear, squished into the third row of seats and sitting directly behind me. "Just say thank you, dumbass."

"Thank you," I grind out, not feeling the words but not looking to have Bear smack me in the back of the head either.

"You're welcome," Joe tells me, probably loving the shit out of my misery.

"We're five minutes out, but the Disciples are running behind. Morris said they ran into some shit but will be there in twenty," Thomas announces.

"Fucking bikers," James groans.

"Watch it now," Bear growls under his breath. "We're not all dipshits."

I respect the hell out of every man in this SUV. They've come to my rescue before, setting aside whatever's going on in their lives to help. They never asked for anything in return and haven't given me too much shit—besides Joe. That's more than anyone in my family has ever done for me.

"Keep your eyes out as we get closer," James warns, scanning the sides of the dirt road at the endless trees.

"You think we're being set up?" Thomas asks, looking out the side window, eyes trained on the brush.

"No, but something doesn't feel right," he admits, slowing the SUV as we get closer.

Those words are enough to set off alarm bells. Thomas and James have been in more shit than I'll ever be able to fully comprehend.

"Get locked and loaded," Bear orders, the familiar sound of the metal of his gun clicking behind me.

I glance toward the ceiling, shaking my head. "What a shitshow. This is why I should've come alone."

That statement earns me a backhand to my chest. "Stop with your bullshit already. If something's off, it's best we're all here to make it out alive, rather than sending your ass in there to get killed."

"What do you care?" I mutter, glancing over at Gigi's father, who's done nothing but hassle me since the moment he found out I'd slept with her.

Joe sucks in a breath, his blue eyes narrowing as he runs his hand through his dark hair. "I deserve that. I've been an asshole to you on more than one occasion."

"Ya think?" I raise an eyebrow, peering at him out of the corner of my eye.

"Put yourself in my shoes, kid. The last thing I want is for my girl to be staring down the barrel of a gun."

"Me either, Joe. I've told you that. I'll do everything I can to protect Gigi."

He nods. "I know, and I believe you. But I'm also not going to hold my little girl in my arms as she cries because her boyfriend had to be a goddamn hero and take a bullet when he could've made it back alive with our help."

I swallow, thinking about dying and how Gigi would react. "I don't ever want to be the cause of her tears," I tell him.

"Then we do this together."

I nod when he glares at me, waiting for some kind of affirmation that I'd heard him. "Understood," I mutter.

James pulls the SUV over near the same spot in the abandoned parking lot where they dropped Gigi and me when the shit with DiSantis was about to go down. Night is coming, the navy skies are moving toward us with each passing second, casting shadows in the trees and the fields surrounding the patch of cement.

James cuts the engine, turning around in his seat to face us. "Don't let your guard down. Guns out, but keep them tucked in your waistband and be ready for anything."

"Shit can never be easy," Joe groans.

"I live for this shit," Bear brags with a hint of laughter, which makes him seem all the crazier than I've always thought he was.

Joe turns his head, giving Bear the glare he'd just been giving to me. "We're not as old as you, fucker. We're not looking to die today."

"I ain't dying, fool. I'm like Iron Man. The bullets bounce off." Bear pounds on his chest, trying to prove his manhood.

God, I really love these crazy assholes. They are so much like the guys in the Disciples, minus the drugs, whores, and constant partying, of course.

Joe rolls his eyes. "I don't even know why we're friends, Bear."

"You love me," Bear teases, letting his crazy show even more because shit's about to get real. "And we're not just friends. I'm your uncle."

I chuckle to myself, but my laughter dies when Joe cranes his neck and turns those hardened eyes on me.

"I need out. I gotta piss," Bear grumbles, pushing between us as he moves to my row, reaching for the door handle as he leans over me.

"Don't," James starts to tell him, but Bear's out of the SUV, almost kicking me in the junk in the process. "Goddamn him."

"Prostate," Bear mutters before the sound of his zipper followed by a loud sigh are the only noises besides the birds squawking in the distance. "You'll understand when you're older."

"Everyone out." Thomas opens his door, boots touching the gravel, creating a cloud of smoke. "Eyes peeled."

I step out, ignoring Bear as he moans, doing his business near the tire of the SUV.

"If you get piss on my tire, I'm going to make you lick it off." James stares at Bear's back, shaking his head and snarling.

"Don't worry, Sally. I'm in complete control," Bear tells him, swaying his body from side to side, fucking with James and always looking to get a rise out of everyone.

James moves to the front of the truck, leaving Bear to finish his business. "Fuck you and your Sally shit."

"It's quiet," Thomas whispers, scanning the trees in the distance. "Too quiet."

Joe's eyes are on me as we make our way to the front of the truck to join Thomas and James. We're all on high alert, except for Bear. The man is perpetually doing his own thing, not giving a single fuck about anything else around him.

There's movement to the right, and our four sets of eyes follow, drawing out guns. This isn't the Disciples. There was no roar of their engines, no familiar rumble in the ground below our feet.

Our guns are drawn, raised out in front of us as a small army of men clears the trees with their guns drawn too.

"Fuck," I hiss softly, locking my arms straight out, drifting slightly from side to side, not sure where to point my gun.

There're so many of them. At least two dozen to our five. We're completely outnumbered, and my stomach plummets, knowing there's a strong chance we're not getting out of here.

This is my fault. The bullshit of my family is following me, spilling over onto the only family that's shown me any love.

"Goddamn it," Thomas fumes, eyes locked on the men advancing through the field.

"What do we do?" Joe asks, gun out in front of him like the rest of us.

My heart's pounding, slamming into my chest like it's trying to escape. My palms are sweating, but my hands remain steady because this isn't the first time I've been in this fucked-up situation.

"Um, guys," Bear calls out with a quiver in his voice.

"Shut up, Bear," James growls, not bothering to turn around.

We don't have time for Bear's antics. This shit is life or death. There are dozens of guns filled with hundreds of bullets, waiting to draw blood.

"Put your guns down," a voice threatens from behind us, coming from Bear's direction.

Thomas turns his head, and his eyes immediately narrow. "Goddamn it, Bear."

"This is no time for games," James barks, turning his body and gun in a semicircle because we're no doubt surrounded.

The hair on the back of my neck stands up, and my arm tenses, finger tightening on the trigger. *Stay calm.* Gigi's words, words she's told me so many times, float through my head.

"Put your guns down," the man warns again, but closer and louder than before.

"Guns!" Thomas yells out, still facing Bear, back to the others making their way toward us. "They have Bear."

"We don't want to hurt anyone. We're only here for the kid," the man behind me explains.

I turn, knowing they want only me.

I'm the kid.

I'm the one they're after.

The men at my side, Gigi's family, are innocent in this entire thing. They never should've been here, but I let them talk me into the pack mentality, believing it was better to come in numbers than breeze into the Disciples' compound on my own.

"I'm here," I grit out, dropping my arm and the gun at my side because if they want me, they can have me. "Let him go."

The man at Bear's side has a gun to his head, snarling at me as his beady eyes land on my face. "I knew you were a pussy."

I take a step forward, holding out my arms, letting the gun twirl around my finger before it falls to the ground. "Let him go, and you can have me," I beg, somehow keeping my voice calm.

"No!" Joe yells out, stepping in front of me, blocking my movement with his back.

"What are you doing?" I yell as my stomach rolls. "They want me, Joe. I'm not worth losing your life."

"Shut up, kid," Joe barks back, not moving a muscle and not lowering the gun.

This is so fucked up. More fucked up than I ever could've imagined. How would I go back to Gigi and explain her father died because of me? She'd never forgive me. Never love me again. No matter what, she is a daddy's girl, loving this man more than anything else in her life.

I place my hand on his shoulder, squeezing gently. "You have too much to live for. Don't be a fool," I whisper, my voice cracking because, goddamn, no one has ever stuck their neck out like this for me before.

He's rock solid, frozen and not moving. "You can't go."

"We have thirty guys to your five and another thirty waiting behind. You really want to die today?" the asshole with the gun to Bear's head asks.

No. I'm not into dying today or any day soon, but I definitely am not into letting these men, the ones I've grown to respect, die for me today either.

I stalk next to Joe, glancing at him, pleading with him with my eyes. "Let me do this, Joe. You have a wife and kids to think about. I'm not worth it. Your life isn't worth the trouble my family has brought here and has always given me."

There's a softness to Joe's blue eyes as he studies me, jaw tight with anger. "If they take you…"

I touch his arm, knowing I need to get these words out because I may not have another chance. "I'd rather they take me than you. I love your daughter. Love her more than my life, but I can't let you take a bullet for me. I can't leave her and the rest of your family knowing I was the reason we died today. Not when I can do something to stop it. I'm willing to give my life for her, for you, and for them." I angle my neck backward. "Just tell her I'm sorry and that I love her."

Joe sighs, pain written all over his face as his clenched jaw pulses. "We'll figure this out."

I push down, making him drop his hand. "I'll figure this out. Just make sure the girls and my brother are safe."

"If anything…" he says, and his voice cracks, "…happens to you, we'll make sure Austin is taken care of."

His words give me solace and a sense of peace. I never thought I'd live to be this old. I figured I was dying that day Morris put a bullet in my shoulder. I've been living on borrowed time, and now it's up. My card is being punched, but at least I won't take my last breath for no reason. I'll be saving four men, returning them to their families to keep on living and loving.

"I'll go with you, but only if you leave them be!" I yell, holding out my hands at my sides again, showing I mean no harm.

"Goddamn it," Thomas groans.

The man with the greasy hair, Viper cut, and grizzly beard ticks his head toward the SUV. "The kid is ours, and so is everything that comes with him."

No one moves. It's like they're frozen to the ground, unsure what they should do. This is their time to run. Their way to escape. Their fucking freedom.

"Let me go!" I yell, turning to face three shocked faces, wide-eyed and ready for a gunfight. "Please. I beg you. Just leave. Go home. Go back to your family."

"You're lucky we don't want your head instead, Thomas. We know what you did to the Sun Devils. You're a traitor and a snitch. If he—" the man dips his head toward me "—wasn't so valuable, we'd be coming for you instead."

Did Morris sell us out? Would he do that? He's told me time and time again I'm like the son he never had but always wanted.

"Goddamn Morris and Tiny," James growls, thinking exactly what I am.

"Take him," Bear tells the guy still pressing the end of the gun to his head. Bear raises his hands higher in the air, and I'm praying like fuck he doesn't pull his Iron Man bullshit, thinking about getting cute and hitting the guy.

The man pushes Bear forward and motions for me with his gun. I look back, trying to give Joe a smile. "Tell her I did this for her," I plead before taking a step toward what I know will be certain death.

He nods with a scowl, not saying another word.

I step forward, head held high, walking forward without regret. I saved the life of four men today and sacrificed myself for so many others.

CHAPTER 17
GIGI

I COVER MY MOUTH, holding back the bile that's climbing up my throat and the cry threatening to break free.

They took Pike.

The words my father uttered on speakerphone replay in my mind on an endless loop, taunting me.

"You better not come home without him," Mom whispers into the phone, peering over at me before turning her back.

They took Pike.

Rocking back and forth, I whisper to myself, "He's going to be okay. He has to be okay."

Pike always finds a way out of trouble. He has his entire life. Why would this time be any different?

The drop was supposed to be simple. At least that's what they told me when they said I couldn't go.

I should've known better.

I should've begged to be there.

It wouldn't have been the first time I faced danger, but at least I would've been there, and things could have been different.

"What's the plan?" Mom asks as I start to hyperventilate, unable to stop myself as I can't get the air into my lungs easily.

They took Pike.

My vision blurs as tears fill my eyes, and the bile in my throat inches higher.

Pike's going to... I shake my head, not allowing myself to think the worst.

"That's so dangerous," Mom whispers, looking over her shoulder at me again and grimacing.

"Oh my God," I groan, running toward the bathroom, hand clamped against my lips before everything escapes all over my mother's hardwood floor.

I lift up the seat, throwing myself over the top, and open my mouth, letting whatever's coming work its way out. I groan as my chest heaves and my stomach lurches, the nerves taking over and rationality leaving my body with it.

Tears stream down my face, plopping into the bowl and splashing as I pull away.

This is it.

This is what it feels like when you're in love with someone and you know their life is going to end. I won't get to say any final words, reminding him of how I feel. How I'll always feel.

My mother walks into the bathroom, dropping to the floor next to me, her knees hitting the marble tile. "Baby, your daddy wants to talk to you."

I take the phone, and then she grabs a hand towel, wiping my lips like I'm a baby. "Daddy," I croak, unable to keep the panic from my voice. "What happened? Where's Pike?"

"Baby girl." My father's always calm, deep timbre comes through the speaker. "I don't know how it happened, but there were other men there. But don't worry, sweetheart, we're going to find him."

Don't worry?

"Oh my God," I whisper as the tears continue to fall because my father's words aren't making me feel any better.

"We're with Morris and the Disciples, making a plan. I promise, baby." His voice cracks, and I know he's tearing up, something my father rarely does, "I swear to God, I'll bring Pike back to you."

I know my father. I know he's a man of his word, but he's not Superman. "You don't know that," I snap, my anxiety and sorrow getting the better of me.

My dad blows out a breath, no doubt feeling the weight of my pain. "I'll do everything in my power to make it happen."

"How did this go so wrong?" I wipe the tears away from my cheeks and glance at the phone. "I thought Pike said this would be easy."

"Nothing's ever easy, baby. Especially when you're dealing with criminals." He pauses as I sniffle, feeling a fresh wave of tears coming on. "The men would've killed us all if it weren't for Pike, baby. He was brave today. Dumb, but brave."

"He's a good man, Daddy."

I've told him this a million times. He never believed a word, too blinded by his rage about me growing up.

My mom rubs my back, swaying from side to side as she tries to comfort me and humming a song she used to sing to me every night before bed.

Dad grunts. "I know, baby girl. I know. I have to go now. We're making a plan, and then we're hitting the road. I'm going to bring him home." There's rustling and yelling in the background. "I'll call as soon as we have him."

"Daddy!" I yell before he has a chance to hang up. "I love you."

"Love you too, Gigi. Hey, sugar?" His voice is so sweet and quiet as he asks for my mom.

Mom gives me a sad smile, trying to put on a brave face for me. "Yeah, sweetie. I'm here."

"I love you too," he breathes.

"I love you. Just come home safe, City. Don't be a hero," she tells him. Her face pales as soon as he hangs up, even though she tries to hide it by turning her head.

I drop the phone onto the rug and wrap my body around hers.

"Shh," she whispers, cradling me against her chest, rocking me like she used to when I had nightmares. "If anyone can save Pike, your daddy will do it."

If.

She said if anyone can.

No matter how scared I was at the Disciples' compound when DiSantis was after us, at least I was there.

I knew what was happening, but to not know anything is so much more frightening.

"They'll come home to us." She runs her hand down the back of my head in slow, steady strokes. "I know your daddy, baby, and he'll stop at nothing to make you happy."

"I don't want Dad to get hurt either," I whisper, choking back the tears that are lodged in my throat.

My dad's always been my hero. He seems immortal in my eyes, but I know he's like every other man.

He bleeds the same.

Feels the same pain.

Can die just like every other living thing on the planet.

"He'll be fine. They're smart. He has all the guys with him, baby. Don't work yourself into a panic."

Don't work myself into a panic? There isn't any work involved. I am there. My entire body feels the weight of what is happening.

I lie there, letting my mother's gentle rocking dry my tears, but the panic...it still grips me as I think about Pike.

Is Pike hurt?

Is he alone?

Is he afraid?

Are they torturing him?

Is he already dead?

There're so many questions, each one filling me with dread, knotting my stomach into a tighter ball.

"Hello!" Tamara yells out before I hear the front door slam so hard, I'd be shocked if the photos in the foyer are still hanging. "We came as soon as we heard."

I groan, not feeling like company or putting on a fake smile, pretending not to be completely terrified.

"Come on, baby. Let's go talk to Tam," Mom says, lifting me off the floor as she tries to stand. "It's not good to sit in here too long. I know you're already thinking the worst."

I climb to my feet, swiping at my cheeks with the backs of my fingers, spreading the tears around more than wiping them away. Everything around me is fuzzy like I'm dreaming, but I know I'm very much awake. This isn't a nightmare, but my new reality.

Tamara's in the hallway of my mother's house, holding a bottle of Jack Daniel's in one hand and a box of chocolate in the other. "I came prepared," she says, giving me a small smile, using the glass bottle to push her dark brown hair away from her face.

"I'll leave you guys be. I need a moment alone," my mother mumbles, heading in the other direction without even giving Tamara or Austin a hug.

I turn, following Tam's gaze as she gawks at my mother. I wish I could comfort my mom in the same way she just comforted me. I know she's going to cry. I know my mother better than anyone in the world. She consoled me, but she's just as fearful for my father's life.

How could she not be?

He's her everything and has been for decades.

"How bad is it?" Tamara asks as I turn to face her.

"Bad, Tam. Really bad." I shake my head, twisting my lips and blinking to stop myself from crying again.

"Izzy called and told me to get my ass over here because shit went south. I'm not sure what that means, but I grabbed Austin and headed here..." She holds up the Jack, shaking it, but thank God, she doesn't smile. "Want a drink?"

"I want all the drinks," I tell her, stepping toward the kitchen in heavy, slow movements like the weight of the world is on my shoulders.

Austin's on the couch, hunched over, holding his head.

She goes to the cabinet, opens the door, and grabs two glasses as I slide onto the same barstool I'd been sitting on earlier. "What happened?" she asks.

"They were ambushed, and they took Pike." Saying the words still doesn't make it all feel real. My gaze moves to Austin, and he doesn't move, doesn't even blink.

Tamara's eyes widen as she sets down the glasses in front of her and freezes. "No shit. That is bad."

I nod, fighting back the tears. I will not cry again. I always tell Pike to keep calm, and I have to too.

"They're making a plan to rescue him." I choke on the word rescue, but I somehow rebound, getting the last word out.

"They'll get him. Our guys never come home empty-handed," Tamara reminds me.

"Yeah," I mumble, but I'm not even convinced by my answer. "You okay, Austin?"

Austin grunts, not even looking up at us. "I'm fine," he snaps, but we both know he's lying.

"It's okay to be worried," I tell him. "But I know my dad and uncles—they'll stop at nothing to get Pike back." And that's exactly what I'm worried about too. Not only is Pike's life in danger, they're all in danger.

"This is all my father's fault," Austin whispers before climbing to his feet and storming out of the house.

"Leave him," Tamara tells me when I start to move. "He needs time to process everything." She presses the meaty part of her palms into her eyes and blows out a breath. "I'm not sure Jack was right for this situation. I think this is more a tequila type of crisis. You need to be completely shit-faced."

I'd laugh if things weren't so grave. Breakups always called for the hard stuff because who wanted to remember their broken heart? But this is different. I don't want to be passed out when…

"Jack's good," I tell her, grabbing the bottle from her hands, not needing a glass. Her eyes widen as I twist off the top and lift the entire bottle to my lips.

"Maybe you should…"

I glare at her, opening my mouth, letting the amber liquid wash over my tongue and slide down my throat. I wince a little as my throat burns from the mix of hard liquor and vomit.

"Damn, girl. You're not playing," she teases as her eyebrows shoot up, and I keep guzzling mouthful after mouthful.

I pull the bottle away, gasping for air as I wipe my lips with the back of my hand.

She motions for the bottle, because Tamara is never one to be left out of a party, even if it's not a happy occasion.

I narrow my eyes and hold out the bottle to her, knowing damn well she isn't going to take it. "I just puked and didn't rinse my mouth. You really want to share?"

She shakes her head as her lip curls. "Bitch, you should've used a glass. Gross."

I climb off the stool, taking the bottle with me as I walk around the couch and plop down. "I've never felt so helpless, Tam. They don't even know where he is."

She's next to me a moment later, tearing off the plastic wrapping on the cheap box of chocolates I'm sure she picked up at the drugstore. "What happened exactly?"

I tell her the limited details my father shared, leaving nothing out. Her eyebrows move around as if they have a life of their own as she gawks at me like I've just told her the craziest tale.

"Well, Jesus," she mumbles, holding a piece of chocolate near her lips but not taking a bite. "Doesn't he have one of those fancy-ass watches? I mean, why don't they just track him through GPS?"

I gasp, leaping from the couch and immediately regretting all the Jack. My knees wobble as soon as my feet touch the floor, but I catch myself on the armrest before my face has a chance to get up close and personal with the floor. "You're a genius," I tell her, crouched over, waiting for the room to stop spinning. "A goddamn genius."

She shoves the chocolate into her mouth, smiling at me. "I know. I've always known," she replies while chewing.

I glance around, my eyes blurry from the tears that still haven't stopped and dizzy as a motherfucker. "My phone. Oh my God, where's my phone? I have to call my dad and tell him."

Tamara pushes the chocolates to the side, running toward the kitchen. "I'm on it," she snaps as she grabs my phone and starts tapping away at the screen.

"Yeah, baby?" Dad asks before Tamara's made it back to me.

"Daddy, I know how to find Pike." I speak so fast, it comes out like one single long word.

"Tell me," he replies, and for the first time in what feels like hours, I don't feel so useless anymore.

CHAPTER 18
PIKE

"JUST KILL HIM," a man orders like he's not talking about taking a man's life.

My life.

The voices are muffled and distant like I'm dreaming, but I know I'm very much alive.

I can't see anything, but I feel *everything*.

The dampness of the blood that's pooled near my hand after they decided a hammer to the pinkie would make me talk.

The cold cement against my cheeks as I lie on my side, gasping for air after they used my stomach to clean their boots, kicking me so many times, I lost count.

"He could be useful," another man replies somewhere behind me.

"We have the key. What more do we fuckin' need?" the asshole who wants to kill me asks.

"I know he means something to the Disciples. Maybe we could…"

"Don't be a dumb fuck," the asshole snaps. "The Disciples aren't going to give us shit. They wanted the key, but it's a good thing this kid's father is such a fuckin' talker."

"Doesn't hurt to have Chev spying either," the dumbass says, and I know exactly who they're talking about.

Chev earned his cut after I left. He wasn't very talkative, but he took orders without question, always delivering what was required. When the Disciples find out they have a rat in their ranks, they're going to kill him in the most painful way possible.

If they find out.

I try to open my eyes, but the swelling is so bad, nothing's clear.

All I have is the darkness for solace. "Just kill me," I groan the plea, my voice barely loud enough for anyone but me to hear.

I'd rather die than be a pawn in their sick game.

"Shut up!" a man yells, before something connects with my jaw, snapping my head backward.

The searing-hot pain quickly follows, slicing through my system from my face to my lungs. I gasp, choking on my own blood, wishing they'd just put me out of my misery already.

"He's heard too much. Seen even more," another man explains, his voice icy and calm. "Drop him in the Everglades. You know the spot."

"Should we kill him here?" Dumbass asks.

"No. He can walk into his watery grave," Asshole replies.

I'm sorry is my silent apology to Gigi, knowing I'll never get to see her beautiful face again. The pain I've endured at the hands of my captors is nothing compared to the agony she'll feel from my death.

I swallow down the metallic taste coating my tongue, fighting through the pain, reveling in my final hours of being alive.

There's so much about my life I'd change if I could, but if living longer means never being with Giovanna Gallo, I wouldn't change a goddamn thing. I'd die today to know her love. I'd willingly end my life early for an ounce of her softness. She is everything I ever wanted and never had until recently.

I may be taking my last breaths, but I don't have any regrets. The men who live on because I'm here, lying on the ground, have families, and they'll do everything in their power to make sure Gigi carries on. She'll marry someday and have babies.

My chest aches, thinking of their tiny faces looking so much like their mother and knowing I won't be their father. It's a selfish thought, but one I can't stop myself from having.

Hands slide over my arm, gripping me roughly. "Up you go, princess. You're about to get your wish."

I groan, finding my footing but still unable to see more than a thin line of light. "Fuck you," I snap, twisting my shoulder as he tries to pull me upright. "Get your damn hands off me."

"He's a live one," the asshole adds. "He would've been a good soldier."

A loud explosion throws me backward, sending my knees and face back against the cement. I groan as the metallic taste of my blood fills my mouth again, and the shooting pain from hitting the concrete ricochets up my legs.

Gunfire and yelling ring through the room, along with the ringing from the explosion echoing in my ears that I can't seem to stop. I collapse, sprawling out on the cool, damp floor, letting the sweet ache of my injuries remind me I'm still very much alive.

But not for much longer.

"Take his ass outside!" someone yells, a voice I know. A voice I've heard a million times. "Get him out of here quick."

The gunfire doesn't stop as heavy bootsteps come near. "Pike, holy fuck," Morris groans. "Jesus Christ." ·

Yeah. I'm pretty sure I look as shitty as I feel.

"Come on. Let's go," he orders, touching my arm gently like there aren't bullets whizzing near his head.

I lift myself to my knees, wincing as pain shoots up my thighs and causes me to gasp for air. I reach out, finding his hands in the darkness, still unable to see. "Morris," I whisper, thinking I'm imagining he's here.

"Yeah, shithead. Get up, or I'm going to poke you in the eyeball to get your ass moving."

That's Morris. He's such a sadistic fuck. I have no doubt, in this moment, bloodied and busted as I am, he would fucking poke me. He punched me when I was shot; why wouldn't he do the same now?

Even with the pain, I muster a crooked smile. "You came."

"If you don't get your ass moving, we're both going to be dead," he tells me, pulling my entire body weight forward until I find my footing.

I hold on to his arm, letting him be my eyes because no matter how hard I try, I can't see a fucking thing. When the warmth hits my skin, I know we're outside but nowhere near safe.

"The guys," I wheeze.

"They're big boys with even bigger guns." Morris pats my hand. "They'll be okay."

"Leave me and go back." I stop walking, letting my hands fall away from his arm. "Don't save me and risk their lives. Go, Morris. If you ever loved me, go save them," I plead.

"Always a fuckin' problem," Morris groans, placing his meaty hand on my shoulder. "Don't move. Stay here."

"Fucker, go!" I yell, crumpling to the gravel.

Where the hell would I go? I can't see six inches in front of my face, let alone far enough to wander off like some lost kitten.

Morris doesn't say another word, but the sound of gravel crunching under his boots makes it clear he finally listened for once.

I lean back, letting the hard rock bite into my skin as I lie flat, relishing the warmth the stones have soaked up from the sun. I let myself drift because the reality is just too much to take.

"Man, he looks like shit," Bear murmurs from above me, waking me. "I mean, he wasn't anything special to look at before, but now..."

"Fuck you," I mutter and wince.

The gravel crunches near my head, followed by gentle hands touching my battered face. "Call an ambulance."

"No." My answer is immediate and firm. "No cops. No hospitals."

"Put him in the truck. We'll have the doc come to the compound and check him out," Morris commands. "I'll call her now and have her meet us there."

"Can you walk?" Joe asks, his hands moving to my hand, lifting my palm upward. "Fucking hell."

"It's fine." I pull my hand back to my body. "I'm not left-handed."

"I wasn't worried about work, son," he says softly, and I can hear the sincerity in his voice. "Help me carry him."

"No," I groan as I push myself upward with the one hand I have that they didn't smash into pieces. "I can walk on my own."

"This should be fun to watch," Bear teases, always the complete asshole.

"Shut up," Joe snaps. "Come on, Pike. Let's get you out of here, and I'll call Gigi from the truck."

"Gigi," I whisper, thinking about my girl and the level of panic she has to be experiencing. "Call her now."

"No," he tells me, the light shifting back and forth as he moves in front of me. "Truck first, and then you can talk to her. We don't need to be here when the cops show up."

He's a bastard, but he's right. The sound of the blast had to draw someone's attention. No doubt the place will be swarming with police soon.

I reach out, and Joe immediately slides his hand in mine, helping me to my feet.

"James, bring the truck!" he yells as we take a step forward, and I gasp for air.

"My fuckin' ribs," I wheeze. "They're broken."

Joe slides his arm behind my back, and I lean on him, letting him guide me through the darkness. "A lot of you is broken, son. A whole hell of a lot."

"In ya go, kid," Thomas orders, one hand on my arm while Joe keeps me steady.

I climb inside the truck, being given the front seat, and collapse backward, sucking in the little breath my broken ribs will allow.

I'm going to live.

I've never been one to cry, but in this moment, with the men piling into the SUV with me, I could. They put their lives on the line to save mine. No one has ever done that. No one has ever cared enough to do something so profound and selfless.

"Daddy?" Gigi's voice comes through the truck speakers.

"We got him, baby girl. He's okay."

"Pike?"

"I'm here, darlin'," I manage the words, not sounding as completely shitty as I feel.

"Oh my God, baby. I've been so worried. I thought you were…"

"I'm not. I'm okay, love."

I'd say more, but I'm too choked up and moved by everything Gallo.

"He's a little banged up," Joe tells her.

Banged up? That's one way of putting it.

"We'll call you when we get back to the compound, okay, princess?"

"Pike?"

"Yeah?"

"I love you," she says softly, her voice cracking.

"Love you too, darlin'," I tell her, unable to keep the emotion from my voice.

"Talk soon," Joe adds, and then there's silence to match the darkness.

———

"How does that feel?" the MC's doctor asks as she presses a towel against my eyelid after slicing through the skin. "It'll help reduce the swelling and should make it easier for you to see."

"Feels great," I lie, taking the towel from her hand and holding it against my face.

I feel like one-hundred-percent absolute shit. I've never felt this bad in my entire life, but at least I am alive. That's what I hold on to as she checks me over, patching up my busted parts.

"There's not much I can do for the ribs. They'll heal, but it'll be a few months before you feel normal again. Luckily, your jaw isn't broken, but you should get to a dentist soon to make sure your teeth aren't damaged from the boot you took to the face."

She's blurry, but her shape is clearer with each passing second. I can see the shadow of her body and the bright red of her top.

"The pinkie, I stitched and set. You may need surgery on it if it doesn't heal straight. Keep an eye on it. As for the rest of you, I cleaned any wounds, but they're minimal."

I almost laugh. Minimal?

"He gonna live, Doc?" Morris asks, stalking into the room, scrubbing the back of his neck with his hands.

"He'll live."

Morris exhales, sounding relieved. "Thank fuck."

There are a few clicks before she moves away from me, leaving me on the table.

"Thanks, Doc."

"I'll send you the bill." She pats him on the chest, giving him a bright smile before disappearing out the door.

"This is my fault," Morris admits, stalking across the room and pulling out a chair in front of me. "I fucked up."

I glance down, dropping the cloth next to me so I can see him. "It's my father's fault—and Chev's."

"Chev?" Morris raises an eyebrow, cocking his head to the side.

"He's a rat, Morris. A fuckin' rat." I wince and grab my ribs. "That's how the Vipers knew about the drop."

"I'll take care of him." He nods, and I know what that means. Chev is a dead man walking. "You're one lucky SOB," he says, changing the subject.

I shrug, but I know it's the truth.

"Those men, the girl's family, they weren't leaving without you."

I try to smile, but I grimace, hating everything about today. "They're good people."

"The best," Morris agrees and touches my leg. "I knew you were something special."

"Was that before or after you sucker-punched my shoulder?" I ask him.

He barks out a laugh. "Never going to let me live it down, are ya?"

I shake my head. "Never."

Morris studies me as his laughter dies. "I didn't think I'd see you alive again, Pike. I'm happy I was wrong."

"Me too," I mutter.

"You have a whole room of people who want to see you, and then we'll let you rest. You're staying the night and all heading back tomorrow. Tiny's having your room made up so you're comfortable."

"Thanks," I whisper, taking in a man who's been more of a father to me than mine ever was. When he goes to stand, I know there need to be more words. There may not be another chance. His life, the MC life, isn't known for its longevity. "Morris."

He turns around, his dark eyes gazing at me with intensity. "What's wrong?"

"Thank you for always being there for me. I would've been honored to call you brother."

He smiles. "I would've been happy to call you a son," he replies, knowing exactly what those words mean to me.

I don't say anything else. Morris isn't the type of guy you gush to too much about your feelings. I've never heard him utter the words *I love you* to another man, and I'm not going to force him to say them now.

A minute after he leaves, the four men who came to my rescue walk into the room, their gazes sweeping over my body.

"She patched you up good," Joe says, but he's lying. "You don't look too bad."

Bear winces as his eyes soak me in. "He looks like hell," he argues.

James glares at Bear, slapping him in the chest with the back of his hand. "Now's no time for jokes, asshole."

Bear shrugs. "Wasn't joking. Look at him." He throws out his arm toward me. "If hell had a look, it would be that."

Joe ignores him, stalking toward me and stopping only a few inches away. I crane my neck back, somehow stopping myself from wincing again.

"You scared the shit out of us," he admits, running his hand through his hair. "I thought I was going to have to tell my little girl you died. I thought I was going to have to live with the guilt that I let you go instead of me."

"I went willingly."

He places his hand on my shoulder, regarding me with something I've rarely seen from him—respect. "It was honorable, Pike. Something any of us—" he shifts his head toward James, Thomas, and Bear "—would do for one another, but you didn't have to give your life for ours."

"I did," I tell him, holding his gaze. "I love your daughter, sir, and I couldn't have looked her in the eye if something had happened to any of you. Her world revolves around her family."

He gives me a pained smile. "We'll always be her family, Pike, but you're her world now."

How does someone respond to something like that? Thank you doesn't seem right. It's too monumental from a man who wanted to see me exit her life as quickly as I appeared not too long ago. I have no words. Nothing that can adequately convey how I feel.

"Izzy's going to have my balls," James tells Thomas, cracking his neck toward the door. "I told her I'd avoid killing someone this trip."

"Never make those kinds of promises, brother. I've told you this," Thomas chastises him, shrugging it off.

They're still two scary motherfuckers. Family or not, my ass is never crossing them. Never.

"You better get your woman under control," Bear orders, and just like that, everyone's forgotten I'm a bloody mess.

CHAPTER 19
GIGI

"YOUR LIFE IS like a goddamn soap opera," Tamara quips as we stand in the parking lot of the apartment. "I'm almost jealous."

I turn to her, narrowing my eyes. "You're an asshole. This shit isn't fake, Tamara. Pike could've died."

She frowns, glancing down at her sandals. "I know. I'm sorry," she whispers.

My body's buzzing, and every second that passes, I find it more impossible to stand still. "It's fine. I know you were scared for him too."

She was too. She loves Pike just as much as I do. Not in the same way, but he's grown on her. At first, she wasn't convinced he was a one-woman man. It's not like I have the best track record when it comes to relationships. I probably would've thought the same thing if I were in her shoes.

"They here yet?" Austin asks, coming up behind us, hair a mess because he's just crawled out of bed.

I shake my head, turning back to the street and seeing nothing. "They'll be here any minute. Dad said they were at the light."

"Ever feel like you need an epic adventure?" Tamara asks, earning herself another glare.

"Are you for real?"

She shrugs, giving me a smile. "My life is so boring. Like, if white paint had a life, the shade would be Tamara."

I giggle because the stupidity of her statement is too much for me. "You're…"

"TamTam, I can brighten your world," Austin offers, sliding his arm around her shoulder. "Just give me a shot."

"When you become a badass biker man, give me a call," she teases, elbowing him in the ribs. "Read my shirt, kid. Nothing else needs to be said."

"Tattooed boys are my favorite toys," he says slowly, ogling her chest more than the stark-white lettering. "Gigi can tattoo me tomorrow." He smiles, winking at her. "I got you."

She rolls her eyes and groans. "It's a way of life, Aussie, not a decoration. There's nothing sexier than a man covered in ink, riding a Harley," she sighs. "Am I right?"

"Sure. Yeah," I reply without really listening. I'm too busy staring at the street, waiting for my favorite tattooed boy. "Where are they?"

Austin's strong hand is on my shoulder. "They'll be here. He's fine," he reminds me, something he's been doing for the last twelve hours.

"I know." I twist my hands in front of me, shifting from side to side to keep my sanity in check. "But I won't believe it until I see him with my own eyes."

Suddenly, the roar of dozens of motorcycles fills the air, and we all lift our heads, watching as the motorcade enters the apartment complex.

"Holy fuck!" Tamara yells.

"It's like the president has arrived," Austin jokes over my shoulder.

"Damn," I whisper, seeing James's SUV surrounded by bikes, progressing at a steady pace in the middle. I hold my breath as time seems to move slower than usual.

I've never been a patient person, but standing here now, waiting to see Pike again, feels like torture. The ground rumbles under my feet as the line of bikes stops near the curb.

"Breathe, Gigi!" Austin yells in my ear, reaching forward to hold my hand.

I squeeze his fingers, sucking in a deep breath before I pass out as I release them.

Calm down. He's fine.

I don't remember the last time I was this excited and petrified at the same time. Probably never.

When the black SUV rolls to a stop in front of me, I take a step forward, shaking out my hands and the fear that's been plaguing me.

My dad is the first one out, rounding the SUV, barely making eye contact. "Hey, baby," he whispers. "Now, don't panic."

"Don't panic?" I jerk my head back, widening my eyes. "What's that mean?"

"Oh, dear God," Tamara whispers. "That's never good."

She's always quick with the uplifting comments. *Bitch.*

Dad smiles, touching my cheek gently. "He's fine. He doesn't look great, and I don't want you to freak out."

I shrug off my father's touch and take off toward the SUV. My fingers shake as I grip the handle, flinging the door open. The flinch is immediate. The gasp is next.

"Fuck," I hiss, tears filling my eyes at the horror of his battered face and the happiness of him making it home.

"Missed you too, darlin'," he drawls, turning slowly to swing his jeans-covered legs out of the truck.

I want to rush forward, pepper his face with kisses, but I can't seem to move. It's like I'm frozen to the ground, the reality of what happened written all over his face.

"Baby," I whisper, my voice cracking as I cover my mouth.

"You said I was pretty, Joe. She doesn't seem too impressed with my makeover," Pike laughs as his boots touch the ground.

"I tried to prepare her." Dad shrugs.

"Didn't work," Pike tells him, grimacing as he straightens and starts to take a step.

I move forward, reaching for him. "Can I touch you?" I ask.

He nods, giving me a smile. "I'm not going to break."

"It looks like you're already broken, yo," Tamara, the comedian, taunts.

"Ignore her," I groan, but Pike's smile never falters.

"I am, but I've never been happier to be alive," Pike confesses, holding me close with one arm.

"We're going to go," Dad says, watching as I help Pike up on to the sidewalk.

"What about them?" Austin ticks his chin toward the bikers.

"They'll be nearby for the night."

I lift my gaze, finding Morris planted on the front bike, watching us. I smile at him, happy as hell he's here. He immediately sends a wink back my way.

Pike turns, taking me with him. "Joe?"

"Yeah?"

"Thank you," Pike says simply.

My dad looks at me and then toward Pike. "No thank-yous are needed for family, kid."

I gape at him, wondering what in the hell happened to change his attitude. I get Pike almost died, but it sure as hell wasn't the first time. Dad wasn't all kumbaya after the shootout at the Disciples' compound. Granted, Pike didn't look like absolute shit then either.

"That was some crazy shit right there," Tamara says, blinking at my father like she thinks she must've been hearing things too.

"We went through a lot," Pike tells us. "More shit than I'll ever tell you."

I grab a better hold of his belt loop, careful not to put too much pressure on his ribs. "I want to know everything."

He shakes his head. "Some things are better left unsaid, darlin'."

"Our place or hers?" Austin asks, walking slowly at his brother's other side.

Pike glances over, smiling at his little brother. "Ours. I want my bed and my girl tonight."

Amen.

———

I tuck my hand under my cheek, trying to hold back the tears. "I was so scared, baby. So, so scared."

"Come here," he breathes, motioning for me to scoot closer.

"I don't want to hurt you."

"You won't."

I move an inch closer, but still far enough away I don't cause his side of the bed to move.

"Darlin', I need you against me." He smiles.

"You're all…" I motion to his bare chest with my hand, wincing.

"I know, but you can't hurt me any more than I already am. Just come here and stop being so stubborn."

I snort, pushing myself up on my elbow. "I'm not stubborn."

He reaches up, brushing my hair away from my face with his fingers. "I thought I'd never see you again." His eyes search my face, and I do my best not to cry, but fail. "Don't cry again," he pleads.

"I'm a mess," I groan, wiping my cheek on my shoulder. "I'm sorry."

I've cried more tears today than yesterday. Every time I looked at him, a fresh wave would overtake me. His swollen eyes and bruised jaw are a constant reminder of everything he went through.

He slides his fingers across my cheek until they're in my hair, my face resting in his palm. "Don't ever be sorry."

My lips find his wrist, one of the only places on him that isn't busted. "I just love you so much."

"Come here," he orders again, digging his fingers into my neck. "I want to hold you."

I don't argue this time, needing the skin-on-skin contact as much as he does. I press my chest against his side, the one without the broken ribs, and place my head on his shoulder.

"We need to talk," he says with so much seriousness, I gaze upward into his green eyes, quickly sobering.

"What's wrong? Am I hurting you?" I start to move, but he holds me down with his hand on my shoulder.

"No, you're not hurting me."

"Then what?"

"When I was lying there, sure I was a dead man, I did a lot of thinking."

"Yeah?"

Oh my God. Is this the moment? The one every girl dreams about? The one I'll tell my children about someday?

"If I were to die..." he starts.

So wrong, Gigi. So fucking wrong.

"Stop," I whisper and push myself upward and away from him. "I don't want to hear anymore."

"If I were to die..." he repeats.

I shake my head and close my eyes. "It's not happening."

"Darlin', listen." His touch is whisper-soft but unmistakable. "I need to say this."

I take a deep breath and open my eyes again, knowing it's only fair to let him say whatever's on his mind. He almost died, for shit's sake, and no matter how badly I don't want to hear what's about to come next, I have to let him say it. "I'm listening."

"I don't plan on going anywhere anytime soon, but I need to know that if something happens to me, you'll keep on going. You'll find a husband, make babies, grow old, and be happy."

I twist my lips, blinking at him. "Are you for real right now?"

He nods.

"If I were to die, would you ever be happy?" I question him.

"Well, no," he confesses without batting a fucking eyelash.

"Neither would I. So, can we talk about something else?"

"Only if you lie down again."

"As long as you don't talk about dying anymore." I place my hand on my chest, trying to calm myself down. "My heart can't take it."

He nods, grabbing my arm and pulling me toward him. "It's the last thing I want. I don't think I can ever have enough time with you."

I curl into him and press my lips to his shoulder. "I know this is a strange thing to say, but I feel like I've known you my entire life."

"I don't want to remember what life was like before you." He runs his fingers through my hair, and I can't hold back the moan. "I wasn't livin' until you came into my world, darlin'. I was existing. There's a difference."

"I can't imagine my life without you, Pike."

"I love you," he whispers.

I gaze up and smile. "I love you too."

We lie there in silence, lightly touching each other.

If I didn't know better, I'd swear I was dreaming.

CHAPTER 20
GIGI

TWO MONTHS LATER...

I turn in my seat, Pike's warm hand resting on my knee, to glare at Austin in the back seat of my pickup. "If you say a word to our parents about our first stop, you're not going to make it to your eighteenth birthday."

Austin swallows, his Adam's apple bobbing. "Come on, ladies," he says, sliding his arms behind Lily and Tamara. "Would I do something like that?"

"Yes," all three of us answer in unison.

Lily elbows him in the ribs. "We may not kill you, but I'll hold you down and let Tamara pull your fingernails out."

Austin pales, and I bite my lip to stop myself from giggling. Lily's hard-core and gives zero fucks. I adore the bitch so much and wish she'd gone to college near us instead of venturing out on her own. Fuckin' scholarships.

"You wouldn't do that." Austin's voice cracks, but he keeps on rolling. "You love me."

Tamara runs her palm across his hand. "That's why we'd only do your fingernails and leave you alive, Aussie. We'd never kill you, but we're not above torturing you." She smiles, and it's so beautifully wicked, my heart grows three sizes like the Grinch at the end of my favorite Christmas movie.

"You bitches are vicious," Austin groans, pulling his hand back and tucking his fingers between his legs. "So fucking vicious. I won't say a word. Jesus, give me some credit. I memorized the story, practicing it and spitting it back perfectly when they questioned me at the shop."

It's not like they can tell us no. We are all adults after all, living on our own. And even though our families are nosy, they don't have the right to tell us what to do.

But that doesn't mean any of us want to hear their shit either. God, if my dad found out we were stopping by the compound for a night, I'd get a freaking earful until I went deaf. He'd probably still keep yelling, figuring his deep, husky voice would penetrate somehow.

Lily winks at me, knowing just like I do, there's no harm in scaring the piss out of the guy. We've learned one thing in our two decades together—we never snitch on each other.

"Loosen up, Aussie. This is going to be a fun weekend." Tamara reaches up and pinches Austin's cheeks, trying to get him to relax.

He shakes his head, digging his fingers deeper. "I just wanted to see some T&A. Someday, you'll trust me."

Lily drags her finger down his other cheek, smiling when he starts to squirm. "You're going to see some T&L, and that's about it, li'l guy."

"T&L?" Austin asks.

"Tamara and Lily," Lily laughs.

Austin rolls his eyes. "You two are like my sisters." He pretends to gag, but I know he's lying. The horndog hasn't let up, and even though he's nervous as fuck between the two of them right this second, he's loving the attention they're giving him.

"Here's the rules," Pike tells us, glancing in the rearview mirror and squeezing my leg. "This is for everybody and not just Austin, ya hear?"

"Yes!" the four of us groan, knowing Big Daddy Pike is about to lay down the law and it's going to be boring as fuck.

"I lived with these people. I know their ways. This is one of the tamest parties of the year. The kids will be there, but that doesn't mean there isn't bad shit happening if you go looking for it."

"Oh yeah?" Lily asks, scooting forward. "What kind of shit?"

"You won't go lookin' for it, so don't worry about it, Lily," he tells her before bringing his eyes back to the road.

"Drugs?" Austin asks with a little too much enthusiasm.

Pike's steely gaze slices to the mirror. "If you go within so much as five feet of drugs, I'm cutting your dick off and shoving it down your throat."

I wince, imagining the horror and pain. Pike can say what he wants, but I know he'd never lay a finger on his brother...drugs or not.

"You're just as bad as Gran," Austin mutters.

"That goes for all of you. No drugs. No hard liquor. I don't want to be dragging your sloppy asses out of some asshole's room or rescuing you from a crazy gang bang that sounded like fun because you were too drunk to realize they weren't talking about pounding rocks."

"What?" I ask, glancing at him, so fucking confused.

He shrugs but keeps on rolling. "Don't embarrass me, and for the love of God, don't embarrass yourself."

"You have a way with words, Shakespeare," Lily teases, covering her mouth immediately to snicker into the palm of her hand.

"Sure thing, Joe. Whatever you say," Tamara adds because she's a shithead and loves pissing off Pike.

Pike wrinkles his forehead. "What did you call me?"

I place my hand on his forearm, somehow managing not to laugh. "We hear you, boss man. Calm down a little. It's Labor Day weekend, and we're supposed to have fun."

"Fun," he mutters, glancing toward the top of the truck cab. "I don't care about fun, Gigi. I didn't even want to go to this damn party, but you just had to jump at Morris's offer."

I bristle at his choice of words, tightening my grip on his arm. "These people were your people once, Pike. They saved your life twice," I remind him. "Relax a little. We had fun the last time we were here. Remember?"

He turns his head so slowly, eyes so icy, the hairs on the back of my neck stand up, looking for a quick exit. "Last time we were here —" he points toward the compound "—we almost died."

I nod, remembering it well and still happy as shit we lived. "But we didn't." I put a smile on my face, hoping to make him chill out. "We were whisked away without even being able to say thank you to the men who put their lives on the line to save us. I think we could at least have a beer with them and let them know their bravery didn't go unappreciated."

He groans. "You know I love these guys. They were my family for years, but damn, Gigi. They're not the fun-loving bunch you think they are. They're one-percenters."

"Damn," Lily squeaks, "they're that rich?"

"You seriously need to get out more," Tamara tells Lily, leaning over Austin, giving her a *you're a freaking idiot* stare.

All I can do is roll my eyes, ignoring the cute, clueless bitch in the backseat. She's such a brainiac; she knows her chemistry way better than her MC lingo. Poor, poor Lily.

"What?" Lily asks, glancing around the truck like we're supposed to clue her in, but I don't have time for all that.

"Don't worry, babe," Austin tells her, finally removing his hands from his legs to tap her hand. "I got you."

"Now," Pike barks, turning around, facing the three goofballs in the backseat. "Am I going to have to go into Gallo witness protection after this trip because one of you assholes has to act like a tool?"

Three headshakes are immediate, and then he brings his eyes to me. "You going to behave too?"

I smile and shrug. "Don't I always?"

Pike blinks, but the corner of his lip twitches, and I know I have him.

———

I lean back in the chair, comfortably sandwiched between Pike's thighs, gazing up at the sky. "I take back what I said before."

"What?"

"About this place being like Disney World for crack whores and criminals." I laugh, resting my head on his shoulder as he strokes the bare skin of my shoulder with his fingers.

"What do you think now?" he asks in a husky voice, and my skin tingles with each pass of his fingers.

"This—" I lift my hand, pointing toward the bounce houses and all the other family shit all over the compound's yard "—is totally the Disney World for them bitches. Before was more like Chuck E. Cheese."

My body shakes as Pike laughs, the deep, rich sound sending shivers down my spine. "Darlin', you're beyond fucked up."

"But you love me?" I ask, turning my face to look up into his beautiful green eyes.

He nods without hesitation. "More than breathing," he tells me, and my stomach flutters.

I snuggle into him as he drops his hand, sliding his arms around me. "Are you relaxed yet?" I ask, watching as the club whores prance around, showing their goods to whoever will look. "You were wound pretty tight before."

His lips brush the skin near my ear, and I close my eyes, getting lost in his touch. "I'm just scared," he admits, and my eyes snap open.

Pike rarely says those words. He hasn't uttered them since the last time we were here.

"There's nothing to be scared about."

He tightens his hold, his warm breath skidding across my neck. "Any time we're here, we're a target. They're an MC, Gigi. This isn't a hobby. Bad shit happens all the time." He exhales, pulling me with him as he leans back into the chair. "There wasn't a day when I lived here that something crazy didn't happen. And just being here with you guys has me on edge. I won't relax until we're at least thirty miles away from the gates."

"We can go now," I offer.

"We'll stay. It's dark, late, and I'm tired as fuck. We'll crash here tonight, but we're gone first thing in the morning."

"I asked for an early check-in in Daytona."

"Good, darlin'. I could use a little downtime. We've been going nonstop for what feels like an eternity."

"Pike?"

"Yeah."

"I'm about to sweat my face off, so do you mind if I have a beer since we're all about relaxing now?" I smile into the darkness.

"Beer's fine, but not tequila," he teases with a hint of laughter.

I push myself up, leaving the safety of his arms, and roll my eyes as soon as I turn around to face him. "Don't forget, without the tequila, we wouldn't be where we are now."

He's out of his seat, hands on my hips, before I have a chance to react. A slow, small smile crosses his lips. "Darlin', you were mine the moment I laid eyes on you. Tequila or no tequila, we'd still be right where we are now."

I gulp, taking in those endlessly deep eyes. "Yeah," I whisper, knowing what he's saying is true.

"Yeah," he tells me, gripping my hips rougher. "I wasn't letting you walk out of that bar without me."

"You're really cocky."

One corner of his mouth moves higher. "I got my girl, didn't I?"

"Mr. Cuervo got you this girl," I tease.

Pike slides his hands to my ass, pulling my body against his cock. "Keep lyin' to yourself, beautiful."

"Pike!" Austin's voice comes from behind me.

Pike lifts his head immediately, eyes searching through the crowd to find his brother.

"Over here," the same pain-in-the-ass teenager says again.

Pike dips his face, bringing his lips so close to mine, I can't breathe without taking him in. "Promise me we won't have kids for a few years. I don't like dividing my time."

My belly flops again because, holy freaking hell, he's talking about babies. "I promise." I nod.

"Pike!"

"Jesus Christ," Pike growls, turning me around and tucking me under his arm, resting his hand on my shoulder. "Let's go see what he wants."

"Dude." Austin runs his hand through his hair, eyes wide and panicked. "I can't find Tamara. She was here one minute, talking to some guys, and then..."

Oh. Freaking. Hell. Pike's body stiffens, and my eyes widen. "I will fuckin' kill..."

"Baby," I beg, grabbing his hand before he has a chance to curl his fingers into a fist. "Tam's a smart girl. I'm sure she's just using the bathroom or something."

I'm lying.

I know that little badass-biker-seeking whore is off sucking face with some guy who, no doubt, has a death wish.

Heaven help us all.

CHAPTER 21
PIKE

"WHERE THE HELL IS TAMARA?"

Lily's eyes widen as soon as she turns around to look at me. "Um…" She looks everywhere but at me, twisting her hands in front of her body. "Around," she lies.

Gigi's hand tightens around my bicep. "Calm down, baby. She's just having fun."

"Fun?" I snap, sucking in a breath as I turn my face up to the sky, growling like a wild animal.

"People are looking at us," Gigi whispers.

"I don't give a shit who's looking," I tell her, bringing my gaze back to her face.

"Lily." Austin steps between Lily and me. "Which way did she go?"

Lily points toward the clubhouse and stands on her tiptoes, casting her gaze over Austin's shoulder. "Just don't freak out on her, Pike."

I run my hand through my hair, concentrating on my breathing because I'm already freaking out. I'm responsible for these women. It doesn't matter how old they are; they're still here with me. I can't go back to Tamara's father and say "She's a grown woman" if shit goes bad. They're going to blame me and only me for anything and everything.

"She alone?" I ask, somehow managing to speak without sounding like I'm ready to murder someone.

Lily's fingers twist around a few strands of her hair as she eyes me. "No," she squeaks, "but she's safe."

I bite out a bitter laugh.

Safe? There's not a man in this compound I'd call safe for a girl like Tamara Gallo. I don't care how wild she is; there's a difference between college boys and biker badasses. She's never waded into this territory, and no matter how sweet a brother can be, he's always after the same thing.

"Maybe Lily and I should go find her," Gigi offers when I don't give a reply. "It'll only take us a few minutes."

"No." My response is immediate. "I'm going in there, and the three of you—" I sweep my gaze around to them "—will stay here and not move."

"I'll keep an eye on them," Austin promises, trying to be the man.

He has a good heart. My parents didn't fuck him up, thank god. And when he actually becomes a man, he's going to be the best one in the family. But for now, he's still a kid.

"Doofus, you're, like, ten." Lily rolls her eyes at Austin.

Gigi's hand is on my arm again, holding on tight. "We won't move, baby. But promise me something."

"What?" I growl, unable to unclench my jaw.

"Don't kill her. Don't start a war about whatever's going on in there." She throws out her hand toward the building. "She's just being Tamara, and she's an adult."

I grit my teeth, trying to give my girl a smile but failing miserably. "It's not her you have to be worried about."

"Well, shit," Austin drawls, running his hand through his hair, spinning in a circle like he knows what's about to happen. "Want help?"

I shake my head, leaning forward and placing my fingers under Gigi's chin, bringing her large, scared eyes to me. "I won't start a war and I'd never hurt Tamara, but whatever asshole she's with is fair game."

"Shit," Lily mutters, inching toward the car and away from our small group. "Maybe we should wait by the car in case we need a quick escape."

Something about her words breaks through my anger, and I laugh, shaking my head. "We're not going anywhere, Lily. Relax. I'm just going to go in there and bring Tamara out. She shouldn't be inside with anyone, especially not someone from the club."

"He looked really nice," Lily adds, giving me a big, fake smile. "Like, really sweet and a great guy."

Somehow, I don't roll my eyes at the naïveté in her statement. Ted Bundy looked nice too, and that didn't turn out well at all for any of his victims.

Gigi glares at her cousin. "Shut up, Lily. You're not helping anything," she tells her before tipping her head back to glance up at me. "Go. We'll wait here, but keep calm, baby. Calm."

I kiss her quickly and leave, knowing the three of them are staring at my back as I walk toward the clubhouse. I remind myself of Gigi's words in her sweet voice.

Keep calm.

"Where ya headed, brother?" Morris asks when I'm within a few feet of the door and am reaching for the handle.

I swing my head around, not moving the rest of my body. "I'm lookin' for someone."

Morris raises an eyebrow, waiting for me to explain.

"Gigi's cousin is in there with one of the brothers."

Morris nods and laughs. "Just don't start something unless your ass is ready to finish it."

I stare at him with a straight face. "I never start anything I can't finish. You know this."

He studies me for a second, the laughter still on his lips. "I know, Pike. But remember, she ain't your kid either." He opens the door and steps inside, holding it open for me and ticking his head to the side.

My eyes follow his movement, and my body stiffens. Tamara's at the bar, sitting in the lap of some guy I don't know, his hands a little too close to her ass for my liking.

She tips her head back and laughs loudly. "You are just too much, Crow."

"Yeah, doll?" he asks her, eyes sweeping down her neck and straight to her tits.

The clubhouse is virtually empty. Everyone's outside waiting for fireworks except for a few stragglers milling around the public space near the bar. Crow and Tamara are the only two sitting down, looking like they're having a great time.

I let out a shaky breath, happy as fuck I didn't catch him balls deep inside her. I would've had to pound his face in and probably get my ass kicked in return by a few brothers too.

"Pike!" Tamara screeches as soon as she sees me, waving her hands high in the air like she's excited to see me. "Come meet my new friend."

Fucking women.

Crow cranes his neck, glancing at me over his shoulder, hands tightening around Tamara. "Ah. The man. The myth. The legend," he mutters, his eyes raking over my body like he's sizing me up, waiting for me to strike.

There're two ways I can handle this—I could march over, drag Tamara off his lap, and yank her ass outside, dealing with Crow afterward, or I could try to be civil and coax her outside without making a huge scene and getting Gigi mad at me.

I stalk forward, hands clenched, shoulders tight. "It's just Pike."

Tamara lifts her leg, kicking out the stool next to her and Crow.

"Come talk with us," she says, and she's in such a cute and playful mood, I hate that I'm going to rain all over her happy parade.

I slide onto the stool, resting my elbow on the bar, eyeing the guy who's now her ass cushion. "You look familiar, Crow."

He gives me a toothy grin, the white of his teeth a stark contrast to the black in his beard. "We've met a time or two," he mutters casually before glancing back at the girl in his lap.

I narrow my gaze, locking in on his hands and the ink covering them. The solid black wings with the tips grazing the top of each finger. "Weren't you out of New York?"

He nods but doesn't bother looking at me. "After all the shit went down, I took Tiny up on his offer to join the Disciples. So far —" he slides his hand up higher on Tamara's waist, fingertips way too close to her breasts "—it's been fucking perfection."

I'd met Crow a handful of times, and he seemed like an all right guy. Different from the others, even. Quiet like me. Reserved yet not, when the time was right. But he is still a biker. Still wrong for Tamara, no matter how nice he makes himself sound.

She blinks at him like she's drunk on his gaze. "It's worked out great for me, handsome." Tamara winks at him, sliding her arm around his neck like they've been friends forever.

"Gigi's looking for you," I blurt out, and Tamara's head snaps back.

"Well, shit," she mutters, never missing a beat. "Tell my girl to come in here."

I lift an eyebrow. "I think you should go see her," I emphasize the word go, but she just blinks at me like I'm speaking another language.

"Don't be a party pooper, Pike. I'm having so much fun, and Crow's legs are..." She trails off, blushing as he winks at her. "So comfortable."

"Doll," Crow says softly, almost sweetly. "Give us men a few minutes to talk. Go grab that cousin of yours, and the four of us can have a drink and hang out, yeah?"

Tamara's eyes widen as the smile on her face grows. "Baby," she croons, and I almost vomit. "I'll do whatever you want."

I cough, barely holding my shit together. *I will not kill him. I will not kill him.* I repeat the words to myself in a slow, steady rhythm so I don't lunge toward him, doing something Gigi will make me regret.

Tamara climbs off his lap, running her fingers through his beard as her feet find the floor. "Promise me you won't go anywhere."

He glances down at his lap. "I'm not moving a muscle, sweetheart. My thighs are going to miss your sweet ass. So, do me a favor and make it quick."

Tamara doesn't even blink or seem to care that he just bossed her around because he twisted it up in a nice way. She nods, not even hesitating as she takes off toward the door.

"What?" I growl with my jaw clenched so fucking tight, my teeth ache.

Crow tilts his head to the side, a smirk playing behind his beard. "Calm your shit, brother. We're just flirting. I know that girl," he says, motioning toward the door with his chin, "is not a club whore. She's sweet. A little naïve, but still sweet."

"First, I'm not your brother." I glare at him because so help me God, I want to murder him. "Second, she's very naïve. Third, she is sweet, but you'll never know how sweet as long as I'm breathing."

He stands up, reaches over the bar, grabbing a few beer bottles that are sitting there. "Relax," he tells me, offering me a beer. "I know where to dip my wick, and it isn't in her."

I take the beer, eyeing him as I twist off the top, throwing it onto the bar. "She's my family, Crow. I won't let you or any of the other guys here near her without a fight."

He leans his head back, drinking half the bottle down his throat before he speaks again. "I'm still finding a place here with the Disciples. I'm the new meat, and from what I've seen so far, I'm not impressed by the buffet."

"Why Tamara?" I ask point-blank.

"She's sweet and pure. Ever have something so perfect, you want to do whatever you can to hold on to it?"

"Every fucking day," I admit.

"I ain't looking to cause problems. I found her in here an hour ago talking to Lefty, and I did whatever I had to do to get her away from him."

My stomach drops at the mention of Lefty's name. The scariest and fucking nuttiest bastard in the club. Lefty has more kills to his name than anyone else, and he doesn't always think clearly, too fucked up on coke most of the time.

"I did you a solid by talking to that girl. Didn't know I was doing me a solid too." He smiles, going back to his beer and turning his face away from me.

"Fuck," I groan, knowing I could've walked in on something so much worse than Tamara in Crow's lap.

"Yep," he barks. "I think you owe me a thank-you."

"Never fuckin' happenin'," I snarl, even though I should say thank you to him for rescuing her from a madman.

Crow laughs, fisting his hand before punching me in the shoulder like we're long-lost friends. "Just let me flirt with the pretty thing. I'm harmless, and tomorrow, I'll be nothing but a memory. I could use a little good in my life, even if it's only for a few hours."

I inhale, tightening my hands around my beer bottle, about to tell him to fuck off when Gigi, Tamara, Lily, and Austin walk through the door, sounding more like twenty people with all their chatter than four.

"This is Crow," Tamara tells Gigi, looking at him like he walks on water, fluttering her pretty black eyelashes his way. "He's my guy."

I almost choke on my beer, pounding on my chest as Gigi gives me the side-eye.

"Gigi," Gigi says, holding out her hand to him, elbowing me because I can't stop coughing on the goddamn beer.

"I see pretty and sweet runs in the family," Crow flirts, lifting Gigi's hand up to his lips like I'm not fucking sitting there.

"Watch it," I bite out, finally clearing the beer from my throat.

He drops Gigi's hand, glancing over at Lily. "And who's this beautiful creature?"

Lily blushes immediately, lifting her shoulders with wide eyes like she's a baby lamb headed to slaughter. "I'm Lily," she chirps, all bashful and nothing like her cousins.

Tamara climbs back into Crow's lap, staking her territory before he can say anything more or reach out to touch Lily in any way. "I missed you," she whispers, reaching up to touch his beard with her long, thin fingers.

His eyes twinkle as he looks at her. "Missed you too, dollface."

"Oh, good lord," Gigi whispers. My hand goes to her waist, pulling her against me as she gawks at them.

"Hey," Austin adds like the forgotten one of the group because he's a dude and doesn't have the right parts to get noticed around here. "I'm this one's brother." He tips his head in my direction.

Crow's eyebrows shoot up. "For-real brother?"

"For real." Austin smiles, looking genuinely proud of being related to me for the first time ever. "At least that's what my birth certificate says."

I know one thing in this moment. I will never tell him we don't share the same father. It's nothing he needs to know. I'm all he has left in this world, and I don't want to fill his head with any doubts or questions. I went most of my life thinking that cold bastard Colton Moore was my daddy, and telling the world the opposite wouldn't change a goddamn thing after all the hell he put me through.

"I can see it," Crow says, turning his attention back to the girl in his lap.

"This isn't good," Gigi whispers as she tucks her face into my neck, trying not to be heard by her cousin.

"We talked. He knows how to behave."

"I'm more worried about how Tam's going to behave."

I laugh, running my fingers up her arm. "We just won't let her out of our sight, darlin'."

"Great," Gigi grumbles with a frown as she looks up at me. "I've turned into my mother."

CHAPTER 22
GIGI

WE HEADED to the beach while the guys stayed behind, crashing in the beds as soon as our rooms were ready. This is just what I needed after a sleepless night at the compound, watching over Tamara and Crow like I was my parents.

Ugh.

"Who are you talking to?" I ask Tamara, glancing over as she feverishly pecks away at her phone screen.

She hasn't put the damn thing down since we left the compound. She's taken her phone everywhere, even to the bathroom, and is giddy every time the damn thing vibrates.

"Crow." She smirks, giving me the side-eye. "He's just too much fun."

I know the allure of a bad boy. Pike sucked me in from the moment I met him. Damn it. I always told myself I'd never fall in love with someone like my father.

And what happened?

Boom. Joe Junior fell right into my lap.

Not really. I fell into his bed, planting my ass there for a solid week because he was just too good to walk away from.

And now... Now, I can't imagine life without him.

"Fun's one word for him," Lily grumbles on my other side, stretching out her body on her towel. "I'm so fucking tired because of you two assholes."

"We didn't need babysitters," Tamara spits back, not bothering to look in Lily's direction. "We're both grown adults."

Instead of cuddling up in Pike's old room like we did last time, he and I stayed on the couches in the common area with Tamara, Crow, Lily, and Austin. I tried my best not to think about all the shit that went down on those couches before I sat on them.

"Ha," Lily snaps. "I swear you're just trying to do whatever you can to make everyone around you crazy-worried and stressed as shit."

Tamara rolls her eyes, dropping her hand near her hips. "I'm just trying to have some fun. We're only young once. I mean, look at our parents. It's all bills, crying kids, and the same old bullshit every day. This is our one chance to live life and be free before adulthood sucks the life out of us."

"There's a difference between living and having a death wish," Lily tells her, scooting her ass down on the towel to block her face with the nearby umbrella.

"Tam has a point." I can't believe I'm agreeing with Tamara about this, but I keep going and try not to put too much thought into it. "I'm done with college, and you two will be after next year. We're going to be old before we know it."

Lily sighs. "I wish we could go back to high school and do it all over again."

"Fuck no," I spit out, thinking about the heartaches and bullshit we all went through during those four years. "Maybe back to freshman year of college, but there's no way I'd go back to high school."

"Ugh," Tamara mutters, wiggling her toes as her silver glitter polish twinkles in the sun. "I hated those years."

Lily sits up, resting her upper body on her elbows. "They weren't so bad."

Tamara and I both turn our heads, gawking at our cousin because she must have amnesia if she thinks those were golden years we'd ever want to relive.

"It sucked ass, Lil. Are you ill right now?" Tamara laughs.

Lily shakes her head. "Life was simple then. What was our biggest headache? Homework. I mean, come on. No job. No responsibilities."

"Curfew. Parents. Rules. What about that sounds like fun?" I ask.

Lily lifts a shoulder, staring out across the rolling waves. "Time just moves so fast, and for the first time ever, we're all going to be in different places."

My heart aches for a moment because she's right. When Tamara and I were at FSU, Lily would come up on weekends and breaks, and we'd party our asses off. But now... Now, I'll be home, and they'll be far, far away from me.

"In a year, you'll both be home, though, right?" I ask, looking between my two sisters from other misters.

I can't imagine going very long without seeing them. They are as much a fixture in my life as my two little sisters. We grew up together. Got into trouble together. Started dating around the same time, totally not telling our parents about that either. We know one another's secrets, and there aren't two other girls on the planet I am closer to than them.

Lily sighs and Tamara shrugs.

I sit up quickly, spinning around on my ass and clutching the towel between my hands. "What the hell? You two have to come back. You can't leave me."

"You have Pike now," Tamara admits like he's a replacement.

I blink. "Tam, be serious now. He can never replace you."

Lily brushes her hand against mine before linking our fingers together. "I'm trying to get into USF to work on my doctorate and I hope to do my residency at a hospital in Tampa, but you never know, Gigi."

I can feel my eyes starting to water as my nose tickles. "You have to come home."

"We're trying, babe. We're trying," Tamara says, lifting her phone back up to her face as soon as it vibrates. "Jesus Christ," she gasps, eyes going wide as saucers.

"What?" I smack her legs, trying to look at her screen, but she turns her phone the other way.

"When is it too early in a relationship for a dick pic?" she asks, keeping her eyes trained on the screen with a smirk.

I wince, knowing there isn't a cock in the world that looks good in a selfie. "It's always too early," I tell her, shaking my head and totally judging the super-dreamy—her words, not mine—Crow. "Pike's never sent me one."

Lily lunges over me, ripping Tamara's phone from her hands and stares at the screen. "You fuckin' liar. It's just words." Lily tosses the phone back toward Tamara. "Boring."

"I just wanted to see what you'd do. You guys ever ask for a dick pic?" Tamara raises an eyebrow, staring at us.

I shake my head. "Why the fuck would I want a dick pic?"

"You're such a weirdo," Lily scoffs, scrunching up her nose at Tamara. "I don't know how we're related."

"If you weren't dating Pike," Tamara teases, looking right at me, "I'd say Mallory was right about you. But he gives you some points in the cool column."

What? Mallory was the biggest asshole, and if it weren't for her sister Mary, we wouldn't have been friends. Tamara knows this. She hated Mallory just as much as I did.

I cross my arms, twisting my lips and glaring at my cousin. "I'm cool, and Mallory's a tool."

I mean, I am. I've never been the nerdy type. I'm not too uptight to party. I could hang out with just about anyone and have a good time. I'm not afraid to get drunk and let loose. Hell, I slept with Pike, and I didn't even know the man. Maybe not my best moment and it could've ended much differently, but I wouldn't change a goddamn thing in my life.

She shakes her head. "So not, but you think you are. And you." Tamara tilts her head, studying Lily. "You used to be pretty badass, but now your nose is always stuck in a book, worried about that perfect GPA."

Lily smiles, running her fingers down her legs like she's trying to calm herself. "The world couldn't handle three Tamaras."

"Someday, you're going to bust free, Lil, and I'm going to be there cheering you on."

"I don't have time to bust free," Lily sighs, falling backward on the blanket and spreading out her body. "I'm so exhausted."

"Maybe we need to go on an epic adventure." Tamara taps her chin. When she starts thinking up crazy shit, I know we're in trouble. "Gigi can't come because she has to work, but you and I could totally do it."

I grind my teeth, hating that somehow, I'm the adult in the group. "I hate you two."

"No, you don't." Tamara smiles. "Plus, if I had a hottie like that in my bed, I wouldn't be going anywhere except to pick up more birth control."

I roll my eyes. "Adulting sucks."

"I can't go on an epic adventure," Lily sighs. "Maybe next summer."

"Maybe Crow will be my adventure," Tamara comments, not looking at us when she speaks.

"Don't," I warn her. "Don't get into something you'll regret."

"Do you regret meeting Pike?" she throws back, lifting one perfectly plucked eyebrow.

"Of course I don't."

"He's no different from Crow."

I blink at her. "Yes, he is."

She leans back, placing a rolled-up towel under her head, looking cool as a cucumber. "How?"

"They just are," I tell her, lying back too, ready to pass out.

"They're both badass biker dudes. They're both Disciples."

"Pike was never a Disciple."

"Semantics," she says. "They both ride Harleys."

"You're talking nonsense." I wave her off with my hand. "Pike is more than a biker."

"So's Crow."

"Do you literally want your father to shit a brick?" I ask her point-blank.

Tamara laughs. "Anthony will survive."

"I'll remind him of that when you're off on your epic badass biker adventure."

There's a shadow suddenly covering us before we hear, "Who needs sunscreen?" coming from Austin's mouth.

I tip my head back, seeing the horny teenager almost drooling from all the skin. You'd think we were naked with the way his eyes are almost popping out of his skull. Our bikinis are modest compared to some of the others on the beach. It's not like our tits are completely hanging out, even if he is acting like it.

"Close your mouth, Austin," Tamara tells him, pulling her sunglasses back down over her eyes. "Coffee." She lifts her hand, snapping her fingers.

"As you wish, my queen," he says, falling to his knees at her side.

I grumble at how completely annoying Tamara and Austin are.

"Babe, come in the water with me," Pike orders, walking up behind Austin, carrying a cardboard carton filled with coffees.

"Coffee first," I groan, lifting a hand, being overdramatic.

Fuck. I feel like a tractor ran over me, leaving me for dead. I used to be able to stay up all night, party my ass off, and pop out of bed for class. But now it's all roadkill city.

Pike sits down above my head, pushing one of the cups in front of my face. "Drink up, sunshine."

I take in his ink and bare skin. The way the rays of sunshine bounce off the crevices of his muscles is so damn beautiful. "Maybe you should cover up," I tell him, taking the coffee from his hands.

Pike glances down, eyebrows furrowing. "I'll cover up when you do." His gaze flickers to my breasts, but it's so freaking hot, there's no way in hell I'm putting on any more layers.

I look around the beach, noticing the women eyeing my man, totally fantasizing about him. "Women are staring at you," I tell him before taking a sip of the iced coffee my body and mind need to function.

"Um—" he glances around "—the men are eye-fucking all three of you in your string bikinis, but you don't hear me complaining."

I roll my eyes, and Tamara giggles, followed by Lily's laughter. "We aren't wearing string bikinis," I tell him, moaning right afterward as I take another sip.

"Darlin', make that noise again, and the ladies are going to see more than my chest," he warns me, giving no fucks about the other women around us.

I raise my eyebrows before my eyes go right to his crotch. "Maybe we should go in the water. It's getting a little hot."

He waggles his eyebrows with a smirk.

"You two are gross," Tamara teases. "I'm not coming in there if you two fool around."

"There was more come on that couch last night than there is in that ocean," Pike tells her, not able to keep a straight face when she winces.

"Fuckin' gross," she mutters.

"Biker life," I tell her, hoping to warn her off Crow as I set my coffee in the sand and follow Pike toward the water.

"What's that about?" Pike asks, tipping his head back.

I link my hand with his, walking as fast as I can across the sand, which is as hot as lava from the sun overhead. "She's texting Crow."

Pike stops, and I almost fall forward as his hand locks around mine, holding me in place. "What did you say?" he growls.

I pull him forward, dancing in place because my feet are practically on fire. "I'll tell you once we're in the water unless you don't like my feet with skin."

"Skin's good," he mumbles like he's thrown.

Pike is never thrown. Never at a loss for words. But I can tell something is weighing on his mind.

"What's wrong?" I ask him, letting out a loud sigh when my toes finally hit the wet, cool sand near the water's edge.

"I don't like her with Crow," he admits. "A girl like her with a guy like him is nothing but trouble."

I wade into the water, letting my fingertips graze the tops of the waves as we wade deeper. "Tell me about him."

I don't ask about the *a girl like her* comment because I know he doesn't mean anything bad. He knows Tamara has a good heart, but he also knows she's much, much wilder than I ever could've been.

He doesn't say anything, just stares straight ahead as the waves crash nearby.

I tug on his arm, wanting his attention and his words. "Tell me." I smile, dipping my lower body into the water until just my breasts are bobbing on the surface.

He glances down, seeing my sweat-dotted breasts moving across the waves, and smiles. "Darlin', how am I supposed to say anything when you're tempting me like that?"

"Be a good boy and tell me what you know about Crow, and maybe you won't have to walk out of here sporting that hard-on I know is under the waves." I wink, being totally playful because there's a darkness in his eyes.

He lunges forward, wrapping his arms around my waist and smashing my breasts into his chest. I gasp, trying not to swallow the salty water as his lips find my neck, sucking the spot that always makes me pant. "I love when you think you're the boss," he whispers against my skin.

"I am the boss," I tell him, wrapping my legs around his

middle, grinding my pussy against his hard cock. "Now tell me about Crow."

"Bossy as fuck," he murmurs against my skin, and I laugh, hooking my ankles and digging my heels into his ass.

Damn, I love this man.

CHAPTER 23
PIKE

"THIS PLACE BRINGS BACK MEMORIES," Tamara says, winking at me across the table. "Am I right?"

I laugh even though it feels like a lifetime ago. Watching Gigi for what felt like hours, waiting for the girl to finally make her move. "Great memories," I mutter behind the mouth of the beer bottle in my hand.

Gigi snorts. "I remember nothing."

"You're a shit liar," Tamara tells her, shaking her head. "You weren't that drunk."

"Drunk enough to pass out," I add, earning me a glare from Gigi.

"Shut up," she tells me, but she's totally being playful. She's relaxed since our talk about Crow yesterday and then having words with her cousin about the man.

Maybe they worked shit out. Hopefully what I said to Gigi that she then passed on to Tamara put things into perspective.

"It's a shame Austin and Lily aren't here," Gigi says softly, turning the beer bottle in her hands.

"They're lightweights. I mean, who wants to stay in the room and binge-watch *Game of Thrones*?" Tamara blanches.

"They're nerds, Tam, and it's probably best that Austin isn't here. Kids really shouldn't hang out in bars."

Tamara bends her head back, slapping her hand on the table. "Jesus fuck, when did you turn into Suzy?"

I close my eyes and dig my fingertips into my eyes, knowing Tamara said the one thing that can set Gigi off quicker than a firecracker.

Gigi jerks her head back. "You're an asshole."

"Well." Tamara shrugs. "You just referred to Austin as a child, and the last time I checked, he's almost a grown man."

"Almost," I grumble, lifting my head and opening my eyes. "He's still in high school, and if I catch him at a bar…"

"You going to spank him?" Tamara raises an eyebrow, and I swear to God, the girl is just trying to get a rise out of me.

"Are you perpetually bored?" I glare at her.

She snorts, scrunching her nose. "You two are like two old biddies. I swear you're a perfect match."

Gigi slides her warm palm across my arm, making it impossible for me to keep the sour look on my face. "Ignore her. We know we're awesome." She smiles, and that face could light up an entire room.

"You know who's awesome?" Tamara asks, looking over my shoulder as a smirk plays on her lips.

Gigi turns, her fingers tightening around my arms.

"Don't say it," I mutter, knowing exactly who they're looking at. *Goddamn this girl.*

Gigi's head snaps back to her cousin, dropping low to the table. "You invited him?" she hisses and somehow avoids yelling, even though I know she wants to.

Tamara nods. "Just for a few drinks. The compound isn't too far away, and he said he was missing me."

My jaw tightens as I curl my free hand into a fist, every muscle in my body so tight, I could snap.

"Fuck," Gigi hisses. "You're such a dumbass."

"Just be nice. We leave tomorrow, and I'll never see him again." Tamara pouts like that shit will work on me, but I'm not her parents, and it has no effect.

"You're not leaving with him," I tell her, pointing at her across the table with one finger, while the others are curled around the beer bottle.

"Yes, Dad," she groans and rolls her eyes. "Don't get your granny panties in a wad."

This has to be the painful agony of what being a parent feels like. The constant push and pull of doing the right thing and trying to give your child enough freedom to live, but not enough to hang themselves with. Tamara had to be a trying kid. I don't know how Anthony is still alive after twenty-one years of her constant need to be an asshole.

"Hey, sexy," Tamara greets him, rising to her feet as soon as Crow's within a few feet of our table.

He slides his bare arm around her waist, pulling her in like they're long-lost lovers. "I missed you, doll," he says softly, rubbing his beard against her neck, causing her to break out in a fit of girlish giggles.

"I'm going to vomit," Gigi mutters, placing her hand on my knee and squeezing hard.

They embrace for far too long, nuzzling into each other's necks, touching like they're more than just friends. "I'm so happy you came," Tamara adds as she grabs at his beard, holding his eyes. "So, so happy."

"I'd come anywhere for you, sweet lips." He winks.

"Crow." I interrupt their conversation when Gigi groans again at my side.

"Her father's going to murder us first," she says, shaking her head. "We're so dead."

"What are we drinking?" Crow asks, glancing down at the table with his arms still wrapped around Tamara. "Next round is on me."

"Isn't he sweet?" Tamara looks right at me, but I give her nothing, so she goes back to gawking at the bearded man with eyes as dark as coal. "He's the best ever. Come on, baby. I'll help you carry the beer for Grandpa and Grandma."

Crow furrows his eyebrows, but he just shrugs, letting her pull him into the crowd.

Gigi sighs, resting her head on my shoulder. "She's really trying to kill us."

I let out a small laugh and lean over, kissing the top of her head. "It'll be fine. A few drinks and his eyes will wander. He'll forget about her by tomorrow."

Gigi peers up at me, those blue eyes searching my face. "Did you forget about me so easily?"

"Fuck no, darlin'. I missed you the moment you left."

She gives me the biggest smile, making my insides warm. "Me too," she lies.

"You didn't call," I remind her.

She coughs, glancing down at her hands. "I was embarrassed."

"About?" I ask.

She shrugs. "I'd never had a one-night stand."

"It wasn't one night," I say, unable to wipe the smile off my face, remembering the endless days we spent wrapped around each other.

Gigi giggles, and it's still the sweetest sound I've ever heard. "I remember, old man. Will life ever be that easy again?"

I sigh, wrapping my arm around the back of her chair, playing with the ends of her hair with my fingertips. "I don't know, baby. But as long as you're at my side, I'll weather the bad any day to get to all the good."

"We got beer," Tamara announces as Crow sets down a metal bucket of beer and ice in the middle of the table.

"Drink up," Crow tells us as he turns a chair around, wrapping his upper body over the back as he sits, holding a glass of water in one hand.

"You're not drinking?" Tamara asks, mouth hanging open as she looks at the man at her side.

He shakes his head. "I'm driving tonight. Booze and bikes don't mix, doll."

That's the first thing to come out of his mouth that has me thinking maybe he isn't the biggest tool in the shed.

"You can crash in my room," she offers, pushing the bucket in his direction.

He glances my way and shakes his head. "I think it's best if I don't."

And again, he's being smart. There was no way in hell I was going to let him stay in her room. I don't care how old she is; it would've been a hard no. Well, I would've put Austin in there too, which would've been an instant mood-killer.

"I understand," she says, eyeing me across the table. "Maybe next time."

"Sure, doll. Next time," he mutters.

"So, Crow," Gigi mutters. "Did you grow up in New York?"

He shakes his head, smiling as Tamara touches his arm and runs the tips of her fingernails back and forth. "I was a military brat. We moved around a lot."

"Have any brothers or sisters?" she asks immediately after he answers.

"One brother, no sisters."

"Do you have a job?" she asks as she reaches into the bucket, fishing out a fresh beer.

Crow dips his hand into his back pocket and tosses his wallet near Gigi. "Tamara told me about your uncles. Feel free to have them check into me."

Gigi scrunches her nose. He called her out, knowing she was interrogating him.

Tamara snorts. "She won't do that, baby."

Gigi takes the wallet, flipping it open and scanning the contents.

"Logan Taylor," she says, pulling out his driver's license and tapping her index finger against the top.

"That's my name," he says to her, still smiling as he runs his fingers over his beard.

"Logan's a sexy name too, baby," Tamara adds. "But Crow's totally badass."

Crow turns his face toward Tamara, smile never wavering. "You call me whatever you want, sweet lips."

I take his wallet and driver's license from Gigi's hands, putting everything back the way it was when she opened the damn thing. "Leave the man alone."

She gapes at me in total disbelief.

I toss the wallet back in his direction. "They're just friends."

Gigi blinks before shaking her head. "What are you doing?" she whispers in my ear.

I place my fingers on the side of her neck, turning her head so I have her ear. "You want to drive her into his arms?"

"No," she whispers against my skin.

"Then stop being a cockblock. What happened when your parents hated someone?" I ask her.

"Point taken," she groans and backs away, gaze moving toward her cousin. "Want to go dance with me, Tam?"

"No," Tamara replies, too busy with her hands all over Crow.

Gigi stands, rounding the table before pulling on Tamara's arm. "Yeah, you do. You love to dance. Don't you want to show Crow all your moves?" Gigi shakes her hips.

I want to pull her back into the chair, tell her she's not shaking that fine thing for all these bastards, but I don't.

"Do you care?" Tamara peers down at Crow, looking for permission.

"Shake away," he says, tipping his chin toward the small dance floor.

"Want to come?" She wiggles her fingers at him, but he shakes his head. "Your loss, baby."

I glare at Crow, watching him as he gawks at Tamara's ass. "Why are you here?" I ask him as soon as the girls hit the dance floor.

He shrugs, lifting his water to his lips, giving zero fucks that I don't want him here. "Just trying to hold on to that goodness."

I lean forward, setting my beer to the side and clearing a space in front of me. "While I understand wanting to hold on to that goodness, there's definitely a line you're crossing."

"A line?" he asks, slinging his arm over the chair and placing his glass of water down in front of him. "She asked me to come and have a drink. It was either come here or hang with the guys, watching them as they got shit-faced. What would you have done?"

"Crow, baby. Watch!" Tamara yells, turning around as soon as he glances in her direction and shaking her ass in a way that doesn't say friends at all.

"Fuck," he hisses, but not from being pissed off.

"Crow, listen." I take a deep breath, trying not to be a hypocrite because, fuck, I've been there. I've been drawn in by all the sweetness, almost getting Gigi killed in the process. "Your life doesn't mesh with hers." I turn my head toward Gigi and Tamara, laughing and bouncing to the old eighties metal song coming out of the oversized speakers. "She's everything you think. Sweet and all that shit, but she isn't for you. She'll never be for you."

He narrows his eyes, studying my face as he tosses his thumb over his shoulder. "And your girl?"

"I don't deserve her. I don't think I ever will. But we've been to hell and back together."

"Tamara said you two work together."

Tamara's a little too chatty, especially with a complete stranger. "We do now."

"And you used to live at the compound."

I nod, keeping all emotion from my face.

"She told me all about you, Pike. All about her family too."

My knee starts to shake as I force myself to stay seated. "They wouldn't like you either."

He gives me a shit-eating grin. "Never met a family who didn't love me."

"What are you doing with a kid like her?"

"Kid?" He laughs. "She's not a kid. Look at her. Isn't she the same age as your girl?"

I scan the dance floor, catching sight of Tamara and Gigi shaking their hips and tits for everyone to see. There's nothing childish about them besides their ability to bicker and sometimes be annoying as fuck.

"They're a year apart," I tell him, swallowing because I know I'm being an asshole.

"I get where you're coming from. I know you don't want my dirt to blow back on her, have her running for her life."

I know that's a dig at me. I'm sure Crow knows all about the men who were lost in the Disciples from the attack by DiSantis's men.

"I'm not like most of the guys in the club. I stick to myself. I do what's needed when I'm asked and am loyal as fuck, but I'm not into the club whores, drugs, and drinking every day scene. I work my ass off working on cars, saving my money for when I get an old lady." He turns his head toward Tamara, the smile back on his face. "I want some goodness in my life someday too. But I know that girl —" he pauses for a second and looks back at me "—is a wild one and isn't looking to settle down. I'm not here to break her heart. I'm not here to turn her bad. I saved her from some bad shit with Lefty, and you know it." He points at me, and I resist the urge to bat his hand away. "She asked me to come, so I'm here. Tomorrow, she'll move on, putting her crazy love on someone else. But tonight, I'm soaking up her sweetness, storing it away for the times I need to remember I'm more than just a soldier in someone else's army."

"Get your fuckin' hands off me!" Gigi screeches from the dance floor, her voice carrying over the music.

The guy has a lopsided smile, not seeming to care that she's batting his hands away.

I'm out of my seat before she can say another word, Crow's loud bootsteps right behind me.

I grab the guy by the collar, hauling him backward until he stumbles, almost falling over. "The lady said hands off."

"Who the fuck are you?" he croaks, slurring his words and spitting at the same time.

"Her man," I tell him, twisting the material around his neck so tightly, I know he's losing oxygen.

"Incoming!" Crow yells out as Tamara and Gigi are pushed backward, and a small group of men steps forward.

"The fuck you touchin' him, man?"

Here we go. There's never a dull moment. Never a simple evening out. Never any peace.

The guy in my clutches swings on me, and I sweep my leg out, taking his feet out from under him.

"Oh fuck," Gigi hisses, eyes wide as the other men move toward us, fists in the air.

"I got you," Crow says at my side.

Mass chaos breaks out. Fists, legs, chairs, and just about everything movable goes flying in the bar. It's like something out of *Roadhouse*.

As my fist connects with a guy's face, I search the crowd while Tamara and Gigi head toward the door, hands over their heads to protect themselves.

"You messed with the wrong motherfuckers," Crow tells one of the guys before landing a wicked uppercut, causing the man's head to snap back in a completely unnatural way.

In this moment, I've never been happier to have the bastard by my side.

———

"Son of a bitch."

My eyes snap open, and I wince as the sunlight streams through the open curtains. "What's wrong?"

I turn, seeing Gigi holding a small sheet of paper, her eyes wide and mouth hanging open.

"The bitch did it. I'm going to kill her." Gigi starts pacing, shaking her head.

"Did what? Who?" I ask, rubbing the sleep from my eyes before lifting up on my elbows.

"Tamara," she whispers as she stops moving, gaping at the paper in disbelief.

"What did she do?" I ask again.

Gigi shoves the piece of paper in my face. "Read it."

Cover for me!
I'm chasing my
epic adventure.
— Tam xoxo

WILDFIRE

A MEN OF INKED HEATWAVE NOVEL

USA TODAY BESTSELLING AUTHOR

CHELLE BLISS

WILDFIRE COPYRIGHT © 2020

No part of this book may be reproduced or transmitted in any form, including electronic or mechanical, without written permission from the publisher, except in the case of brief quotations embodied in critical articles or reviews.

This is a work of fiction. Names, characters, businesses, places, events, and incidents are either the products of the author's imagination or used in a fictitious manner. Any resemblance to actual persons, living or dead, or actual events is purely coincidental. This book may not be resold or given away to other people.

Publisher © Chelle Bliss March 3rd 2020
Edited by Lisa A. Hollett
Cover & Model Photo © Kevin Creekman

CHAPTER 1
TAMARA

"WHATEVER YOU'RE SELLING, sweetheart, we're not interested," the badass biker guy says as he starts to close the door in my face.

"Crow's expecting me."

He grunts, slowly pulling the door back open. His gaze sweeps over my body, taking a little too long on my chest before getting a good look at the rest of me. "Yo, Crow! You got company!" the burly man yells, blocking the entire doorway and making it impossible for me to get inside.

"He told me to drop by anytime. So, I'm here. Yay." I throw up my hands, looking like a complete moron, but I'm trying to put on a good show.

The corner of grumpy's mouth twitches, and I think I'm getting somewhere until he yells, "Crow! Get your ass out here before this girl makes a bigger fool of herself."

The smile on my face falls, and I narrow my eyes, wishing we were close to the same size because I'd sock him right in the jaw. "You're so rude."

"Babe, you show up on my doorstep, claiming to be a guest of

Crow's, throwing your tits around like it's going to earn ya something. I'm just being as real as those beautiful tits of yours."

I open my mouth to tell him to fuck off, but I snap it shut because he said I had *beautiful tits.*

"Goddamn it," Crow says, his boots pounding the cement floor as he walks up behind the grumpy guy.

My stomach knots, but I plaster a smile back on my face, pushing my jitters away. I know Crow's going to be excited to see me. He has to be. Last night before he left the bar, he told me to drop by sometime and he'd show me a good time.

"What the hell?" is all Crow says as our eyes lock. "What are you doing here, doll?"

"Surprise!" I say, lifting my arms up, along with my tits, ready to throw my arms around the hot badass biker's neck.

But before my hands get anywhere near his shoulders, he wraps his fingers around my wrists. "What the shit?"

I blink, furrowing my brows. "What the shit?"

"Yeah?" He dips his chin, his black hair falling in front of his dark eyes. "What. The. Fuck?"

My arms are still in the air, my body tilted toward him as he holds my wrists captive. "You told me to drop by."

"Yeah. So?" He rakes his eyes down my body as he lifts my hands higher, making my tits a little perkier. He steps outside, pushing me backward by his grip on my wrists. "I figured you'd call or some shit. You can't just *show up* at the compound."

"Well, I did." I yank my arms backward, glaring at him. "Why the fuck are you being the world's biggest cocksucker right now?"

The grumpy fucker who opened the door snorts, but he quickly stops as soon as Crow glances over his shoulder.

"Go the fuck inside, Eagle," Crow growls before facing me again. "Want to say that again, doll?" he asks, raising an eyebrow like maybe I'd rethink my statement.

I don't. "You're being a cocksucker," I snap, staying true to what I said just a second ago.

He is being an absolute and complete, first-class cocksucker. The version of Crow I'd met a few days ago, the one who called me doll, is gone. Now, I am stuck with this prick who's acting as if he doesn't even know who the hell I am. As if he didn't tell me to stop by for some fun sometime and I'm nothing more than a nuisance.

Crow reaches back and pulls the door shut before grabbing the cigarette from behind his ear. "I get that this is all new to you and you don't know how shit goes down around here." He places the cigarette between his lips, rolling it around as his dark eyes narrow. "So, I'm going to let that slide just this once, but call me it again—" he pauses as he reaches into the front of his jeans pocket, fishing out his lighter "—and I won't be so nice."

I blink, staring at him as he flicks his thumb across the lighter and lifts the flame near his face. "Nice?" I snap, blinking a few more times as he inhales the smoke. "This is you being nice?"

"Doll," he says, his full mouth curving around the smoke tucked between his two lips, "this is me being really nice. So, I'm going to give you thirty seconds to walk your fine ass back through the gates, climb in your car, and get gone."

I curl my fingers into a fist until my nails bite into the skin of my palm. I glare at him, breathing heavily, wishing I were a guy so I could knock him on his ass. "That's it? Get gone?"

"Yeah," he mutters, throwing up a shoulder like it's no big fucking deal.

"I fuckin' left everyone behind to come to see you. They went home already, goddamn it. I grabbed a taxi here. You promised me an epic adventure, and I figured I'd cash it in early."

God, I'm such a fool. I thought I meant something to him. I thought he'd follow through on all the promises he made, but I should've known better. I'd known plenty of men like him, and they were all the same. Every single word out of their mouths, total lies.

"Babe," he says the word short and not so sweet. "We were just bullshittin'. Didn't think you thought I was serious. You were babbling on about wanting an *epic adventure*, and I figured why the fuck not indulge you, maybe get in your pants last night, but got nothing. I'm not into cockteases, and I sure as fuck don't have time for your *epic adventure* when I have club business to deal with."

Every time he says the words epic adventure, he raises his voice, making me sound like a Valley girl. "Cocktease?" I shake my head, pulling my arm back like I'm about to hurl my fist right in his smug-ass face.

"Two times I saw you. Two times I left without so much as a hand job. If that ain't a cocktease, I don't know what is." He takes the cigarette from his lips, tapping the ash to the ground. "You going to hit me or just stand there, pretending like you're a chick of action again?"

I blink again, dropping my arm back at my side, confused as shit by the change in his attitude and the shitty way he's acting toward me. "Fucker," I hiss.

"Good girl," he says, placing the butt of the smoke back between his lips. "Now get that fine ass of yours moving before I take matters into my own hands."

I gape at him, wondering if I'd imagined the sweet guy from the few days before. Was I drunk the entire trip and totally misread the entire situation? Um, that was a hard no. Then there were the sweet text messages, soft touches, sexy whispers—all of which I remember very clearly.

"I'm going to count to ten, and if you're not…"

The door swings open behind him, and my eyes widen. Morris, Pike's friend, is standing in the doorway, shoulders high and hard, looking like he's about to leap off the steps and strangle me.

"Hi," I squeak, taking a step backward. "I'm going to go." I pitch my thumb over my shoulder, shuffling my feet in the cinders. "Just wanted to say hey to Crow before I head home."

"Stop!" Morris barks so loud, I jump and stop moving. "Tamara, get your ass inside."

My gaze moves to Crow and then back to Morris. "But Crow

said I needed to get gone. So, I was..." I rub the back of my neck, grimacing. Jesus Christ, this is embarrassing. "...gonna get gone." I smile, lifting my shoulders higher, wishing I could freaking crawl inside my own body and disappear.

"What the fuck?" Morris snaps, glaring at Crow and pointing his finger at me. "You know who this chick is, and you're just going to send her off by herself?"

Crow shrugs, rolling the cigarette between his traitorous lips, eyes never leaving me. "Don't give a fuck who she is, Morris. She isn't my problem, and she sure as hell isn't my guest."

I grind my teeth together. "Still a fucker."

"Leave us," Morris says.

I step back, lifting my hands. "I'm going. I'm going," I say, glaring at Crow as he gives me a smug smile.

Morris groans, shaking his head. "Not you, Tamara."

I stop moving, stop breathing, as my gaze flickers to Morris.

He ticks his head toward the compound, narrowing his eyes on Crow. "Go the fuck inside," he mutters. "Before I lose my temper and do something I'll regret."

Crow throws down his cigarette, smashing the paper into a pulp under his boot. "Are you going to let some bitch cause problems?" he sneers.

"I'm going to pretend you didn't just call her a bitch because you're going to walk inside and shut the fuck up," Morris tells him, crossing his arms over his chest, eyes becoming slits.

When Crow moves toward the door, I gulp and my knees wobble, but somehow, I stay upright. "I can just go. It's not a big deal."

"Stay," Morris snaps, but it's not in a pleading tone. He's commanding me like I'm one of the club's soldiers or, hell, like a dog.

Damn. I've done some dumb shit in my life, but man, this takes the cake. At least no one's here to witness my misery. I'd never hear the end of this stunt if Gigi were here. And if Pike were around, I'd be ripped a new asshole.

Morris and I stare at each other in silence until the door slams shut, leaving us alone.

"I'm sorry," I blurt out, moving backward as he comes down the stairs. "I didn't mean to cause a problem. Just let me leave, and I promise to never come back."

He sighs, stopping a few feet away. "Where the hell have you been?"

I tilt my head, thinking I heard him wrong. "Excuse me?"

"Pike called twelve hours ago looking for you." Morris rubs his forehead slowly. "So, I'll ask again, where have you been?"

"I, uh…" I think about running, but I know I won't get too far before Morris catches me. He's too close. "I spent some time on the beach, working up the nerve to get here. Then, I took a taxi until I got close. The guy wouldn't drop me off at the compound gates." I shrug. "So, when he left me at the main road, I walked the rest of the way."

"That's a three-mile walk."

I nod, feeling every step of those three miles in the soles of my feet.

"Fucking hell," he mutters.

"It's not a bad walk. I'll just head back to the main road and call an Uber." I twist, starting to make my way back to the gate. "Just please don't tell Pike I was here."

"Don't move," Morris says, taking a step toward me. "You're not leaving."

"Please," I beg. I'm too young to die, and for what? An asshole who probably didn't even have a memorable cock. "I won't tell anyone I was here."

His hand comes toward me, and I flinch, squeezing my eyes shut, waiting for the pain. "What are you doing?" he asks.

I open one eye, noticing his hand near my arm, frozen in midair.

"Just make it quick. If you're going to kill me, just please use a bullet," I beg.

Morris lets out a gravelly laugh. "I'm not killing you, li'l girl. I was just going to…" He throws his hand behind his head, rubbing his neck. "I don't know. I was just going to try to comfort you, put my arm around you, and bring you inside until I can get you a ride."

I blink, taking in everything he's just said, craning my neck to look into his eyes. "You were going to comfort me?" My voice cracks when I say the last two words. "You weren't going to kill me?"

He shakes his head, grimacing. "Why would I kill you?"

"I showed up here without being invited." I cover my face with my hands and mumble into my palms. "Because you're a badass biker dude, and that's what they do."

His hands touch mine, peeling my fingers away from my face. "I'll never hurt you. Never."

I let out a shaky breath. "Okay," I whisper.

"Come on, sweetheart." Morris ticks his head toward the compound. "Let's get you inside and find someone to drive you home."

I don't move at first, but then I remember all the things Gigi and Pike said about Morris. They raved about the man, talking about his honor and loyalty. I don't have a reason not to trust him to help me. "I just need a ride back to Daytona."

"They're not there anymore. They headed home."

"I know." I smile, looping my arm in his when he offers it to me. "I'm not going home yet."

He raises his eyebrows. "You're not going home?"

"I have a few weeks before school starts again, and I'm going to enjoy the hell out of the time I have left."

Morris curses under his breath. "We'll call them to let them know you're safe, then."

I shake my head, pausing before we're by the steps. "Only if you promise to tell them I left, and you don't know where I went."

"Whatever you want as long as you let me get you somewhere safe."

"That's a deal, Morris."

CHAPTER 2
TAMARA

"HEY, LITTLE GIRL."

"Not happening," is all I say, keeping my eyes forward, twirling the little straw in my drink, ignoring the guy at my side.

"But, baby…" He slides onto the stool to my right.

I take a deep breath, reminding myself this isn't a college bar. I'm at the Disciples' compound surrounded by bikers, and an unwelcome guest at that. "While I appreciate the offer, it's a hard no."

"But you haven't even looked at me, baby. You might like what you see."

Every muscle in my body tenses at the way his voice sounds when he calls me baby. I turn my head to the side, taking in the creep. The bottom of his beard touches his old Guns N' Roses T-shirt, and his smile is missing a few teeth. In his younger days, he probably wasn't half bad, but now, sitting next to me, he's not even close to fuckable.

I smile, hoping to make my delivery a little more palatable for the guy because I've never been one to beat around the bush. "I saw, I looked, and it's still a no, man."

His piano-keyed smile falls as he strokes his beard, throwing daggers at me with his eyes. "Nothing but a stupid bitch anyway," he bristles, scooting off the stool as quickly as he sat.

I shrug, not giving two shits if he thinks I'm a bitch or if I hurt the douchebag's feelings. I'm sure I'm the only girl he hit on tonight, and I won't be the last one ever to tell him to fuck off either.

"Ballsy," a hot guy mutters as he reaches for something under the bar.

I lift my drink, holding the flimsy straw between my fingers, gawking at the sexilicious dick-stick in front of me. "Truth is sometimes the best policy."

He leans forward, resting his elbow on the bar, holding a beer, and smirks. "And when isn't the truth the best policy?"

The dingy, low-hanging overhead lights let me get my first real look at the hottie.

Holy mother of God.

Hottie isn't even the right word for his level of sexy. The light-gray eyes, the color of the sky just after a storm, study me.

I do my best to pretend he's just like the guy who slunk off the stool and that his level of hotness has no effect on me. "When you're protecting yourself or someone else," I reply, somehow keeping the lust out of my voice.

"What's your name, princess?" His smirk grows, exposing a dimple. Yep, a freaking dimple.

God...I know we've had a shit relationship at times, but give a girl a break.

"Tamara," I breathe and instantly wrinkle my nose.

Shit. I sounded like a whore moaning my own name. Why in the world does this guy get to be so hot? He makes Crow look average, and by no means would any woman turn him away.

"Tamara," he repeats in a deep, silky tone.

I blink, feeling my cunt twitch. *Behave.* Jesus, it's been so long since I've been touched by anyone, a single word sets my body on fire. I'm the lamest of the lame at this point.

"I'm Mammoth."

I'm sure you are, I think to myself. Or at least, I think I do until he leans closer, bringing those stormy eyes level with mine. "You're cute."

Oh shit.

Way to go, me.

I've never had a filter, and the small one I do have seems to be failing me a lot lately. My head and mouth are going to have a talk soon, and it's not going to be pretty.

I don't lean back to avoid his penetrating gaze. Show no fear or, in my case, horniness. I can do this. I don't have to throw myself across the bar and suck his face. I can hold a normal conversation with a hot guy without screwing his brains out, right?

"You're all right," I mumble and don't so much as blink through the lie.

And by all right, of course, I mean off-the-charts hot. He's the type of guy who would make you do a double take or a long, slow blink, thinking your brain's playing tricks on you because there shouldn't be a man this hot in the world. He's tatted everywhere. Well, at least everywhere I can see that isn't covered by the black T-shirt he's wearing. His hair's pulled back with just a few strands falling at the sides, begging for me to fix them, but I don't.

One of his eyebrows rises, and that sexy-as-fuck smirk doesn't go away, taunting me. "Just all right?" he asks.

"Yep," I snap, driving that P home, as I look him right in the eyes.

"Still fuckin' cute," he mutters again, lifting the bottle to his thick, full, and very kissable lips.

"I am not cute," I bite out.

Bunnies are cute.

Kittens are cute.

Babies are cute.

But I, Tamara Gallo, am not cute.

I'm hot, and there's a huge difference.

"Y'are."

"Nope. Not cute," I argue, but my body's disagreeing, going all warm and squishy with his compliment.

"Yep, so damn cute." He chuckles, throwing me a wink.

"What the fuck are you doing?" a familiar voice snarls behind me, killing all the sexy fun.

"None of your business," I reply, not turning to look at the asshole because I have the new hottie in front of me.

Mammoth's eyes flicker to Crow. "She yours?" he asks him and not me, like I don't even matter—or at least, my opinion doesn't.

"Yes," Crow growls.

That lie has me spinning around on my stool so fast, the liquid flies right out of my glass, splashing over my hand. "Does lying come naturally to you?" I glare at the bullshitter.

"Whose name did you use to get your luscious ass on that stool?" Crow taunts with a smile hanging on his lips.

I narrow my eyes, wanting nothing more than to wipe the happiness right off his face. "Some asshole I thought I knew."

Mammoth's laughter is low but there.

"The fuck you laughin' about?" Crow questions him, eyes squinted and dark as he takes a step forward, gaze locked on Mammoth.

"You're such a tool, man. This fine piece of ass shows up looking for you, and what do you do? Fuck it up. What a shock. Once a fuckup, always a fuckup."

The compliment coming from Mammoth's lips washes over me, turning the tense situation even hotter.

Here I am, sandwiched between these two hot bikers, both men I'd fuck in a heartbeat, and they're arguing over me.

God, maybe I am a little slutty.

My sexuality isn't something I'll ever apologize for.

Men never do.

They get a slap on the back and an "attaboy" from their buddies for their sexual prowess.

As women, we're judged—even by our friends—for sleeping around. The conquests aren't notches on a bedpost, but slashes in our Scarlet Letter cardigans.

But not me. I'd never hang my head in shame, and it doesn't hurt that I've never given a fuck what anyone else has thought about me.

Crow growls, inching forward, shoulders bunched up near his head. He's pissed by the shit Mammoth said, and I'd be lying if I didn't admit, at least to myself, his anger makes me so damn happy.

"Fuck you, man," Crow thunders, earning him my free hand slamming into the middle of his chest before he comes any closer.

"Stop it, Crow." I hop off the stool so we're almost eye-to-eye. He's a good six inches taller than me, but my killer heels make us equals. "You pretended like you didn't know me. Like you didn't want me here. So now, I'm minding my own business, having a talk with this guy—" I pitch my thumb over my shoulder at the big guy, holding Crow's steely glare "—and leaving you the fuck alone. That doesn't mean you get to be an asshole and insert yourself where you're not wanted!" I holler, getting the attention of more than one biker, including Morris and Tiny.

"Incoming!" someone shouts as the two men stalk across the room, heading toward us like they're ready to throw down.

Oh my God. Oh my God.

I stepped over the line.

Yelling at a brother and being a woman do not mix.

I knew that.

I don't have a ton of experience around motorcycle clubs, but I know enough, or have seen enough television, to know I'm supposed to be seen and not heard.

"I'm so, so, so, so sorry," I plead, stepping back with my hands in front of me until my ass hits the bar. "I didn't mean…"

"What the fuck, man?" Morris barks, crossing his arms over his wide chest, looking scary as all get-out.

"I-I..." I stutter, wincing and waiting for...I don't know, but I figure it isn't going to be pretty.

Tiny's eyes flicker to me, and he shakes his head before they snap back to Crow, going icy freaking cold. "Crow, in Church now."

"This is bullshit," Crow hisses, glaring at me like he wishes I'd burst into flames and cease to exist. "This bitch comes in here, talking trash, and I'm getting hauled into Church. She should be tossed out on her ass for..."

"Stop right there!" Morris roars, moving toward Crow's back, placing his giant palm on the asshole's shoulder. "Don't say another word unless you want to be sipping your beer through a straw tomorrow."

Crow snarls, looking like he wants to bite my throat open, watch every drop drain from my body before he can bathe in my blood.

I widen my eyes as I practically hyperventilate, never more scared in my entire life. When Crow turns his back to me, I finally let my body go slack, gripping the bar to keep myself upright. "Fuck," I whisper as softly as possible, not looking for any more attention than I'm already getting.

Morris studies me for a moment, lips twitching, before he finally unfolds those thigh-sized arms from across his freakishly massive chest. "Mammoth, you busy tonight?"

"No, brother. Just enjoying a beer and talkin' to this sweet thing."

"'Sweet'?" Morris barks out a bitter laugh, making me smile even though I'm still scared shitless. "There's nothing sweet about this one."

"I was talking more about her ass than anything coming out of her mouth," Mammoth replies.

I glare over my shoulder at the hottie, putting on a show, when in reality, my stomach flips like there's an acrobatic performance going on inside my body. He thinks my ass is hot. It freaking better be with the number of squats I do in a day to keep the bitch firm and tight.

"Finish your beer," Morris orders him, throwing his large index finger toward me, "and take her sweet ass back to her family."

"It's a three-hour ride," I croak, biting down on my lip as soon as Morris's eyes snap to mine.

Morris scrubs his hand down his face, muttering a very creative string of curse words behind his palm. "Get Pike's room made up and keep an eye on her. Tomorrow, you can give her a ride home."

"I'm housekeeping now? Do I get one of those fancy uniforms too?" Mammoth teases.

Morris sighs, pinching the bridge of his nose and closing his eyes for a second. "Don't be a dick. Ask one of the women to make the bed for her, and make sure she gets there unharmed and without stirring up any more shit tonight."

"Got it," Mammoth replies. "I'll make sure she gets where she's meant to be."

"Don't screw her," Morris warns, killing any hopes of a fun, playful evening.

"Great," I mutter, but I squeak as soon as Morris swings his eyes back my way. "You're the best, big guy." I smile, trying to stay on his good side...if he has one.

"Fuckin' Gallo chicks. Total pains in the asses, full of trouble, and crazy, stupid beautiful. Deadly combo," Morris mumbles before stalking away, heading toward the room Crow and Tiny disappeared into.

I slide back onto the stool, grabbing a napkin from the bar to wipe the soda I'd spilled on my hands, but I don't dare look at Mammoth.

I can't.

Not after all that just went down.

"I'll just crash on the couch," I tell him, not wanting to saddle him with my problems. "I don't want to be a burden."

Mammoth's hand lands on mine, stopping my movements. "A

cute chick is never a burden," he says with a slight squeeze of his fingers.

I peer upward, almost melting into a puddle when that freaking dimple makes an appearance, and so does that goddamn smirk too. "I'm pretty sure a cute chick you can't screw is, in fact, a big-ass burden."

One side of his mouth moves higher, deepening the dimple. "He never said we couldn't fool around in that bed after I put you in it," he murmurs.

I dip my eyes to his luscious lips, thinking about kissing him. I squeeze my legs together, trying to quench the ache, but I find it impossible. "What makes you think I want to kiss you?" I rasp, my gaze still locked on his mouth, betraying me.

He drags his tongue across his bottom lip as he leans closer, swiping his thumb across the top of my hand, and sending goose bumps up my arm. "Tell me what you want, princess, and I'll make it happen."

"I...uh..." I stammer as my head swims with all types of dirty ideas. I'm not only thinking about making out, but sex and the filthiest kind. The type that stays with someone for a lifetime, burned into your brain as well as on the skin.

"Still cute," he teases, instantly snapping me out of my pornographic fantasies.

I flick my gaze upward, scrunching my nose. "You're killin' your chances." I push my mostly empty glass toward him with my free hand. "I need something stiff."

His eyebrows shoot up, and that freaking panty-melting smirk slides back. "I like a chick who knows what she wants."

I cough as soon as I process what my dumb-ass mouth just vomited. "To drink," I insist, trying my best to recover from my slip of the tongue, "I meant something stiffer to drink."

"Uh-huh." He laughs, lifting his hand away from mine to grab my glass. "What do you want?"

You.

"Tequila," I blurt out, needing the strongest shit I can handle. If my mouth isn't going to fall in line, I might as well do everything I can to make this evening impossible to remember.

He lifts the bottle, twisting off the top slowly. "One finger or two?"

I blink, suddenly breathless and forgetting for a second he's talking about tequila. My eyes dip to his hands and the ink covering the backs and down his slender fingers almost to his nails.

"Princess," he murmurs when my mouth opens and closes like the words are stuck in my throat.

I swallow hard, never having felt thirstier than I do now. "Two fingers," I whisper before I can ask for a Mammoth-dick-width amount, just to see what he'd give me.

He looks down as he pours the tequila, giving me a break from those sexy gray eyes, but he's still smiling.

I stare at him, soaking in every inch. From his dark brown hair, his chiseled jaw, right down to the veins popping up from his inked forearms.

This isn't how I thought this night would go, but hell, maybe it's not a complete waste after all.

CHAPTER 3
MAMMOTH

"YOU'RE REALLY PRETTY, BIG MAN." Tamara almost purrs the last word, standing so close, I can feel her body heat on my back.

I fluff her pillow, finishing making her bed myself because all the women in the compound were *busy*. "You're cute as fuck, princess." I laugh softly, trying to remind my dick she's off-limits, but wanting nothing more than to bury myself inside her.

"I don't want to be cute as fuck," she whines as I turn around to face her, "I want to be hot as fuck." She gives me a lopsided frown with glassy, tequila eyes.

I reach out, placing my hand on her cheek, slowly sliding my thumb across her jaw. "You are hot." I stare at the lips I've been fantasizing about for the last hour, knowing I'm crossing so many lines.

Her mouth curves as she blinks those hazel eyes, each one closing out of sync with the other. She's definitely shitfaced and somehow cuter than she was when she was being mouthy as hell at the bar. "Thank you." She leans toward me and brings her plump, pink lips closer, tempting me.

I can't take my eyes off her beautiful mouth, especially the high arches and deep V in the middle. "But still fuckin' cute too," I add, knowing she's going to get pissed again.

I've never cared for chicks with tempers, but there's something about this one's ability to fly off the handle that makes me want to aggravate her over and over again.

"Mammoth," she warns, swaying as I hold her cheek in my palm.

"Tamara," I tease, unable to keep the amused smile off my face.

"You're a jerk."

"But you want me."

"Yeah," she replies before her tongue pokes out, sweeping across those lips I've done nothing but think about being wrapped around my cock since the moment she opened them. "So, you going to kiss me or what?"

"You fucked Crow?" I ask, needing answers. The last thing I want is a chick who's had every dick in the compound inside her. I'm not into club whores or messing with anyone else's woman.

"Nope." She beams.

"You make out with him?"

She shakes her head.

"You kiss him?"

She pauses, staring at me for a second before she shakes her head again.

I sweep the pad of my thumb across the bottom of her lip, studying her beautiful face and soaking in her hazel, gold-flecked orbs. "Why'd you come here for him, then?"

Her chest heaves as her gaze sweeps across my face. "I thought we were friends." She shrugs, looking so adorable and lost. "But again, I was wrong."

"Men and women can rarely be friends, princess. Especially when the woman is as hot as you are," I admit, knowing this from personal experience.

"I'm hot," she repeats my words as pink fills her cheeks. "You asking about Crow because you want him for yourself?"

I bow my head, pulling her against me, bringing my mouth closer to hers. "Does that feel like I want Crow?" My cock presses into her, twitching at the warmth of her belly.

She draws in a long, shaky breath as her eyes blaze with nothing but need. "No, but your dick isn't screaming cute right now either," she teases, sliding her arms around my body, groping my ass. "You gonna keep playing twenty questions, or kiss me already? You're killing me, smalls." She plasters her tits against me, smiling up at me like she's the dirtiest fucking angel I've ever seen.

"You're trouble, princess," I rasp, wanting to rip off her clothes, showing her just how much I want her.

But I can't.

Morris cockblocked me for the first time ever.

He said don't screw her, but he never said I couldn't have a little fun.

"But the best kind." She smiles, batting her eyelashes like she's innocent.

I tighten my fingers around the back of her neck, pulling her face closer as my eyes search hers, needing the affirmation she isn't just all talk and tequila. "You want me, Tamara?" I ask, never wanting to take advantage of any woman when she's drunk.

Her fingers dig into my ass as she grinds against me, making it clear she wants more than a kiss. "Yes," she moans before licking those pretty lips. "But do you want me?" She raises an eyebrow.

I crush my lips down on hers, done with the games, wound so tight I could probably come in my pants if she'd grind against me a little longer. The girl is that freaking hot. Not only is she beautiful, but the attitude on her could bring any man to his knees, begging for a taste of her sweet pussy or to be put out of his misery.

Her lips taste like tequila and feel like the softest velvet I've ever touched. I want to lose myself in her sweet softness and forget all the bad shit in my life.

She's the perfect distraction, and from the way she's kissing me back, rubbing up against me, she wants this as badly as I do.

I tangle my fingers into her wild, dark hair, tipping her head back, giving me complete access to kiss her deeper, harder. Her moan passes between her lips, sliding into my mouth along with her tongue.

My entire body tingles like I'm being shocked by nothing more than her touch. The hand I've had on her back drifts lower, roughly cupping her round ass cheek over her skirt.

"I want you," she whispers into my mouth between kisses. "I want you so fucking bad."

"Shh," I tell her, not needing to hear those words coming from her lips. It's taking everything in me to go slow, savoring the moment, and most definitely not screwing her brains out. I pull away, only far enough to see her eyes. "I'll give you what you need, princess."

Her legs are instantly around my waist, clinging to me and leaving no space between my jeans-covered dick and her...

Is she wearing underwear?

I'd thought once or twice about the tiny skirt she was wearing and if she had anything on underneath. All night, I tried like hell not to fixate on something I'd probably never get the answer to.

I groan when she moves her hips, crushing my cock between my jeans and my pelvis. All the cuteness I thought she had is nothing in comparison to the hot-as-fuck sex kitten currently riding my cock.

Her fingers are under my shirt and then in the back of my pants, digging those claws into the meaty flesh of my ass. The mix of pleasure and pain has me panting and kissing her harder, deeper.

I walk backward, toeing off my boots, with my arms holding her tight and our mouths fused together. When the backs of my knees hit the small bed, I say, "Watch out, princess. We're going for a ride."

Her eyes flash before she untangles her legs, but she doesn't climb down, holding herself against me with one arm wrapped around my neck. I fall back onto the mattress, taking her with me, gasping when her pussy slams down on my cock with so much force, I actually lose my breath. She doesn't miss a beat, grinding against me, tits almost to my chin, giving me the air I'd lost from her own sweet lips.

Warm wetness soaks through my jeans, coating my cock as she swivels her hips, torturing me. I slide my hand up her leg, moving over her hip, searching for the edge of her panties, but I find nothing but soft bare skin.

Sweet Jesus.

My cock twitches, earning me a moan from Tamara as my fingers dig into her ass cheek, pulling her down harder, controlling the pace.

"I want to come," she pleads, shifting back to stare down at me and fighting the rhythm I'm giving her.

I roll over, putting her under me, my cock still pressed against her sweet cunt. "Not like that," I murmur against her lips, praying I have enough strength not to fuck her brains out.

This will be a test of will. But she isn't just any chick... She's a fascinating mix of pure sweetness and total wildcat.

I'm totally fucked with her, but not in the way I want to be.

A girl like her could mess with a man's mind as well as crush his heart, laughing in his face the entire time he's pleading for his soul back.

She blinks up at me when I pull away, that cute smile playing on her lips. "You gonna fuck me?" she taunts, knowing damn well I was ordered not to sleep with her.

"With my mouth and my fingers, baby, but nothing more."

Her pout is immediate and fierce. "But..."

I shake my head and press my lips to hers again before she can beg for my dick. A guy can only handle so much before he snaps. And right now, I'm hanging on by the thinnest of threads.

My hand is under her skirt a second later, caressing the skin of her inner thigh as she lifts her ass off the bed, begging for more. I smile against her lips, liking the way she kisses and loving how needy and greedy she is.

A few inches higher, I glide my fingers across her slick skin, and I can't stop the low rumble from building in the back of my throat.

Fuck.

I want her.

I'm not sure I've ever wanted anyone more in my life.

Her fingers grip my shoulders as she pants against my lips, lifting those lush hips higher, granting me access. My fingers only graze the outside of her pussy, up and down, up and down, until my fingertips are coated and she's frantically chasing my hand, wanting my fingers inside.

"I need you," she moans, dropping her knees to the bed, spreading herself wide open.

I pull away, crawling down her body and stopping to kiss the round peaks of her breasts sticking out from her tank top. The girl is mint, and her rack is something a man could spend hours admiring and still never get enough.

But there's no time for that now.

She *needs* me, and fuck, I have to taste her.

Nestling between her legs, I flip up her skirt, exposing her golden-brown skin. My mouth waters at the sight of her sleek, bare cunt, glistening in the dim lighting of the room, open and waiting to be devoured.

I gaze up the length of her, locking eyes as I lift myself up on one elbow and tuck a hand under her thigh to hold her. My touch is whisper-soft just above her clit, drifting downward as slowly as I possibly can.

She sucks in a breath, her hazel eyes rolling back as the pad of my thumb crosses over her sensitive skin, finding the target. I bend my neck, keeping my eyes on her as I place the flat of my tongue against her clit, getting my first taste.

And holy mother of God, the sweetness of her exploding across my taste buds is nothing but pure ecstasy.

She gasps as I close my lips around her, sucking her softness into my mouth, worshiping her pussy with my tongue. I moan my appreciation, sliding a single finger around her opening, wanting to crawl inside her. She licks her lips, eyes locked on me, panting as I push inside.

When her hand slides up her stomach to her chest and she tweaks a hard nipple with her fingertips, I almost lose it.

God is fucking with me.

Plain and simple.

He's paying me back for some dumb shit I've done in my life, and there's been plenty.

Nothing like throwing this hot-as-fuck girl at me, totally comfortable in her sexuality, tasting like heaven and looking like sin, and making it so I can't bury myself so deep in her I never want to leave.

She lifts her hips, pressing her pussy against my face as I bury a second finger inside her, thrusting deep and rough. I'm a man on a mission. Possessed and driven to do nothing more than give this girl the best damn orgasm of her life and make sure she never forgets me.

I curl my fingers every time I pull out, stroking her G-spot, driving her closer to the edge and digging my grave of misery even deeper.

"Oh. My. God. I'm gonna come." She rocks those sweet hips toward me, smashing her pussy against my face. "Fuck. Fuck. Fuck." She gives me no room to breathe, grinding against my lips as I push my fingers deeper.

If I were any less of a man, I would've come right then and there. The way her mouth falls open, her golden-brown skin peppered with sweat, gasping for air as her body twitches, coming all over my fingers.

Goddamn.

More than her pussy slams into me in that moment. I am struck by the realization that I want nothing more than to watch her shatter from my lips, my fingers, and my cock over and over again.

"Baby—" she lifts herself up on her elbows "—it's my turn to get the real mammoth." She smiles, licking her lips.

Yeah, I'm so, so, so fucked...and not in the way I want to be either.

CHAPTER 4
TAMARA

I WINCE as I roll over, the pounding inside my head almost unbearable, and collide with something hot and completely naked. I blink through my sleepy haze and pain—until I see his face.

Mammoth's eyes are open, staring down at me. "Mornin', princess," he rasps in a sexy-as-hell, first-thing-in-the-morning tone, which has probably melted more panties than I care to think about.

"Morning." I nuzzle into his warmth, flashes of last night coming back to me.

The dimple, the one that started all the trouble, peeks out as his mouth tips upward at one side. "Sleep okay?"

"I did." I give him a lazy smile and immediately scrunch my nose, regretting the tequila.

"Tequila got you?" The lines near his eyes deepen, no doubt loving my misery.

"No," I lie.

"Still fuckin' cute."

"Mammoth." My lips flatten, trying not to find him irresistible, which is pretty damn hard because in the dictionary, there's a picture of him as the perfect definition.

"Princess." He lifts an eyebrow with that fuckin' smirk firmly planted on his gorgeous face.

I chew on my lip as he gazes at me with those smoky gray eyes, just smirking that hot, smug smirk he's perfected. "Hey, Mammoth?"

"Yeah?" he grunts.

"Why didn't you let me return the favor last night? I mean, I know sometimes after drinking, older guys have problems getting it—"

He reaches up, pressing his index finger against my lips. "Stop."

"Up," I add, saying the word against his skin with a smile because that smirk, the one that got me into so much trouble, is gone.

He's on me in a flash, rolling me to my back, hovering above me. "I'm not old, princess, and I've never in my life had trouble getting it *up*." There's a growl to his voice, a defensiveness that makes my inner cheerleader give me sparkle-fingers. I broke the façade, insulting his manhood.

"Don't be ashamed, baby. It happens to everyone," I tease, but my smile falters as soon as his hard, thick cock presses against my middle.

"Does that feel limp to you, baby?" He leans forward, nipping at my bottom lip with his teeth.

"Well..." I try not to push myself down, impaling my body on his hard shaft, "Not necessarily. I can definitely feel there's something there."

Without another word, he crashes his lips down on mine, sucking all the smartass right out of me. I'm panting within a second, rocking my pussy against the underside of his cock a few seconds after that.

Oh God, he feels so good.

So hard.

So thick.

So Mammoth.

"You want me, Tamara?" he murmurs against my lips, eyes blazing with so much heat, it's a miracle he doesn't burn me with his touch.

"I do." I gasp as the head of his cock slides over my clit, sending a shock wave through my system. "I want you so fuckin' much right now."

He pulls his mouth away, rubbing his beard against my jaw, growling. "We can't," he says just as I'm reaching between us to palm his dick.

"What?" My eyes snap open as I gape at him, shocked and confused. "Why? Who cares what Morris says? He's not my father."

He shakes his head, sliding down my body, dragging that goddamn beard across my skin before he and the coarseness of his hair is gone. "We can't," he repeats as if I didn't hear him the first time.

I lift myself up, gawking at his naked body as he stands at the end of the bed, not trying to cover himself at all. The artwork on his skin is nothing short of amazing. There's not an inch that isn't covered by black ink. "I promised Morris," he sighs, running his fingers through his hair, "I can't break that trust."

"I won't tell," is all I can say because, holy fuck…he's a piece of ass, looking better naked than he ever did with clothes. If I wouldn't look like a complete idiot, I'd cry from the sheer beauty of him.

His cock twitches, catching my eye because I've been too busy gawking at the rest of him to check out his package completely. When it sparkles, I propel myself forward, needing a better look.

"You have piercings?" I ask, my eyes never leaving his giant, bedazzled dick. "Lemme see." I wiggle my fingers, begging for him to step closer.

How did I not feel that when I was rubbing against him like a cat in heat?

"Don't touch," he warns and doesn't move as I'd asked. "I can't have you touching my junk right now."

"Big pussy," I mutter, finally looking up to his face. "Fine. I promise not to touch your junk. Happy?" Rolling my eyes, I curse under my breath, calling him another name as I come face-to-face with Mr. Mammoth himself in all his freaking glory.

And, goddamn, is it glorious.

It's a work of art.

If I could have a poster above my bed, something to pleasure myself to every night, it would totally be Mammoth's cock.

"How long ago did you get this?" I scoot closer so I'm only a couple inches away.

"Four years ago," he says in a strained voice, hands on his hips like he's trying to hold himself back.

"I'd love to get my hood pierced," I admit, having never told anyone that before, but feeling the need to tell him everything.

Mammoth coughs, grabbing on to his hips so tightly, his knuckles turn white. "So, get it."

I snort. "My father would kill me."

His knees lock, sending his cock a little closer to my face. "Why does your father need to know? I mean, that's weird. Do you have some sick relationship I need to know about?"

I shake my head, squeezing my eyes shut. "No," I groan, knowing that's exactly how it sounded when the words flew out of my mouth. "He owns a tattoo and piercing shop. If I did it anywhere in the lower forty-eight states, I guarantee that shit would get back to him before I could hobble out the door and gingerly climb in my car."

"That makes more sense," he laughs, causing his long, hard, straight-as-an-arrow prick to wave in my face, taunting me.

"Stop it," I hiss, glaring up at him. "You can't say I can't touch and then wave it around like some forbidden prize I'll never be able to win. Be fair."

He grunts, locking his knees again as he squeezes his eyes shut like he's physically in pain. "Be quick. I can't stand here all day for you to stare at my dick. It's torture, princess. I can feel your warm breath across my skin, and it's taking everything in me not to shove my cock right into that pretty little mouth of yours right now."

I gape at him. "I should've sucked your dick last night."

He shakes his head, setting the dick into motion again. "Last night was about you. Not me."

I jerk my head back, totally thrown off by his selflessness.

No guy, and I mean not one that I've fooled around with in my twenty-one years, has ever worried about my pleasure. "You have an old lady?" I ask, figuring maybe he made a promise about where his dick could go, and it didn't include other women's mouths.

"No."

"Celibate?" I raise an eyebrow.

The laughter is immediate, sending his body and cock into a tizzy. "Definitely not."

I reach out, grabbing on to his thighs and hauling him forward so I can keep staring at the magnificence. "Then why didn't I at least give you a handy?" I ask, holding him still and dropping my gaze back to the promised land.

"A handy?" he asks.

"You know, a hand job," I whisper in complete awe of the giant hunk of metal in his cock. "This Prince Albert is something else in person. So much scarier." I thought I'd at least thought the last words instead of speaking them, but I didn't.

That much is clear as soon as he says, "But it feels oh so good when it's deep inside."

"Fuck," I hiss, totally embarrassed and turned on. "So again, not even a hand job?" I'm changing the subject, trying not to think about how the cool metal would feel sliding in and out, in and out, in and out.

Shit.

"I haven't had a hand job since high school," he confesses, and my head snaps upward, meeting his eyes.

"For real?"

He nods, the smug grin back on his lips. "Princess, why would I need a hand when there're pussies and mouths out there?"

Flashes of dozens of chicks filled with his cock go through my head, playing like a porno on fast-forward. I hate them all immediately. I want them all to die cruel and horrible deaths because they've feasted on a cock that wasn't meant to be mine. "But my mouth and pussy aren't good enough?" I grind out, glaring daggers at him.

He's out of my grip, stepping back, cock waving like it's saying goodbye.

We could've been great friends. Had such an amazing give-and-take relationship, sharing everything.

But no.

The hottie isn't that into me or else he'd be *in* me already.

"Damn it." He stalks across the room and grabs his pants off the floor, giving me a sweet view of his fine, toned ass. "Why do you have to make an impossible situation even harder?"

I'm on my knees, breasts exposed to his hungry eyes, not the least bit bashful about my nudity. "I didn't know offering a hand job was going to set you off. Jesus." I throw up my hands as I crawl toward the edge, giving him a better look because fuck him. If he's going to tease me, I'm sure as hell going to tease him too.

"Stop," he demands, his voice deep and dangerous.

I lick my lips, thinking maybe I'm finally going to get a taste of the jewelry.

He yanks his jeans up his legs, tucking the work of art into the denim.

Goodbye, Mr. Bedazzle.

"Get dressed," he tells me, striding toward the door without pulling up his zipper. "I'll meet you by the bar." He shows me his tatted back, opens the door, and storms out, slamming the heavy wood behind him.

"Well, okay," I whisper with wide eyes, talking to nobody but myself. "Whatever the fuck that was. Goddamn bikers. Bunch of pussies."

"What the fuck!" a voice comes from the hallway. A voice that most certainly was not Mammoth. "What the fuck did I tell you?"

Uh oh.

Morris.

I tiptoe off the bed, careful not to make a sound as I make my way to the door, pressing my ear against the wood.

"I didn't fuck her, man. A promise is a promise."

"You think I'm going to buy that bullshit?"

"I slept in there, but I swear nothing happened."

Liar.

"If I find out you're lying, I'll…"

"Have I ever lied to you? I told you I wouldn't fuck her, and goddamn it, I didn't do it. I wanted to, for fuck's sake. I've never wanted any chick more than that one, but I didn't take her."

I fist-pump the air, celebrating. He didn't fuck me, but he wanted to at least. I mean, that's the good news even if he didn't act on it.

"What crawled up your ass and died?" Mammoth asks Morris. "You always know I'm a man of my word."

"I know, or else I wouldn't have asked you to babysit."

I give Morris the middle finger for the babysitting comment, thankfully hiding behind the door so he can't see. I'm not a baby, and the last thing I need here or anywhere is a fucking babysitter.

"Word on the street is the Vipers are headed this way and they're out for blood," Morris tells Mammoth. "We're going on lockdown."

I gasp, covering my mouth quickly so they don't hear me. "Oh shit."

I've watched enough television to know what that means. Plus, with all the shit that went down with Gigi and Pike, hearing the horror stories afterward, I know more than I ever wanted.

I scan the room, wondering if this is where I'll take my last breath.

Local girl in search of an epic adventure dies in a biker battle.

I can see the local headlines already.

"Where ya want me?" Mammoth asks without an ounce of fear or hesitation.

"Tiny said to stay with the girl and keep her safe. Anyone comes after her, you take them out."

Take them out? I know he's not talking about sharing a meal or a friendly conversation over an ice cream cone. Morris just told Mammoth to *kill* anyone who came after me.

Kill, as in murder. *Oh my God.*

"I'll protect her with my life," Mammoth promises. "Can I fuck her, at least? You know, so if I die, I don't die for nothing."

And in the middle of all the craziness, my head spinning and my knees shaking with fear, a freaking laugh bubbles out of my throat because he's begging for permission.

"Nope. No fucking her," Morris orders. "She's an innocent."

I roll my eyes, laughing at the stupidity of their words.

Innocent?

Freaking hilarious.

I haven't been innocent since I was fifteen and let Tony Mandello finger me under the bleachers after cheer practice. It all started with that asshole, who finger-banged me like he was Woody Woodpecker and my cunt was a tree. My pussy still aches when I think about the way he pounded into me, clueless in all the ways of pleasing a woman.

"She's not innocent," Mammoth argues. "She's a hellcat in heels."

"She's not a club whore or your old lady. I know her family, Mammoth. They'd have my balls if I let anything happen to her. That includes your ass knocking her up."

"I didn't know I needed permission for my cock, old man. I did you a favor last night, behaving out of loyalty, but my willpower only goes so far."

"If we live through the weekend and you fuck her, you're going to wish the Vipers got you instead of the Gallos."

"Oh, please." I wave him off.

What was my father going to do besides have a massive stroke? Yell, for sure, and probably wring my neck for being at the compound in the first place, but he wasn't the murdering kind.

"You're both grown-ass people, but there are consequences for sleeping with a girl like her. Put some thought into it with your head and not your dick. I know she's beautiful, but sometimes the deadliest things are the most appealing."

I dance around the room, celebrating the carnal victory we've been handed, when reality slams me right in the face.

We're on lockdown and might not live another day.

CHAPTER 5
MAMMOTH

"WHAT THE FUCK ARE YOU DOING?" Crow leers at me as we stand boot-to-boot.

"Don't know what you're talking about." I somehow keep a straight face.

He can't be serious with this bullshit. He made it damn clear to her and the entire club that she wasn't welcome here. Now, he's pulling some macho bullshit, making it seem like I stole his girl when he didn't have her to begin with.

"She isn't yours," he tells me. His dark eyes blaze with anger, trying to intimidate me, which is laughable.

"She isn't yours either," I throw back. "And by the way you treated her, she'll never be. Do us all a favor. Fuck off before you and I have more than words."

"You really want to fight me over some bitch?"

I narrow my eyes. "I'm going to let your words slide, figuring your feelings are hurt and because of the brotherhood, but call her that again, and you're going to get your ass beat," I growl.

"You two dipshits done?" Tiny asks as he walks up to stand at our side.

Neither of us moves. Our eyes are locked, and the anger coming off us is like an electrical storm, charging the air.

"Crow, you were wrong how you treated her. Case closed. You invited the chick here and then didn't so much as try to take care of the situation to not draw any attention to yourself or the club." Crow's eyes slide to Tiny as he opens his mouth, but Tiny keeps on talking. "You fucked up. Own it."

I smirk, loving that Crow's getting put in his place for being a jackass. The guy has been nothing but a dick since he strolled through the door like he owned the joint and his shit didn't stink.

"And you," Tiny says, and I know he's talking to me before I glance in his direction. "You're responsible for her while we're on lockdown. You, along with a half-dozen men, will stay here while we go out and take care of club business. No one gets in, and no one goes out. You're in charge. Understand?"

"Got it." I nod. "And him?"

"He's going with us," Tiny replies.

Thank fuck for small miracles.

"I should really stay. She's here because of me. She's my problem," Crow offers, trying to seem like the bigger man, but we all know he's not.

One of Tiny's salt-and-pepper eyebrows rises. "Are you shitting me right now with this?"

Crow shakes his head. "I'm putting the club before myself. It's my fault she's here, and I should be the one to deal with her."

"He stays." Tiny points at me.

I smile, wishing I could do a victory lap around the parking lot, kicking up dirt right into Crow's ugly mug.

"We're not done," Crow threatens.

"You know where to find me," I taunt the motherfucker.

His eyes never leave mine until he's forced to turn around to follow Tiny across the parking lot. The guy seriously needs his ass beat, and I'd be more than willing to be the one to do it. Tamara or not, he's been asking for trouble since the moment he walked through the door.

I stalk into the clubhouse, finding a handful of women huddled on the couches, talking softly. I tip my head to them, not bothering to stop. The last thing I want to do is talk to last night's trash.

"Mammoth, baby," Sadie's voice slithers over me like a snake.

I stop, eyes pinned on the bar in front of me, and don't turn to face her. "What, Sadie?"

Her hand slides over my shoulder before her tits press against my back. "Since we're stuck in here together," she purrs into my ear, "maybe we can keep each other company."

I peel her hand away from my chest and turn, sliding my hand to her wrists, holding her tight so she hears what I'm saying. "It's never happened, and it'll still never happen, Sadie. I don't care if the world's coming to an end, you're not getting anywhere near my dick."

"But…" She blinks, yanking her arm back and her wrist from my grip. "I thought…"

"I've always been nice to you, but don't mistake my kindness for lust. I'm not sticking my dick where the entire club's already been. You're never going to be my old lady. Never."

She flinches, her head jerking back. "I knew the nice-guy act was total bullshit. You're the worst kind of man, Mammoth." She stomps back toward the women on the couches, leaving me be like she'd just delivered a wounding blow.

"I'm devastated," I mutter to myself, shaking my head at Sadie's bullshit.

"Gates are locked," Dog says as he marches through the front doors, followed by five other brothers. "You want first shift or second?"

"Second," I tell him. I have a hot chick who's supposed to be out here waiting for me and isn't. "We'll do three-hour shifts until nightfall, and then it's all hands on deck."

Dog nods, slapping Brute on the chest. "Let's go. You're with me in front. And Mac, you got the back."

A second later, they're gone.

"You two," I say to the two remaining guys, Eagle and Ginger, "get some rest. It's going to be a long fuckin' day and night."

Ginger nods. "I'll be in my room. Holler if you need me."

Eagle glances over his shoulder, giving a toothy grin to Sadie, who hasn't stopped giving me the stink-eye. "I'm going to use my time a little more wisely," he says before slapping me on the shoulder, stalking toward the waiting and very willing Sadie.

When I finally turn the handle on the door of the room where I'd left Tamara, nothing could've prepared me for what I see. "Hey, big guy," she says, buck-ass naked, spread-eagled on top of the bed, wearing nothing but a smirk.

My dick is instantly hard.

Goddamn.

She's like every man's wet dream. But as much as I want her, I'm so fucking pissed, my fingers curl inward. "What the fuck are you doing?" I kick the door closed before someone walks by and sees, catching more than an eyeful.

She pushes herself up against the headboard, leaning back, her tits perky and nipples hardening. "What's it look like I'm doing?"

I start to open my mouth to tell her she's a fucking fool, but then she slides her hand between her open legs, putting on a show. "I've been waiting for you." She lets out a little moan, eyes locked on me as she glides her fingertips through her folds. "It's been so hard too." Her gaze dips to my crotch.

"Motherfucker." I want nothing more than to slide between those sweet thighs and bury my dick in her softness.

She pats the bed with one hand, fingering herself with the other. "Come here," she pleads. "Let me make you feel as good as I do."

I grab a blanket off the dresser and throw it at her, not trusting myself to get within five feet of her without leaping on top of her. "Cover up," I bark, sounding cold and unappreciative.

And I do appreciate her.

I appreciate every delicious inch of her body, along with her unabashed sexuality.

Her smile falls. "You don't want..." She blinks, tears filling her eyes. "I thought..."

God, I'm a prick. "I'm sorry," I say, stepping forward to sit on the edge of the bed. Again, not getting any closer than I have to.

She grabs the blanket, covering her body quickly. "You're sorry?" she snaps.

"I'm sorry," I repeat, shaking my head. "I didn't mean..."

She crosses her arms, holding the blanket against her chest. "To be a dick?" She lifts her chin, challenging me to disagree with how she finished my statement.

"I am a dick, princess." I blow out a breath and study her beautiful face as she swipes at her cheek, wiping away a tear. "I didn't mean to get pissed, but what if I wasn't the one to walk in this room first?"

She opens her mouth and then snaps it shut, blinking at me with those butterfly lashes. "Well, I..." She swallows, probably running through the reality of what could've happened if it had been someone like Lefty or, hell, Crow.

"What if Crow had walked in?" I squeeze my hand tighter, harnessing my anger just thinking about that prick seeing her naked.

"But he didn't."

"He could've," I growl, the anger slipping.

She bows her head, hoisting the blanket up higher, covering her tits completely. "I just figured I'd make you happy."

I scoot next to her, placing my fingers under her chin, forcing her to look at me. "We're not in a dorm. It's not safe around here for someone like you."

"Someone like me?" she repeats, her hazel eyes flashing with anger.

"Yeah." I smile, soaking in her beauty.

Chick without a man, stuck inside the compound with a handful of horny fuckers. There's so much that can go wrong. That doesn't even take into account the jealous bitches whispering on the couches about her being here.

"You have some fucking nerve." She yanks her chin away from my touch and slides across the bed like she's going to run. "Someone like me," she mutters.

"Hey." I reach out, latching on to her wrist, stopping her as she climbs to her feet. "What the hell, princess?"

She glares at me as her lush top lip curls. "Someone like me," she repeats, raising her voice and dropping the blanket, exposing her chest. "I don't know what the hell that's supposed to mean, but if you think I'm an innocent flower, you're wrong. So fucking wrong!"

I blink, gaping at her. "That's not what I meant. I know you're not innocent. We just met, and I've already had my mouth on you."

She tries to pull out of my grip, but I'm not letting her stalk away all pissed off and naked as fuck.

Not happening. Never.

I tighten my hold, careful not to hurt her. "I wasn't calling you a whore, Tamara."

Goddamn it. She gets me flustered so easily.

She raises her chin, eyes narrowed, the rage still there. "Then what the hell were you talking about?" she snarls.

I haul her against me, chest-to-chest, eye-to-eye, needing her full attention when I speak the truth. "I was talking about a hot little thing like you being at the compound, spread-eagled, waiting to be fucked. There're women out there who will never be your friends and some assholes you definitely need to run away from. The only thing I want is for you to be safe. If something happened to you…"

"I'm a hot little thing?" she mumbles, clearly not hearing the rest of my statement.

I nod, releasing her wrist to touch her face. "Princess, I've never met a woman who sets my body on fire the way you do."

"So, you like me for me?"

"I like you for you. If someone asked me who Tamara is, so many great adjectives would come to mind." I smirk.

"Like what?" She smiles, finally relaxing against me.

"Ballsy, sassy, tough, funny, stacked, sexy, and a little crazy."

She laughs, running her hands up my chest to curl her arms around my neck. "Wanna add freaky to that list?" She waggles her dark eyebrows and rubs her nose against mine.

"I'm adding troublemaker to the list," I murmur against her lips before taking her mouth hard and fast.

"Mammoth?" Ginger says quietly, knocking on the door, always having shit timing.

"What?" I growl, kneading Tamara's ass in my palms and turning her away from the door so my body blocks her.

"Dog needs you," he replies, smart enough not to come in.

"Damn it." I sigh. "I'll be right there!" I yell, fucking hating being on lockdown like I've never hated anything in my life.

"Go." She smiles, pushing against my chest. "I'll be right there." She points at the bed before waving her hand in front of her body. "Waiting like this."

I swallow, trying to think of sick puppies or my parents fucking to kill my hard-on, but nothing helps. "The door stays locked after I leave. No one comes in except me, and you don't leave this room unless you're escorted by Ginger. You understand?" I'm unable to take my eyes off her fucking unbelievable body.

She nods, giving me a small smile. "You're the only thing coming in and out of here. Don't worry," she says, dipping her fingers back between her legs as she sits on the edge of the bed, knees spread wide. "I'll find some way to keep myself company."

"Add tease to that list too," I growl, storming out of the room to nothing but the sound of her wicked laughter.

CHAPTER 6
TAMARA

"WHAT THE FUCK ARE YOU DOING?" the very angry voice on the other end of the phone screams, making me wince. "Have you lost your goddamn mind?"

Eagle chuckles and runs his hand across his face, trying to hide his amusement as I get my ass chewed out.

"Thanks." I take the phone from his hand as I hide my naked body behind the door. "You can go now," I tell him.

"Leave the phone outside the door when you're done talking to your mommy," he teases, still laughing his ass off.

Fucker.

I can't believe my parents called the compound looking for me. Actually, I take that back. I totally can. They'd stop at nothing, especially embarrassing me, by calling a motorcycle club. Who does that? Maxine and Anthony Gallo, of course.

I close the door in Eagle's face, take a deep breath, and try to prepare myself for my mother's tirade. "Hey, Mom," I say casually, like we're having a normal conversation about what's new in our lives.

"Don't 'hey, Mom' me, child," she grumbles, breathing so heavily, I'd think she just finished working out. "You're lucky I'm a hundred miles away because if I were there, I'd..."

"Mom," I interrupt her oncoming threat to end my life. I know that's where she's going before she says it. We've been down this path once or twice before. "I'm safe."

"Safe!" she screams so loudly, I have to pull the phone away from my ear. "You're at a biker compound, filled with criminals, and you want to tell me you're safe?" She cackles like a lunatic. "I never knew you were so dumb, Tamara."

"I'm a grown woman now. I know right from wrong, and I know how to take care of myself. I knew you and Dad would flip your shit if you knew where I was going. I had to see a guy about a thing."

"A guy about a thing?" she asks, breathing heavier now with her voice lower and somehow scarier. "What the hell is a thing?"

"I can't believe Gigi ratted me out," I groan.

"She didn't. Pike told your father."

That freakin' tattletale asshole. I figured Austin or Lily would open their big fat mouths way before Pike ever sang like a canary to my father about my whereabouts. "He's an asshole."

"He's concerned and acted like an adult, which is more than I can say for you," she rants. "He was concerned that you took off, and he didn't know where you went. I had to call James to track your ass down. Imagine my shock when he found you hiding out at the Disciples' compound."

I fall back onto the bed, figuring this isn't going to be a quick or easy phone call. Maxine Gallo is just gearing up, and once she gets started, there is no stopping her until she is good and ready.

I stare up at the ceiling, memorizing the cracks in the paint, trying to ignore my mother's tirade. "They're nice people, Mom. They're not criminals," I argue when she finally stops long enough to take a breath.

"Do you hear yourself?"

"I do." I close my eyes, throwing my arm over my face, wishing

I could hide. I've never had a problem with confrontation when it comes to anybody but my parents. They're my weakness, especially my father.

My mother scares the hell out of me, but my father, I never want to see disappointment in his eyes.

"Now, back to the *thing*. Are you doing drugs?"

"What? No," I blurt out. "I've never done drugs, Mom. You know this."

We've had long conversations about drugs and the dangers. So long, I thought my ears would bleed from listening to her go on and on about the long-term effects and damage they could do to my body. I got the message, and to avoid any further "long talks," I avoided drugs throughout high school and college because of her.

She grunts, and I can picture her shaking her head, stalking around the kitchen as she paces the same path over and over again. "I also never thought my daughter was the type who would run away and hide out at a biker compound either."

"Run away?" I laugh into the crook of my arm. "I'm twenty-one, and I don't even live at home anymore. How can I run away?"

"You may think you're grown, little girl, but I gave you life, and I can take it away too," she warns, giving me the same old spiel she has given me since the first time I challenged her authority.

It's such a mom line, and it's hilarious.

I bite down on my lip, trying to quiet my laughter. "You can't ground me, Mom."

"Your father's so pissed, he can't even talk to you right now. You're going to wish for a grounding when you come back. That would be merciful, and we're not feeling so generous."

Well, damn. My laughter dies when I know my father's disappointed. "I'm sorry."

I thought he'd understand. Hell, at my age, he was so much wilder.

"I'm grabbing Nita and Malia, and we're coming to get you."

"Like fuck you are!" Dad yells in the background, causing my mom to growl into the receiver. "James and I are going to get her as soon as we're allowed."

"Allowed?" she asks him.

I cringe because the real shit hasn't even hit the fan. She doesn't know about the lockdown.

Lucky me.

"They're on fucking lockdown!" Dad howls. "Fucking lock-down and my kid's there, waiting for her ass to get shot. She better hope she lives, or else I'm going to..." He keeps talking, but I can't understand what he's saying because my mom covers the phone.

If my dad weren't so pissed, I'd laugh again. If I died, what would he do then? He couldn't spank me or send me to my room to think about my shittastic behavior. But then, I'd be dead, and I could never imagine my parents getting over my loss.

"Tell him I'm safe. I'm not in any danger," I say softly, trying to calm everyone down.

"She said she's safe and not in danger," my mother repeats, no doubt rolling her eyes as she delivers the message to my dad.

"Is she fucking out of her mind?" Is his response. "She's at the same place Gigi was when men with guns came blazing in, shooting up the place. Oh, don't worry, Dad. I'm safe," he says sarcastically, "What a bunch of horseshit. Turn your goddamn phone on, Tamara. You're not sixteen, hiding out at Blake's house. You're in real danger, and I'd like to know you're okay without having to go through a biker to find out if you're still breathing."

I shuffle off the bed and fish my phone out of my purse. "I'm turning it on now," I tell them, feeling like shit. "I'm sorry."

"It's on now, baby," she relays my message, adding the baby, probably trying to calm down the raging inferno that is Anthony Gallo.

As soon as my phone starts up, a litany of over one hundred messages, twenty missed calls, and ten voice mails fills the screen.

"Next time I call, she better goddamn answer it," Dad barks, and I flinch, having never heard him so pissed off in all my life.

"I will." I swipe away the notifications immediately.

"She will," Mom repeats. "If she knows what's good for her."

"I'll text her when we're on our way," Dad says in a little bit calmer tone. I mean, he's still pissed. I can hear it in his voice, but he's not yelling anymore.

"Mammoth is going to bring me home," I say, thinking I'm being helpful. It's a long drive, and Dad and Uncle James are busy men with better things to do than to come and pick me up.

"Oh lawd," Mom mutters. "I can't with this one. You talk to her. I can't deal with her bullshit."

"What did you say?" my dad asks after my mother obviously hands over the phone to him.

"Daddy, I just said I have a ride. There's no need to drive this far for nothing." I wince, waiting for the blowback because there's always blowback when my dad's pissed.

"Crow's bringing you back?"

I scrunch my face as soon as the asshole's name is mentioned. Man, Pike told my parents everything. "Not Crow. He's a jerk, and he isn't even here anyway. He's off doing…" I pause, realizing I don't know what the hell any of the men do during a lockdown. "Whatever he does."

"Wait, you aren't there with him?" I can hear the shock in his voice. "I thought at least he was there protecting you."

I shake my head like Dad can see me. "He wasn't happy when I showed up here and has been the biggest asshole in the world to me. He's out on patrol or whatever he does during lockdowns."

"You're there alone?" He sucks in a quick breath and then starts to hyperventilate. "We'll be there in three hours," he tells me like it's that easy and I'm in need of a rescue.

"I'm not alone, Daddy." I throw the Daddy in there again, trying to butter him up and calm him down. "They have a guy assigned to me for my protection, and when this is all over, he'll bring me home too."

I expect an immediate response, but there's only silence. Well, in reality, there's his heavy breathing as he lets the information settle.

"Okay?" I ask when he doesn't reply after a few more seconds.

"Who's protecting you?"

"Mammoth."

"What's his real name?"

"I don't know. He's just Mammoth here, and I didn't ask him for identification."

"Have kids, they said," he mutters. "It'll be fun. Biggest fuckin' lie of my life."

"I love you." I know those three words usually melt Anthony Gallo into someone a little more agreeable.

"I'll text you as soon as James runs a background check on Mammoth and let you know if he's allowed to bring you home."

"Allowed?" I chuckle. He's so cute sometimes. "I'm not fifteen, Dad. And Mammoth's a solid guy." Like so solid, you could bounce a penny off his abs, but I leave that little bit out. "He's not what you'd think he'd be like from looking at him. You'd probably even like him if you ever met him."

"If I allow him to drive you back, I expect to meet him. But first, I'm going to have James do some digging. Keep your phone on, and I'll text you. Don't leave the compound without texting me first. Don't head home until I give you the go-ahead."

"I'll let you know when we're leaving," I tell him because I'm not going to wait for the go-ahead to do anything. Not at twenty-one years old...that much is for fucking sure.

"Tamara."

"Daddy."

"If I text you, for the love of God, text me back so I don't start to panic, thinking you're dead."

"Start?" I ask, teasing him a little.

"Don't be a smartass."

"I learned from the best." I smile, loving my dad and mom so much, even if they're overprotective weirdos sometimes.

"You're going to be the death of me."

"You've been saying that for nine years."

"Fuckin' kids."

"Tamara," Mammoth says on the other side of the door, giving me a warning knock.

"I got to go. I promise I'll leave my phone on. Try to relax. Just know I'm safe."

"I love you, baby," he says, talking so softly, I know he's finally calming down. At least for now, he is almost normal, but my dad's emotions are like a tide. But instead of being driven by the moon, his are steered by my mother.

"I love you too, Dad. Talk soon," I say and tap the screen, ending the call before Mammoth comes inside.

The door creaks open, and Mammoth peeks his head through the opening, surveying the room. "I heard voices," he says, eyes darting around like he thinks someone's hiding in here with me.

I hold out the phone as proof that he wasn't hearing things and I most definitely do not have company. "My parents tracked me down and chewed my ass out for being here."

The door closes, and a moment later, Mammoth is in front of me. "Can't blame a guy." He places his palm against my cheek, stroking my skin with his thumb. "If you were mine, I wouldn't let you pull the shit you did."

I stare into his smoky eyes. "Oh yeah?"

"Yeah."

"You wouldn't *let* me?" I somehow hold in my laughter because he's freaking serious.

His lips don't even twitch as he says, "I'd take you across my knee and spank that pretty little ass of yours."

My eyes widen. "You'd...do that?" I swallow hard, suddenly unable to breathe.

Then he smirks. "Want to test me?"

I slap his chest, snorting. "I thought you were totally serious. Jesus."

"I was." He winks.

I gape at his handsome, rugged face. "Well, it's a good thing I'm not yours, then."

"Imagine what fun we could have, princess. Your need to cause trouble would have my palm working overtime."

"You're still fucking with me."

"Still fuckin' cute," he whispers before his lips are on mine, pushing me back into the mattress and giving me a night to remember.

CHAPTER 7
MAMMOTH

TAMARA STARES UP AT ME, head on my chest. "So, what's your real name?"

I stroke the soft, golden skin on her shoulder, loving the way her skin feels against my body. "JD."

"JD what?"

"JD Saint."

She lifts up on one elbow, hovering above me. "Mr. Saint?" She laughs.

"That's me, princess."

"And the JD?"

I shake my head because no one but my birth parents, the army, and the people in the hometown I left behind know what the initials stand for. "Mammoth," I reply.

She rolls her eyes and slaps my chest playfully. "JD does not stand for Mammoth."

"Try me." I pull her back down into the crook of my arm when she rolls her eyes again. "You know my last name, which is more than most people do."

"So, I'm kind of special?"

"Yo, Mammoth!" Ginger yells, pounding on the bedroom door so loudly, Tamara jolts against my body.

I kiss her forehead before rolling out of bed and grabbing my T-shirt off the floor. Her eyes are on me, never leaving my flesh as I yank on my pants and move toward the door. I turn, raising an eyebrow when I see she's frozen, sitting up, breasts exposed.

"Cover those up." My gaze dips to her bare chest. "Unless you want Ginger to get an eyeful and you to get a red ass later."

Her face flushes as she giggles, lifting the sheet over her chest, hiding her body. "Red ass," she whispers, thinking I'm kidding.

I crack the door to Ginger, who's leaning against the wall opposite with his arms crossed. "Tiny called. They're meeting with the Vipers in the morning, trying to work out a deal without bloodshed. So, either shit's about to get real in a hurry, or we'll be out of lockdown tomorrow night."

Knowing Tiny, he'll work out a deal and find a way to make peace, which will benefit all parties involved. No one will walk away empty-handed or shortchanged as long as there's no bloodshed or bullets flying before the deal can be finalized.

"Got it," I tell him, holding the door against my shoulder, making it impossible for the greedy-eyed redhead to get a glimpse of Tamara.

"You two coming up for air?" he asks as he tries to glance behind me but sees nothing.

"No!" Tamara yells out.

Ginger's mouth breaks out in a giant smile as he shakes his head. "You got your hands full with that one, brother."

"You have no idea," I tell him, "And you never will."

"Figured as much," Ginger mumbles, knowing well enough I won't be sharing this one. "A guy can dream."

"Keep that shit in your head and PG," I warn him.

Ginger gives me a grin before stalking down the hallway. "Pussy-whipped already," he says, loud enough for me to hear as I'm closing the door.

"Fucker," I mutter to myself as I close the door and turn around to a very naked and completely uncovered Tamara. I raise an eyebrow as I rake my eyes over her bare skin. "You don't like to follow directions, do you?"

"Are these the problem?" she asks, cupping her breasts in her hands, knowing exactly what she's doing as she kneels toward the end of the bed. "Why don't you teach me a lesson?" There's a faint smile on her lips and a twinkle in her eye. She's testing me, loving to push boundaries and not even just my own.

I close the space between us quickly, and she swallows, craning her neck to look up at me. "Princess, you could tempt an angel."

"Or a Saint." She gives me a playful wink, running her thumbs across her nipples, drawing my gaze away from her face.

I bend my head forward, brushing my lips against hers, listening to her ragged breathing. "Put on some clothes and meet me by the bar. I need to feed you."

"But," she murmurs against my mouth. "I'm horny, baby."

I laugh softly, digging this chick so much and wondering if I'll ever get my fill. "Food first, then fucking, princess."

She bats her eyelashes like those are her magic wands that'll have me bending to her will. "Fucking then food," she argues, trying to barter a deal.

One that isn't going to work. Not on me, at least.

I cup her cheek, staring down into her hazel eyes. "You need energy for what I have planned for you."

With those words, she's out of bed, searching for her clothes. "Food first," she says to herself. "Lots of pleasure after."

I chuckle, watching her as she grabs the T-shirt I wore yesterday and pulls it down over her head. But when she moves toward her skirt, I grab her by the wrist, stopping her.

"No," I tell her, shaking my head.

"No?" she asks, eyebrows high.

"No."

"Why?" There's a smirk on her face. She knows why, but the girl likes to fuck with my head, among other things.

"Don't move." I release her wrist, needing to get something more for her to wear than a flimsy skirt with no panties.

"I won't." She raises her hand, lifting two fingers. "Scout's honor."

I'm out of the room a second later, stalking toward my room to grab a pair of sweats that could fit her. Even if they don't, they'll be baggy as hell, leaving everything to the imagination for anyone who sees her.

"What are these?" she asks, holding out the gray sweats when I place them in her hand.

"Your pants."

She scrunches her nose, staring down at the material like it's the most hideous thing she's ever seen. "Are you giving me some skank's clothes they left behind after you tossed them out?"

I bark out a laugh. "They're mine, princess. There're no other clothes in my room but my own. And how many chicks have you seen around here in sweats?"

"Well, none, but..." She holds them out, the waist almost as wide as her shoulders and the legs nearly as long as her entire body. "What the hell am I supposed to do with them?"

"Wear them. Roll them up. Hell, pull them up over your tits. Whatever you need to do to cover your body."

Her eyes snap to mine, her eyelids narrowing to slits. "What's wrong with my body?"

I touch her face, sweeping my thumb across her chin. "Your body is perfection."

"Then why these?" She lifts up my pants, shoving them in my face.

I push them down, staring her right in the eyes. "That body is only for me to see. You want to flaunt it for the guys, then you're not mine. You want to save it and wear the sweats, trust me, I'll totally make it worth your while."

She studies me for a moment, lips parted, breathing heavy, turning over the words I've just said. For once, she doesn't argue or give me lip. She steps back, sticking her little feet into the legs and pulls up the pants to her waist. "Now what?" she quizzes me as she holds her arms wide, showing me the giant-ass gap caused by her tiny waist.

I grab the cording at the waistband, tying the sweats as snugly as possible as the material pools around her feet. "There."

"I look ridiculous," she huffs, kicking out her legs to drive the point home, again, that the pants don't fit.

I'm on a knee, rolling up the legs so she can walk without falling. "You look beautiful," I tell her, gazing up her body, loving the way she looks in my big T-shirt and favorite sweats. "I'd eat you." I wink.

She places her hands on my shoulders, stepping closer, making sure my face is right in the promised land. "Who needs food when I'm on the menu?"

Grabbing her around the knees, I lift her upward as she squeals. "First, food," I say, placing her over my shoulder so her ass is level with my face. "Then, pussy."

"You're no fun sometimes." She sags over my shoulder as her fingertips find the top of my ass. "The view from here is great, by the way."

"Mine too," I tell her as I carry her out the door, heading down the hallway. Before we make it to the common area, I sink my teeth into her ass cheek, holding her legs tightly so she doesn't try to shimmy down my body.

"Ouch," she hisses, slapping my ass with what I assume is all her might and then wiggling her ass closer to my face because I know she liked it.

"Don't worry, princess. I'll kiss it and make it better later."

"Promises, promises," she grumbles as her fingernail skates up the bare skin of my back, sending goose bumps everywhere.

"I'm a man of my word."

"Looks like you found yourself a new toy," Eagle says as soon as he sees us. He's parked on a barstool, nursing a cup of coffee, probably laced with something more than caffeine.

I glare at him as soon as Tamara's body stiffens in my arms. "Fuck off, man."

"*New* toy?" she whispers, those fucking fingernails which had just been giving me pleasure now biting into my flesh, about to draw blood.

"Ignore him." I throw him a look that tells him I hope he chokes on a big cock and dies a slow death.

"Put me down," she demands, kicking her legs, but I'm not having any of it.

"Stop." I tighten my hold, leaving Eagle on the barstool, praying no one else is in the kitchen.

Eagle is a motherfucker and a troublemaker, always talking before thinking.

My private life has always been that...private.

And he knows better than to talk shit about relationships, casual or otherwise, when there're women around. I never mention his old lady and wife, Linda, when he's trying to bang two chicks at the same time, neither one of them her.

Tamara's quiet, nails still planted in my skin, but otherwise not moving as we make it to the kitchen.

I loosen my grip and ease her down my chest until we're eye-to-eye. Her feet aren't on the floor, but my arms are around her waist, holding her there, suspended.

"What?" she growls, the playful, happy mood from earlier gone.

"Princess." I look at the girl all filled with piss and vinegar. "Are you havin' fun?"

"Yes," she says, but she looks behind me instead of in my eyes, digging those goddamn fingernails into the skin of my shoulders.

"Baby."

"JD," she throws back, attitude oozing off her like lava.

"You want to be my old lady?"

Her eyes snap to mine, flashing with anger, joy, and sadness. "I don't know, but I know I don't want to be a new toy. Toys are replaceable and temporary."

I smirk, staring at the beautiful creature who wants a good time but doesn't want to feel like she's just another chick in a long line of endless, faceless, nameless pussy going in and out of my life. "There's only one, Tamara."

Her fingernails relent, and she slides her hands to my neck. "How many women have you called princess?"

I know if I answer this wrong, she'll dig those sparkly claws right into my face. Thankfully, I can be honest and come out without a scratch. "Only you."

She blinks. "Only me?"

"Only you."

She smiles, the compliment seeming to do the trick. "Smart man."

"An honest man. Now, you want pancakes or eggs?"

Her eyebrows draw down. "I'm a shit cook."

I laugh again, never expecting her to cook for me. "I'm cooking. Now pick."

Her face brightens immediately. "Big, bedazzled dick and cooking skills. You're like a dream man."

"You forgot about my mad tongue skills, baby."

"They're all right," she teases, earning her my mouth against her neck, biting gently into her skin. "Why don't you lay me on that table and prove me wrong?"

"Food then fucking," I remind her, murmuring into the soft, sweet warmth of her neck and lowering her feet to the floor. "Lots of fucking."

"Fine." She turns her face to take my lips.

The kiss is long, deep, and filled with promise. My hands find her ass, kneading the round cheeks in my palms. She moans, pressing her breasts against me, no doubt trying to tempt me to go back to the room.

I push her away, panting. Another minute longer and I would've done just that. "Sit," I tell her, moving her to a stool near the countertop. "And don't move."

She pouts as she slides onto the hard wooden surface, looking so small in the extra-large clothes but still damn hot. "You don't have to worry about that. Nothing I make is ever edible. So, where'd ya learn to cook?"

"First off, eggs and pancakes are the easiest damn things to make."

"Trust me, I fuck up toast." She snorts.

Somehow, I believe her, but I don't share that. "My mom taught me. Most nights, I'd cook for us both when I lived at home," I say into the refrigerator, grabbing everything I'll need.

"And home is where?" she asks, sitting up a little straighter when I turn back around.

"Ohio, but I've lived everywhere."

She scrunches her nose. "Never been to Ohio."

"What's the face for, then, beautiful?"

"It's cold there."

"That's why I'm here," he says.

"Where's home for you?" I ask, forgetting if she told me before or if I'd overheard it.

"Grew up in Tampa. It's where my family lives and where I'll be for the summer, but I'm going to school in Tallahassee."

"FSU?"

She nods, watching me like a hawk. "Yep. Did you go there?"

"You're cute." I laugh, cracking the eggs and dumping the contents into the bowl.

"What?"

"If I had a degree, I'm pretty sure I wouldn't be living at the compound, doing the shit I'm doing."

"It's never too late," she tells me. "You should apply and go there with me. I mean, you have the GI Bill to pay for it and everything, right?"

"Yeah, but I'm too old for college shit now."

"I have a year left. We could hang out, fuck like bunnies, study for class, ya know...fun shit."

I shake my head, unable to stop laughing because this girl is the best kind. "They should really have you write their brochures."

"How old are you?" she blurts out of freaking nowhere.

"Thirty."

She doesn't even flinch. "I'm twenty-one."

"Figured you were older," I reply honestly, especially since she said she had a year left.

"I graduated high school a year early." She shrugs like it's no big deal.

"Smart chick. I like that."

"So, you don't care I'm only twenty-one?"

"Do you care I'm thirty?" I throw back.

She shakes her head. "I like my men a little older." She smiles. "Men my age are..."

"Pussies," I throw in because, fuck me, they shouldn't be called Gen Z or Millennials or whatever shit they're on now. They should be called Gen P for pussies or pansies.

"From your lips to God's ears." There's a minute of silence as she watches me prep the pancakes and then whisk the eggs. "Are your parents still in Ohio?"

"No, she moved here a few years ago to be closer to me."

She frowns. "Can I ask what happened to your dad?"

I grab the pans from the rack above the stove, placing them on the burners. "Never knew the man. He died in Desert Storm before I was born."

"I'm sorry," she whispers, covering her mouth with her hand.

I throw a smile her way, because there's no need for her sadness. "Baby, don't be sad. My father died a hero, and in my mind, he'll always be my hero. I don't know what I missed. My mom stayed single until I was grown and out of the house. I'm sure having a dad would've been great, things would've been easier, but I had a great life. My mom made sure of it."

"It's still sad." She glances down at her hands as she sets them in her lap, twisting her fingers together. "I can't imagine not having my dad in my life."

"Tell me about him," I ask, working on our breakfast, done with talking about myself and my sad past.

"Well, my mom is insane." I glance her way, but she waves me off. "Not literally." She laughs. "She's just...intense. My dad is cool sometimes, and he's really my best friend."

"Brothers or sisters?"

"I have a younger brother, Asher. He's a little asshole, but I love him too. Then there're my cousins. There's so many of us, your head would explode."

"Must be nice to have a big family."

"Didn't you have aunts and uncles?" she asks me, watching in fascination like she's never seen a man cook before.

"I had a few, but they all lived so far away, we only saw them at holidays or funerals."

"That would be awful." She slides off the stool, coming to stand at my side. "We're together all the time. Every weekend, my grand-parents have dinner at their house, and then my dad and his siblings own a tattoo shop together. Gigi, my cousin and Pike's girl, and I went to FSU together. This is really the first time I've ever ventured off on my own."

I turn my attention away from the pancakes to her sweet face. "And you showed up here, and it could've ended very badly."

She places her hand on my upper arm, peering over the stove. "But it didn't. I got this hot, shirtless guy, cooking for me, giving me orgasms. I'd say it worked out pretty damn great."

"You got lucky."

"So did you," she says, winking.

"When I bring you home tomorrow, how much danger am I going to be in?" I ask, partially joking but mostly serious.

Her eyes widen. "Tomorrow?"

I nod. "Lockdown's probably going to end, and then I'm under strict orders to take you back to your family."

The sadness in her eyes weighs on me before she releases her grip on my arm and moves back toward the stool. "It'll be fine. They'll be fine. I'll be fine."

But the real question is... Will I be?

CHAPTER 8
TAMARA

THE MC COMPOUND during a party versus during a lockdown are two very different places. Gone are the music, laughs, and general good time.

Boring is an understatement.

If it weren't for Mammoth, I probably would've scaled a wall by now. Possibly got my ass shot while doing it too, but danger and a dash of stupidity never stopped me from doing anything.

Mammoth's been outside for two hours, leaving me with nothing to do except nurse a beer, play on my phone, and return Sadie's heated glare.

The bitch hasn't stopped watching me, throwing me shade the entire time because in her messed-up head, Mammoth is hers. Or at least she'd like him to be, no matter how many times he's set her ass straight.

"Mammoth will be in in another hour," Eagle tells me as he slides onto a barstool near me.

Not next to me.

Somehow, it's like I have the plague. The other members in the MC won't risk coming within more than a few feet of me because of some invisible contagion I'm carrying.

"Good." I nod, not bothering to look at the older man who's been nothing but sweet to me.

"You all right, girl?"

I don't know why, but I giggle. There's something about him calling me girl that just brings out the giggles full force. Maybe it's the way he says it. It's not sweet. It's not mean either, but it most definitely is funny.

"I'm fine, boy," I reply through my fit of giggles, giving him the side-eye as his face crumples.

"Boy?" he asks and grunts like I've punched him right in his big, beer-belly gut. "I'm hardly a boy."

"Well." I run the back of my hand across my lips, wiping my mouth and trying to stop my laughter. When I turn to face him, somehow I've sobered, but just barely. "I'm hardly a girl either, Eagle."

He eyes me, gaze sweeping across my face, soaking me in. "You're closer to a girl than I am to a boy. You're a babe in my eyes."

I take in his mostly gray hair and salt-and-pepper beard, knowing he's way older and probably cashing Social Security checks monthly. "Do you call every woman who's younger 'girl'?" I question him. The conversation is mostly to pass the time but partially out of curiosity.

The corner of his mouth twitches as he lifts the beer bottle to his lips, eyes narrowing. "Honestly?"

I nod.

"I'm shit with names. I'm all about using girl, baby, sweetheart, and shit like that because I have less of a chance of getting my ass in trouble."

The laughter that had died comes roaring back. "Do the women know this?"

He shrugs as he takes a swig of beer, still staring at me down the neck of the bottle. "Don't think many of them care."

He's probably right. I'm pretty sure Mammoth could call Sadie anything, and she'd still jump on his cock like her very life depended on the impalement.

"So, you don't know my name?"

He slides the mostly empty bottle onto the bar, resting his thick forearm on the wood. "I know you're a Gallo and Gigi's cousin, but beyond that...I got nothing. So, you're 'girl.'"

"Makes sense." I smile at the older man, loving his laid-back and easy nature. I'm sure there're times he's scary as fuck, but now, sharing a drink, shooting the shit, isn't one of them. "Lord knows I've been called worse."

"Eagle." Ginger's voice echoes through the common room. "Can I have a word?"

And in the blink of an eye, Eagle's gone.

No goodbye.

No quick nod.

He just slides off, stalking across the room, and disappears out the front door with Ginger right behind him.

I turn back around and grab my phone, giving Sadie and the other bitches still gathered on the couches my back.

I know they're talking about me. I can hear little bits and pieces of what they're saying, but I'm not engaging. I can throw down with the best of them, but biker bitches are complete unknowns.

Gigi: OMG. I heard you're on lockdown. R U okay?

Me: You sold me out, bitch.

Gigi: Pike sold you out. I had your back.

I send her a picture of my middle finger, the anger and betrayal I felt after talking to my parents now gone.

Gigi: Whatever, asshole. You just disappeared. What the hell was he supposed to do?

Me: Keep your cute lips sealed.

Gigi: There are no secrets in this family.

Me: I know a few about you that may shock more than just your parents.

I sent the message with a winky face.

Gigi: You'd have to tattle on yourself to share those secrets, smarty-pants. So, if you want to play dirty...I'm ready.

Fuck. She's right. Every dumb-ass thing she's ever done, I've been at her side. Lily too. We were like the three musketeers of dumb shit and antics.

Gigi: How's Crow?

Me: A complete tool and bastard.

Gigi: Fuck! What the hell are you doing there?

Me: Not Crow.

Gigi: So, you're just playing Candy Crush?

Me: Fuck no. There's another guy. A new guy.

Gigi: God, you're so wonderfully slutty. I think it's what I love most about you.

Me: Where are you?

Gigi: At the shop. Your dad is so fuckin' moody too. You're going to get a complete ass-chewing when you get back.

Me: Fun times.

Gigi: I hope it was worth it.

Me: 100%

Gigi: Bitch, spill the beans. Who's the other guy?

I stare at my phone, watching the cursor blink, wondering if I should tell her. I know whatever I say will filter right on over to Pike.

What if Pike hates Mammoth?

He knows all the guys in the club, at least the ones who were here when he lived here. I'd hate for him say something shitty, trying to kill my good time.

Me: Mammoth.

Gigi: I don't think I ever met him.

I can just imagine her right now, leaning over in her chair, talking in Pike's ear, questioning him about Mammoth.

Gigi: Pike said Mammoth wasn't there when we were there for the party.

Gigi: ...

After the first Pike statement, there are three dots for a long time. She is typing up a dissertation on Mammoth, and it probably isn't going to go in his favor.

Gigi: Pike said the guy is solid, but that he isn't someone to play around with. Pike said mind your own business, keep your hands to yourself, and stay in his old room. Mammoth isn't someone a girl like you should be hanging out with.

I blink at the screen, reading over her words and shaking my head. *A girl like me* is a statement I've never liked to hear or read. The easiest way to end the conversation…agree to do what Pike says. I only have a few hours left here anyway, and then I'll be back in Tampa, getting my ass reamed for trying to live life.

Me: You got it, boss. Gotta run. I'm heading to the kitchen to grab something to eat.

Gigi: Don't burn the place down with your mad cooking skills.

Again, I shoot her back the middle finger. I don't know why Gigi thinks she's Betty fuckin' Crocker. She is just a step above me in the cooking department, only able to make ramen edible. Just because she's never fucked up ramen, while I have, she thinks she can host her own cooking show.

I don't make it to two steps away from the bar when Sadie's at my back, skank-ass heels clicking against the hard, concrete floor. I spin around, coming face-to-face with her, not letting her bully me.

She tosses her blond hair over her shoulder as she glares at me. "Tomorrow when you're gone, Mammoth's mine. Let those words sink in. Have your fun while you can, but within twenty-four hours, I'll make sure you're barely a memory."

I plaster a fake smile on my face. The bitch will not get to me. She's trying hard. Hasn't stopped since I walked through the doors and Mammoth picked me over her. "I'm pretty damn sure that even after I walk out that door, you're not getting in his pants. Say what you want, Sally," I sneer, getting her name wrong on purpose because fuck her. "But I know he's not into your fake tits, fake hair, or fake personality."

She leans her upper body back as her hateful eyes travel down and then up, taking in everything that's me. I'm still wearing Mammoth's clothes, looking not one bit hot in the baggy ensemble. "I know his taste, sweetheart. I've been here long enough. Seen the parade of women on his arm. You aren't it."

"I may not be his usual taste, but honey—" I give her the same look she's throwing my way, full of hatred and disgust "—you're not it either. You're never riding the Mammoth train, no matter how many tickets you buy."

I don't know what the fuck I'm saying. I'm pretty sure she doesn't either. Sadie doesn't seem like she's playing with a full deck anyway because she doesn't even blink at my bullshit.

"You think you can hang with him?" she laughs, tipping her head back, but somehow her hair doesn't move. The bitch has to have a lifetime supply of Aqua Net somewhere to keep her hair looking more like a perfect helmet than individual strands. "You're getting watered-down Mammoth. The real Mammoth, you've never met, sweetheart. He needs a real woman to satisfy his hunger and cravings."

Now it's my turn to not even fucking blink. I break down her statement word by word, wondering what in the fuck she's talking about, but I figure she's just right of the sanity line. "He looked pretty damn satisfied after I sucked his cock, Sadie." I shrug, adding a smirk when her face reddens. "He looked even more satisfied after he fucked me…repeatedly."

She steps closer, glare turning fiery. "You want to know the real Mammoth?"

"I do know the real Mammoth, bitch."

"Been in his room yet?"

I shake my head, and I am suddenly pissed. Has Sadie been there?

"Why don't you go to his room and find out who the real man

is. Not the teenybop version you've been playing with. See if you can hang with the real guy once you see what's inside. After you realize you're in over your head, I'll be here to make sure he has a real woman to meet his needs and tastes." She turns on her heel, stalking back toward the couch where all the women are staring at us with their mouths gaping open. "Fourth door on the right."

"You shouldn't have fucking done that," one of them says.

"You know Mammoth doesn't like his business out there," another one adds as Sadie takes her spot right in the middle of all the bitches.

"He's going to be so pissed at you," a third states, wincing.

"Fuck her and him," Sadie replies as I make my way toward the bedrooms. "She thinks she's what he wants, but she couldn't be more wrong. It's time for the little girl to go back to wherever she came from and let the big girls handle Mammoth."

I had every intention of going back to my room. Well, Pike's old room. I even have my hand wrapped around the handle, turning the knob, but Sadie's words and my own curiosity get the better of me.

I glance down the hallway, first to the right and then the left, before I shuffle down to Mammoth's door. I stand outside, staring at the dark, rich wood, telling myself to stay out and mind my own fucking business. I've never liked people going into my room uninvited, and I'm pretty sure Mammoth feels the same way.

But then again, I've sucked the man's cock and let him fuck me ten different ways, giving him orgasm after orgasm. I feel like I have a right to know. I earned it, right?

I'll just take a peek.

In and out.

Make it quick.

Don't touch anything.

A total recon mission.

At least that's what I tell myself anyway before I step into his room, closing the door quickly and quietly behind me.

At first glance, Mammoth's room is just a bedroom. There's nothing out of the ordinary besides how neat and tidy it is for a badass biker guy's space.

Inside there is a sleek metal bed against the wall, a leather bench at the end, a dresser, and an old travel trunk like I've seen in some antique shops. The walls are painted black, and there are no pictures anywhere. No photos of other women or even one of his own mother hang on the wall or sit on top of his dresser.

I don't know what Sadie was talking about. There's nothing crazy inside Mammoth's room except for his cleanliness. I don't think I've been with a single man who's ever even made his own bed. There isn't even a sock lying on the floor, tossed away and forgotten like I've seen in every dorm room I've ever been in.

I don't know if Sadie thought this would scare me away, but it doesn't. The last thing I want is to pick up after a slob for the rest of my life.

I blink, almost choking on the thought.

What the actual hell?

The rest of my life isn't something that should even be entering my mind when thinking about Mammoth—or any man, for that matter.

I'm too young to be tied down.

Too young to promise myself to only one guy.

I have life to live.

Oats to sow.

Epic adventures to have.

Before I leave, I know I'm missing something. My Tamara senses are on overdrive, telling me to dig, snoop, and do all the things I'd kick Mammoth right in the junk for doing to me. I figure I have ten minutes before he'll come back, which leaves me only a few minutes to figure out what crazy shit Sadie was talking about.

So, I do what any girl would do, I start with the closet and find nothing except for dozens of T-shirts sorted by color, along with at least ten pairs of jeans and a leather jacket. I sweep my fingertips over the black leather, wondering what he looks like when he wears it. He couldn't get much use out of it in Florida. The weather never seems to get cold enough to make it necessary.

My gaze dips, soaking in the boots on the floor of his closet, placed into neat rows and in matching pairs. It isn't like my closet where I just throw shit in there, figuring I'll find what I'm looking for when the time comes.

If Sadie thinks a clean man is scary...she's way crazier than I ever imagined, and I make a mental note never to listen to another word the nutty bitch says.

When I close the closet door and step backward, I almost fall over the big-ass chest I'd forgotten was against the wall behind me. After I let out a slew of curse words because fuck, the metal on the bottom hurt like a motherfucker when I jammed my heel into it, I kneel down and run my hand over the top of the chest, knowing I should just leave. The man has been nothing short of amazing, and I am invading his privacy, which is wrong.

So freaking wrong, but I can't stop myself.

"What are you doing?" Mammoth asks, walking into the room like a silent ninja as I lift the top.

I freeze, eyes wide, knowing I'm in so much trouble.

CHAPTER 9
MAMMOTH

TAMARA DROPS the lid to the trunk, falling back on her ass and scrambling backward like she's been stung by a bee. "Nothing, Mammoth. I swear. I was… I'm sorry. I didn't mean to…" she blurts out, speaking fast.

"Princess." I know she's scared.

Tamara is a talker, but she never talks this damn fast.

I drop to my knees behind her, placing my front to her back, and wrap my arms around her. "Breathe, baby."

She's practically hyperventilating, her chest heaving with each short breath. "I'm so, so, so sorry." She shakes her head, not relaxing in my arms.

My lips find her neck, kissing the soft skin near her jaw. "I'm not mad," I tell her, but I should be. She was snooping around my room, looking for God knows what and finding something she probably doesn't understand.

"Sadie told me." She swallows, tilting her head, giving me access to the full length of her neck. "I knew I shouldn't."

My arms tighten around her, my hands on her stomach and lips on her skin. "It's okay," I tell her again because the words I'd spoken before didn't seem to have sunk in. "Relax."

She turns her head, gazing at me. "You're not mad?" She sounds surprised and, hell, I'm a little shocked too.

If it were anyone else in my room going through my things, I would've lost my shit.

I shake my head softly, nuzzling her neck. "No, I'm not mad, but we need to talk about personal boundaries."

"I didn't have any right to invade your personal space. I let Sadie play with my head."

"Fuckin' Sadie," I grit out through clenched teeth. "Don't ever let anyone fuck with your head, especially someone like her."

Tamara turns in my arms, hooking her legs over mine to sit in my lap. "She told me I wasn't your type. She told me I didn't know the real you. She said tomorrow I'd be nothing but a memory, and you'd move on to someone who was more your taste."

My hands are on her waist, holding her tight, keeping my features gentle. "Sadie's the one who's not my type. She's a bitter bitch because no matter how many times she throws herself at me, I always push her away. I don't like fake people. I don't like to play games either, and Sadie's only about the games."

A frown pulls at Tamara's full lips. "But am I your type?"

"You're in my bed, aren't you?"

She snakes her arms around my neck. "Technically, we've been in Pike's old bed and not yours." She smirks.

"Not anymore," I tell her, lifting her chin so she's looking straight at me. "Tonight, you're in my bed."

"Maybe." She swallows, blinking those hazel eyes at me. "Maybe we should stay in Pike's bed."

"Why?"

"I like knowing you've never been with anyone else there." She glances at my bed before giving me her eyes again. "I kind of like knowing I'm with you somewhere you've never been with anyone else before."

I can't stop the smile from spreading across my face. "Princess, no one's ever been in my bed except me."

She blinks, chewing on her bottom lip, staring at me like I'm yanking her chain. "No one?"

"No one."

"But you're…"

"I'm not into club pussy. I'm also not into sharing. I don't stick my dick into any chick who's willing just for the sake of getting off. Before you…" I pause, not believing I'm going to admit this, but I know it has to be said. "I've never fucked anyone at the compound. When I'm with someone, it's never here. I never have anyone in my bed to fuck, sleep, or anything else."

"Why?"

"I like to keep my professional and private life separate."

She nods like she understands, but I'm not sure she believes me or really knows what the fuck I'm talking about.

"Can we talk about what's in the…" She ticks her head toward the chest.

"What'd ya see?" I ask, not wanting to go into too much detail, especially if she didn't see anything.

"Nothing much." She shrugs, unable to meet my eyes. "You walked in and scared the shit out of me before I had a chance to…"

"Snoop?" I raise an eyebrow.

"Well, um, yeah," she mumbles with a small smirk. "I'm sorry."

"I have nothing to hide." I brush her thick black hair over her shoulder, slowly dragging my finger back over her shoulder to her collarbone. "Not from you, at least."

"Mammoth, yo. You in there?" Eagle's voice booms, followed by a pounding on my bedroom door. "Get your dick out of that chick. We got club business to handle."

"Fuck," I hiss and slide my hand down from her waist to her ass, giving her two quick pats on those luscious cheeks. "I got to handle this."

She scoots off my lap and sits cross-legged on my bedroom floor before I rise to my feet. "Don't let me stop you," she tells me, smiling like she just dodged a bullet of some sort.

"What is it?" I ask before the door is even fully open, finding Eagle with his arms crossed over his chest, pulling at a toothpick between his lips.

"Lockdown's over. Shit's cleared up. Guys are headed back. They'll be here in ten. Orders from Tiny are to wait until after the meeting before taking the girl home."

"Got it," I tell him, starting to close the door before his big palm slams into the wood, stopping me.

"Word is Crow's pissed about—" Eagle lifts his chin toward my room where Tamara's sitting, watching and listening to every word "—what's been going on between you and the girl."

"It's none of Crow's business what's happening."

Eagle nods like he agrees, but it's not his opinion that matters, and throws up his hands. "Not my business or my problem. I'm just passing along what I'm hearing because you're a friend, Mammoth. What you do with that information is up to you."

"Thanks," I tell him because I was a dick. The very mention of Crow and Tamara makes my blood boil, and no matter what, Eagle did nothing to earn my anger.

"I'll meet you in Church," he says as he walks down the hallway away from my room. "Ten minutes."

When I turn around, Tamara's on her feet, standing in the middle of my bedroom. "So, that's it, right?"

I rub my hands together, blowing out a breath, trying to ignore the knot in my stomach. "Afraid so, princess."

Her lips immediately turn downward. "I was hoping we had longer. I'm not really ready to leave..." She kicks at the hardwood floor, staring down.

I stalk toward her, grabbing her by the waist and hauling her body flush against mine. "It's been fun, yeah?" I whisper against her lips, wanting nothing more than to kiss her...forever.

Forever?

Damn.

Never in my life have I ever thought that word. Not about

anyone or anything. My life, inside the club and out, has never lent itself to thinking about anything too long term. But there's something about this chick, something I can't put my finger on, that has my mind going where it shouldn't.

She doesn't look at me. Doesn't give me those hazel eyes that have my cock itching to be inside her every minute of every day. Owning her. Possessing her. Wanting her. "This is no place for someone like you. My life is…"

How do I explain to someone outside the life what it's like to be inside it? Especially a sweet little thing who was raised so differently.

"I get it," she says into my chest.

I place my fingers under her chin, forcing her to give me her eyes. "You don't."

She blinks, shoulders sagging forward as she sighs. "I do. We had a good run, didn't we, handsome?"

"The best," I tell her, wishing I could give her more. "Don't go pulling shit like this again, though. Got me?"

There's a halfhearted smile on her face. "But I wouldn't have met you if I hadn't."

She has a point. But then again, what if I hadn't been here when she showed up at the door? "Promise me you won't do it again, Tamara?"

"Ooh," she says in a singsong voice. "Pulling out my real name. Shit's getting serious."

I tighten my hand on her waist, gripping her just above her hips. "You could've been hurt. You're lucky Morris and Tiny like your family, or shit could've gone an entirely different way."

She stares me straight in the eyes, not even blinking when she says, "I'm a big girl. I would've been fine."

The fire that's been simmering in my belly boils over, spreading through my veins like molten lava. "Baby," I whisper, trying not to yell, "big girl or not, this shit is no joke. Any other MC, any other biker, and shit could've ended badly. I don't care how big or small you are, if there's a gun pointed at your head, you're never going to be the one in control."

"Fine, JD. I promise," she murmurs, trying to placate me but failing miserably. The roar of the engines has her stepping out of my arms. "You better get to Church and meet the guys."

"We're not done," I tell her, leveling her with my gaze.

She turns her face, staring out the window above the trunk, dismissing me. "We've hit the end of the road, big guy. You don't need to bring me home. I can get a ride from someone else."

"Like fuck, princess. Your ass is gonna be on the back of my bike, heading toward Tampa in under thirty. I don't want to hear any bullshit from you about it either."

Her eyes snap to mine, narrowing into little slits. "I don't know who you're talking to, but although this has been fun, I'm not yours to boss around."

I close the space between us before she has a chance to react, grabbing her chin, done with her attitude. "Listen, I get you're all badass and don't need anyone, including me, but that's not how I roll."

Her hazel eyes flash with anger, but she does nothing to pull away from me.

"So, have your cute little ass ready in thirty. You got me?"

"I got you," she hisses, scrunching her nose. "Loud and fucking clear, JD."

I love her sass and her inability to let that chip on her shoulder fall, even for me. "Still fuckin' cute," I mumble, knowing it'll piss her off and not giving a shit either.

She growls, pulling her face away from my hand. "Don't you have somewhere to be?"

"So do you. Grab your bag and meet me by the bar," I tell her, opening the door, waiting for her to leave my room.

"Fine," she snaps, stalking past me without so much as a sideways glance.

"Fine," I reply, locking my room up tight, avoiding a repeat of her snooping through my shit.

"Thirty," I call out as she disappears into Pike's old room, slamming the door behind her, shutting me out.

Man, the woman had so much attitude. Maybe more than anyone I've ever met.

Entitled? Completely.

A pain in the ass? One hundred percent.

Worth it? Totally.

"We need to have some words," Crow says before I even make it out of the hallway. He's waiting for me, leaning against the counter at the end of the bar, glaring at me like I stole his favorite toy on Christmas.

"There's nothing to say." I stalk past him, almost making it by him before he reaches out, grabbing my arm. I stop, turning to face him, glaring at the asshole I've never really liked. "You better get your hand off me if you want to keep it, motherfucker."

He snarls, hand still firmly planted on my forearm. "You took something that didn't belong to you."

I bite out a laugh, gaze dipping to where he's left his hand. "Can't take something that wasn't already claimed, dumbass." I yank my arm away from his grip, turning to stand toe-to-toe with the asshole. "You threw her out like a piece of trash and lost all claim to whatever fucked-up thing you thought you had."

He passes his fingers over his lips, watching me. "She's a good kid, Mammoth. She doesn't belong here. She shouldn't be around men like me and you."

I grind my teeth, holding myself back from decking him. "Speak for yourself, man. You're the asshole. I haven't done shit to her that she didn't want done. I didn't turn my back on her, trying to send her away in the darkness like you did."

He shakes his head, closing his eyes. "I did that shit for her own good. I never thought she'd show up here, looking for me. Never in a million fucking years did I think we were more than just a flirtation. That girl's dying for some danger in her life, but I wasn't about to be the one to give it to her. I promised Pike I'd never hurt her, never sleep with her, and I kept my word. But you—" he twists his lips "—are going to have some hell to pay for what you've done to her."

"Crow, I know your life is as fucked up as your head, but brother, listen carefully." I pause, letting his festering anger grow, knowing the man's a loose cannon waiting to blow. "I didn't do anything to that girl that she didn't want done. I was a gentleman about it too. I never once made her feel like a piece of shit or unwanted. I wanted her. Hell, I still want her. I know your ass has some trouble ahead of you and that's why you were turning her away, but you could've been a man about it instead of a little bitch."

"Enough!" Tiny's voice booms through the room, catching wind of our conversation. "Get your two dumb asses in here. We have business to discuss before Mammoth heads out."

"I'm taking her home," Crow argues.

I roll my eyes. This asshole never stops. He'd give anyone whiplash with his back-and-forth, especially about Tamara. "Your ass is staying here," I tell him before turning my back, heading toward a watchful Tiny.

"Mammoth's taking her, Crow. Stop being a bitch, and get your ass in here. We have shit to do, and I need some fucking sleep. We all need some rest after that shitshow."

Crow doesn't open his mouth.

He doesn't argue with Tiny.

He doesn't say another thing as he follows me into Church, probably throwing daggers into my back with his eyes.

The Prez had spoken, and there is nothing more to argue about —at least not with Crow.

Tamara...she's another story.

CHAPTER 10
TAMARA

ME: Lockdown's over. I'm heading home.

Gigi: From one shitshow to another.

Me: WTF. That bad?

Gigi: Remember the meltdown your parents had when you disappeared for a weekend last time?

Me: Yep.

Gigi: Child's play.

Me: Fuck. Maybe I should stay gone longer.

Gigi: No! Just time it so you come to Grandma's for dinner today. Drag your feet. Grandma will make sure your parents don't murder you.

Me: FML!

Gigi: Yeah. Just about.

"Ready?" Mammoth asks, scaring the shit out of me as I stand by the bar, leaning over the top, texting back and forth with Gigi.

"What time is it?" I ask, wasting another few seconds with a question I already know the answer to.

"Ten."

"Can we take the back roads? I don't like being on the highway on the back of a bike." Another lie.

There's nothing like a highway with the hum of a motorcycle under me to get the blood pumping. But back roads would easily add another hour, if not more, to the trip, putting us at Grandma Gallo's door just about the right time.

Mammoth rolls his neck and glances at the ceiling, blowing out the loudest breath. "If it'll make you happy, princess, we'll take the back roads."

"Thank you," I say, grabbing my small bag off the stool next to me and starting to walk toward the door.

Mammoth's hands are on the handle a second later, taking the bag from me, and I hand it over without a fight.

"See you, doll," Morris says, giving me a quick kiss on the cheek before I make it to the door. "Maybe I'll see you around sometime."

I touch his cheek, running my fingers across his stubble. "Maybe you will, Morris. Thanks for being so kind."

"Don't tell anyone. Wouldn't want my reputation to get ruined." He gives me a kind, toothy grin, followed by a wink. "Don't give that one too much trouble. I know how you Gallo girls can be."

I throw him an innocent smile. "I don't know what you mean."

"Nothing but trouble," Morris mutters, waving his hand at me as I step back toward the doorway through which Mammoth disappeared.

I squint when the sunlight hits my face, blinding me as I step outside and away from the compound. I scan the parking lot and the endless line of bikers until my eyes land on Mammoth. He's straddling the sexiest bike, all chrome and black. Big like him. Sleek and sexy, looking like the perfect match.

His eyes are on me, watching me as I walk his way, hips swaying, head held high, trying to show no emotion.

In reality, I'm bummed. I really like Mammoth. He's solid, strong, and sweet.

He reminds me of the men in my family and of Pike too, whom, if Gigi hadn't snatched him up, I sure as hell would have.

"Ready?" he asks, holding out a helmet for me as I get closer.

"As ready as I'll ever be," I say, staring down at the helmet because there's no way I'm wearing it. "What's that for?"

"So your face stays pretty, princess." He keeps a straight face as he says that, but I don't.

I shake my head, pushing the helmet and his hand back toward him. "I don't do helmets, baby."

He levels me with his gaze, not even cracking a smile. "No helmet. No ride."

This could work in my favor. I could easily spend a few more minutes or, hell, an hour arguing with him. With pissed-off parents waiting on me, every second I can waste is one more I'm still breathing.

I cross my arms, cocking my head at the sexy biker. "So then, should I ask someone else to take me home?"

His jaw ticks. "Serious?"

"Dead."

Somehow, I say that without cracking a smile.

Goddamn, he's hot. Even when he's pissed, he's the most handsome man I've ever laid eyes on. If I weren't so pissed at him, I'd hop in his lap, trying to tempt him into another round before he takes me home. But then again, there's some time along the way, a rest stop or a deserted spot where we could fuck. Mammoth's the type of guy I could ride forever and never grow bored. The way he looks at me...I feel like there's no other girl in the world.

I'm so lost in thought, I don't even notice his arm swing out, snagging me by the wrist. "Listen. You're cute. Too cute to be riding a bike, including mine, without protecting all that cuteness. Ever see someone's face hit the pavement?"

I scrunch my nose. "Um, no."

"That's because they don't usually live. Now, you're going to wear the fucking helmet. No lip. No back talk. I care about getting you home safe. If I didn't, I'd let you roll the dice, but you're too important for all that."

"But if you care…" I don't finish the statement, snapping my mouth shut. I'm letting my aggravation show. Somehow, I've turned into a needy asshole. I've never been that girl. I've never wanted to be wanted as badly as I do now with Mammoth.

"I care." He brushes his fingers against my cheek, and my breath hitches. "This isn't a goodbye."

"It's not?" I ask, my voice so filled with hope and shock.

He shakes his head, sliding his hand up my arm, causing goose bumps to break out across my skin. "Do you want it to be? Do you want me to drop you off and never look back?"

I shrug, trying to play it cool.

Don't be a dork, Tam.

Do not lose your shit because this hot-as-fuck badass biker guy wants to see you again. I'd thought the same thing about Crow, and that was a hot mess. "I'd see you again. I mean, you're not hard on the eyes, and you're a pretty good fuck."

He coughs before his lips slide into a smile. "I'm a pretty good fuck?"

I pick at my fingernails, not meeting his eyes. "Better than most," I lie.

He's the best.

If they could give out awards for best fucks, he'd win the gold fucking medal.

No man has ever made my toes curl the way he did.

No one's ever had me wanting more, ready to beg like he has. And I've never begged before. I was better than that, or at least I thought I was.

His hands are on my ass, his knee between my thighs, sending shivers down my spine. "I think I need to remind you of just how magical my cock is."

I smirk, batting my eyelashes at him. "We could go back inside for another round."

"Put the helmet on, and get your ass on the back of my bike. I know just the spot on the way, and I'll make sure you walk away never forgetting I've been inside you."

My knees wobble, and I probably would've fallen onto the cinders around my feet if he weren't holding my ass, grinding his knee in between my legs. "Okay," I whisper, suddenly thirsty and needy.

A second later, his hands are gone and the helmet is on my head. He makes quick work of adjusting the straps, making sure I can see and breathe. "Now climb on and wrap that tight little body around me."

I move without hesitation. Snaking my arms around his chest, I slide forward, straddling his hips with my thighs. Our bodies are flush, my tits to his back, body heat on body heat. A quick rev of the engine and we're off, the wind brushing against my hot skin but making no effort to cool the need Mammoth stoked inside me.

After what seems like hours pressed against him and the steady hum of the motorcycle doing nothing to stop the need for him from deepening, he pulls off the side of the road. He turns his head, giving me those beautiful gray eyes. "Change your mind?"

I shake my head, lost for words and so damn excited about getting my brains banged out in the middle of the woods. It seems naughty. Maybe the naughtiest thing I've ever done, and I've done some pretty bad shit in my life.

He pats my hands, and I tighten my grip, holding on as he takes us forward, moving down the dirt road into a national forest somewhere in the middle of the state. It's desolate. There's not a soul around. And the only sound is from the birds perched somewhere in the trees around us as he cuts the engine.

I pull off the helmet, shaking out my hair as soon as he climbs off. We're hidden by the lush brush around us, tucked away from the road and any stragglers who could wander by.

Mammoth comes to the back of the bike, pulling me backward, spinning me around to face him. Before I can say anything, his lips are on mine, kissing me deeply and stealing the little bit of breath I've been able to catch since we stopped.

His hands are on my legs, hiking up my skirt, tearing at the flimsy cloth of my panties. In the blink of an eye, they're gone and I'm bare. I spread my knees, giving him access to everything I have as I work at the button on his jeans, tearing the zipper down before yanking the denim down his thighs, exposing his beautiful, thick cock.

His strong hands wrap around my thighs, hauling my hips almost off the seat as he leans over, pressing my back into the leather and metal of the bike. We're doing this. In the middle of nowhere, out in the open, where anyone could see.

"Mammoth," I moan into his mouth, my voice quivering with need and fear.

What if we get caught? What if someone sees us? Every sensation and sound is heightened by my paranoia.

Mammoth doesn't seem to be the least bit concerned about being caught, stroking the tip of his cock through my wetness before thrusting deep inside me.

I'm momentarily winded as my body adjusts to the fullness of his long, thick dick being fully seated. As if sensing how I'm feeling, Mammoth doesn't move at first, kissing me deeper as his hand slides up my leg between us, finding my clit.

I rock against him, needing his movement with each swipe of his thumb pad against me. Mammoth pulls out, thrusting into me deeper the second time. I gasp into his mouth, tangling my fingers in the back of his hair, and I hold his face against mine as I squeeze my eyes shut.

The strokes are long and hard. The seat bites into my back, mingling the pain and the pleasure only his cock can deliver. Within seconds, I'm moaning and my body's sprinting toward an orgasm I can't stop.

One wave of pleasure passes over me, seizing my muscles and my ability to breathe, but that doesn't stop his unrelenting pounding into me. As my body goes limp, Mammoth lifts me, his mouth leaving mine, turning me onto my stomach so my tiptoes are on the ground and my tits are flat against the seat.

He lifts my hips, lining up our bodies again before thrusting inside me from behind. I cry out, the pleasure so intense, I can hardly catch my breath. He curls his fingers into my hair, pulling my head backward as his upper body flattens against my back.

"I own this pussy, princess," he murmurs against my mouth, driving that point home by thrusting so deep inside me, my toes leave the ground.

I can't respond. I can barely breathe. But then his lips are on mine again, giving me the air I so badly need. In and out, in and out. I lie there like a rag doll as he fucks me from behind while I'm bent over his bike, skirt hiked up, exposed and open.

His strokes become faster, each thrust so hard, I'm forced up as far as I can go on my tiptoes and still stay upright. My scalp tingles at the gentle pulling of his fingers, my mind blank from the sensations, and my body humming from the hard fucking as he pulls me into a second orgasm while his crashes over him.

Spent, I go limp against the seat. My mouth falls away from his as I gasp for air, speared on his cock in middle-of-nowhere Florida. His chest is flush against my back, his breathing ragged and harsh against my ear as he tries to find his breath.

"Don't ever think I don't want you," he growls. "I could live inside your pussy for a lifetime and never have enough."

His words send goose bumps across my skin and have me shivering underneath him. I like what he says. I like how he says it. I like feeling possessed. I like feeling wanted.

"Your pussy was made for me, princess."

I don't argue.

I can't.

His cock slips out of me, replaced by his hand cupping me between my legs. "I own this," he tells me, whispering the words low and deep in my ear. "Don't forget that."

Forget Mammoth? Hardly. There are other guys in my past who are nameless, and recalling their faces is almost impossible. But Mammoth… He's someone I'll never forget, and that scares the shit out of me.

I turn my head, our lips almost touching. "I'll never forget."

How could I?

A guy like Mammoth is totally unforgettable and not because of his giant dick or hauntingly beautiful gray eyes.

CHAPTER 11
TAMARA

WE'RE at the top of my grandmother's driveway, and there are no fewer than ten sets of eyes watching us from the front porch.

"Maybe I should drop you here."

I tighten my grip around his waist, glancing over his shoulder. "You're probably hungry. Why don't you come in for a bite to eat?" I'm grasping at straws here, but the last thing I want is to be here alone.

From the way my mother's arms are crossed and she's tapping her foot, I know I'm in deep shit. I mean, I knew that before we ever left the compound, but now after seeing her, I'll need a ladder to get out of the steaming pile I've thrown myself into with my little epic adventure stunt.

"I am hungry," he says.

Relief washes over me, knowing I won't die at my mother's hands within the next five minutes.

"I could eat."

"My family's great," I tell him, which is true, but right now, they look pretty damn scary. At least to me, but maybe not to a badass biker like Mammoth. "My grandma will love to feed a big guy like you."

Again, not a lie, but I'm using Mammoth as my human shield, praying my mother finds mercy in her soul not to go crazy on me.

Who the hell am I kidding?

He cuts the engine and puts down the kickstand. "You scared?" he asks when I don't loosen the grip I have on his body.

"Nah," I lie, peeling myself off his back and finally removing my helmet.

Damn. The only people in the group who look happy to see me are Gigi and Grandma. Everyone else looks pissed. Not just a little pissed, but nuclear-level angry.

Freakin' great.

"Are you sure your grandma won't be upset?"

"She'll be happy to have another mouth to feed." I give him a tight smile. "Trust me."

I climb off the bike, moving slower than any senior citizen I've ever seen during snowbird season as I try to tame my hair after it was held captive by the helmet.

"Princess, stop being so dramatic. You're just making it worse."

I crane my neck backward to take in his rugged face and piercing gray eyes. "Baby, you don't understand my family."

He turns his head, surveying the group that hasn't moved an inch. "They look nice," he says seriously.

"It's all a ploy," I grumble, knowing full well how angry they all are and what that means for me. I'm going to get my ass chewed out, especially by my mother. And my father will probably stand behind her, nodding, too angry to even form words. "They look sweet, but they're vicious."

Mammoth grabs my bag from my hands. "You look like your mom," he tells me, glancing down as I peer up at him. "You have her beauty."

I've always thought I was a perfect mix of my parents. My mother's big eyes, but a combination of their eye colors. My nose is my father's, my high cheekbones purely Maxine, along with my plump lips the boys always seem to rave about.

Gigi's the first one off the porch, running toward me. "Damn, I've never been so happy to see your crazy ass." She throws her arms around me, ignoring Mammoth. "They're not as upset. I think you'll live until at least dessert."

I hug her back, trying not to laugh because it'll only set my mom off. "Thanks for the heads-up."

"Good job on the timing. Pure perfection," she tells me as she backs away, and her gaze swings to Mammoth. "Oh. Well, aren't you a big one." She giggles.

"Mammoth, this is Gigi, my BFF and most favorite cousin. Gigi, this is Mammoth, the best fuck I've ever had, and he is indeed a big one." I wink at her.

Mammoth mutters a slew of curse words under his breath. "Princess, can you not talk about my dick to your entire family? I'm pretty sure it's not what they'd like to hear."

"Baby, I promise not to talk about your cock to everyone, but this is my girl. We have no secrets."

And we seriously don't. We're open books, and that's the way it's always been.

"Come on. Let's get this over with. I'm pretty sure your mom's going to burst your eardrums with the amount of anger she has swirling in her gut," Gigi tells me as we weave through the long line of cars down the even longer driveway.

"Great," I groan, wishing I could've avoided the entire freak-out that's about to happen.

"Tamara," my mother says in a clipped tone. "It's nice of you to show your face again."

"Hi, Mom," I reply, giving her a big smile, but not leaving Mammoth's side. I'm too scared to let go. Too frightened of her seemingly quiet anger simmering under the surface, ready to break free.

Dad's right behind her, but his eyes aren't on me. They're locked on Mammoth, soaking him in, appraising him, probably knowing I've slept with him because men, especially my father, have a way of knowing shit they have no business knowing.

"I have so many things to say to you," Mom says almost in a whispered tone, and she takes a deep breath like she's gearing up for something big. The same tone has the little hairs on the back of my neck standing on end, telling me to run. "You're lucky I'm too old for prison, because right now, it's taking everything in me not to put your ass down."

I ignore her theatrics, trying to change the subject because Maxine Gallo wants to go full-blown crazy momma on my ass. "Mom, this is Mammoth. He saved me," I tell her and the rest of the family who's looking at him like he's an oddity.

Pike's glaring at Mammoth from near the doorway, silently stewing like the rest of them.

Typical.

Mammoth drops my bag to the sidewalk, holding out his hand to my uncle Joe since he's the closest to him. "It's nice to meet you, sir."

Uncle Joe eyes Mammoth's palm, but before a handshake is exchanged, Grandma steps through the crowd, pushing them apart and coming to stand in front of me.

"Tam, baby. I'm so happy you're home and you brought a friend." She tips her head back, the bloom of gray hair bobbing as she soaks in the wideness of Mammoth's frame. "Well, aren't you a tall drink of water."

"Lemme see," Aunt Fran, the complete horndog who seems to have a hot biker guy tracker inside her, says, forcing her way through the crowd of people and coming to stand next to my grandma. "Well, isn't he…"

"Yep," Grandma says, like they have some silent language or are communicating telepathically.

"He's…"

"Uh-huh."

I glance up at Mammoth and shrug, but he has nothing but a

smile on his face. He's looking at them like they're two sweet old ladies, but he's so wrong. Dead wrong. Grandma is sweet, but damn it, don't cross her. She'll make your life miserable, and even though her children are grown, she's still the boss.

Then there's Fran. She's the handsiest old lady I've ever seen. She gets away with groping strapping strangers because of her age too. They think she's just nice and probably feeble, but she's smart as a whip and horny as fuck. She's my spirit animal and everything I aim to be when I get old.

"Let me get a better look at you, son," Fran says, motioning with her hands for him to step closer.

He goes without hesitation, thinking she's just blind, but the woman could spot a hot guy from a mile away. "Hi," Mammoth says to her before her hands are on his chest, feeling up his pecs with all the *Oohs* and *Aahs*.

"Not bad," she adds, sliding her hands to his arms and over his ink. "Not bad at all."

"Fran, get your hands off that boy," Uncle Bear barks from the doorway, watching his handsy wife feel up another guy. "If you don't stop, I'm going to have to teach you a lesson."

Fran licks her lips, smiling up at Mammoth. "I like his lessons," she rasps, throwing Mammoth a wink.

"Fuck me," I mutter.

"Dinner's almost ready. I hope you have an appetite to match your size, Mammoth, 'cause I'm going to feed you like you've never been fed before," Grandma says as she pulls Fran away from him.

"You know the way to a man's heart, ma'am. I'm starved," he tells her, making the woman happy as she loops her arm through his and starts to move him toward the front door.

"A word," Mom says before I have a chance to go with them. I almost thought I'd made it. Almost thought I'd gotten off scot-free. But nope. Maxine wouldn't make it that easy on me.

"Sure, Mom." I smile nervously. "I'm so happy to be home and safe. Phew. That was a tense few days, yeah? I mean, I could've been killed." I throw that in, hoping to cool her anger

The few family members who were still outside follow Mammoth and Grandma into the house, leaving Mom, Dad, and me alone on the porch, where I'll probably meet my maker. I'm being dramatic, of course, but in the end, I'll probably wish for a quick death instead of Maxine's tongue.

She doesn't find amusement or solace in my words. There's no hint of a smile or a *You're so right, baby. I'm happy you're okay.* There're just her appraising eyes, searching my face, anger brewing in the darkness.

"So, I'm sorry," I blurt out, hoping to head off whatever can of verbal whoop-ass she has planned for me. "It was a dumb thing to do. I know. I know." I throw up my hands, ready to get on my knees and beg for my life. "I could've been really hurt, but I'm okay. I made it back safe and sound. I learned my lesson, and I'll never do that again."

Mom steps forward, lips flat, eyes trained on me. "I'm too pissed to talk to you about how irresponsible, stupid, and careless you were this weekend. I won't remind you of all the ways you could've been hurt or killed with your little stunt. I won't..."

"You kind of are," I whisper and bite down on my lips as soon as her eyes widen.

If Maxine were a hitter, she would've slapped the shit out of me right there. "Get your ass inside, feed the guy, and get him on his way. We'll finish this talk at home."

"I don't live at home, Mom," I remind her, which probably wasn't my best response, but it's the first thing that came to mind.

"Tamara Marie," my father growls, and I jump.

I completely forgot he was standing off to the side, silent and even scarier because my father has never really been the quiet type. Not with me, at least.

"We'll finish this conversation after your friend leaves. I don't want to embarrass you in front of him," Dad says.

"Fuck that," Mom adds immediately. "I don't care who witnesses this. If you don't live at home, we'll finish this now. I have shit to say, child, and you're going to listen."

I suck in a breath, pissed off but relieved that I'll have a few more hours before my parents really lay into me for my shitty behavior. But then, I don't want to wait. I don't want to have their anger following me around all day like a dark cloud over my head. So, I do the only thing I know how to do in a situation like this—throw myself at their feet and beg for mercy.

"I know it was wrong of me to turn off my phone and not tell anyone where I was going. It was selfish and childish of me to do something so stupid and irresponsible. I'll never do that again. But," I say, touching my hand to my chest, giving them the reality of the situation too, "I'm twenty-one years old, I don't live at home anymore, and I'm in college. Ninety percent of the time, you don't know where I am or what I'm doing. At some point, you need to realize I'm an adult."

My dad's arm is around my mother's shoulders now as they both gape at me, suddenly rendered speechless. I'm not being harsh, just truthful.

"But I am sorry. I promise not to do something so stupid again. If I ever go back to the Disciples, I'll make sure you know where I am first."

My father's eyes flash with anger, and I realize I had been winning the argument until the last statement. "I forbid you to ever go back there," he tells me like somehow he's still in control of my day-to-day life, which he's not.

"Daddy, I love you. You're my best friend," I tell him, being partially truthful. "But you can't forbid me to do something."

My mother steps forward, and I step back, avoiding her hands, which were no doubt going to grab my arm and tell me how life was really supposed to go.

"Kids," Grandma says, popping her head out of the doorway like she sensed shit wasn't going well. "Get in here and finish this later. We have a guest, and the food's ready. You're embarrassing me."

I smile at her, thanking her silently for the save.

"Fine," Dad snaps. "But this conversation isn't over."

Yay!

"Not by a long shot," Mom mutters, giving me the stink-eye before peeling away from my father and following my grand-mother inside.

"I love you, Dad," I whisper, looking for a glimmer of hope.

He grabs my hand, sliding our fingers together before bending over and kissing my cheek. "I love you too, peanut. You scared me," he admits. "Your mother will calm down. Just give her some time." He stops walking, and so do I. "Look at me, baby."

I glance up, staring into the eyes of the first man I ever loved and will always love.

"We know you're grown. We're having a hard time dealing with our baby growing up and trying to spread her wings. But we were scared." He shakes his head, closing his eyes for a moment. "When we couldn't find you and then we heard about the lockdown, I nearly shit myself with worry."

"That's not an image I'll ever get out of my head, Dad." I snort.

"Tam, be serious. Remember how scared you were for Gigi when she was there, and you didn't know if she was okay or not?"

"Yes, but she texted me often, so I knew she was okay." I regret the words as soon as they're out of my mouth. I know why they're pissed. I turned off my phone, ignoring everyone.

I was selfish and inconsiderate of their feelings.

"I'm sorry, Dad. I won't do that again. I didn't think about how you were feeling or if you were worried. I just wanted a little fun before school started. I should've at least let you know I was okay."

"Yoo-hoo!" Grandma yells from somewhere in the foyer because we didn't follow along with them into the house.

"We better go, but we'll finish this later," he tells me. "We can't ground you or punish you, but you need to look at this from our perspective and start thinking about someone other than yourself all the time."

"I know. I'm sorry," I say again and mean every word.

I've always let my good time trump everything else. I've only thought about myself and how something will make me feel, but things are about to change. They have to.

CHAPTER 12
MAMMOTH

I HAVEN'T SAT down with a girl's family since I was in high school. I forgot how awkward the experience is. Years haven't changed anything except the comfort I feel in my own skin. For the most part, they've kept their eyes on the television, throwing a glance my way every few minutes. They've been nothing but kind to me since I walked through the door, uninvited and most likely unwanted.

"Well, Mammoth, why don't you tell us about yourself," Tamara's grandfather says, eyeing me curiously.

"What would you like to know, sir?"

I'm out of my league here. I have a big family, but we are scattered across the country, only exchanging Christmas cards at the holidays or catching up at funerals. But the Gallos, they know everything about everyone in the house. That much is clear.

Grandpa slides up the sleeves of his plaid flannel even though it's ninety degrees outside. "Where do you come from?"

"Here and there, but originally Ohio." I lean forward, resting my elbows on my knees, giving the man my eyes out of respect. "We moved around a lot when I was a kid."

"Military?" he asks, tipping his head back like he's taking me in through new eyes. Mentioning the military always earns me respect from even the wariest soul.

I know how I look. There's nothing clean-cut about me anymore. Head-to-toe tattoos, piercings, long hair, my worn-in jeans and T-shirt, and my boots that are standard issue and I'm never without. Rain or shine, heat or cold, they're the thing I could never leave behind from the military.

"My father was in the army, and me after him." I gaze toward the foyer where Tamara stayed behind with her parents.

"Honorable," Tamara's grandfather says, while the other two men in the room stay silent.

"How do you go from the military to a motorcycle club?" the big guy on my right asks, wrinkling his nose like somehow the two could never mix.

"That's what you ask, Mike?" the dark-haired guy asks the bigger one.

I blow out a breath, knowing it's not the path most bikers take. "After I left the army, I felt lost. Tried to find my place for a while and failed. I was in Daytona one weekend, visiting an old friend, and ran into Tiny and Morris. A few beers later and I felt a connection. I saw their brotherhood, the family they built, and it called to me. Reminded me of my days with my platoon. Missed that shit. Wanted it back. So, I took it."

The dark-haired guy stares at me, not moving a muscle. "What was your rate?"

"MP."

"Can we speak English?" the big guy who I now know is Mike asks, looking from his brother to me.

"Military police," I tell him, unable to hide my smile because there's something about the guy I like.

"Joe, you ever wished you had a son to serve our country?" Mike asks.

"Part of me wants to say yes." Joe smiles, finally showing an emotion other than pissed off or indifferent. "It's honorable for sure. Hell, life with boys would've been easier in so many ways, but I love my girls and wouldn't trade them for anything in the world."

"I'd love it if Stone joins the military when he graduates. Mia's against it, which isn't shocking. She's a softy. But me, I want my boy to be a man." Mike flexes, and I almost expect him to kiss his biceps by the way he looks at his muscles. "The kid has my genes after all."

I keep my mouth shut. Not passing judgment on their conversation. Everyone thinks their kid would make the best soldier, when in reality, the life isn't for everybody. Most of the dumbasses who sign up to serve have no idea what they're in for until it's too late and they have *Property of the United States* practically stamped on their ass.

"Thank you for your service, Mr...." Tamara's grandfather says, ignoring his sons.

"My name's JD, sir." I lean back, liking the old guy more and more. He's calm, cool, and appears to be genuinely curious and kind. "JD Saint."

"Sir," the old man laughs. "Sal, please."

"Yes, Mr. Sal."

Sal shakes his head. "Just Sal."

"Wasn't raised that way, sir. Old habits die hard."

Between my mom and then the military, especially when it comes to my elders, sir is standard. I can't shake it. In the club, I don't give a fuck, but outside, in the real world, I am always respectful. Always.

"How did you end up in Florida, JD?"

"I was assigned to United States Southern Command near Miami. And after I got out, I never left, sir."

"Sal," he reminds me, shaking his head, but I'll never call the man by his first name.

"Where the hell are Thomas and James?" Tamara's grandmother

asks, holding a spoon in her right hand with an oven mitt covering her left. "I can't hold dinner much longer."

"They should be here any minute," Joe tells her, glancing down at the watch on his wrist. "Said they were only a few minutes away when they called."

"They have five more minutes, and then we're eating without them," she announces before spinning back around and marching toward the kitchen.

"Tamara's other uncles," Sal explains. "James and Thomas were tying up some loose ends on a case."

I'd heard about them. More like I'd heard of them from the guys in the Disciples. I'd never met them, always out of town on business when they were around and when all hell broke loose back in the spring. But I knew their reputations and their willingness to straddle the law when necessary.

"We need to talk." There's a hand on my shoulder, and I crane my neck back to see Pike's face. "Now."

Anger's not a look I'm used to seeing on his face. He was never really pissed off and was usually pretty even-tempered about everything. He was so chill, I wondered what it would take to really set him off. Based on his face, I'm about to find out why his anger is pointed at me.

The three men in the room stare at us as I stand, excusing myself, and follow Pike past Tamara and her parents, and out the front door. He doesn't stop on the front porch, stalking down the walkway toward the driveway before weaving in and out of the cars until we reach the road.

"What the fuck are you doing?" he asks, running his fingers through his hair like he's about to yank every strand out by the roots.

I stare him straight in the eyes and shrug a shoulder. "Nothing, man. I wanted to make sure Tamara made it home safely."

His eyes never leave mine, and neither does the fire inside them.

"She's here and you've done your duty, but I don't know why you're still standing here."

"Tamara asked me to stay, and so did her grandmother," I tell him, not understanding what the big fucking deal is. "What the hell's your problem?"

"What the hell happened to Crow? I figured he'd bring her home. Tamara went to the compound looking for him, but somehow she's on the back of your bike."

I blow out a breath, trying to keep my cool so I can explain the reality of the situation to my old friend. "Crow turned her ass away."

He cocks his head like he didn't fucking hear me. "Say that again."

"She showed up, looking all cute and shit, bag in hand, looking for the asshole, and he told her to fuck off and turned his back on her."

Pike's jaw ticks, and his fingers curl into tight fists against his palms. "He did what?" he grits out through his clenched teeth.

"Yeah, man. Threw her out like trash. It was dark outside, and he was just going to leave her out in the parking lot all by herself."

Pike closes his eyes, nostrils flaring, looking like his head is about to explode. "I will fuckin' kill him."

"Crow's an asshole," I mutter, but Pike already knows that.

Everyone does.

He's pacing now, wearing a path in the grass near the edge of the driveway. "He was so nice to her, led her on, and then went to turn her out like that."

"He's about to do some solid time, Pike. The man didn't want her tangled up in his bullshit. I think, for once at least, he thought what he was doing was best for her and not him."

Pike stopped moving. "He's about to do time?"

I nod. "Facing ten to twenty. Trial starts next week, and the evidence is solid. If he takes a plea, he'll be in for five."

"That's why that fucker kept talking about holding on to the good and to just let him soak her in," he says, rubbing his forehead. "I thought it was so strange."

"He wasn't so into soaking her in when she showed up out of the clear blue. I'm pretty fucking shocked he didn't sleep with her as a last hurrah. Crow's never been one to think twice about breaking anyone's heart."

Pike slides his hand to his neck, tipping his head toward the ground. "So, what? You brought her home out of the goodness of your heart?"

"Well..." I spread my hands apart, knowing I have to be up-front and frank. "The girl had a mouth on her and had an attitude to boot. I was trying to mind my own damn business, but I couldn't."

"You fucked her." He levels me with his gaze. He isn't asking me a question. He already knows the answer and wants confirmation.

I raise an eyebrow, crossing my arms over my chest. "How is that any of your business?"

A small growl escapes his throat, and he balls his fists at his sides again. "She's like a little sister to me. The last thing I want is for her to get mixed up in the Disciples' bullshit. I like you, Mammoth, I always have, but you're not right for Tamara."

I jerk my head back. His words strike a harder blow than his fist ever could. "What the fuck does that mean?"

The vein near his temple bulges as he takes a step toward me, but I don't move. "She's not the type of girl you can just throw out with the trash. She may seem like a party animal and a little crazy, but damn it, she's more than that."

"You really care about her," I observe. I can see it on his face and in his eyes.

There's respect there and even love. An emotion Pike showed as rarely as he did anger.

"Not only am I in love with her cousin, but Tamara's my neighbor, and I work with her father." He throws his hand toward the house. "I love and respect this family. The last thing I need is someone coming in here, fucking up everything I've worked so hard to get."

I rub my hands together, clenching my jaw, knowing I need to set his ass straight. Either that or I'm going to knock his ass out for implying I'm using Tamara like the other guys use and throw women away on a whim. "First," I say, stepping forward until our boots are touching. "I know she's not a whore, and I've never treated her like one. Second, I like this girl—hell, I like her more than I've probably ever liked anyone before. She's sassy, smart, and totally not afraid of anything, including me." I take in a breath and quickly continue before he can interrupt me. "Third, I'm not here to fuck anything up. Tamara asked me to stay, so I stayed. Simple as that. I don't need to explain myself to you or anyone else in this world, but out of respect, I'm going to clue you in on a few things because I've always thought of you as a friend."

He grunts, but he keeps his mouth shut as he glares at me.

"If she asks me to stay longer or wants to see me again, I'm not going to ask you for permission, and I'm sure as fuck saying yes."

His forehead wrinkles as his eyebrows draw down. "If you break her heart…"

I jerk my thumb toward the house. "You think I'm going to break that wild thing? If anything, she has the ability to crush me, brother."

He draws his lips back, snarling. "You've spent, what, two days with her? I think you're both wading into dangerous territory. You're in the Disciples, and Tamara isn't cut out for club life. Her family wouldn't stand for it and, frankly—" he lifts his jaw, eyes narrowing "—neither would I."

"Let's not get ahead of ourselves here. Tamara wants me around, I stay. She wants me gone, I go. She wants to see me again, I'm there. She wants to cut me off, I move on. It's entirely up to her. Not me. Not you. Got it?"

He inhales before blowing out a long exhale. "Don't fuck shit up. Not for me. Not for her. Not for anyone in that house."

"It's not my plan, Pike. And just so you know…" I rub the back of my neck, ready to tell him something I haven't told anyone yet. "I'm growing weary of the life."

He rocks backward, eyes wide. "Never thought I'd hear those words from you."

"They helped me during a time I didn't know my ass from my head, but I've got my shit together now. I know what I want out of life, and it isn't prison time. I want a family. I want a normal job where I don't have to look over my shoulder every day, wondering if someone's going to put a bullet in the back of my head for something I didn't even do. The life gets old."

A Challenger with blacked-out windows hurtles into the driveway, coming to a stop right next to us.

"These two motherfuckers," Pike mutters. "Scariest men you'll meet outside the MC."

I move my gaze to the car. "Really?"

Pike laughs. "You'll see. You know they're in tight with Tiny and Morris. They're ex-DEA, but they have some shit going on around them I can't quite put my finger on. Just be prepared for the inquisition because, no doubt, they already know everything about your life. They seem to know everything and everybody. Their reach is far and wide, Mammoth."

"So, now we're friends again?" I snap, my eyes still glued to the Challenger.

"You're not my enemy unless you fuck Tam over. If you do, then it's game over. Plus, if her family hates you, nothing else will matter."

The Challenger's engine cuts off.

"Hey, baby," Tamara says, coming up behind me before the men have a chance to get out of the car while Pike walks back to the house. "Everything okay?"

I wrap an arm around her, staring down at her beautiful face.

"We're good. What about your folks?" I tip my head toward the house, knowing it wasn't all pretty. I didn't hear much when we walked by, but enough to know it wasn't smooth sailing.

"I think my mother's finally calmed down. We should be good." She smiles up at me, slowly wearing away the calluses around my heart. "Wait until you meet my uncles. They're freaking amazing."

"I've heard."

The doors open, and I turn my head, zeroing in on one man.

A man I know.

A man I never expected to see here.

Someone who knows too much about me and can destroy whatever Tamara and I have before it has a chance to get started.

Fuck.

CHAPTER 13
TAMARA

MAMMOTH'S BODY stiffens next to me, and I gaze up, finding his eyes locked on my uncles, jaw tight.

"Saint?" Uncle James says, drawing my attention away from Mammoth and straight to him. Uncle James's gaze sweeps from our faces to where our bodies are touching. "What the fuck are you doing with my niece?"

Mammoth's hand is at my waist, his fingers tightening against my skin. "Fuck," he hisses softly, closing his eyes for a moment.

"You two know each other?" I ask, my eyes moving from Uncle James back up to Mammoth's face.

Holy shit. This isn't good.

The look Uncle James is giving Mammoth is nothing short of murderous. Maybe they know each other from the Disciples or from a case Uncle James worked in the past, but either way, there's no love passing between their glares. But James called him Saint, not Mammoth. He knows him from outside the circle of the MC. No one there called him Saint. Only by his nickname, something they all do like they don't even know each other's real names.

"Do we know each other?" Uncle James repeats my words, moving around the Challenger and coming toward us. His footsteps are fast, and his stride is long. "We've known each other for close to ten years."

I do the math in my head. That puts Mammoth close to twenty. He was stationed near Miami, Uncle James's hometown. "Ah. So, you know him from the army?"

"Princess." Mammoth peers down at me.

James clears his throat, standing so close and tall, he casts a shadow over me, blocking out the afternoon sun. "Princess? You've got to be shitting me."

"It's not what you think," Mammoth says quickly, and it's my turn to stiffen because like hell it's not what he thinks.

"What the hell, man?" Uncle Thomas asks, coming to stand next to Uncle James, forehead wrinkled and eyebrows drawn down like he's just as freaking confused as I am.

"We have...history," Mammoth says, eyes locked on Uncle James, muscles still tight and grip still firm on my body.

History could be good. It usually is. But based on Mammoth's body language and the way Uncle James looks like he's ready to rip Mammoth's throat out with his bare hands, I'm thinking there's a lot of bad.

"She know?" Uncle James asks, talking in code as he dips his head toward me. "Everything?" He's speaking around me but not to me, which is odd. Uncle James has never been the type of man not to be up-front and especially not to treat a woman like she's invisible.

"Hello," I say, waving my hands. "I'm right here."

Uncle James's glare snaps to me, and he grunts. But the recognition is short-lived before he's back to Mammoth. "Does she?"

Mammoth shakes his head. "She doesn't."

I immediately start conjuring up the worst possible shit imaginable. Murder. Drugs. Kidnapping. Extortion. All the ways my uncle and Mammoth could know each other and why Uncle James is so pissed Mammoth is touching me.

I push away from Mammoth, craning my neck back to stare up

at my uncle. "If you have an issue, you should probably talk to me instead of around me." There. I found my balls, talking to my uncle like I've seen Aunt Izzy do my entire life.

There's only silence, and for a moment, his eyes don't leave Mammoth. But then they do. If I'd had a full bladder, I would've literally pissed myself at the way my uncle's head turns slowly, eyes narrowing even more. This is the scary, badass side of my uncle I rarely see, but when I do…I want to hide.

"I know he's in the Disciples, Uncle," I say, trying to calm his fears and get his hard, angry shell to crack just a little bit. "It's not a big deal."

Uncle James tilts his head, staring at me, not blinking and certainly not looking amused or at ease. "How much do you know about him?" He says *him* like the word is glass in his throat.

I turn my head, glancing over my shoulder at Mammoth, smiling at the big guy. "I know enough," I say before giving my full attention back to my uncle.

"Enough?" He raises an eyebrow.

The man is impossible, but I shouldn't be surprised. I don't know any man who isn't exasperating and exhausting, especially in my family. "I know he's in a biker club. I know he served in the army and lived near Miami. I know his dad was in the army too. I know he moved around a lot as a kid. I know his name is JD Saint." I leave out some stuff, like I know the way he sounds when he has an orgasm or the way he smells just after having sex. They sit on the tip of my tongue, wanting to push my uncle over the edge, but I also know I want to live to see another day.

Mammoth's hand is back on my waist, giving me a soft squeeze. "Give us a minute, princess. Your uncle and I need to have words."

"No," I answer quickly, hating that I'm being dismissed.

"Tamara, listen to the man," Uncle James tells me.

Uncle Thomas steps forward and touches my shoulder. "I'd like to talk to you about what happened at the compound. Think you can debrief me before we walk inside? If we're any later, Ma will have our heads."

I know what Uncle Thomas is doing, but at least he's being nice about it. He's excluding me from a conversation but using more tact. It's always been his way. He's less dismissive of everyone, always taking into account other people's feelings, while Uncle James is more concerned with getting what he wants.

"I'll be fine," Mammoth says when I don't move right away. "I'll be right behind you."

"Fine. I'm going," I say, rolling up on my tiptoes and kissing Mammoth's cheek right near his lips. "But not because *he* told me to go."

Uncle James grunts, but I ignore him. He deserves as much for the way he dismissed me, talked around me, and generally acted like an asshole.

I'm not two steps away from Mammoth when Uncle Thomas hooks his arm around my shoulder, drawing me closer to him. "I don't know what it's about, but it's best to let them work it out, kid."

"Why's he such an asshole, Uncle?"

Thomas sighs and shakes his head. "He always is when he thinks someone he loves is in trouble."

I stop walking, turning up my face to look at Uncle Thomas. "Mammoth isn't trouble. The MC, for sure, but not Mammoth. He was nothing but a gentleman to me."

It's a lie. I know it, and from the way my uncle's nose wrinkles, he knows it too.

"You pulled a dumb-ass stunt the other day, taking off without letting anyone know where you were going."

"On any given day, no one knows where I'm at, Uncle. I don't even live within one hundred miles of here. So, unless you have a GPS tracking device on my car..."

He laughs, but I don't.

"Wait, do you have a..."

He shakes his head. "No, sweetheart. We don't have anything on your car. All I know is you scared the shit out of Gigi, and Pike sang like a canary."

"Asshole," I mutter, remembering Pike deserves payback for ratting me out.

"What happened at the compound?" Thomas asks as we start walking again, making our way toward the house.

I shrug. "Nothing. They went on lockdown soon after I got there, Mammoth was left behind to make sure I didn't get hurt, and when it ended, he brought me home."

"Did you hear what the lockdown was about?"

I think a minute, trying to remember if there was anything I'd overheard, but the days passed in a blur. "Honestly, I don't remember."

He pulls me closer, kissing the top of my head. "No worries, Tam. I'm just happy you're home safe. What happened to Crow?"

My eyebrows rise, and I almost trip. "Pike," I grumble, knowing he spilled a whole lot of details to my family and not just general information. "Such a dick."

My uncle laughs again. "Don't be too hard on the guy. He was worried, and we're not an easy group to keep a secret from. We have a way of working information out of someone even if they don't want to speak."

"Sure," I mumble, knowing they are a mighty force when they come together, but I'd thought Pike was stronger than that. I figured he could withstand a Gallo grilling after living with the Disciples. Hell, Gigi and I had mastered resistance at the age of fifteen. Pussy.

The front door opens, and Gigi's standing there, staring at Uncle Thomas and me before her eyes go to Mammoth and James. Her eyebrows shoot up, and I can practically read her mind.

"I better go see Angel. I'll let you two talk," Uncle Thomas says before releasing me, then giving Gigi a quick kiss and disappearing into the house.

Gigi comes out onto the front porch and stands next to me. "What the hell is that about?" She throws her hand out toward the two men in a heated conversation.

"Hell if I know. They didn't say shit to me, but they know each other somehow."

Gigi has a look of horror. "They know each other?" Her mouth gapes open as she eyeballs the men across the yard.

I nod. "Apparently." I sigh. "Uncle James called him Saint."

"No shit," Gigi whispers, shaking her head. "That's not good, Tam. Not good at all."

I shrug and purse my lips. "It shouldn't matter if they know each other. Mammoth's a solid guy. He's been nothing but nice to me since we met."

Gigi bumps me with her hip. "Explain *nice*."

I snicker, staring at the tall, well-built man who had my toes curling repeatedly and delivered orgasms like he was a freaking expert. "We fucked a few times."

"News flash, I wouldn't expect anything less," she teases, bumping my hip again. "I want details, and what happened with Crow?"

I roll my eyes. "Hell if I know."

"He seemed to really like you."

"Seemed is the operative word," I mutter. "I thought he'd be happy to see me again, but I was wrong. So wrong. He treated me like a piece of shit when I showed up thinking we were going to have a good time. He acted like I was a nuisance and not someone he'd spent days flirting with."

Uncle James and Mammoth are now standing closer, their bodies a little more animated as they speak. But their voices are too low, and I'm too far away to make out any of the words.

Damn it.

"And him," Gigi asks, pointing at the object of my current attention and infatuation. "How did you end up with that man?"

"Dumb fucking luck." I laugh, remembering the way he looked

at me from the other side of the bar, smiling with those sexy gray eyes and amused by my attitude. "But girl, let me tell you, that man…" I fan myself. "No one's ever lit my fire the way he does."

Gigi's mouth falls open. "This isn't a hit it and quit it."

I shrug. God, I hope it's not, but who the fuck knows. He's a biker who also lives on the other side of the state. I can't see him uprooting his life for me, and I still have a year of school left. The upside is that my dorm room isn't that far from the compound if he's game for more. "I don't know, babe." I sigh. "I'm not the only one making that decision. If he wants more, I'll happily spread my legs for that man again."

"What's going on?" Pike asks, coming up behind us.

Gigi turns around, but I keep my back to him. I have so many words to give him. None of them nice. But now's not the time, and I'm too worried about whatever Mammoth and Uncle James are still arguing about to give two shits about the traitor.

"Uncle James is having a little chat with Mammoth," Gigi tells him, moving farther behind me. She's probably nuzzling her boyfriend because she can barely keep her hands and body off him.

"What are they talking about?"

"We don't know," she answers.

Suddenly, the two men break apart. Mammoth stares at me as Uncle James stalks toward the front porch. I take a step forward, moving away from the house and toward my sexy biker.

Uncle James puts up his hands and says, "Don't."

I stop walking, rocking backward on my heels. "Excuse me?" I ask, glancing at Mammoth as he starts to climb back on his bike. "What the hell did you do?"

"What did I do?" he asks, touching his chest and glaring at me like I just robbed a bank or some shit.

"Mammoth!" I yell, leaving Uncle James standing in the middle of the driveway because he's not my father and I'm a grown-ass woman. Ain't no man, especially not my uncle, going to send any of my friends or lovers away without my okay. And right now, he doesn't have my okay to send Mammoth packing. "Stop!"

"Tamara, let the man go," Uncle James calls out.

I keep moving forward toward Mammoth, shaking my head as he reaches for the key he's already stuck in the ignition. "What the hell?" I ask when I'm within a few feet and no longer need to yell. "Where ya going, baby?"

Mammoth ticks his chin toward something behind me. Or should I say someone… Uncle James. "James and I have," he says, moving his hand to the back of his neck, "history."

I put my hands on my hips, tilting my head, wondering where the badass biker I met has gone. "So fucking what? Whatever happened between you two has nothing to do with us."

Mammoth shakes his head before reaching for me, grabbing me by the hips. "Princess, you don't understand."

"Did you sleep with him too?" I'm trying to be funny, but the look on Mammoth's face tells me it's really not a joking matter. "Did you?" I ask, confused. Other than him having a very intimate relationship or being a felon, I don't understand why it would matter how they know each other.

Mammoth pulls me closer, his thumbs toying with the skin on my stomach. "We know each other from a club."

I snake my arms around his shoulder, tangling my fingers in the back of his hair. "He already knew you were a Disciple, and so does everyone else in the house. Who cares?"

Mammoth laughs sweetly, his gray eyes twinkling in the sunlight. "No, princess. Not that kind of club. A very different kind of club."

I blink, more confused than I was a moment ago. "A different club?" I blink again, letting his words settle, and then I gasp as realization finally smacks me in the face.

Ding. Ding. Ding. We have a…Dom?

Shittttttt.

CHAPTER 14
MAMMOTH

BY THE WAY Tamara's eyes widen, she finally understands exactly what I'm telling her. "Wait, you're a…" Her voice trails off, and she blinks those beautiful hazel eyes at me again. "And you know my uncle from a…"

I nod. "Yeah." I squeeze her sides, waiting for what I'm telling her to finally sink in.

Her eyes widen for only a moment before she pulls her shit together like she's not entirely put off by the idea. "But you didn't seem *that* way at the compound." She draws her plump lip between her teeth, gazing down at me, chewing on the soft skin. "Are you a sub, then? That's what it's called, right? A submissive." She's dead fucking serious when she asks me that. There's not even a hint of a smile or a playful blink.

The bark of laughter that bubbles out of my throat can probably be heard for blocks. I shake my head, never imagining she'd go there, but finding it cute as hell when she does. "Do I really look like a sub?"

She shrugs, eyebrows raised, her beautiful mouth turned up on one side. "Kinda."

My lips flatten, but I know she's yanking my chain. This chick is such a ballbuster and she's trying to fluster me, but I'm used to a challenge. I'm used to attitudes. Hell, I'm used to people testing my limits as much as I do theirs. This is child's play. "You're fuckin' with me, princess. And this time, I'll let it slide."

"Or else you'll..." She cocks one perfectly black eyebrow, always pushing the limits.

I pull her body against mine, our eyes lock, and our lips are barely an inch apart. "Spank your ass," I murmur softly against her mouth.

Her breathing's shallow and fast, matching my own. What I wouldn't give for a few hours alone with her right now.

"Baby." She wraps her arms around my neck, straddling my leg, taunting me with her pussy. "Get off your bike and come inside."

"I should go." *Fuck.* I don't want to, but I know it's the honorable thing to do.

I've known James for years and have always respected the hell out of the man. The last thing I want to do is literally fuck someone in his family and cause issues, but I like this girl. Hell, I more than like her. She's like a drug I can't get enough of. She could quickly become an addiction if I'm not careful.

"Fuck my uncle," she says softly, brushing her tits against me, practically putting them in my face. "He doesn't get to decide my life or yours, yeah?"

The pull of her words, the smell of her body, and the warmth of her skin have me moving her back and my body untangling from around the bike. "I'm not ready to give you up yet."

I wasn't ready when we started the drive, and even after my heart-to-heart with James, I'm sure as fuck not ready now. Nor am I willing. Even though I was in the military, I'm now shit at taking orders. I spent enough of my life being told what to do, and I am done. Over it. Finished.

Being a Dom has been a way for me to have control during a time in my life when I had very little. That's military life. But now…now, I want my freedom, and I want Tamara, no matter what James or anyone else has to say about it.

Tamara takes my hand, pulling me toward the house. She almost stumbles when she looks up, noticing her parents standing on the porch, watching us with James at their side. Her mother's eyes are raking over me.

Hating me? Most likely.

Her father, he's easier to read. If he could murder me, he'd do it in this moment. James must've told him everything, including my past and my sexual tastes. Not something I'd do to him, but I see he has no problem talking shit about me to his family.

They turn their backs, heading into the house before we make it within twenty feet of the front porch.

"This should be so much fun," Tamara whispers, clutching my hand even tighter. "If I die today, know you gave me the best dick ever." She looks up at me with those big eyes and a small smile. "Okay?"

"No one's dying, princess." I lift her hand to my mouth and kiss her skin. "And Tamara, I gave you Mammoth Light. You've never gotten the best stuff."

Her eyebrows rise immediately, almost meeting her dark hair above her forehead. "You were holding out on me?"

"You've never met Saint," I say, teasing her mostly, but serious too. There's Mammoth the biker, looking to get laid, and then there's Saint, a whole different side of me only a select few ever get to meet.

"Well, fuck me."

"Is that an invitation?" I cock an eyebrow.

"Do you need one?" she asks.

"I'm not sure you can handle all this," I tell her, taunting her, wanting nothing more than to have my way with her.

The light fucking of the last few days, the sweet fucking we'd done, was nothing compared to what I wanted to do with her. And if I have my way, it'll happen.

Tamara stops walking, turning her body toward me, gazing upward. "Baby," she whispers, a smirk on her lips, "I'm not sure you can handle all this." She throws my words back, and I know above everything else, I'm going to love the hell out of the challenge.

———

"So." James hasn't taken his eyes off me, and by the way he's holding the fork in his hand, I'm pretty sure he wants to jam it right into my eye.

"So," I say back, staring across the table at the man I've known for years and always thought was a friend.

"This is so weird," James's wife, Izzy, whispers at his side, moving the food around on her plate like she's not sure what to do. I've seen the woman almost completely naked and never expected to be sitting at the dinner table across from her. "Isn't it?"

The room has emptied. Everyone finished their food and is cleaning up, except for the six of us. James, Izzy, Tamara, me, and her parents. Awkward is an understatement. Weird doesn't even begin to cover what the mood in the room is.

"Let me get this straight..." Anthony, Tamara's dad, says, rubbing his chin as he narrows his eyes. "You go to those kinky-ass sex clubs and sleep with total strangers to get your freak on."

Those words have James and Izzy stiffening. The fork could now easily go toward Anthony and not just me.

"Do you honestly think everyone is fucking each other? That it's just some crazy-ass orgy?" James asks Anthony, finally not giving me the death glare.

Anthony shrugs. "Listen, we've been in a few to watch. I'm not a total idiot, James. I've seen what goes down there. It's hard enough for me to think of my sister in a place like that with her husband, but to think of my daughter..."

"Hold up," Tamara says, pushing her plate to the side before resting her hands on the table. "I've never been to a sex club. Let's get that straight right now."

All eyes are on her, including mine. This is her family. Her time. Her information to give or hold on to and not my place to make shit worse for her.

"Well, thank God for small miracles," her mother whispers, running her hand across her thick black hair.

"I'm also not a virgin," Tamara announces. "Haven't been for a long time."

If I could crawl under the table, I fuckin' would. What kind of family has an open conversation about sex like this? Sure as fuck not mine.

"Motherfucker," Tamara's father curses, tipping his head back to look at the ceiling when he does it.

"Oh, please," Tamara says, pursing her lips. "You were a complete and total manwhore, Dad. I know all about your days in the band, banging your way around Tampa Bay. By the time you were twenty-one like me, how many women had you slept with?"

I rock back in my seat, and Tamara's hand moves to my knee, locking on to me. I'm captive, forced to stay here, witnessing one of the most uncomfortable conversations of my entire life. But I do it. I stay. For her.

"We're not talking about me," he replies, waving her off, dismissing her question.

"Because you're a man," she challenges him, cocking her head to the side, staring him down.

James blows out a breath, and I move my eyes to him and Izzy, his beautiful wife, who's just as quiet as the last time I saw her. But that time, she was half dressed, collar around her neck, kneeling near his feet, and a perfect work of art.

"Stop!" Izzy says, slamming her hands down on the table. "All of you need to stop the bullshit." She pushes herself up, palms flat on the wood, glaring around the room and at the five of us. "Anthony, you were a manwhore."

Tamara's mother opens her mouth to speak.

Izzy turns her attention toward the woman. "Maxine, I know you weren't a saint either, so don't even bother with the bullshit. You two were single for years and didn't enter into your marriage as virgins. As for James and me, what we do, kinky or not, is none of your business. Just like it's none of our business that you like it in your—"

"Shut up, Isabella," Max says quickly, not letting Izzy finish the sentence.

My mouth is hanging open. The insanity going on in this room is shocking me, which is pretty damn near impossible because I've seen some crazy shit in my day.

"She likes it in her..." Tamara asks, gaze moving back and forth between her mother and Izzy.

Izzy shakes her head, holding the room's attention. "It doesn't matter. Is Tamara grown or a child?" Izzy's hands are on her hips now, and she's glaring at everyone, including her husband, waiting for a reply.

"She's grown," Maxine mutters, but not happily.

"And what about you?" Izzy asks James, who looks just as unsatisfied and pissed as Tamara's father.

"She's an adult, but that—"

Izzy shakes her head. "She's an adult. End of story."

Anthony waves his hand toward his sister, who's still standing. "It's not that easy, Izzy."

"It is that easy. Jesus," she mutters. "This girl—" she waves her hand at Tamara "—has dated some real dipshits over the last few years. She finally brings around a solid and honorable man, and you're all losing your minds."

Her kind words have the corner of my mouth pulling upward.

"Do you want her to be alone her entire life?" Izzy asks seriously.

"Well, no," Maxine says, toying with her diamond wedding ring. "Of course not."

"And you?" Izzy asks Anthony, who immediately shakes his head. "Then calm your shit, enjoy dessert, and be happy your kid is healthy, safe, and seems to be enjoying her life a little bit."

"You were always my favorite," Tamara says immediately, earning a wink from her aunt before she sits back down.

"Listen." James blows out a long breath, running his hand over the top of his short dark hair. "I can't say I'm thrilled about this. I still think of Tamara as a little girl with crazy beautiful hair, playing with dolls. It's hard for me to wrap my head around the fact that she's grown up. And seeing her here, with you, someone I've known in *other* circles, is jarring. I need time for it to settle. Information like that isn't easy for me to digest."

"For you to digest?" Anthony asks, shaking his head, laughing. "What about me? I mean, do you want to think about Rocco being spanked or whipped by some chick?"

James blanches. "It would take one helluva chick to wrangle that crazy fucker."

Izzy covers her face, slowly shaking her head as Tamara's grandmother walks in with the handsy older woman from earlier.

"Strawberry shortcake?" Grandma Gallo asks, holding out the cake plate, showing everyone the dessert and totally clueless about the conversation.

I feel like I've been through battle, dodging bullets at every turn, but I've only had dinner and a totally awkward conversation. Jesus Christ. Is this how this family always is? Up one another's asses, talking sex, sharing secrets, and bossy as fuck?

"Hey," the old woman says, sliding her hands on my shoulders and digging her fingertips into my muscles. "I'm sure after a long ride, you could use a little rubdown."

"Fran," Izzy warns, glaring over my shoulder.

Tamara's ignoring the woman who currently has her hands on me, not coming to my aid at all. "It looks delicious, Grandma," she says, leaving me to fend for myself.

"Hey, ma'am," I say, tipping my head back, looking at the

woman who I know was gorgeous in her youth because she's still beautiful, even if she's old enough to be my grandmother. "While I appreciate the offer, I don't think it's appropriate or necessary in this moment."

"Appropriate." The older woman snorts. "I've never been appropriate a day in my life."

"A piece?" Grandma Gallo asks, holding a plate, staring right at me.

"Yes, please, ma'am," I say softly, wondering how I'm going to get the woman off me.

"He's so respectful," the woman behind me says, kneading my shoulders harder. "I like that in a man."

"You got a man," her husband says. His arms are crossed, and while he looks annoyed, he doesn't seem shocked to see her pawing me. "You better be moving that sweet ass over here, sweetheart, and putting those hands on me."

The woman leans forward, bringing her mouth close to my ear. "You're a looker, kid. A total hottie. I just like getting my husband all worked up and angry. He's a wild man in the sack that way."

A little vomit rises in my throat, but I push it back down, trying to force a smile on my face. She's gone before I have a chance to reply and at her husband's side, sliding into his lap.

"What happened at the compound?" Bear asks me, changing the subject away from sex and to something a little more comfortable, for me at least.

Tamara's grip on my knee slides higher, but I don't flinch. "Same old stuff. Just an issue, but it's been dealt with." Tamara's grandmother pushes a plate in front of me of the best-looking strawberry cake I've ever seen.

"It's homemade. I hope you like it, Mammoth." She smiles kindly, and I see hints of Tamara in her features.

"I'm sure I'll love it, ma'am. And my name's JD."

"And that stands for?" Anthony asks.

"JD," I reply, picking up my fork, knowing I'm not giving him what he wants.

"Like John David."

"Something like that," I mutter, jamming a forkful of cake into my mouth to rescue myself from having to answer any more questions.

Tamara laughs as I moan around the fork, loving the fuck out of the cake. "I think he likes it, Gram."

"I'll give you the recipe, baby." Grandma winks at Tamara. "The way to any man's heart is through his stomach."

"Lies," Bear mutters, squeezing his wife. "All lies. Fran can't cook worth shit, but I still love her."

"You okay?" Tamara asks as I sit silently, eating the cake, watching the craziest group of people I've been around in a long time.

"Great," I tell her as soon as I swallow the bite that's in my mouth. "Just freaking great."

"Good, baby." She pats my leg, smiling like the sun and the moon revolve around me. "I know they're a lot to take in, but they're good people when you get to know them."

I have to agree with her.

For all their insanity, there's nothing but love around this table. Unconditional love in every form and so much goodness, it's hard not to want to hold on to a little of the craziness.

CHAPTER 15
TAMARA

"OH MY GOD, sorry I'm so late," Lily says, almost running on to the patio and talking so fast, it all comes out like one word.

We sit on a chaise lounge near the pool, flanked by Gigi and Pike, with Austin on the other side of us.

Her eyes widen as soon as she sees Mammoth. "Who the—?" Her mouth hangs open, and I laugh because the look on her face is priceless. "What the—?" She twists a few strands of her hair around her fingertip, gaping at me.

"Lily, this is Mammoth," I tell her, touching one of his legs as they straddle my side. "Mammoth, this is Lily, my nerdy cousin who's going to be a doctor someday."

"No shit," he mutters, sounding impressed. "Hey, Lily."

"Damn," Lily whispers as her eyes move over Mammoth, soaking in his tattoos, long hair, and general hotness. "It's nice to meet you, Mammoth."

Austin leans forward, patting the end of his lounge chair. "Where the hell have you been?"

Lily groans as she slides onto the chair, hunching over and hugging her knees. "My goddamn piece-of-shit car died on me again. I don't know what the hell is wrong with it, but I want the damn thing to last for one more year at least."

"What kind is it?" Mammoth asks from behind me.

"Some fancy foreign piece of shit," Austin says, always ragging on Lily for her automobile choice because he thinks there's nothing better than a good ole shit-kickin' pickup truck.

Lily snaps her head to the side, and she gives Austin the death glare. "Shut up."

Austin throws his hands up, pretending he'll relent, but he never does. He's easily fallen in as part of the family and worked his way into what used to be our threesome, but so did his brother. Times have changed fast. We are no longer solo, three chicks out to cause trouble and chaos, breaking hearts everywhere we go. We are growing up, and I'm not sure how I feel about it either.

"I can take a look at it," Mammoth tells her, ignoring Austin's jab about her car.

She gasps. "Would you? You know about cars?"

Mammoth nods. "I do. I've been tinkering since I was a kid."

I smile at him, liking that he's willing to help my cousin who doesn't know a lug nut from a brake pad. For being so damn smart, she's dumb in so many basic things. Her brilliance has limits and doesn't include anything mechanical. "You'd do that for her?" I ask Mammoth, my smile widening as he nods.

"Of course," he says like I'm insane for thinking otherwise.

I've never been with someone so willing to help others, especially my cousins. Thinking back, I've always been with selfish pricks. Guys who cared about busting a nut and not much else. I'm not even sure a few of them knew my name, but at the time, I didn't care. I used them as much as they used me.

"I'll help," Pike says, rising to his feet before Mammoth even has a chance to stand up. "We'll get you sorted, Lily." Pike stares down at Gigi as she lies back, stretching. "Wait here, darlin'. We won't be long."

Mammoth's up, leaning over and pressing his lips to mine. "You don't mind, do you?"

I shake my head, gazing into those eyes that make me a big pile of pliable goo. I've turned into one of those girls who melts at the mere sight of a man, and I don't think I like it either. "Nah, baby. You go do your man things and bond with the tattletale."

A moment later, his lips are gone, and he and Pike are walking through the sliding glass doors, disappearing into the house.

"What the hell did I miss, and where the hell is Crow?" Lily asks as soon as we're alone...well, except for Austin, but he doesn't count.

I sigh, covering my face with my hand, wishing I could sock that asshole right in the nuts. "He's a tool."

"Well, yeah," Lily mumbles. "We all knew that except for you. But why isn't he here, and where the hell did you find that hottie badass?"

I slide across the lounge chair, and Gigi follows, moving to my chair so we're all sitting in a huddle. I look at my girls, wishing we could turn back the clock a few years and start the insanity of our college years all over again. "When I showed up at the compound, Crow acted like he wanted nothing to do with me. So, I said fuck it, and voilà." I pitch my thumb toward the house. "I found myself a new one. I upgraded. Supersized. But in the end, I think I ended up with a way better deal."

Lily's lips curl. "I never liked Crow. There was something not right about him."

"You never like anyone, Lily baby," Austin says, piping into our conversation like he always does. "No one's good enough."

She grabs his sandal off the cement and tosses the damn thing at him, but he catches it and laughs. "Hey, buddy, I like you, and you're not even that likable," she tells him.

"You love me," he teases her. "You all love me."

"We do, Aussie," I tell him, always feeling the need to reinforce his ego. The kid has been through some crazy shit. More shit than

I'd be able to deal with and still be capable of sitting here laughing and smiling like life is carrying on as usual. "What's not to love about you?"

"How long do I have? I can make a list," Gigi says, busting Austin's balls like she always does.

"You love me the most," he tells her, knowing she's full of shit.

"Hello." Lily waves her hands, calling our attention back to her. "The big guy. I want details."

Before I can open my mouth and tell Lily everything, Gigi throws her hands up and says, "Get this shit. He's like Uncle James."

Lily's nose wrinkles. "He's like what?"

"Like Uncle James," Gigi repeats, shaking her head and laughing. "A bossy fucker like him. A Dom."

Lily's blue eyes widen, and the pinched expression on her face is replaced by shock. "He's a Dom?" she whispers like she's trying to keep a secret under wraps.

"Wait," Gigi says, scooting over a little more and leaning forward toward Lily. "It gets better. They know each other."

Lily's big eyes get even bigger as she glances over at me. "They know each other?"

Gigi nods. "Yep. It's like there's some super-secret club 'Doms R Us' or some shit. And to say Uncle James wasn't happy to see him with Tamara on his arm is an understatement."

"Damn it," Lily mutters, grabbing at her ponytail and smoothing down the strands in front of her shoulder. "How do I always miss the good shit?"

"You're too busy with your nose stuck in a book, babe," I tell her, knowing my cousin wasn't out partying last night, but studying her ass off for some imaginary exam she thinks she has to nail as soon as school starts.

Lily raises her chin, staring down her perky little nose at me. "Am not."

"Are too," I throw back. "Life's passing you by, and you're missing it all."

"Both of you bitches are going to spend your lives working your asses off for someone else, when there's a family business sitting right in front of you, waiting to be taken over. I can't believe you two aren't going to work with me at Inked. Imagine the fun we could have for the rest of our lives," Gigi says.

I sigh, knowing she's right, but I can barely even draw a heart without fucking it up, making it look like a five-year-old drew the damn thing. "If I had an artistic bone in my body, I'd be there, babe."

"You think her"—Gigi points at Lily—"dad is an artist?"

Lily snorts. "The man is all muscle and heart, but Picasso he's not."

"You should take over for him, Lily. Take some time off school after next year. Come work at the shop. Learn the craft. I mean, do you really want to go to school for another bazillion years?"

Lily curls over her knees, hugging herself. "I hate school," she announces, and Gigi and I gawk at each other, shocked by Lily's admission. "Hate it!"

The girl has always been a straight A student, priding herself on her perfection and book smarts. She's never once complained about studying or her impossible college schedule, seeming to thrive on the difficult course load.

Gigi's eyes flash with concern. "You hate it?"

Lily peeks up from her knees and shakes her head. "I don't want to be a doctor," she whispers, like it's the dirtiest secret she's ever told.

I rock backward as if she's punched me. "You don't?"

"Fuck." Gigi practically slaps herself on the forehead because we both thought...

"I want to drop out."

Austin scoots off the chair and places his hand on Lily's shoulder. "Wait. Let me get some popcorn before you drop that bomb-shell. The fireworks are going to be better than the Fourth of July."

"You're not helping," I grind out, glaring at the playful little prick. He knows, even in the short amount of time he's been here, Uncle Mike and Aunt Mia are going to lose their proverbial shit over this revelation.

Lily swats his hand away. "I'm not telling them now." She rolls her eyes and groans. "I don't want an audience for the shitshow that's going to go down."

"What the hell, Lily? Why now? What happened?" I ask, wondering if my cousin is having a midlife crisis at the ripe old age of twenty.

She shrugs, twisting her lips. "I want more out of life than studying." She flings out her arm, waving at Gigi and me. "You two are really living, while I'm stuck in the library all weekend, study-ing, wasting my life."

Gigi touches Lily's knee. "But being a doctor isn't a waste. Think of all the people you could help. The lives you could save."

"Or the people I could kill," she admits like she's talking about nothing serious. "I don't want that kind of responsibility. I don't want the pressure of knowing one little mistake could be the differ-ence between someone living or dying. You know?" Lily rests her face in her hands, elbows on her knees, staring down at the ground. "I just don't want it anymore. The last year, I stayed in school for my parents, but I want to stop living for them and live for me for once."

Gigi stares at me, shrugging when I mouth *What the fuck?* at her. "I'm sure they'll understand," Gigi tells her, trying to soothe her fears, but we all know she's lying.

Her parents will care. Uncle Mike, probably not so much, but Aunt Mia... She's going to lose her freaking mind. She's been grooming Lily since she was a little girl to take over the clinic, thinking they would work side by side until Lily would one day take over her passion project and help the underserved members of the community.

"They won't, but they'll just have to deal with it. This is my life. My choice. My time. They did what they wanted to do. Dad has his piercing and his fighting. Mom has her clinic and people who adore her for helping them, but I don't want it. I don't want any part of it." Lily shakes her head, muttering something under her breath. "I have some shit to figure out."

"Tam's heading back to school, and you can crash in her room. We can totally be roomies, cousin. Think of the fun we could have."

I glare at Gigi. The bitch is giving my room away without even so much as asking me.

"What?" Gigi asks, throwing her hands up. "Your skanky ass is slinking back to college, right?"

I nod. "I am. One more year and I'm done. I just wish the compound was closer."

"You're serious about this guy?" Lily asks, studying me like I'm the one with the biggest fucking news of the day.

"I am." I smile as my stomach flips just thinking about him.

"Do what makes you happy." Lily bobs her head, giving me a small smile back. "Just do you, babe."

"Or do Mammoth," Gigi snorts. "'Cause I'm pretty sure he's what's making her happy right now. It's like he fucked the bitch right out of her."

I give Gigi the middle finger. "You can fuck right off."

"And she's back," Gigi teases, laughing. "There must be an expiration period on the niceness his cock delivers."

"It is pretty magical." My statement is met with grunts and giggles. "Now—" I clear my throat, ignoring the assholes "—back to my room. If you promise me you're going to have some fun and finally get your fill of cock, you can use my room and keep my bed company when I leave."

Lily covers her face. "I don't think I can do it. I can't drop out. I most certainly can't tell my parents."

"It's up to you, Lily. It's your life, and you know we'll support you," Gigi tells her as she moves to the spot next to Lily where Austin had been. "Just tell them. I bet they won't be that upset."

Gigi's lying her ass off. She knows it. I know it. Lily knows it too. They're going to go from angry to nuclear in under two seconds as soon as they hear the news Lily's dropping out of college to do...cock?

"Let's go see what the boys are up to. Maybe they've fixed your car," I tell them before Lily can start crying. The girl is petrified, but although I know her parents will be mad, they love the girl like she shits rainbows.

We don't cut through the house, wanting to avoid our parents and a barrage of questions. As we walk around the side of the house, opening the gate at the fence, we see Pike and Mammoth leaning over the hood of Lily's little black car, asses sticking out, looking mouthwateringly good.

"Fuck, that's hot right there," I mutter, enjoying the hell out of the view. "You see that kinda shit at your school, Lil?"

Lily shakes her head, but her eyes are firmly on their backsides. "Nope. Just a lot of khaki."

Gigi and I gag in unison, shivering like we couldn't deal with the horror of such a fashion crime.

"There's nothing sexier than a pair of snug jeans on a man." I fling out one arm, pointing at their perfect bodies, and snake my other arm around Lily's shoulder. "I mean, look at that ass. Amirite?"

Lily smiles next to me as if the stress of her earlier admission has been washed away. "I could use a little bit of that right now. I mean, not them exactly, but someone like them."

"Girl," Gigi says in a singsong voice, "men like that will break you."

Lily snorts. "I'm not as delicate as I look."

"Didn't your last boyfriend wear a pocket protector?" Gigi asks her, rolling her eyes. "No respectable man wears that."

"They're very practical," Lily tells her, showing her nerd even more. "And super sexy sometimes."

God, my cousin is drop-dead gorgeous. Between her blue eyes, long curly brown hair, and killer rack, men would be falling over their own feet to get a taste of her beauty.

"Come on, nerd girl. Let's go start living life," I tell her, pulling her by the neck toward our men in black.

CHAPTER 16
MAMMOTH

SO, there's an issue with sleeping with younger chicks. So many fucking issues. More than most men, even ones close to their age, want to deal with.

First, they're talkative. I don't mean they like to casually chat. I mean they never shut the hell up. They can talk for hours about the same bullshit, never seeming to tire about the topic.

Second, there's no off-switch. None for the talking or everything else. They're full of energy and always looking to party. Doesn't matter what kind of shindig it is; they're down for just about anything.

Third, they can't keep a secret worth shit. If there's something you want the world to know, just tell a woman under the age of twenty-five, and you might as well publish the information on the front page of the newspaper.

Fourth, most likely...you need to meet their family. This includes parents and anyone else who's nearby.

Of course, there are exceptions.

I did have to meet Tamara's family, but they weren't assholes. Besides James, who I know is just trying to look out for his niece, they were all pretty fucking chill. The grandma could cook her little ass off, and the older aunt, the handsy one, she wasn't even too bad on the eyes. All in all, the Gallos were solid. I could see why when Pike found Gigi, he held on to the girl like the world revolved around her.

Sure, Tamara's talkative too, but not to the point where I've tuned her ass out.

But as for the secrets... Fuck. There are none.

Tamara can't keep one worth shit, at least not from her family. And her family seems to know everything about everyone, so there's no keeping my life private from them. There's not much left to keep either. By now, I'm sure James and Thomas have run my name through every background check they have at their disposal, finding I'm clean and probably scratching their heads or at least wishing they'd uncover something.

I stare up at the ceiling, Tamara curled up next to me, wondering how I got here. I mean, I know. But still...how?

I never get involved with anyone at the club. Those bitches are the cattiest, most ruthless women I've ever met. The last thing I want to do is fuck one of them and have them hounding me for more cock. So, why Tamara?

She was an outsider. A complete unknown. I knew she was there for Crow and that he turned his back on her, but I had no idea why. I liked her sass and "go fuck yourself" attitude, which, unlike most of the clingy women hanging around the compound, was a breath of fresh air.

"We're fifty-five minutes away," Tamara says, her face awash in light from her phone.

I turn my head, glancing down just as she hides the screen. "From what?"

"A sex club." She waggles her eyebrows, and it takes everything in me not to laugh.

This chick.

I pull myself up, resting my back against the headboard, smiling. "We can't just drop in to a place like that, princess. That's not how it works."

Her forehead wrinkles as she drops her phone on the comforter, staring up at me. "How does it work, then?"

It's time for a little lesson. Something I'm not used to doing. Typically, I'm not into people looking to explore the lifestyle, but I'm not usually into younger women either.

I slide an arm under her back and lift her up, planting her on top of me. "You have questions?"

"Tons," she says, straddling my waist, knees locked against my hips as her hands find my chest. "I want to know all the dirty things." She rakes her nails across my pecs, finding my piercings and toying with them.

I dig my fingers into her hips, steadying her as she starts to slowly gyrate her hips on top of me. "You want to talk or fuck?" I ask, because this can go either way, and I'm perfectly happy with whatever her answer is.

"I get a choice?"

"You always have a choice. Being dominated by someone isn't about them taking away your choices or doing something to you against your will."

Her fingers stop moving, but the death grip she has on the barbells in my nipples has my cock aching to be inside her. "It's not?" she asks, her eyebrows high.

I shake my head, stroking the soft skin above her hips. "No, baby. It's not. I've never forced someone to have sex with me. That's rape. Always has been, always will be."

She nods like she's comprehending. "But sometimes you'll do stuff to me that I don't want you to, right?"

I sigh softly, remembering to be patient. She's a newbie. A clean slate. "Dom/sub relationships, even only sexual ones, are about trust, communication, and of course, pleasure. I would never do something to you if I knew you wouldn't enjoy it. I don't get off by making you hurt. That's not my style."

Her lips twist, and I can almost see the questions piling up in that pretty little head of hers. "This is going to make my head explode." I roll over, covering her body with my own as her legs wrap around me, locking at her ankles. "Will you teach me?"

Nothing would give me greater pleasure than testing Tamara's limits. I remember being lost, trying to find my way and figure shit out, but I was lucky and had great mentors. If she wants to learn more, figure out if she has a sub bone in her body, I'll be more than happy to teach her, mold her, fuck her.

"Of course. If that's what you want, I'd be more than—"

"I want it," she says in a husky tone, pushing her sweet cunt against my cock. "I want it all."

I can't hold back the laugh that comes from deep in my chest. "You're greedy."

She runs her hands up my arms before resting them on my shoulders and giving me a smirk. "Is that so bad?"

"And impatient." I move my face closer and my cock farther away from her, which gets me a small whine in return, but I continue, "Demanding, selfish, and wild. So fuckin' wild you need taming."

"Tame me, baby. Tame me," she murmurs against my lips before smashing her mouth against mine, taking what she wants, showing no restraint.

I pull away, taking my mouth from her and lifting my body higher and farther. "First lesson, princess. You don't control things anymore. I do. Kissing included."

Her eyes flash, but there's no anger. Just need. "Do I have to earn them?"

"Still fuckin' cute."

Her eyes narrow, and she digs her heels into my ass, trying to get the friction of my cock back. "Baby," she whispers, tracing the outline of my jaw with her fingernail, "I'm not cute. If you'd fuck me, I'd show you exactly how cute I'm not."

"Even cuter," I tell her, teasing her, pissing her off because she's even hotter when she's angry.

"What the fuck?" Gigi's voice breaks through the silence we've been enjoying for the last hour since we made it back to Tamara's apartment from her grandparents'. "They what?"

Tamara slaps at my arms, trying to slide down my body and through my legs. "Move it," she demands, swatting, and not so playfully. I roll away, letting her go, lying with my back on the mattress and my cock straight up like a flagpole. "What's wrong?" I ask her, staring down my dick as she moves around the floor, picking up her clothes.

"I don't know," she says as she pulls her tank top over her head, not bothering with a bra. "But I'm sure as hell gonna find out."

"Pants!" I yell out as she moves toward the door in nothing but a G-string.

She throws up her arms, cursing under her breath before snatching a pair of shorts from a drawer and pulling them on. "Better?" she asks, all full of attitude, looking to have her ass smacked and hair pulled because sometimes she's wound so fucking tight, she needs something to unwind her.

"Better," I tell her, smiling, dreaming about making her ass pink from my palm.

She rolls her eyes and is out of the bedroom a moment later, leaving me behind. I grab the sheet, pulling it over me since she didn't bother to close the door. I don't care about public nudity when I'm at a club, but in the privacy of her apartment, around others, even I have standards.

"They threw you out?" Tamara's voice echoes down the hallway, and I know a really fucking great night just went off the rails. What I had planned and wanted wouldn't happen because whatever hell is breaking loose in the living room will take precedence over my cock.

"They needed a minute to talk and cool off. They went totally batshit crazy. My mom had to give my dad a Xanax so he'd calm down. I told them I was going to leave for the night, let them talk, and I'd come back tomorrow if they were willing to listen."

The girl losing her shit in the living room is Lily. I know the sweet, perky voice anywhere, and based on what Tamara told me, she was about to drop out of college and try to find herself. Guess that didn't go over too well with her folks, but talks like that rarely do.

"Jesus, Uncle Mike is such a fuckin' pansy sometimes," Gigi says, not sounding as panicked as she did a moment ago.

Maybe there is hope for my cock after all.

"This calls for tequila," Tamara says in return.

DOA. That's what my cock is. Instead of complaining, I roll out of bed, slide on my pants, and head toward the living room to at least get in on the action.

Tamara's eyes find me as soon as I walk out of the hallway, finding her setting a bottle of tequila on the counter. "You in, big guy?" she asks, smirking at me, begging for that spanking I'm so badly in need of giving.

"I'm down, princess," I tell her. "What's wrong?" I act like I don't know, but I'm pretty sure the entire apartment complex heard them screeching about Lily's situation.

"Lily's parents lost their shit. So, we're going to cheer her up." Tamara fills one shot glass and moves on to the next. "Maybe head to the bar after this. We do a few shots before going to save some cash."

Gigi and Lily are sitting across from Tamara, waiting for their drinks, nodding in agreement as Pike comes to stand next to me. "You don't have to stay," he tells me like I'm going to listen to him and leave because there's a chick crisis.

"Fuck off, man. I'm here to stay." I walk away from Pike and head toward my girl. She's filling the glasses so much, the tequila is spilling over the sides, pooling at the base of the glass. "It's all about moderation. Something you don't seem to know anything about," I tell her, taking the bottle from her hand.

She rolls her eyes as she turns toward her cousins, ticking her head my way. "This one's bossy."

"That should go over well," Gigi says, giggling and elbowing Lily in the side, but I know they're full of shit. "She's always been great at listening and following directions."

Tamara isn't one who's hard to peg. The moment I laid eyes on her and she opened her mouth, I knew she had no discipline. Maybe when she was little, but as an adult, she's making up for being caged.

"If Aunt Izzy can put up with Uncle James, there's still hope someone can tame Tamara," Lily adds before downing a second shot of tequila right after the first.

"Izzy seems pretty damn tame." I pull Lily's glass back without looking up, but when I do, I see three girls with their mouths hanging open. "What?"

"Izzy is not tame, Mammoth. She's the boss of everybody, right behind my grandmother. If you do wrong, she's going to have her foot so far up your ass, you'll be shitting Louboutin for a week."

"Loub-a-what?" I ask, staring at her in confusion. "You mean Louis Vuitton, like the purses?"

Tamara's eyes sparkle with laughter as she slides her hand behind my back, groping my ass. "Louboutin. It's a fancy shoe and very different from Louis Vuitton."

I pour myself a glass now, needing something to stop me from hauling her ass back into the bedroom, finishing what we started. "I swear to shit, you just said the same names."

"Doesn't matter." Tamara shakes her head. "Just know Izzy is not meek, mild, or tame. The girl is fearless. She had to be, growing up with four brothers."

"She's always been my idol," Lily says, surprising the fuck out of me. The little bit of time I've spent with her, she seemed more like a quiet little bookworm than a badass.

"Man, you don't know shit about Izzy," Pike tells me, grabbing a shot glass off the counter, helping himself to the tequila. "That woman has given me nothing but trouble since I walked in the door. She busts my balls every single day at the shop. But James—" Pike smiles before slamming back the tequila and wiping his mouth with the back of his hand "—he walks in the door, and she changes in a freaking heartbeat."

"That's bullshit," Gigi says, pointing at Pike with her long, thin finger. "She doesn't bow to him."

"She kind of does, darlin'," Pike says, looking to me for confirmation.

Tamara takes the shot glass right from my hand and places it back on the countertop, but she's looking at her cousins. "Fuck this. I'm done talking about old people having sex, especially my aunt. Let's head to the bar, dance, get shitfaced, and see what kind of trouble we can stir up in this small, boring-ass town. We need to get Lily's mind off her parents for a few more hours until she passes out, and tomorrow, all will be well again."

"Who said drinking?" Pike's brother, Austin, whom I met earlier today, asks, strolling through the door already dressed and ready for a night out. "You ladies weren't going without me, were you?" he pouts, earning a collective response of *Never!* from the three cousins.

This kid is good. Smooth as shit for being so young. Impressive, really, but it shouldn't surprise me since he is Pike's brother. Pike isn't a dipshit. For not becoming a Disciple, he held his shit together under some situations in which even the most hardened of criminals would've wilted or at least pissed themselves like a baby. But he didn't. He was solid, and I've always respected him for figuring out his path and chasing his dream.

"Let's get this party started," Austin announces, dangling a set of keys from his finger. "I'll be the designated driver."

Tamara's arm moves around my waist. "You guys go with Austin. I'm going with Mammoth on his bike."

"TamTam," Austin says, touching his chest. "You're really going to trade in time with me for…" His eyes slice to me, raking over my face. "…this guy?"

Tamara nods quickly. "I'll always love you, Aussie, but we never would've worked. It's best this way."

"You slept with him?" I ask, ticking my chin toward the kid who can't be more than eighteen.

Tamara laughs. "No fuckin' way, baby. I like my men—" she clears her throat, running her hand up my chest "—a little bigger."

"You mean older," Austin corrects her. "We know I'm way prettier. You're missing out, babe. Missing out on the best thing ever." After those words, he's out the door, keys in hand, heading toward the parking lot.

"He's a dipshit," Gigi mutters, taking Lily's hand and leading her toward the front door.

"Ready?" Tamara asks me when I don't move right away.

I almost say no. *What the hell am I doing here with this group?*

My world and theirs are miles apart. Mine is filled with mayhem and violence, while theirs consists of partying and the easy life.

But then Tamara's hands find my ass and her lips my mouth, and everything, including our differences, disappears.

CHAPTER 17
TAMARA

"YOU HEADIN' back soon?" Gigi asks me, not hearing the conversation I'm having with Mammoth.

I turn my attention to my cousin, snuggling into Mammoth's large side and placing my hand on his knee. "I should. I really need to get ready for the last year of classes. Get my books and meet whatever chick's going to be my roommate this year."

"Classes," Lily mutters, staring at the glass she's turning in her hands. "Drop out of school. What the hell was I thinking?" She's talking to herself, doubting her decision, but I think she's making the right one.

My cousin has always done everything everyone around her has wanted. She's always been the doting daughter, doing whatever her parents asked. She's barely lived life, her nose usually stuck in a book, scared to fuck up because she'd end her illustrious medical career before she even got started.

"Babe," I tell her, waiting for her to look at me. When she does, I tell her what I need to say. "You do you. As long as you're happy, you're making the right decision. You have to live life for you. Not for us. Not for your parents. Not for anyone except yourself. If you don't want to be a doctor, be whatever the hell you want to be. You want to sell hot dogs outside the local hardware store, I'll be there to cheer you the fuck on. You want to hold a sign on the street and shake your hot little ass to generate some business and call yourself a marketing director, I'll be your biggest fan. I don't care what you do, but at least be fucking happy about all the possibilities you have before you now."

"Hot dog stand?" she whispers, her mouth tipping into a lopsided smile because she's drunk off her ass.

I nod. "You know what the hell I'm talking about."

"For real, Tam? I know you're trying to cheer me up, but Jesus, I don't want to be the wiener lady."

"Maybe you shouldn't go into inspirational speaking," Gigi tells me, laughing her ass off until I narrow my eyes at her. "What?" She throws up her hands. "She was going to be a doctor, and now you're talking to her about hot dogs and twirling signs on the street. She's going to work at Inked with me. End of story."

"Oh my God!" Lily howls, throwing herself forward and laying her face in her arms. "I fucked up."

"You did not," Austin tells her, rubbing her back. "You're following your heart. You get one life to live, a short as fuck one too, and you need to live that shit to the fullest, babe."

I smile at the kid. The one who knows how precious time is after losing his mother in a tragic way. Everything can change in a second. When I'm taking my last breath, the last thing I want to feel is regret.

"What if they never forgive me?" she whines into her arm, being overdramatic like the rest of us.

"Uncle Mike and Aunt Mia will forgive you, Lily. They love you more than anything in this world. Just give them a few days to get over the shock, and they'll be fine. You'll see," Gigi says to her, pushing Austin's hand out of the way, glaring at him.

For once, he wasn't trying to get fresh. He was just being sweet, something he does often, but it's usually covered by a flirt because it's easier on his heart and better for his ego.

Gigi leans forward, bringing her face close to Lily's, talking in a soft, soothing tone. "Your mom was a big-time doctor at the hospital, but she quit, following her dream to open a clinic. Your parents know what it's like to want something else, something better. You'll see, babe. It's all going to be okay."

"She always like this?" Mammoth asks before sipping his beer.

"Not always," I lie.

We're all dramatic. Even the guys in my family are over the top about the smallest things. Tough guys? Sure. Attention whores? Completely. It's part of our DNA. We do nothing small, even drama.

"We'll all end up at Inked someday. It's our legacy. You're not going to sell hot dogs to hot construction workers, Lily. You're going to be with me, Pike, Austin, maybe Tamara." Gigi looks at me when she says that, always hounding me to work at the shop even though I refuse. "And now you. Our parents need to retire. Imagine all of us together every day, working, talking, living the best life we can. It'll be like old times."

Mammoth's hand is on my shoulder, stroking the skin on my neck, making me ache for him. "It's still a no for me. I haven't figured out what I'm doing next week, let alone for the rest of my life," I say, but my voice is deep and husky because he's distracting me with his touch.

Austin and Pike give each other a look before turning their eyes to Mammoth, passing some ESP shit back and forth about us. It's like men are special, unaffected or unworried about shit in life. They act like they're never dramatic, but hit their bike with your car door and watch them turn into the world's biggest crybabies.

"No one knows what they're doing for the rest of their life. Shit, we're too young for all that," Austin says, rubbing the back of his neck with his hand as he stares down at his soda. "I mean, I never thought I'd be sitting around a table in a bar with my three girls, sipping a freaking Coke, instead of boning some Betty in a bathroom, drunk on vodka in the backwoods of Tennessee."

"Some Betty?" I raise an eyebrow.

Austin nods. "Listen." He smiles, dropping his hand from his neck to the table. "I'm a guy. I'm not overly picky either."

I gag a little, covering my mouth because the thought of him boning anyone makes me a little sick. "You're going to get a disease if you keep sticking that dick into anything that moves."

He shrugs, the smirk not leaving his lips. "Gotta live life on the edge, but I always, and I mean always, wear a rubber."

"Thank God for small miracles," Pike mutters. "Last thing you need is a kid."

"Shit. As soon as I'm old enough, I'm getting a vasectomy."

"Shut the fuck up, you idiot," Lily finally speaks up, still cocooned in the safety of her arm. "You're not going to do that. You're going to want babies someday."

"You want babies with me, Lil?" Austin asks, scooting a little closer to her and covering her hands with his. "I'll keep my balls intact for you, sweetheart."

She doesn't even lift up her head. "Um, I'll never sleep with you."

He pats her hand. "Keep telling yourself that."

She groans, ripping her hand out from under his like his skin is burning her. "Vasectomies aren't easy to reverse. How many times do you want them to cut your balls open?"

Austin pales immediately. "Maybe a vasectomy is a little too drastic after all."

"Uh-huh," Lily mumbles.

Austin keeps his gaze on her. The boy has been head over heels in love with Lily since the moment he laid eyes on her. He's scared of her too. Even more scared of her father, but that doesn't stop him from dreaming. "See, Lily baby. Look at how you just changed my life. I would've had fucked-up balls, and we would've had no kids if it weren't for you talking sense into me now."

Lily lifts her head, mascara streaming down her face along with tears. "We're never having kids, Austin. Got it?"

Austin rocks back, the sight of Lily's face all splotchy red and makeup a complete disaster scaring him and everyone else at the table. "Got it, love. A guy can dream, yeah?"

"Jesus," Gigi grumbles. "You're a mess, Lil. Let's go to the ladies' room and give the men a few minutes of silence."

"Thank fuck," Pike and Mammoth whisper under their breath, almost in unison.

The glares that turn their way as the three of us stand are nothing short of ice-cold. "You better hope we come back," Gigi tells Pike, poking him in the shoulder with her pointy-ass fingernail.

"Darlin', you're coming back," he tells her, cocky smile on his face like he knows she can't get enough of him.

"Hurry your pretty little ass back, princess," is what I get from Mammoth, who opts to cut me off before I have a chance to make a crack about his comment.

"We'll see." I shrug. I don't make it two feet before he wraps his arm around my waist, hauling me backward and into his lap.

His lips are near my ear, breath warm against my skin. "I know you're testing me. I know you're trying to push my buttons. But let's remember, if you want to play the game with me, I'm gonna win, Tamara."

My body shivers when he says my name, but that doesn't stop him from talking.

"You play hard to get, I'll chase. You pretend you're walking away, I'll follow. You want to meet the real Saint, I'm ready to play, princess."

I turn my head, our mouths so close I can smell the sweetness of the beer on his breath. Our eyes are locked. His gray to my hazel. My body's humming in his lap, begging for more than just a simple touch. "I'm game, baby. But just know, I always play to win."

His hand comes up, cradling my face. "I never back down from a challenge."

"Me either," I whisper, sounding a little less confident than I wanted.

"Gonna tame you yet."

"You can try."

"Fuckin' cute," he says against my lips before taking whatever smartass thing I was about to say and completely erasing it from my mind.

The man has a way of doing that. Making me stupid. Making me forget I'm the badass chick who takes no shit from anyone and gives people hell. He makes me someone else. He makes me want things I never wanted to want before. Damn it.

"Hey, asshole, you comin', or you sucking face all night?" Gigi asks behind me.

I wave my hand, lips still locked on Mammoth's mouth, taking the air he's giving me.

"Such a whore," Gigi says before the sound of her boots and Lily's high heels pound the wooden floor, growing softer.

"I gotta go." I pull back from Mammoth, breaking the kiss. "I have to be here for my girl tonight. But tomorrow, I'm all yours." I smile, staring into his fiery eyes.

"Don't write checks your ass can't cash." He smirks, his eyes sliding down my body. "I always follow through."

"Baby." I slide off his lap, keeping my hand on his shoulder as I gaze down at him. "I'm a sure thing, but we'll see who tames whom in the end."

Mammoth smiles as I walk away, and I quickly turn my back, mouthing *dumbass* to myself. I've never said such stupid shit to a man before.

Never.

"What the hell is wrong with me?" I ask as I push open the bathroom door, finding Lily and Gigi standing near the sink.

Gigi laughs as she carefully wipes the mascara from Lily's face. "You're in love or at least lust." She glances at me as I flinch like I'm having an allergic reaction to the very thought of being truly in love.

"How did this happen?" I cover my face and shake my head. "I just don't understand."

"Magical cock, babe," Gigi replies even though I wasn't really looking for an answer.

I groan and stare at myself in the mirror. "It's the piercing, isn't it?" I glance at Gigi's and Lily's reflections in the mirror and wave my hand in the air. "It's like one of those medallions magicians wave in the air to hypnotize a person."

"Oh my God. His penis is pierced?" Lily's mouth falls open.

I nod with a stupid grin on my face. "It sparkles, Lil."

"I've never seen a pierced penis," Lily admits, and neither of us is shocked by this because it's Lily.

"And that's surprising how?" Gigi asks, moving Lily's head back so she can finish cleaning her face.

Lily sighs. "I'm going to die all alone, never seeing a pierced penis, surrounded by a hundred cats. Aren't I?"

"Never," I tell Lily. "You'll always have us."

Gigi nods in agreement, dabbing the Kleenex against her tongue, which is just gross, but Lily doesn't seem to care. "And if you come work with me at Inked, I guarantee you'll see plenty of pierced penises."

Lily pushes Gigi's hand away from her face. "I know you're trying to sell me on Inked, but I don't know if it's a good fit or what I want to do for the rest of my life."

After tossing the Kleenex in the trash, Gigi leans her hip against the counter and crosses her arms. "None of us know what we want to do with the rest of our lives, but for now, you can work there. Learn piercing and spend a little more time with your dad while you're training. Once you figure out your life plan, then you can move on. But—" Gigi pauses and grabs on to Lily's shoulders "—imagine the fun we'll have for a little while until you figure shit out. Izzy and I could use another girl around the shop. There's a little too much testosterone."

"Yeah," Lily murmurs. "I guess I can."

"See." Gigi smiles. "Things aren't so bad, are they?"

"Well." Lily winces. "I don't have a place to live, I don't have a degree, I don't have a man."

Gigi shakes her head and places her finger against Lily's lips to shut her up. "You have us. You have a job. You have…"

"Yeah?" Lily tilts her head when Gigi pauses. "And?"

"Us," I repeat. "Who needs anything more?"

"I love you guys," Lily says without tearing up.

For the first time since stepping foot in the bar, I think she's ready to face her future, and so am I.

CHAPTER 18
TAMARA

ONE WEEK Later

Mammoth pulls off his boots, looking massive in my small dorm room. "I think I should stay the night."

I stand in the doorway to the bathroom, wearing nothing but his T-shirt I snagged during the week and claimed as my own. "You can't," I tell him, wishing things were different. "I'll get kicked out."

His arms are out before I get to him, pulling me to stand in front of him. "Well, at least I know there won't be any other men staying in your bed, princess." He slides his hands up my thighs, finding me bare underneath. "I'm going to miss this," he says, stroking the crease under my ass cheek with his thumb.

I tangle my fingers in his hair, soaking in his touch. "Is this the end of us?"

We've only known each other for a little over a week, but I feel like I've known him longer. I can't imagine him not in my life at this point, and I'm more than a little freaked out by that too.

He tips his head back, staring at me with soft eyes. "Do you want this to be the end?" he asks, not answering my question, but deflecting.

"No, baby. I don't want this to be the end."

The roughness of his palms squeezing my ass has my body swaying, wanting him. "Then this isn't the end."

I crave him, and after a week of him avoiding sex, I'm ready to pounce. "But do you want to see me again? This relationship, or whatever it is, is a two-way street."

He pulls me down, positioning me in his lap so we're eye-to-eye and I'm straddling his legs. "I've never wanted anything more."

"Yeah?" I smile.

One of his hands is up the back of my shirt, caressing my spine, and the other's still firmly planted on my ass. "Yeah. I haven't had my fill."

Does that mean there's a limit to our relationship? Once he's had enough of me, enough pussy, enough time, he'll leave and never look back? The very thought has my stomach flipping. "When will you have your fill?" I ask, figuring I might as well know now so I don't set myself up for heartbreak later.

"I'm not sure I ever will, princess," he says softly, and the flipping of my stomach intensifies, but for very different reasons.

I shift my hands on his shoulders, finding his hair and burying my fingers in the softness. "This is kind of crazy, ya know?"

"If someone would've told me two weeks ago I'd be crazy in love with a chick, I would've told them they were fucked in the head."

I swallow, suddenly breathless. "You're in love with me?" The words almost stick in my throat.

He nods and splays his hand against my back, making me feel tiny in comparison. "It's illogical, but nothing feels more right than being here with you. I'm sure people will think we're crazy, but sometimes, the heart, body, and soul know when they find their other half."

I lean my forehead against his, inhaling the scent that's completely his and totally masculine. "Mammoth?"

"Yeah?" he grunts.

"I won't share you."

He pulls back, gazing at me with those smoky gray eyes that caught my attention the first time I saw him. "I'm not sharing you either. Let's make that clear. If we're in this, we're in this. No one else. I don't want to be in Daytona, wondering what you're doing or who you're doing. And the same goes for me. If I need a piece of ass, I'll hop on my bike and be here in a flash to get a taste of my princess."

My insides go warm and squishy because Mammoth's mine and I'm his, but there's a sadness too, because I don't know when I'll see him again. It could be months, but I pray, with his sexual appetite, it'll be at least once a week. "Can you just stay here?"

He slowly shakes his head. "I can't. I have shit to take care of with the club. If I ever want out, I have to start putting things into motion now. Can't just do that on the fly."

"Are you leaving the club because of me, because of us?"

"I knew the time was coming. I felt that deep. But now, I have a reason to go. A reason to start over. A reason to move on and go forward."

"So that's a yes?" I tease him, which earns me a playful swat to the ass. My skin tingles and heats from the impact, and I totally dig the sensation, especially when his palm soothes the very same spot.

"You're a tease," he says in that deep, honeyed tone. All full of promise and lust.

"I'm a sure thing, baby," I tell him, moving my hands down his chest and cupping his cock through his jeans. "A very sure thing."

"Yes, yes, you are," he whispers, dipping his face closer and brushing his lips against mine. "How long until your new room-mate gets here?"

"She'll be here in the morning."

"That gives me all night to get what I want and need to get me through the next few weeks."

I suck in a breath, knowing an entire night alone with no one listening, interrupting, or trying to kill our good time is just what I need too to get me through the next couple weeks. Weeks? He said weeks. I don't have time to think about anything, especially time, as his lips crash down against mine, stealing the breath I'd just inhaled.

My fingers make quick work of the button and zipper on his jeans, ready to see that bedazzled cock I've missed for the last week.

But before I can reach inside, his fingers are at my wrists, pulling my hands away. Opening my eyes, I pull back, taking in his rugged face and the playful smirk hanging on those beautiful lips.

"Sweetheart, this night is mine just like you are. You're not in charge now. You do as I say, and I'll give you everything you want," he says in such a serious tone, my insides quiver.

"I'm yours," I whisper, not able to talk any louder because my voice would totally betray the need that's building inside me.

"You are mine," he repeats, and my cunt twitches in excitement. "Lift your arms."

I lift them immediately, and a moment later, the T-shirt I've been wearing is gone and discarded on the floor.

His gaze never leaves my eyes even if my tits are fully exposed. "Put your hands behind your back."

I move quickly, placing my arms behind my back, which also makes my tits stick out, moving them closer to him. "Like this?" I rasp, licking my lips.

"Just like that." He moves one hand behind my back, capturing my wrists between his fingers.

I feel naked. I mean, I am naked, and I've been naked in front of him before, but I feel completely and utterly exposed. His gaze leaves my face, traveling down my neck, before landing on my breasts.

"Sheer perfection," he murmurs.

My nipples instantly harden like they're begging for his fine-ass lips to be wrapped around them. No other man has ever been able to elicit such a reaction from me. I'm like a bitch in heat whenever Mammoth's around, willing to do whatever he asks.

I take a deep breath, trying to stay calm when my body's anything but. "Am I getting the full-on Mammoth treatment?"

He shakes his head as he shifts his legs outward, spreading mine wide open. "Not yet, princess. Soon, though."

I hold in the complaint that's hanging on my tongue. I want to see the man in action. See what all the fuss was about back at my grandmother's house. I've read shit. I've watched even more, but I've never experienced anything above average sex... Well, that was before Mammoth rocked my world.

He lifts his free hand, tracing my collarbone, gaze moving from my eyes to my skin and back. "Do you want to go to a club? Do you want to learn what it's all about?"

"Yes," I pant. "I want to know everything. I want to experience everything." His simple, featherlight touch sends goose bumps all over my skin, causing my nipples to harden even more like they're begging for a piece of the action.

"Let's see if you can follow basic commands. If you can, I'll think about taking you. There's a lot to absorb and learn, but I'm a patient man—if you're a very willing student."

"I'm willing."

God, am I willing. I want it all. I want all of him. Every piece and morsel, every ounce of sin and pleasure he's able to give me. I'm not sure I've ever wanted anything more than I do him now, in this moment, in this breath.

His eyes flash as soon as the word is out of my mouth, but I figured he'd like hearing it just as much as I liked saying it. "Good girl."

The warmth of his compliment, one a lesser man could never get away with, washes over me like never before. I bask in it, loving the way he makes me feel with such sweet words and the look of lust in his eyes. I want to please him, because I know in the end, he'll bring me pleasure too.

The hand near my collarbone traces a path between my breasts, to my navel, and slides between my legs. "Always so wet, princess," he murmurs as he leans forward, sinking his teeth into the fleshy part of my neck.

I nearly collapse from the pleasure, overcome by sensations of pain and pleasure as his fingers rake through my wetness. I tip my head back, giving him complete access, and move my hips forward, trying to get more.

"Greedy," he says into my neck before he takes his hand away, robbing my body of the contact. "Lesson number one, I give you pleasure. You do not take."

I'm about to apologize or possibly argue—because it's me—when his hand comes out of nowhere, slapping against my pussy and causing my body to shoot upward using nothing but the bottom of my legs against his. "Fuck," I hiss, feeling the sting between my legs as it ebbs and flows, finally coming to a simmer with an even more intense throb.

Before I can say another word, his fingers are back, but this time, they're against my clit, circling the now overly sensitive spot, still aching from the slap. "Give up yet? Want the light stuff, baby?"

I twist my fingers together, unable to move my hands still held captive in his grip. "No." Fuck no, this is intense. More intense than anything I've experienced in my life. And the slap against my pussy? It threw me for a loop, but goddamn, the way my body's on fire and my clit's pulsing like my heartbeat, all I want is more.

I glance down, seeing the smile on his lips as he moans into my skin. I can't take my eyes off him as his mouth moves down, down, until it's so close to my breasts, I can feel his warm breath caressing my flesh.

It takes everything in me not to rock against his fingers. Not to chase the pleasure his hands are giving. But I stay still. Captive in his grip, unmoving in his arms, and a wide-open, willing sexual toy in his lap.

He traces his tongue around my nipple, and I close my eyes as my pussy convulses, begging to be filled. As if by some unspoken miracle, his fingers that had been circling around my clit slide through my wetness again and press against my pussy.

Yes! I want to scream, beg, plead to be filled, but again, I stay silent. My feet dangle off the floor, and there's no part of my body that's grounded to anything except Mammoth.

When he finally closes his lips around my nipple, sucking hard, I gasp through the pleasure and relax into his touch, almost swaying backward, but his arm stops me. He holds me in place, open and available, as his fingers push inside me, filling me in the most delicious way.

He's gentle at first, the softness of his thrusts mingling with the hardness of his mouth against my breasts, but the ache is still prevalent and almost overwhelming in my clit from the earlier slap.

He slides his thumb against my clit again with each thrust in, and it disappears as he pulls out. Over and over again, driving my body upward and closer to the orgasm I so badly want and need. I'm gasping and panting as he sucks my nipple harder, using his teeth to change the sensation and biting down with just enough pressure to send a tingle of pain into the pleasurable mix.

I'm so close. So, so close, I'm straining, trying to find the floor with my feet, but I can't. My toes are too high off the floor, his legs too long for me to get any real traction. My greediness, as he'd call it, earns me a harder nip of his teeth against my nipples, making me cry out in pleasure and pain. Jesus fucking Christ. This is the most decadent mix of sensations, pushing me closer, feeling the air in my lungs evaporate as my skin dampens and my pussy spasms, begging for more.

Mammoth pulls his lips away, leaving my breasts wet and throbbing as he adds another finger to my pussy, thrusting in and out of me harder. "You like this?" he asks, his voice deep and needy.

"Yes!" I chant, wanting more. Needing more. "Yes! Yes!"

"Take my cock out," he says, releasing my wrists as he finger-fucks me.

It's not easy to work around his arms, but I do. My gaze moves to his face as soon as his cock is in my palm, hard and steely.

"Stroke me, princess. Show me how you'd fuck me."

I don't hesitate. My thumb slides up the bottom of his dick and over the sensitive spot I know drives every man wild. I don't get more than a few pumps in before his fingers leave my body again. "I want that sweet cunt fucking me instead of your hand. Get on the bed on all fours."

Yes! Fucking finally. I want nothing more than to be filled by his glorious prick covered in jewelry stroking my insides, pounding into me until I'm screaming in ecstasy. I move like my ass is on fire, hopping off his legs, climbing onto the bed on my knees, ass high in the air, waiting for that big dick to rock my freaking world.

He lines up behind me, but I keep my face forward, not daring to look because I'm not sure if I'm allowed. I'm not doing anything to mess this up. I'm wound so tight, the orgasm right there, just out of reach. I know a few powerful thrusts and that damn piercing hitting my G-spot will send me over the edge into an orgasm that'll rock my world and leave me dizzy and spent.

His hand is on my ass cheek, his thumb so close to the place I've never let any man go, I instantly tense. "Any man ever take you here?" he asks, lightly brushing his finger over my asshole.

"No," I whisper, unable to talk any louder. "Never."

"Want to be taken here?" he asks.

"I don't know," I answer honestly. I've heard ass play is great, but most of the guys I'd been with weren't even all that amazing with a vagina, so there was no way I was letting them near my ass. No freaking way. But with Mammoth, the possibility is there, and I have no doubt he'd make me feel good.

The bed dips and his hands disappear. I sneak a look behind me, watching as he pushes his pants down his legs, kicking them off to the side before reaching behind his back, lifting his T-shirt over his head. Seeing him naked, covered in piercings and tattoos, never gets old. I could stare at him forever and not once be bored, studying the lines and dips and ridges of his muscles.

He wraps his hand around his cock, stroking the length as my mouth waters, wishing I could wrap my lips around the swollen head. "Turn around and put your face against the mattress," he tells me.

I look at him funny for a second. When he doesn't move, just stares at me, I press my face sideways into the comforter, pushing my ass higher in the air and my pussy out, inviting him to enter.

I don't wait long before his hand is on my ass again and his cock is pushing into me, filling me. Inch by inch, he slides inside slowly, torturing me with the most delicious pleasure. He grips my hips, fingers biting into my flesh as he seats himself fully and stops. He leans over my back, bringing his mouth next to my ear. "I'm going to fuck you hard, princess. So hard you won't be able to breathe. If it becomes too much, tell me to stop. Understand?"

I lick my lips, salivating at the idea of him fucking me like a wild animal. "I understand." I seal my eyes shut as his tongue swipes across my cheek like he's tasting my flesh.

He moves his hips away from my body as his cock slides out of me. I tense, expecting him to slam into me immediately, but he doesn't. I open my eyes, careful not to turn around, but watch him the best I can to see what the hell he's doing. He moves his hands to mine, lifting them to the mattress and pulling me backward only slightly.

When he slams into me, I have nowhere to go. My pussy takes the full force of the thrust. He doesn't relent. Thrusting in, pulling out, pumping inside of me as I rise off him only an inch before I'm pulled backward by my arms and impaled on his cock.

I'm practically bouncing off him, mumbling words that make no sense as the climax I've been on the edge of for what feels like hours starts to build higher, root itself deeper. I cry out, unable to hold my tongue, screaming, "Yes!" This kind of pounding is something I could get used to and never go without.

He grunts, pumping harder, deeper as the piercing on the head of his cock strokes just the right spot to send me spiraling over the edge, unable to breathe, tears streaming down my face and... pissing myself?

I'm soaked.

The bed's soaked.

Everything below my waist is covered in wetness as my lungs empty and air seems to be something I can't get enough of. My body quivers, wave after wave of pleasure washing over me as my eyes roll back in my head. I don't have time to think or care that I may have just pissed all over him, and from the way he's pounding into me, grunting through the pleasure, cursing through each thrust, he doesn't care either.

I lie there limp, a prisoner to his hold as his strokes go deeper, turning faster and more frantic like he's chasing the orgasm as desperately as I was. A moment later, he howls. Fucking howls like a wild beast, throwing his front against my back, panting.

The only thing I can think in this moment is... I want more.

CHAPTER 19
MAMMOTH

THERE ARE things I always wanted in life but never had. Wanting a close and large family wasn't one of them. That was until I met the Gallos. Peeking into their lives, seeing the way they interacted with each other, made me want a sliver of that goodness in my world.

I never wanted anything much as a kid besides my father. My mother was amazing, but she couldn't replace the hole left in our small family by his death. It didn't matter to me if he was a hero or not; I missed out on a hell of a lot by not having him in my life, molding me, teaching me, showing me how to be a man.

I turned out okay even though we moved around a lot, my mother jumping from one job to another to keep the family afloat. Sure, she had his military death benefit, but in no way was it an easy ride for her being a single parent to my dumb ass. She always wanted the best for me. Best schools. Best clothes. Best toys. Maybe because she knew there was a void in my life and tried to fill that darkness with material things, hoping I wouldn't feel the pang of sadness about my father's missing presence.

The void lessened when I joined the service, but then opened back up, almost swallowing me whole after I left. The Disciples made me feel welcomed after that. It wasn't about the riding, the pussy, or the money. For me, being a member of the motorcycle club was more about the camaraderie and brotherhood above anything else.

But after meeting Tamara's family, watching how they interacted with one another, seeing how much they loved one another, I realized I wanted everything they had. I wanted that big family, filled with love and laughs, always knowing someone would have my back.

Two weeks ago, I left Tamara in her dorm room, promising her I'd be back as soon as I was able. I had a lot to work out in my head, in the club, and with my brothers. I'd played shit off, pretended like leaving the club would be easy, but I knew it rarely happened. And if someone was able to leave, they weren't often left breathing for long.

Princess: Are you coming tomorrow?

Me: Hell yeah.

I wouldn't miss her family reunion for anything in the goddamn world. Her parents tried to scare me, acting like her mother's side would be enough to send me packing, but they're wrong. They don't know what it's like to stare down the barrel of a gun, but I do. Between the army and the club, I've had more shit hurled my way in the past decade, and the last thing I am scared of is a family barbecue.

Princess: I've missed you.

Me: You too.

Fuck. I had too, and I'd never missed anyone in my life before she walked her fine ass into the club, a mess of hair and a wicked mouth. She was like a hurricane, changing the landscape around her, including me.

"Mammoth," Morris barks out across the room, taking my attention away from my phone and the conversation with Tamara. "In Church."

"You ready for this?" Eagle asks, standing across the bar from me, nursing a beer. "You might not be breathing tomorrow."

I set my glass on the bar top, staring back at Eagle. "It's a risk I'm willing to take."

"She's worth your life?"

I nod as I stand, ready to face Morris and Tiny. "She's worth every damn last breath."

Eagle's smile is immediate. "Never thought I'd see the day you'd go all stupid over a chick, man."

"Me either," I mutter as I jam my phone in my back pocket, ready to face whatever Morris and Tiny will throw my way about wanting to leave the club.

It's now or never. I can't start planning a future when I'm at a standstill. And that's what I am as a member of the Disciples. Unmoving. Not going anywhere in a hurry but to a cold jail cell someday because everyone gets popped eventually.

"Good luck," he tells me before lifting the beer back to his lips, swallowing whatever else he wants to say but doesn't.

Very few have ever gotten out of this life without ending up in jail, in the ground, or in witness protection… None of which are an option for me. I'd never rat out my brothers, but I sure as hell didn't want to end up in prison or dead. I want nothing more than to live life, love a good woman, and be part of a family I've never had.

If Tamara and I don't work out in the end, I'll be okay with that too. Leaving the club is the first step in getting my life back and putting myself on the right course for my future. It's now or never. If I don't make the break now, there'll be no escaping this world. I can't stay because Tamara isn't an old lady, and she'd never fit into this world no matter how hard she'd try.

All eyes are on me as I walk toward Church. Everyone in the club knows what I am going into the room to talk about. Secrets aren't easily kept, especially with this group and when they involve leaving the life.

When I enter, Morris and Tiny are seated at the end of the table, talking to each other, but their eyes are on me.

"Close the door and sit," Tiny tells me, dipping his chin toward the chair right in front of me.

I try to read their faces but fail. They're stone-cold, devoid of all emotion as I close the door, sealing us away inside the room where so much of our lives within the brotherhood is decided.

I sit as soon as the door closes, ready to fight for my future. I'll do whatever they ask, within reason, as long as it gets me my freedom in the end.

"Morris said you wanted to talk about the future," Tiny says, rubbing his beard as he speaks. "So, we're here. Talk."

I lean forward, placing my clasped hands on the table, staring straight at them and say, "I want out."

Tiny leans back, tilting his head, staring right back. "Completely?"

I nod, and Morris leans over, whispering something in Tiny's ear as Tiny keeps his gaze pinned on me. I don't dare look away or fidget. Not when sitting in front of these two, looking for my freedom. They know weakness. They can spot it a mile away. They also know me, having found me six years ago after I left the military.

"Why?" Tiny asks when Morris moves away from his ear.

"I want to start a business and move to the other coast."

"Fucker," Morris mutters under his breath, shaking his head. "The girl got to you. Didn't she?"

"Reality got to me, and the girl a little too." I'm being honest with them. Sure, Tamara's part of the reason, but not all of it. I never planned on staying here forever. I've never stuck to one place for too long and never saw myself changing in that way either.

Morris sighs, cracking his neck like I'm causing him physical discomfort. "Gallo girls are all the same. They twist your brains and dicks. The lot of you. Pike and now you run straight into their arms and never look back."

"I've been thinking about this for a while. You know my past.

I've always been searching for something, trying to fill the void I've had since I was a kid."

Morris nods like he understands, but Tiny, the bastard, doesn't move a muscle.

"I've loved being part of the brotherhood, but I think it's time for me to move on, spread my wings, find my place in this world."

"You think we're just going to let you walk out that door, wave us goodbye, and disappear?" Tiny asks, eyes narrowed, looking like the callous bastard I know he can be.

"I hope, but I'll do whatever you need me to do to make it happen," I tell them, knowing there's always a price.

Nothing in life is free, even freedom.

"All this trouble for some pussy," Tiny says, shaking his head, judging me and assuming I'm weak.

I'm the furthest thing from weak. But I'm also not stupid. Finding a good woman, someone who can make me laugh and piss me off within a second of each other, is something I'm not willing to let pass by. I know she could never be in this life. Her family wouldn't allow it, and I wouldn't feel safe.

"Give us some time to discuss how to handle this, and we'll call you back in. Letting someone leave, especially you, has consequences and comes with a cost."

"I'm aware," I say before standing and exiting the room, while they sit in silence, staring at my back, waiting for me to close the door.

Eagle's waiting for me at the bar, still nursing the same beer. "And?"

"And nothing," I tell him as I slide back onto the barstool I'd been sitting on before Morris called me into Church. "They're discussing my future."

Eagle nods slowly, smiling at me. "Well, that's a good sign. They could've shot you in the head and ended the discussion right there."

When he puts it that way, I suppose it is a good sign. I didn't walk into Church thinking they'd kill me, but the possibility was there. I wouldn't have been the first man killed within these walls, and I sure as fuck wouldn't have been the last either.

"I hate feeling like I need permission to move on with my life. It's like being in the army but worse," I grumble, leaning over the bar to grab the beer I know he has stowed in the wings for his next round.

"You knew that was what you were signing up for. You weren't signing a contract with Uncle Sam. You took a different oath. A deadlier and more long-term one than you did for the army, man. If you didn't want this life forever, why the hell did you prospect and even get involved?"

I twist off the cap, flicking the metal into the trash can behind the bar, making the shot like I'd done it a million times. "My head wasn't right back then. Shit was all mixed up, and I was lost. The military life fucks with you, and then when you're out, you're out. It's a clean break. A life you've known for years just vanishes. The family you had is gone in a flash. I was searching for something, anything really, when I found you guys. If I had been thinking right, I wouldn't have joined. But I was pretty fucked up."

"Still are," he mumbles with a smile. "Fucked up for that fine piece of ass. Just like the other ones. There's something about those girls."

"I've never felt this way about anyone before, Eagle," I admit, rarely ever sharing my feelings because the guys here never talk about that shit.

Eagle's different. He's always been my friend. Someone I could share things with without judgment. The same goes for him. We were a team within the club, but I hadn't even taken him into consideration and how my leaving would affect him.

"I'm sorry I'm leaving you behind. You know you're my best friend here. Someone I know will always have my back."

"You chase your happiness, kid. I'm fucking happy here. I have no family, no kids. Without this club, I don't have much. Just because you're leaving doesn't mean I'll cut you out of my life. I'm sure we'll share another beer together unless they..."

"Yeah." I lift the beer to my lips, downing half the bottle because, goddamn, I may not get out of here alive. The possibility is real, even if I want to pretend it's not on the table. I took an oath, a pledge to these men, and now I'm breaking it.

My phone vibrates in my pocket, probably a text from Tamara, but I ignore it. There's too much happening, and my head's not in the right place right now to talk to her. I want to be able to tell her I have an answer before we speak again.

A moment later, Eagle's phone goes off, and my gaze dips to the screen, seeing Pike's name flashing.

"Well, this should be interesting," he says before grabbing the phone and tapping the screen. "Yo." Eagle's gaze is fixed on me as Pike speaks for over a minute. "I think you better talk to Mammoth about this shit."

My eyebrows rise and my heart starts to pound as I tighten my grip around the bottle. "Talk to me about what?"

"Here." Eagle gives me the phone before lifting his hands and excusing himself from the spot behind the bar. "It's not my business or my chick."

"What's up?" I ask Pike, holding Eagle's phone up to my ear, ignoring the growing knot in my stomach.

"I tried calling your dumb ass, but you didn't answer."

"Kind of in the middle of something, Pike. Spit it out. I'm meeting with Morris and Tiny."

"It's Tamara."

"What about her?"

"She's going to see Crow today before they ship his ass out of state to start serving his time."

I rock backward on my stool like I've been punched straight in the face. "She what?"

"I overheard Gigi talking to her. I guess Crow called and wanted to talk to her, apologize for the shit that happened, and asked her to visit him before he leaves. I thought you should know."

"Motherfucker."

"She's on her way to Gainesville, maybe. I think that's what I heard. I have no idea where he's being held right now. I'm hours away, or I'd stop her."

"I'll handle her and Crow," I bite out, tasting the bile that's rising in the back of my throat.

"Take it easy on her. She doesn't understand things like the club."

"She should know loyalty, though."

"She's loyal, Mammoth. As loyal as they come, but when she has a friend in need, she'll do anything she can to help him too."

"A friend?" I let out a bitter laugh. "Crow's no one's friend."

"They had a connection that day. Not a sexual one. I told him I'd murder him before I'd let him touch her. You just need to explain the way she's fucked up by going to see him, without at least letting you know she was doing it."

"I'll finish with Tiny and Morris and head that way."

"Good luck, and don't be too hard on her."

Hard on her? She'll be lucky if she can sit for a week after pulling shit like this. I've been too easy on her. I didn't lay the proper groundwork for our relationship. She needs rules, guidance, and boundaries, and I'm just the man to give them to her.

"Later, Pike," I say before disconnecting the call, not needing him to mother me on how to treat women.

"That's pretty fucked up, brother. You may get yourself killed over this chick who's going to visit Crow. How well do you know her? Can you really trust her?" Eagle asks as he takes the phone back from my death grip.

"Mammoth," Morris calls out, but his tone is even and unreadable.

"Fuck," I hiss again, wondering if this day is about to go from shittastic to completely fucked up.

"If you die, it was great knowing ya, man," Eagle tells me, and he's completely serious.

"You too," I say, moving away from the bar, my entire body tight and my mind reeling with nothing but images of Crow's face and my girl sitting across from him.

I march into Church, pissed off, ready for whatever's coming. Tiny and Morris are already back in their spots at the head of the table, staring at me with those fucking unreadable faces.

"We've talked." Morris gestures to the same seat, wanting my ass in it. "We've also come to a decision."

I move into the seat, fisting my hand tightly on top of my knee out of sight. The anger that's coursing through me, anger at Crow and Tamara, is so strong, I'm ready to fucking punch anyone and anything, including the two men sitting in front of me.

"We can't let you go," Tiny says first, swiping his index finger across the wooden table where all the major club decisions are made.

"Not completely," Morris adds when my back stiffens and I'm just about to tell them both to fuck off. "But we've come up with a compromise."

"When were you planning on leaving?" Tiny asks.

"About nine months."

"She knocked up?" is his reply.

I shake my head. "It's when she graduates."

"You're ours for the next nine months. After that, you'll be available to us when needed. If we want to move something on your coast, you'll move it. If we need something taken care of over there, you'll make it happen," Tiny explains. "You'll be free of the compound, but nothing more. If we decide to open a chapter over there, you'll be a member."

"Done," I say because at least they're giving me an out, even though it's a small one. All I care about right now is finding Tamara and figuring out what the fuck's happening with Crow. "That it?"

"That's it, kid," Morris tells me as I stand again, ready to get the fuck out of there. "Where you headed in a hurry?"

"I got to go see about a girl," I tell them, marching out of the room, heading straight toward my bike.

CHAPTER 20
TAMARA

THE ROOM IS EXACTLY like I've seen on television. We, the free people, are all lined up, phones to the side, with the inmates on the other side of the glass. There's a coldness to the space. The walls are covered in matte gray paint, and the white linoleum tile looks like it hasn't been cleaned in weeks. I don't even want to think about the phones and the hundreds of people who've touched them since the last time they were sanitized.

I don't know what I'm doing here. The last time I saw Crow's face, I wanted to give him the biggest black eye. He treated me like a piece of shit, turning me out like I was trash. But when he called today, confessing that he was being shipped out of state to serve time in prison and asked to see me, I couldn't refuse him.

How could someone? Even if the guy was an asshole when I last saw him, what guy isn't an asshole at some point? He and I, we had a connection of some sort. A friendship, maybe, that I read wrong, blowing it up into something bigger in my head. It doesn't matter now. He is about to serve hard time.

My family could forgive a lot. They were those types of people. They knew everyone messed up at some point, but if things were different and I hadn't met Mammoth, I know they wouldn't have accepted me pining over a guy serving prison time.

I fidget in my seat, toying with the edge of my skirt, unable to sit still because I can hear the whispers around me filled with sadness and tears. Girlfriends and wives have come to see their other halves, unable to touch them for God knows how long.

As if out of nowhere, Crow's standing on the other side of the glass, wearing standard prison orange, hands in cuffs, looking nothing like the man I'd been flirting with just a few weeks ago. He's flanked by a prison guard, who pushes Crow into the empty seat before starting to unlock his handcuffs. Crow's gaze is locked on me and filled with something I've never seen there before. Sadness.

He ticks his chin toward the phone on my side before reaching for the one to his right. My lip quivers, sorrow overcoming me because whether I'm mad at him or not, seeing someone taken down and held captive is a hard pill to swallow.

He gives me a soft smile as I lift the phone and bring the receiver to my ear. "Hey, beautiful," he says so sweetly, he sounds like the Crow I flirted with not too long ago.

"Hey," I reply, not willing to give him any compliments, especially after the way he treated me.

"Thanks for coming."

I look down when the reality of where we are and what's about to happen to him hit me. "I figured we had things we needed to say to each other." I lift my face, staring into his eyes, and tighten my grip around the phone. "A chapter we needed to close."

"I knew this was going to happen."

"What?"

"I knew I was going to be serving time, and not just a little time, but more years than I could ever ask you to wait."

"You could've told me. I wasn't looking for a relationship, Crow. I didn't want to be your old lady. I thought we could have a little fun. That's it. You didn't have to turn me away like an asshole."

He nods like he understands while his gaze sweeps over my face as if he's trying to memorize every detail. "I couldn't, babe. Couldn't have a taste and then nothing at all. A greedier man would've taken that. Would've taken your sweetness and stolen it, pulling from those memories to get through the shit years ahead. But I couldn't."

"You wouldn't have stolen anything since I was going to give it to you freely. I could've handed you some memories to relive over and over again while you're there."

Crow scoots forward, bringing his face closer to the glass and directly underneath the dim overhead light. It's the first real glimpse I've had of him since he sat down. He looks like shit. His once soulful eyes are framed by dark circles and a few lines I hadn't noticed before. It's like he aged overnight. "I promised Pike I'd never touch you, but goddamn it, babe, you sure as fuck made it hard on me."

"Fuck Pike," I hiss, moving closer too, trying to hide away in the cubicle so I can try to forget there's a room full of people around us. "He's an asshole."

Crow shakes his head. "He's not, kid. He's solid. He's only looking out for you, and a man doesn't do that unless he loves and respects a woman. Cut him some slack. He was just trying to save you from heartbreak later."

"Heartbreak?" I snort, shaking my head. "Crow, babe, you're hot and I'm pretty sure we would've fucked like bunnies, but I wasn't falling in love with you."

He raises an eyebrow like I'm full of shit, but I know the truth. "I just wanted a good time. I didn't want forever."

"I would've ruined you for any other man, sweetheart." He smirks like he actually believes his own shit.

"How long are you going away?"

"Seven years. Maybe five if I get early release." Somehow, he answers without so much as a twitch.

"Seven fucking years?" I repeat, trying to even think back seven years. I was fourteen and in high school. Seven years is a long damn time, especially to be locked away with no escape.

Crow nods slowly, gaze still moving around my face and slipping to my breasts. "It is. Could've been more, but I pleaded down to a lesser charge for a lighter sentence."

"What the hell did you do?"

"Killed a man," he says like he's talking about the weather.

My eyes widen, and for a moment, I can't breathe. I flirted with this man. I was going to sleep with him, adding him to the notches on my bedpost. I never thought to ask him about his criminal record and most certainly not if he'd ever offed a man before. I lean forward and drop my voice. "You killed someone?"

He shrugs. "He wasn't just someone. He was an asshole and deserved what he got."

"Seven years for killing someone?"

"We were fighting. I didn't set out to kill him, but it happened. So, since it wasn't premeditated, I got seven years if I'd forgo trial."

"If it was an accident, why didn't you fight? I mean seven years seems like it would feel like for-fucking-ever behind bars."

"Babe, when a man has a record as long as mine, you realize which battles you can win and which ones you can't. I was going to prison, no matter what. Why fight something that was inevitable? All I could do was control how long my ass would be rotting in a shithole like this."

"It seems unfair," I whisper.

"Life's unfair, babe."

"Yeah."

"If it were fair, I'd be out there, sinking between those beautiful legs instead of that asshole Mammoth."

I cringe when he says his name. I didn't tell Mammoth I was coming here. I knew he'd be pissed, and even though I knew I should've at least mentioned I was making the trip, I still didn't bother to open that can of worms. I'll tell him tomorrow and deal with the consequences of his disappointment or maybe anger. But Crow was a friend. Sure, I showed up at the compound looking for him and not Mammoth, but I most certainly ended up with the right man.

"What's wrong with Mammoth?" I lift my chin, feeling the need to defend the man who's not here to defend himself.

"He doesn't deserve you."

"And you do?" I cross one arm over my chest, twisting my lips to stop myself from saying anything more.

He lifts his hand, the wings on his skin on full display before he pushes his fingers back through his hair. "I don't." He blows out a long, ragged breath. "I'm a complete piece of shit, but he doesn't deserve you either. You should stay away from a man like him, babe. You're too strong for him. You're too badass to be kept down by a controlling pervert like him."

"Controlling pervert?" I raise an eyebrow. I'm pretty sure both of those words could be used to describe Crow and just about every man on the planet.

"He's into some kinky shit. Some shit you wouldn't be into. I don't want to see you get hurt."

"Now you're concerned for my safety?"

Crow looks around before there's a muffled voice in the background of his line I can't quite make out. "I only have a minute or two left. So, let me talk, and you just listen."

I nod because there's no time for a smartass reply, and I'll never see him again. At least not for another five years at a minimum.

"I'm sorry I was a jerk. I'm sorry if I hurt your feelings. I'm sorry I turned you away that night. I'm sorry for so many things when it comes to you. I'm sorry I listened to Pike and didn't take what you were offering, but I want you to know..." He covers the receiver and yells something across the room before locking eyes with me again. "I never meant to hurt you, Tamara. Write me sometime, kid. Remind me of the good things in life. Can you do that?"

I nod as tears start to fill my eyes. I don't know why I'm crying. It's not like we had a *thing*. He was an acquaintance at best, and we only spent a handful of hours together, but I still feel bad for him. "I will, Crow. I'll write to you."

He slides back in his chair before standing. "Fuckin' Mammoth." He shakes his head as he gives his hands to the prison guard. "That asshole doesn't deserve you, babe. When you see that side of him I'm worried about start to come out, you run, babe. Run far."

I blink, washing away my tears as Crow's hands are bound with metal and he warns me about Mammoth like he's the crazy, murderous type instead of Crow.

Crow lifts his chin, giving me a sweet smile. "Bye, doll. Until next time." He throws a wink at me.

"Bye," I say as I stand and wave at him.

His orange-clothed back disappears through a door. He doesn't look back. Doesn't give me anything else. Just the apology and a warning about Mammoth being a kinky asshole, which I already knew.

Mammoth is going to be a very pissed-off kinky asshole after he finds out I came here, to the prison, without so much as mentioning the trip. Especially since I was visiting Crow and the two had history together. It wasn't like I had to tell Mammoth every time I visited a friend because I certainly didn't know everything he was doing or who he was doing at the compound.

"Ma'am," a lady says near the doorway I'd walked through earlier. "It's time to go." She smiles when I look her way, still in shock over seeing Crow like that, knowing I'd never see him again.

Even when he got out, we'd still have nothing in common. No reason to be friends. We didn't run in the same circles or live in the same town. Even if I were still with Mammoth then, the two of them did not like each other. That much was clear.

I follow the line of people through the dingy waiting room, everyone wiping the tears from their faces but me. Thank God nothing happened between Crow and me. I wouldn't want this to be my life, my future, my world. But then there's Mammoth. He's a member of the same club as Crow. Being with him, am I risking the same inevitable heartbreak?

I squint as the sunshine hits my face, and I start toward my car in the parking lot. I'm staring at the ground, pondering what could've been and what could be. A long, thick shadow covers the ground, the outline of a bike attached, and my heart stops. I snap my head up, finding Mammoth resting against the seat of his bike, eyes locked on me. He doesn't say a word. He just stares at me with those icy gray eyes.

"Hey, baby," I say, trying to keep the worry out of my voice.

His arms are crossed over his massive chest, and the look on his face says it all. He's pissed. Not just a little upset, but so angry, I'm wondering if his promise of an ass spanking is going to happen and soon. "Princess."

I keep walking, careful not to miss a step or pretend like I was caught doing something I wasn't supposed to do. "Whatcha doing here?"

"I was just about to ask you the same thing." His eyes bore into me, making my belly flip, and not in the way that makes me want to jump into his arms and right onto his dick.

There are a few feet between us. Not enough space for him to touch me because although I trust him, I've never seen him this mad. I lift my chin and give him my best poker face. "Crow wanted to apologize before he left. Figured I'd let him say his piece, I'd say mine, and there'd be nothing left unspoken."

He studies me for a moment, eyes sweeping down my face to my body, soaking in the very tame outfit I'd picked out just for this occasion. I wasn't going to come in an overly sexy outfit. This was Crow, but by no means did I want to send him the wrong signal. "We need to talk. Some lines were crossed."

I move my hand to my hip as I scrunch my nose. "Lines were crossed?"

He nods with a scowl. "We made promises to each other, and you've already broken one. My word is my bond, my promise, my law, but what's your word?"

"Are you for real?" I ask, my eyes wide as I throw a hand toward the cold, brick building behind me. "I came here to say goodbye. Not to fuck the man. He's nothing but a friend, and as with any friend, when they ask for my help or for me to visit, I do what friends do." I glare at him, ready to spank his ass if need be. "I show the fuck up!"

Mammoth's off his bike, stalking toward me as I start to back up, retreating from his towering presence. But my legs are shorter and his stride is longer. He's on me in an instant, reaching out to touch my face, and I flinch. "Princess," he says, but this time more softly. "I'm not mad you're here. I'm not even mad it's Crow you came to see." His palm is on my cheek, gently cradling my face in his hand. "I'm more concerned you didn't even bother to tell me where you were going. Our relationship is nothing without communication and trust. Without communication, there can't be any real trust either. I don't want to be in a relationship where I can't trust you to be honest."

"I'm sorry. I figured you'd tell me no."

"I'm not going to run your entire life. When you're going to do something that may hurt you or us, I'll speak up, but a little faith in my ability not to be an angry asshole would be nice. But there will be consequences for this," he says with a hint of a smile on his face.

I swallow roughly, gripping his T-shirt between my fingers. "Consequences?"

His thumb moves across my jaw, grazing underneath my bottom lip. "I'll follow you back to your place. I'll grab a hotel room nearby, and we'll head to the reunion tomorrow. We'll finish this conversation there."

"Um," I mumble, thinking maybe this was a bad idea. "You don't have to come. I'm sure you're a busy man."

"I'm coming, princess. I promised your family I'd be there, and trust me, there's no punishment without a reward."

My eyebrows rise. "So, then how is that a punishment?"

"You'll see," he says, brushing his lips against mine before taking a step back. "I'll be right behind you."

"Okay," I whisper, my head dizzy from all the wicked possibilities along with fear.

But this is Mammoth. He's never been anything but generous when it comes to pleasure. I just hope he isn't as generous with the punishment.

CHAPTER 21
MAMMOTH

"COME HERE." I pat my leg, sitting on the edge of the bed, watching Tamara as she fidgets nervously.

Tamara twists her hands in front of her, staring at me from under her eyelashes. "Do we really have to do this?"

I nod. "We're just going to talk, but I don't want you all the way over there when we do it."

"You aren't going to spank me?" she whispers.

"Not yet," I answer honestly. "Not until we talk, get shit straight, and come to an agreement. Now, come here."

She's in my lap a moment later, her hands gliding along my bare chest until her fingers find my piercings. "I'm sorry," she says for the tenth time since she spotted me outside the jail.

"I know." I move my hands to her waist, turning her so we're eye-to-eye for the conversation we need to have. I've always lived life by a code and a set of rules, keeping shit simple. Gray areas have never been my thing. They leave too much to be misinterpreted. "It's okay, princess. You can stop apologizing."

"Why do we have to talk?" she whispers, glancing downward like she's embarrassed.

I tip her chin up, wanting nothing more than to look into those beautiful hazel eyes. "You have one year of college left."

"Nine months," she corrects me before biting down on her lip like I'm going to be pissed she interrupted.

"Nine months." I give her a small smile, brushing my thumb across her cheek, trying to ease her nerves. "Do you want your freedom for those nine months?"

Her eyebrows draw down immediately, and her nose wrinkles. "My freedom?"

"Yeah. Maybe you don't want to be in a relationship right now. Maybe we're moving too fast. Hell, we've only known each other a few weeks."

She shakes her head. "It feels longer."

"Is that a good thing or bad?" I ask with a hint of laughter to my voice.

"Good," she adds, smiling her beautiful smile. "I feel like I've known you forever, or at least, I don't want to remember a time you weren't in my life."

I tighten my grip on her hip. "Me too, Tam, me too. But I'd also understand if you don't want to be in a committed relationship too. You're still so young. Maybe too young to be saddled down by an old asshole like me."

"You're young," she lies, running her fingers over my pecs until her hands are on my shoulders.

"Don't bullshit me, sweetheart. You're the young one. I don't think at twenty-one I would've been ready to settle down. Hell, at thirty, I didn't think I was ready until I met you."

"I don't want anyone else, Mammoth. Only you."

"Then we need honesty and transparency in all things."

She raises an eyebrow. "All things?"

"All things."

She blinks, chewing on the side of her lip for a few seconds before she asks, "Like what?"

I flatten my palm against her back, holding her closely, leaving very little space between us. "I talked to Morris and Tiny. I have to stay with the Disciples for the next nine months. Even after that, I won't be completely out. I'll still be on the hook with them in some fashion until they no longer have a use for me. Can you live with that?"

"I think so." She swallows as her lips turn down at the corners. "Does that mean you're going to be doing illegal things?"

I shrug and stick with honesty. "I don't know what they're going to have me do. I can't promise to walk the straight and narrow as long as they have their claws in me, princess."

"I couldn't stomach visiting you in jail like I did with Crow. It would rip my heart out, Mammoth. Totally and completely devastate me."

"I won't end up like him. That, I can promise you."

"How?"

"Just trust me. I promise you'll never have to visit me behind bars."

Her gaze dips again, and she scoots her bottom half closer, right over my dick. "While we're on the honesty train... Can you promise me, I mean really promise me, you're not going to fuck Sadie or anyone else? I mean, can you go weeks without sex?"

"Can you go weeks without sex?" I throw back because I may be a man, but I'm not a nymphomaniac.

"Of course."

I brush a few strands of her hair away from her face and behind her cheek. "If you need my cock, just ask, and I'll be here. Same goes for me. If I need you, I expect you to be open to a visit."

"Can I come to the compound, or is it off-limits to me?"

"You can come to the compound whenever you want."

She smiles. "There's not a lot of privacy here." She jerks her head to the roommate's shit that's all over the place like a squatter has moved in, taking over the place.

"The compound isn't private, but at least I have my own room."

"And about what was in your trunk..."

"You want to play, baby? We can play."

Her cheeks flush. "I wanna play."

She knows the magic words. The ones that set me on fire. "Want the full Mammoth treatment?"

"Can we do a trial and see how it goes? I mean, I'm interested in trying everything once. I've never been a pussy."

I laugh, loving that she's so willing and eager. "We can try it, and if it's too much or you want to dial it back, we'll adjust. Or hell, I'll try to adjust for you."

"Can we go to a sex club? Please," she begs.

I laugh harder. "Of course."

"Then, hell yeah, I'm all about this."-She waggles her eyebrows. "'Cause that shit's hot as fuck."

"Don't think this is going to be easy or fun and games, Tamara. I'm not easy. I don't put up with shit like the stunt you pulled today. Going to see Crow would've been a hard limit."

"Well," she announces, sitting up straighter, pushing her beautiful cunt against my cock. "My hard limit is Sadie and just about every bitch at the compound. No talking to, touching, or texting any of them."

"Done," I say quickly. "I never did any of that anyway."

"If you go to a club, you can't go without me...ever."

"Not an issue. Now let's talk about your sexual hard limits. They're important. The entire relationship is built on trust and communication. Other than today, we've had that, but I need for you to be totally open about sex with me. Can you do that?"

She smiles. "Talk about sex?"

"Yeah."

"For sure." She winks. "It's my favorite subject, especially when it involves you."

"I'm going to give you a list to look over, and then we'll talk about each item before we start exploring your sexuality and limits."

"Mammoth..."

"What, princess?"

"We need to pick safe words, right?"

"Not so newbie now, are you?"

She laughs with an innocent shrug. "I know a little, mostly from sexy books I used to steal from my aunt Izzy."

"Why am I not surprised? But yes, we need safe words. What do you want to use for stop?"

"Um." She nibbles on her lips, searching my eyes. "Stop?"

I shake my head. "It has to be something you wouldn't say by accident during sex. Like pineapple. Something you'll remember."

"Hmm, not pineapple. It's too long. How about boat?"

"Boat, it is. And what about if something is happening you're unsure about, or I'm reaching your limit?"

She looks upward, like she's searching deep for the answer. "Spoon."

"Spoon works too. So, boat means stop, and spoon is a warning, mostly for me to make sure we're on the same page."

"Now," she says, sliding her hands back down my chest to my crotch. "Can we start? I'm anxious. I want to learn how to kneel right. I know Aunt Izzy does this. I've heard my family whispering about it. My aunts seem almost jealous at times."

"Sometimes giving up control can be the most freeing thing of all," I tell her, patting her on the ass until she climbs off.

Her eyes widen. "That's what my aunt says too."

"We're about to find out, princess. Take off your clothes," I tell her, watching her every movement and facial expression, making sure she's willing and not just trying to make me happy.

She pulls her tank top over her head, dropping it to the floor next to her feet before she reaches behind her back, undoing her bra with one hand.

I sit, watching in fascination, having missed every inch of her body after being apart for a week. I hadn't forgotten how beautiful she is. There is no way that could ever happen. But seeing her flesh, touching her skin, kissing her lips, slams home the reality of how much she has me hooked. How badly I want every inch of her body and her mind.

She keeps her eyes on me as she unbuttons her jean shorts, slowly lowering the zipper, exposing her completely bare mound. My mouth instantly waters as the memory of her sweetness slams into me like a ton of bricks.

"On your knees."

She licks her lips as her breathing slows, and her pupils dilate as I climb to my feet in front of her naked body, somehow resisting the overwhelming urge to touch her.

"Remember your safe words, and say them as soon as you need to. Don't let me go beyond because it'll break the trust and set us back."

She nods, staring at me, looking like she's about to jump into my arms and fuck me.

"Now, kneel." I push down on her shoulders when she blinks, shocked at the sternness in my tone.

She bends over, kneeling in front of me. "Like this?" she asks, head tipped back, already forgetting one of the rules.

I reach forward and pinch her nipple hard enough to get her attention, but not with so much force she'd cry. I'd sucked on them enough, had my teeth on them, too, to know her pain and pleasure limit. "No talking," I remind her, twisting my fingertips until she sucks in a breath and her back straightens.

She nods in response, and I take a knee in front of her, manipulating her body into the perfect kneeling stance, showing her how I want her to present herself to me. "Like this," I say, running the backs of my fingers from one knee, across her core, to her other knee, causing her to shudder. "Open to me. Always open to me."

I push on her shoulders, straightening her posture and placing her arms so her hands are resting near her knees. She stares at me, studying my face as I maneuver her body.

"Getting into this position with grace will take some time and practice, but I know you'll do it, princess. Now..." I stand, gazing down at her beautiful body, open and waiting as I step closer, bringing my crotch to her face. "Undo my pants." Without hesitation, she reaches for my pants, making quick work of the button and zipper. "Take out my cock." The sex kitten's hand is in my pants, fingers wrapped around my dick, fishing it out of my pants like she's starving and my cock is her next meal.

"Put your hands behind your back and lock your fingers together."

Her eyebrows draw down for a moment before her face goes blank and her hands go to where I've instructed her. She looks so beautiful like this. More beautiful than anyone I've ever seen in my life. Tits pushed out, waiting for me to play. Body on full display. Pussy glistening, already dripping with need. Fuck. I don't know what I did to be such a lucky son of a bitch, but whatever it was, I hope I did enough to earn this woman forever.

I fist my cock, stroking the shaft, paying close attention to the way her eyes light up as she watches every movement. She's into watching. A voyeur, maybe. It's something we'll address at a later date once I get her safely within the walls of a club I feel comfortable enough to bring her to.

I move forward until my cock is almost pressing against her lips and aching for her soft warmth. "Open your mouth."

She complies without hesitation, parting her sweet lips, eyes on me and blazing with need as she sticks out her tongue, offering me her mouth.

I breathe deeply, trying not to let her see how much she affects me as I place the head of my cock on her tongue before slowly pushing deep into her mouth. I nearly rock backward when my cock hits the back of her throat and she doesn't so much as gag but almost smiles around my cock as she closes her lips around my shaft.

Reaching down, I tweak her nipple between my fingers, feeling her moan against my cock as her eyes close. She likes it. She likes it rougher than I ever imagined, but I shouldn't be surprised; she's a wildcat, plain and simple.

I could stand here all day, fucking her mouth, playing with her tits, but I know her roommate will be back in an hour, and there're so many things I want to do with Tamara and to her. I want to fuck her, make her feel me there, buried deep for days.

A few more thrusts and I rock backward, letting my cock fall from her lips completely. Her eyes fly open, but I touch her cheeks, trying to alleviate any anxiety. "On the bed, princess. Face in the mattress, ass in the air, pussy out."

Like the greedy little tiger she is, she's quick to move and get into position. We'll have to work on grace, but hell, I'm a happy man.

"Wider," I tell her, wanting her pussy wide open as I bend forward, placing my face in front of its beauty. "Hold your ass cheeks open."

She pauses, but when I swat the side of her thigh, she moves quickly, grabbing her ass and parting her cheeks. There's a quick intake of air from the top of the bed, but she bites down on her lip, stopping herself from saying what she's thinking. "Boat or spoon?" I ask, soothing the spot of skin I'd just swatted.

She doesn't answer.

Good girl.

"Answer me, Tamara. Boat or spoon?"

"Neither."

I place a hand on each hip, caging her arms against her legs as I lean forward, running my tongue through her wetness, getting my first taste of Tamara in a week. And sweet Jesus. She's just as delicious and glorious as I remembered.

She squeaks, squirming as I bury my entire face between her legs, my nose practically in her asshole, but who gives a fuck.

Sex is sex.

Holes are holes.

A body is meant to be worshiped.

And I plan on having her everywhere. I'll know every inch of her body within a short time, making sure there isn't a patch that's untouched or a spot that isn't mine.

I hold her tight, dragging my tongue through her folds, across her pussy, and right along her backside. She nearly melts into the mattress, back bowing deeper, lifting her ass to my lips like she wants more.

I slide my tongue higher, over the small of her back, following the line of her spine to her neck. I move my mouth near her ear, leaning my body over hers until my entire front is plastered against her back. "I want to claim you everywhere, princess. Even here," I say, touching my finger to her asshole and circling the rim. "Do you want that?"

Her asshole contracts against the pad of my finger. "Yes," she whispers, sealing her eyes shut.

"Soon, princess. I'll use my fingers tonight, go slow, and see if you like the sensation. Remember to use your safe words if it becomes too much."

"Yes."

"Hands down and at your sides," I tell her, wanting nothing in the way of her pussy and my cock.

As soon as her hands are on the mattress, I push down on the middle of her back, causing her ass to rise higher. With one hand, I hold her hips upward, taking some of the pressure off her until she gets used to the position. With the other, I run the head of my cock through her wetness, coating my skin before I thrust in deep and hard, in one single stroke.

Her body rocks forward, the impact of my pelvis slamming in, and pushing her forward on the mattress. She gasps but otherwise remains silent until my thumb finds her asshole, pressing lightly against the tiny opening.

I spit on her ass, letting my saliva slide down to her hole, covering my finger. On the next thrust, I push the tip of my finger against her ass, letting her muscles relax and move until I'm barely inside. Her ass tightens and loosens, over and over again with each pump until the entire tip of my thumb is inside her up to the first knuckle.

Not even a whimper escapes her lips as I deepen the strokes and pull my thumb out before pushing back inside, sliding a little farther. Her entire body shudders from being filled with my cock and fingers. Double penetration is an entirely different feeling. A heightened level of pleasure she doesn't seem the least bit put off by, and the thought of all the possibilities sends a thrill down my spine.

I pull my thumb out of her ass but keep pounding into her in a steady rhythm. Lifting my hand to my mouth, I lick my index, coating it with spit, ready to see if she can handle deeper penetration.

She lets out a moan as soon as I touch her asshole again, pushing my index finger inside, fucking her ass. She groans, and her mouth hangs open, drool pooling on the mattress near her lips.

I'm pounding into her. When my dick's moving out of her sweet cunt, my finger's pushing into her tight ass, and vice versa, creating a whole new level of sensation. Her body shudders, her insides quiver, and she moans louder with each pass and swipe of my cock and fingers on her insides.

Within minutes, I can't hold back, thrusting harder until her body inches forward with each push and our bodies are covered in sweat. She screams through an orgasm, her cunt and ass squeezing my cock and fingers, milking me through each wave and crest of pleasure until she is gasping for air. I follow, unable to stop the orgasm from ripping through me before I collapse on top of her, our bodies sticking together.

"Just perfect, princess. Completely perfect," I whisper in her ear, barely getting the words out as I try to catch my breath.

She hums her agreement, unable to move—or maybe not sure if she should. The only thing I know for sure in this moment is I am right where I was always meant to be.

CHAPTER 22
MAMMOTH

"I SEE YOU CAME," Mrs. Gallo says, watching me as we walk up the walkway to Tamara's grandma's front porch.

I know she's talking about the reunion, but all I can think about is the countless orgasms I've given Tamara since yesterday.

"Of course, Mrs. Gallo. I wouldn't miss this for anything in the world," I tell her, holding Tamara by the waist, speaking before she can answer, or maybe speaking in her place.

Her mother studies me before her gaze moves to Tamara. "Why aren't you speaking?"

I squeeze her side, giving her the cue to speak because we're trying different things to test her abilities to obey. "I'm speaking, Mom. I just didn't think you were talking to me when we walked up."

Mrs. Gallo stares at me funny, blinking her long eyelashes a few times. "Something's up. What happened?"

"Nothing." Tamara glances at me. "Anything wrong with you, baby?"

"Nothing, princess. Life couldn't be better."

"What's wrong?" Tamara's father says, peeking his head out

from behind the door. "Everyone's waiting, and you three are out here chitchatting."

"Hush," she tells him, waving him off. "I was saying hello and trying to warn him."

Warn me? If I can handle the guys of the MC and military life, I think I can handle a family reunion.

Mr. Gallo steps outside, placing his arm around his wife's back like I have mine around Tamara's. His eyes are on mine, though, watching like a hawk how I'm gripping her. "No warning will prepare him for the Washingtons, sweetheart. The man will either sink or swim."

I laugh, smiling down at my girl. "Should I be worried?"

She shrugs, nuzzling into my side. "Nah. They're just trying to scare you. This side of the family is just like the other. They're both insane, but nothing you can't handle, baby."

Mr. Gallo gags. "I think I just threw up a little in my mouth."

"Dad," Tamara groans. "Stop being dramatic. It's not like I have my tongue down his throat."

Mr. Gallo staggers backward, grabbing his chest. "My heart can't take it. Stop talking, Tamara."

"Again, not a virgin, Mr. I Banged-Most-of-Tampa-in-My-Heyday."

Mr. Gallo blanches, dropping his hand to his side but pulling his wife closer at the same time. "There has never been anyone but your mom." That remark gets him a backhand to the chest courtesy of his wife. "Fine. Fine. I need a beer to get through this day. Who's with me?"

"I am." Tamara glances up at me as soon as her parents turn their backs. "Is that okay?" she asks quietly.

"Two beers maximum and no other liquor. I want you lucid tonight."

"We going to the club?" She waggles her eyebrows.

"No, but we have more training to do." I smirk, winking at her.

Her cheeks turn bright pink, but the smile on her face says it all. "Two beers. Got it," she whispers again.

"Fuckin' cute."

She opens her mouth to tell me off, but when I raise an eyebrow and squeeze her side, she snaps her mouth shut quickly.

"And who do we have here?" a man about the same age as Tamara's parents says as we walk into the tiny foyer of the modest home in downtown Tampa.

"Don't be an asshole, Denzel," Max tells him. "Behave yourself."

"Wait," I say, looking from the man to Tamara. "Is his name Denzel Washington?"

"Uh, yeah. So lame." She laughs, and I join her, wondering at the misery the man has had in his life with such a notable name.

"Uncle Earl's going to shit a brick," Denzel says, shaking his head. "When he sees this one—" he motions toward me, swiping his hand through the air "—covered in those tats and piercings without much skin left untouched, he's liable to have a heart attack and die."

"Stop being a dramatic dumbass."

Denzel throws up his hands. "I'm just saying, this is going to be fun."

"Where's your wife, Brenda?" Max asks.

"She's around here somewhere. Probably trying to get Ruth to stop giving her cooking lessons. The woman is good for one thing, and it isn't biscuits." Denzel winks. "If you know what I mean."

"Ew, Uncle D. You're gross," Tamara tells him, pretending to gag. "Don't talk about Aunt Brenda that way. For the love of God, I can't take all this sex talk with you people. You're old. Too old to still be doing it."

"Baby," her uncle says, stepping closer and placing his hand on her shoulder, glancing my way for only a moment. "When you're in love with someone, age is just a number. And no matter how much your hips hurt, you'll find a way to express that love."

"Dear God, someone save me," Tamara mutters.

"I could really use that beer," I say, trying to give the rescue I know she wants and needs.

"This way," Max says, suddenly being nice. Kind of like a cult leader before they feed you the magic Kool-Aid that'll make your insides melt and come pouring out of your mouth in a stream of foam. She is feeding me to the wolves, and she knows it, enjoying every goddamn moment of it too.

The smells in the house are something out of this world. My stomach rumbles as we move through the kitchen to the back door and finally onto the porch. As soon as the door opens and we step outside, Tamara on my arm, everything and everyone stops moving.

Everybody at the party turns our way, gawking at us—well, actually, at me.

"What's happening?" an old man asks, squinting in our direction, holding a cane in one hand. "Someone talk to me."

"Shut up, you idiot," an older woman, maybe his wife, says, slapping him upside the head.

"You're lucky you're fragile, Clara, because I'd take you over my knee and remind you who's in charge," he tells her, rubbing the spot she just hit.

"Jesus, they never change." Tamara squeezes my side. "Sorry," she tells me, staring up at me with worry all over her face.

"Princess, don't be sorry. This is your family. I'm sure it'll all go fine. Just breathe."

"Breathe," she repeats, sucking in a breath and holding it for a few seconds. "Just breathe."

"Come on down here." The old man motions for us to move forward, while the rest of the party is at a standstill. "I want to see you better."

"If he thought I had a lot of tattoos, he's going to shit when he sees Mammoth," Anthony tells Max, and I know I'm in for an earful from Earl Washington.

"Well, my word," Clara, the older woman at Earl's side, says as I get closer, standing so tall, I create a shadow over her and the rest of the table. "My. My. Aren't you a big one?" The woman reaches out, groping my biceps. "A really big one."

"They call him Mammoth, Auntie," Tamara says, smiling like she won the door prize or the fucking lottery because she is on my arm, but it is really the other way around.

"Girl," Clara says, "the name fits."

The two women giggle as Uncle Earl grunts. "I can't see shit with the sun. Can someone give me a little shade, please? An old man could die in this sunshine, and no one would care."

I scoot over, giving him what he wants, using nothing but my body to accommodate him. His jaw drops as he catches sight of me, tattoos, piercings, and long hair. "Does she braid your hair?" he asks me, giving no fucks about my size.

"Earl," a new woman, somewhere between Earl and Maxine's age, says as she moves toward us. "Do you always have to be an asshole?"

"At my age, I can be whatever I want, Ruth. Someday, you'll realize who's in charge, and it isn't you."

Ruth rolls her eyes as Tamara turns around, leaving my side in a flash to run into the arms of the woman. "Granny. God, I missed you."

Max's mother. I can see the family resemblance passed down from generation to generation. The beauty of the Washington women is unmistakable and undeniable.

"Baby, I missed you too." Her grandmother holds her out, studying her. "You're looking well. Better than I've seen you in a long, long time, child."

"It's because of him," Tamara says, throwing her thumb my way over her shoulder. "He brings me happiness, Granny."

Granny's eyes are on me, staring at my face, traveling down my body, soaking me in. She's appraising me, making a determination by looks alone if I'm worthy of her granddaughter.

"Ma'am, it's lovely to meet you," I say, heading off any wrong thoughts about my being a disrespectful asshole before she has a chance to form that opinion. "It's an honor to be in your home."

Her gaze moves back to Tamara, not even replying to my statement. "I can see why you have that love-sick puppy look written all over you. You finally found a man who's willing to put up with your crazy, wild ass?"

"He's so much more than that, Gran. Mammoth," Tamara says, turning toward me, motioning for my hand. "This is my granny. And, Granny, this is Mammoth."

"I can see that," her grandmother says playfully before winking. "I can only imagine, child."

"Granny," Tamara gasps. "Behave."

"I'm old. Not dead. I can appreciate a good-looking man when I see one, and this one—" she steps back, eyes raking over me again "—is fine, honey."

If I blushed, I'd be red right now. But lucky for me, I am used to women saying crazy shit to me. I'm not sure if it's my size, the tattoos, the long hair, or the combination that always sends them into a hormonal tizzy.

"I approve of this one," her grandmother says.

"For fuck's sake," Anthony, Tamara's father, mutters off to the side. "For me, they were rude. But for this one…" He rolls his eyes. "They're all, he's beautiful, welcome to the family."

Earl turns his attention toward Anthony. "Well, your ugly mug was a hard pill to swallow. You've grown on us, though."

"Liar," Anthony shoots back. "You just never thought I was good enough for Max."

"Still don't, even if you gave us some beautiful kids," Earl replies, "and somehow managed to keep this one happy and healthy."

"At least I get credit for something," Anthony says.

"I'll give you credit for one more thing. You're really good at fetching this old man a beer. Why don't you show me how much you love me and get me a cold one?"

"Old asshole," Anthony mutters.

Earl moves his cane around, dragging his tongue along his bottom lip. "If I die now, it's your fault I overheated."

"Dramatic old man."

"Whiny white boy."

"They always like this?" I ask her.

"Yep. They're like oil and water, but there's love there too."

I'd take her word on it. I don't see it, but I haven't been around for the last two decades to observe how their relationship has changed and grown.

"So, sit, Mammoth." Earl turns his whole body, too old to turn just his neck. "Get a cold one for the boy too."

"Thanks, sir." I smile even though Tamara's father growls and gives me the evil eye.

"He knows his manners. I like that. Too many young kids have no manners anymore. This one never had any." Earl motions toward Anthony, and it takes everything in me not to laugh.

This family is ruthless toward him, but for me, they've been gentle. Maybe they're breaking me in, trying to catch me off guard before the hammer comes down.

Anthony gives Earl a beer before handing one to me, grumbling under his breath the entire time about one of us being an ungrateful asshole. I'm guessing Earl, but it could go either way.

"Heard you were a military man," Earl says as he lifts the beer to his lips. "What branch, son?"

"Army, sir."

"Sit. We have a lot to talk about."

Tamara pats my ass, smiling up at me. "Relax, baby. I'll go help with the food while you and Uncle Earl swap army stories. He loves nothing more than talking about when he served during the war." She practically pushes me into the seat.

"No one else around here served. They went to college instead.

No one truly understands the dedication, sacrifice, and pride a soldier has after serving this nation. It's nice to have someone to talk about this with for once. Only took decades for someone to bring home a military man."

Tamara's still at my side, staring at Uncle Earl like she's debating if it's a good idea to leave us alone.

"Come on, baby. They'll be fine. Uncle Earl will bore him to death, but he's otherwise harmless."

Tamara leans forward, bringing her mouth next to my ear. "Is it okay if I leave you?"

I turn my head, our lips almost touching. "Go, princess. I'll be fine, but you keep using that language, and we'll have to leave the party early."

Her eyes twinkle with glee. She knows what she's doing. She always does. She's a tease, but in the end, we both come out satisfied.

"Earl, behave," Clara warns before she heads toward the house, with Tamara, Ruth, and Max not far behind.

Anthony leaves too, wandering toward Denzel, who's seated a few tables away.

"It's all an act," Earl tells me, lifting his beer. "The older I get and the crazier I act, the more they leave me alone. The women in this family can drive a man around the bend, but if you act like you're only half there, life's easier."

I laugh and raise my beer bottle. "I like your style, sir."

"So, soldier, where did you serve?"

"I was stationed at SouthCom near Miami and did a few deployments to Afghanistan."

Earl bristles. "I served in Korea. A war that's often forgotten, but the devastation to the military was tremendous."

I wince, knowing that even though war is war, I never would've wanted to trade places with him. I'd known a few veterans from Korea, and many of them never wanted to talk about their service. It wasn't that they weren't proud, but the memories of what they'd lived through were painful for them to relive, even if only through words.

"I've heard the horror stories, sir. I can't imagine what it must've been like for you."

"Back then, the units were segregated."

"They were?" I ask, shocked and appalled. "I thought that ended after the Second World War."

He shakes his head. "Sure, the law changed. Truman signed the order, but the commanders in the field had other ideas. Times were different then, son."

"I can't imagine living in a world where we're divided by color, especially when we're all willing to die for the same nation that's divided us."

Earl shakes his head. "We did what we had to do for the nation we loved, which didn't always love us back."

"I'm sorry," is the only thing I can say, even though it's not my fault.

"Don't be. You weren't the asshole commander sending the young men to be slaughtered, thrust out first to be sacrificed."

I wince at the reality he lived. "No, but they still don't care. We're just a number sometimes, a warm body able to hold a gun. It was my greatest honor to serve my country, but the nightmares of the things I saw still follow me."

"They'll always haunt you. Always. You just have to learn to realize your nightmare made the lives of others better. You sacrificed a piece of your sanity for the people who are sitting around you today, happy and oblivious."

"Everyone?" I ask, ticking my chin toward Anthony, Tamara's dad.

"Even him. I like that man. Liked him since the day I met him. He's been good for my little Maxie. I'll never admit it to his face, but I'm thankful he came into her life when he did. She was in a dark place, and he gave her life again," Earl says.

Someday, I'll learn the story there, but it isn't my place to ask or Uncle Earl's story to tell.

An hour later, Tamara's at my side again, a plate full of food that looks so good I know I'll need more than one workout to burn the calories. "Gran made this plate just for you," she says sweetly before setting the dish in front of me. "She said you'll need your energy to keep me under control." Tamara winks. "If she only knew."

I pull her into my lap, kissing her cheek and neck, tasting the salty sweetness of her skin. "I love you, princess, and I love your family too. Both sides. All of them."

Tamara's smile widens. "You love my families?"

"I do. You're so lucky and blessed." I wrap my arms around her, nuzzling into her neck. "So fucking lucky to have them all in your life."

"They're in your life too now, Mammoth. You're not alone anymore. I hope you're ready for a lot of family dinners and reunions, because my family doesn't just catch up at holidays and funerals. This is your last chance to run."

I touch her chin, holding her gaze. "I'm not going anywhere. I've never felt more at home, at peace, than I do when I'm with you."

"I love you," she whispers back. "And I never thought I'd say that to anyone until I met you."

I know then I'm home. My life of wandering no longer appealed to me.

I want roots.

I want a place to call home.

I want family.

I want Tamara Gallo forever.

CHAPTER 23
TAMARA

ONE MONTH LATER...

Things are still going strong. Mammoth's been patient, teaching me, molding me, awakening a sexual part of myself I never knew existed.

If someone would've asked me two months ago if I'd be okay submitting to a man, being told what to do, not only in the bedroom but at other times, I would've told them to fuck right off with their nonsense.

But I would've been wrong. Dead fucking wrong.

There is a power and a freedom in letting go. I no longer worry about pleasing him, questioning what he likes or what he wants. He tells me, making perfectly clear his desires.

I've never felt used or abused, only loved and adored. Sure, he's bossy, but I push back, earning some punishments just for the fun of it.

I'd talked with Aunt Izzy about how she handles her relationship with James, especially since she's one of the strongest women I know. She laid it out for me, explaining the power I hold even as a submissive. She changed my view, putting things into perspective for me.

I like being cared for. I love that Mammoth does everything he can to make me happy, giving me pleasure and looking out for my well-being. Sure, I fuck up a lot, and he seems to understand, but I always end up with a red ass in the end.

The spankings are the best, though. Who the fuck would've guessed I liked the sting of his palm before the pleasure of his fingers? I sure as fuck wouldn't have.

For the first time in a long time, I am excited for the future. I no longer give two fucks if someone looks at us funny, only caring how Mammoth looks at me. The issues people have with us being a couple is their problem, not mine.

I am loved. That's all that matters. Loved by a good man who respects my family and is openly embraced. Maybe not by Uncle James, but even he's softened up a bit on Mammoth, realizing I am right where I want to be with the man I want to be with. Uncle James has to relent sometime. No one holds anything over his head about what he does in the bedroom with Aunt Izzy, not even Thomas, who is James's best friend.

"Princess, we're late. What the hell is taking you so long?" Mammoth asks from the other side of the bathroom door as I apply one last coat of mascara.

I stare at my reflection, soaking in the new version of me. The happier one who's more comfortable in my skin than I've ever been before. Mammoth's done that. I've never felt as home as I do when I'm with him. I feel a sense of belonging and purpose with him at my side.

"We have a reservation at eight, and the party won't wait for us."

"I thought we were going for drinks?" I yell back, running my finger over my red lipstick, smoothing it out across my bottom lip.

"No, princess, we're going to the club."

My eyes widen as I gasp, dropping the mascara wand to the counter and running to the door. "You mean a sex club?" I ask, opening the door quickly, almost knocking myself over.

Mammoth laughs, leaning against the wall, looking so handsome, I almost don't want to leave. Almost. But he said sex club, and I've been begging to go to one since I found out he was in the lifestyle.

"I got us passes for the weekend and filled out all the paperwork, getting us approved. Had to pull a few strings, but we're in if you're game."

"I'm game." I throw myself into his arms, peppering his handsome face with red kisses. "I'm totally game."

He gropes my ass, grinding his hard cock into me. "Then finish up and let's jet. We have a big night ahead of us."

"I'm ready." I push past him, but he catches me by the arm, gently pulling me backward.

"You're missing something."

"What?" I ask, glancing down at my outfit, wondering what the hell he's talking about.

He slides his hand into his front pocket, fishing out something from inside. When he opens his palm, there're two thick silver bracelets. "I'm not into collars, but these are necessary for tonight. They'll be enough to let everyone know you're taken. My name's carved on each one, leaving no question of who you belong to."

My insides quiver and my stomach flips. This is official and a big fucking deal in the BDSM world. I know that much, studying my ass off and learning everything I can when I find time in between reading for classes. "They're so beautiful," I whisper, holding out my wrists immediately, wanting nothing more than to wear his mark.

"They're more than decoration, princess. They're a commitment."

"I know. I've never wanted anything more than this."

Mammoth's smile is easy and immediate. "I promise to give you a night you'll never forget."

"I promise to give you a life you'll always want to remember," I tell him, knowing the future is full of nothing but possibilities.

I gaze down, watching as he closes the bracelets around my wrists, locking them. Each one has a tiny loop, but for what purpose, I don't know. It doesn't matter anyway. They're a work of art and a gift from Mammoth, the first one I've ever received.

His hands stay around my wrists, covering the silver bracelets. "Ready, princess?"

"I think so." I swallow, realizing we aren't playing anymore.

He slides his hands up my arms, resting them on my shoulders, caressing my skin to soothe my shaky nerves. "You'll do fine. Just remember the things we've gone over. Things we've practiced. Everything you've learned."

"I'll do my best." My insides are a mess. I've been begging him to take me to a club for over a month, and now that he's finally made it possible, I wonder if I've made a huge mistake.

He ticks his head toward my bedroom. "I left an outfit for you on your bed. Put it on and then we'll go."

"You bought me clothes?" I blink, wondering who this man is and where's Mammoth?

His hungry gaze travels down the black cocktail dress I'd picked out especially for tonight. "You need something a little more accessible." He smirks, and my insides liquefy. When I don't move right away, too stunned that he not only bought me clothes, but slutty clothes, he pats me on the ass and barks, "Now, get that sweet ass moving. I'm only patient for so long."

I don't hesitate again. I'm out of his grip, rushing into my bedroom. I stop dead when I see the outfit laid out on the bed for me. Slutty? Yes. But freaking tasteful, if that's such a thing.

The miniskirt is simple, white, and short as fuck. If it covers my ass cheeks, it'll be a freaking miracle. The tube top is cute and white too, without much material, but enough to cover my breasts. Then there're the shoes. Nothing fancy. No high heels. They're sandals which kind of throws me. They're not the shoes I'd wear with an outfit like this, but from what I've read, most of the girls are barefoot. Either way, he picked this out for me, and if it's going to get him to bang my brains out until I'm incoherent, I'll freaking wear it all day long.

"Leave your underwear off," he says, and I chuckle to myself because I haven't worn underwear since middle school.

Changing takes me less than two minutes. It's not hard when I'm only putting on scraps. When I step into the hallway, Mammoth's leaning against the wall, eyes trained on my doorway, waiting patiently.

He hums his appreciation as his gaze glides up and down my body. His eyes blaze with so much hunger and heat, I know he likes how the outfit looks on me. He's always been a fan of my body, making sure I know it at every opportunity. He doesn't waste any time, taking my hand, and leading me toward the door.

As soon as we're in the living room, Gigi looks up from the couch, her eyes raking over me before widening. "What kind of restaurant are you going to?"

Pike glances my way, almost choking on his tongue, not out of lust, but shock. "Fucking hell," he mutters under his breath as he shakes his head, going back to looking at his phone.

"Don't wait up," I tell her, ignoring her question. "We'll be late."

"It's your long weekend home, Tam. I thought we'd all hang out." She gives me a faint smile, disappointed that I'm ditching her for some dick.

"Tomorrow, Gigi. I promised Mammoth tonight, but tomorrow, the four of us will do something fun."

"Lily too," Gigi adds because I keep forgetting she's in town instead of away at school.

"Lily too, but the girl better be ready to party."

"She's a totally different person," Gigi tells me. But I've known my cousin my entire life, and Lily's always been as straitlaced as they come.

Mammoth tightens his hand on my waist, a cue for me to wrap it up without sounding rude. "We'll figure it out then. We're off.

Wish me luck." I smile nervously, toying with the bracelets, and Gigi's eyes narrow in on my new jewelry.

"Sweet Jesus," she mutters, waving at me as I rush toward the door, not wanting to answer too many questions right now.

"We're taking your car, princess. Give me the keys."

I hand them over, not even thinking twice, because my hands are shaking so badly, I'm not sure I could drive without causing a wreck. Mammoth takes the keys before opening the car door for me. "Your night of pleasure awaits."

This may not be a coach and I'm sure as hell no Cinderella, but I do feel like a pampered princess and the luckiest woman in the world.

I barely speak as we wind through traffic, making our way to downtown Tampa in record time. Mammoth doesn't drive slowly on a bike, and it's no different in a car.

By the time we're in the parking lot of the club, the jitters I had earlier have turned into a full-on, body-shaking anxiety attack.

"Baby," Mammoth says as I hunch over my legs, breathing so fast, I think I might pass out. "Maybe we shouldn't." He rubs my back, soothing me, letting me freak out.

"No." I inhale, closing my eyes, trying to calm down. "I want this."

"When you walk through those doors, pretend you're a different person. This is the one time in your life you don't have to think. I won't let you fail. I won't let anyone touch or hurt you. This is about us, your pleasure, your experience. But if you want to leave, we'll go. Just say 'boat' at any time, and I'll take you home."

I take two more deep breaths, squeezing my hands together, knowing I want this. He's right. I don't have to think. For once, I can let go and be free. No one knows me inside those walls. The only thing that matters is us. I'm all about new experiences, and nothing usually rattles my cage. Tonight shouldn't be any different.

I straighten my back, slowly opening my eyes. "I'm ready."

"Tonight, we'll watch others and, if you're comfortable, maybe get a private room."

I nod, not speaking, knowing he hasn't given me permission. It's easier this way. The less I have to talk tonight, the better.

He's out of the car a second later, rounding the back.

"You can do this." I take one last deep breath before the car door opens and Mammoth's hand appears.

I don't even stumble as I climb out of the car, hooking my arm in his. I'm doing this. We're doing this. I'm about to step into a world I don't fully comprehend but am dying to know more about.

"Good evening, Sir," a man says when we walk through the front doors and into a dark, lush foyer. "Name?"

"Good evening," Mammoth replies, handing the man two passes. "Reservation is under Saint."

When the man gazes at me, I immediately tip my head, staring at the floor.

"You can leave her shoes with me unless you'd like her to keep them on."

"You can hold them," Mammoth tells the man before dropping to one knee and carefully removing my sandals. The cement is cool under my feet but not cold. A welcome sensation because I'm almost sweating from being so nervous.

"Enjoy your evening."

"Thank you." Mammoth slides his arm back around me. "Come on, princess. I'm about to rock your world," he whispers in my ear, sending goose bumps scattering everywhere.

CHAPTER 24
MAMMOTH

THERE'S something about being surrounded by a large family, even one that's not my own, to put things into perspective. I never looked at my life like I'd lacked anything, but after being with the Gallos, I know I was robbed.

Maybe if I'd had a family like this, I wouldn't have felt as lost when I left the service, and I'd never have ended up with the Disciples. I wouldn't be under their thumb, doing their dirty work for God knows how long. Things would've been different. I would've been different.

Looking around the room, I can see the love these people have for one another. Sure, they fight like cats and dogs, but at the end of the day, they'd all take a bullet for one another.

I want what they have, and since meeting Tamara, I've been welcomed into the family by everyone, even her parents. After they gave me half a chance, they saw a change in their daughter. She is more settled, probably feeling some of the same way I did once I found her. She is like a tether, anchoring me to something more than myself and giving me purpose.

Fuck. When did I turn into this sappy asshole? Tamara did it and so did the Gallos. Pike had warned me about how they fuck with your head, especially the women. Gone were the days when the men ruled the roost like at the MC, because in this household, Mrs. Gallo, Tamara's grandmother, is the queen bee.

James, who had tried to throw my ass out, has even started to warm up to me. Not grumbling under his breath every time I enter a room. We keep our conversations to a minimum and never speak about our past.

Bear's fingers toy with the hairs near his chin. "What about the club? They givin' you shit?"

I shrug, wondering how much I should say. I am still a Disciple. Don't see that changing, no matter how far away I move. They are always going to be an issue. "We have an agreement."

"I'm sure you do," he mutters. "What about..."

He snaps his lips shut as soon as Gigi, Tamara, and Lily walk into the room.

"Hey, Uncle Bear," Gigi says, ruffling the man's hair. "You givin' Mammoth a hard time?"

"Always, kid." Bear winks at her.

"Hey, baby," Tamara says, sliding in my lap. "When're you leaving?"

"In a few minutes, princess. I have to get back to the compound."

She places her face in the crook of my neck, smelling me. It's a new thing she does, claiming my scent drives her wild. "When will I see you again?"

My hand finds her hip, holding her tight, wishing we had longer. "In a few weeks. I have to take a run up north."

"North?" she whispers. "For what?"

"Can't say. Club business."

She pulls away, staring at me with her big hazel eyes. "Be careful, okay?"

"I promise. You can't get rid of me that easy, sweetheart." I smile, moving some of her hair away from her face before holding her cheek. "I love you, Tamara."

"Love you too, Mammoth," she whispers, cheeks turning pink.

"You two are like a regular Hallmark card," Bear teases.

"Shut up, Uncle. I think it's super sweet," Lily tells him, leaning with one arm on his shoulder, but her eyes are fixed on us. "Someday, I hope to find that."

"You better get your nose out of those books, then, girl. You aren't going to find that—" he waves his hand at me "—in a library."

"I didn't mean him." She slaps his shoulder. "I meant a man."

Bear flinches even though the impact couldn't have hurt. Lily's small, gentle, and doesn't pack a hard enough punch to hurt even a small man. "I don't care if you want a woman, baby. You gotta get out more. Put yourself out there."

"She's not dating," Mike says, walking into the kitchen from the living room and heading right to the fridge. "She's never getting married either."

Bear laughs first, followed by the girls.

"You're a fool," Bear tells him, shaking his head. "Your little girl is growing up, and you're just going to have to deal with that fact, Mike. You can't control her anymore."

"Never fuckin' could," Mike mutters, glancing toward the ceiling.

"Don't worry, Dad. I'm not going anywhere anytime soon. I mean, even when I move out, you'll see me every day at the shop."

"Move out?" Mike pales. "You can't move out."

"So, when I find a man, should we just move in?" Lily asks him, chuckling behind her palm.

Not that long ago, Lily was in tears at Gigi and Tamara's apartment because her parents had lost their shit about her quitting school. They seemed to get over it, accepting her decision, and have already moved on.

"I better run," I say, patting Tamara's ass, wanting to avoid chasing the sun. "Call me when you get back to school, yeah?"

"Yes, bossy." Tamara winks, and I laugh, sliding my arms around her back, leaning forward to kiss her.

"Walk me out."

"Bye, Mammoth," Gigi says, followed by the rest of the group. I wave instead of speaking because in this family goodbyes can take forever. It's one thing I learned about them, and something I'm not sure I'll ever get used to either.

Tamara's mother is at the door, waiting for us with Anthony at her side. "We just want to say something."

"What's wrong, Mom?" Tamara asks, tucking her finger into the waistband of my jeans.

"Nothing, baby." Her mom smiles at her before turning her gaze toward me. "This is for Mammoth."

"Yes, ma'am?" I smile nervously because the woman would scare any man. She is that fierce. Just like her kid.

"I was wrong about you. I judged you unfairly based on your outside and not your inside. Sure, you're a badass biker, but you're more than that. You're more than your tattoos and piercings. I've seen the way my daughter's face lights up when you're in the room. I feel the way her soul is happy when you're nearby. I sense her peace with who she is and will always be." Her mother smiles as tears form in her eyes. "You did that for her, and I'll always be grateful you came into her life."

"Am I dying?" I ask because Max Gallo isn't usually filled with so much kindness.

"No, child, but they were things that needed to be said. I should've said something sooner, but I couldn't find the words. I want you to know we think of you as family. You're ours now. One of us. You need anything, you call. You need help, you holler." She opens her arms, steps forward, and wraps herself around my body. "We're your family now."

If I were a guy who cried, I'd be in tears. Never have I felt such love and acceptance than I do in this moment.

EPILOGUE

LILY

THERE'S ALWAYS a moment in my day when I want to punch someone. I'm just about there, but I'm doing my best to hold it together, because today, that someone is my father.

He's taken me under his wing since I dropped out of college, teaching me everything there is to know about Inked and the piercing of every type of body part imaginable—and even some I never thought possible.

The man is the quintessential helicopter parent, hovering around me every second of the workday and even at home. I thought it was cute when I was a little girl. It didn't even bother me when I was in high school because the big lug loved me and he showed it.

But now, at twenty-one, it's old. Really old.

Then there's the fact that I'm Lily. The sweet one. The good girl. The only person in the family who doesn't say how I feel, always wanting to keep the peace—or at least, not draw extra attention to myself.

"Dad, I know. You've watched me do it hundreds of times

already," I huff, resting my chin in my palm, staring out the front windows of the shop. "I seriously can do this on my own now."

His eyes widen as he jerks his head back like I've slapped him with my words. "I know, sweetheart." He nods. "I know."

I know there's a but in there because there always is. My father doesn't know how to agree with anyone without adding the big old but, throwing in his opinion whether he's right or wrong.

"But..." And there it is. Predictable.

I roll my eyes.

"Fine," he says quickly after he glances down, catching me. "You can do the next client through the door all by yourself."

I sit up straight, mouth hanging open, because my dad's never this easy. "Really?"

He taps his finger against the large calendar sitting on the front desk. "It's a simple nipple piercing in an hour. You could do those in your sleep."

"At this point, I can do them all in my sleep," I tell him, pushing his finger out of the way so I can see the other appointments for today. The shop has only been open an hour, but so far, it's been extremely quiet. The rest of the day is booked but not over-booked...nothing I can't handle on my own. "Why don't you take the day off, take Mom somewhere nice, and let me handle this today?" I bat my eyelashes, begging for him to say yes, because if there's one thing I know about my dad, he's a sucker when it comes to me.

He reaches back, rubbing the back of his neck as he glances around the empty waiting room. "I don't know, Lily. That's a big step."

"Everyone's here." I motion toward the back area where every-one's busy setting up or working on their first client of the day. "If I have a problem, I'll ask Uncle Joe or Anthony. And—" I smile, placing my hand on his chest "—Mom's off today, and the house is empty."

Barf. I can't believe I'd stoop so low as to entice my father with an empty house and my mother to get a little space. But times like this call for drastic measures, even if that includes your parents doing the nasty.

Dad's face brightens. "She'd probably like to grab some lunch."

"Yeah," I mutter as he kisses the top of my head, no longer concerned with leaving me alone for the first time ever. "You'll make her day."

"Mine too," he whispers in my hair.

Still gross, but it's working.

"It's just easy piercings today. A few nipples, a couple ears, and two belly buttons."

"Sounds like a blast." I don't even try to hide the lack of enthusiasm from my voice. Who knew so many women had their nipples pierced? Not me, but the number is staggering and growing each day.

The front door opens, and I gasp. The man walking inside is like a ghost. Someone I haven't seen in over five years because he's been away, serving in the military. Or at least, that's what I heard from Aunt Suzy.

"Oh my God, Jett!" I screech, pushing out of my father's arms and running toward the boy I had the biggest crush on as a kid. "You're alive."

"Babe," he says, holding out his arms to me, catching me as I smash into him, almost climbing his body. "Why wouldn't I be alive?" His laugh is deep, rich, and damn…it's sexy too.

When he left, he was a boy. One I had a very serious crush on, but I never said a word to anyone. He was the older, cool kid, and I was…not. If it weren't for Tamara and Gigi, I would've eaten lunch in the library, opting for solitude and fiction over the sad reality of my real life.

But Jett was popular. The girls wanted him, and the boys wanted to be him. He always had that cool factor. Something I never, even to this day, could figure out how to get a piece of for myself.

"No." I laugh, slapping him on the chest when my feet finally touch the floor. "You left, and we never saw you again." I shrug and snort all at the same time. I grimace and take a step back because, fuck me, why in the name of God did I have to sound like a little pig when I laughed?

As soon as I peer down at the floor, trying to avoid his haunting gaze, he moves his fingers under my chin, forcing my face upward. "I never had an extended enough leave to stick around town for very long. When I was home, you guys were away at school, getting smarter and prettier, while I was getting my ass kicked."

Oh my God. Oh my God. Did he just say I was prettier?

No. He can't be talking about me.

He's just being smooth, Lily.

This is Jett after all, and he's a world-class flirt.

Of course he's not talking about me.

Maybe Tamara or Gigi, but not me, because I'm Lily, the nerd and the least cool chick in high school or, hell, the entire city, for that matter.

"I dropped out," I blurt, having no filter around him just like back in high school.

Some things never change. That's why I avoided him back in the day. Any time he was around, I literally had verbal diarrhea, saying the most embarrassing shit I'd ever heard come out of any girl's mouth when a hot guy was around.

His fingers tighten near my neck as his eyebrows rise. "You what?"

"I dropped out of college," I whisper like it's a dirty secret I can't bear to say any louder.

"Jett, Jesus. Look at you, kid," my dad says, stalking across the room until he's at our side.

My father's shadow, along with his outstretched hand, causes Jett to drop his hand away from my face. "Mr. Gallo. You never change. It's great to see you, sir." Jett smiles, and I swear to God, the whiteness of his teeth and the sparkle of the sunshine off those babies could light up a room.

My dad shakes hands with Jett, and with his other hand, he totally feels up Jett's bicep. "The military made a man out of you, son. A real man."

Jett's mouth twitches as my father gropes him because the man is obsessed with muscles. Back in the day, Dad was a total meathead and a hotshot fighter. But now, he's all about his family and Inked.

"Thanks, sir," Jett tells him.

Dad cranes his neck toward the back as he finally releases his hold on Jett's ample arms. "Joe, Jett's here."

"Jett?" Uncle Joe yells out from the back like he heard his brother wrong, but he didn't.

He's here, all right. Live and in the flesh and looking more delicious than ever. There isn't an ounce of the man that isn't drop-dead gorgeous. Even his feet are cute, and I *hate* feet. His face is tanned and covered in the most perfect five-o'clock shadow even though it's early afternoon.

I stand there, staring at Jett like he's a celebrity and I'm an awkward fan too starstruck to form words. Jet peers over at me, winking, and I nearly faint.

"Holy fuck," Uncle Joe says as soon as he walks into the waiting area at the front of the shop, catching sight of Jett. "It's been two years since I've seen your ugly ass."

"Uncle, you're no prettier either, but you sure as fuck are a lot older," Jett teases him, giving my uncle a quick bro-hug.

Uncle Joe holds on to Jet's shoulder, soaking him in like he's one of his own kids he hasn't seen in forever. "Sophia didn't say you were coming home."

"I surprised her and Dad this morning."

"Lily, want to go over the books one more time?" my dad asks, but I shake my head and wave him off, not answering with words. "Or would you rather me stay here all day?"

That's all he has to say to get me moving. Pretty boy or not, I don't want my father sticking around here, hovering over me like a rain cloud.

I turn my back, leaving Uncle Joe and Jett to talk as my father goes over the schedule one more time. I sneak a peek at the hottie, pretending to be staring at the books, but I am really watching his hands move and the muscles on his arms as they flex.

"What are you doing here? I don't have any openings today, but I could probably fit you in."

"No, Uncle. I didn't come for some ink, but if I did, I'd only want you to do it."

"We're good, Dad. I got it. Now go home and spend time with Mom," I say, finally turning my attention to my father, trying to push him toward the door.

"If you run into trouble, baby, just call me." He kisses my cheek and is one step closer to being gone.

"Then what's up?" Uncle Joe asks Jet.

"I wanted to get pierced."

My father's foot stops in midair like someone grabbed the damn meat stick and held him there. He turns, eyeing Jet, with one hand on the door handle.

"Well, Lily's here." Uncle Joe ticks his head my way. "Do you know what you want to get?"

Holy shit. Holy freaking shit. Jett wants to get pierced. That means me. I'm going to pierce the hottest boy in school. The one I daydreamed about on the regular.

Jett smirks, glancing in my direction. "A Prince Albert."

My eyes widen.

My father's eyes do not just widen, they almost bug out of his eye sockets. "I'm staying," he announces, dropping his foot back to the floor and letting go of the door handle.

"Like hell you are," Uncle Joe says, coming to my rescue. "You were leaving, so leave. Lily can do this. She's trained and has done them before."

I blush, thinking about the times I've done it with my dad watching over my back while I held a cock in my hand. Talk about awkward. Besides being walked in on while having sex with someone or taking a poop, I can't imagine anything more embarrassing.

Uncle Joe pitches his thumb over his shoulder. "If she needs help, Anthony's here or Pike can assist."

My dad shakes his head. "Jett's junk is too important to let someone like Lily do it alone."

I giggle—hearing my dad talk about Jett's penis just sets me off, and me doing *it* alone.

"Listen to yourself, man." Uncle Joe swats my father's shoulder before pushing him backward. "Don't worry about Jett's junk. I know Lily can handle just about anything, including a penis."

"Lemme die," I whisper, covering my face with my hands to hide my red cheeks.

"It's Jett's penis," my dad argues, shaking his head.

Uncle Joe crosses his arms, glaring at my father. "And his penis is special because?"

I peek through my fingers, still too mortified to look anyone in the face, especially Jett, who's staring right at me.

"Because it's Jett." My dad shrugs.

"Get out of here, or else I'm calling Mia and telling her you could've spent the day with her but decided to babysit your twenty-one-year-old daughter instead because she had to touch a penis."

Oh my God. I wish everyone would stop saying penis. Especially when they're talking about Jett's penis.

My dad throws his hands up. "I'm going, but I want a full report and expect some text messages too."

"What details you want?" Uncle Joe sighs, rolling his eyes. "You want to know his length or some shit?"

"I'm out," Dad says, pushing through the front door, arms flailing around as his mouth moves.

I drop my hands from my face, gawking at the front door as it swishes and my father storms out. I can't hear him once the door closes, but the string of curse words spilling from his lips before was fierce, creative, and nothing short of profane.

"You got this?" Uncle Joe asks me, ticking his chin toward Jett.

I nod, still mute and embarrassed.

"Good." He smiles and grabs Jett's shoulder. "Are you okay with her doing the piercing?"

Jett moves his gaze to me again. "As long as she knows what she's doing and it won't lead to me getting an amputation, I'm game. How about you, Lily? You up for it?"

"I know how to handle a penis." I smile, not realizing what the hell I just said and how freaking dirty it sounded.

That's until Jett's smile widens, and he winks at me again. What the hell did I say?

I know how to handle a penis? Fuck my life.

When Jett's around, it's like my brain disconnects from the rest of my body. This is going to be a long, long day, and it's barely started.

"Well, she's your girl." Uncle Joe ignores my idiotic statement as he moves toward me with a straight face. "Just holler if you kids need help."

I stand there, gaping at Jett. My mouth is opening and closing like I'm a goldfish out of water, gasping for air.

"Jett?" Gigi's voice is filled with shock as she stands next to me, gawking at Jett too. "Am I seeing things? Are you really here?"

All I can do is blink. It doesn't matter that Gigi seemed to come out of nowhere. I never saw or heard her walk into the waiting room. All I can think about is Jett. Jett's penis. My hands. The needle. Oh my God. I am finally going to see the one body part I've dreamed about on this guy but never seen.

"Hey, sweetheart." He runs his fingers through his beautiful hair, doing the smooth, cool thing he always has.

She's in his arms a second later, kissing his cheeks frantically. "I didn't think you'd come back alive."

Jett moves his head to avoid her kisses. "Stop, Gigi." He laughs, gripping her arms, trying to put some space between them. "You're killing me, smalls."

She swats his chest. "You disappear for years—no letters, no phone calls, nothing. You just vanish into thin air, and now I'm not supposed to kiss you." She wipes her cheeks like she's crying and being overdramatic. "You're like seeing my long-lost brother. I'm getting my kisses before you disappear again."

Jett's parents, Sophia and Kayden, have been best friends with Aunt Suzy and Uncle Joe since way before any of us were born. From what I understand, Sophia and Suzy were roommates before she met Uncle Joe. I find it hard to believe because Sophia's kind of kick-ass and Aunt Suzy...well, she's more like me.

Jett smiles. "I'm not going anywhere. I'm back for good."

My heart almost leaps out of my chest with the news. Not that it should matter because it's not like we've ever run in the same circles. And then there's the fact that he's Jett and I'm boring Lily.

Gigi slaps Jett's shoulder and nearly vibrates with excitement. "We have to celebrate, then. Tamara will be home this weekend from school. You game for a little party like old times?"

Like old times. I never had any old times. The parties they went to in high school, I didn't attend. I stayed home, knowing my dad wasn't going to let me go anyway, and read books. I studied on weekends or helped my mom at the clinic. Talk about boring. I could've been the poster child.

Jett looks over Gigi's shoulder. "Only if Lily's coming," he says, staring straight at me.

I blink like I'm in a trance or daydreaming, trying to wrap my head around what he's saying. Maybe I'm imagining things. Why in the world would the town hottie want me there? I'm about as fun as watching paint dry on the walls. I know it too, and I've accepted my blandness.

"She's totally coming," Gigi answers for me.

"Maybe she has a date or something," he tells me.

Gigi snorts. "Lily doesn't date."

"I date," I grumble, giving Gigi the death glare.

"Oh. Okay," she laughs, rolling her eyes in my direction. "Are you free this weekend?"

I don't answer right away as I stare at Jett, our eyes locked and my body beginning to overheat. "I think so." I shrug, trying not to commit to anything in case I chicken out.

Gigi hugs Jett one more time. "We're doing this, and it's going to be epic."

"Yeah," Jett says as Gigi wraps her arms around him, but his eyes are on me.

"I better start prepping," I say, stepping backward toward the piercing room. "So much to do." I smile nervously, feeling the heat of his gaze.

"What are you doing at Inked?" she asks him when I turn my back, almost running away from them.

"I'm getting a Prince Albert."

Gigi gasps. "No. Fucking. Shit. Are you shittin' me?"

"I never joke about my dick, sweetheart."

Once inside the small room, I close the door, plastering myself against the cool metal for support. I can do this. It's just a penis. I've seen so many at this point, I've lost count. What's another one, right?

Ready for more? Blaze is now available to devour.

Perpetual good girl Lily is caught off guard when her high school crush, playboy Jett, struts into her family's business. But when they become roommates, their chemistry proves just how much opposites attract…

Read Now>> Tap here to read Blaze

What to read next...

MEN OF INKED HEATWAVE VOLUME 2

Learn more at *menofinked.com/heat2*
or visit *chelleblissromance.com* to purchase a
signed copy to add to your personal collection.

BE A GALLO GIRL...

Want to be the first to hear about the next Men of Inked book or everything Chelle Bliss? Join my newsletter by tapping here to sign up or visit *menofinked.com/inked-news*

Want a place to talk romance books, meet other bookworms, and all things Men of Inked? Join Chelle Bliss Books on Facebook to get sneak peeks, exclusive news, and special giveaways.

MEN OF INKED
FAMILY TREE

MENOFINKED.COM/BOOKS

Please visit *menofinked.com/gallo-family-tree* to see a larger version.

Welcome to the family!

LOVE SIGNED PAPERBACKS?

Visit *chelleblissromance.com* for signed paperbacks and book merchandise.

ABOUT THE AUTHOR

I'm a full-time writer, time-waster extraordinaire, social media addict, coffee fiend, and ex-history teacher. *To learn more about my books, please visit menofinked.com.*

Want to stay up-to-date on the newest Men of Inked release and more? Tap here to join my newsletter or visit *menofinked.com/inked-news*

Join over 10,000 readers on Facebook in Chelle Bliss Books private reader group and talk books and all things reading. Tap here to become part of the family or visit at *facebook.com/groups/blisshangout*

Tap here to see the Gallo Family Tree or visit *menofinked.com/gallo-family-tree*

Where to Follow Me:

facebook.com/authorchellebliss1

instagram.com/authorchellebliss

bookbub.com/authors/chelle-bliss

goodreads.com/chellebliss

amazon.com/author/chellebliss

tiktok.com/@chelleblissauthor

pinterest.com/chellebliss10